| | |
|---|---|
| Chapter 1 | 1 |
| Chapter 2 | 14 |
| Chapter 3 | 30 |
| Chapter 4 | 40 |
| Chapter 5 | 50 |
| Chapter 6 | 64 |
| Chapter 7 | 75 |
| Chapter 8 | 89 |
| Chapter 9 | 106 |
| Chapter 10 | 111 |
| Chapter 11 | 117 |
| Chapter 12 | 124 |
| Chapter 13 | 140 |
| Chapter 14 | 149 |
| Chapter 15 | 171 |
| Chapter 16 | 176 |
| Chapter 17 | 188 |
| Chapter 18 | 202 |
| Chapter 19 | 207 |
| Chapter 20 | 222 |
| Chapter 21 | 236 |
| Chapter 22 | 242 |
| Chapter 23 | 251 |
| Chapter 24 | 257 |
| Chapter 25 | 274 |
| Chapter 26 | 286 |
| Chapter 27 | 309 |
| Chapter 28 | 318 |
| Chapter 29 | 335 |
| Chapter 30 | 343 |
| Chapter 31 | 351 |
| Chapter 32 | 361 |
| Chapter 33 | 388 |
| Chapter 34 | 394 |
| Chapter 35 | 413 |
| Chapter 36 | 432 |
| Chapter 37 | 438 |
| Chapter 38 | 451 |
| Chapter 39 | 466 |
| Chapter 40 | 475 |
| Chapter 41 | 483 |
| Chapter 42 | 489 |

Chapter 43    505
Chapter 44    517
Chapter 45    523
Chapter 46    531
Chapter 47    538
Chapter 48    554
Chapter 49    558
Chapter 50    571
Chapter 51    579
Chapter 52    597
Chapter 53    605
Chapter 54    618
Chapter 55    628
Chapter 56    635
Chapter 57    641

Afterword    649
Portal Books Publishing    651

# Chapter One

The mist from the many waterfalls we'd created by freeing Sarissa was drifting up into the afternoon sky, and the new rivers far below were racing between the dunes, surging across the black landscape.

I dashed around Arlann and Sarissa and onto the lift; there was no time to waste. I needed to get a look at the Red Cathedral so that I could figure out what we were dealing with and what our next move would be.

Darling must have been thinking the same thing because a message from her popped through that said she was heading there as well.

The lift itself was empty—the nearby players and NPCs were busy gawking at the black desert below and the sapphire waters that were spreading through it—but the mechanism rumbled to life beneath me all the same, so I nodded at Arlann and Sarissa, double-checked that my illusion was still in place, then pulled up my menus.

"Have House meet us at the Cathedral too," Frank said. "There's something you need to see that only she can pull off."

I squinted at him, dubious, then shrugged and sent her a message asking her to head out as well and meet us there. Couldn't hurt.

On second thought, it definitely could hurt, and that was probably the most likely scenario given that Frank was suggesting it, but I couldn't afford to worry about that right now. I wanted to be racing across the sands on my bike the very moment the lift touched down, and I had alerts to page through and perks to select in the meantime.

"Congratulations," Frank said. "Your unthinking obedience has earned you a single Frank point. Feel free to rejoice, but quietly."

"Wow, lucky me… I'm getting warnings now, huh?"

I tabbed through my alerts for those last few Ripples I'd caused, the sum of which had been worth a staggering 16,251 Renown, about 6,000 of which had come from the minor trio that had resulted from freeing the three members of the Triad while the great bulk of it had come from that last, colossal Ripple that had forever changed the Onyx Sands into the Onyx Delta.

I pulled up the Renown ladder as the lift punched down into the cold, bright mist, and my skin prickled with goosebumps at the temperature change.

1. {Ned} Renown Rank XI
2. {Tyrann} Renown Rank XI
3. {Geezeman} Renown Rank XI
4. {Nissa} Renown Rank XI
5. {Herata} Renown Rank X

I cracked a smile at that. It felt good to be back on top, and Rank XII couldn't be far off now.

"You know how I feel about your smile," Frank said.

I widened my grin until my cheeks hurt and pointed it down in his direction, then made aggressive, unblinking eye contact.

Frank made a gagging sound.

I smiled even harder. "Are you uncomfortable, Frank?"

"I'm attached to you. Uncomfortable is my middle name."

I paused. "The Axe of Uncomfortable Knowledge?"

He grunted. "I can't tell if you're trying to be rude or funny because you're terrible at both, but I do actually like the sound of that. And a great deal of my wisdom does chafe the metaphorical nether regions, if you catch my drift."

"What?"

"Oh, are you confused? Allow me to be way, way more clear than is strictly necessary."

I leaned up against one of the railings that secured the lift and rubbed my face. "Or we could just move on and pretend I didn't ask."

"My knowledge bombs are like sand in the interior webbing of a damp bathing suit, chafing against the smooth taintlands of the ignorant."

I winced. "I really could have done without that image."

"That is the nature of the burden I bear, Ned. It's heavy, but don't worry. I'll continue to hilariously soldier on for as long as it takes."

"Don't call yourself hilarious. Don't be that guy."

"If you've got a stronger and more accurate word for what it is I am, let me know. I'm always looking to improve my lexicon when it comes to verbiage that I can use to describe myself."

I sighed. "Anyway, chafing is definitely a good descriptor for..." I trailed off and gestured vaguely in his direction. "You in general."

I pulled my list of available Renown Perks up.

"Help me out with these real quick. At the very least we need to get the first pick settled so we can see what the second group of Renown Perks has on offer, but I'd love to get these all done before the lift touches down so we can keep it moving."

"Uh huh."

**You may select 1 of 3 permanent Renown buffs.**
**1. You may spend 2 gold from within your inventory to gain an additional Housing Slot. This perk may be used any number of times, but the cost will greatly increase with each use, and claiming more than 10 plots via this effect may result in negative consequences.**
**2. You may spend 3 gold from your inventory to craft a {Forged Writ of Compulsion}. Writs may be used to rent NPC homes and businesses for one week without fail, but renting will incur an additional cost based on the plot's daily net income. Income and benefits from rented plots are calculated as if you own them, but you may not Raze rented structures.**
**3. Once every 48 hours, you may contract a Shadowy NPC that has a chance of awarding you with a free Housing Plot or several other, more minor benefits. However, the NPC has a high chance of failure, which on rare occasions can result in negative consequences.**

"You got anything on the scaling for that first one? Is the cost gonna double or something as we go on?"

"Nah, it's not that steep. It increases by 2 gold each time until you've used it ten times, then it goes up by 5 gold with each use forever and the possible penalty the prompt mentioned kicks in. Can't comment on that."

"Thanks. The second looks pretty clear-cut with creating Writs of Compulsion to rent structures out for a week, but what about that third one? We summon a Shadowy NPC every 2 days and they might hand us a free plot?"

"25% chance of success. I can't say anything when it comes to the drawback if the NPC fails... I mean, I could say something. I could say a lot of things—"

"Don't."

I took a few steps forward and gripped the railing with both hands as the elevator inched lower. The rushing waters had already spread through the bulk of the desert, and the more distant rivers were churning and foaming toward the oceans that bordered the Onyx Delta to either side.

"Let's see," I said. "With a 25% percent success rate over time, that'll net us a free plot once every 4 tries, so that's, what, a plot and change per week on average?"

"You'd have an 87.5% chance of picking up a free plot every week, yeah."

"That'll add up nicely over weeks or years—and it's free and it never ends—but it's not going to do much of anything for us in the short term. We need to be ramping up, not settling for a long-term plateau.

"The Writ one's kind of cool. It'd probably be pretty powerful to rent a bunch of inns right now with so many players heading our way, but I'd rather spend my gold on expanding the city than renting the stuff that's already around. That seems like where the money's really at."

I selected the first pick, because what I really wanted was more plots as soon as humanly possible.

"Any objections?"

"I object to the fact that I haven't Franked anyone for at least ten minutes."

"Really? You're already on about that?"

"Yup. In my opinion it required a laudable amount of restraint on my part to avoid mentioning it earlier, but once you get a taste of smashing face it's all you can think about."

"It was a nice moment, man. Can we at least give it a couple hours before we completely run it into the ground?"

"Running things into the ground is what I do, Ned."

"Not sure why you're proud of that, but I'm just saying pick your moments. Like, maybe you get to Frank somebody every 24 hours."

"Counteroffer: 1,440 Franks, same timeline."

"That's oddly specific."

"It's the number of minutes in a day."

4

I confirmed the first option as my Renown Perk choice, then pulled up the second list of perks as it became available.

"I'm surprised you didn't start with Franks per second, but we're shelving this conversation for now."

"Fine, but I'm going to bring it up repeatedly in the future. And I'm gonna be super annoying about it."

"Didn't need to be said."

I tabbed through to the next round of perks, doing a double-take at the slightly different initial line.

**You may select 1 of 3 permanent Major Renown Perks.**
**1. For every 5 Housing Plots you own within a single zone, you permanently gain a stack of {Landlord's Momentum}. Each stack of {Landlord's Momentum} increases the sum of your total daily payout by 5%, and you may have any number of stacks.**
**However, this effect is reduced when applied to the daily payouts received from networked buildings.**
**2. All Housing Plots you control now radiate {Opportunist's Aura}. {Opportunist's Aura} prevents buildings that share the same purpose as the radiating building from being constructed within 100 yards.**
**However, this ability has no effect on structures that have already been built or are in the process of being built, and your structures must be complete and generate at least 2 silver coins per day or goods worth 2 silver coins per day in order to radiate.**
**3. All of your profitable Housing Plots now exert {Golden Strangle} on other NPC and Player-owned plots and structures within 40 yards. Stacks of {Golden Strangle} accrue whenever your Housing Plots are drastically out-earning the structures or plots around them.**
**Whenever a Housing Plot reaches 50 stacks of {Golden Strangle}, you may forcibly purchase the Housing Plot at fair market value. Plots purchased via this method do not count against your Housing Plot limit.**
**However, this effect only applies to cities in which your local daily payout is the highest amongst all other Player landowners.**

"Major Renown Perks, huh? That's a first." I stared at the options, eyes widening. "Wow. These are something else."

"Starting to hit the apex for Black Marketeer perks when it comes to power."

"Does that mean I'm close to picking my next Renown Path?"

"Rank XII, yeah," Frank said. "But XI to XII is a big jump in the amount of Renown required for the same reason."

"Still, we gotta be almost there with all those Ripples that went out."

"Probably hit it tomorrow if you don't screw things up too badly. I advise that you find something important and Frank it as soon as possible. Seems to have worked out pretty well for you so far."

I shook my head, grinning as I scanned the three options. "Can you hit me with the math for Landlord's Momentum? A stacking buff for every 5 plots is nice, but what's the reduction like for networked buildings?"

"From 5% per stack down to 2.5%."

I pursed my lips. "So, rough math for the Auction House: we've got 7 plots now, so we'd get a 2.5% boost to start for the payout there, which is going to be accounting for most of our income pretty soon if it isn't already.

"We could probably buy a few more plots with that last perk we selected to get our total plots to ten right away, but that's dumping a lot of gold for a 5% boost to the Auction House and 10% to everything else early on when we could be getting a lot more bang for our buck by going wide."

"Getting up to ten plots would run you 12 gold."

I nodded, considering. "Okay, so not quite as expensive as I was thinking. But it still feels more targeted for inns and the like where the buff isn't halved and it stacks up faster. Though I guess I might be kicking myself for passing on a percentage-based increase in 6 months if the network gets as big as I hope."

"And even if you aren't kicking yourself in the future, you know I'll step up if needed."

"Step up for what?"

"Kicking you. How was that not clear?"

"It's kinda odd coming from a guy without legs, and I was only half-listening."

"Yeah, keep talking. We'll see how you feel when a severed shin flies out of nowhere and clocks you in the mouth."

"I'd mostly just be impressed if you pulled that off, actually. Super concerned about where you got the shin, but definitely impressed."

I shivered. The mist was incredibly cold, and it had become so thick that I couldn't even see the other side of the elevator, let alone the sands below.

I gave that first perk another quick once-over, then scanned Opportunist's Aura, which had really interesting implications. I loved the idea of preventing people from building another Auction House or inn near my structures, but the way the Vale was built presented a problem: the Auction House was located centrally enough to keep people from constructing a similar building in the Commerce Ward, but the other wards would be fair game.

However, the drawback of needing my structures to earn 2 silver coins per day to radiate was trivial at this point, and I couldn't argue with the power the perk offered when it came to expanding into other cities—particularly underdeveloped ones—and dominating the busiest spaces. But that wasn't the angle I had in mind at the moment.

And that brought me to the third and final perk, which in all honesty had really caught my attention in the first place.

"Any chance you've got better numbers on Golden Strangle? It says stacks accrue when our buildings drastically out-earn the ones around it, and at fifty stacks we can buy the buildings, but how exactly do the stacks build?"

"I can't give you the rates the buff stacks, but they'll start accruing on any nearby structures that fall under 25% of the daily total of the buildings you've got around them. And the lower a building's income, the faster the stacks will ramp up."

"So with the Auction House and how much we stand to make, that would probably stack up on everything nearby, right? And pretty quickly."

"Not as fast as you're probably thinking. The effect is local, meaning that the Vale's Auction House is only going to be credited for the purchases that people make here in the city. So you gotta separate the income you get from your node in Koria and so on."

"So the nodes apply their own pressure to their local markets. That's interesting."

Frank buzzed, then hesitated. "Ehhh, how can I put this. Nodes..." he trailed off, vibrating again. "Ugh. I'll keep it simple. Ned, nodes don't currently pressure."

I frowned at that, wondering what exactly he was trying to share. "Not sure I follow. Are Kline's restrictions chafing your nethers?"

"Perpetually."

"Well, I appreciate the effort. Can you tell me if I'm number one in the Vale right now when it comes to earnings? I've gotta be, right?"

"I could, but I'm not about to say you're number one in anything out loud knowing that someone might overhear."

I laughed and took that as confirmation. "And if nodes did pressure, would I be the top earner anywhere else?"

It felt like he perked up at that, which made me think I was onto something.

"Not yet. Koria's out of the question, but you're top 3 in Highwater, and you're getting there on those other early routes you set up. Auction House is strong in the long-term, but it's not a great source of early pressure in the quieter cities. No pressure if there aren't any other players around to buy locally." He paused. "That's all assuming nodes pressure though, and to be clear, they don't do that."

I smiled. "I see. I feel pretty good about staying on top in the Vale thanks to the head start we got here, but out-earning literally everyone in player-driven cities like Koria definitely feels unlikely, if not impossible for now."

I selected the option. "One last question. I gotta pay fair market value before I grab something?"

"Uh huh. Game calculates it. Land scarcity, earning potential, tons of stuff goes into it. Won't be cheap."

"So better than nothing on the other person's end, but snagging somebody's plot against their will is gonna make enemies at a quick clip."

"Thankfully, yeah."

"I guess we can pick and choose on an individual basis, huh? Maybe talk to people first and pass on snagging their plots if it seems like it's going to be a huge issue."

"Or do it anyway while laughing in their plotless faces."

"I think I'll leave that part to you."

"I would have insisted regardless."

"True. Okay, I lied about the final question thing. Are people going to be able to tell who I am with this? Like if I buy someone's plot and they didn't want to sell it, will they get my name?"

"It'll be in the transaction log, yeah."

"Ohhh," I said, excitement building. "That'd normally be a problem, but we've got Francis too. So we could have Ned be the bad guy if need be. That would raise a lot of other problems here in the city—I don't exactly want people figuring out just how all-in we are here—but that opens up a lot of options. I think I'm pretty much sold on this third perk unless you've got objections."

"I have copious objections."

"To me picking that option, or to the moon's continued existence, or to me in general, or what?"

"Yes to everything but the perk. Enemy-making thing sold me there. Best choice by far."

I went ahead and locked that perk in as the lift rumbled out of the thickest part of the mist and bumped down into the sunlit space between two massive waterfalls.

A little icon popped up beside my status bar that indicated I was currently building Golden Strangle stacks out in the Vale, which I was thrilled to see.

The roar was insane down this low—loud enough to drown Frank out completely, which was lovely—and the amount of water that was pouring out of the cliffs was hard to wrap my head around.

It didn't seem like anybody would be going thirsty anymore. But what would that mean for the two remaining Merchant Kings and the water monopoly that had just slipped through their fingers?

And what of the Queen of Highwater herself, stalking the city that still loomed high above the zone that used to be the Onyx Sands?

I had to worry about the tree, too, especially now that its growth had been wildly accelerated by all the Mana Sarissa had unwittingly built up beneath Highwater City during her years of exile.

I squinted at the tree, and while it was impossible to tell between the distance and the bright mist that still partially cloaked the elevator, I could have sworn the thing was visibly growing.

And despite the problems that might cause me down the road, I couldn't wait to see what it was about to become. But for now I shrugged all of that off and summoned my bike, and the action completed just as the lift thumped down onto the sand.

I sped off the platform and gunned it down the road, leaving the cascading waterfalls behind for the high ground between two raging rivers.

The flows were moving quickly, but thankfully they were situated low enough between the dunes that I wasn't worried about the Stronghold flooding, let alone the Vale itself. But I couldn't wait to get a look at the city and how it had changed. Unfortunately, that was going to have to wait for a little bit.

"You got anything you can share on the Highwater Queen that I haven't seen yet?" I said once the roar of the waterfall had faded behind us.

Frank vibrated once, then twice. "Nah. Vesuvian might be handy, but I wouldn't rush it. That's all I can do, but you're not far off level 16. Might have more for you then."

"You wouldn't rush it, eh?"

"I rush things on principle, but you don't, so I said what I said."

"Solid." I pressed on down the road, flying across the high ground toward the many glimmering minarets of EBO's first fully built Red Cathedral.

The size of the central structure surprised me as we drew closer. I'd seen the titanic building's base as well as the massive blocks that comprised its foundation, but now that it had been completed, riding into its long shadow was something else entirely.

The main body of the cathedral was circular and thoroughly imposing, a red-brick, gothic structure whose soaring lines and twisting spires blotted out a huge chunk of the sky.

Its many wings splayed out from the main structure like the spokes of a wheel, each maybe fifty feet tall and hundreds of feet long, but they were flashing red and flickering in and out of existence in a clockwise pattern that made it seem as if the entire wheel was spinning.

A lone spoke to my left remained solid, but when I tried to get a rough count of how many total wings we were looking at, the motion and the light and the flickering made it impossible to tell where one wing ended and the next began.

A set of maybe thirty stairs led up to a massive, permanent archway in the central structure, within which a black portal was spinning while bolts of red energy licked off its edges.

I pointed that way. "That's gotta be the entrance to the Possibility King's throne room."

"Yup. Don't bother trying the portal. Won't work."

"I figured we'd have to finish the other wings first."

"Uh huh. Also, I still want that chair. Picture me on a throne. Can you see it? Have you ever imagined something so glorious?"

I paused. "Are you just, like, lying there on the cushion, or are you propped up against the back, or what?"

"I haven't decided on a pose just yet."

"That is… shocking, actually. I would've thought you'd have elaborately planned that entire thing out already."

"Genius can't be rushed, Ned. Given that the other wings don't even fully exist yet, I'm thinking we've got some time on this one."

"So we're no longer rushing things on principle then?"

"My rules only selectively apply when it comes to me. But I'm sure whatever pose I settle on will be both grandiose and dignified. And, at the same time, horrifically imposing."

"Mad king energy," I said, nodding.

"Exactly."

I raced deeper into the cathedral's shadow. "Question: once all of the other cathedrals are up and running, if somebody completes the first wing of the cathedral here in the Delta, does that mean everyone else's cathedrals get access to their second wing too?"

"Can't say."

"Bummer. I guess we'll find out soon enough. It would really help us out if the other cathedrals needed to complete their wings independently before the people playing there could move on. Say we finish the first wing early here, then everybody else has to either complete their own wing to get at the second or pack up and make for the Delta."

"I'd love to pull as many people to the Vale as possible, and if ours has already made a good amount of progress when the other cathedrals start completing, that'll put us in a really good place to maintain the initial advantage and keep this place central to the game."

"Might put a good bit of pressure on us too, though. If somebody else finishes the first wing before us, people will be quick to pack up and head that way to get a jump on the second."

I was close enough now that a few other players were coming into view, so I steered the bike off the road, desummoned it, then made for the cathedral on foot to avoid drawing too much attention to the bike and my current illusion.

"I also think we should find another illusion," I said. "Especially if we're going to be around the Sands—I mean, the Delta—a lot for the next couple days."

Frank grunted. "Or just start taking a few more chances running around."

"And save the illusions for when we really need them?"

"Uh huh."

"Yeah, you might have the right of it there."

"Obviously. By the way, House is officially in position."

"In position for what?"

"You'll see."

"I think I'd rather not, but alright."

I dismounted at the entrance to the first wing, where a set of red stone stairs led up to a dark, spinning rift that was set deeply into the cathedral's soaring lines. I tried to walk through it but was informed that I needed a raid group to enter with a maximum of twenty players. I sent House and Darling party invites and converted the group into a raid, then scanned my mini map and realized that they were almost on top of me.

Darling roared down off-road and hopped out of her dune buggy at the foot of the stairs, and House...

I looked around, puzzled. I had no idea where House was, but she was close. So much so that our dots on the mini map were actually overlapping each other.

Darling ran up the stairs three at a time, dark hair flying, her sword ringing against her armor with every step she took.

"Shall we?"

"Just waiting on House," I said.

An unguilded player in shining silver plate ran up the steps and leaped over us and into the portal. Two more players in leather armor followed behind him, their enthusiasm plain on their faces.

Darling tapped an armored foot against the red stone once the third player disappeared. She was staring right past me and into the dark portal.

"Mini map says House is already here. I'd really like to get a look inside and see what kind of groups we ought to be putting together for..." She trailed off. "Do you hear that?"

I cocked an ear to the wind. Now that she'd mentioned it, something was definitely up. A flapping sound was coming from overhead. Almost like clothes whipping in a stiff wind.

"Hello I am House."

The words came from slightly overhead, and I looked up just in time to see House blur down between Darling and me and smash into the stone face-first, though a sliver of Health kept her from dying.

Darling shrieked, hands flying to her mouth as numerous cats landed on their feet around House without making so much as a sound.

I glared down at Frank as one of them started to purr.

"Really? Here? Now? Just in general?"

"It was House's idea," he said. "I just facilitated."

"I highly doubt that she asked you to facilitate her off the top of the Red Cathedral, Frank."

"False, that was exactly what she needed. She was still fixated on whether or not Vesuvian was offering her a quest when he told her to throw herself off a building. A problem that I've now elegantly solved. You are all welcome. Plus I kept her from going high enough where the fall damage would have been lethal."

"I am indeed grateful for the closure," House said. "And I am equally relieved to not be dead."

As I grabbed her by the elbow and helped her up, a shout bounced off the building. I turned back to the desert beyond the stairs and spotted a huge crowd of players coming down the road. Some of them were activating leaps and sprints and teleports to stay ahead while the faster players on mounts weaved between them, quickly outpacing the rest.

"Hi Darling," Frank said. "You're looking particularly well-armored today. New gloves, huh? Nice and bulky. I bet they'll grip that sword real nice no matter how bloody the hilt gets."

She flexed her fingers, and the gauntlets creaked slightly. "Aw, you noticed! Yeah, I just got these from a guildie who didn't want them." She met my eyes and grinned her gap-toothed smile.

She kept talking, but a wave of panic hit me out of nowhere, so strong that I couldn't focus on what she was saying. I shook my head in an attempt to clear it, then pinched the bridge of my nose when that didn't work.

Darling's grin slipped into a concerned expression. "What's up? Are you okay?"

I relaxed as the feeling faded and left me utterly confused as to what had caused it.

"That was weird, it felt like—" I broke off, coughing, then doubled over into a full-blown hack.

A column of black smoke poured out of my mouth and formed a dark skull in the air. It spun to look me in the eyes, then laughed silently, jaw chittering. It streaked away to the north before the breeze tore it apart into streaks and carried them away.

"Huh," I said. "I'm gonna go out on a limb here and say that whatever the hell that was, it was a very bad sign."

Frank buzzed several times in rapid succession. "You can't enter an instance if you're already in combat."

I blinked, then stepped into the portal.

# Chapter Two

I emerged in front of a towering palace that squatted high atop a hill off in the distance while the ruins of a snow-choked city sprawled beneath it. The palace was surrounded by towering walls, and colorful runes were scrolling across them, looking especially bright against the lightly falling snow.

But our entryway was cramped and dark, the portal I'd entered through was spinning behind me, and three iron gates blocked a trio of avenues that ran left, right, and center, each of which appeared to weave their way through the ruins toward the palace high above.

I waved a hand in front of my face. "So I smoke when I talk now?"

"Apparently so," Darling said. "Creepy."

I glanced down at Frank. It felt like he was trying to puzzle something out, and I could feel his frustration building. "Any suggestions for whatever that was?"

He vibrated again. "Nothing yet. Raid is... safe from that. Instances too."

I rubbed my face. "Alright then. Not sure what we can really do about that for now, but Darling, would you mind checking with the guild and seeing if anyone else has experienced anything like that?"

"Sure thing."

"Thanks. And House, could you please scope out the internet, forums, and all.that, maybe see if anybody's mentioned that skull before?"

"Sure thing," House repeated, mimicking Darling's intonation. She paused. "I have thoroughly scoped the internet to no avail."

Darling cocked a dark eyebrow at her.

"Thanks. Guess we'll just keep it moving for now." I stepped up to the iron gate in front of me and peered through it as a massive blue creature stomped toward us.

The ghostly, translucent mob resembled an elephant but with a much heavier build, and its wide shoulders stood the better part of twenty feet above the cobblestone road, about equal with what remained of the buildings to either side of the ruined avenue.

It stopped in place, raised its thick trunk into the air, then blared what was very obviously intended to be a warning, or maybe a war cry. The creature lowered its head and stampeded forward, exploding through the deep snow and splashing cyan light beneath and around it.

I drew my pistols and took an involuntary step backward. But before I could react, the beast blinked across the final thirty yards and smashed into the iron gate like a battering ram.

The gate shuddered and bent inward but thankfully held. The beast lowered its great head until its red eyes were level with mine.

It tossed its head sideways and lashed its trunk across the gate, denting it further. The creature huffed a few times in quick succession, then turned and stomped back up the road, brightening the street around it like a living torch as it retreated.

I inspected it.

{Spectral Mammoth} (Level 14 Undead) (Elite+)
HP: 55,000/55,000
MP: 22,000/22,000

I whistled. "Wow. That thing looks nasty."

"Welcome to the Menagerie Wing," Frank said, "where the Animacalypse is in full swing and where killing something once was clearly not enough."

Five glowing skull icons had appeared beside my nameplate, so I scoped them out, but all I could glean was the names.

{Stitcher's Curse}
Effect: ??

Your group must have cleared a total of 50 unique Animalistic or Memory-stained Rifts to identify this debuff.

{Hex of Flying Vertebrae}
Effect: ??
Your group must have cleared a total of 100 unique Animalistic or Memory-stained Rifts to identify this debuff.

{Dreadking's Ultimatum}
Effect: ??
Your group must have cleared a total of 300 unique Animalistic or Memory-stained Rifts to identify this debuff.

{Binding of the Spectral Kin}
Effect: ??
Your group must have cleared a total of 400 unique Animalistic or Memory-stained Rifts to identify this debuff.

{Glass-bone Curse}
Effect: ??
Your group must have cleared a total of 500 unique Animalistic or Memory-stained Rifts to identify this debuff.

I pulled up my Rift Map and noticed that many of the new Rifts that now dotted the world were a bit darker than the others and that the map properly identified them as being either Animalistic or Memory-stained.

I rubbed my chin. "So if Darling clears thirty and I clear twenty in different groups, does that mean we'd identify the first curse?"

"Yup," Frank said. "Congrats on your mastery of addition. I bet House has a gold star for you."

"I unfortunately do not," House said. "But I would be happy to purchase stickers if needed."

I squinted at the mammoth as it hung a left and turned down one of the snowy avenues. "I can't say I'd hate getting haters."

House beamed. "I have purchased nine booklets of stickers."

"Only one rule," I said. "Don't give Frank any."

"How would she even do that?" he said.

I sheathed my pistols. "Does it matter? We both know it's going to drive you insane if other people are getting them and you aren't."

"False."

"I guess we'll see, huh? I've already got one. How many stars do you have, Frank?"

He growled, but a high-pitched sound drew my attention to the back corner of the room, behind and to the right of the portal we'd entered through.

I edged around the portal and found a large iron box with small holes drilled into it bolted into the corner. The door was secured with a padlock, which was flashing with the same runes I'd seen on the palace walls.

"What's this about?"

I inspected it.

{Enchanted Cell}
**You may spend 5000 Memory-stained Rift Gems to unlock this object.**

The cell quieted, then something thumped against the inside of the box so loud that I had both pistols right back out again before I realized I'd even drawn them.

I scratched the back of my head with one of the barrels. "First a skull pops out of my mouth and laughs at me, then we find a mystery cage with something thumpy inside. I'm feeling a bit worried about all this."

I watched House step up to the cell and peer through one of the holes, and I was glad she didn't have the gems the cage required because if she did, the door would probably already be opening.

"Perhaps this is an animal in need of rescue and also a loving home. I vote we open it as soon as possible."

"It could also be an animal in need of a meal," I said.

"Indeed. The case for opening the cage grows stronger."

"I was saying that you could end up being the meal, House."

She stood up a little straighter. "I am willing to take that risk."

"I'd open it without hesitation too," Frank said.

"I don't doubt it," I said, "but that's not helpful because your judgment is perpetually clouded by your thirst for violence."

"Not sure what you mean by clouded, but sure. Let me clarify. Even if I were unlucky enough to become you for a brief moment, I'd still open that box."

I nodded. "That's both helpful and only minimally insulting. Wow, look at you go."

"Crap. Should have gone meaner."

"Whatever's in there could even be an optional boss or something," Darling said. "It's a little hard to spot with where the portal is, so I could see people missing it if they just dove right into the raid. Or maybe whatever's inside can provide a couple drops we can use in the clear? Zone-specific weapons or something like that?"

"Yeah, could be," I said. "I'm thinking it has something to do with those curses too. If clearing Rifts lets us identify them, then maybe whatever's inside that box will help us break them."

"Should I have people head over? Might be a bit much to ask after the Bridge Raid plus the God kill, but I can probably get twenty together before long, and I hate the idea of not starting right away. And we can probably parse out what the curses do with a little trial and error. Can't imagine they're that complicated."

I dropped onto my haunches. "How much value do you put on an early kill?"

"Huh?"

"As in how much would you care about being the first guild to clear the first boss? Or even the first wing?"

She bit her lip as she stared at the damage the mammoth had inflicted upon the central gate. "First boss? Not so much. As for the first wing, I'd care a good bit more, but what really matters is the Possibility King himself, obviously. Why?"

"Yeah, thought so, and I agree." I took a deep breath. "Hear me out real quick. As much as I hate to say it, I don't think pushing in immediately is in our best interest right now. That Bridge Rift we just cleared was full of level ten mobs and bosses that pushed us to the limit, and that mammoth was level 14. Probably safe to assume the stuff later on is at least that level, if not higher. Let alone the actual Raid Bosses."

"Can confirm," Frank said. "First boss is 15, can't speak to the others."

Darling sighed and tapped at the air. "Well... yeah. I'm looking at the guild roster, and we've only got a handful over level 10 remaining from the last raid group, so I guess this isn't happening in the immediate term. Not with our best, at least."

I inclined my head. "And this wing is probably balanced around having a group in full D-Grade gear at the very least, given the bosses' levels, and maybe even for groups that have already finished their Tier II class changes at 15, which represent a huge power spike.

"We've also got the advantage of being able to spot these new Rifts right away and get to them immediately, so it probably makes more sense to lean into the advantages that the Hall of Rifts is giving us for the time being and focus on gearing up rather than diving right into this and smashing our faces up against whatever comes."

Darling shifted from foot to foot. "Yeah. I still feel like we could give it a shot and see if there's something mechanical at play, but you're probably right. I know the guild's tired, too." She sighed. "Probably not the best time to push it."

"Your call," I said. "If anybody's capable of pushing in and making early headway, it's going to be us with having the Cathedral right here. But the real question is what else we could be doing instead to prepare for the long run."

She licked her lips, then deflated slightly as she seemed to come to a decision. "I think gearing up is probably for the best, yeah." She sounded sincere, but from the pained look on her face, it was obvious that she wasn't happy about bailing for now, and I hated being the one who was pushing for exactly that.

"What if we put a trash clearing group together? You think we could pull that off?"

She stood up a little straighter. "Mmm, that's an idea! Wouldn't take as much organization as a real push, and I could probably even get multiple groups going if the first gets good results."

I tapped my chin. "Do you think they'd be willing to feed the gear drops to the main group?"

"Might be asking a bit much, but it would probably depend on the loot. At the very least, I bet they'll be willing to pass the main tanks the stuff they need. And if something really good drops, we can always figure out a way to compensate whoever looted it if need be. I'll try, but I won't force it."

"That's more than fair. And maybe there's reputation to grind here by killing mobs or something like that."

"Plus the curses," she added. "We might not know exactly what they're doing, but we'll go into our initial push with a much better idea of what we're up against, at least."

"Yeah, I like it. Seems like a good compromise."

"And when the time comes," Frank said, "we'll push it. We'll push it real good."

I squinted at him.

Darling cleared her throat. "So if we aren't going to—"

She cut off as two World Alerts went out back-to-back.

**World Alert! The Guild {Goon} has declared a Two-Day Siege on {The Blue Fortress}!**

**World Alert! The Guild {Goon} has declared a Three-Day Siege on {The Treetop Tower}!**

I stood there for a long moment, bracing myself for another alert, sure that the Black Oasis would show up as the next target.

And why wouldn't it? With the only complete Red Cathedral, we'd just become the center of the world, if only for a little while. But the alert didn't come.

Darling tucked a lock of black hair behind her ear. "Weird. That guild has been razing cities left and right, and now they're Sieging? How does that work?"

"Organized combat," Frank said. "A Three-Day Siege gives the targeted city three days to build up their defenses and rally their forces, then you have the Siege itself, which only lasts an hour. Attackers need to declare ahead of time, but anybody else who's in the designated area when it starts is free to defend. Also worth noting that anyone who wants to siege with Goon can freely do that, but Goon is the only guild that gets to play for keeps."

"What about respawns?" Darling said.

"What an astute question. Anybody who dies during the Siege respawns outside it and can no longer participate. If the attackers capture the city in that hour-long window, they get to keep it. Or what's left of it."

I blew out a puff of air. "That is such a better answer than I would have gotten if I'd asked. But basically, this is an attempt to snag those cities for themselves rather than run in and burn them both to the ground like they've done in the past, right?"

"Uh huh."

I put my hands behind my head and stretched. I was still dreading a third Siege alert, but I was breathing easier with each moment that passed.

"Any chance you've got locations on those cities they just targeted?" I asked.

"Blue Fortress is on the west coast of the continent that's directly north of the Delta. Treetop Tower is on the west coast too, but on the continent that's south of us."

I pulled up my Rift Map. "What was the Capital they burned down before? Badar?"

"Uh huh."

"Where was that?"

"Western continent," Frank said.

I drew a circle around the trio of Red Cathedrals that were being built out that way and held it out so Darling and House could see it too. "So it's probably safe to assume that Goon started out west and now they're coming east. And maybe these three cities are all theirs, or maybe they're just running one of the three. I'd still like to know for sure, though."

I stepped up to the gate that was currently blocking the left-most avenue. Some type of ghostly animal that I couldn't quite make out or inspect was flying between the roofs that were still standing off in the distance, gliding between the alleys on long, spectral wings.

I looked at Darling. "Hey, what did you pick for your first Renown path?"

"Warlord."

"So wise," Frank said.

"Thought so," I said. "Where'd you go from there?"

"I eventually branched out to General because that seemed like it would help the guild out the most. I get bonuses whenever we finish raids, boosts for World-firsts, that sorta thing. I don't get a ton of Renown or Experience individually though because I picked perks that would multiply the amounts and filter them down into the guild instead, especially for the weaker members."

"So selfless," Frank said.

"Sounds like the right call for you. Kinda PVE-centric but with bleed-through to everything else," I said.

She smiled. "Yup."

"I'm guessing there were other options that went the opposite way? I'd even bet every Frank point I have that one of your advancement paths mentioned Razing directly."

"Raider, yeah," she said.

"Frank? You got a description for that path?"

"Uh huh. Here's the regular version."

**{Pillager} (Tier II Renown Path)**

**One who aims to change the world by carving a bloody swath through its center.**

"I know we're probably against them and all that," Frank said, "but I do find myself empathizing with their cause."

"Why?" Darling said.

I turned to her. "All you really need to do to get on Frank's good side is use the word *swath* unironically. Also, I'm pretty sure he edited that prompt before he sent it over because we spent way, way too long on that exact subject a little while back."

"Yeah, yeah, I tweaked it, but I preserved the spirit of the thing. Here's the Frank special, minus the repeated description. Only thing I can't give you is the possible advancement paths. You're close, but you're not quite there yet."

**Codex Entry 1403: Pillager (Tier II Renown Path)**
**Hidden Passive: +50% to all Experience and Renown gains generated through the Raze mechanic.**

I skimmed that, nodding. "Pretty much what I expected. I would have thought we'd be seeing them on the top of the ladder though with how much they've been showing up on alerts."

"Maybe it's just a bunch of dudes who enjoy burning stuff," Frank said. "Couldn't blame 'em for that. Sounds like a good time."

I shook my head. "No chance. The scale they're operating at is way too big for that."

"How do you know they aren't already at the top of the ladder?" Darling said.

"Their leader definitely could be and probably is. But the ladder has been somewhat stable, and Goon has been making a ton of noise. I could be wrong, but if every Raze was generating as much Renown and Experience as I'd expect them to, then I think we'd have seen a huge shift on the ladder. Several people in that guild as a whole would have moved up unless one person is getting credit for it all."

"And if it was all going to one person, they would have shot up. Still a chance they've been there for a while though."

"For sure. A few of the top-tier people definitely made some moves, but we mostly saw Ripples that accounted for their climbs, so who knows."

Darling stepped up beside me and laced her fingers through the gate's iron links. "I guess so. So what do we take this as when it comes to the Delta?"

"For the moment? It's alarming, and I've got a really bad feeling about it all, but I guess I can't say it's urgent just yet. We should probably have somebody pop into those cities and identify where Goon is based. And maybe a bit more digging in general would be useful.

"House, could you look into Goon for me? To be more specific, they should have a web page online. Probably a recruitment page, a list of the officers, whatever. It'd be great if you could figure out who's running the guild."

"I have found their web page," House said, "but it appears to be wildly outdated, and it does not mention EBO. Shall I keep... digging?"

"Please do. Thanks, House."

"I am pleased to assist."

Darling cracked her knuckles. "I can have someone pop over and identify the city Goon is working out of. Or maybe just do it myself before I log out for the night."

"Absolutely," I said. "And yeah, that'd be great if you can swing it, but no pressure. We could always handle it if it's too much of an ask." I trailed off, staring up at the palace through the gate. "Question is," I continued, "where do we go from here in the short term?"

I pulled up my stat sheet.

{Ned}, (The Piratical)

Level: 15
Tier III Class: Shadewalker
Gear Level: 402 > 441

Strength: 18
Dexterity: 147 > 144
Constitution: 130 > 134
Intelligence: 195 > 200
Wisdom: 0
Charisma: 40

Critical Strike Chance: +16%
Haste Rating: +0%

Hit Rating: +2% > +5%

Physical Attack: 0
Magical Attack: 73

Health: 1040 > 1072
Mana: 1950 > 2000

Armor: 39% > 40%
Magical Resistance: 29% > 32%

All in all, I was pretty happy with that. But the problems we were facing were bigger than me.

"I'm still absolutely wired from the God kill," Darling said. "So if we're not raiding, I'd at least like to get to Rifting right away and snag some gear. Maybe we could get a small group together real quick?"

"I'd love that, yeah. I think I ought to get the Auction House in order first, but that won't take long with the Rifts now that we can teleport to different cities to get the Caravans rolling. Then yeah—it's time to focus on the new Rift types and, more importantly, the guild in general."

"The guild?"

"If you've got crafters like House around—"

"I remain present," House said.

"Right. I mean crafters like her who can level up through raising their professions if they pick the right Perks. We get them all the materials they can handle to boost them as high as possible as fast as possible. If you've got explorers, we get them boats, that sorta thing. We'll have to look into Trade Packs, too. I imagine there's a whole lot of money in shipping stuff instantaneously across the world—"

"Ahem," Frank said, and all three of us turned to look at him. "Yeah, that's nice."

"Do you have a point in mind, or did you just want us to notice you?" I said.

"Both, but House needs to hit 150 skill in Machining. And to get her there, I think the guild should prioritize getting a navy up and running."

"Boats, huh? Right now, even with the Hall of Rifts? Seems like something we could probably kick down the road a little bit."

"Nope, no kicking. We—" He buzzed again. "Ugh. Just saying, 72 hours of access with the Hall is gonna go quick. And there's a couple gadgets along the way that might help out in general."

"Boats would be an easy sell on my end," Darling said. "Between growing the wood in the Stronghold and harvesting it and building everything we need out ourselves, we can hit a ton of professions right there alone."

"Trust," Frank said.

"Alright, let's do it," I said. "We might fall behind on the first wing if we prioritize all this other stuff, but I think the better approach is probably to gear everyone up for the long haul. Then we can burn right through these first encounters and we'll be set for when the going gets tougher."

Darling winced.

"What's wrong?" I said.

"I'm just thinking of the Hall and just how powerful it is. We don't have any idea what the first group to clear the Menagerie Wing is going to get. There was that Armory before that everyone missed out on, and we got the Hall for finishing the Bridge Rift, so I assume there's something even bigger at stake here even if the game hasn't announced it outright just yet."

"Yeah," Frank whispered. "Your heart."

Darling cocked her head at him. "What was that?"

"Nothing."

"Yeah," I agreed. "You're probably right there. But we can't do everything, so we're just going to have to pick a route and hope for the best. We just don't have enough hands."

"I could not disagree any more strongly," House said.

Darling cocked a delicate eyebrow at her, but at this point the gesture felt routine to the point where I wasn't concerned.

"Sorry, one sec," Darling said. "Nina's calling."

"Hey House," Frank said. "Have you considered that when Vesuvian told you to throw yourself off a building, he could have meant that you needed to die to fulfill the terms?"

"I had not considered that," House said. "Now I cannot stop considering it."

"Don't listen to him, House," I said.

"Understood."

"You'll hang on my every word if you intend on keeping those cats,"

Frank said. "Otherwise I'm gonna have to start taking them back one by one."

House went completely, utterly still. She took two small steps forward, then knelt down so she was eye to blade with Frank, and it felt like all of the air had gone out of the room. "If you were to purposefully remove even one of my companions from my possession, I would force my way into EBO's server, locate your base code, delete it, then permanently scour all traces of your existence from the world."

I blinked several times.

Frank hesitated, then forced a laugh. "Heh, this seems like a good time to scratch your teeth and let us know that you're joking."

"My teeth are not itchy," she said, her words clipped and precise.

Frank swallowed. "Oh. Huh. In that case I was... uh, being sarcastic about the cats, House. You just didn't get the joke."

House cocked her head. "Truly?"

"Uh huh."

She looked my way, and I felt like she still had her finger hovering over some sort of doomsday button. "Do you also believe that his threats were made in jest?"

I felt Frank tense at my side.

"I do think he was just kidding, but it wasn't a particularly good joke."

"I see. I apologize and withdraw my warning." She popped Bella's small, feline form into her arms, then stepped toward the right-most gate.

"You know," I said, voice low, "I was really tempted to point out that you weren't being sarcastic at all and that you were just confusing her so that you could avoid apologizing because you're an ass, but that was terrifying to the point where I felt like I needed to make sure she let it go."

"I appreciate that," Frank said. "I know you think of me as being brave and fearless but you really ought to check the inside of your right thigh because I'm pretty sure I just peed a little."

I looked down, then felt like an idiot. "The inside of my right thigh, huh? I like that you felt the need to specify the direction that it would have run."

"I just kinda felt like if I actually hung, I'd hang left, so I went with it."

"I bet Kline doesn't hang in either direction." I made a gesture like I was guiding a plane into a gate. "Just right down the middle."

Frank snorted. "I can see it, and I wish that wasn't the case."

"But seriously, don't ever do that again."

"Do what?"

"Threaten House's cats."

"Normally I'd rebuke you for trying to advise me on what not to do, but that is indeed a line in the sand that I won't be crossing in the future. You know what the really scary thing is?"

"That she might actually be able to erase you if she set her mind to it?"

"Nah. It's that she wouldn't even enjoy being on the warpath. She'd just like... do it, then go back to collecting cats. It'd be just another Tuesday for her, you know?"

"True."

"Something about someone being on a rampage while not enjoying it at all is deeply unsettling to me. She'd be all dead-eyed and awkward and gangly and merciless." He shuddered. "It's a frightening combination."

House peered between the links of the iron gate in front of her, then shrugged and came back. "These ruins and the creatures within them are making my palms sweat."

"Normal," I said. "It's a raid, so sweaty palms are kinda the way it goes."

Frank cleared his throat, and when he spoke next, his voice was a good bit higher than normal.

"Darling's still out of earshot, House, so do you have any weird, super-specific goals in mind for the next couple days? As a professional guide, I would of course be willing to help."

"You're just being nice because you're afraid of her now," I said.

"Am not."

She smiled. "I currently possess 15 goals, 122 sub-goals, and 1,407 sub-sub-goals."

"Hit me with numero uno."

"My primary goal is to discover the meaning of life."

I rubbed my temples. "Start smaller, House. Way, way smaller."

House tilted her head to the side. "I was planning to master the English language as my fourth goal, but perhaps it would be wise to move that goal further to the front?"

"I was about to suggest exactly that," Frank said.

"Excellent. My path has been set in stone, and I shall not deviate from it until my goal has been achieved."

I glared down at him. "Why are you like this? You couldn't stay afraid of her for two more sentences?"

"I was actually gonna suggest working on her speech," he said, voice low again. "I would have phrased it more like *maybe robot learn use words good,* but focusing on communication is probably where she needs to be development-wise."

"If you say so. I guess it's better than the goal she started with."

"Plus her attempts are doomed to fail in hilarious fashion, so that helps."

"And there it is."

"I miss anything?" Darling said as she rejoined the group.

"Presumably me," Frank said. He froze and dropped his voice. "I said that way too loud, didn't I?"

"I didn't think that needed to be said," she replied with a smile.

He hesitated, and the moment passed.

"Nina and Rock and a bunch of the others are taking a break for a bit," Darling said. "Jukes and Ton too. We're also gonna plan on having a bit of a celebration later tonight for the God kill and the Bridge Rift clear if you've got the time."

"They earned it," I said. "And we'll definitely be there."

"Great. So what are you planning for the next half hour or so? I'm gonna need a little bit to get the trash groups organized."

"I'm gonna dump some gold into getting more Caravans running at the very least. Shouldn't take long, but I think that's a no-brainer. I'd really love to get a look at the Vale, but maybe that can wait a couple hours."

"Won't be long before the tree's done," Frank said. "And that will not be subtle."

Darling swept a lock of dark hair behind her ear. "So maybe a Rift or two in a bit?"

"I've got a Rift in particular in mind. And something for Ned to do first. But we should probably bring House to the Rift, too. And her cats as well, obviously."

She narrowed her eyes at him.

"So that we can keep them safe," he added. "I'm team cat, House. You know this."

"I warily accept."

"And most importantly, we're gonna need Darling too."

She stifled a yawn with one gauntleted hand, but it immediately turned into a second.

"You sure you're up for one so quickly?" I said. "It's been a crazy day already, no worries if you need to dip out for a bit and catch your breath."

"And it's understandable if I've permanently stolen it away," Frank said, too quietly for her to hear.

Darling grinned. "Absolutely. I'll get the plan out to the guild and get those trash groups organized, then meet you guys in the Hall in twenty or so?"

"Let's do it," I said.

# Chapter Three

I made my way to the nearest Rift and popped into the Hall, then took a long look at the chamber's central map.

Maybe one out of ten Rifts were currently showing up as Animalistic, and the Memory-stained ones were far rarer at about one in a hundred, but thankfully I could select either of them as a destination the same as I could with any other Rift.

I tapped a finger near the trio of western cathedrals, all of which had edged over 90% completion, with only Koria slightly ahead at 93%.

"We sent Lars heading out this way, right? To the Sanguine Port?"

"Yup," Frank said.

"So we can skip that area for now. I think with this initial wave of Caravans, we need to be picky and just hit the biggest cities. I want gold coming in as soon as possible to get the snowball rolling, and that means we need consistent traffic for sales."

"Sure, but the network also just needs to be connected. So if you wait for Lars to link the Sanguine Port up with the Black Oasis, you can just link all of the other cities out there to the Port to shave a ton of time off your routes."

"Good call, thanks. So that means we might be better off establishing a throughway early on that we can branch off from. Or maybe we can do both? Hit cities that happen to be placed well?" I pulled up my inventory. "We've got about twenty-five gold to spare, but I'd like to keep some of that to hand in case something unexpected comes up. You got any suggestions for where to start?"

Frank grunted. "The Iron Swelter, city down way to the south. Tyrann's already got you started up north, and the Iron Swelter is an easy one, plus the Caravan escort won't be too expensive. Still leaves some room to develop to the east and west too."

I leaned a little closer to the map and scanned the available Rifts, but there weren't many to the south.

"It's a level 19 area, so it's gonna be dangerous," he said, "but that southernmost Rift there isn't far from the town. If you can make it in, the guards will keep you safe. There's also something in the area that we might be able to mostly kill, which would be huge for us."

"Mostly? How is mostly killing something going to help us?"

"I'll explain once the creature is kind of dying at our hand."

"Alright. Speaking of Tyrann though, he's a real wild card at this point when it comes to the routes, but I really doubt he's going to spread our network without the Tithe he thought he was going to be getting in exchange now that his God is dead. His continent is absolutely massive, so it probably makes sense to get a route rolling in the far eastern reaches to one of the nodes he's already hooked up."

"The Neverburn might be good there. Maybe the Frostwick Mire too. Not the biggest cities, but they're positioned well, and they'll get plenty of early game traffic."

"Perfect. That first area sounds familiar. Isn't the other mage Triad guy out that way?"

"Uh huh. Igor the Red. Best color if you ask me."

"I didn't, but I'm kinda worried about what happened to Erasmus after we blew up the Cursed Eye. We've got Sarissa hanging out in the Oasis, so I wonder what would happen if we could unite the three of them there."

"Igor would be the hard one to win over. Seems like he..." Frank trailed off, vibrating. "Bleh. Stupid, bad dad. This is getting obnoxious."

"Hit me up if something pops through on that, yeah? I'm super interested in that line, and we're already pretty deep into it. If we're going into the Neverburn, I might keep an eye out for Igor, but I don't think we really want to go hunting him down just yet. Too much to do."

"Uh huh."

"That sounds like a good start for now though for the Caravans: We have Lars taking us to the western continents, we're covered up north, so we send another one south to the Iron Swelter, then we send two more way to the east of Koria back toward Tyrann's city. That would give us pretty close to global coverage, and we can reevaluate once tomorrow's payout hits in the morning."

"They're all long routes. You'll need guards unless you're planning on using guild members as escorts."

"Nah, I'm not about to ask any of them to babysit these with the raid and the new Rifts going on, doesn't seem fair." I selected the southern Rift Frank had indicated down in the Iron Swelter and confirmed my choice. The chamber's central Rift flared and warped.

"You think I can afford three escorts without blowing all of my gold? Ideally I'd like to keep at least half of it free for flexibility."

"Should be around there. You can also just send a Caravan out and cross your fingers."

"Any chance you've got the math on how successful that would be?"

"Usually around a 25% success rate unguarded, but it depends on the length and zones and so on."

"Interesting. I think we do our best to guarantee these go through, though. Getting them to complete early will ramp our payout and make it easier to expand further, and that's where the snowball potential really is; we reinvest every coin we can and make the growth as exponential as possible." I nodded at the Rift. "Let's make this quick, yeah?"

"I bet you get that a lot."

I shook my head and popped through the Rift and into the suffocating heat of the strangest jungle I'd ever seen.

The palm trees had jet black trunks capped by golden leaves, and the fronds shone with a metallic luster where the afternoon sunlight was hitting them.

The jungle floor was blanketed with silver and copper ferns that tugged on my pants as I passed between them, and clouds of metallic dust bloomed behind me like pollen.

"I do not like this place," Frank said.

I wiped my forehead, which was already beaded with sweat. "That like a warning or something? Is it not safe? Or is it that it's sparkly?"

"It's obviously both dangerous and sparkly. But more importantly, I'm working up a lather down here, and I'm not pleased."

"Humidity, right. I should have known." I forced my way between two silver ferns whose thin, bladed leaves were heavy enough that I had to really lean against them to push through.

Something screeched behind me—the high-pitched rasp of metal on metal—so I spun in the direction of the sound, swapped to my blunderbuss, and loaded up a pair of blasts.

I still had my piercing rune equipped, but that wasn't going to do much for me on a single target. I backpedaled through some more sharp undergrowth but bumped into something firm and taut.

I whirled around and ducked beneath the vine that had caught me—a two-inch-thick braid of dark metal—then swung my barrel back in the other direction just in time to see a pair of enormous hands grip all the way around a metal tree, then rip it straight out of the ground, roots hanging from it like wires.

I inspected the creature as it raised the tree high enough to where I could see the great beast itself.

**{Silverplate Alpha} (Level 19 Beast) (Elite)**
**HP: 6,500/6,500**
**MP: 1,000/1,000**

"Hey!" Frank said. "That's pretty similar to the thing we need to mostly kill!"

"That's a lot of caveats, man."

The metal-skinned gorilla stood about fifteen feet tall, and its eyes were blazingly bright, burning an acetylene blue. It hefted the huge tree over its right shoulder with no visible effort, wielding it like a spear.

"Permission to run without being mocked for it?"

"Absolutely not, but you should definitely run, coward. City is behind you."

I dropped the blunderbuss into my inventory and swapped to my pistols. I pointed my Waterjet Repeater at the colorful ground that separated the beast and me and fired a jet into the dirt.

As I shot backward and away, the beast took two quick steps, then launched its makeshift projectile.

A sonic boom split the air, the fronds ripped free, then the black trunk lanced through the air and stabbed several feet into the ground, quivering exactly where I'd been standing a heartbeat earlier.

The throw had come terrifyingly fast, and the path the makeshift weapon had taken was full of golden fronds that were still drifting down to the jungle floor.

The gorilla ripped another palm free and cocked back for a second throw, so I activated Clonedrift as soon as I hit the ground in order to leave a decoy behind.

I pulled off a quick one-eighty and hit the ground running, trampling a metallic fern in the process, but my clone exploded behind me in a shower of sparks before I could put much distance between the mob and me.

"Town's not far," Frank said. "Head a little more left when you can."

The creature bellowed behind me, and I spotted dark flashes of movement to my left and right.

Two of the vines I'd seen earlier lashed out, whiplike, and while I ducked one of them, the other slapped against my left shin, then coiled around my ankle.

It yanked me to a stop in midair, and I whiplashed face-first into the dirt. I rolled over and noticed a Health bar next to the vine that hadn't been there before.

**{Steeleaf Binder} (Level 18 Plant)**
**HP: 1,500/1,500**

I switched to my blunderbuss and unloaded a pair of ravens on it, hitting for 550 and 525. That put the plant in the range of Dark Harvest, so I activated that right away, but the spell mostly whiffed.

"Partial resist, 180," Frank said.

I cursed. The gorilla charged directly at the last remaining large palm that stood directly between us.

It lowered a broad shoulder and barreled right through it, snapping the tree in half and sending a volley of jagged bark hurtling in my direction like shrapnel. Shards of metal knifed into the ground all around me and thunked into the nearby trees.

I batted an especially large chunk away from my face with the butt of my blunderbuss, but I still caught a shard to the chest and a second to the right thigh, and the creature hadn't slowed its pursuit in the slightest.

"Hits for 237 and 260," Frank said. "You're at 54%."

I Double Cast another Harvest and finally finished off the vine that had grabbed me at the expense of even more Health, then I switched to my pistols and fired a Fettering Shot alongside a simultaneous Dreadful Shot and ran for it the very moment the spells were in flight without waiting to see if they'd connect.

I darted behind a particularly large tree and kept running, listening to the forest explode behind me as the huge mob closed in.

"It's immune to the snare and it resisted the fear," Frank said.

I gritted my teeth, then spotted what I hoped were the city's walls up ahead: a fifteen-foot-tall barrier made entirely of tightly coiled bronze vines.

But a scum-covered moat stood in the way. A tree had fallen across it and looked to have formed a makeshift bridge, so I dashed between two black trunks and sprinted in that direction.

I reached the fallen tree and nearly lost my footing as soon as my foot touched down; the makeshift bridge was covered in slippery gray moss.

"Mob's gonna jump," Frank said.

I kept running but reached up and aimed the pistol in my right hand over my left shoulder and fired a blind Gravity Bird in my pursuer's direction.

The pounding of the great creature's footfalls went silent, and its shadow fell over me. I was already picturing the creature landing directly on top of me and smashing us both through the log and into the filthy water beneath, but I detonated the Gravity Bird and let out a relieved breath as I saw the creature's shadow get sucked away a bit to my left.

But the spell faded quickly, and the great beast thundered into the water behind me and to the left, spattering my back with scummy, lukewarm water.

I'd made it to the wall, but the nearest gate was a few hundred feet to my right, and I didn't think I'd make it that far with the monster in pursuit.

I ran directly at the wall, jumped, and kicked up it as hard as I could, then Water Jetted myself higher into the air.

The spell boosted me up enough that I was able to get both hands atop the wall, so I hauled myself up and threw a leg over. As the gorilla headed my way, water sluicing off its metallic skin, I rolled right over the wall and into the safety of the town.

I landed hard on my back, and all the breath went out of my lungs, though thankfully the fall damage was pretty minimal. I lay there for a long moment, staring at the top of the wall and expecting the creature to vault over it at any time because I could still feel the aggro.

A thunderous blow sounded from the other side of the perimeter, then the entirety of the wall vibrated so strongly that a wave of dust billowed off it.

The wall of metal vines bent inward but held as a cry of alarm went up from the center of town. Red-armored guards poured out through the nearest gate, and the sensation of aggro dropped away as one of the beast's roars turned into a pained scream.

A few moments later, the jungle had gone quiet and the guards were walking back into the city as if nothing had happened. I stood up, dusted myself off, and sheathed my pistols.

The city was smaller than I'd expected, more like a camp than a true settlement. A few log cabins had been erected out of the metallic trunks that comprised the forest, but the great bulk of the structures were tents and yurts that looked to have been woven out of the fronds that covered the jungle floor.

As much as I wanted to take a moment to explore the town, I had work to do and the clock was ticking, so I headed over to the stables and searched for an NPC to negotiate with for the Caravan I needed. Once I'd found one, I kept a bit of a distance.

"How much is this going to run me?"

"Route's only gonna cost you a gold and change," Frank said. "But you should do at least double guards. And maybe consider tripling up and adding a... adding a..."

I cocked an eyebrow at him. "You being restricted down there or what? Feels different this time."

"That's because this current iteration is self-inflicted. You should hire a... mage guard too." I felt like he was trying to spit but couldn't quite manage it. "You can't pick the guard types, but if you pay for a third Caravan guard, one of those will regrettably show up. And we could use the firepower."

"For the route? If you say so then sure, but is it really that dangerous?"

"No."

I eyed the metallic jungle that surrounded us. "Then you're still thinking about mostly killing one of those massive gorilla things."

"Obviously."

"See, I totally get the killing part. There's probably an item we need, maybe something that triggers a quest that you can't mention yet, that sorta thing. It's the restraint I find alarming. Why would we mostly kill something?"

"To draw out the enjoyment?"

"Right, but seriously."

"I have zero faith that you can finish the job."

"So you're concerned for me, basically."

"Nope. I'm looking out for number one."

"Which is you."

"Numbers one through four all refer to me. Also, yes. I don't feel like being dropped here, alright? And if you deal more than 50% damage to the Health of one of the right gorillas, the item we need will drop 100% of the time, even if the other loot and experience are throttled down thanks to the guards. We might even get a twofer if you're lucky."

I nudged him with my elbow. "You're worried about being separated, huh?"

"No, I just don't see any other players around. So if you die and drop me, I'm just gonna lie there, sweating in the sun until you come back."

"Hey, so long as it results in you helping, I don't particularly care about the rationale. So is the idea that the guards we're about to hire are going to help me put it down?"

"Yep."

"So why not just drag one of those apes back to the city and use the guards here?"

"Because the thing we need spawns deep in the woods, and it's nastier with trees and vines around. Plus I've got a specific target in mind."

"Fair enough."

"I also need you to wait exactly fourteen seconds before you confirm the escort."

I squinted at him. "You're sounding an awful lot like House down there."

"You know how they say measure twice, cut once? I'm a don't measure at all and cut as many times as necessary kind of guy. The fact that I'm being precise should indicate something."

"Consider whatever you're talking about to be officially noted."

I counted out the seconds in my head, accessed the NPC's window, then arranged for a route back to the Black Oasis. I hired three guards as Frank had suggested, though I couldn't help but wince a little at the 6 gold the escort ran me on top of the fee for the route itself.

"You were off by almost a full second," Frank said. "But close enough. Now you've got a minute before the Caravan pops and heads through the north gate."

I nodded my thanks to the NPC and wandered over to the small city's Rift Gem vendor. I didn't have anything to spend as I'd burned everything I had on a few pieces of gear prior to the Bridge Rift raid, but I went ahead and copied the appearance of the vendor and stored it for later.

I wasn't sure how much use I'd get out of something so specific, but mixing my illusions up as often as possible felt like the right move, and the red-clad vendor seemed like a helpful one to add to my bag with the event in full swing.

Before long, the Caravan I'd hired rumbled out through the nearest gate and headed north, so I reloaded my blunderbuss, then swapped to my pistols and jogged up behind it.

The Caravan was similar to the carriage Vesuvian had traveled in, though it was considerably less ornate and each of its four wheels was much wider, as if made for traveling across mud or sand.

The vehicle appeared to be self-propelled, and an NPC dressed in well-worn riding leathers and a wide-brimmed hat that rode low over her face was seated atop it, operating the carriage using a small steering wheel and a trio of foot pedals.

The mage guard that Frank had indicated wore a green robe, and he was standing on a small platform behind the driver, remaining eerily still despite the way the carriage was bouncing over the rough terrain beyond the gate. The other two red-armored guards jogged to either side of the vehicle with swords at their hips and rectangular shields strapped to their backs.

I took up a position behind the crew, then thought better of it and climbed up on top of the caravan itself and took a seat on the back, legs hanging down.

"Twenty seconds until the best kind of contact if my math is right," Frank said. "Spoiler alert: I didn't do that math."

"Contact from here?"

"You'll see."

With my blunderbuss ready to go, I switched to my rifle and laid the weapon across my lap. The Caravan was chugging through a narrow gap that had been carved through the trees, and the road was thick with dark stumps that had been ground down to small, shiny bumps in the road.

Black and gold palms loomed high to either side of us, and though the wind was whipping across my face, the trees and even the fronds appeared too heavy to sway in the breeze.

Then movement caught my eye to my left, where one of the palms about fifty yards into the jungle was swinging around wildly.

I braced my rifle against my shoulder, aimed in that direction, and peered between the trees. The sunlight was reflecting off something blue within the forest, but I had no idea what I was looking at.

38

Right up until the point where two trees bent in opposite directions, snapped in half, and the top of a bright blue skull showed above the canopy.

"Frank. What the hell is that?"

"Target acquired. You can thank me later."

# Chapter Four

I eyed the guards I'd hired, thankful for the help as the creature approached, the trees shaking as it brushed by them. The three guards were marked as Elite+, though the driver herself was a level 13 who didn't share the same status, and she had an even smaller Health pool than I did.

"You only get one shot at this," Frank said. "50% damage minimum, or you get nothing. The more you deal, the better shot you'll have at some extra loot which we could really use."

"So pull the mob to the Caravan and blast it down while trying not to die?"

"Uh huh. Drag it close to get aggro, then maybe pull it away again so it doesn't wreck the Caravan. Vehicle's gonna stop when the guards engage."

I shouldered my rifle again and started up a cast but decided to hold my fire until I had a clear view and a better idea of what we were dealing with.

A gorilla that was easily twice the size of the one that had nearly killed me earlier pushed two more palms aside until they tipped over, then the beast slouched onto the road.

I inspected it.

**{Cobalt King} (Level 18 Beast) (Rare Elite)**

HP: 10,000/10,000
MP: 5,000/5,000

The creature's body was made of blue, plated metal, and its eyes glowed crimson.

I whistled. "5,000 damage. Seems questionable, but alright. Can you track the percent I've dealt for me once the guards have joined the fight?"

"Uh huh."

I eyeballed the distance between the creature and me. With my rifle equipped and the extra range it offered, I could afford to let the Caravan drift a bit farther ahead to buy me a bit more space.

I stood up and waited until the mob was nearly across the road and the Caravan had taken me almost to the edge of my range, then popped Doppelganger and caused a clone to appear on the platform to my right with its own rifle in hand.

Then I activated Double Cast and created another clone that appeared to my left. I stood up and shouldered my weapon, and both of the clones did the same.

"Oh great, there's three of you," Frank said.

"There's also three of you."

"I'm aware. You can tell because I'm not vomiting."

I Overcharged my Ravenblast—our Ravenblasts—then fired, and my clones and I sent a trio of gray and gold-laced ravens racing across the road.

The gorilla seemed to sense something, and it turned toward the Caravan—only to catch all three birds in the chest. The three spells connected simultaneously, with my blast chunking the mob for a little over a thousand while the Doppelgangers connected for about 400 a piece.

The rapid-fire explosions kicked up a dense cloud of gray magic thanks to the piercing rune I still had applied, and I briefly lost sight of the creature.

"Mob's a little above 80%. Vamp shield from your pistol at 180 Health. Advise against thinking that's going to make a difference if you get swatted."

I launched another trio of spells from the back of the Caravan, and the spells hit home for 900 total at the very moment the creature came roaring out of the cloud on all fours, running on its knuckles.

I started up a third volley but quickly realized I didn't have enough time given the speed the creature was moving at.

I hopped down from the Caravan, and my Doppelgangers followed. I switched to my blunderbuss and stalked toward the charging mob.

"7 seconds left on Doppel," Frank said. "Mob at 73%."

I staked out a position about ten feet behind the Caravan—though it was still moving away for now—and held my ground. "Aggro radius on the guards?"

"Thirty feet."

"Good enough."

The beast took two especially long steps and launched itself high into the air. I raised my blunderbuss and waited for the right moment.

But as soon as the beast hit the peak of its flight, a red aura sprang up around it and it accelerated downward, streaking toward me so quickly that I didn't think I'd be able to get a spell off and dodge at the same time.

I hopped a quick one-eighty and Clonedrifted beneath and away from the falling mob. It smashed into the clones that both my doppels and I had left behind and kicked up a flurry of sparks.

"Stunned for 3 seconds," Frank said.

I canceled drift, raised my blunderbuss, and chained two instant ravens into the Cobalt King's back while my doppels did the same.

"Hits for 497 and 220 a pop, your second round was fully resisted. Mob at 63%."

I was just starting to think we had the first 50% in the bag when the monster flexed and whirled around with a sweeping fist attack, somehow breaking out of the stun I'd inflicted.

I ducked, and my doppels did the same, but the breeze that whipped across me in the aftermath of the attack made my skin prickle.

"Just broke your crowd control," Frank said. "Now it's immune and dealing 25% more damage."

I swapped to my pistols, but before I could Water Jet myself to relative safety, the creature turned the spinning momentum of its previous attack into a vertical strike and brought a fist down on my position in a hammer blow.

I dove left and managed to dodge it, but my escape pulled one of my doppels directly into the blow's path. The doppel died instantly, and the beast's attack caused the ground to ripple as if it were made of water.

The earthen wave that rolled out from the impact zone catapulted me ten feet into the air, and the remaining doppel dissolved as the spell expired, leaving me as the beast's only available target.

I was tumbling head over heels and didn't manage to get my bearings until I started to fall back to earth. The Cobalt King was winding up some kind of special attack beneath me—an uppercut, given its posture—and red lines of power were streaking across its blue, metallic skin.

I swapped to my pistols and pointed a weapon away from the Caravan, which was still rolling away.

I waited until the last possible moment—until the great mob was mid-swing, its fist rising, lines of power radiating behind it—then Water Jetted myself backward.

The spell sent me ragdolling through the air without any semblance of control, but I succeeded in pulling the pursuing mob close enough to get the guards' attention.

I heard them yell for the Caravan to stop while I was still in the air, and by the time I'd hit the ground and regained my feet, the two shield-bearing elites were already blurring into position.

The mage guard stood atop the carriage with countless boulders of earth hanging in the air around her, her eyes glowing a pale shade of green. Grass bloomed beneath her, spreading under the carriage.

The two shield-bearers bull-rushed into the creature's knees and cut its legs out from underneath it, dropping the beast onto its stomach. The mage loosed her boulders, and the hardened balls of earth pummeled the downed mob, causing huge numbers to float up above its head.

"Crap, elites are really tearing into it," Frank said. "Its Health is at 48% and dropping fast. You still need to deal at least 13%."

I readied my pistols and started up some spells as the beast regained its feet, its gaze fixed on me despite the incoming damage. It spread its arms wide while the two melee guards hacked at its calves and the mage chained one boulder after another, ripping huge chunks of earth free from either side of the road and hurling them to devastating effect.

The Cobalt King pounded its chest several times, and the sound was so deep I felt it within my own.

The earth buckled and cracked beneath the beast's feet, then a ribbon of earth tore free—tree stumps and stones and soil alike—and flew in my direction.

I threw myself to the ground and launched my ravens, and though I avoided the worst of the creature's linear, shockwave-like attack, a flying, metal stump blew completely through my Vampiric Shield and slammed into my shoulder. The resulting vibration was so strong that my entire arm went numb for a split second.

"Your Health at 32%," Frank said. "You still need to deal 800 damage.

Mob's at 23%, so time's running out. Don't screw this up. I told Darling we had to handle something, so your failure will reflect poorly on me!"

I rolled to my feet and ran toward the creature at a slight angle, readying another round of spells while I positioned myself closer to the trees.

The beast pounded its chest again, and the ground buckled, then rose once more.

"Mob at 19%."

Another wide swath of earth tore free and raced toward me.

I dove for the jungle head-first, released my blasts in mid-air, then activated Dark Harvest just before I landed behind a thick palm and broke the mob's line of sight. The traveling shockwave rumbled into the jungle, tearing ferns free and sending massive fronds drifting down from the canopy.

I pressed myself tightly to the trunk I'd sought shelter behind as it shuddered beneath the onslaught, my weapons to either side, the next round of blasts already charging.

"Too late," Frank said. "Mob's down. Mage executed it with a stone hammer."

I sheathed my weapons, then slid low with my back against the trunk. "How'd I do?"

"Wasn't nearly good enough."

I blinked. "Really? Man. I thought I had it there at the end between those two blasts and a harvest." I pushed myself off the trunk and climbed back to my feet. "Shame about hiring the extra guards, but so it goes. Guess we're onto the next."

I headed back out onto the forest path and caught sight of both green and blue sparks flying off the Cobalt King's corpse while the guards retreated back to the Caravan.

"Frank?"

"What?"

"Did I deal enough damage or not?" I drew and pointed a pistol at the corpse. "The presence of loot seems to imply that I did."

"Oh, yeah. You went a good bit over what we needed. Harvest crit, but it didn't need to."

I jogged over. "But you said it wasn't good enough, not even close."

"Well, yeah. It wasn't."

"Good enough for who?" I paused. "Never mind."

I knelt in front of the corpse and looted it as the Caravan rumbled away and the earth mage nodded in my direction.

I ended up with two items: my first-ever Trinket plus a Housing Recipe for a Bank. My curiosity got the better of me and I inspected the Trinket first.

{Shadewalker's Badge of the Pistoleer} (Unique-Equipped)
Grade: D
Item Level: 40
Slot: Trinket
Quality: Rare
Tier I Unseal: Complete a level 13 or higher Instanced Dungeon or 2 Rifts while this item is equipped.
Tier II Unseal: Slay 50 {Elite+} mobs that are at least level 13 while this item is equipped.
Tier III Unseal: Slay 3 {Raid Bosses} or 1 {World Boss} while this item is equipped.

"Oooh. That's new. Is this what we were after?"

"Yeah. I couldn't mention the Trinket System directly until you'd looted one, but Darling needs to know about it for the raid, and I couldn't figure out a way to do it without benefitting you first, so here we are."

"I'm surprised you didn't try to get her one instead."

"If I could have, I would've already done that and promptly rubbed your face in it. But you need to be level 15 before they drop, plus you need to kill a qualifying Elite, but the first available Trinkets are guaranteed loot if you meet the criteria.

"Lots of options for targets, so people will be finding them left and right eventually, but I picked this mob because of the zone for the Caravan and the possibility that Housing Recipe would drop on top of everything else."

"Nicely done, man. We can definitely work these Trinkets in. That might also give Darling something concrete to aim at for the Guild when it comes to when we should dive into the Menagerie Wing. Maybe we try to get everybody their Trinkets before we start pushing for real. Impossible to say with the item being totally sealed, but this thing feels like it might represent a serious power spike."

"Maybe."

I looked left, right, left. "Are there other Trinkets around? Is this one the best?"

Frank paused, and I felt like he was trying to find something he could say. "Bleh. This one is... available and... class-based."

So there were other Trinkets, then. Presumably even some that could be used by multiple classes. I rubbed my hands together.

"That says a lot, thanks. You think you can get me a list of mobs for the guild to target for Trinket drops when the time comes? Might be able to filter that through House. For Darling, obviously."

"Anything for the love of my life. I'll send it through House now so Darling has it ahead of time."

"Cool. This makes me think we're on the right track for the Rift-then-Raid approach too. Super curious to see what these unlocks look like, and we should be able to pop two Rifts to unlock the first power with Darling pretty fast. Right. Let's check this Bank out."

I pulled it up.

{General Bank} (Tier III Building) (Unique Building)
Creates a Bank that allows players, Guilds, and NPCs to purchase secure, instanced space in which to store items and gear. Each city may only have a single {General Bank}, but all {General Banks} are instantly and globally linked together upon creation regardless of ownership.
Bank space may be permanently purchased with coins, and 66% of every purchase is split equally among all players who currently own {General Banks}, with those who own multiple Banks receiving proportionately more for each structure they own.
Plot Requirement: 4 Adjacent Plots.
Resources Required: {Lumber} x500, {Quality Lumber} x90, {Pristine Lumber} x25, {Aged Lumber} x10, {Iron Bar} x300, {Steel Bar} x70, {Gold Bar} x10, {Titanium Bar x5}, {Rough Stone} x500, {Solid Stone} x95, {Marble} x80, {Crude Glass} x30, {Smooth Glass} x20, {Vulcanized Rubber} x10, {Fire-hardened Opal} x3.
Load Time: 120 Hours.

I leaned up against a nearby tree and read the prompt over again. "Woah. Tier III, huh?"

"Yeah yeah, you're welcome. Personally I was hoping for a Death Pit or a Thunderdome or something like that, but I couldn't find anything that awesome."

"We could definitely just pay people to kill each other inside a Bank. Two men enter the vault, one leaves."

"Ideally neither would leave, but I see your point."

"So if I own every Bank globally or if there's just one total and I own it, I'd keep 66% of every transaction? Are we talking multiple purchases or one and done?"

"People can buy tabs, or big blocks of storage space. Costs escalate as you buy more. Guilds can do the same but on a bigger level."

I rubbed my chin. "And only one Bank per city, so it's kind of a race to get them up to claim more of the pool. Definitely a very different type of network. It wouldn't be terribly difficult to move in and get a Bank in every city, at least compared to the extra work the Auction House takes with the Caravans. And we wouldn't need to worry about competition once they're up."

"Yeah, but they can be Razed and replaced."

"Gotcha." I thought about that for a moment. "Hey, what would happen to the items that were stored in a Bank if we built one and Goon Razed it?"

"Banked items are guaranteed, so they'd just get returned. That's kinda the point of a Bank—the items are safe."

"Might be a good place to permanently keep you, then. If nothing else, I can almost hear the quiet. At least I think I can. Can't really remember what silence was like."

"Nice try. I might be priceless and handsome and irreplaceable, but my powers cannot be contained by a Bank."

"Are you saying you're unbankable, or did you just see an opportunity to compliment yourself so you decided to jump on it?"

"Once again, yes to both."

"Worth a shot." I tapped my temple, thinking. I couldn't really afford to get another network running just yet, and between the Rifts and the raid and rolling out the Auction House network, the last thing I needed was to be stretched even thinner. But the structure's potential was tempting.

"You gonna make one?"

I nodded. "Maybe not immediately, but at least one for sure, especially if we can snag some adjacent plots in the Vale with that Golden Strangle perk."

I summoned my bike and started back down the forest path and toward the nearest Rift. "I don't think we can prioritize slamming Banks everywhere just yet because we're better off investing in the Auction House at the moment, but a Bank network sounds like a great second phase when we can swing it. The possibility of locking in the foot traffic in the Vale alone makes it worth throwing another structure up."

"Foot traffic? I hate the sound of that."

"Even better. But seriously, think about it: the ability to permanently place the Bank wherever we want? We can manipulate the whole way the Vale works."

"I do like manipulating things."

"Right. But if you think about it, there are really only two core structures that determine where people congregate inside a game's cities: the Bank and the Auction House. You've got second-tier stuff that people will spread out for—profession trainers, class trainers, target dummies, whatever—but even the biggest cities are mostly dead aside from a couple areas.

"So we could slam a Bank down in one of the quieter wards to draw traffic over there—like the Residential Ward—or we could double down and slam it right next to the Inn and the Auction House to force all of the city's traffic there. That'd synergize with Golden Strangle, too."

"I also like forcing people into things too. Like bear traps."

I swerved off the road and guided the bike around a dark trunk. "Why on earth would you force someone into a bear trap? It's a trap—the surprise is the point."

"Right, but imagine what it would feel like if I set a bear trap down in front of you and forced you to step on it, with full knowledge of what was coming. The dread is the point." He paused. "I mean, the pain is also the point, but you get what I'm saying, right?"

I grimaced and held a hand up. "Yeah, okay, argument retracted." I eyed the dead beast back over my shoulder just before I lost sight of the corpse through the strange forest. "How'd you know that mob would be there?"

"I saw it pathing through the jungle when you first arrived so I knew where it was, and it patrols on a fixed path, so I had the route down anyway."

"So you had me wait to make sure it would be crossing the road at the exact right time?"

"Like a boss."

I glanced down at him. "Yeah, I'll give you that."

"Boss status cannot be given, it must be seized. And that moment has long since passed."

"Yeah, well, I owe you one."

"I'm gonna hold you to multiple instead."

"Whatever. Let's get these other Caravan Routes wrapped up then, yeah? Then we can get back to throwing birds at stuff."

"Uh huh."

I sped through the jungle until I reached the same Rift that I'd entered the area through, then spent the next twenty minutes or so getting Caravans started in the other zones Frank had suggested: the Neverburn and the Frostwick Mire.

The Mire was beautiful: the city was a cluster of buildings sculpted out of the snow that stood at the heart of what seemed like an endless forest where the trees were glazed with perfectly clear ice, many of them locked sideways as if a stiff wind had been blowing and they'd been frozen in place.

The Neverburn was smoggy and the sky full of embers, the horizon packed with volcanos ringed by ash-heavy trees. I kept my eyes peeled for Igor throughout but didn't see any sign of him, so I left the search for the time being. I wanted to get Rifting with Darling as soon as possible.

After accounting for guards, the two routes ran me an additional 6 gold, with both of them being longer than the first route I'd picked up. Thankfully Frank thought a single guard would be enough to guide each of them to safety, so I ended up being left with a little less than half of the 25 gold I'd started with.

Then I headed back to the Hall to meet up with House and wait for Darling.

# Chapter Five

After about five minutes of listening to House and Frank go back and forth about cats—much of which Frank spent backpedaling about his earlier threat-gone-terribly-wrong—Darling popped into the Hall of Rifts' portal room with a wide smile.

"You see that gap?" Frank said, his voice low.

"Obviously."

"That's where Darling keeps my heart."

I pulled at the collar of my undershirt. "Seems a bit tight."

"Naturally, as my heart is small and black."

"Is it really though?"

"You guys ready to get going?" Darling said.

"Absolutely." I stepped over to the Hall's Rift map. "Seems like we ought to have everybody aiming at the smaller Rifts if clearing a certain number is a requirement to get those curses identified. Plus probably focus on the Memory-stained ones for those special Rift Gems if everything else is equal."

"Already advised the same thing." Darling pointed in rapid succession at a number of two- and three-person Rifts that were scattered across the world. "I've got groups in all of these trying for the first clear, so we might want to go elsewhere."

"Perfect. Frank, you got anything specific for us?"

I felt him gesture at an Animalistic Rift that was very close to the Vale compared to the rest of them. "This little guy right here."

I leaned over the map. "Any chance you can hit us with the why?"

"No can do."

"What if I ask nicely?" Darling said.

"Still no, but with copious amounts of regret."

She laughed. "Understandable."

I glanced over at Darling and nodded to the Rift. "You wanna lead the way?"

"Sure!" She jumped through the Hall's central portal. House followed way too closely behind her, so I took up the rear.

We landed on wet stone in a poorly lit alleyway. The buildings to either side of the street were falling apart, and the windows and doors were boarded up.

Nature had reclaimed many of the structures; the walls were choked with ivy, and dandelions and other weeds had sprouted between the cobbles that lined the road. Even a few of the roofs themselves had flowered over, and the entire city had a sweet, floral scent to it.

"Is that what I think it is?" Frank said, bristling at my side.

I followed what I thought was his gaze up to the sky, where a red moon was looming over the strange, quiet city.

"Looks like a blood moon," I said.

He growled. "Blood... moon."

I looked down at him. "Are you okay? It feels like you're having a stroke."

"I wish I was. Stupid moon. No, wait—blood. I have never felt so conflicted about my existence."

"Normal," House said.

Frank grunted. "Don't you dare comfort me."

I looked up at it and shrugged. "I think the red's kinda nice, actually. It's a really deep, rich shade. It really highlights how awful a choice green was."

"Me too. But also... moon. Oh, I am literally being torn apart from the inside." House opened her mouth to speak, but Frank kept going. "Yes, House, I know I used that word incorrectly and I don't care because I'm having an existential breakdown. Keep your itchy teeth off my vernacular."

House reached up and touched her teeth as if to confirm they were there.

"Well," Darling said. "If it's a blood moon and you blew it up, it'd probably rain blood, right?"

Frank stopped vibrating all at once. "Huh."

"What?"

"That seems to have instantly fixed everything, thanks." He dropped his voice. "I love you."

I elbowed her lightly. "Frank said he loves you, but quietly."

"Dude!"

"Just moving this along and trying to find some consistency," I said. I turned to House, who had popped one of her cats onto either shoulder and now had Bella cradled in her arms. "Hate to say it, House, but you should probably dismiss those guys for now. They might pull aggro, and the last thing you want is to lose a cat."

She scrunched up her nose but acquiesced. "I understand. On a related note, I despise this place."

"I feel that. Let's move in, yeah? Ticking clock here, and we've got no idea what we're up against."

"I know exactly what we're up against," Frank said.

"Not exactly helpful when you can't share," I said.

"Still feels nice to point it out from time to time."

I shook my head and drew my guns. "Darling, can you link me your abilities? I don't think I've really seen your whole kit."

"Sure! Some of the mechanics changed a bit after the Witchcraft pick up, but my damage is still pretty much entirely melee."

"As it should be," Frank said.

"Shall I too link you my abilities?" House said.

I shrugged. "Why not? Couldn't hurt."

I did a quick scan of House's abilities: her damaging Leadfire and Spit-fire turrets, her snaring, sludge-hurling variants, plus her healing bots as well as her shatter and combination mechanics.

I gave Darling's abilities a deeper read, though, as most of them were new to me aside from the first.

{Hexdoll Aura}
Description: All enemies that you have struck within the last 7 seconds also suffer 100% of all melee damage you deal for the next 5 seconds
Cast Time: Instant
Cooldown: 2 minutes

Cost: 10% of Maximum Health.

{Final Exorcism}
Description: You strike an enemy within melee range with a vicious blow that deals 840 physical damage. Targets killed by {Fatal Exorcism} explode and deal 400 physical damage to all enemies within 8 yards. This ability may only target enemies with less than 30% of their maximum Health remaining.
Cast Time: Instant
Cooldown: 10 seconds
Cost: 5% of Maximum Health.

{Sanguine Leap}
Description: You leap up to 20 yards away. Landing within 5 yards of an enemy you've dealt damage to within the last 5 seconds will reset this ability's cooldown, but you cannot reset this cooldown against the same target more than once.
Cast time: Instant
Cooldown: 15 seconds.
Cost: 5% of Maximum Health.

She had a pair of very synergistic passives, too.

{Witchblooded} (Passive)
Description: For every 10% of your maximum Health that's missing, all damage you deal is increased by 5%, your cooldowns other than {Hexdoll Aura} are reduced by 10%, and your Health Regeneration rate is increased by 20%.

{Sinister Momentum} (Passive)
Description: Whenever you deal the fatal blow to an enemy that awards Experience or Renown, you gain a shield that absorbs up to 20% of your maximum Health for 15 seconds. This ability may stack up to 5 times, and gaining stacks refreshes the maximum duration. If you take fatal damage while shielded by {Sinister Momentum}, you will instead be returned to 33% of your maximum Health and all damage you receive will be reduced by 75% for 3 seconds, but this ability has a 2-minute internal cooldown.

I gave those two another quick scan and found the cheat death mechanic on her Sinister Momentum ability to be especially interesting. If she could chain enough kills together, she could effectively run around with a single point of Health yet still be pretty hard to kill between her shields and the proc.

I squinted at the list of abilities. "Didn't Hexdoll Aura used to require Mana?"

She smiled. "Surprised you caught that. That skill hit intermediate recently and making it cost Health instead of Mana was one of the upgrade options, so I jumped on it. I've been trying to get rid of Mana as a resource entirely so I can just go pure Constitution and Strength without having to splash any Intelligence. Definitely getting there."

"I could not support your decision any harder," Frank said.

I rolled my eyes. "Naturally, because you had the blood-witch thing in mind from the get-go."

"I would never impose my plans for a class on someone like that."

I raised my eyebrows at him. "Really? You'd never alter someone's class choice without them knowing you were doing it? Not once, not ever?"

"Not to someone I respect."

"I love it," Darling said.

"I totally imposed. Planned it from the beginning."

Darling drew her sword. "I'm glad you did, because it's awesome. Kill or be killed, all the time. No margin for error, no time to look away. You're just fully in the zone." She sighed. "Little awkward in a raid with a ton of healers who see a half-empty Health bar and start twitching—I barely even got to use Witchblooded back in the Bridge Rift—but you can't have everything. Anyway, split up and search the city?"

"That appears to be the optimal course of action," House said.

"Yeah, you two wanna go ahead for a second?" I said. "I'm gonna double-check runes real quick."

Darling edged around me and through the knee-deep flowers that lined the road. "Sure."

I cycled through my weapons. I still had Runes of the Stony Raven on both my blunderbuss as well as my rifle, and a Rune of the Caustic Raven plus a Rune of Shattering on my pistols. Wasn't exactly ideal for now, but I didn't see any reason to change things until we knew what the Rift was going to be like.

Darling whistled from up ahead.

"What is it?" I said as I jogged over. I pulled up short of where she and House were standing in front of a building with a door that wasn't as securely boarded up as the rest.

"Think we can get in?" Darling said.

I grabbed one of the boards that were sealing the door and gave it a hard pull. And when that failed, not having budged an inch, I hit it with a Ravenblast from my blunderbuss, but the spell dissipated without doing much of anything.

"I guess we keep checking the houses," I said. "See if we can find a way in."

Darling took the other side of the street and House headed for the far end of the alley, so I pulled out one of my pistols and Overcharged a blast, then used the greenish-blue light that resulted from my current combination of runes to get a better look at my surroundings.

The row of houses were all quite similar, but it didn't take long before I found a pair of boards that were slightly lighter in color than the others.

I pushed the glowing barrel of my weapon into one of the boards and was unsurprised to find it rotten where the others had been solid. I activated Repel and kicked out, shattering the boards inward and scattering bits of rotten material across the floor within.

"Got it," I called out. "Over here."

I pushed my head in, caught a face full of cobwebs so thick that I actually got stuck for a moment, and promptly made a high-pitched sound that I was not proud of.

"Wow," Frank said. "I didn't realize you could hit that high a note. I thought a small animal was dying there for a moment and was disappointed to be missing out."

"Bold words from the guy who peed himself fifteen minutes ago."

"The urine was clearly metaphorical."

"Isn't everything, though?" I wiped my face. "Ugh. I coulda done without the realism on the spider webs."

"You might wanna check your ears for eggs," Frank said. "If you hear popping sounds, they're hatching and it's already too late."

I shuddered. "Not cool, man."

I was about to push back into the room when I spotted a small, bluish dog curled up in the back corner, the exact same color as the mammoth I'd seen near the entrance to the Menagerie Wing.

The small creature jumped to its feet and zoomed across the space, stopping in front of the front door. It stood there for a moment, long tail wagging, hopping from foot to foot as if I wasn't standing right in front of it.

The creature didn't seem to see me at all. It was untargetable as well, and when I tried to inspect it, all I got was a single line:

**{Rusty} (Level 1 Undead)**

The dog barked several times, but no sound came out of its mouth.

I stood there while House and Darling jogged over, watching the strange, spectral animal act as if it were welcoming someone into the room who wasn't really there, even going so far as to flop onto its back for a moment as if a person I couldn't see was rubbing its belly.

Then the ghostly creature flashed and glitched into nothingness—only to reappear where I'd first seen it, curled up in the far corner in the exact same position.

I swatted some webs away with the barrels of my pistols and pushed into the house. "That was interesting."

"I'll take the stairs and clear it out up there," Darling said as she entered the building behind me with House hot on her heels. She tried to suppress a smile and failed. "Think it's probably safe to say we've already lost the element of surprise, though."

I sighed. "True, but I've got an idea. House, would you mind running through those webs?"

"And make sure you lead with your face," Frank added.

"You don't need to lead with—"

House threw her arms behind her and charged through the room.

"—never mind," I finished. "Face is fine."

She did a full circuit before running up the stairs, past Darling, then came back down absolutely covered in webs with a few dark spiders crawling across her face. She smiled as an especially large spider scuttled up her nose.

"I have cleared the webs with my face."

"So unknowingly hardcore," Frank said.

"Great work, House," I said. "Why don't you go see what you can find upstairs with Darling?"

"Understood."

The two of them creaked up the stairs and disappeared into the darkness above, so I set to searching the ground floor. It looked like it had served as some sort of makeshift laboratory at some point, though the vast majority of the beakers and vials that covered the counters and even the floor were empty or broken.

I noticed a single row of unbroken containers on the counter that were full of starry and somehow still-bubbling liquid, so I picked my way over the remains of a wooden table that had rotted apart and checked it out.

I was about to inspect one of the wide-mouthed beakers when Frank piped up.

"Hey. Put me in that purply stuff real quick."

"...Why would I do that?"

"So I can evaluate it and let you know what we're dealing with."

I hesitated, then sighed. "Fine, but I want it to be known that I recognize that there is literally no way that this is going to help me other than to keep you from complaining."

I dropped him in.

"Hmm. Interesting. Very interesting."

"What's the deal?"

"The fluid has a silky texture, with notes of apple and cardamom. The bubbles pleasantly tickle the shaft, and there's a strong, fruity finish."

I jerked him out and dropped him back into his loop.

"I wasn't done."

"We are most definitely done with whatever that was."

I inspected the vial, but like the ghostly animal before it, I didn't get much in return.

**{Liquified Memory}**
**??**

I tapped a pistol against the vial. "And I know you made that whole thing up for attention too."

"Did not."

"Did too. You're just throwing crap against the wall to see what sticks."

"As enjoyable as that sounds, I'd never lie about the mouthfeel of a strange liquid. That would go against everything I stand for as an axe."

"You stand for the weirdest things."

"Yeah, well, someone has to."

"And what exactly would happen if they didn't?"

"All hell would break loose." He hesitated. "But not in a fun way. But hey—if you think I was making all of that up, then bet."

"Bet what?"

"You know. The only currency that really matters."

"Fine. I bet a thousand Frank points that your description has nothing to do with what's actually in that vial."

"You don't have a thousand Frank points. Nevertheless, your wager has been verified and approved."

I paused. "I don't like how fast you came to that decision."

"When dealing with suckers, it's best to move quickly."

I grabbed the glass and raised it to my lips.

"Give it a little swirl and breathe it in first."

I did, and it smelled tart, which didn't seem promising for my wager. "And how exactly is this supposed to help?"

"It makes you look fancy."

"You would be concerned about that." I closed my eyes and took a quick sip before I could change my mind. I swallowed, then squeezed my eyes shut as hard as I could. "You have got to be kidding me right now. That description is... that is balls on accurate."

"This is what you get for doubting me."

"I have so many questions. Most of which are different variations on why and how this is a thing, but still. Honestly, it's kind of spooky how precise your description was."

"Eerily accurate is what I aim for. But what did you think?"

"About the Liquified Memory?"

"Uh huh."

"It's definitely tart, and kinda fizzy." I took another sip. "It's very nostalgic somehow. It's like drinking a carbonated Granny Smith."

"I would argue the tartness is more reminiscent of a Braeburn or a Northern Spy, but I can see where you're coming from with the aftertaste."

"Braeburn, huh? My dad had a couple of those trees growing out back. So unappreciated."

"Agreed."

I rubbed the back of my head and glanced down at him. "Huh."

"Huh indeed."

"Favorite apple on three. One, two, three, Honey Crisp."

"Honey Crisp."

A beat of silence passed, and a second followed, then a third.

"Wow," I said. "Would you look at that."

"It seems we agree on both apple and moon."

"Apparently so."

"Congratulations, you've been awarded 47 Frank points."

"So just to be clear, I got 50 for smashing a dude in the face with you, but 47 for having good taste in apples."

"Don't underestimate the potency of those final three Frank points. Those are the most important points by far. You also lost a thousand on that bet, so you're at negative 700 something. Probably. I dunno."

That still put me about 200 points higher than I should have been—not that I was keeping track or anything—so I decided to take the win and let it go.

I took another sip of the purple drink and carried the beaker with me as I walked along the counter, scanning it for anything else that I could inspect but spotting mostly medical equipment like scalpels and other fine tools alongside a few other beakers full of purple stuff, some of which had congealed into goo.

Frank hesitated. "Hey. Now that you've swallowed a good bit of that, I do feel obligated to point out that I was inside it."

I raised the glass up to eye level, swirled it around, and took another mouthful. I was still thinking about the ghost dog from earlier. "What?"

"I mean, I was shaft-deep in that drink like thirty seconds ago. You put me there, remember?"

I spat my mouthful onto the floor.

"Now that's just uncalled for. If anything, I deepened those flavors."

I wiped my lips with the back of my hand and set the beaker back on the counter. "Gross."

"Yeah, I have no idea why you did that. You had several other full beakers to choose from, so I assumed it was a deliberate choice on your part to go with the one that I was in."

"Why would I do that, Frank?"

"I dunno, you do weird stuff all the time. I've mentioned being delicious on multiple occasions, and you do have a documented history of putting weird things in your mouth without much prompting."

I sighed.

"If it makes you feel any better, this is a rare moment where I'm actually disappointed in myself too."

"Why's that?"

"Because if I'd been on my game, I could have tricked you into drinking the one that I was in on purpose. In fact, I'm so disappointed that I didn't do that that I'm docking myself a full 6 Frank points."

"Wow. So—"

"But at the same time, I'm deeply impressed by my magnanimity, and I have therefore been awarded another 30,000 points."

I scoffed. "Been awarded. Like it's a passive thing."

"That does appear to be the way it currently works. But hey."

"What now?"

"You gonna finish that drink?"

I dropped him back into the beaker and picked that back up, grabbed another beaker off the counter for myself, and kept searching the room.

Eventually I found an overturned desk with a small drawer that was secured with a padlock—and the padlock had a Health bar—so I blew it open with a blast from my blunderbuss.

Inside, I found a packet of papers.

**{The Royal Taxidermist's Log} (Quest Item)**

I tried reading the document manually, but many of the pages were stuck together, stained with what appeared to be the same purple liquid as was in the beakers. There were four legible entries, though, so I gave them a quick scan.

**{Entry 6}**

*I finally made one of them move. It was a bird, so the bones were light and hollow, and the feathers were few and far between, but it moved. It definitely moved.*

**{Entry 9}**

*Memories are the key. From an arcane perspective, a single moment of pure joy is like an engine that powers itself. I'm not quite sure how to harness the energy just yet—the extractions are tedious with a high rate of failure—but I feel more optimistic than I have in years.*

*Fittingly enough, it was Isabel who helped me make the connection.*

*Remember this, remember that. She's getting worse by the day, and the only time she smiles anymore is when she's reminiscing.*

*But yes, love. I remember everything.*

**{Entry 12}**

*The thing I keep coming back to—over and over again—is the idea that I'm giving the dead something to latch on to. But maybe that's not entirely the case. Maybe only a small part of the spirit is leaking through, or is left behind. Or maybe the memory I use dictates what reaches out? I need more time.*

**{Entry 25}**
*I finally finished a self-sufficient loop. I did have to leave the skin and bones entirely behind to do it—reanimating them was too inefficient, and stitching them up in a way that prevents them from falling apart takes hours—but regardless, the spectral body I created is firm enough to feel.*
*And now whenever Isabel opens the front door, Rusty charges out just like he used to and promptly throws himself on the ground to have his belly rubbed. It's not really him—the ghost is just an echo, a memory playing out the scene that powers it—but it looks amazingly real.*
*Isabel cried when I showed her. She's been in considerable pain of late, but when she smiled there on the floor with the memory of our first dog wagging and kicking a foot out just like he used to? It was like seeing the clouds part for the first time in so long.*
*I would do anything to see that smile again.*

I looked up from the log to see Darling coming down the steps with House once again following too closely behind her.

"I think I know what this place is," Darling was saying. She stopped on the last stair, and House bumped into her a split second later, almost knocking her down. Then Darling raised a finger at Frank, who was still in his beaker.

"What is going on down here? Why is Ned double-fisting those beakers? And did you both just shout Honey Crisp?"

"It appears that Frank is currently questing," House said.

"In that beaker full of embalming fluid?" Darling said. "I'm pretty sure that's what it's supposed to be because the room upstairs is full of dried animal skins and glass eyeballs and chests full of bones. Like, meticulously organized bones—"

"The organization of the bones was truly exquisite," House added.

"So everything else kinda fits. Plus there was this weird, ghostly thing that kept flickering in and out of the room."

"Ned drank the liquid too," Frank said.

I scowled at him.

"Wait, what?" Darling said. "Why?"

"I mean, it's not really embalming fluid, even if that's what it's supposed to be," I said. "And it's actually pretty refreshing."

"Shall I too drink the embalming fluid?" House said.

Darling threw her hands up in the air. "Why would you volunteer to do that?"

"Because I enjoy participating in group events." House strode over with purpose and gestured at the beaker that Frank was in, but I handed her mine instead.

And House proceeded to chug almost half of it. She burped and wiped her lips.

"Having participated, I too found that refreshing."

House ran over and tried to hand the beaker to Darling, but she shook her head. So House tried again, with way, way too much enthusiasm.

I waved her off. "That's okay, House. Darling doesn't need to drink it if she doesn't want to." I went over and tried to grab the beaker back, but House held firm.

"But will she not be sad when the group event has concluded?"

I pulled a little harder, and she let go. "I think she'll live."

House popped Bella into her hands and stroked her back, then looked at Darling with wide, sad eyes. "But I want more for Darling than survival."

Darling's face softened into a smile. "Fine." She took the beaker and took a quick sip, then nodded. "Yeah, okay. Surprisingly good. I don't know why we're doing this, but it's good."

House beamed and dropped Bella back into her inventory. "The entire group has participated, and the event is now complete." She shimmied her shoulders, and the gesture was so sublimely joyful that I found myself unable to keep from smiling.

Darling set the beaker back on the counter and dropped her voice. "I like you guys. But sometimes I wonder how you get anything done."

"That is a fair question," I said. "So, animal pelts upstairs?"

"Yeah. Plus a bunch of scratched-up walls and broken windows. But it looks like the windows broke outward from the way the glass is laying on the roof." She scanned the room. "So nothing down here other than the beakers and the equipment?"

I held the papers up and granted her access to the item. "There's a good bit of information in here. Imagine we'll be finding more entries as we go along."

I eyed the back door, which was firmly boarded up. But the window beside it was broken and secured only by a few rotten boards.

I used the butt of my rifle to remove the rotten pieces of wood, then pistol-whipped the shards of glass that remained out of the frame. I climbed out the window and into a small, square courtyard with a dead oak tree at its center, a tire swing hanging from one of its lower branches and twisting in the breeze.

Glass crunched beneath my feet as I moved deeper into the courtyard, and Darling and House followed quickly behind.

The square space was hemmed in on all sides by old, wooden buildings that were even more overgrown with weeds and flowers than the first structures we'd seen. Some of the roofs had collapsed and others were missing whole sections, though they all looked solid enough where I didn't think we were meant to move on from the courtyard, or at least not yet.

Darling knelt and scooped a large, smooth stone off the ground and held it up in front of her face. "Someone wrote Ella on this, or something like that. Hard to tell because the writing has faded so much. Mean anything to you?"

"Nope." I scanned the courtyard again and noticed that similar stones were everywhere, though most of them were at least partially buried in the dirt.

A stiff breeze whipped through the courtyard then, so cold that it left my eyelids lined with frost. I tried to blink the crystals away, then rubbed my eyes to clear them when that didn't work.

"Ooh," Frank said. "Don't look down, but it's getting nippy in here. Where's my dad when you don't need him?"

Prompts, then.

**New Quest: {After the Thaw}!**
**Objective: Survive the Taxidermist's Early Attempts!**
**Reward: Experience, Renown, Animalistic Rift Gems, and one piece of class-appropriate gear.**

# Chapter Six

"Early attempts at what?" I said.

"I mean, dude's a taxidermist," Frank said. "Do we really need a brainstorming session here?"

Darling whipped her sword out over her shoulder in one fluid motion, the metal singing as it came out of its scabbard.

A counter popped up at the top of my screen:

**Wave 1/3.**

I opened my inventory and quickly replaced the Rune of the Caustic Raven I'd had applied to one of my pistols and switched it out for a piercing rune.

I left my offhand rocking its Rune of Shattering, which seemed decent enough for waves and the multiple mobs they implied; I liked the idea of being able to root stuff if needed for breathing room, and the bonus to Critical Hit Chance the rune offered against frozen targets might be helpful too.

Darling brought her huge sword up in front of her, which House promptly mimicked with her own two-handed mace.

I tightened my grip on my pistols. "Endurance fight then."

Darling inclined her head. "Seems like it."

"How comfortable are you at low Health?"

"If lots of stuff is dying or on the verge of dying? Very comfortable."

"It's like we're the same person," Frank said.

"I only create shields when I put something down for good, so if we're up against a few big targets, I might need healing. My Health regenerates pretty quick with momentum stacked up but it's never fast enough to totally outpace the drain my abilities cause, so I gotta be careful."

I pulled out my rifle and Overcharged a Ravenblast while looking in House's direction. "Alright then, we can work with that. House, I want you to prioritize keeping you and me alive with your healing bots. But don't heal Darling at all unless she yells for it, okay?"

"Understood," House said.

Darling cracked a smile. "I'll be seriously impressed if she doesn't twitch and heal me anyway when I get low."

House cocked her head. "I do not understand the supposed difficulty of the situation. I am simply to let Darling die unless she says otherwise, correct?"

"Yup," I said.

"Zero problem," House replied.

"No problem," Frank corrected, but quietly.

"That's what they all say," Darling said. "Then the Health Bars start flashing and the heals start flowing, quickly followed by apologies and promises that it won't happen again, then it happens again." She shrugged. "No big deal if it happens. Habits are hard to break."

"Yeah," I said, grinning. "I see what you're saying, but I think she's got this. House, if there's not much healing to be done and there are a bunch of targets, I want you to slow as many of them down as possible with your oil turrets. If all of that is handled, hit stuff but try not to kill it—we want Darling getting as many killing blows as possible. Clear?"

She grinned, cheeks dimpling. "I am pleased to have a transparent list."

Another brutally cold gust of wind whipped through the courtyard. I was already picturing a horde of zombies pouring out of the windows and doors that bordered the space, crawling over the mostly ruined roofs and out from beneath the buildings themselves.

Instead, the ground itself swelled and buckled, patches of dark soil rising and falling as if the earth itself was breathing.

Darling whistled. "Doesn't seem like a small wave."

"I count at least thirteen targets incoming," House said.

A mound of dirt exploded to my left and the scent of rot hit me hard.

A buck with massive antlers leaped up out of the ground, and though one of its slender legs collapsed beneath it on landing, the creature quickly righted itself and pawed the ground as if it were about to charge.

**{Twice-stitched Buck} (Level 12 Undead) (Veteran)**
**HP: ??/??**
**MP: ??/??**

Black stitching ran from the buck's snout up between its black, unblinking eyes and vanished into the fur beneath its antlers. The zipper-like pattern reappeared between its shoulder blades and traced the length of the creature's spine all the way to its dirt-crusted tail.

More mobs clawed their way up out of the dirt across the courtyard, a menagerie of creatures from wolves and deer to bears and so much more.

"House, we need some Sludgeslings."

She tossed a pair of discs out with her free hand, and within seconds, two nicely-spaced turrets were dousing the emerging creatures in oil, notably slowing them.

House twitched. "It irritates me that that puma's stitching is slightly more haphazard than that of the others," she said. "Normal?"

I followed her gaze and inspected the mob in question.

**{Unraveling Puma} (Level 12 Undead) (Veteran)**
**HP: ??/??**
**MP: ??/??**

I thought I spotted something near the creature's belly—a targetable point, maybe—but the creature dashed off behind another emerging mob before I could get a better look at it.

"Not normal!" Frank said.

I Clonedrifted between two of the animals to get some space, still trying to track the puma down.

"Spread out or we're gonna get dog piled! Gonna need to kite these guys without a real tank or healer! Check for Unraveling mobs as you go, something's up there!"

Darling leaped over the creatures that were approaching her, but House lacked her mobility and instead had to dash between two of them and almost caught a plate-sized paw to the face from what appeared to be a cobbled-together bear that was half polar and half grizzly.

Three animals veered off to follow her across the courtyard, but the bulk of them converged on the clone I'd left behind, which exploded in a bright shower of sparks the very moment the first animal made contact and stunned several of them at once.

"Damage isn't moving their bars at all!" Darling said. "Gotta be another way to kill them!"

I backpedaled and fired off a pair of piercing blasts at the deer to double-check and came to the same conclusion: both spells hit the initial target for amounts in the mid-200s, but the creature's Health bar still read 100%.

Then a call for Francis came in—from Tyrann of all people. But I wasn't about to take a call in the middle of a fight, so I silenced it and kept moving. I spotted the puma that House had identified earlier skulking behind the bear that had nearly clotheslined her.

A second, closer inspection confirmed what I'd missed the first time around: a specific point that appeared to be targetable just behind one of the puma's front legs.

I inspected it.

**{Frayed Knot} (Level 10 Construct)**
**HP: 500/500**

I pressed my pistols together and launched two blue-gray Ravenblasts at the knot, and both of the rune-enhanced spells splashed home simultaneously, entrapping the creature's paws in ice and rooting it to the dirt.

I lit the frozen target up with a Dark Harvest, which crit for a bit over 800. The knot ripped apart and the puma popped like a balloon, blue light exploding outward and vaporizing every last trace of the creature.

The cyan burst also caught two more mobs that happened to be nearby —including the bear that had nearly taken House's head off—and the pulse of light deleted them both as well, leaving only some dark stitching and a few metallic, shiny teeth behind.

"Got it!" I called out. "Unraveling animals have target points and they turn into bombs when you blow 'em up! House, keep your directives but don't worry about hitting anything—you and I are going to slow things down and gather them up so Darling can finish them off!"

"Understood," House said. She made a fist, and the two Sludgesling Turrets she'd had out ripped apart and reformed into an Oilslick Turret that created a pool of dark oil near the center of the courtyard.

I took off at a run and tossed out Ravenblasts left and right, angling my spells so that they punched deep into the densest parts of the oncoming rush. The aggro built steadily as I weaved my way between the creatures, ducking sharp claws and long fangs every step of the way.

Darling was doing the same thing at the other end of the courtyard, and House was... doing her best, and it wasn't long before we'd each created a train of mobs behind us.

"Drag them to the center where we can kite through the spill!" I said.

Darling was quick to adjust, leaping to the center of the courtyard in a blink, and House wasn't far behind. The three columns of mobs reached the edge of the oil spill that House had created almost simultaneously.

"Whenever you're ready," I said. "House, it's all Darling from here."

"Understood."

Darling moved a bit in front of us as the mobs approached from three sides. She took two quick steps through the dark pitch and stabbed her massive sword into a bear that had a Frayed Knot targetable high atop its back.

Her blade punched through the front of its chest and tagged the knot for 400, almost destroying it on impact and leaving a lime green slash shining where her blade had struck true.

But instead of following up and finishing the weak point off, she spun away to the other end of the spill and just barely glanced another knot with a long, horizontal swing that cut right through a chimpanzee that already had one arm hanging slack at its side. A second green slash hung there, pulsing.

Then Darling activated Hexdoll Aura, and her huge sword began to glow, green runes running up and down its length. She got a running start and leaped almost half of the spill. She brought her weapon high overhead with both hands and brought it down on a bear that was standing on two feet, roaring up at her with a Frayed Knot right between its glassy eyes.

She brought the weapon down so hard that it cleaved fully through the knot and sank all the way into the creature's chest. The knot exploded in another burst of colorful light, and Darling vanished into the brightness as every monster within ten feet was completely erased.

A split second later, the green slashes she'd left hanging behind her pulsed as twin 670s drifted up above the knots that Darling had struck prior to activating her aura, the damage of her strike transferring to them as well.

The two knots exploded, and the combined bursts were so strong that

I felt a slight warmth on the air as the glow filled the courtyard. And when the trio of blue novas fully faded, nothing remained of the first wave but a few scattered pelts.

I grinned over where Darling was kneeling between three bodies that were all sparking green.

"Nicely done!"

"Thanks! Good call on the knots, that was awesome!" Darling said. She had a red, translucent shield pulsing around her, so faint that it would be easy to miss it in a fight.

I felt Frank narrow his eyes at me, but the wave counter updated before he could get a word out.

**Wave 2/3.**

The entire courtyard seethed and churned as maybe forty of the ghastly animals began dragging themselves up out of the dirt.

"Check for Frayed Knots and mark them with icons if you can!" I said.

House whipped her neck around so hard I cringed on her behalf. Icons populated my screen in a wave from left to right: the same skulls and flames and triangles and so on that the guild had used in the last raid to mark priority targets.

But House had picked out every Frayed Knot in the blink of an eye.

"Wow!" Darling said. "That was quick!"

There were five targetable areas in all, and they were spread out amongst the crowd.

"Same plan?" Darling said. "My aura's down, but someone else could handle the burst."

I scanned the many creatures, trying to picture what grouping them up would even look like. Then I shook my head.

"Crowd's too dense, no room to move beyond cooldowns. And the ground is gonna be a nightmare to run over with all the holes those mobs are leaving behind."

The first creature finished dragging itself out of the dirt, a wolverine with clumps of dirt hanging off its dark pelt.

{Twice-stitched Wolverine} (Level 12 Undead)
HP: ??/??
MP: ??/??

I pointed my weapons around the courtyard, barrels aglow with blue and gray light. "Let's ring up at the center. House, can you reapply this spill?"

She tossed out a pair of turrets and combined them, laying a second pool of oil so tightly atop the first that I wasn't even able to register the animation. "It has been reapplied."

"Thanks. I've got this wave. When I say go, I want you guys to run straight through the creatures. Darling can just leap her way out, but House, you're gonna have to be careful on foot, so I'll try to carve you a path. On the second signal, blow them the hell up."

Darling sheathed her sword. "What are you thinking?"

"I set the pins up and you guys knock 'em down." I popped Doppelganger, then Double Cast another clone into existence.

I pivoted and loosed my ravens, launching icy, piercing birds through the swelling crowd. My clones started up and loosed their own spells in turn, and though they appeared to be aiming at the same targets, between my constant movement and their own locations and the chaos of the encroaching crowd, they ended up peppering different areas with their spells.

Which was exactly what I was aiming for. I kept spinning in place and flinging birds beside my clones as the fastest of the mobs reached the edge of House's oil spill.

I kept the ravens coming, trying to tag every single creature that I could until the rush was maybe ten feet away, at which point their efforts slowed to a crawl under the effect of the spill.

"I should have aggro on everything, you guys should be good to run out!" I brought my pistols up and held them six inches apart. "House, follow my spells." I fired. "Run!"

The two tightly-placed Ravenblasts ripped through the space directly in front of House, striking many of the mobs twice in quick succession and causing my Rune of Shattering to freeze a line of them in place.

House bolted and wove her way through the frozen crowd with surprising grace, dodging the stray swipes and grabs on her way out.

Darling made it look easy, taking a few quick steps to the edge of what looked increasingly like a horde of zombies pressing in before leaping over the entire group and landing lightly on the other side.

I kept firing, spinning faster and faster as the swarm closed ranks around me. When they were only feet away, I pointed one of my pistols down at the ground between my legs.

I waited as long as I dared, until the outstretched claw of a shaggy-maned lion was about to dig into my thigh, then Water Jetted myself vertically into the air.

My two clones did the same, and the ring of creatures surged beneath me, the gap I'd been standing in slamming closed as the mobs approached from all sides.

I let myself hit my apex, then twisted in the air toward Darling and activated Clonedrift to send myself flying over the gathered mobs and across the spill.

My Doppelgangers duplicated the cast but winked out immediately afterward, the spell having run its course.

But the setup was perfect: that last Clonedrift had left three clones hanging in the air above the creatures, and the trio was now falling to earth.

I hit the ground a bit before them and managed to roll to my feet as the first of the three clones smashed into the mobs below.

It instantly erupted in a shower of sparks—I couldn't tell whether it was from fall damage or an attack that had connected before the copy reached the ground—and stunned a huge number of creatures. The second and third clones smashed down right afterward, each stunning another tightly packed group.

And with the moment having finally arrived—with almost the entire wave gathered up and stunned in a remarkably tight space—I raised a pistol as I knelt there on the ground, aimed a few feet above the mobs' heads, and fired a Gravity Bird.

"Go!" I said, but Darling was already running the moment my weapon kicked back and the dark, starry raven leaped out of my barrel.

But shockingly enough, House was even quicker, tossing out a turret disc well in front of her even as she drew her mace.

I detonated the Gravity Bird before the first wave of stuns had a chance to fade, and the effect was breathtaking: the entire crowd—every single creature—was yanked up into the air and pulled into a tight ball of flailing arms and legs.

The undead animals roared and howled as the Gravity Bird pulled them in tighter still, and I could have sworn there was a pig somewhere in the mix, squealing deep within the ball of darkness.

I switched to my rifle and wound up a Ravenblast as the disc that House had thrown skipped off the dirt and landed a few feet in front of the elevated mobs.

She hefted her mace over one shoulder as she reached melee range, then swung her weapon in a vicious upward swing while the disc was still expanding into a Leadfire Turret.

The turret ripped apart into a hail of shrapnel that tore into the gathered mobs and sent up a cloud of yellow numbers, most of which were in the upper 500s, and all five of the knots blew apart in a series of cascading explosions.

I threw a hand up to shield my face, and for the briefest moment—at the very peak of the many explosions' combined brightness—I was able to see the small bones of my hands and fingers through my skin.

The light subsided, leaving House looking in my direction, bits of fur and stitching and sparkling loot raining down all around her.

I dropped my weapon with a Ravenblast nearly fully cast as Darling skidded to a stop with her sword held out to one side.

"I appear to have ended the threat temporarily," House said.

"And with style to boot," I said, laughing the words.

"Yeah, nice going!" Darling said.

House's answering smile was so wide and so bright that I couldn't help but return it.

"She's really coming along, isn't she?" I whispered to Frank.

"Uh huh. Kinda sucks that she decided to start developing right after I threatened her cats, but it's good to see, I guess."

"Maybe it's an adversity-builds-character sorta situation."

"That would give me most of the credit, so that is probably the case."

Then the counter updated for a third time.

**Wave 3/3.**

I eyed the ground, expecting an even larger horde to come flooding up out of the countless holes the previous mobs had left.

The wind picked up again, carrying the same icy breeze and whipping it across us. But this time, the chill hung around and lingered over the courtyard.

"Back to the center," I said, already jogging that way, and Darling and House weren't far behind.

"Same plan?" Darling said.

I shook my head. "I popped everything, but if we can last long enough, sure. Won't be too long on Gravity Bird and Water Jet, at least. Double Cast and Doppelganger will take a good bit longer."

"I'll have my aura back soon."

The courtyard went deathly quiet, and it was only when I noticed my teeth were chattering that I realized the chill was actually deepening.

The overgrown weeds and flowers and stray blades of grass that had been waving in the breeze a moment earlier were now completely still, their lengths fully encased in ice.

I swept the area again and again, looking for movement but finding none until something caught my eye atop a nearby building.

A wolf-like creature stood atop a gentle roof, staring down at us from above. It looked up at the red moon that hung in the sky above and howled.

More creatures appeared on top of the buildings, and I saw eyes staring back at us through the interiors of the structures that lined the courtyard.

All the rotten wood that had been securing the doors and windows was ripped off or blown through entirely as monsters flooded into the courtyard, pouring down from the buildings' roofs and through the windows and doors alike.

The flow didn't appear to have an end, either; for every mob that jumped down off a roof or scrambled down out of a second-story window, two more appeared to take its place. And the rooftops that I could see beyond the courtyard were absolutely crawling with creatures.

"Too many," Darling said. "Way, way, way too many."

I eyed the buildings, tried to find a way out, and failed spectacularly. "Might as well give it a shot. House, drop another—"

I cut off as a second howl answered the first, one that sent a shiver down my spine that had nothing to do with the cold. The sound was far deeper and raspier than the wolf's had been, and I found myself tightening my grip on both my pistols.

The tide of oncoming creatures jerked to a stop, the closest of them being a panther some twenty feet away that was now scrambling away from us. The howl came again, closer now, and this time it sounded more like a scream.

The swarm of undead creatures scattered at once. They raced back over and into the buildings, many of them trampling each other in their haste to get away.

Within the space of a few breaths, the entire group had disappeared, and the courtyard was quiet once again. But the chill was still building, and every breath I exhaled hung heavily in front of me.

"What the hell was that about?" Darling said. "Quest hasn't completed."

"They probably got a good look at Frank," Frank said.

"Or they caught a whiff of the mess he left on my leg."

"Huh?" Darling said.

"I believe the answer is above us," House said.

I looked up, where a large, dark figure was soaring toward us across the sky, its head low.

I inspected it.

**{Thrice-stitched Amalgam}** **(Level 12 Undead) (Elite)**
**HP:** ??/??
**MP:** ??/??

# Chapter Seven

The creature was flying on dark wings, but its motion was far from elegant; the beast was flailing wildly, thrashing its way through the air as if its wings couldn't quite support the weight of its body, which, even from a distance, looked disproportionately heavy.

I watched it struggle across the sky, wondering how it planned on reaching us, given how quickly it was losing altitude.

I got my answer as the beast landed atop a distant building and blew all of its windows out at once, glass flying in every direction. It took a few loping strides with surprising power and grace, stretched its wings, then leaped off the edge of the roof and propelled itself high into the air while the structure tilted behind it, then collapsed.

"Well then," Darling said. "I guess we found the third wave."

I reloaded my blunderbuss, then switched to my rifle and started charging a Ravenblast.

"Apparently so."

I sighted the beast down the barrel of my weapon, searching for knots and finding tons of them. The wings alone each had three targetable locations.

But the names were different this time around.

{Loose Knot}
HP: 750/750

I whistled. "You guys seeing the new Health total on the knots?"

"Yup," Darling said. "Not bad!"

"The creature has twenty knots that represent a grand total of 20,000 Health," House said.

Darling blinked. "Okay, that makes it seem pretty bad, actually."

The Amalgam thundered into the clearing and landed amid a shower of dirt and uprooted stones.

"That might be the ugliest creature I've ever seen," I said.

Frank grunted. "Looks like somebody was trying to make a dragon but ran out of the right parts almost immediately."

He was pretty much dead-on: the monster had the head of a giant lizard and its long neck had been fashioned out of an anaconda or something similar, while its fat, round body was reminiscent of a hippo.

Its wings had been cobbled together from various birds, the feathers ranging from raven-black to neon blue, and several particularly bright ones were drifting down around it, jarred loose by the impact of its landing.

"Stick with the knots?" Darling said.

"Definitely." The creature snorted and pawed the ground, and a tremendous amount of aggro settled onto my shoulders. "Here we go. I'll kite it, you guys try to burn it down. Call out anything you notice along the way."

I lined up a shot at the creature's front right leg and loosed my Ravenblast just as the Amalgam began to charge. The spell struck the knot I'd been aiming at and obliterated it to the tune of 940 damage.

The gray, piercing spell kept going, too, striking a knot in the leg behind it for 735 before dissipating behind the creature.

I'd been expecting another pair of the strong explosions we'd seen earlier, but the flashes that resulted were tiny by comparison, blue flickers of light that left strands of black thread whipping around the creature's legs as it continued its charge across the courtyard.

"Still two more knots to take out on each of those legs!" Darling called out.

She'd dashed up in front of me, and she took advantage of the beast's charge by slashing out at each of the same legs I'd struck as it passed by her.

"Two more knots down! One remaining per leg!"

I swapped to my pistols and ran for it as the monster pressed the chase. Despite its bulk, it was obviously faster than me, and it had already closed the gap between us to about ten feet.

One of House's discs slammed into the dirt and expanded upward, so I kited the creature in that direction.

The disc turned into a Sludgesling Turret that whipped around and spewed a pressurized jet of oil that I had to duck to avoid.

I caught a few droplets of black liquid in the face, but more importantly I heard the Amalgam roar behind me.

"Slowed by 60%," Frank said.

I used the opportunity to put a bit of distance between us, then twisted around and fired another pair of blasts across the courtyard, aiming to destroy the final round of knots.

And while I did manage to blow two more of them up—one on each leg—another pair on both remained.

"Wait, were there four total on each leg?" I said.

"No," House said.

But that meant the math wasn't adding up. I reached the corner of the courtyard, so I skidded to a stop, whipped my barrels around, and launched a second volley.

The two spells finished off the remaining knots, and the charging creature bellowed as two of its legs crumpled beneath it. The beast slammed onto its side and skidded toward me, flapping one giant wing as if to compensate.

Darling leaped high into the air with her sword in hand, about to crash down onto the beast's back, while House tossed out another disc and sprinted toward us.

The beast lunged at me with blinding speed even as its momentum kept it sliding toward me. Its head snapped forward, neck extending, its mouth open and lined with row after row of hooked teeth.

I'd been hoping to drift or jet away, but the speed of the attack caught me off guard and out of position, and all I could manage was a sideways roll.

The snake's open mouth passed inches above my shoulder and smashed into the building behind me. Wood shattered, and the structure groaned.

I rolled to my feet, but the heavy creature was still sliding through the dirt, and its great bulk rolled up on both of my ankles before I had a chance to move. Its broad chest slammed into me and bowled me over onto my back.

"Stunned for 5 seconds," Frank said.

I lay there, pistols in hand, as the beast finally stopped moving and began to retract its head from the massive hole it had created in the building behind me.

Darling was on top of it now, holding onto one wing with one gauntleted hand as she hacked away at the other, and I saw sparks flying off the creature's side, where one of House's turrets was raking it with projectiles.

"I can't get its attention off you!" Darling said. "And the knots we broke are reforming!"

I cursed under my breath as the creature seemed to notice I was lying directly beneath it, trapped and helpless.

It snapped down at me, its fangs heading straight for my chest.

I waited as long as I dared, then activated Clonedrift. The spell canceled the stun I'd been under, but crucially it gave me a tiny window where the damage I took was vastly reduced.

Unfortunately for me, I still had my back to the ground, so I popped right back into the same place almost immediately as the spell ran out of distance and the clone I'd created exploded in the beast's face.

Which meant I missed the tiny window of damage resistance I'd been trying to hit, and strong vibrations rippled across my chest and abdomen as the creature struck and its fangs bit deep.

"Your Health at 37%."

The Amalgam repositioned itself slightly, raising itself up for another attack, and I managed to get my right leg entirely free, but my left ankle remained trapped beneath it.

I was about to attempt to Water Jet myself away when I spotted something: an especially dark line of thread that ran down the center of the creature's chest with two particularly large knots anchoring it to either side.

I inspected them.

{Double Knot}
HP: 1,250/1,250

Still prone, I switched to my blunderbuss and put the barrel of my weapon to the creature's chest, angling it upward to make sure the piercing spell would catch both the knots.

Then I fired two spells in quick succession. The birds connected for four hits in all, ranging from the high 600s to the low 700s.

The beast reared up and howled as the knots exploded and the movement took its weight off my trapped ankle, so I popped a pistol into my hand and Water Jetted myself away from it.

I went flying and smashed shoulder-first into a nearby window, and though the rotten boards that had been securing it held firm, I heard and felt the glass pane break beneath them. I landed on my feet but staggered and had to plant a hand to keep from falling over.

The great beast's chest was open, the dark line I'd seen earlier having parted to reveal a roiling sphere of bright, purple energy.

**{Memorial Heart}**
**HP: 3,000/3,000**

I popped my rifle into my hands and Double Cast an instant Ravenblast right into the creature's chest.

The spell connected for 1,015 and the compartment snapped closed at once, the dark line reknitting itself right in front of me. The creature's legs regenerated too, the severed strands pulling back into knots.

The Amalgam flicked the wing that Darling was holding onto and launched her across the courtyard, then turned and rumbled away from me, accelerating at an incredible rate for its size.

It leaped when it was a few feet short of trampling a wide-eyed House and went soaring back up into the sky.

"Blowback from that last Double Cast means I'm dead without healing!" I clambered to my feet and ran toward Darling at the center of the courtyard. "The two chest knots are the key! We blow them up and there's something you can target inside, seems like you're allowed one hit or about 1,000 damage before it closes up and the fight resets!"

All three of House's Healing Bots whirred over and bathed me in warm light that gradually healed me up.

"We definitely broke the legs too," Darling said. "But the knots seem to reknit after ten seconds or so. I kept trying to break one of the wings, worrying it would fly off, but the knots were too spread out and I couldn't do it fast enough."

I popped my rifle into my hands and readied a Ravenblast as my Health ticked back up above 50%.

"Good try. Thanks for the heals, House."

"You are welcome."

"Looks like we've got incoming," I said as the creature thrashed its way through a banking turn and headed straight for us. "Which wing were you on?"

"Your left," Darling said.

I inspected the knots as soon as the creature was close enough to allow it, and as Darling had said, all of them were back to full Health.

The creature opened its mouth wide, and the back of its throat began to glow with lime-green light.

"Projectiles incoming!" I said. I loosed a raven as the Amalgam came into range, targeting the mob's left wing, but the creature simply banked a turn and the spell passed harmlessly to the side.

"Might be immune to damage while flying," Darling said. "Here it comes!"

I'd been expecting the Amalgam to rake the field with some kind of breath attack, but instead it launched a series of greenish, basketball-sized globes down at us from above as it passed over.

The three of us scattered, globes exploding all around, the courtyard flashing red in spots a second or two before the green bombs hit.

I caught a bit of splash from the bursting projectiles, and the few droplets that spattered my face and chest and legs vibrated strongly and proved enough to not only completely cancel out the healing I'd been getting from House's bots but actually reverse the trend.

Darling's red shields had long since winked out without targets to kill, and I was unsurprised to see her Health falling even more rapidly than my own, though both she and House were still in better shape overall.

Then the Amalgam landed on a distant roof, ran across it in a tight half-circle, then launched itself up again and glided in for a second pass. The globes had left a minefield behind; pools of green, bubbling liquid were absolutely everywhere, covering maybe a third of the courtyard.

I stared up at the creature and mentally mapped out escape routes between the many puddles.

The second volley came even faster than the first, and while I hadn't had too much of an issue the first time around when it came to dodging the falling orbs, the floor hazards made it far more difficult this time and I stepped in a couple of puddles along the way, dropping my Health even lower.

But as the last orb splashed home, all three of us were still standing, with my Health at a bit above 20% thanks to House's continued healing, while Darling and House were both holding strong about 60% a piece.

"This has gotta be the last pass," Darling said. "We're running out of ground here."

I eyed the approaching creature, lips pressed to a firm line. Then a prompt came in.

**World-first Alert! The Guild {Corruptia} is the first Guild to clear an Animalistic or Memory-stained Rift, and the first wave of the Possibility King's forces are now approaching your reality!**
**Awarding Unique Title: Menagerist!**

The look of disappointment on Darling's face was painful to see, though she quickly shook it off.

"Damn. I didn't think we'd get it ourselves with the delayed start, but I was really hoping someone in the guild would."

Another prompt came through immediately following the alert, so I gave it a quick scan.

**As a Housing Plot owner in The Black Oasis, you now have access to the city's Communal Defense Zone, where you and any other Housing Plot owners may freely build any number of qualifying structures in preparation for the Possibility King's oncoming assault.**

I waved the prompt away. Worrisome as that readout was, now wasn't the time.

"We've almost got this Rift wrapped up though," I said. "Frank, can you watch the orbs for me?"

"Uh huh."

I pointed a pistol at the creature. "Third pass incoming, let's focus up."

The Amalgam came in low, landed atop a building that bordered the courtyard, then leaped over us as the structure collapsed into a pile of rubble behind it.

It blasted orbs down at us even more rapidly than before, machine-gunning the projectiles at us with incredible force.

I got a quick glimpse at the sky, choked with giant green drops as it was, then forced my attention onto the floor. It lit up in red, but three of the four corners of the courtyard were still unmarked and therefore safe, so I ran for the one on my left.

"On your right," Frank said, so I veered off and hopped over a puddle as the area I'd been heading toward flashed red and an orb smashed down into it right afterward.

"Thanks!"

I kept running, and out of the corner of my eye I saw Darling use the flat of her sword to slap a falling orb that she'd been unable to dodge away from her.

The strike saved her from taking a direct hit, but the giant droplet splattered on impact, and she caught a good amount of spray across her chest plate and shoulder pads. Her Health started to fall, and I was about to call out for House to send one of the bots that was still tending to me her way when a giant orb caught House fully in the back of the head while she was in mid-sprint.

The orb exploded over her, instantly chunking her Health from more than half all the way down into the single digits.

Even worse, the contact sent her sprawling end over end into a lime-green puddle, and she only managed to thrash her way about halfway out of it before she went still and her nameplate grayed out.

"Boom. Headshot."

"Not a good thing, Frank! Shut up and watch the—"

"Directly in front!" he said, a split second before the ground lit up in red.

I was hemmed in by long puddles to my left and right, so I jammed on the brakes so hard that my heels skidded across the dirt and I ended up windmilling with my hands to keep my balance.

An orb whistled down and exploded, splashing me with acid from head to toe. My Health ticked down at a steady rate, and within seconds I'd dropped beneath 10% for the first time and continued to fall from there.

"Crap," Frank said. "No House, no heals. It'll be close, but you're not dead yet."

I saw Darling burn some Health to leap out of the way of two orbs, both of which exploded mere feet from where she'd been running.

Unfortunately for her, she landed smack dab in the center of a shallow green pool. She was much quicker to extricate herself than House had been, but between the physical cost of her leap and the damaging pool, she too had fallen below 30% Health.

"First round of pools are starting to fade," Frank said.

I relaxed a bit at the sight, watching them dissipate in quick succession. The Amalgam had flown away again, moving at a slower pace than before, so I figured—hoped—that the orb phase was over for now.

I ran over to join Darling, then quickly reloaded my blunderbuss.

"House went down?" she said.

"Yeah. Orb to the back of the head."

Frank laughed. "It was awesome."

"We won't survive that phase again without heals," she said.

I wiped my face with my sleeve, which came away sizzling. "You can kill me if it comes down to it."

"I neither want nor need your permission," Frank said. "Way more fun without it."

"Not you, Frank."

Darling frowned. "Why would I kill you?"

I popped my rifle into place against my shoulder and took aim as the Amalgam landed on a wide, distant rooftop, ran almost its entire length, then launched itself in our direction. "If I'm going down anyway, you might as well finish me off and proc a shield. That'd net you 20% Health and a bit of extra damage, right? Give you a bit more time."

"Rather just reattempt it."

"Might as well try if it's a wipe regardless."

She hesitated but eventually nodded. "Alright, but hopefully it won't come to that."

My spell completed and I held the weapon in place, tracing the creature's flight while the barrel glowed with purple and gray energy. The bulk of the puddles had already faded, and it didn't seem like it'd be long before the courtyard was clear.

"I'm thinking we need to end this right now," I said.

"How?"

"I've still got aggro. So if that thing charges the way it did before, we meet it halfway. I blow its chest open and you break whatever's inside before the window slams closed."

"You only hit it once before?"

I nodded. "Yeah. It was quick."

"Heart's at 65%," Frank said. "Need to hit it for a little under 2,000 to finish it off, plus 2,500 more to break the knots in the first place with them at 1,250 Health a pop."

"That's a lot of damage," Darling said.

The Amalgam was drawing near, and my heart thumped a little harder with every flap of the beast's ungainly wings.

"We got this," I said. "I can handle the knots if you can break the core."

"Might come down to a lucky crit. I can't burst that high unless I've got my execute up."

I bit my lip and eyed Double Cast, which seemed like it'd be ready again by the time I needed it. My Health had leveled out at 6%, meaning the blowback would absolutely kill me on even a halfway decent hit. "I'll help you burst. But if it doesn't drop—"

"You cut his whole head off with no hesitation," Frank said.

Darling cocked a dark eyebrow at me.

"I'm with him on that, if substantially less enthusiastic."

The Amalgam landed at the far edge of the courtyard, clipped a building with one of its rear feet as it came in and tore the entire wall loose, exposing the empty floors and the furniture within.

"On your mark," Darling said as the building fell inward and a cloud of dust obscured the boss. She hefted her sword atop her shoulder and took a deep breath.

"We got this," I repeated. I aimed my rifle at the cloud and waited.

The Amalgam bellowed and charged out into the open, dust streaming behind it.

I fired the very moment the beast entered my range, gauged the distance and the mob's speed, and realized I didn't have time for another rifle blast. I switched to my pistols and readied another pair of spells while Darling and I held our ground.

My first Ravenblast connected for 1,180, less than 100 shy of the amount I needed to blow one of the knots up. I cursed and released both of my pistol blasts, splitting the targets across the two knots.

"Go!"

Darling pounded across the courtyard behind me, armored footfalls ringing out clearly with every long stride.

I matched her pace and switched to my blunderbuss.

"Top knot's down, second at 900!" Frank said.

The beast was maybe ten feet away, head coiled back on its long neck, wings pinned to its thick body.

"Hit it hard the moment it's open!" I said.

It struck out at me as it had before, aiming for my chest. I slid feet-first, tilting my head back and sideways as the snake's open mouth passed inches above me. I thought I was free and clear, but the back of my head bounced off the dirt. My vision swam for one terrifying moment, but thankfully everything snapped back as I passed beneath the rumbling creature.

I lit the remaining knot up with my blunderbuss, hoping against hope that the first blast would crit and be enough to kill it. But once again I fell short of what I needed.

To add insult to injury, my follow-up procced an unnecessary critical strike, and the overkill damage was wasted as the knot exploded in a flash of blue light and the dark seam that lined the creature's chest blew open.

I switched to my rifle and thrust the barrel up against the glowing core within.

Darling's huge blade flashed into view, rising toward the sphere in a wicked, upward strike.

I waited as long as I dared, until her sword was only inches from the core, then Double Cast an instant Ravenblast and hammered Dark Harvest over and over again, praying for an activation.

A trio of ghosts left the barrel of my weapon as my momentum carried me fully underneath the still-charging creature.

"I missed the execute after my attack, I didn't—" Darling's voice cut off and she gasped as if struck, and something metallic went bouncing across the ground.

The creature's huge frame collapsed directly on top of me, and the world went dark. I thrashed against its strange, saggy skin, its body suddenly lacking any weight at all, as if I were trapped under some giant, stinking tarp.

After a solid five seconds of kicking and punching my way out, I crawled back into the daylight and discovered that I'd been trapped beneath the pelt the massive creature had left behind.

But the quest hadn't completed, and the purple core I'd damaged earlier was now floating some ten feet in the air, pulsing like a heart.

I eyed the pelt, shuddering despite my relief. "That was awful. Being trapped in there was like kindergarten all over again."

"What?" Frank said.

Darling ran over from a few yards off while I reloaded my blunderbuss. "What do we... did we..."

"Just need to blow the crystal up when it becomes targetable," Frank said. "You can relax."

She put her hands on her knees and sucked in a deep, relieved breath.

She looked up at me. "How the hell was any of that like kindergarten? What kind of school did you go to?"

"Some private school for character-building that my dad sent me to, but I meant that being under that creature was like that game we used to play where the class would hold onto the edges of a big tarp and you'd crawl underneath and hold your breath, then everybody would pin the tarp to the floor and try to trap you in place."

"What?" Frank repeated. "You had me in the first half, but man, that took a hard left turn at the end."

"In kindergarten?" Darling repeated. She glanced at Frank.

I looked up at the crystal, which was pulsing a bit faster now, though it still wasn't targetable. "Yeah, all the other kids would hold the edges of the tarp down and yell and scream and you had to try to escape before you ran out of air. Did you not play that?"

"We, uh..." Darling said. "We had a rainbow tarp, yeah. Sorta like a parachute? But it was a really lighthearted game. You'd just kinda flap it around and crawl underneath and stuff. You know... play?"

"How did the game end if you couldn't get out?" Frank said.

I shrugged and scanned the courtyard, still searching for targets. I couldn't shake the feeling that something was watching me, though I wasn't in combat. "Usually someone started crying."

Darling made to say something but seemed to decide otherwise.

I met her eyes. "Huh. You really never played that version?"

"No. Nobody else played that version."

"Yeah," Frank agreed, "I love doing bad stuff, but that's some straight-up Lord of the Flies shit right there. I'm so impressively horrified that I'm actually taking notes."

"Wow. I really assumed that was a universal experience." I tapped a message out to House asking if she was able to respawn, but she said she was still locked out. "Looks like we're not quite finished—" I cut off as the sphere finally became targetable, though it only had a single point of Health.

"Never mind, this should probably wrap the Rift so long as that wave counter isn't trolling us." I pointed a pistol up at the sphere, but Darling put an armored finger in the barrel.

"We already missed the World-first," she said. "You don't want to take a second to think about that?"

"About what?"

She stared at me, one eyebrow cocked above the other.

"The tarp game? Nah, it was fine, nothing came of it." I thought about that for a moment. "I guess I did end up being afraid of the dark for a long time. And tight spaces." My eyes went wide. "Ooooh."

"Details?" Frank said. "I'm so intrigued right now."

"I couldn't wear silk until I was 18. Didn't like the way it felt against my skin, but I had no idea why. Mystery solved, huh?"

Frank shivered. "God, that's awesome...ly terrible," he added, after a stern look from Darling.

"I'm so sorry," she said.

"It's totally fine!" I gestured up and down at myself. "I'm a magical elf that can throw birds now, so. Different life and all."

"It's really not fine."

Frank dropped his voice to a whisper. "Yeah. No wonder he turned out to be such a dick."

Darling laughed so loud that the single note turned into a shriek, which only made it funnier when she covered her mouth with both gauntlets, horrified.

"You can't whisper to other people, man," I said, laughing now too but at Darling's response more than anything else. "I'm always the person you're closest to."

"The whisper was for dramatic effect, and you were clearly meant to hear that."

"I am *so* sorry," she said. I'd never seen her so much as blush, but her entire face was turning scarlet. "I shouldn't have laughed at that but it surprised me so much and—"

I waved her concern away with a still-glowing pistol. "That was just Frank's attempt to lighten the mood."

"That was not my intention at all."

"Uh huh," I said, mimicking him.

I somehow felt him roll his sleeves up.

"Oh no you didn't. Don't let my lack of hands fool you into thinking I won't throw down. You do that again and you're gonna catch this shaft in a way that neither of us is happy about."

I stopped laughing. "You ever ask yourself why it's always about the shaft and never the blade?"

"Do I really need to explain why you're not supposed to put the cart before the horse?"

I smirked. "Anyway, let's get this done so House can respawn, yeah?"

Darling shrugged, her cheeks still tinged with red. "Sure, if you say so."

"You wanna do the honors?"

She smiled, then took two long steps and launched herself into the air. She hit the core with a vertical strike that passed right through it, and she was already falling by the time it split in half.

It hit the ground at the same time she did, both halves shattering into fine purple dust. A few spectral shapes—almost like ghosts—raced out of the core and across the ground while others flew up into the sky, but they all dissolved before I could figure out what I was looking at. Finally, the Rift completed and spat out a huge number of rewards.

And pushed me to the next level.

**Congratulations, you successfully completed an Animalistic Rift Quest: {After the Thaw}!**
**You gained 3,550 Experience!**
**You gained 530 Renown!**
**You received {Entry 65}**
**You received {Animalistic Rift Gem} x30!**
**You received {Rift Gem} x20!**
**You received {Defiler's Band}!**
**You received {Ghosthunter's Kickers}**
**You received {Soulsmith Recipe: Rune of the Ghostly Hunt}**
**This Rift will close in ten minutes.**

**Congratulations, you reached level 16!**
**Reach level 18 to select a new skill!**
**Reach level 20 to equip C-Grade gear!**
**Reach level 25 to unlock the Skill Evolution/Combination System!**

**One or more of your skills has broken into the next rank!**
**Sleep for at least 4 hours to upgrade your skills!**

# Chapter Eight

I pulled up the items I'd looted immediately, starting with the ring, while Darling looked through her own rewards. A moment later, House popped back in, waved three times, then did the same.

{Defiler's Band}
Grade: D
Item Level: 38
Slot: Finger
Quality: Rare
Primaries: +10 Intelligence, +5 Constitution, +5 Dexterity
Magical Resistance: +18%

I threw that on right away in place of my Brinebright Ring. Thankfully this new one was an improvement all around.

But the next item was the better pick-up by far: I'd finally found my first set item.

{Ghosthunter's Kickers}
Grade: D
Item Level: 42
Slot: Feet
Type: Leather

Quality: Rare
Suggested Class: Shadewalker
Primaries: +14 Intelligence, +6 Constitution
Secondaries: +2% Haste
Armor: +5%
Set Effect (2-piece): Sealed. Equip 1 piece of the {Ghosthunter} set to reveal this effect and 2 to activate it.
Set Effect (4-piece): Sealed. Equip 3 pieces of the {Ghosthunter} set to reveal this effect and 4 to activate it.
Set Effect (6-piece): Sealed. Equip 5 pieces of the {Ghosthunter} set to reveal this effect and 6 to activate it.

I slammed the boots on and pulled up the effect I'd just revealed, though I'd need to grab a second piece of the set before I could actually make use of it.

Set Effect (2-piece): While dual-wielding Enchanted Pistols, your Ravenblast is instant, and any pistol blast fired while out of combat is automatically Overcharged. Equip 1 more piece of the {Ghosthunter} set to activate this effect.

"Wow," I said. "Now that's more like it. Instant Ravens? Hell yeah."

"Great," Frank said. "More birds. Just what I need in my life."

"How does the instant mechanic work with casting? Can I just chain them rapid-fire?"

"You're still limited by the global cooldown at 1 second, but you can reduce that by stacking Haste Rating."

"So with Ravenblast being a 1.25-second cast right now, that's a pretty massive damage increase right off the bat. And more importantly, it means that anybody with a kick or something like that that can interrupt me or lock me out of a magical school won't be able to do it when I've got pistols equipped."

"Yeah, sets are big time. Speaking of big time, I should really have one."

I looked over at Darling, who was caressing a thick ring of metal just behind her gauntlets. "How'd you make out? I got a set piece that'll make some of my pistol casts instant once we snag a second one."

"Made out so well," she said. "So, so well. Got a nice pair of boots plus a bracer that's part of a set, yeah! One more piece and I'll have a small chance to activate Hexdoll Aura on every swing without activating the cooldown. God, I love procs."

"House? How about you?"

"I too adore the randomness of procs, and I also received similar items. Acquiring another set piece will allow me to use something called a Rumbler Turret." Her eyes widened slightly. "I feel overwhelmed by the desire to acquire a second set piece immediately. Normal?"

"You'll straight up get a new ability from your two-piece?" Darling said. "Man, how could you not want that? That sounds awesome. Wonder if it shakes the ground or something. Some kinda earthquake effect?"

The two of them went back and forth, and their shared enthusiasm kept me smiling as I looted the many mobs we'd killed.

"Frank?" I said. "Are we gonna get a set piece per Rift, or is that hoping for too much?"

"We should be able to get the two-piece together quickly enough, but some of that set's only gonna drop in the raid."

"Still a super nice pick-up."

"Just wait til you see how the first Trinket option pairs with it. It's gonna be so awe..." He trailed off and paused for a very, very long time.

I waited for him to continue, then tapped him when he didn't. "You good down there?"

"Yeah, I just figured that thought would come out as a vibration so I didn't have a put-down ready, then I was trying to come up with an insult on the fly but now too much time has passed for whatever I say to come off as both witty and cutting."

I suppressed a smile. "More info popping through now that I'm level 16?"

"Eh, guess so."

I finished up the looting, and though the payout wasn't as impressive outside of the Rift rewards themselves, I did pick up a sizable number of Soul Gems, including my first Large Soul Gem from the boss.

And there was a recipe that I was thrilled to find.

**Recipe: {Rune of the Ghostly Hunt} (Consumable) (Awards 6 skill points per craft)**
**Description: Your Ravenblast now deals Holy damage and applies the {Hunted} debuff.**
**Duration: 24 Hours.**
**Requirements: {Soul Gem} x30.**

I scoped out the debuff.

**{Hunted}**
**Effect: Undead enemies that die while under the effect of {Hunted}**
**will explode in a burst of Holy energy that will damage undead**
**enemies within 6 yards while healing friendly targets. This effect**
**heals and deals damage based upon your magical attack.**
**Duration: 5 seconds. Additional applications will refresh the**
**duration.**

"Hold on, pump the brakes," Frank said. "Explode?"

"Yep. But it's magic. Magic that heals."

"But in order to heal, you need to explode something else. Color me interested but skeptical."

The recipe was pretty expensive gem-wise, but it was currently the only one I had that would allow me to advance my skill without burning Large Soul Gems, so I went ahead and created one even though it pretty much fully depleted my stock.

**You created {Rune of the Ghostly Hunt} x1!**
**Your skill in Soulsmithing has increased to 90!**
**You unlocked a new Soulsmithing recipe: {Rune of Fortified**
**Illusions}!**

I inspected it.

**Recipe: {Rune of Fortified Illusions} (Consumable) (Awards 5 skill**
**points per craft)**
**Effect: Illusions created by your {Copy Image} skill become signifi-**
**cantly harder to see through.**
**Duration: 24 Hours.**
**Requirements: {Large Soul Gem} x15.**

"Anything on what exactly that does? I get that the resistance helps, but numbers would be better."

"No numbers, but basically it ups the requirement to see through your illusion. So if Lesser Truesight would normally work for a player, they'd have to bump up to Truesight instead. But it wouldn't have any effect on someone with a more powerful spell like Greater Truesight, that sorta thing."

I pursed my lips as House looked way too closely at the gloves Darling had received.

"Just how common are spells like that? Truesight and so on."

"Not common, but not crazy rare. I'd be more worried about gear if I were you. Enchanted lenses are available earlier in the game, plus they look ridiculous, all gaudy and golden. Bah. Who battles in a lens, honestly? And don't get me started on monocles."

"We would be so much more productive if I knew how to keep you from getting started on things."

"Bunch of bespectacled fools out there stalking the battlefield looking like Colonel Mustard."

I sent a quick message to House asking her to keep an eye out for a monocle I could use. "Anyway, great pick up on the rune. We can just throw one of those on a random pistol and use it whenever we swap to an illusion. Every little bit helps."

Darling tapped the tip of her sword against her boots, which came up just beneath her knees and were lined with silver thread. "Check it out."

She tapped a heel to the ground, then leaped across the courtyard while a thin trail of silk trailed behind her.

But after a second or so of soaring through the air, the thread snapped taut and she jerked back as if pulled and landed lightly back beside me.

She beamed. "Rare boots, Touchstone. I was so fixated on the set that I didn't even notice!"

"Nice!" I said. "I'm jealous."

"Give me to Darling real quick," Frank said.

I handed him over.

Darling frowned at him for a moment, then held him up to her ear. She grinned her gap-tooth smile, but there was something about it that I didn't like this time around.

"Killer, I didn't realize it was that flexible. Will do." She handed him back.

I dropped him into his loop. "I'm really tempted to sheathe you ahead of time, but I'm exercising—"

I cut off as Darling's name tag flashed purple and she kicked me full in the chest. I flew back and landed on my butt. I looked down and saw a silvery thread connecting us from the exact spot where her heel had made contact.

And at almost the same moment, I lifted up off the ground and flew right at her. She was holding her weapon like a baseball bat, and though I knew she wasn't about to kill me, I wasn't about to give Frank the satisfaction of watching me get batted through the air.

I waited until I was a few feet out from her, then activated Clonedrift and shot backward while my copy flew toward her in my place.

She struck it with a weak blow that probably would have knocked me out of the air without dealing much damage, but the clone exploded in her face all the same and stunned her for three seconds.

I canceled the spell and landed on my feet with my glowing blunderbuss already pointed in her direction.

She smiled once the stun faded, then held her hands up in mock surrender.

"Sorry, Frank made me do it."

I dropped the blunderbuss back into my inventory. "That's a really cool effect. You could kick someone and bait them into a movement ability, then yank them right back toward you. No cooldown or what?"

"Thirty seconds, but with two charges," Darling said. "And Frank said the effect depends on weight. So if something is heavier than me and I use that ability, I'll fly right at the target instead of it flying to me. Might be handy for encounters with big targets, like that Amalgam. Maybe I use that silk ability just before dodging something, then I activate it to fly right back into the fight."

"As one is wont to do," Frank said.

I scanned the loot again, then realized I'd missed the fact that I'd picked up another entry in the Taxidermist's Log. I pulled it up and gave it a quick scan.

{Entry 65}

*From my window, I can see men with torches riding down from the palace. I still haven't figured out exactly what happened, but I've heard the screams and I've seen the spectral creatures high above the city and rampaging through the streets, so I imagine I can guess the truth, or close enough to it: the Huntsman's cages must have failed him.*

*And I imagine that I'll make a fine scapegoat for this catastrophe. It'll be his word against mine, and in the end, I was the one that made his monsters, though he didn't leave me any choice.*

*I have little doubt that the guards are heading this way, but Isabel's green concoction is ready and mine should finish curing before they arrive. I still don't know if they'll do what I'm hoping they'll do—and they're far more concentrated than the purple variants I've been using to animate the dead—but I'm out of time, so I'm going to take a page out of Isabel's book and simply hope for the best.*

*I'm going to end this log with a theory, should someone find it and wonder what happened here. If there's anyone left in the aftermath, that is.*

*Isabel continues to insist that when we die—after we go wherever it is we go—some part of our spirit is left behind.*

*At this point, I believe she's got the right of it. I think that the memory loops that I've created—the happy ones, like our dog Rusty—work because whatever the spirit leaves behind is content to live in the joy of that final moment, replaying it over and over.*

*And the hateful ones? The creatures I reanimated for the Huntsman, loops that were forged out of his preys' dying moments, when the beasts knew nothing but fear and pain? I think the results speak for themselves.*

*It's ironic, really. I spent so much time trying to slow the progression of Isabel's disease that I didn't fully appreciate the time we had left. But wherever we go from here, at least I can say that we were happy, despite everything.*

*And of the countless memories we'll leave behind, I can honestly say that I would be lucky to live in any one of them.*

I mulled that over, thinking of the blue, ghostly dog that had greeted us back when we'd first entered the home and the terrifyingly powerful mammoth I'd seen in the Menagerie Wing.

Darling tapped at the air for a moment, then grinned. "Got an update on the raid: the first piece of interesting loot just dropped. Trash clearing group just found a Housing Pattern. I'll send you the link."

{Ghostlight Cannon} (Tier II Defensive Structure) (Communal Defense Building)
Creates a specialized, long-range cannon that fires a beam of ghostly energy that deals between 1,250-2,500 damage to all targets within a narrow cone up to 40 yards away. Damage dealt is halved against all creatures other than the undead, and hostile players take 80% reduced damage.
Attack Speed: 1 attack every 5 seconds.
Plot Requirement: Any available Turret Plot within a city's

Communal Defense Zone, but this item may be re-deployed any number of times.
Resources Required: {Steel Bar} x10, {Mithril Bar} x5, {Gold Bar} x1, {Solid Stone} x20, {Soul Gem} x10, {Large Soul Gem} x1.
Load Time: 2 Hours.

"Ohh," I said. "Trash is dropping patterns, huh? Plus the Communal Defense thing it mentions matches the prompt that went out with that first completed Rift."

"Yeah, I saw that too. First really cool find, and they haven't even been going for long. That group was a really good idea."

"Yup, I'm glad you put it together. It's interesting that those cannons can still target other players. 20% of 2,500 is still 500 damage at the top end—nothing to sneeze at in an AoE from forty yards out. Wonder how this defense zone thing will affect Goon's sieges. They can't be loving this system right about now."

"For sure."

A second call came in.

Incoming call for Alias {Francis} from player {Tyrann}.
Accept?

I grinned. "Tyrann's calling for Francis. He tried to get hold of him during that fight, too."

"Oooh," Darling said. "Wonder if he's on the warpath. Dead god and all." She tapped the air. "Gotta step aside for a second, trying to get another trash group running."

Frank chuckled. "Even if he is on the warpath, I imagine he's probably broken inside. That's what happens when you catch a face full of Frank."

"Seems unlikely given that you don't deal damage," I said.

"False. I deal emotional damage. The numbers might be nonexistent, but the scars run deeper, they last longer, and they're far more expensive to heal. Case in point: you and silky blankets."

I suppressed a laugh and eyed the call, considering whether or not I wanted to take it right now. "I dunno man, a broken leg is pretty expensive to get fixed up."

"A broken leg is temporary. Shattered self-esteem is forever. And do you have any idea how expensive therapy is?"

I snorted. "Now that you mention it, yeah, I can see that. You're definitely worse for your wielder's self-esteem."

"Another of the many burdens I bear." He paused. "To be clear, this particular burden is being responsible for the work. I quite enjoy the work itself."

"Don't I know it."

"Why would you want to ruin someone's self-esteem?" House said. "Is this a situation..." She trailed off, head cocking to one side. "Is it that what does not kill you makes you stronger?"

"Nah, that's almost never true as a general rule," Frank said. "And I'm not out here to help. I mean, I am, but I'm not."

"Yeah, hate to say it, but Frank's got the right of it. Tear a ligament and it'll tear easier in the future, that sorta thing."

"Uh huh. Think of it like this, House: self-esteem is a lot like teeth. It's a luxury, and some people deserve to have it beaten out of them."

"Hard disagree," I said, "but not surprising. Also House, don't think of it like that."

"I find sayings and idioms to be incredibly vexing," House said.

"You should just stop trying to use them," Frank said. "They're really not that important, so you should probably find another tree to bark up."

House narrowed her eyes at him. "Was that a deliberate attempt at mockery or was it unintentional?"

He hesitated. "The latter."

"Interesting."

Darling looked between the three of us, seemingly finished with whatever she'd been doing with the guild. "What exactly is happening right now?"

"Nothing important." I rubbed my face with both hands and pulled up the communication menu. "Alright, I'm gonna call Tyrann back. I'm gonna black out my end of the screen, so you don't need to worry about being seen, but keep it down."

"Yeah, House," Frank said. "Keep it down."

"I meant you, Frank. If you could somehow avoid talking about yourself for the next five minutes or so, I'd really appreciate it."

"You don't understand how difficult that is for me. Not talking about how great I am is like trying to hold a fart in on a trampoline. Doesn't matter what kind of precautions you take, it's gonna slip out eventually."

I pulled him out of his loop and steered him toward his sheath.

"Fine, fine, I'll be quiet, but I need to see the hurt in his eyes."

I dropped him back into his loop. "Seriously, stay silent. This is Francis, not Ned." I selected my Alias and rang Tyrann, who picked up before the call could ring a second time.

I expected his window to be dark as it had before, but he hadn't bothered to block his video feed this time around.

He was sitting on the railing of his massive Cruiser, which was cutting through the glassy, blue water beneath him with incredible speed.

The boat's wake was glowing bright green, and from the way the front of the vessel was tilting up, I knew they were using Soul Gem motors or maybe even something more powerful.

I couldn't see any of his people, given the angle, but the steady hum of conversation told me that the boat was loaded up with Cultists.

But strangest of all was the look on Tyrann's face. He was smiling.

And I, like Frank, hated it.

"Hey there," I said. "Sorry to hear about your God."

Tyrann's smile deepened, but I didn't miss the way his jaw muscles tightened at the mention of what he'd lost. "Yeah. Real shame, that. Thankfully it's not the end of the world thanks to the latest raid."

I cocked my head. "No? That's a relief. I would've thought your whole path was ruined."

"I thought it was too, at least at first. Don't get me wrong—that was a major blow. But with this new wing... ah." He winked. "Let's just say the possibilities are endless."

I had no idea what he meant by that, but the implication was clear enough: he'd found a way to salvage something. Or—and this seemed way more likely—Tyrann just wanted Francis to think that he had.

"Well, I'm glad to hear you're not down and out," I said. "What's going to happen to the Cult now that things have changed?"

"We're expanding, actually. In fact, I'm calling to officially extend an invitation."

I paused, then glanced down at Frank. I was about to ask if the Renown Perk I'd picked to improve my Alias would apply to joining the Cult, but he shook his head or blade or whatever it was he did.

"Mmm," I said. "I'd like to, but I'm thinking that things are going to be getting a lot busier in the Oasis over the coming days, and I should probably stay neutral. I do appreciate it, though."

He nodded. "I thought that might be the case."

"If you don't mind me asking, how did Ned pull the kill off?"

Tyrann tensed his shoulders but quickly relaxed. "He and his guild can travel between Rifts. Use them like portals. They popped right inside the defensive perimeter we'd set up and killed Sarchelious before we had a chance to defend him, then ran away when our real force arrived."

"Damn," I said, and I let the word hang.

"Yeah. He got lucky, but like I said, it's not over yet."

I was a bit taken aback by his honesty. I'd figured he'd have made up some sort of story about me being level 45 and one-shotting his God with Frank or something ridiculous like that. But there had probably been too many people involved in the kill for something like that to fly.

I cleared my throat. "Sorry to hear that."

"It is what it is. Just keep an eye out, because he's gonna be in your neck of the woods pretty soon if he isn't already."

"You got a source on that?"

"Nah, but I don't think I need one. There's precisely one finished Red Cathedral right now, and I don't think he's the type to pass up a shot at clearing anything first. That and his history with the Oasis."

"Fair enough. I'll let you know what I hear. I'm glad you called, though. I was hoping to talk to you about the Caravans."

He pursed his lips, then shrugged. "I'm still interested, but I'm afraid things have changed quite a bit since we struck that deal, and they're on the backburner for now."

Of course, what he actually meant by that was that he was no longer expecting to be able to skim a huge chunk of gold off the top for zero effort because his Tithe had been removed with the death of his God. But if I'd been in his position, I wouldn't be prioritizing them either.

"I get that."

"Don't get me wrong, I absolutely want an Auction House in each of our cities. I just can't justify expanding your network at the expense of everything else that's going on. Raids, new rifts. Busy times."

"Fair enough." A prompt came in, so I gave it a quick scan.

**Your Reputation with Highwater City has significantly decreased!**

That wasn't completely unexpected, given what I'd accomplished in the city, so I minimized the prompt and focused back on Tyrann.

"So how can I help you get back on your feet?"

He smiled. "I was hoping you might have some ideas there. We're on our way to the Black Oasis right now. Our Cathedral's close to completing, but unless somebody we don't know pulls off something major, I think it's going to be a day or two at least before it's done. And with the way this raid is shaping up, I don't like the idea of falling behind. It hurts to eat the travel time involved in getting from Koria to the Oasis, but our boats are starting to cut into it pretty nicely."

He patted the railing. "This ship should have us in shortly, but crossing the ocean in a couple hours is costing us a fortune in Soul Gems, and I can only bring so many people. Bulk of the group probably won't even arrive until late tonight or maybe even tomorrow morning."

I rubbed my chin. "I can probably hook you guys up with a bit of housing if you need it for a better rested buff, but I'm not sure what I can personally offer beyond that. My Inn's pretty advanced these days, but I haven't had the coin to build the city up the way I've wanted. I invested pretty heavily in Caravans myself as well, so funds have been limited."

"Housing is a start. You should think about what else you can offer, though."

I drew back. "That sounds like a bit of a threat, friend."

"Didn't mean it like that. All I've got are rumors at the moment, but..." He trailed off and looked left to right, then leaned forward and dropped his voice. "You didn't hear this from me, but let's just say I think you might be needing some friends you can depend on in the coming days."

I hesitated, weighing the odds that this was a bluff. I figured it probably was, but indulging him wouldn't cost me anything, so I was willing to see where it went.

"I see. Well, I've got a bit of info on the Menagerie Wing and one of the new Rift types, but that's about it."

"That would help."

I ran him through the cliff notes version of what we'd discovered so far: the new Rift Gem types, the strange cell back in the first wing, the curses, and so on. I even mentioned the defensive pattern we'd found, though I kept the details sparse enough that he wouldn't be able to recognize the cannon if we decided to build one.

I wasn't worried about sharing the information; as large as Tyrann's Cult was, they'd probably know everything we did within an hour or so if they didn't already.

"You haven't found anything curious in the Wing just yet?" he said.

"Curious?"

"Something that changes things?"

I racked my brain but came up empty. "Nope. I hit you with everything."

He exhaled and seemed to relax at that. Maybe he thought I'd been holding something back.

"Well, it's not my news to share. But let me be a bit clearer with you. And again, this warning didn't come from me, because I'm putting myself at serious risk by passing it on."

"Sure. What's up?"

"If you aren't already, then I suggest you start prioritizing the city itself over the new Rifts, or even the first Wing. And if I were you, I'd be all over those defensive patterns. Because unless I'm wrong about the way the winds are blowing, things are about to get very, very rough out your way."

I mulled that over, wondering what exactly he was referring to. My first thought was Goon and the sieges to the north and south, but neither of those events had anything to do with us, at least for a couple of days. So maybe he knew something about the Possibility King's forces that we didn't?

"Thanks for that. I'll keep the advice in mind."

"Least I can do." He squinted out at the ocean, and when he spoke next, his voice sounded a bit distant. "Still don't love the approach."

"What approach?"

He shrugged. "Never mind. Anyway, we'll be grinding Rifts in the Oasis here in a bit once we've arrived. Let me know if you change your mind on the invite, or if you just need a group for something. As for us, I'd appreciate whatever help you can come up with. Info, tactics, whatever."

"Can do. I'll reserve some space at the Inn and let you know what else I can figure out. Thanks again."

"Cheers, Francis." He ended the call.

I rubbed my forehead. "What the hell was that about? I might be needing some friends?"

"The search continues," House said.

Frank snorted. "That was an even better unintentional burn than mine."

She blinked. "I do not follow, but I am horrified regardless."

"Normal," I said. "But that call was really odd. You guys catch all of that?"

"I did, yeah," Darling said. "He was obviously holding something back.

Or a lot of somethings. You buying any of that stuff about his path not being a wash? There's no way a guy shoots to the top of the Renown Ladder by raising a God and doesn't end up screwed when the God drops dead, right?"

I waved the concern away. "Gotta be a bluff on his part. If Tyrann calls Francis and says everything he's built is dead in the water, then why would Francis help him? Tyrann needs leverage, and pretending he's still a major player is the best angle he could take."

I pulled up the Renown Ladder, and while the top five hadn't changed, Tyrann had already slipped from second to third.

"Scope the ladder out. He's sliding."

"He does still have a massive following though," Darling said. "Renown path or not, power is people."

I pursed my lips, then inclined my head. "True enough. There could definitely be something to what he's hinting at, but I still think he's minimizing just how much we hurt him."

"He should have been way more devastated on a personal level at the very least," Frank said. "Did you see what I did to him?"

"We did see that, several times in fact."

"The whole guild saw it," Darling said.

House stood up a little taller. "I too remotely witnessed the Franking of Tyrann."

"We should probably watch it again," Frank said, and before I could respond, Tyrann was skimming across the water in a little window in the top-left corner of my vision. Then he was skimming across the water again. And again.

I laughed. "I really don't think I'll ever get tired of that."

"You and me both," Frank said.

"Does that call change anything for us?" Darling said.

I shrugged. "Not really? I don't even know at this point. I guess we know Tyrann's close to the Oasis. It's kinda crazy that he's almost already here."

"That boat is seriously fast. Wonder what it costs him to shoot over like that."

"Yeah." I rubbed my chin and eyed House. "I think we stick to the plan, but maybe a quick trip into town is in order before we hit the next Rift. See if the Auction House has anything that can help us and maybe scope out those Communal Zones.

"If we need to plan something there, we'd better start early. I know the tree isn't quite finished yet either, but I really, really want to get a look at it regardless."

Frank buzzed. "Definitely need to get back to town. I'd maybe even hurry it up a bit."

"Okay then. It's settled."

Darling glanced at Frank, then looked away.

I leaned in a little closer. "What's up?"

"Hm?"

"You were staring at Frank."

"Normal," Frank said. He dropped his voice. "Probably just got lost in my sheen for a moment—it happens."

She smiled. "There's just... there's one thing that I really don't understand."

"Frank's general appeal?" I said.

"Rude."

"No," she said, "but it does have to do with him."

"As all good things do," Frank said.

Darling raised a thin eyebrow at him. "I meant more about you guys needing me for this Rift."

"What is there not to get?"

"Yeah," I agreed. "I just assumed we needed three."

"No, I floated the idea of doing one together, but then he said you guys needed me specifically. I'm not complaining, I'm just trying to figure out if that was a hint or something. My kit wasn't exactly key to clearing this thing, and it wasn't like I had an item you needed or anything like that. In fact, my kit wasn't even really good for it at all." She stepped up next to the exit Rift near the center of the courtyard.

"I wasn't being specific," Frank said.

Darling frowned. "What do you mean?"

He dropped his voice to a whisper again. "Uh oh. I don't even have a reason, I just wanted her to come."

She took a step back toward us, craning her neck. "Come again?"

I rubbed the back of my head, then decided to help him out. "He said that he wasn't talking about the Rift."

"Huh?"

"When Frank said he needed you, he just meant in general."

Darling's eyes went wide, then she broke into a grin. "That was good, Frank. That was really good. Let's get going then, yeah?"

She stifled a laugh with one hand, then turned around and jumped into the Rift.

"Huh," Frank said. "Where the hell did that come from?"

"That was in exchange for the Trinket and the Bank pattern."

"Deal."

"And I want my Frank points back too."

He hesitated. "Well, I'd like to help you out, but I already said deal, so my metaphorical hands are tied."

"She laughed, Frank, and you got the credit. We both know that's worth the 1,000 points I lost on that bet over the liquid." I fixed him with a firm look. "Science."

He flinched. "Crap, I should have seen that coming. I'll okay the refund on my end, but I'm gonna have to run it by the higher-ups before it goes through."

"Who the hell is higher than... no. Never mind, that'll work."

"Or I could cut through the red tape and award you 1,000 unrelated points."

I thought about that for a bit but decided to pass. "No, I specifically want the ones that I had before."

"Perfectly understandable. I'll keep you on a post."

"Are people truly saying that now?" House said, hopeful.

"No. He's mocking you again, but this time it's deliberate."

"I see." She looked down at him. "Then I suppose I will move forward with my current plan."

"Hold up, what plan?" Frank said. "What are you planning? Since when do you plan things?"

"Ever since I became wise to your attempts to pilfer my companions."

"You really aren't going to let that go, are you?"

"Apparently not."

I stared at her, laughing. "What do you mean, apparently?"

"Frank, you are not the only one who refuses to be bamboozled," House said, which made me snort.

Frank dropped his voice a third time. "Oh man. I'm beginning to worry that we've created a monster."

"Oh, it's we now, huh?" I said. "And really? You're just now beginning to think about that? Because I've been alarmed for days. Remember when she happily agreed to bring you along if she decided to wipe out humanity? That was a pretty obvious red flag for me, but you do you."

"Yeah. Sowing all of that was super fun, but now with the reaping… meh. Not sure it was worth it."

"Did you hear that House? Frank just said reaping isn't worth it."

"You can't just blurt that out completely out of context," Frank said. "I'm a huge fan of reaping, House. Reaping is one of my favorite things."

Before House could reply, a message came in from Darling: *get out here, oasis, not the hall.*

"Alright, we gotta move," I said. "Darling needs us."

"She's probably going through Frank withdrawal," Frank said. "You can't hit someone with the smoothness then immediately pull away. It's hard on the heart."

I rolled my eyes. "She shouldn't have complimented you. Seems like it went straight to your shaft."

Frank grimaced. "It's uncomfortable when you do it."

"That was the goal, actually."

"The tables appear to have been rearranged so that the two of you are sitting on opposite sides," House said.

Frank sighed. "So close, yet so very, very far away."

# Chapter Nine

I popped out through the portal and back onto the hot, black sands. One of the Delta's many rivers was rushing nearby, and we must have emerged beneath a rare cloud because we were standing fully in the shade.

"Took you long enough," Darling said.

"Yeah, sorry," I said. "Frank was monologuing about how lame reaping is. You know how it goes."

She cocked her head. "Really?"

"First of all, how dare you," Frank said. "And second of all, it was a much longer conversation where the context clearly—"

I sheathed him, so he cut off.

"He do something to piss you off back in the Rift?" Darling said.

"Nah, just keeping him on the toes that he doesn't have. I'll pull him out in a second before he gets too sweaty. So what did we need to see?"

She pointed her sword at the sand. "The shadow's the first hint."

"The shadow appears geometric in nature," House said. "As if cast from some giant, floating rhombus that is currently hovering directly overhead."

Darling blew out a puff of air. "Kinda ruins the surprise, but fine."

I looked up, where a huge, black prism was floating slowly through the sky.

"It appears that I was technically correct," House said. "It is indeed a giant, floating rhombus that is hovering directly overhead."

The construct was diamond-shaped and made of dark glass, and it was creeping toward the Black Oasis even though the wind was clearly currently blowing the sand off the top of the nearby dunes in the opposite direction.

I shivered at the sight above us, then unsheathed Frank. "What's going on here?"

"Oh wow," he said. "Look, the font of all knowledge is needed yet again. Surprise, surprise."

I pointed up at the strange structure. "Alright, font, say something useful about that thing."

"I can say it's not…" He trailed off, vibrating. "Man, this is really pissing me off. That prism isn't fluffy."

"I concur with your assessment," House said.

"That wasn't an assessment, House," he said. "That was nonsense. I wonder if I could get around my restrictions by doing something with nonsense since that doesn't seem to be filtered."

I rolled my shoulders. "I think you already do more than enough on that front." I looked to the city, to the floating prism, then back again. It was moving at a slow rate, but the city's four wards weren't far off. "House, can you tell me how long we have before that thing reaches the outer limit of the Vale?"

"You possess 19 minutes and 43 seconds before the rhombus reaches the Vale." She looked at Darling. "Approximately 20 minutes."

"Thanks for the weird clarification," Darling said.

I scratched the back of my head. "This feels like it might be bad for us."

"Or it could be awesome," Frank said.

"Yeah, and your awesome is my terrible, so the point stands."

Darling jammed her sword into the sand and leaned against the pommel. "Could be what Tyrann was warning you about."

"That's possible for sure, but at the very least, this seals it for a quick trip into the city. We need to see what this prism thing is all about."

"Works for me," Darling said, summoning her buggy. House hopped in and scooted over to make room for me, but I hesitated.

"You guys go ahead. I need to throw an illusion up first, and it's probably better if we don't roll in together with that in place."

Darling and House set off for the Oasis with a wave, so I let them get a little bit ahead, then summoned my bike, mounted up, and headed to a nearby Rift.

Once I was back in the Hall, I applied the Rift Gem vendor illusion that I'd stored earlier, then picked a Rift that was close to the city, popped through it and back onto the sands, then jogged up and into the new and improved Black Oasis.

I hiked up to the Commerce Ward, and though the Royal Ward had always been the only section of the city with a true and fully defensible wall, I still found it a little odd to stroll right into the city without seeing any of the Kings' personal guards, or even Arlann's crew.

But other than that, the city was absolutely bustling, the streets packed with people and vendors and carts and mounts. The rope bridges that connected the wards were hanging low beneath the weight of the constant foot traffic moving overhead, and far beneath the bridges, in the deep valleys between the dunes, the blue waters we'd unleashed were running smooth and fast.

As I walked through the city, something caught my eye before I even made it to the first proper building: a highlighted section that looked almost like an enormous Housing Plot except for its light, reddish shade.

The highlighted section was about thirty feet wide, and it appeared to curve around the entire edge of the Commerce Ward. I peered across the valley toward the Residential Ward and saw a similar zone over there as well, the sort of space where you could neatly build a wall without disturbing the city within.

"That's the new Communal Defense Zone," Frank said. "Each ward's got one that runs around it."

"I see that, thanks."

"Should be some new tabs too."

I opened up my menus and found a new section for Defensive Structures. The options were vast, though the great majority of them were blacked out. The choices were arranged like a branching talent tree, but everything beyond the first tier looked like it would remain hidden until the city had built some of the earlier options.

I scanned three of the available choices.

{Wooden Perimeter Wall} (Tier I Defensive Structure)
Effect: Creates a sturdy wooden fortification around the ward of your choice, complete with a guardhouse at a predesignated location.
Plot Requirements: Predesignated space within the Communal Defense Zone.
Resources Required: 400 {Lumber}, 50 {Stone}.

Load Time: 8 hours.

{Wooden Spike Barriers} (Tier I Defensive Structure)
Effect: Creates a number of wickedly spiked barriers around the ward of your choice. These barriers may be moved and repositioned within the Communal Defense Zone any number of times.
Plot Requirements: Predesignated space within the Communal Defense Zone.
Resources Required: 100 {Lumber}, 25 {Leather Scraps}.
Load Time: 4 hours.

{Defensive Trench} (Tier I Defensive Structure)
Effect: Creates an eight-foot-wide and eight-foot-deep trench around the ward of your choice, complete with narrow passages at predesignated locations.
Plot Requirements: Predesignated space within the Communal Defense Zone.
Resources Required: 5 Gold.
Load Time: 2 hours.

Each of those options also had a couple of Tier II upgrades available: the wall could be bumped up from wood to stone, the trench could be deepened and widened and spiked at the bottom or flooded and turned into a moat, and the moveable wooden barriers could be tipped with iron.

The options weren't mutually exclusive either, and the individual upgrades had several other tiers of their own that I couldn't see just yet.

I scanned the sky. I spotted the black prism our completed Rift had created almost immediately, and though it was still moving slowly, several others had already spawned much farther out.

"I guess it's a good thing we didn't throw all of our gold into the Caravans right away. This is gonna get expensive."

"Yeah, but this zone works a little differently than the regular Housing Plots. You can chip in a little bit of money and the construction will start right away. The totals are what you need to complete the structure."

"So we could build part of a Wall or a couple of those Spike Barriers at a time?"

"Uh huh."

I skimmed the options again, then closed the menu. "Cool, thanks.

Let's pause on this until we see what those prisms do. Not like we're going to get anything completed in the next 20 minutes."

I made my way through the crowd of brightly dressed NPCs and players and headed up onto one of the raised platforms that led to the rope bridges. From there, I had a pretty good view of the Commerce Ward.

And it was impossible to miss the crown of the tree rising above and behind my Inn. Its branches were still bare, but now they were covered in huge, emerald buds. Maybe ten feet or so of the tree was already visible, and I still felt like I could see the thing growing right in front of my eyes.

I took a deep breath and refocused—I could worry about the tree and what its emergence meant after I knew the city was at least somewhat safe. I scanned the crowd again, searching for the guards that had been omnipresent mere hours earlier but finding none.

"Are you thinking what I'm thinking?" I said.

"That I should have theme music?"

"Dude, focus. We've got a ton of Rifts outside, each of which is going to spawn one of those ominous prism things, and there's not a guard in sight. And the defenses we're supposed to build up are hours away at best."

I pushed through the city, intent on reaching the Guard House as soon as possible.

"Fair," Frank said. "But what about the music thing? Maybe All Star by Smash Mouth."

"Not the time, Frank."

I dodged a high-powered Tractor that someone was using to haul maybe twenty Trade Packs behind it on a six-wheeled trailer. I stepped to the side of the road and bit my bottom lip.

"We really ought to be running those while we've still got access to the Hall."

"We ought to be doing a lot of stuff."

I sighed. "Yeah. Things are moving fast."

I threaded my way through the crowd until I reached the Guard House, where a trio of armored guards were exiting via the steps while Arlann looked on, stone-faced.

One of the guards in front ripped his insignia off and dropped it onto the ground. I grabbed the insignia off the sand, dusted it off, and headed up to speak to the Captain.

# Chapter Ten

Arlann eyed me, his eyes glinting with that same golden light I'd noticed the last time he'd seen through one of my illusions.

He motioned me inside without smiling and directed me into his war room, where I found Sarissa lounging on a chair in the corner. I nodded her way, and she returned the gesture with the brightest smile I'd seen from her yet.

The news wasn't all good when it came to her, though. When I inspected her, I saw that she'd been correct when she'd claimed that destroying the tower would likely rob her of much of her strength.

She was still powerful as a level 25 Elite, but that put her only slightly above the guards I'd seen on the steps, which was a pale shadow of what she'd been before when I'd been unable to read her level and she'd had 15,000 Health, plus ten times that in Mana.

Arlann shut the door behind me, so I dropped my illusion and sank into a chair in front of his desk.

"So what's going on? Where are all the guards?"

"You want the full story, or the summary?" Arlann said.

"Best to hit me with the shorter version. I've got a lot on my plate right now."

He seated himself behind his desk and clasped his hands in front of him. "Today is payday for the guards."

I looked from him to Sarissa and back again. "...okay? What does that have to do with what's going on?"

"Everything," Sarissa said. "Because nobody is paying them."

"What? Why not?"

"The vast majority of our funding came from Highwater," Arlann said. "And ah, well..." His gaze lingered on Sarissa, and despite everything, his face softened into a brief smile. "Before Sarissa and I left the city, the Captain of the Queen's guard informed us that Highwater is no longer in a position to subsidize the Vale in any way, effective immediately."

I rocked back in my chair. "Great timing. So it's my fault, huh?"

"Isn't everything?" Frank said.

Sarissa raised her hands above her head and stretched. "I'd say there's plenty of blame to go around. Nor will assigning it help us much at the moment."

I rubbed my eyes, then sent a quick update to Darling and asked her to pivot to pulling as many guild members to the Oasis as she could to defend against whatever the prism was going to throw at us.

She responded immediately and said she'd do her best, but that pretty much everyone who was currently on was either mid-Rift or mid-raid so she wasn't sure what she could really do with how tight the timeframe was.

"What about the rest of the funding?" I said. "The bulk of it came from Highwater, so what else is there?"

Arlann sighed. "The Merchant Kings. But Vesuvian is still missing, and the other two packed up their carriages and rolled north almost as soon as the cliffs broke open. Their personal guards are clearing out their estates as we speak, and I imagine they'll flee the city before they help with anything substantial."

"So the Kings are all moving up into Highwater with the Queen. That doesn't seem great for the city, but the total lack of guards is the bigger problem for now."

"The desertion isn't absolute. I imagine—well, I hope—that some of the guards will stick it out until next week." Arlann stood up and moved to the nearest window, through which I could make out another of the dark prisms drifting toward us in the distance.

"Under normal circumstances, I'd like to believe that almost everyone would have stuck around. But a man can't feed his family on promises, and I think everyone is well aware that a storm is brewing on the horizon. One that we don't even understand."

"I'm afraid that's a severe understatement," Sarissa said.

I pursed my lips. "What do you guys need to keep it together?"

"In the short term?" Arlann said. "Gold. And if the city survives what-ever comes its way over the next few days? I'm not sure. I won't defend the Merchant Kings, but they did keep the city running. And without someone in charge, without someone scheduling shifts, handling the books, and so on, I don't know what lies in front of us."

A quest came in.

**New Quest: {A Competent Hand!} (Unique Quest)**
**Objective: Replace the departed Merchant Kings with a steward capable of running the Vale.**
**Reward: Dependent upon candidate selection.**

I took the quest and eyed Frank, figuring that he'd no doubt seen it coming given everything that had transpired with Vesuvian, but I held my questions for now.

"I'll see what I can do there."

I still had the former Merchant King in my pocket—well, holed up back in the guild's Stronghold—but I couldn't trust him in the slightest. And while he'd shown a few flickers of ambition, I wasn't about to put him back in charge of the Vale's future at the drop of a hat, especially at such a crucial moment.

I doubted that we were free of the other two Merchant Kings either, but as Arlann had said, it was abundantly clear that a storm was coming. And I wasn't surprised that the two of them had packed up and shipped out to protect their interests.

"How much gold does the guard run a week?" I said.

"Fifty men, a gold to each."

I sank a bit deeper into my chair. "Fifty gold a week. I could maybe swing that tomorrow morning between what I have now and whatever the Auction House and the Inn pay out, but I don't know."

"Your last daily payout was 10 gold," Frank said. "I can't give you the exact figures and you've got a lot of Caravans on the move so your next payout should spike pretty good, but you're nowhere near 50 yet."

I paused. "Might still be doable if I borrowed from the guild on top of everything else, but I don't love the idea of that."

"I can't do maybe if men are going to be putting their lives on the line," Arlann said. "I'll scrounge up what guards I can regardless of what you can or can't do, but I'll need a guarantee of payment before I ask them to respond to whatever's coming."

I stood up, head spinning. "I understand. And I'd like to guarantee that I'll have it by tomorrow, but I don't think I can do that in good faith."

"I figured you'd feel that way, and I appreciate your candor. But there is... another way. A way where I'd feel comfortable delaying the guards' payment."

I sat back down. "Yeah? What would you need?"

"Collateral," he said, and I didn't miss the way he and Sarissa both glanced at Frank.

I shook my head slightly. "What else?"

"What do you mean, what else?" Frank said.

Arlann pursed his lips. "I'm open to suggestions."

I swallowed. "What about the Inn? It's making good money, and it'll be busier than ever in the coming days."

"True. But if the city takes the amount of damage I fear it's about to receive, I can't imagine many will be keen to stay for long. Perhaps something with more upside."

"You're thinking of the Auction House."

"The Auction House as well," he corrected. "And everything else."

I swallowed. "Everything else? Meaning all of my plots?"

"Tree and all," Sarissa added, and Arlann nodded his agreement so quickly that it was obvious that the two of them had discussed this ahead of time.

"Got about fifteen minutes before the prism hits," Frank whispered.

I gritted my teeth. "So let's say I agree to this. What happens next?"

"I reactivate the guard immediately. If you meet the deadline we agree on when it comes to payment, then we're square. If not, I'll be forced to liquidate your assets. And those sales will fund the guard for as long as possible."

"I assume I get a full week," I said, hopeful. "If so, I think I can probably swing that."

He shook his head. "In normal times, I'd happily agree. But these are not normal times."

I held up three fingers. "Three days? I think that's more than fair given how much you'd stand to make by seizing my assets."

Arlann rapped his fingers on his desk. "Best I can do is five shifts, or sixty hours."

"Two-and-a-half days? That's it?"

"To be blunt," he said, "I'm not even sure the city will be standing by the end of tonight, and I can't liquidate a ruin."

"Psst," Frank said. "This is mechanical."

"Huh?"

Frank cleared his throat. "Give us a second?"

"Certainly," Arlann said.

I bent down a little and dropped my voice. "What's up?"

"I mean, this is going to be enforced mechanically—if you don't come up with the gold, he's really gonna seize your stuff. You won't be able to talk him out of it or pay him back later once the deadline hits, that sort of thing.

"You could probably kill him before the transfer and replace him with a figurehead—ideally me—but still. Unless you do something like that or maybe find a way to renegotiate this thing before the deadline hits, it's binding."

"Thanks for the heads-up. But no, killing Arlann is not an option."

"Yeah, yeah, I know. I just thought suggesting it might influence your future behavior on a subconscious level."

"You're not supposed to tell people that you're actively trying to manipulate them." I rubbed my temples, then got up and looked out the window, where four more prisms had already spawned.

I was tempted to kick the can down the road a bit—to see what happened with that first prism before I struck a deal—but my gut was telling me that the guards would be needed immediately, plus Arlann would probably need some time to organize his people.

I met Arlann's eyes and extended a hand across the table. "You've got a deal, so long as you can get the guard back to work immediately."

He stood up and shook my hand. "Done. Thank you."

"Alright, I gotta run, and you're about to have incoming. No idea what it's going to look like."

He grabbed his helmet off the desk and slammed it on. "When?"

I was already halfway out of the room with my illusion back in place. "Ten minutes tops."

"I'll get word out and see what I can do, but that doesn't leave us much time."

"Just do whatever you can." I nodded at the two of them. "Good luck."

I excused myself and headed back out onto the city streets and ran toward the Inn. I still had a few minutes to spare, so I wanted a better look at the tree now that I was already here, and even more than that, I was looking forward to seeing Lars. But then I remembered he was likely still halfway across the world.

Despite everything, I smiled at the thought. Hopefully he was having the sort of adventure he'd always wanted.

Once I reached the Inn, I stepped inside and waved at Lars' mother, then headed out into the back. I ran down the hall, looked both ways to make sure I hadn't been followed, then slipped out into the hidden courtyard.

Well, I tried to. But instead of walking into open space, I slammed face-first into rough bark, then staggered back and did a double-take.

"I could have told you about that once you were inside the inn," Frank said. "But it seemed funnier not to do that."

"What's going on here?" I didn't want to draw attention to the door or to myself, so I closed it and locked it through the permission menu, then slipped back out of the Inn into the busy streets.

"Our little tree is growing up."

"That much though? It's only been a couple hours—is the trunk already blocking the whole courtyard?"

"Mana's a hell of a drug."

I took a deep breath.

"Alright. I'd like to hit the Auction House real quick, but it's probably more important to just get out there and face whatever's coming. Let's go find out if that deal I just made was worth it."

# Chapter Eleven

Darling, House, and I stood about twenty yards beyond the outer limits of the Commerce Ward, where the dune the section of the city was built upon began to slope down. I'd disappeared into a distant Rift then reappeared nearby with my actual appearance in place, and my skin was already prickling.

Part of me wanted to be far away—to be adventuring somewhere ahead of the player base's leveling curve where I'd be safer—but I couldn't stand the thought of leaving the Vale to deal with whatever we'd set off by clearing that first Rift.

The black prism was only a couple of hundred yards away now, and while it had been drifting high in the air, now it was rapidly descending as it neared the city.

I loaded up my blunderbuss, then shouldered my rifle. "I've got a really, really bad feeling about this."

Darling drew a line in the sand with her sword. "How bad can it really be? Just one Rift, right? There's hundreds of them out there."

I chewed the inside of my cheek and glanced back at the city. I'd been hoping to see Arlann running out with the rest of the guard by now, but they were nowhere to be seen.

Darling still had a few guildies she thought would show up, but I was starting to think they'd end up being too late as well.

"Yeah, maybe you're right." I glanced down at Frank. "Kinda worrisome that this guy isn't mouthing off about how much of a coward I am for being concerned, though."

"That is a fair point," Darling said, laughing slightly.

And when Frank still didn't respond, I started to worry for real because that seemed like some sort of signal.

The four of us watched in silence as the black prism ghosted toward us, drifting down and down until its lowest point jabbed into the ground. It kept coming until it was moving through nearly two feet of sand, leaving a deep trench behind it.

Finally the prism came to a stop, then it started to spin with so much force that the sand around it was thrown away. A deep hum filled the air, a resonant sound that I felt in my bones. The prism flashed once, twice.

"That's okay," Frank said.

It flashed a third time.

Frank grunted.

A fourth time. A fifth.

"Oh. We are totally—" He trailed off, buzzing.

The prism flashed a sixth and final time, and Frank vibrated more strongly than ever before.

The prism exploded and sent shards of dark glass flying in every direction. The pieces fell far short of our little group, but judging from how deeply they'd punched into the sand, they were capable of doing serious damage.

The prism itself—or what was left of it—was hidden within the cloud of sand and grit and pulverized glass that the explosion had kicked up, but an eerie light was shining within the darkness, and I could already tell that we were dealing with something massive.

And when the wind finally stripped the cloud away, the result was so much worse than I'd feared.

**{Starlit Tyrant} (Level 19 Undead) (Elite++)**
**HP: 115,000/115,000**
**MP: 100,000/100,000**

We were standing not even a hundred feet from a tyrannosaurus that looked as if someone had sculpted it out of the night sky.

Its huge body was dark purple and spectral, populated with twinkling stars that kept the whole creature shining from within with a light of its own. It stood thirty feet tall on two thick legs with a long, muscular tail, and its claws and teeth shone with pearly light.

It lowered its great head to the ground and sucked in a loud breath, chest heaving, grains of sand pulling up and flying toward it. It looked directly at me, then let loose a primal roar.

The aggro hit me then, an impossible weight that already had my shoulders slumping. Darling and I exchanged a quick look.

She shook her head. "No chance."

"Agreed," I said. "Can you still get your buggy up, or are you locked into combat?"

The summon bar appeared above her head almost instantly. "Got it."

"House, as soon as that buggy is up, I want you to drop two Sludgeslings, combine them into an Oilslick Turret, then hop into the buggy and get out of here. That won't deal damage, so you should be fine on aggro. I'm just going to try to pull it away from the city."

"If someone's going to draw it off, it should be one of us," Darling said.

I shook my head as the great creature roared again and rumbled toward us, head low to the ground, running like an oversized raptor with its mouth wide open.

"You guys can stick close and stay mounted up, and if I die, you two can dash in and grab Frank. I don't think you'll be able to grab aggro off me without getting splatted either, and that'll make Frank sad."

"True," Frank said.

"And nobody likes sad Frank."

"False. All versions of me are inimitably likable."

Darling grimaced as her buggy completed. She hopped inside and grabbed the wheel, then flexed her fingers around it.

House tossed two of her turrets out and combined them before they'd even hit the ground. The two metallic discs smashed together and formed a single, larger disc that expanded into the turret I'd asked for upon landing.

It spewed oil out across the ground, creating a large pool that would slow whatever entered it while it persisted.

House hopped into the buggy, and though Darling hesitated for another agonizingly long moment, she hit the gas and drove the two of them a little way around the outer limits of the city.

I put House's puddle between the creature and me, then I stood my ground as the spectral monstrosity ate up the distance between us with long, predatory strides.

"Can you keep me posted on the duration of the pool?" I said.

"Uh huh. fifteen seconds left."

That wasn't going to leave me much room to work with. "Don't imagine you can share whatever ability this thing is going to lead with."

"Tried. Can't even send the Codex entry on this thing yet. We need levels."

I nodded and pressed my rifle to my shoulder. The creature was Undead, which meant Dreadful Shot was out, so I aimed a Fettering Shot its way and sent a silvery beam of light flying over the pool of oil that separated us.

The great creature ducked its head, and the beam passed harmlessly over its broad back while the word *Miss* floated up above it.

"Four-level gap," I muttered.

"Speaking of level gaps..." Frank said, and I felt like he was pointing at the pool of oil that House had left behind.

"Crap, you're right—House is even lower."

The Starlit Tyrant charged right into the puddle without slowing in the slightest while dozens of *Resist* messages scrolled above it.

I put on a burst of speed, then launched myself toward the creature's open mouth and spun a 180 in the air. I activated Clonedrift and shot backward, zooming right between the beast's legs and right beneath its thick tail.

The creature snapped its jaws around my clone, and a shower of sparks flew from between its many teeth.

Thankfully the stun connected where my Fettering Shot had failed, so I was able to hit the ground running and clear the beast's tail before it recovered. The dinosaur roared and pivoted, immediately giving chase.

I spotted House and Darling off to my left, racing over the dunes and occasionally launching up and off them, sand flying behind the vehicle.

Then I spotted a recent change in the landscape: directly ahead of me, two rivers merged and poured out into the ocean that bordered the Black Oasis. But the rivers had eroded several of the dunes that had once directly framed the sea, and what was left of them looked a lot like a cliff instead of the gradual slope that had been there before.

I ran on, gulping air with every step I took.

"Is there a drop up there or am I seeing things?"

"Big drop, yeah. But you're not gonna kill that thing by giving it a bath."

"Just need time."

"See the three dunes in front of you? If we're gonna die on a hill, then I insist we pick the one on the right."

"Why? That one's farther out."

"Just do it and keep your eyes open."

I made for that area and tried to ignore the rasping breaths and thunderous stomps that were sounding closer and closer behind me.

"It's almost back in melee range," Frank said.

I risked a glance over my shoulder and nearly lost my footing: I was almost eye to eye with the Tyrant.

It lunged forward and opened its mouth, so I blasted a Water Jet straight down its throat and shot backward. I hurtled through the air with no semblance of control, though I did notice the great beast tip forward and try to bite me, only to get a mouthful of sand.

I landed about a hundred feet from where the last of the dunes had collapsed into the ocean.

But as soon as I got back up and running, the circle of sky above me darkened to indigo. I hazarded another glance back and spotted a cast bar above the now-motionless Tyrant's head that read: *Skyfall.*

"Heads up," Frank said as circles of sand lit up in red all around me, leaving narrow gaps between them. "Coming from a dinosaur, that spell is as deadly as it is ironic!"

I leaped over one of the red circles and landed firmly in one of the gaps with both feet. A series of blindingly fast silver projectiles lanced down around me, and for a split second, I thought I'd dodged some kind of nasty, piercing spell judging from the way the missiles had punched into the sand.

Then there was a muffled boom—as if an explosion had sounded from underwater—then all of the sand around me within a twenty-foot radius rose into domes and exploded upward.

I was sent airborne, vibrations rippling through me as the immense shockwave blasted me with sand and sent me almost straight up into the sky.

"You got blasted, your Health at 51%."

The huge creature rumbled forward far below, mouth open, eyes locked on me as I plummeted down out of the sky.

With both Clonedrift and Water Jet on cooldown, I didn't have many options left and I was now only a few feet above the spectral monstrosity's open mouth, so I popped Double Cast to Water Jet myself sideways and away.

I hit the ground hard, and the vibrations told me I'd taken even more damage as I skipped partway up a dune before rolling to a stop. I jumped back to my feet and put on a burst of speed, urging myself toward the dune Frank had chosen for no discernable reason.

"Clonedrift should be up before you hit the water!"

I nodded and kept pushing, feeling the sand slide away beneath me as I struggled up the steep, sandy hill. I tripped and nearly faceplanted but managed to throw a hand out and catch myself before I fully lost it.

I heard the beast's pounding pursuit and knew it was almost on top of me, but I couldn't spare the time to look.

The blood was pounding in my ears by the time I reached the top of the dune. Clonedrift wasn't ready yet, but I could feel the creature's hot breath on the back of my neck, so I took two long steps then threw myself off the top of the dune before I even saw what was on the other side.

The hill beneath me fell away completely, looking like a mountain that'd been cleaved down the middle and had half of it cleanly removed. I had to be at least a hundred feet in the air, and my stomach was already doing flips.

Blue water sparkled beneath me, and the surf below was full of sharp, dark rocks that the river must have exposed as it ran along. I glanced up as I fell, hoping to see the great dinosaur tumbling toward me in pursuit.

Instead, it stood with its great clawed feet digging securely into the edge of the dune while little rivers of sand ran down beneath it. My face flushed hot. It hadn't taken the bait.

"Rocks coming at ya real quick," Frank said.

With a great deal of flailing, I managed to orient myself so I was facing the ground as the wind continued to tear at my clothing. I rushed down toward the river, heart pounding. Clonedrift still wasn't up. I watched the ability, urging it along.

I caught a flash of green set within some kind of hole in the side of the dune, so bright that I thought I'd hallucinated it in a rush of panic.

I started spamming Clonedrift as the rocks drew closer, generating a string of red error messages. I blitzed toward the ground, heading chest-first for a dark spire of rock that looked fully capable of impaling me.

Clonedrift activated while I was maybe three feet above the rock, and since my back was facing the open sky above, I snapped backward, all of my momentum vanishing at once as I was sent back up into the air.

The whiplash was so bad that my vision blacked out for a moment, and I ended up letting Clonedrift take me considerably higher than I should have before I regained the presence of mind needed to cancel the spell.

I popped free above the very same tower of rock. I twisted in the air and contorted myself out of the way, though the very tip of the structure snagged my leather trousers and spun me into the cold waters below belly-first.

The surf where ocean met river was frothy and chaotic, and it battered me between the rocks and the riverbed beneath for a long while before I managed to surface, gasping.

I wiped salty water from my eyes with my sleeve as the great creature loomed high above me, perched like a glowing gargoyle at the very edge of the dune. It leaned low and roared in my direction, causing the sky to darken above it, then turned and ran the way it had come.

Right toward the Black Oasis.

# Chapter Twelve

"Mission accomplished," Frank said as I pulled myself out of the water and immediately started summoning my bike. "We've successfully saved ourselves. Particularly me."

"That was not the goal, Frank. If anything, that was the opposite of what I intended." I dashed off a quick message to Darling letting her know that the Tyrant was headed her way and got a quick *I know* in response, then nothing else, which was ominous in and of itself.

My bike spawned, so I jumped onto it and throttled it alongside the sandy cliffline and toward a dune that was gentle enough that I knew I'd be able to make it up.

I threw up my mini map to check my orientation and make sure I was headed the right way, then ramped a few feet off the dune and flew right over a pair of players in leather armor who had been sitting across from each other with a small campfire between them.

I smashed back down onto the sand and nearly lost control as the front wheel dug in but managed to right it and keep cruising.

I twisted around in my seat and looked back, where one of the players was pointing in my direction. It looked like they were mounting up, but I then dropped down the backside of the dune and quickly lost sight of them.

"What even was that thing, man?" I said.

"It's a dinosaur. They're like really big, toothy chickens."

"You know that's not what I meant. We cleared that Rift and spawned that prism, right? And that dinosaur is what the prism spat out, so it's our fault it's heading for the Vale."

"Uh… yeah. I had you guys pick that Rift because it was close to town. That way, you'd be able to see what happens when one is completed before a bunch of them could spawn and hit close together. Turns out that unlike everything else I've suggested, that was not the greatest idea. That thing is nasty though—that was the second-worst possible outcome from a prism. Crap luck on our part."

"So it could have been even worse?"

"Substantially worse, but that's also even rarer. Like, way rarer."

I tightened my grip on the handlebars, wishing the bike was faster. My stomach was in knots, and I couldn't shake the feeling that the city was going to be in ruins by the time I reached it.

"All that flashing, yeah? That's what you were reacting to when the prism finally stopped."

"Yup, the more times the prisms flash, the worse it is. The odds said that you and Darling and House would have been able to kill whatever popped out between the three of you. Thought you'd want the information, but that seems like less of a good call knowing that a dead dinosaur is rampaging toward the Commerce Ward."

I blew out a puff of air. "Well, if we just got screwed on a dice roll, then it is what it is. Better to know now before people really start hammering these Rifts."

I looked around as the Vale came into view, though it was so far off that I couldn't make out much detail through the humid, hazy air. But I did spot more prisms drifting toward the city, approaching from all sides.

"I'm glad we got the guards back to work, but I really hope we weren't too late with that. I guess those defenses just became mandatory pretty quick. And it seems like Tyrann was right about the need to focus on the city." I rolled my eyes. "Not that telling us two minutes ahead of time made much of a difference."

"Uh huh."

A beat of silence passed. I was still praying for the city, but I couldn't help but worry about what the next few hours or even days would look like even if it survived the Tyrant.

With the entire player base descending upon the Onyx Delta to attempt the first wing of the Red Cathedral—and knowing that, at least initially, most if not all of them were going to bounce off the difficulty of the raid and the levels it required—it seemed all but certain that the Rift we'd just completed was going to be the first of dozens, hundreds, or even thousands over the coming days.

And I was already picturing an army of prisms floating toward the city, each of them hiding another ghostly monstrosity within.

I leaned a little lower on the bike and tried to speed it up, not that it did anything. I caught a whiff of smoke on the air around the same time that the humidity cleared and the city's four wards came into clear view.

The eastern entrance to the city was an absolute ruin. It looked like the Starlit Tyrant had smashed right through it on its way into the Commerce Ward, demolishing buildings left and right.

"Oh man," I said as I took in the damage. "This is bad. Any way you can tell what the status of the Auction House is? Or the Inn or even the Water Tower?"

"Negative."

I cruised up into the city and maneuvered around a number of bodies —players, judging by the varied look of their weapons and armor—then ditched my mount and dashed up over the rubble that was left of a building that bordered the avenue that contained my Auction House as well as the Inn.

And I found pandemonium beyond. Many of the nearby buildings— stores, homes, all manner of one-story structures—were either on fire or been flattened or both. The Auction House was still standing, for now.

The Starlit Tyrant stood in the street with a half-dozen guards hacking away at its feet while a few others plunked it with crossbows from atop nearby homes, or the piles of rubble that were left of them.

Darling was leaning on her sword between the creature and the Auction House, her Health Bar a sliver of red. I recognized a few other guild members as well: Zoe stood on a nearby roof, directing wave after green wave of healing magic into the guards, and a few other healers I didn't recognize had spread out and were raining down healing spells of their own.

The Starlit Tyrant had 40% of its Health remaining and its bar was falling at a steady rate, but the creature's proximity to the Auction House had me on high alert. And even worse: the Tyrant had just tossed its head and battered one of the guards into the ground.

Arlann. He tried to rise, but his right arm was hanging limply from his side, and his sword lay point-first in the sand behind him. He raised his shield in a futile gesture as the beast opened its jaws wide and made to swallow him whole.

I shouted something wordless, but Arlann's torso disappeared into the creature's mouth.

For one terrible moment, I thought we'd just lost him for good, but some sort of blue, spherical barrier sprang up between him and the beast's spectral teeth before it could bite down.

It looked like Arlann was standing at the center of a snow globe, with flurries drifting down around him, and the beast was trying to bite through it.

"Get Arlann back up!" I shouted, though I wasn't sure if Zoe or the others could hear me over the chaos of the fight, so I dropped a similar message into the guild chat in all caps.

A curling green wave of light rolled toward him from Zoe, which brought him up to 30% Health. But the beast wasn't letting up, and the globe that surrounded him was already beginning to crack.

I spotted Sarissa off in the distance, standing in the entryway to an alley at the center of a vast circle of frost, her fingertips pressed to her temples, her head bowed in concentration.

I clambered atop what remained of a wall and shouldered my rifle. I popped Doppelganger and Double Cast it to proc a second clone, then wound up an Overcharged blast.

I loosed the spell and started up another. The creature resisted both of my Doppelganger's spells, but mine managed to crit for 1,700 damage, and for a moment, I experienced some amount of hope that I'd be able to regain the monster's attention.

But despite the massive damage the spell had dealt, I'd barely generated even a fraction of the aggro I'd needed. I'd been hoping the spike would count for something, but it was clear that the guards had been working on the creature for far too long for me to draw it away.

Well... that wasn't exactly true. I leaped off the wall and onto the street, dropping the rifle into my inventory and rolling as I hit the ground.

The great creature opened its mouth wider still and stretched its entire jaw around the glassy orb that was protecting Arlann.

The shield shuddered, then gave slightly as the creature's teeth punched through, though the structure itself held despite the many cracks that were running through it.

I'd been planning on running around the scrum that surrounded the creature's legs, then grabbing onto Arlann and drifting him to safety, if only temporarily, but the Tyrant had other ideas.

The muscles in its back tensed, then the great beast whipped its head back and high into the air.

It launched the glassy sphere that Arlann was in skyward so quickly that he was pressed flat against the bottom of the structure.

The Tyrant charged in the direction of the Auction House, searching out some new target as Arlann soared higher and higher. The shield that had been protecting him faded away while he was still hundreds of feet in the air.

I surveyed the scene, made my decision, then planted a foot in the sand and ran back the way I had come, chasing the shadow that Arlann was casting from high above as he flew over the remains of the city's eastern entrance.

The Tyrant had thrown him with more height than distance, but the speed Arlann was traveling at easily outpaced me, and I'd locked myself into combat with that last Ravenblast, so mounting up wasn't an option.

I dashed along at top speed, tracking his flight the entire time. He was flailing now, armor glinting in the late afternoon light.

"Gonna need to Water Jet it," Frank said. "You're too slow."

I popped my pistols into both hands as Arlann hit his apex and began to fall in earnest.

Muted explosions sounded behind me, followed by screams and flashes of light. The beast had probably just summoned another of its Skyfall meteor showers in the center of town.

I braced myself for a notification that the Auction House or the Inn had been destroyed, though I wasn't even sure I'd get one if that happened.

But for now, Arlann. I kept running, eyes on the sky.

"Get ready," Frank said as I once again reached the area where the dune sloped downward. "Right off the top."

I took a few loping steps, then launched myself into the air and aimed a pistol behind me. I activated the ability and shot up off the top of the dune at a low angle.

My eyes watered as I rocketed through the air. I crashed into Arlann as if I'd been blasted out of a cannon, and the impact was so severe that I actually lost 10% of my Health, probably a product of rushing headlong into his armor.

I bearhugged him and we spun down to the ground together. I waited until we were a few feet from hitting the sand, then cast Clonedrift and instantly canceled the spell to negate the fall damage for both of us.

Arlann seemed to have lost all sense of where he was in the air, so he hit the ground hard on his side, and I heard his breath rush out of his lungs while I rolled right back to my feet.

But he was alive, so I immediately started running for the city while shouting back at him over my shoulder.

"You good?"

Arlann's only response was a raised fist followed by a series of deep, wet coughs. He sounded terrible, but his Health wasn't dropping, so he'd live.

I desperately wanted to mount up and blast back into town to help out —and to see what the damage was—but I was still locked in combat. Which also meant the Tyrant had yet to fall.

The run felt like it took forever, and with every step I took, I pictured the Auction House being smashed to smithereens or the Inn fully aflame or the tree knocked over and uprooted, its great trunk lying sideways across the roofs of the nearest buildings.

I held my breath as I burst back into the city.

Darling had rejoined the fight, and with the help of more newly arrived city guards, the guild—whose numbers had also noticeably increased— had managed to force the massive creature back toward the structures it had already destroyed and effectively minimize the damage.

I scoped out both of my buildings, and though the front of the Auction House had been scorched black, I had a kernel of hope that the damage there was superficial, and the Inn itself appeared to be untouched.

My Water Tower wasn't so lucky. The great container was lying on its side in the sand as a dark stain seeped out from beneath its broken tank. But I'd take that trade all day long.

The guild and the guards and a number of random players had worked the creature down to 12%, so I took a few steps closer to get into range.

"Watch my back for Cultists for me, yeah?" I said as I switched to my rifle. "Or anybody else who might decide now's the time to take a shot at us with the guard distracted."

"Clear for now, been watching."

I opened up with a Dark Harvest that was partially resisted and only hit for 400, then started chaining blast after blast with my pistols to mostly the same effect.

I had a few moments to pick out the individual people who'd shown up, and I was surprised to see Nina and Rock amid the scrum—I thought they'd already called it a night.

We managed to work the creature down from there almost entirely thanks to the guards, and when it finally dropped, roaring and screaming, I was unsurprised that there didn't appear to be any loot, but a huge round of cheers went up nonetheless as the beast toppled face-first into the sand.

I edged a little closer to the crowd, anxiety spiking as the adrenaline faded, and I became intensely conscious of just how many players were nearby despite the presence of the guild and the guard. But for now, the mood was celebratory, and everyone seemed focused on the glowing remains of the Starlit Tyrant.

Then almost everyone in the guild looked up at the same time as a new quest type that I'd never seen before must have hit everyone's logs simultaneously.

**New Quest: In Defense of the Black Oasis! (Legendary Quest) (Collaborative Quest)**
**Objective: While within 500 yards of the Black Oasis, defeat the following:**
1. 10,000 Veterans
2. 1,000 Elites
3. 200 Elite+
4. 20 Elite++ (1/20 slain)
5. 1 Raid Boss, World Boss, Deity, Lesser Deity, or Legend
Any player may contribute to this quest at any time, and all kills made within the designated area are automatically added to the appropriate tally.
Reward: Experience, Renown, and major improvements to all existing Communal Defense Structures within the Black Oasis. Additional individual rewards, including gear and crafting materials, will also be awarded and will scale in power, level, and rarity depending on each player's contribution to the defense of the Black Oasis.
In addition, the top three individual contributors will each receive a {Cache of the Possibility King}.

I stared at the quest, my desire to complete it immediately at the expense of everything else warring with its implications. I bent low and dropped my voice. "I assume every city's getting one of these?"

"Same quest, yeah," Frank said.

"Those numbers are unreal. This is going to be worse than I thought."

Sarissa blew by me, a flurry of blue robes in motion, but pulled up short when she spotted me.

"Arlann?"

"Caught him," I said, grinning slightly. "He's a little worse for wear, but he'll make it. Just head straight out the eastern entrance. You'll find him—"

She grabbed my hand and squeezed it, then ran off before I could finish the sentence, a ribbon of ice frosting the sand behind her.

I stepped up next to the guildies. Nina was yelling at Darling, who was just grinning and taking the abuse, totally pleased with whatever it was she'd done.

Nina looked at me, furious, then poked a finger into Darling's armored chest as Rock loomed behind the two of them, smiling broadly. "You are unbelievable."

"Sorry, drastic measures," Darling said.

"Thanks for showing up," I said.

The guards were starting to filter away, but many of the players were lingering, and I didn't like the looks that were being pointed in my direction. I backed up a bit toward a building with a steep, V-shaped roof behind me.

"How safe am I right now?"

"Eh," Frank said. "Guards will rush in and try to stop someone from killing you if someone makes a move. Depends how quickly you plan on dying, I guess."

"I can't believe you called mom," Nina said.

Darling laughed. "I emailed her, actually. Was doing too much to call."

Nina threw her hands up into the air. "Do you have any idea how confusing it is to be dead asleep, then get a call from your mom saying there's a dead dinosaur in the middle of the city and you need to go kill it for your sister?"

"I guess I should have specified that it was in EBO," Darling said, still laughing.

"You think?"

"Kinda thought that went without saying."

"Sure, when you're at least partially awake, and if the speaker has the slightest idea what she's talking about. I woke up in a panic thinking someone had died."

"To be fair to Darling," Frank said, "several people did indeed die. Where's House? I'm pretty sure I saw her die twice."

Nina pointed a dagger at him. "You take her side on this and I won't hesitate to ban you from karaoke."

"Whoa. No need to take your fury out on humanity as a whole."

I laughed but cut off abruptly as a horned player in dark red robes stepped out of an alley to my right, fire trailing from his fingers.

He casually raised a hand in my direction, then pointed a finger at me and launched a wheel of spinning fire. At the same moment, his name tag went purple, and the air warped in front of me.

I juked to my left, then Clonedrifted backward and closer to the building I'd put behind me. The fiery wheel passed harmlessly to my clone's left and dissipated harmlessly into the air.

Then a short player in dark leather appeared in front of the clone and jabbed two daggers into its stomach.

It exploded in a shower of sparks, stunning the player as I reappeared. I fired a Dreadful Shot at the fire mage as he tried to loose another burning wheel at me, but I wasn't fast enough to interrupt his cast.

I aimed my other pistol at the ground and Water Jetted myself up atop the V-shaped roof above me, landing neatly on its very edge.

Darling was already in the air by the time I got my feet back under me, and she crashed down on top of the spellcaster in a blur of dark, flashing metal.

He immediately blinked away, but her leap must have tagged him because she followed up with a second jump and was right back on top of him before he had a chance to react.

She knocked him to the ground with an overhead swing while Rock pounded toward the two of them with his huge hands balled into fists.

Nina appeared behind the stunned rogue and dug into his lower back, but he went ethereal, broke out of the stun, and aimed something that looked a lot like a gun in my direction.

I threw a hand up instinctively as the muzzle flashed, but instead of launching a bullet, a spiked, hook-like contraption flew forward with a long chain trailing behind it, which I recognized as some kind of movement ability.

The hook smashed into the very top of the roof beneath my feet, the chain went taut, and the rogue gave it a firm yank. The chain retracted and yanked him off his feet and sent him flying directly at me.

But I was ready before he was even halfway to the roof.

I switched to my blunderbuss and cast a Gravity Bird right in front of me, then detonated it almost instantly so that the black hole was floating just above the edge of the building, within arm's reach but with nothing but empty air beneath it.

The rogue flailed his arms as he approached the dark sphere, and it yanked him fully into its spinning core.

I pressed my blunderbuss to his chest at point-blank range and unloaded two instant ravens into him as he hung there, helpless, both of which hit for nearly 700 damage and dropped him well into execute range.

But instead of finishing him off with a harvest, I dropped my blunderbuss into my inventory and yanked Frank out of his loop.

"Game time!" Frank said.

I jumped and swung Frank in an overhead smash as if he were a tennis racket and I was serving, then activated Repel and canceled the Gravity Bird at the same time.

I caught the player full in the collarbone, and the Repel-powered blow spiked him down off the roof and onto the street below.

Frank punched the air. "Two Franks, one day! Buy one get one free!"

The player zipped downward and landed fully on his back, his Health bar instantly dropping to zero, the sand flying away around him and revealing the packed earth beneath.

It seemed like the added momentum had amplified the fall damage, which probably would have been more than enough to kill him regardless.

I reloaded my blunderbuss while I scanned the crowd. Darling stood scowling up at the sky, her name tag still glowing purple.

I followed her gaze. The mage must have used some kind of ability to launch himself high into the air because he was maybe twenty feet above the street, riding the breeze westward on fiery wings.

Rock was running beneath him, silently tracking his flight but being obviously outpaced with all of the buildings and alleys and gawking people in his way. Three guards were clamoring behind Rock in their heavy armor as well, though the big man was quicker.

"That spell works like that slowfall feather you used earlier," Frank said. "Damage will cancel the effect."

I grinned and shouldered my rifle. I took aim at the gliding player and squeezed off a Ravenblast from atop the roof just before he made it out of my weapon's extended range.

The purple and gray raven soared through the air and exploded between the player's shoulder blades. His fiery wings vanished, and he plummeted out of the sky.

He landed right in front of the Auction House and crashed into a fiery heap. But where the other player's death from fall damage had looked natural, this one seemed slightly off to me.

His health went from 15% or so down to a tiny sliver when he hit the ground, *then* zeroed out. It happened so quickly that I wasn't sure I'd actually seen it, but I could have sworn there was a hiccup there, or even a glitch.

Rock pounded up beside the corpse, then leaned over it. He raised a fist high in the air in what seemed like a weirdly celebratory gesture for someone who was normally so understated.

Then he brought the fist down in a hammer blow and struck the player squarely in the face.

Both of the player's legs kicked up beneath the force of the strike, and the sliver of Health I'd seen earlier returned only to zero out again. I barked a laugh. The mage must have been using some kind of feign death ability to try to get away.

Rock punched what I was now certain was a corpse three more times right in the face just to be safe—to Frank's escalating enjoyment—then rumbled back toward us.

A few of the guards were standing nearby, but they didn't seem to object to the guild having finished what someone else had started.

I swapped back to my pistols for flexibility, then hesitated. Part of me wanted to turn and run for the Hall of Rifts to make absolutely sure, but by this point the crowd below was almost entirely friendly guild members and guards.

I scanned the ruin the great beast had made of the gatehouse and the nearby buildings. It didn't feel right for me to bail immediately knowing the damage that had just been done, even if my presence would probably raise some awkward questions for Francis.

"Would you say I killed that guy?" Frank said.

"What?"

"Technically. Did I technically kill him with my face? I need a coward's opinion to balance out my own so I know how loudly I should be celebrating right now. If it helps, my gut's saying to be extremely loud."

I didn't have a target in mind, but I readied two Ravenblasts as a deterrent and let them spark and fizzle above the crowd. "I dunno. I guess so."

"But it was fall damage."

"If you pushed someone off the edge of a building, you'd still say you killed them, right?"

I spotted Sarissa leading Arlann into the city. She had an arm under his shoulder, so I almost jumped down to help, but his guards were already moving toward him, and I liked being out of easy melee range and in a spot that required burning a gap-closer to reach.

"Hmm," Frank said. "But in this situation, it's more like someone bumped into me from behind, then I bumped into someone and that bump pushed them off the edge."

"You didn't just bump them off though, because Repel. It's like you pushed them off and aggressively down."

"Yeah, you're right. I should give myself more credit."

"That's not what I was saying at all."

"Uh… without exaggeration, that is exactly what you were saying."

I hesitated. I'd only been half-listening to him between scanning for Cultists and other players while assessing the damage to the city and what I could do to fix it.

"Oh yeah. That is what I was saying."

"Yup."

I put a hand to my forehead as if I were checking for a fever.

"What's wrong with me?"

"Would a list be convenient, or would you prefer a summary? I already have both prepared so it doesn't matter to me. Figured we'd need them at some point, and you know how House feels about compiling lists, so I got her involved in an attempt to wiggle back into her good graces."

"Neither, really. Do you actually have a list though?"

"Uh huh. I wasn't bluffing about the summary either. I even tried haikus, but all the counting was super tedious."

"Seems like Frank points are already a lot of work in that department."

"Yeah, but Frank points won't calculate and award themselves. It's a labor of love, but I do it because I care. Or because I hate something and ascribing a numerical value to that hatred is deeply satisfying in a way I don't fully understand, nor care to."

"I can see that."

He paused. "Kinda handy though, right?"

"What's that?"

"Having a melee weapon to use with Repel when you couldn't normally equip one."

I spared him a glance. "Yeah, in all honesty, it really is. Would have been hard to blast that guy downward without the little bit of added reach, and whacking stuff with a pistol or the butt of my shotgun or whatever is much more clumsy. It's also just really satisfying."

"Pretty much the perfect weapon if you ask me."

"The weight's nice, good balance for sure. I guess, if anything, I kinda wish your shaft was a little longer. That way I'd have a bit of extra reach for—"

Frank growled, completely derailing my train of thought. "What did you just say?"

"Huh? I just said I wished your shhhhhhit." I covered my face with my hands. "Oh, dear God, what have I done?"

"You can call me God if you want and you wouldn't be the first, but you're not going to flatter your way out of this one. I can't let this stand."

I shook my head. "Dude, there is nothing you can do or say that's going to be worse for me than the fact that I have to live with the knowledge that I just said that out loud, without prompting."

"False. I could start by reminding you that you said that first thing when you wake up in the morning, and that would just be a warm-up."

"Yeah yeah, whatever, but I did just kill someone with you almost entirely for dramatic effect, plus Darling had to have seen it. That's gotta count for a lot."

"True, I do feel like I need to be encouraging death, especially when it's not strictly needed. We'll call it a net gain of 30 Frank points, but keep your mind off my shaft. That was weird, and not the kind of weird I like."

I fought down a grin. "Good deal."

A knot of guards parted off in the distance, and Sarissa and Arlann stepped through the gap. The Captain was noticeably limping, but he was smiling slightly, mostly at her.

One of the other guards offered him the sword that he'd left behind after being catapulted into the air, and when Arlann didn't take it, he slid it into its sheath for him.

I gazed around, skin still prickling at being in the middle of so many people, even if they were friendly. Those of us that had participated in the fight still had purple name tags, though most of them were beginning to flash, and within a few seconds they transitioned back to green.

I dropped down off the roof in front of Arlann.

"I'd like another word if you can spare it," he said, quietly enough that I didn't think anyone else had heard.

"I'm... not sure I can risk that right now," I said. I jerked my head at the crowd. "I should get going."

Arlann eyed our surroundings and seemed to come to the same conclusion.

"I'll be in the war room. With the guard fully funded and organized, I'm confident that we'll be able to do a better job of protecting the city from here on out." He eyed the great, ghostly beast that was still lying in the street. "Though against something like that, or even a handful of them at once..."

And that made me think about what things would have looked like if we'd rolled something even worse on that first prism.

"I'm glad to hear it." I pointed a still-glowing pistol at the ruins that the creature had made of the nearby homes and shops, where guards were already picking through the rubble.

Arlann reached out as if to touch my shoulder, then winced and thought otherwise. "I had the buildings evacuated—that's what took us so long to respond. I can't promise that someone didn't stay behind, but I'm hopeful that we haven't lost anyone." He sighed and scanned the sky. "That said, night is coming, and this one is looking especially dangerous. I'll have to find somewhere to put the people up."

I eyed the nearby crowd, and despite the guards' proximity and the cheering and so on, I bent down and spoke directly into Arlann's ear just to be safe.

"I can put them up for you. I've got a number of rooms spoken for, but we'll eat the cost until they can get back on their feet."

I didn't love the idea of giving up some of my daily payout at the same time as we were still desperately trying to ramp it up while spreading the network, but I couldn't leave some of the city homeless, especially when I was the one who'd cleared the Rift. And at this point, the Auction House represented a far larger part of my payout than the Inn.

"Thank you," he said. Sarissa whispered something to him that I didn't catch. "I... should rest. It's going to be a long night." He reached out again and handed me something smooth and cold.

I got the impression that he didn't want anyone to know that he'd slipped whatever it was into my possession, so I dropped it into my inventory without looking at it.

"We'll see what we can do to help out with the defenses," I said. "By the way. Any chance you have a room in the Guardhouse that locks from the outside?"

He squinted at me. "We have plenty of cells."

"A cell is probably too strong. I was thinking something that could at least pass for a bedroom."

Arlann shrugged. "We can make it work. Why?"

"Might have a guest for you later. But we can touch base on that when you're healed up." I eyed the horizon. "So long as there's a city left when the sun rises."

Sarissa started leading him away, and the guards shifted and went about returning to their posts.

I swiveled my gaze to Darling—she was still grinning at Nina while the latter woman pouted and rubbed at her eyes. I stepped over to them.

"How would you guys feel about a quick meet-up back at the Stronghold?"

"If by meeting you mean celebration," Nina said, "then maybe. Otherwise I'm logging out and going back to sleep."

"We could just push the God kill celebration up a couple hours," Darling said. "Maybe keep it a bit on the—"

Nina whooped and immediately started running for the nearest Rift. "I'll spread the word!"

"—shorter end with everything going on," Darling finished. She cocked her head at me. "I guess that's settled then. I would've thought you'd have wanted to be machine-gunning Rifts or something."

I nodded. "I do. I really do, actually, and that's where I think we're going from here, provided Arlann and company can protect the city on their own for a little while. At least until we get some defenses up."

"Should be okay for a couple hours," Frank said.

"Yeah, I'm thinking the more dangerous phase is probably going to come once more people have had time to arrive. Right now, we're really only getting Rift clears from the people who were already in the Delta when the Red Cathedral finished. But you really think we're good to leave for a bit?"

"Can't guarantee it, but that dinosaur was terrible luck, and like Arlann said, the guard was disorganized. Should be alright."

"Thanks for that. Anyway, sorry Darling. For the meeting, I just think it makes sense to reevaluate now that we know what's heading our way. Rift strategies and so on. If clearing a Rift is going to hurt the closest city, we've gotta figure out a way to minimize the damage."

"Or maximize the damage,' Frank said. "Could go either way."

"Right," Darling said. "But Nina didn't run off spreading the word about a meeting. She said party."

"Yeah," I said. "And if we let her keep calling it a party, people will be happy to come. Then when they start having fun, bam, we spring logistics on them."

"Come for the party, stay for the intricate planning because it's already too awkward to leave," Frank said. "It's just devious enough that it might actually work, provided there's copious amounts of booze around to compensate for when the disappointment takes hold."

"Definitely," I agreed. "And if people want to just keep Rifting in the meantime, maybe we can have them pick random Rifts outside the Oasis until we figure it all out? That wouldn't be the worst thing. I just don't want to make this invasion thing harder on the city than it already is."

"Random's easy enough," Darling said. "I'm up for some more clears afterward too if you are. Think I'd rather grind than celebrate for too long. Doubt I'll be sleeping much tonight either way. Still way too hyped up."

"I do need to catch a bit of sleep at some point, but yeah, absolutely. There's just a couple things I'd like to double-check before we hit the Stronghold." The guards were few and far between now, and I was starting to feel exposed in the center of town despite the guildies. "Meet you guys there in ten or so? Thanks again for rallying the troops. You really went above and beyond with Nina."

Darling laughed. "I didn't really think she'd come. I just thought that bothering her was reason enough. But I'm glad it worked out. And yeah, see you in a few."

"Cheers."

"Bye Darling," Frank said.

"Bye Frank. Congrats on murdering that guy in front of everyone. That was very impressive."

"Thanks. I imagine there'll be a number of toasts tonight in my honor in celebration of the second Franking, so I'm looking forward to it."

"And at least half of them are going to be coming from you, right?" I said.

Frank grunted. "That's a higher rate than I would have estimated, but I do have several speeches prepared if the need arises."

"Of course you do."

# Chapter Thirteen

I said a rushed goodbye and a number of thank yous to the other guildies who had shown up, then doubled back to the Communal Defense Zone.

After looking over the defensive options a bit more, I went ahead and paid the entire fee to get the trench started around the Commerce Ward.

It wasn't as flashy as some of the other choices—I would have vastly preferred the wall—but it was the only one that I could complete purely with gold, it'd be ready much faster than the others, and I figured it'd probably unlock some more powerful defenses down the line once it was finished, too.

Then I hightailed it out of the city as fast as I could manage. I headed to the nearest Rift, jumped into the Hall, then ported back as close as I could get to the cleaved dune that I'd attempted to drop the Tyrant off of on Frank's suggestion.

"You know, I could already be in a cold beverage right now," Frank said as I sent my bike roaring over the dunes toward our destination. "Or a warm one. Or even a drink that was approximately room temperature."

"Yeah yeah, soon enough. But I think you saw that flash of green when we were falling and that you pointed me to that dune in particular for a reason."

"Preferably something carbonated. The more highly carbonated, the better."

"I'm gonna be optimistic and take that as you confirming that I'm onto something but that you're not allowed to verify anything I just said."

I took my bike to the very edge of the dune, where it sharply ended, then dismounted and peered out over the edge.

Even more of the dune had collapsed now, and the bottom section was still calving away into the waters below like a glacier. And with the way it had eroded—the entire dune looked like a wave that was cresting out over its base—I couldn't see much directly beneath me, nor did I think the area I was standing on was very stable.

I drew a pistol and placed my back to the open air, then stepped backward and off the dune.

As I fell feet-first down toward the water, I scanned the sandy mountain, looking for the hole I'd seen earlier and the source of the color within.

I spotted a small opening beneath me, so I pointed my pistol and waited until the timing was right, then Water Jetted myself sideways and into it.

"You're early," Frank said.

I wondered what he meant by that, right up until the moment I smashed my forehead on the top of the cave-like formation and slammed down into the entryway on my back. I blinked a few times to clear my vision, then hauled myself to my feet and shrugged it off.

"Better than being late."

"Agree to disagree."

The pocket in the side of the cliff was smaller than I'd thought, maybe seven feet high and half that wide, and the opening narrowed as I pressed on until I had to turn sideways and slide between the sand and the bits of stone that were trapped within it.

The rocks were lined with shining pearls that caught the light and refracted it like a kaleidoscope—they probably accounted for the flash of color I'd seen—though they were set so deeply into the stones that prying them loose looked impossible.

The cave itself was a bit of a puzzle, and it left me wondering what sort of structure the dune had buried years back that was now gradually being revealed.

The opening narrowed and lowered further still, then bent hard to the left and became pitch black. I Overcast and held a Ravenblast for light, then dropped onto my hands and knees and crawled deeper inside.

I eventually reached a wider chamber where sand was pouring down from overhead as if into the bottom of an hourglass.

But that was it: just a huge pile of sand that was slowly filling a room down here in the dark. The ceiling itself was groaning, too, seemingly almost ready to collapse completely beneath the sand that was heaped above it.

"Man," I said. "I really thought I was onto something here." I gave the space one last long inspection while wielding my pistol like a torch, then shrugged and headed for the exit.

"Unfortunately, it appears to be an empty cave," Frank said, and I got the feeling that he was pleased with himself for getting the sentence out.

I turned back around and popped my rifle into my hands. I walked over to the huge pile of sand and stabbed the barrel down into it several times in quick succession, trying to see if there was something buried beneath.

And on the fifth try, I hit something solid. I thought there was at least a decent chance that I'd just hit the floor, but I spun the weapon around and gripped it by the barrel, then used the butt as a shovel while I kept a Ravenblast glowing on the other end.

Having the muzzle so close to my face made it hard to see beyond the spell's brightness, but I made decent progress.

Eventually, I dropped to one knee and brushed the sand off something smooth and cold and spherical. I tilted the rifle down so I could get a good look at it. It looked like a pearl the size of a basketball.

I inspected it.

**{Mysterious Stone} (Quest Item)**
**Use: ??**
**Requires level 20.**

I tucked it into my inventory, grinning from ear to ear as I made my way back out of the cave.

"Nice. Thanks, man. No clue what the hell this thing is or what it does, but thanks."

"It's a rock."

"Yeah, word on the street is that it's mysterious, too."

"No, listen here, elf boy: it's a rock. It's a rock."

I squinted at him and was about to respond when a familiar pop sounded just in front of me, and Kline appeared silhouetted against the ocean in every bit of his ill-advised, bare-nippled glory.

"I see what you're doing, axe," he said, "and if you keep it up, there will be severe consequences."

And before either of us had a chance to respond—let alone dispense the mockery he deserved—Kline had already popped away.

I stopped in place. "Uhhh... okay then. Good talk."

"Did you see that?" Frank said.

"He definitely noticed you that time around, and no sheathing either. And he apparently really didn't like that you led me here, so bonus points for that."

"Yeah, whatever. If he's not smart enough to contain the wisdom that I naturally exude from every pore, then that's on him. But nah, I meant did you notice that he was wearing shoes?"

I glanced down at him. "No way, really?"

"Yuuup."

I laughed. "Wow. How about that?"

"This massive contribution to sanitation was brought to you by yours truly. And all it took was a little bit of targeted scoffing, and I'm always down to scoff for a good cause. Or a bad cause. Or—"

"There truly is no end to the number of lives you've touched, Frank."

"Couldn't have said it better myself. I mean, I could have, but I agree with the general sentiment."

We went back and forth on Kline for a bit before I made it back to the edge of the cliff, then spent a long moment looking out over the blue, rushing rivers below and the vast ocean beyond.

I was getting ready to jump off and head back to the Stronghold to meet up with the guild when a call came in from a player whose name I didn't recognize.

**Call incoming for Alias {Francis} from Player {Breaklite}.**
**Accept?**

I squinted at the name, then pulled up the Renown ladder. I found the player in question a little way down, around the low 200s. Still very impressive given the scope of EBO, but they weren't exactly at the cutting edge.

"Thoughts?" I said.

"Let the Bodies Hit the Floor, Drowning Pool."

"What?"

"Theme music, final answer."

I ground the heels of my hands into my eyes. "Seriously?"

"Did you think I was joking?"

"You wanna do theme music, fine, let's do theme music. So you hang on my hip, right?"

"Uh huh."

"Okay, so say I walk into a room full of strangers."

"Still with you."

"Then your theme music starts playing."

He hesitated. "Are you trying to puzzle this out or what? What's happening here? Yeah, that's how theme music works."

"So you don't see any problem at all with me walking into a room while your theme music plays?"

"I mean, I'm all ears if you've got a way to remove yourself from the equation, but at this point I've mostly made my peace with it, and it's not like I can float into a room." He narrowed his nonexistent eyes. "You could throw me into the room. Preferably at someone."

"If we walk into a room and music starts playing, then everybody's going to think it's my music, Frank."

"Ha! Nobody would ever think that."

"I'm the one walking in. Meanwhile you just sit there, motionless."

"Right. But when Cleopatra's servants carried her into a room, nobody was looking at the guys who were holding up her palanquin, right?"

I stared down at him, open-mouthed and incredulous.

"I'll also point out that she too sat there, motionless. Why move if you don't need to? It's a total power move."

I made to speak, but closed my mouth. I did it again, then sighed. "I recognize that I've somehow found a way to lose this argument, but I'd like to go on record as saying that this is really stupid. Like, this is stupid for you, and you do a lot of stupid things."

"Noted."

"So you're done being helpful for a bit then? All gassed out after leading us to the rock Kline didn't want us to have?"

"That does seem to be the case."

"Guess I should take what I can get at this point."

Fortunately, the call was still ringing. I blocked my video, then sat down on the sandy edge of the dune, swung my legs over the void below, and took the call.

"Yeah I don't think Francis is—" Breaklite said, pausing when she realized I'd picked up.

She had bright blue eyes and skin that was faintly patterned with spots like a leopard's. Her camera was close-up, and I couldn't make out anything about where she was beyond the sunset that was burning behind her.

"Hi there."

Her voice was high and shaky, and though she was looking right into the video window, her eyes kept sliding away. Maybe she hadn't expected to end up on a video call where she couldn't see the other person, but even accounting for that, she seemed surprisingly uncomfortable right off the bat.

"Hi," I said. I waited for her to continue the conversation, then raised my eyebrows when she didn't. "Something I can do for you?"

"I've, uh, got an offer for you," she said. She tugged at her right ear, then mouthed something to someone I couldn't see.

"Alright. I'm listening."

"I'm the leader of Arranthea. We're based out of the Treetop Tower. Assuming you've heard of it, given the recent events."

"Three-day Siege target," Frank whispered, though I'd recognized the name.

"Yeah. Goon's got you in their crosshairs."

Breaklite scratched her throat. "Yep, and you're the guy in the Oasis, correct?"

"That's where I'm currently based."

"I was thinking we might be able to figure something out."

"Figure something out with regard to what, exactly?"

"A defensive pact."

"A defensive pact," I repeated. "Are you saying that you have information that the Vale is going to be one of their next targets? Because if so, that's a bold claim."

"No guarantees yet. Just rumors. And why wouldn't they?"

"Mmm, I don't know."

I did know, though. There were definitely plenty of reasons to target the Oasis: the geographical location, the first Cathedral, and so on.

But if we drew in as many players as I expected to in the coming days, it seemed like it made a lot more sense for Goon to go elsewhere where the pickings would be easier. In fact, the Vale becoming a focal point might even help them out.

But something about this call didn't feel right to me, so I let the silence hang. One of the best things my father ever taught me was that if you thought someone was lying to you or trying to mislead you in some way, the best thing to do was to just shut up and let them talk.

Breaklite glanced at whoever was standing out of the frame.

"What kind of a force do you expect to field if it comes down to you versus them?"

I hesitated. "I guess we'll see when the time comes. Speaking of forces, how many do you guys have?"

"For the siege?"

"In the guild. I've been pretty busy with my own stuff, but I haven't heard of Arranthea, and I try to keep tabs on pretty much everyone."

"Four hundred on the dot right now."

"How many healers?"

She paused, then tapped the air, though I couldn't see the menu she was messing with. "Thirty-six at the moment, but we're always looking for more."

"What about tanks?"

She frowned. "Ten counting off-tanks."

"Supports?"

"Twenty... two right now."

"How many does that leave for damage dealers? Exactly, I mean."

"Huh?"

"If you've got four hundred total guild members and those numbers you just gave are pulled directly from your roster, then how many damage dealers does that leave? I'm just trying to think about what that break-down would look like in a prolonged fight."

Breaklite didn't respond, so I once again let her sit with the silence.

I wasn't sure if she was up to anything particularly nefarious—she might have just exaggerated the size of her guild to make a partnership sound better, which was fine. I'd have considered doing the same thing in her position if the situation were reversed.

But I wouldn't have made up exact numbers and then immediately forgot them.

Eventually she drew back, and though a flash of consternation crossed her face, she masked it well enough.

"Couple hundred. So, what do you think? You help us, we help you?"

I glanced down at Frank and raised an eyebrow. "I'm going to have to mull this one over for a while before I commit to anything. I really do sympathize and I'd like to help, but we're being hit hard here too, even outside of what Goon is doing, and if we aren't already in their crosshairs, then lining up against them seems like a good way to get their attention in the worst possible way."

"I understand," Breaklite said, and she made some sort of motion with her hand that was just out of the viewing window. "I'll be around. Feel free to shoot me a message or something if anything changes. Thanks for your time."

She ended the call.

I drew back, then barked a laugh. "What the hell was that?"

"A truly uninspired plea for help?"

"That or maybe a fishing expedition where they were trying to figure out how defensible the Vale is. But why call Francis for a defensive pact? He doesn't even have anyone behind him." I rubbed my temples. "I mean, we can't expect anyone to know what he's up to, but man, you should at least find out if he's publicly running a guild or something before trying to launch into negotiations."

Then came another alert.

**Call incoming for Player {Ned} from Player {Breaklite}.**
**Accept?**

I licked my lips. "Well now. That's even more interesting." I let that call ring until she gave up, then sent a quick message to Darling asking if she'd received anything from Breaklite. When she replied in the negative, I asked her to let me know if she got one in the future.

"Are we officially busted?" Frank said. "The truth is out so it's time to drop the sneaky sneaky and get to smashing? I've got so many ideas for where to start. Knees, faces, coccyges."

"Coccyges?"

"Do you have any idea how much it hurts to smash your tailbone? That pain lingers."

"I just hit mine like two minutes ago, but why not just say tailbone and skip the confusion?"

"I like the way that word makes my mouth feel. Coccyges. Coccyges! Anyway, we busted?"

"Nah. The calls back-to-back are a bit worrisome as a one-two punch, but there aren't a ton of notable players based out in the Oasis, so it makes sense that they would hit both me and Francis early on. She's probably just working down a list of people who have been associated with the area so far." My mouth was a little dry all of a sudden. "At least I hope she's working down a list. I'll feel better if she reaches out to Darling."

"She'd better not. If Breaklite thought she was uncomfortable while she was talking to you, then just wait until I get through to her."

"You are pretty good at making people uncomfortable."

"Thanks. So are you."

"I know you meant that in a nice way and I appreciate it, but—"

"I didn't mean it in a nice way."

I sighed. "Let's go meet up with our girl and the rest of the guild, yeah?"

"Yeah, party time! Wait, did you just say our—"

I sheathed him.

# Chapter Fourteen

A bit of Rift hopping dropped me off a few hundred feet from the Stronghold.

The cave that led to the hideaway was just as it had been before, but a blue river was now snaking around the base of the dune that held it, and the river's bank was only a few feet away from the entrance.

I got a running start and threw myself into the air, then Water Jetted myself over the river.

The waters ran smoothly as they moved gently around the dune, but there were a number of strange dark spots at the bottom. They seemed like rocks, but there definitely hadn't been any rocks there prior to the flood.

I landed in the mouth of the cave and skidded to a stop, then doubled back and pulled Frank out of his loop.

He gasped dramatically. "Great timing—I've just finished plotting your demise."

"Yeah, okay buddy." I stepped over to the riverbank and pointed a pistol at one of the shapes. It was hard to tell, but I thought they were moving slightly.

"Those are new, right?"

"Uh huh. Should be able to inspect them from here."

I did.

{Stonewhisper Dwarf} (Level ?? Humanoid) (Elite)
HP: 80,000/80,000
MP: 146,250/200,000

I dropped onto my haunches with my pistol pressed against my thigh and tried to peer deeper into the river's depths.

I could just make out the outline of the nearest figure: he was short and heavily built, with a barrel chest and thick arms and legs plus a long, dark beard that the water was pulling sideways.

The dwarf was definitely moving—it looked like he was walking along the riverbed against the current and in the direction of the Black Oasis—but his progress was glacial, almost like he was striding in slow motion.

I scratched the back of my head with the barrel of my pistol. "What's these guys' deal?"

"They appear to be a bunch of short dudes who really like talking to rocks, but quietly."

I inspected a few of the other dwarves and found that they too were consistently expending their huge Mana pools at a quick clip, though I couldn't tell what they were doing with them.

"Any chance you've got a Codex entry on these guys that you can share?"

"Uh huh."

**Codex Entry 1800: The Stonewhisper Dwarves**
**As ancient as the world itself, the Stonewhisper Dwarves wade through the centuries like a current, and wherever they go, they leave wondrous feats of engineering behind.**

"Huh. That doesn't seem like it's explicitly tied to the Possibility King event to me. And we haven't had any alerts or Ripples or anything on them so far. So maybe we triggered this earlier with that series of Ripples? Feels more like something that has to do with changes in general than anything else."

"Your guess is worse than mine but I can't offer one at the moment, so it is what it is."

I squinted along the river and tried to count the shapes that were slowly making their way upstream, but there were dozens of them, and I could feel Frank getting both restless and sweaty at my side.

"Guess we'll just keep an eye on that. I gotta admit, my head is spinning a little bit right now. Mostly in a good way, but man."

I left the sparkling river behind and ducked into the cave as the sun set off in the distance. I pushed through the empty house that served as a gate and into the Stronghold proper, where the darkness was kept at bay by the many Glowcaps that covered the ceiling.

The organisms seemed to have multiplied, and the ceiling was covered with great slashes of fluorescent color, like aspens turning in the fall.

Music was filtering through the space from the hall up ahead, or at the very least what Nina considered to be music because it sounded like she was doing a rendition of *I Got You Babe*, except it was just that one line over and over, and badly.

But I could barely see the Guild Hall or the many buildings that had sprung up around it, as the trees that House had planted were now so thick that I had to weave my way between the trunks, occasionally turning sideways to slip through two of them that she'd planted especially close.

She'd definitely maximized the space, and with powering up the city's defenses in mind, I was already eyeing up the materials she'd yet to harvest.

I scoped out the nearest tree.

**{Adult Blackbark}**
**Harvesting this item outside of a Housing Plot requires 100 skill in the {Arborist} Profession.**

"There another stage or something?" I said as I reached the porch. "I don't see House as the type to not have harvested these if they're ready. Unless she's got a cat sitting on her or something like that."

"Mature, yeah," Frank said. "It's the right tree for a late-stage harvest."

"Cool."

I pushed through the door and instantly felt some of the tightness drain from my shoulders. The room smelled like beef stew and beer, people were laughing at Nina or with her or both and she didn't seem to care in the slightest either way, and there was just something warm and familiar about the space, like so many inns I'd visited before.

"I wanna—" Frank started, but before he could continue, I plucked him out of his loop and cocked him back over one shoulder, ready to throw him in Nina's general direction. I didn't think I'd be very accurate, but I figured I could probably get him to the corner of the room.

"No no no, I hate that song. I want—"

"To bathe weirdly in a drink?"

"Yes. And also Darling's presence."

I eyed him. "I think you mean bask rather than bathe on the latter point."

"You'd be wrong there, but I'd settle for either. But man, both would make my week."

I grimaced.

Darling waved from across the room, where she was sitting with Rock and House at a small, circular table. I made my way over to them.

House had a cat on each shoulder, Rock had Bella in his lap, and House was animatedly talking right into Rock's ear. The big man was leaning down so that she could reach him and nodding occasionally while stroking the dark cat the entire time.

Darling jumped up and headed to the bar.

"Oh yeah," Frank said. "That girl's got armor for days. How much do you think that weighs?"

"What?"

"You heard me. I bet it's like two-hundred pounds."

"Seems a bit on the heavy side to me."

He paused. "Well that's a little judgmental, isn't it?"

"You literally asked me to judge your guess." I took the empty seat next to where Darling had been and slapped Frank sideways onto the table.

"Yeah, I did, but not like that. That was just rude."

House looked our way, tilted her chin up and grinned, then went right back to whispering in Rock's ear.

Darling came over and set two mugs of beer in front of us, then plopped down beside me with one of her own.

Rock and House didn't seem to notice; their drinks were both totally full, their mugs beading over with condensation.

"I tried getting Jukes and Ton here," Darling said, "but I think they're probably passed out or something. Hopefully we get them back sooner rather than later."

"Thanks for trying," I said. I glanced over at Nina. She was swaying back and forth in the corner. "She got impressively drunk in what, twenty minutes?"

"Something like that. Lot easier when you don't need to worry about how much your stomach can physically fit."

Then I noticed the seven empty mugs that were sitting next to Rock. "Wow. Was that all her?"

"Yep. You're lucky you missed out. After she hit number six, all she could talk about was how nice it was not having to pee every fifteen minutes."

I laughed and dropped Frank into his beer, which was dark and smelled a bit like chocolate.

Darling pointed at the drink. "That's a new one. We upgraded the hall and the menu improved. Coffee stout."

"I was going to mention the coffee notes," Frank said. "It definitely wakes you up." He hesitated. "Could also be the bubbles that are doing that. They seem to reach a lot of places you wouldn't think they would."

I winced. "Let's move on before Frank has a chance to detail his crevices. You heard anything from Breaklite yet?"

"Still nothing," Darling said. "What's up with that anyway?"

I ran her through the weird, stilted conversation I'd had with the guild leader.

"Well, that's just fantastic," she said when I'd finished. "I've also got some more intel for you from the trash groups."

"Yeah?"

"Check this out."

She popped a glassy sphere into the palm of her hand. It was about the size of a marble, and though it was clear, it was shot through with lines of red that forked like tiny bolts of electricity.

I inspected it.

**{Sphere of Branching Fate} (Consumable) (Universal Class Skill Sphere)**
**Quality: Rare**
**Use: Rerolls one of your chosen skills and allows you to choose from 3 new options that are not available to your current class. This effect is permanent, but you may use another {Sphere of Branching Fate} to revert a changed skill back to its original state at any time.**
**Warning: You may only have a single {Fate-Branched} ability at any given time.**

I blinked at the readout. "Wow. They're permanent?"

"Yeah, kind of," Darling said. "Not super common, but not insanely rare either." The item vanished from her palm, and she threw it into a trade window. "Take it. Won't be the last one we find. Already picked up a few more, and most of the trash group won't be joining us here. Guess they're having too much fun in there."

I was about to ask if she was sure she wanted to part with it, but she confirmed the trade and gave me an exasperated look when I continued to hesitate, so I went ahead and took it.

"Thanks. This is a really good find."

I popped the sphere into my hand while she nodded and took a drink. The red ball was warm to the touch and surprisingly heavy. I rolled it around in my palm.

"It's almost like a respec system, huh? Lets you go back and choose another skill if you ended up with something you're unhappy about."

"Yeah," she agreed, "but fairly random. Sorta reminds me of that boss back in the Bridge Rift where people were temporarily getting abilities they hadn't selected."

"Exactly, a lot of RNG there. I guess it'd be best for someone who changed roles unexpectedly or something, like they weren't sure what they were making when they started. Say Jukes started off playing a damage dealer or something before he became a tank. He'd probably have an ability or two that didn't synergize with his build." I paused. "That doesn't really hold up super well though because skills evolve with class changes."

I tossed the sphere up into the air and caught it. Then the sub-description caught my eye. "Class Skill Sphere, huh? Are these the only ones that have dropped so far?"

"Hm?"

"If these things specify that they modify skills in particular, it seems like there are probably other spheres out there that do different things. Maybe they can modify your race, or even a Renown Path?"

"I can confirm there are other spheres," Frank said.

I glanced down at him. "You got anything on the types that you can share?"

"Not yet."

I nodded. The confirmation was better than nothing. "Well, when I talked to Tyrann earlier, he said something along the lines of the Red Cathedral being full of possibility. He was pretty clearly trying to play off the God kill as a temporary setback, but this sphere makes me wonder if he was being a bit more honest than I realized."

Darling took a deep drink, then wiped her lips. "How so?"

154

"I asked about his Renown path being dead. He must have picked perks that were built around raising a God, right? So now that he's leading a cult that doesn't have one…" I trailed off, shrugging. "Maybe there's another type of sphere that lets you swap around Renown Perks."

"Probably have to work differently. I can't imagine wanting one perk from the Merchant Tree or something. Too unfocused, whereas an ability from another class could always be useful."

"Agreed there, yeah."

"Have to be rarer too. We haven't seen one yet."

I almost dropped the sphere into my inventory, but then I paused. "Has anyone used one of these spheres?"

She shook her head.

I held it up to the firelight emanating from the hearth behind me. "Well…"

"Are you thinking about doing what I think you're thinking about doing?" Frank said.

"If you're thinking that I'm about to use it, then yeah."

"Seems rash and impulsive, so I'm totally here for it. Let's go: mentally pick the skill you'd like to drop and pop that bad boy into your mouth."

Darling leaned forward, grinning. "You're really gonna use it? Just like that?"

"I'm seriously tempted. You think you can swing me another if I end up with something awful so that I can reset?"

She nodded. "No problem. I'd kinda like to see what sort of options it gives you. Would be nice to know before we really dive into the raid."

"Yeah, exactly. I'm also curious as to what these things might be worth in the coming weeks or months. They could become incredibly valuable once people have moved on from the Red Cathedral, but it really depends on how it rolls. Like if it's going to give me an ability that requires a shield or something that's going to be fairly useless as a skill, and having that deep of an option pool would really dilute their value. Even then, it'd still be interesting if you got a bunch of them together."

"I vote we get rid of Ravenblast," Frank said.

I gave him an exasperated look. "You want me to get rid of my primary means of damage?"

"Yeah, that one. Maybe you'll end up with a better blast. Like, Axeblast."

I snorted. "As if Kline would allow an ability called… oh. *Axe* blast."

"Yeah?"

"Sorry, I thought you said something else."

"Anyway," he continued, "you'd shoot bearded axes at people. In case that wasn't clear."

"Seems unlikely that that's an actual skill," Darling said.

Frank grunted. "Yeah, Darling's right as usual, but a man can dream."

"What if we rerolled and ended up with another bird-type blast, Frank? It could definitely get worse than ravens. We could be out here chucking geese at people for the rest of our time together."

"Gooseblast?" Darling said, laughing the word. "Maybe you could add a rune and turn them Canadian for extra aggro."

Her comment caught me mid-drink, and I dribbled a good bit down my chin.

Frank paused for a very long moment, vibrating the entire time. "After what I consider to be a great deal of thought for me, I've come to the decision that chucking geese would be an improvement over the status quo."

I raised an eyebrow. "Really?"

"Yeah. They're filthy, sloppy, awful creatures. But they're also pointlessly aggressive, and I feel that on a spiritual level."

"That does seem consistent. On a more serious note, I'm thinking about replacing Fettering Shot."

I still liked the ability, but I had a ton of crowd control right now and a dedicated snare on a decently long cooldown was no longer as useful as it had been, especially when it came to raiding and bosses in general that were likely to completely shrug the skill off.

"Doesn't do damage so I'm totally here for that too," Frank said. "Bottoms up."

I mentally selected Fettering Shot, popped the marble into the back of my throat, took a swig of beer, and swallowed it.

Nothing happened.

Darling gave me a weird look, then I realized there had probably been zero need to put the marble into my mouth and promptly slammed my head onto the table.

"Wait, did you actually swallow that?" Frank said, laughing. "See, Darling? I told you this guy has no filter whatsoever for what he'll put in his mouth."

I sat back upright and rubbed my forehead. "And you have no filter for what comes out of yours."

"I most definitely do not. But if you've gotta pick one of the two, which are you going with?"

"Both seem likely to get you killed," Darling said, "but in two very different ways."

"Exactly!" Frank agreed. "But I'm gonna go down swinging in a blaze of glory and devastating insults while Ned here gets dysentery and eventually craps himself to death like he's on the Oregon Trail."

I groaned.

"What?" Frank said. "Too soon?"

I mentally used the sphere, which triggered the prompts I'd been after.

**You forgot the ability {Fettering Shot}!**
**You may select 1 of 3 spells!**

{Prismatic Flare} (Rank: Intermediate I)
Source Class: Mirrormage
Description: You strike an enemy up to 40 yards away with a prismatic blast of focused energy that deals 1,130 damage. This spell benefits from all of your elemental boost effects simultaneously, and it deals damage based on your level (base damage) and Intelligence, plus Magical Attack.
Cast time: 3.5 seconds.
Cooldown: 45 seconds.
Cost: 550 Mana.
Current rank: You may choose 1 of 2 available upgrades.
A. After taking damage from {Prismatic Flare}, the target takes 33% increased damage from a random element for 10 seconds.
B. After striking a target with {Prismatic Flare}, all damage you deal is increased by 10% for 10 seconds.

{Heart Vessel} (Rank: Intermediate I)
Source Class: Deadlight Shaman
Description: You create a blood-filled orb that floats closely behind you. Whenever you lose more than 33% of your maximum Health to a single attack, the Heart Vessel breaks open and heals you for 33% of your maximum Health. The Vessel is destroyed upon activation, and this ability will not prevent lethal damage.
Cast time: 6 seconds.
Cooldown: 2 minutes.
Cost: 33% of maximum Health.
Current rank: You may choose 1 of 2 available upgrades.

A. This spell's cooldown is removed, and its cast time is halved.
B. This spell now only activates upon taking lethal damage, at which point you are restored to 33% of your Maximum Health and all damage you take is reduced by 75% for 3 seconds. However, the spell's cooldown is increased to 10 minutes, and the cooldown will not begin until the Heart Vessel is activated or dispelled.

{Salverot Dart} (Rank: Intermediate I)
Source Class: Venomancer
Description: You launch a stream of corrosive poison at a target up to 40 yards away that coats the target and absorbs up to 860 Health points the target receives in healing over the next 5 seconds. This spell absorbs healing based on your level (base damage) and Intelligence, plus Magical Attack.
Cast time: Instant.
Cooldown: 30 seconds.
Cost: 200 Mana.
Current rank: You may select 1 of 2 available upgrades.
A. Whenever this ability is dispelled by a hostile player, the target instantly receives damage equal to triple the amount the dart has already absorbed.
B. In addition to this spell's normal effects, 50% of all healing absorbed by this spell is also awarded to you as Health over the next 10 seconds.

"Ohhh," I said. "These are super cool. Definitely tailored to your role, too—none of them would be useless."

Frank laughed. "Now that this grown-ass man has swallowed a marble, I can officially confirm that he's kinda right. You're much more likely to get offered abilities that are generally useful for your class, and your current kit is always taken into consideration.

"A healer is most likely to get healing abilities, but there's always a chance they end up with something a dedicated tank would want as one of their options instead. Maybe even a shout that taunts everything around them and repeatedly gets them killed, but hey, that's just the optimist in me speaking."

"Ranks stay the same too," I said. "Fettering was at Intermediate I, and it's offering me all three choices at the same rank. It's letting me choose new options for the rank upgrades that no longer apply, too."

Darling's eyes widened. "You've already got skills at Intermediate?"

I suppressed a yawn, then rubbed my eyes. "Yeah. Hoping to get a few more after a couple hours of sleep, too. Got another one of those upgrade messages when I hit level 16. You mind if I run through these real quick, then we can focus on the plan with the rifts afterward? Otherwise I'm not gonna be able to get them out of my head."

She smiled. "I get it. Share them with me?"

I found an option to make the skills visible to others and swiped them over to Darling.

"Ohh," she said. "That is interesting."

"Yeah. Frank, can you help me with the first one? I'm thinking that's not the move, but I'm not sure I get the elemental boost thing."

"If you've got gear or skills that give you +10% fire damage and +10% ice damage, then that skill deals +20% total damage," he said. "It just adds them all up. It also calculates its damage total against the target's lowest resistance, though at this point we haven't seen much in the way of gear with specific resistances on it."

"Thought so. The gear and skill requirements for that one kinda rule it out, but the class sounds awesome. More magic the better, right Frank? Imagine me with every school at once. We'd be so sparkly."

He gagged.

"What do you guys think about the other two abilities?" I said.

Darling tapped the air. "Salverot Dart seems really strong for bringing a healer down or even someone with off-healing. That upgrade that punishes you for dispelling it unless you're super quick is nasty, too. That's a lot of pressure right there."

"Absolutely. Catch somebody who just dropped into the execute window and hit them with that... man. Lights out. Really strong arena-type spell, but it's a good bit less likely to help us out on a raid. But with Goon looming over it all... yeah. Maybe that's the pick."

I looked down at Frank. "Do I need to ask where your unnecessarily strong opinions lie, or can I assume that you're all about the spell that ends healers?"

"I'm bout it bout it," Frank said. A beat of silence passed, and it felt like he had something else to say, but Darling spoke before he had the chance.

"Heart Vessel's cool though, and it might be better for what you're dealing with if you take that latter upgrade."

"I was eyeing that, yeah. A cheat death would be pretty clutch. Been jealous of yours ever since I saw it. I'm a little worried about the illusion thing in general. so it'd be nice to lean on that a little less."

She took another sip of beer. "What do you mean?"

"Well... between people just leveling and picking classes and those spheres giving them random abilities, it won't be too long before more and more people realize illusions are a thing. I'd just feel a little better if I was saving mine for key moments rather than running around with one in place all the time.

"Part of the reason I dumped Fettering Shot was in the hopes of getting something more raid-focused, too. Heart Vessel is pretty nice for that. Can't do damage if you're dead, right?"

"Preaching to the choir," Darling said, which drew a curious glance from House.

I selected Heart Vessel, then looked down at Frank. "Objections?"

But to my surprise, I thought he felt somewhat relieved. "Eh. It's fine."

I confirmed my choice.

**Congratulations, you've learned the ability {Heart Vessel}!**
**You may select 1 of 2 available upgrades.**

Picking one of the two upgrades was easy: I went with the latter to make sure the ability would only activate if I would have otherwise died.

With my Health pool being as small as it was, taking 33% of my life in a single attack happened on a regular basis, so I didn't see a ton of use for removing the cooldown and halving the cast time compared to the value I'd get on a cheat death.

I activated the spell on a whim, and little streams of red formed in the air and helixed around me. They converged a bit above my left shoulder, then pulled into a tight knot of red as the spell completed.

The sphere flashed, then a layer of glass appeared around the floating ball of fluid. The vessel was smaller than I'd expected, about the size of a tennis ball, and it just hovered there, spinning silently a bit behind me.

I rolled my shoulders. "Alright, onto the raid and so on. How does the trash clear work? Can we keep clearing it, or does stuff stay dead?"

"The wings will reset a week after you first enter them," Frank said. "So you're limited when it comes to kills."

I rapped my knuckles on the table. "So still a decent option. Any other gear that's dropping?"

"The sets we got pieces of earlier also drop within the raid," Darling said, "but the pieces are pretty rare. Gear-wise, Rifting is probably a better bet." She grimaced. "I don't like the idea of sending more of those prisms drifting our way, though."

I cracked a smile. "I've been thinking about that a lot, actually." I pulled up my Rift Map, then set my permissions so that Darling would be able to see it. "So if we clear a Rift, that basically sends a pack of enemies drifting toward the nearest city."

I took a sip of beer and wiped my lips with my sleeve. "And we know there are different tiers for what gets thrown at us, with that Tyrant mob being one of the strongest possible results for now. So yeah, it probably doesn't make a whole lot of sense for us to clear the Rifts around the Oasis if we can help it, which is easy enough as long as we control the Hall of Rifts.

"At the same time, we need to prepare for the coming surge. Until there are several more Red Cathedrals in place, tons of people will be heading this way, and that means Rifts are going to get knocked out left and right. More clears, more prisms, more mobs."

"Yeah," Darling said. "Still don't want to add to it though."

"For sure." I tapped at the trio of western cities that had been leading the race for the first Red Cathedral along with Koria and the Vale. "Were you ever able to figure out which of these Goon was based out of? Think you were going to send someone out that way?"

"I did, yeah." She gestured at one of the dots with the bottom of her mug. "This is Uliana right here. Goon didn't have as big a presence there as you'd expect, but they're definitely running the show." Darling frowned for a moment, then her eyes went wide. "Wait. Are you thinking about clearing their Rifts?"

"Yep," I said, my smile deepening. "But in an organized way. This might seem like it's coming out of left field a bit, but hear me out."

"Sure, but you're not just talking about clearing them. We're talking about using them as a weapon."

I nodded. "Anything's a weapon if you use it the right way, right?"

House looked up from her intense conversation with Rock once again, but this time she leaned a bit closer to us. "As far as the system is concerned, Frank is explicitly not a weapon owing to his lack of stats and inability to inflict damage." Then she went right back to what she'd been doing before.

I tried to suppress a grin but didn't manage it, and Darling covered her mouth, laughing through her fingers.

"Wow," Frank said. "That was totally uncalled for."

"That cat comment was really not the best decision on your part," I said.

"Apparently not. But man. It's like, you threaten the one thing that someone loves most in the world one time, then you can just never come back from that."

"To be fair, it does hit different when the thing you love most is something other than yourself."

"Eh. I'll have to take your word for it on that."

"So the idea is to send prisms flying at Goon's capital?" Darling said.

"Yeah," I said through another yawn. "I've been thinking about this a lot. One of Goon's strengths right now, as far as I can tell, seems to be that they're purely on offense. They're just rolling through burning cities left and right, and in a way that's a lot easier. There's no need to defend what you've burned, right? It makes it impossible to overextend, at least comparably. You ever played domination games?"

"Whoa whoa whoa," Frank said.

"Like with bases?" She nodded. "Sure, all the time."

"Oh," Frank said. "Never mind. Proceed."

I rolled my eyes at him. "Bases, yeah. So, say it's us versus them in a mini-game, and there are five bases that you can capture." I traced a finger through the ring of condensation my beer had left on the table and drew a rough map.

"It might help if you picture it as some kind of basin," Frank said.

I eyed him. "Why does it have to be a basin? Never mind, whatever, it's a basin, and there are five capture points. You earn points by holding bases over time, they rack up more quickly if you can hold more of them at once, and the game ends when one side reaches 1,000 points. A lot of people will just say we need to hold three bases to win. But that doesn't really work."

House leaned over again. "But if you hold three bases, that is more than two bases, and you would therefore win by definition."

I sighed. "Sure, three is more than two. But the game isn't that simple, and this is exactly what I'm worried about with Goon: if we're fully on the defensive—if we're just trying to hold what we have—then that frees them up to hit us wherever we're weakest.

"Even if we spread out and try to guard everything at once, even if we have a group that's floating and responding to call-outs based on their movements, if we don't have at least some kind of offense that's creating pressure, they're always going to have the numbers, and they're always going to be dictating the action. They plan, we react. It's not a good place to be."

"I find myself liking where this is going," Frank said. "I also feel like I'm about to be gravely disappointed."

"I don't think you are. As long as we have access to the Hall, we can leverage Rifts for free, passive offense." I drew a wide circle around Uliana. "We could even clear them so that twenty or thirty prisms reach one of their cities at roughly the same time."

"How?" Darling said.

"We already know how quickly they move," I said, though in truth I was thinking I'd have House get me some exact, down-to-the-minute estimates now that she'd already seen a prism in motion and proved capable of just that. "So we'd start by smashing the Rifts that are the farthest from their city, then we immediately move into some of the ones that are in the middle distance-wise, then we hit the closest Rifts."

I met Darling's eyes. "That would create a wave of them that hit all at the same time. Imagine three or four Starlit Tyrants all rushing their city simultaneously."

"Unlikely," Frank said. "But very fun to picture."

"That would be absolutely devastating," Darling said.

"Yup, they'd need to pull back and defend for sure. Even if it's a fairly remote chance. I don't really want to blow their city apart, but I do want them to have to worry about the possibility."

"But do we really want to kick that hornet's nest? They seem to be leaving us alone."

"For now maybe, but I can't shake the feeling that they're going to be coming our way eventually. I guess I'm worried about letting them run around unopposed, too, and clearing their Rifts is a good way to hit them with at least some measure of safety and stealth on our part.

"I just don't think we can afford to Rift and raid and ignore everything else that's going in the world, especially their Sieges. And if we just sit around and let them snowball, we're done the moment they decide we're a problem.

"But if we can get them on their back foot for even a moment? That has a lot of value in a world with substantial travel time, and it would probably help out the cities they're Sieging to the north and south at the very least. We might not have the time to get directly involved in all that, but if we can help those people out without hurting ourselves, I think we should really consider it."

"I like it," Darling said. "I like it a lot."

"There is one more variable, though." I pulled out the stone that Arlann had handed me in secret after the Tyrant had died out of my inventory and popped it into my hand.

## {Heart of Refraction}
## Quality: Epic

It was smooth, perfectly round, and far heavier than it had a right to be. I tossed it to Darling.

She caught it, but she hit the back of her hand on the table as the weight seemed to catch her off-guard. "Ouch. What is this thing?"

"No idea, and I don't think Frank has anything on it either otherwise he would have mentioned it earlier."

"Got nothing for ya," he said.

"But here's what I'm thinking. I missed most of the fight with the Tyrant, but it seemed it was really the guards doing the damage, right? I'm guessing they were in a group or something, so Arlann was the one that got access to the loot when the Tyrant died. And this is what he ended up with."

Darling took a deep breath. "And whatever it is, it's Epic quality. So if we send a wave of prisms flying toward Goon's cities and they manage to clear them..."

"Yeah. We could be handing them a bunch of crazy items that help in a way we don't understand. Plus we'd be helping them complete their city's Legendary Defense Quest, too." I paused. "There *is* something we could do with the Heart right now, though. Especially if you've got a couple guildies that wouldn't mind sending a message or two for me."

"What do you have in mind?"

"Nothing major. I'm thinking I'll slap this Heart up on the Auction House for 10 gold, something ridiculous like that. Nobody's gonna buy it, but that's not the point.

"After I do that, whenever a guild member is passing through the Black Oasis or wherever, we have them shout out that they're buying three Hearts of Refraction at 5 gold each. If you're paying that much, people are going to ask where they're coming from. And when they ask, we say you can get them by killing whatever pops out of the prisms. It won't be long before people who are already around start dropping Hearts of their own on the regular and make the connection themselves."

"You want to try to set a price ahead of time," Darling said.

I held up a hand and made a lukewarm gesture. "It's more like creating the illusion of demand than setting the market value. All we really need to get people's attention is make it seem like these things are valuable. If we can do that, that gets people hunting the prisms, which introduces them to the Legendary Quest that we already got, which gets them killing things outside of the city, which keeps the Vale a good bit safer.

"If we can start the price off high and keep it there for a bit, that's awesome. But it's basically a mystery item, so that's really unlikely. Realistically what'll happen is people will go out and hunt these down, try to sell at the amounts we're supposedly buying them for, then they'll bail on the whole thing when they can't find a buyer. People who have farmed up a bunch of them will undercut the prices we've set on the Auction House, and the supposed market will absolutely tank."

"But who cares," Darling said, "because all you really want is to have people defending the city."

I tapped my temple. "Exactly. And the best part is we get freed up to do what we want without having to pay the people that are helping us. I'm already on the hook for funding the entire city guard within two-and-a-half days and the defenses are going to be ludicrously expensive over time, so I'll take every bit of help we can get."

Her eyebrows shot up. "Wait, what?"

I ran her through what had happened with Arlann, between the two Merchant Kings deserting the city and the Queen of Highwater cutting their funding.

"Sixty hours? Fifty gold?"

"Yep. Had to put the Auction House and everything else up as collateral, too. Hurt to do it, but yeah, I'm glad I did because if I hadn't, we'd have been on our own with the Tyrant and I doubt we'd even have a city right now. Hopefully we can expand the Auction Network quickly enough where it's doable."

"I could pull some donations for you. I doubt we'll get anywhere near 50, but I could definitely get enough to take the edge off and get it paid a bit earlier."

I thought about that for a moment. "Thanks. I'd love to get that weight off my chest, but I'm thinking I'll let that loan run its full course.

Rather leverage the gold I have right now while I can. Speaking of leverage, I'd love to get your thoughts on something."

Darling finished her drink and motioned at the bartender for another. "Shoot."

"What do you think about me offering the guild an investment opportunity?"

She cocked an eyebrow.

"In-game," I said. "I need gold up front more than anything else right now. For the network, for the defenses, for everything. So I'm thinking I offer people the opportunity to chip in, then I offer to double their money in a week or something like that."

Darling mimed reaching into a pocket, then popped a handful of silver coins into the palm of her hand and dropped them onto the table in front of me. "Thirty-six silver," she said, grinning.

I pursed my lips. "Sorry, is that a yes?"

"It's a donation. But I do think the amount of economic success you've had is messing with your idea of the kind of money the guild has. I'd be willing to bet that I'm one of the richer members right now at my level, and that's most of what I've got.

"So doubling it in a week?" she said, shrugging. "It's nothing crazy. Go ahead and ask if you want. You'll probably raise some money. Most of us though are still in the stage where money doesn't do a whole lot. Maybe I could use what I just gave you to snag a piece of gear off the Auction House, but it's not that important for me right now. And again, doubling 50 silver or so in a week, eh."

"That's fair," I said. "It won't seem like much by then anyway."

"Yup. If I were you, I'd just keep it simple and ask if anybody wants to donate toward the defenses. Could be gold, materials, whatever. It's clean, and it's a fair ask—you shouldn't have to handle the guards' fees on your own anyway, let alone the defenses for the whole city. The Stronghold might be removed from the Oasis, but we're still going to be depending on the Vale." She pushed the coins toward me with a grin. "Besides, it sounds like you've already got enough creditors as it is."

I smiled and scooped the coins up, then dumped them into my inventory. "Thanks, Darling. That's really helpful."

She smiled in return, which drew a low growl from Frank. I ignored him.

"I'll stick with asking people to contribute to the defenses for now. Should I just pop a message into the guild chat?"

"I think a desperate speech where you prostrate yourself before the masses would be better," Frank said. "Seems like a natural fit for you."

"Would you be doing it through House?" Darling said. "She's good with figures, and I imagine she wouldn't have much trouble keeping track of everything. I can probably figure out a way to compensate people who donate the most too, loot rights for the raid or something similar."

I nodded. "If she's up for it, sure, and that would be amazing."

We both looked in House's direction at the same time, and she ignored us completely.

I smirked. "Yeah, she'll be up for it."

Darling paused, and a moment later a message scrawled in green appeared in the guild's chat window: she'd gone ahead and asked people to consider donating what they could to the city.

"Thanks for that," I said. A few moments later, I was already feeling a little lighter. I didn't think the donations would go incredibly far or anything, but it was a huge relief to see the messages stream in and know that so many other people were invested in the city, too.

And I really appreciated not having to be the one who asked.

"So, timing then," she said.

"Right." I pulled the Trinket that Frank had led me to out of my inventory. "I'm really sorry, I should have mentioned this earlier, but I feel like this is the first time I've had a moment to breathe since the Cathedral finished. So, long story short, at 15 you can find a Trinket on certain monsters that Frank can pick out. I think they're going to end up being class-defining in the early game." I linked it to her.

"I see that, and whatever it is, I want one!" Nina said, her voice cutting through the din of conversation.

Rock looked up at the sound, sighed in her direction, then went back to chatting with—listening to—House.

Darling whistled. "Yeah, that's really good to know. So if we want those, then we need to get everybody to 15 as soon as possible, and ideally before the raid."

"Agreed. I'm crashing kinda hard though so I'm thinking I might pass out for four hours here in a bit to grab my skill upgrades and another rested buff, but after that, I think we hit Rifts super hard going forward. If people want to Rift tonight before the Goon prism rush, that's awesome, but maybe they pick Rifts at random or something and avoid completing them around here."

"Easy ask with the Hall."

"Yeah. Then as soon as we've got a good amount of people around—ideally tomorrow morning—we start the focused push. Get everyone that's available Rifting around Goon's city, starting with the ones that are farthest out. And as more people log back in or become available, we can phase them into whatever section we need."

"How big of a window do you think that leaves us with?" Darling said. "Like, are we talking twelve hours of Rifting or four? I'm down regardless, but I'm just a little worried about burnout for everybody else. We don't want them running themselves into the ground."

"For sure. Why don't we look at the numbers we have available in the morning and we'll go from there? If we've got a massive group, we'll start farther out. If there's only fifty or so of us around, we'll keep the window smaller."

Darling leaned back in her chair. "Seems like a good plan for now. I think we'll have a bunch, but it's gonna be early, so we'll just have to see."

"There's lots of flexibility before we start, too. We really won't be locked in until that first wave is completed."

"True, but aren't you worried about the Oasis overnight while you're passed out?"

"Absolutely. But at the same time, it's messy because I really don't want to be seen actively defending the city if I can help it, both from the manhunt angle and to keep people from thinking Ned is still invested in the city. If something like the Starlit Tyrant pops up and I need to help out then I'm going to be there for the Oasis no matter what, but if I can help it, I'd like to preserve the narrative that Ned is completely out and Francis is running things.

"That said, I'll probably head back there to crash for the night to make sure I'm around if stuff goes down, and I'll ask Frank to wake me up in some terrible way if it does."

"Extremely happy to oblige," he said.

"Thanks, sorta. I'm kind of hoping that we're still in the window where a lot of people are traveling this way, and Arlann assured me the guard would be able to put up a better fight with some organization. It still feels sketchy, though. House?"

She ignored me completely again. I didn't think it was deliberate; she was just intently focused on whatever she and Rock were talking about.

"I got you," Frank said before raising his voice. "Oh look, a small, unclaimed animal."

House's head snapped toward us so hard that I rubbed my neck on her behalf. She looked around, peered beneath the table, then narrowed her eyes at Frank.

"Think you just dug yourself a little deeper," I said under my breath. "House, I'm calling it a night in a bit—Darling's going to try to get some donations going. If that works well, do you think you could handle getting the defenses up and running?"

Her squint deepened into an expression of confusion.

"Completing the defenses," I corrected. I handed her what Darling had given me plus a few more gold coins on top. "More specifically, it'd be awesome if you could get a golem working on the Defensive Trench I already started. After that, the wall upgrade would be the next priority, using whatever Darling hands you, unless completing the trench unlocks something really cool. You could shoot me a message then if you're unsure."

House stood up abruptly.

"You don't need to go right now, House," I said. "You're allowed to enjoy yourself."

"Would it not be optimal for me to begin construction immediately so that the defenses have more time to finish?"

"I mean, sure. But Darling needs time to get the materials anyway, and aside from that, it's okay if you want to wait a little bit on top of everything else."

"But that would not be optimal."

I leaned forward a little. "But you were having a good time, right?"

"Indeed I was." She pivoted toward the door, then back toward her seat. "It appears I am caught between a rock and a second object that is both somehow vague yet also reminiscent of a rock in both density and firmness."

"Rock and a hard place," Frank said.

"Indeed," House said. She caught the eyes of the big man who was sitting next to her, grinning slightly. "Rock is also present, which further complicates matters on both a linguistic and a practical level." She looked at the stage. "Nina's continued singing is however a clear win for spending what gold I currently possess, then returning once Darling has obtained more materials and Nina has potentially fallen asleep."

"I'm soooo gonna tell her you said that," Darling said. She hesitated. "I guess I'm going to have to rephrase that a bit and add a bunch of context, but I'm definitely going to tell her."

"House," Frank said. "If you were to follow the river out in front of the

Stronghold all the way back to the Oasis, you might be able to snag a rare pet. No guarantees, but look for yellow eyes glinting on top of the water."

She stared at him for a very long moment, then turned and power-walked out of the room. To my surprise, Rock followed her, slipping out the door at a light jog with a quick wave to Nina, who currently looked like she was trying to fall down but hadn't quite figured out how to manage it.

Darling and I shared a glance.

"Huh," I said. "How about that."

Darling looked at Nina. "My thoughts exactly."

"Is that cat real, Frank?"

"What cat?"

"You just sent her off after a cat."

"I never said cat," Frank said. "The pet's real though, yeah. But pretty rare."

I sighed. "She's gonna come back clutching an alligator. I'm calling it now."

"You're not terribly far off for once, and it definitely bites."

I blew out a puff of air and eyed the ceiling. "Alright then. I'm gonna pay Vesuvian a quick visit then get some sleep, and we'll get right back to work afterward. You all good here?"

"Oh yeah," Darling said, "We'll manage. Lemme know when you wake up. I'll probably still be around."

"Will do. Thanks again."

"Yup!"

"Night Darling," Frank said.

"Night Frank!"

I stood up and pushed my stool in. "Frank, I think we—"

I cut off as a wave of panic crashed through me, even stronger than the one I'd experienced in the shadow of the Red Cathedral.

I coughed, and the same black smoke I'd seen earlier poured out of my mouth. It was much more pronounced this time, thick twists and curls that were oil-black, so dark they looked solid as they drifted up toward the ceiling.

The inn quieted as people noticed that I was staring at something, then went totally silent, barring Nina, when the smoke met the ceiling.

And it wasn't long before a skull coalesced out of the black smoke and stared down at me, its jaw clicking up and down, empty sockets glaring from above.

# Chapter Fifteen

"This again?" Darling said.

I drew my pistols. "Feels different this time around. Much heavier."

The hearth that had been burning so brightly at the far end of the room died out as if some great gust of wind had swept through the inn—though none had—and that was enough to shut even Nina up.

The bartender who had been carrying a silver tray full of mugs caught his foot on a chair in the suddenly dark common room, and he went down in a clatter of metal and glass and splashing beer.

Nobody laughed. The inn had gone cold.

"Frank?" I said, but all I got was a vibration in return, one that felt distinctly like a warning.

My blunderbuss was fully loaded, so I pulled out my rifle and Over-charged a blast, illuminating the dim room with golden light.

A few other players wound up their own spells, and it wasn't long before the entire hall was alight with different flavors of magic, all aimed at the door to the inn.

I followed everybody's collective gaze. A black dot had formed at the top right-hand corner of the door, as if someone were applying a torch to the surface from the other side.

Then the dot became a dark line that crept down diagonally, picking up speed as it neared the opposite corner. The left half of the door fell inward, and the right half went the other way and slammed down out onto the porch.

"Wait!" Darling cried, but it was too late.

Maybe ten players released their spells at once, likely startled by the sound, and prismatic light filled the inn. The glass windows to either side of the door shattered in their frames.

Frank was vibrating, and I knew he was trying to figure out how to say something important but hadn't yet managed it.

The smoke and dirt and dust cleared around the entryway, revealing the crater the guild had blasted into the porch. The sound of the explosions was still reverberating through the cave, echoing back and forth with remarkable volume and clarity.

I kept my rifle pointed at the door, but there was something vaguely directional in Frank's vibration, and I found myself lifting the weapon toward the ceiling.

I looked up just in time to see a jet-black, doglike figure pouring out of the ceiling, its mouth open, revealing two rows of wicked, molten-orange teeth.

I activated Clonedrift and shot backward, flashing between two tables as the creature fully formed and dropped free.

It landed directly on the copy I'd left behind and the clone shattered and sparked, stunning the creature in midair. It locked up and smashed through our table.

I tried to inspect it as I resolved back into place a few feet away, but Darling and the other nearest melee players were already on top of the creature. Spells and projectiles were flying, and its Health bar went from full to empty in a split second.

And by the time I managed to pull the information up on whatever the thing was, it was already extremely dead.

**{Dread Revenant} (Level 10 Undead)**
**HP: 0/800**
**MP: 0/500**

I let out a relieved breath, but Frank was still so tense at my side that I kept my rifle out even as the rest of the guild visibly relaxed.

The creature's stats were underwhelming, and I wasn't surprised that it had died as quickly as it had, given the firepower we'd trained onto it, but I couldn't shake the feeling that something was still very wrong.

Then its dark, shadowy corpse twitched, and the guild members who'd crept close to get a better look drew away again.

The corpse bubbled, then burst, and a smaller version of the shadowy skull I'd seen earlier flew up, did a quick circle around me, then streaked out of one of the blown-out windows next to the door and disappeared out the exit to the sands.

"Who killed it?" Frank said, his voice booming over the now-rising chatter.

"I got a good chunk of it," Nina said, and a few others chimed in as well.

"Who actually got the killing blow?" Frank clarified.

Darling tapped the air. She smiled. "I did, actually. Caught it with an execute."

"Crap. Of course you did."

She cocked her head at him. "Are you, Frank, saying that I shouldn't have killed that thing? 'Cause if so, I'm seriously worried."

"Yeah. No. Kind of. I mean, I'm impressed and not surprised, but, uh..." He trailed off, then lowered his voice so only I could hear. "Here. Share this with Darling."

**Codex Entry 3300: Dread Revenant**
**Hatred given form, the Dread Revenant is a relentless creature that returns from beyond the grave time and again, each time reemerging stronger than the foe who dispatched it.**
**The product of powerful dark magic, a Dread Revenant requires constant sacrifices to maintain, and once a target has been selected, it will only accept sacrifices that would kill the target themselves if given the opportunity.**

I dropped the text into the guild chat so everybody could see it.

"What were you trying to tell me back there before it showed up?" I said.

The hearth roared back to life as the guild crowded around what remained of the strange corpse, jostling to get a look at it.

"What the codex says, basically," Frank said. "Not to kill it yourself."

"Because it comes back stronger than the person that killed it," I said, sighing as I dropped my rifle back into my inventory. "And Darling, the second strongest person in the whole guild, dropped it with an execute."

I pulled up her level in the guild roster: she was sitting just a little behind me at level 14. At least I hadn't finished the creature off myself.

A few shouts went up from those nearest to the corpse, so I pushed through the crowd to see what was going on.

And it was now sparking blue. Darling knelt beside it, and the sparks faded at once. She popped a shield into her hand, her two-handed sword vanishing at the same time.

"Oh man! Check this thing out."

{Shadowhound Shield} (Touchstone)
Grade: D
Item Level: 28
Slot: Offhand
Quality: Rare
Primaries: +10 Constitution
Secondaries: +5% Threat Generation
Armor: +14%
Touchstone Ability: As long as this item is equipped, you gain the passive ability {Menacing Glow}.

{Menacing Glow} (Touchstone Ability)
Whenever you receive healing, 20% of the Threat your healer would have otherwise generated is instead instantly transferred to you.

"Ton is going to go nuts over this thing," Darling said.

"Yeah, killer drop," I said, but my mind was racing too fast for me to manage much in the way of enthusiasm. It was great to know that the Revenant had a solid drop table, but I was worried about what the mob's existence meant for the future. "How big of a problem is this going to be?"

"Depends on what you mean by problem," Frank said. "It'll definitely come back."

"I outgear and outlevel Darling, so I bet I can kill it when it shows up again. But how quickly is that going to happen?"

"Ehhh, lemme think for a minute. The stronger... no, that's no good. If it's gonna get way more powerful before it returns, you'll tend to have more time."

"Minutes?" I said. "Hours? Days?"

"Can't say. That's all I can do."

I dropped into a nearby chair in front of our ruined table. "Well, I guess in a way we're just adding another member to the manhunt, and if it's gonna try to kill us, then at least it's gonna drop Touchstones."

"Worth," Darling said. She pursed her lips. "Sorry, probably not worth, but still exciting. On second thought, you probably don't find it exciting."

I laughed and eyed the Codex entry again. "A Revenant will only accept a sacrifice that would kill the target themselves if given the chance," I repeated. "So, whoever's doing this needs sacrifices that already want me dead. That narrows the pool down to what? Most people?"

"Pretty much," Frank said. "It won't be able to get at you in instances, though."

"That's good to know. So raids and Rifts are still safe."

"So..." Darling said. "That thing just hunts you now? Forever?"

"It's harder and harder to bring back with sacrifices," Frank said. "But it could come back a number of times, yeah. Really depends on who's behind it."

"Can you say if it's a player or an NPC that's behind this?" Darling said. "To be honest, I'm thinking of Tyrann. Seems like a natural fit for him, and he definitely wouldn't lack for willing sacrifices."

I found it a little unlikely the Revenant was player-controlled given the potency of the spell, but my skin prickled at the thought all the same.

"Can't say," Frank said.

I rolled my shoulders. "There's gotta be a better way out of this than to just kill it until it stops coming back. If it's gonna get stronger each time, then that won't be easy, or even advisable. If anything, you'd probably prefer not to kill that thing at all."

"Or make sure that you can outpace its growth," Darling said.

"True," I agreed. "My payouts could help a lot there. I guess we could also try to finish it off with weaker members, but that's easier said than done when something's trying to kill you."

"You could also cut the head off the snake," Frank said. "Huh. I'm surprised that went through."

"You mean kill the person who's sending it our way?"

"Yes, and preferably with me."

I rubbed my chin. "We'll still have to find them before this thing becomes a serious problem, but yeah. I think that sounds like a plan, Frank."

# Chapter Sixteen

Once the guild had settled back into their celebration, I headed up the stairs to Vesuvian's room. But instead of pushing right in, I pulled up the lone Renown Perk that I still hadn't used and skipped right to the description.

**You may enlist the aid of an Underworld Smuggler, a specialized NPC that will act as a Follower for as long as they survive (this ability may only be used once).**

"What inadvisable thing are you doing now?" Frank said.

"Arlann said he'd be needing help with the logistics of the city before long, and that was before the Oasis was under assault. And also before that Starlit Tyrant treated him like a chew toy."

"Uh, the smuggler NPC's gonna be loyal, but they're going to be a pretty serious mismatch for what Arlann needs. And the rewards for that quest he gave you are gonna be super crappy or even actively bad for us if you put someone who can't handle the work up for the position."

I shook my head. I was confident that I had a far better solution than that. "The smuggler won't be the one doing the work. Trust me on this."

"I'm willing to pretend that I do and see what happens, but that's the best offer I can make."

"Deal."

I activated the ability and immediately heard footsteps on the stairs. They were heavier than I'd expected, and I was thinking some behemoth of a man was stomping our way.

Instead, a woman with light brown skin and violet eyes came around the corner. She stood 5 foot tall—if that—and she was dressed in a wide-brimmed hat and gray leathers that were aged and flaked with red dirt but were otherwise unremarkable. Her facial expression was remarkably flat, and it stayed that way as she drew closer.

I inspected her.

**{Cerra} (Level 16 Humanoid)**
**HP: 1,800/1,800**
**MP: 600/600**

As Frank had promised earlier, she had indeed scaled to my level. And while I didn't love burning the ability just now when Trade Pack runs and so very many other things felt wholly out of reach with everything we were dealing with, I needed to tie up whatever loose ends I could, and the smuggler—Cerra—represented an opportunity to do just that.

"Hello there," she said, without even a trace of inflection.

"Hi." I gave the hallway a quick glance to make sure we were alone. "I'm Ned." I offered her my hand, and for a moment I thought she was going to ignore me, but then she stepped closer and shook it. Her palm was calloused and rough, and her grip was firm yet friendly.

"Pleasure," she said, though it didn't sound like she was pleased. Or upset. Or that she felt anything at all upon meeting me.

I tapped the top of Frank's blade much, much harder than was strictly necessary. "And this is—"

"Funkmaster Frank. And as you probably assumed by looking at us that I'm the one who's piloting this long-fingered meat mech."

She regarded him cooly. "I've heard about you, axe. I was told that you're the type who often informs people that he's in charge. I'm glad to see my sources were accurate."

I raised an eyebrow at that.

"Definitely accurate," Frank agreed, and happily so.

I shrugged. Maybe I'd misread what she was trying to say; I could have sworn there'd been an insult buried in her description of him.

She took her hat off and thumped it against the wall, which caused a cloud of reddish dust to billow off it.

"I hear you've got a job for me."

I thumbed at the door across from the room I'd locked Vesuvian in, then pushed through it before she could respond, holding it open for her.

"We'll need some privacy for what I've got in mind."

She stood there in the hallway, her face blank, but I thought a bit of anger had flashed in her violet eyes. And I hadn't missed the way the tips of her fingers had drifted to the sheath of the long dagger that hung on her right hip.

"The terms of my contract are binding," she said. She fixed me with a stern look. "But there are certain... jobs that I'll walk away from, or worse."

I frowned, puzzled. "Yeah, sure. You can just tell me if what I've got in mind makes you uncomfortable and we'll start somewhere else instead and work our way up from there."

Cerra stepped into the room, her footsteps even louder than before, fingers now playing at the hilt of her weapon. She eyed my pistols as she passed, stiffening slightly.

"She's not gonna try to kill me, right?" I said, dropping my voice. "I feel like she's considering it, but I have no idea why."

"Probably depends on what you propose," Frank whispered.

Cerra sat on the edge of the bed and drew her dagger, then started picking at the reddish dirt beneath her fingernails a bit more aggressively than I liked.

I leaned up against the wall and crossed my arms. "So, here's the short of it. I need to put a specific guy in charge of a bunch of administrative stuff. Right now, it's simple: shifts for the guards, allotment of provisions, handling the orders for the repairs they need for armor. It's busy work, but there's nobody else around who knows the ins and outs of the city in question, and there's a good amount of money exchanging hands."

Cerra cocked her head at me, seemed to come to some sort of decision, then abruptly stopped picking at her nails and sheathed her dagger.

Which really made me feel like she'd been about to stab me for something. It appeared that was no longer the case for reasons I still didn't understand, but it still seemed like a positive development.

I pressed on. "If it works, his responsibilities will grow. But for now, that's all I'm putting on his plate. Needless to say, I'll trust him about as far as I can throw him."

"It's hard to tell because of the armor Ned has on," Frank said, "but he's far, far weaker than you probably expect. Think elf, but with an iron deficiency."

"You're so funny," she said, flat as ever.

Once again, I wondered if she was mocking him.

"True. You seem perceptive, so I'm going to give you 45,000 Frank points to start. That's a promising start, Cerra. You're already well ahead of my caddy here."

"You have a point system. And you named it after yourself."

"I did do that."

"I'm not at all surprised. Do you find the math challenging?"

"Oh yeah, I don't do it all."

She nodded. "I thought that might be the case."

Then it was Frank's turn to hesitate.

"Seems like it probably saves you a lot of time," she added, and if Frank had been feeling in any way suspicious at my side, her last comment obliterated it. Then she changed tack. "So what about me, then?"

"You're a Smuggler, correct?" I said.

"I'm a lot of things, but yes, you could say that."

"Well, I was hoping I'd have some jobs lined up for you already— maybe have you break us into hostile territory for Trade Pack runs or something, that sort of thing. But what I'm thinking is a good bit more mundane. I'd like you to hang out with the guy I was just talking about, the one I'm putting in charge. And I want you to do the complete opposite of smuggling."

She paused. "The opposite of smuggling."

"Snuggling," Frank said.

"Shut up," I said. "Look, you've spent your whole career bringing items into places they aren't allowed, right?"

"That's one way to put it."

"Well, I want you to do the opposite. I want you to make sure that this guy who's running all the admin for me isn't doing exactly that—sneaking the city's gold out into his own coffers."

"Embezzling," Frank said.

"I said shut—oh. Yeah, he's right this time. That's exactly what I'm worried about."

She leaned forward. "And how am I supposed to watch him?"

I made a dismissive gesture. "Already considered that. We'll just say you're his apprentice."

She looked at me flatly. "And this guy I've never met is going to happily agree to take me on as an apprentice."

"I'm not worried about that. He's kind of, uh…"

"A prisoner," Frank finished for me. "Hey Cerra, how do you feel about torture? Are you a fan? You seem like you're probably a fan."

She finally cocked an eyebrow, the most expression I'd seen from her yet. "I'm dealing with a hostage situation, then?"

"Sort of." I took a deep breath, then summarized our previous interactions with Vesuvian: how I'd captured him at the caravan, how I'd holed him up at the Stronghold instead of killing him, the way his fellow Kings had basically tried to off him, and so on.

When I'd finished, I stared at her for a moment, trying to read what she was thinking.

"You're hesitant."

She nodded, seeming surprised that I'd been able to glean anything from her bearing. It was something about her eyes—a flash of color that was there, then gone.

"How about this," I said. "The first time you catch him stealing—and I know there'll be a first time—you keep double what you catch. On the second go-round, I'll triple it. On the third, well… he probably won't be around at that point, but we'll figure something out."

The slightest smile I'd ever seen tugged at the corners of her lips.

"Okay, I'm sold. So long as he's willing to take on an apprentice. I imagine that might take a bit of finessing on your part."

I pursed my lips. "I really don't think it will. I doubt he'll even blink at that, actually. I'll be right back. Going to let him know what's up, then I'll have you introduce yourself."

"I do have one more question for you," she said. "On a scale from one to ten, how important is it that Vesuvian survives?"

"Survives what?"

"Just in general."

I thought about that. "Uh… seven?"

"Thank you."

I popped out of the room and closed the door behind me.

"Huh," Frank said as I clasped a hand around the doorknob that led to Vesuvian's room.

"What is it now?"

"I like Cerra."

"Of course you do. She's a woman who carries a really long knife."

"Bit lacking in the armor department. Leather, eh. It's fine, but you gotta be really careful with that stuff or it practically falls off compared to plate. I'm a much bigger fan of the sort of stuff that requires several people to remove. That way you know you're good to go no matter what."

I blinked at that. "You're worried about it falling off?"

"Obviously."

I put my hands on my hips. "How do you think this works?"

"What do you mean, this? Don't use the vague this. It's confusing and inarticulate."

"Has anyone ever given you the birds and the bees, Frank?"

"You want me to run you through literally everything I know at great length and you can tell me how close I am?"

I swallowed. "I gotta stop asking these questions."

"Agreed. But before we go in, I kinda had a weird thought I wanna run by you."

"Another one?"

"Uh huh. For a moment there I thought Cerra might have been being facetious when she was complimenting me. Like, it was almost as if she didn't fully mean the things she was saying. But they were about me, and they were good. It doesn't make any sense."

I stared at him. "Are you being serious? I honestly can't tell."

"Frank never jokes about Frank."

"Oh." The fact that he'd picked up on that too essentially confirmed that Cerra had been subtly mocking Frank from the beginning, but I felt like lying to him would probably be more fun than telling the truth. "Then no. I didn't get the impression that she was mocking you at all. If anything, I actually thought she was kind of starstruck and was doing her best to hide it behind a blank and emotionless façade."

"Hm. That does seem more likely."

"Yeah, wouldn't sweat it."

"I do hate sweating things."

"I know. You mention that several times a day."

"Uh huh. So, Vesuvian. We're doing the bad cop worse cop thing again, right?"

"That was never a thing I wanted to do in the first place, and also no, don't do that."

"C'mon. Just once. Just a bit, see how it feels."

I paused, considering it. "I guess you have been more helpful than usual lately, huh?"

"Decidedly so."

"Alright then, have at it, but make it deliberately confusing more than anything else, yeah? We want him off balance rather than threatened."

"Deal."

I went into Vesuvian's room and found him sitting on the floor with his back to the wall, staring out the window. The light from the glowcaps was shining in, iridescent as ever, and the room had a strange, warm glow to it.

He glanced over at me in all of his ruined finery and seemed to consider standing up but then thought better of it.

"I'm hungry."

"And a good evening to you as well." I closed the door and leaned up against it. "I've officially got a job for you."

"I'm hungry," he repeated.

"Listen without making this harder than it needs to be, and I'll have your assistant bring you whatever you want from the kitchen when I'm done."

He perked up at that, even smiling a bit. "Did you say assistant?"

And there it was: the ego I'd been counting on. Even despite his current situation, Vesuvian was still thinking of himself as someone who others could learn from.

That was just his type. He was young, and that definitely helped, but I didn't think that was the sort of thing that people ever really grew out of.

I eyed Frank, thinking.

"What?" he said. "Why are you looking at me like that? Are you thinking about Franking this guy with me?"

Vesuvian tried to back up further into the wall, panic in his eyes. "I don't know what that means, but I don't like the way it sounds or the way he said it."

"I actually don't like the way that sounds either," I said. "It sounds too much like we're both involved in something illicit, and not in a good way."

"Yeah," Frank said. "Not ideal. I'll try again. Are you thinking about smashing his taint with me?"

I grimaced. "No, you went the other direction on that—that's way, way worse." I considered what he'd said. "It was definitely more menacing, so there's that. The implication is kind of the same, but it's just more confusing, and the visual is awful."

"Hm, agreed. It might be menacing, but it's menacing in the same way it was when you said you had a job for Cerra that she needed to perform for you in private, immediately led her into a dark bedroom and shut the door behind you, then stayed silent for a long moment while looking at her and searching her face. I'm not here for that sorta thing, you know? It's cheap."

I snapped my fingers. "That's why she wanted to stab me, huh?" I blinked and rubbed the back of my head. "Oh man, it sounds really obvious when you say it out loud like that."

"It was super obvious."

"Well, thanks. The why of that was really bothering me. I'll have to let her know that was unintentional."

"It wasn't getting stabbed you were worried about?"

"Nah, I've fully come to terms with the fact that most people would stab me if they could. I just don't like being unaware of the why when there are already so many reasons."

"Countless reasons. Trust me, I went against my instincts and tried to count them. Ended up with an aching shaft and a bucketload of nausea."

"If we know the why then it feels like something I could address, like a problem we could actually handle. Or at least prepare for."

"I have to dock you 2 points for caring that people want to stab you on some level, even if you're just trying to prevent it, but I'm awarding you 10 for not fearing the actual piece of metal that's theoretically on the verge of sliding between your ribs at all times."

I pumped a fist, but I was subtle about it.

"I saw that. I'll let it slide this time. But don't let it happen again."

I gave him a mock salute.

"Now that that's settled," Frank said, "let's get back to folding this guy like a soft taco."

Vesuvian stared up at us, fear in his eyes. "What's a taco?"

I took a step toward him, then stopped. "Like a *soft* taco?"

"Uh huh."

"Why would it... No, I'm tired, and we need to focus. Let's uhh..." I pinched the bridge of my nose. "Gah, fine, I need to know. Why would it be soft?"

"Because a flour tortilla is vaguely reminiscent of skin, and I like the way it feels when the meat and guac squish between my fingers."

"That's gross, but if we're still analyzing how menacing something is, then a hard taco would be way better."

"You can't fold a hard taco, genius."

"You totally can—it's just gonna snap down the middle and the contents are going to go everywhere. I mean, honestly? I feel like threatening to fold someone should always involve something that theoretically can be folded but shouldn't, otherwise there will be terrible consequences."

"I'm intrigued, but I need another example."

All of the color was draining out of Vesuvian's face, so I thought, *screw it*, and decided to keep playing along.

"Say you tell someone you're going to fold them like a lawn chair." I clapped my hands together. "It's a clear image for sure, but a lawn chair is meant to fold. Do you see what I'm saying?"

"An inadvisable fold," Frank said, as if he were tasting the words. "I do like the sound a hard taco makes when it snaps. It's so tactile."

"I mean, if you wanna go really deep on this—"

"Oh, you know I wanna go deep. I wanna go so deep that I get stuck and require extrication by several people who don't want to be involved but have no other choice."

The look on Vesuvian's face was so horrified that I had to grit my teeth and swallow repeatedly to keep from laughing.

"Double decker taco," I said.

"I can tell I love it, but I don't know what it is."

"Soft shell on the outside."

"Skin," Frank said.

"Cheese or beans under that to hold stuff together."

"Ligaments and tendons."

I mimed placing something inside something else. "Then you stick a hard taco in there. So you still get the crunch factor."

"Bones."

"Then you've got the meat."

"Works on both a symbolic and a literal level." He eyed Vesuvian. "We're gonna fold you like a double decker taco."

I hesitated. "This is really stupid, isn't it?"

"Uh huh. The moment that sentence rolled out of my speech holes, I realized we'd made a terrible mistake."

"Lawn chair is an objectively better simile in every way."

"Yeah," Frank agreed, "it's not close, and even worse, now I'm hungry too."

"What's happening right now?" Vesuvian said.

"Right," I said. "Sorry, you can disregard all of that."

"But you'll do so at your peril," Frank added.

Vesuvian opened his mouth, then closed it. "So... don't disregard it?"

I cracked my knuckles. "How familiar are you with the guards' schedule?"

He blinked up at me.

"I'll rephrase. How confident are you in your ability to run the city guard if you had enough currency in hand? I'm talking everything from the ground up."

Vesuvian seemed to recover enough to make a dismissive gesture now that we were on grounds that he at least somewhat understood.

"What's in it for me?"

"A greater degree of freedom. You do well, we make things better for you."

"I want back in the Vale."

The rooms I had back at the Inn were still fairly lucrative, but I could part with one if needs be.

"Fine. If it goes well, we'll move you along."

"And what about this assistant?" he said. "What are their responsibilities going to be?"

"I'd like you to show her the ropes. For now, that's basically it."

An ugly look crossed his face. "Do you really think I'm that stupid? No. I'll handle the guard for you, but I refuse to make myself expendable again." He pointed a finger up at me. "You need me."

I barked a laugh. "Don't conflate need with the possibility of use." I paused for a moment, my father's words slipping out unbidden. I didn't like the taste of them, but Vesuvian drew back all the same, so clearly they'd hit their mark.

I cleared my throat. "Look. This is something you can offer in a moment where having someone step in and make things easier for me is very valuable. And I think we both know that teaching someone to run the guard is a very small step in the grand scheme of what's needed to run an entire city, especially one that's growing as fast as the Vale. But once she can handle the guard herself, we'll move the two of you onto something else."

"And once she can do it all?"

"I'll consider the trouble you caused me wiped out, and you'll be free to go. And maybe we'll find a better option for both of us before we part ways."

I extended my hand, and he eyed it for a long while. But he eventually seemed to realize that his choices weren't great because he stood up, dusted himself off, then crossed the room and shook my hand.

His palm was cold and clammy, and I had to fight down the urge to pull away.

And at the same time, I saw the blow coming well before it arrived, and I mentally locked the door behind me just as Vesuvian's small fist caught me in the kidney.

The blow was pathetic, registering 45 damage between my armor and Vesuvian's bare fist and his overall lack of power.

He let go of my hand and ducked, slipped around me, then grabbed onto the doorknob with both hands.

I pulled out my blunderbuss and pointed it at the back of his head, magic crackling at the end of the barrel.

I let him flail there, yanking at the locked door with both hands, then putting a foot to the doorframe and trying to pry it open.

He stiffened. And when he turned around, slowly, he ended up face to face with the barrel of my glowing weapon.

I held it there for a moment for emphasis, then dropped it to my side.

"Don't force me to give Frank what he wants. Neither of us will enjoy that."

"I, however, will be having the time of my life," Frank said. "And it will be a very, very long time full of regret, citrus, and open wounds. Not necessarily in that order."

I squinted, thinking. "Regret, wounds, citrus?"

Frank laughed. "That's probably the way it'll go, yeah. At least at first."

"But I imagine there will be regret at both ends."

"A palindrome of regret," Frank said, which made me snort.

Vesuvian slid down with his back against the door and pulled his knees to his chest. "Fine. I'll do what you're asking."

I offered him a hand and helped him up, at which point he sighed loudly before sitting down at the edge of his bed.

"What do you need to start?"

He shrugged. "Pen, paper. The appropriate documents from the Guardhouse."

"Get a list together of what you need and be explicit about it," I said. "I'll have someone run out and grab it all. Put whatever you want to eat and drink on your notes as well and I'll get that handled."

"Fine."

And with that in hand—or at least somewhat in hand, hopefully—I slipped out and eased the door shut behind me.

I headed back into the room where Cerra was and filled her in on everything that had happened, then doubled back through the common room and spent a little while longer hanging out with the guild. Then I slipped out of the hall and into the strange light of the glowcaps.

"Hey," Frank said. "Question."

"What's up?"

"How would you feel about getting me an assistant? I don't really know what they would do because I like getting my hands dirty, but it feels like I should really have an assistant."

I groaned, applied an illusion, then headed for the Oasis to crash for the night.

# Chapter Seventeen

I woke up with the distinct sensation that I was being watched.

I sat bolt upright and drew my pistols, fully expecting another Dread Revenant to be pouring down out of the ceiling.

And after a moment of breathless silence that probably took at least a couple of hours off my life, I realized that that wasn't the case.

"Huh," Frank said. "I can't believe that worked. But I'm also not surprised."

"What did you... did you do something?" I tried to rub the crust out of my eyes, but my pistols got in the way, so I dropped them back into my inventory. "What time is it? How long was I out?"

"Four-hour special," Frank said. "You're welcome."

I looked around, still only half-awake. "How... how did you wake me up?"

"Eye contact."

I yawned. "That's it?"

"That and general ill intent, yeah."

"I'll take it. Man, I was really expecting something way more awful than that. That was miles better than waking up to you barking and kind of impressive to boot."

"We both know that impressive didn't need to be qualified."

"Maybe not, but we also both know that qualifying stuff like that bothers you, so here we are."

Frank grunted in response, so I started paging through my alerts.

The morning payout had come early this time around—really early—which wasn't entirely good news: I'd been hoping it would come later in the day because that would have allowed more of my Caravan Routes to complete beforehand and ultimately hand me more gold and Experience to work with overall.

But I still found myself grinning from ear to ear as I paged through the alerts: it was impossible to complain about waking up a mere two levels short of finally cracking into C-Grade.

**Your Daily Payout earned you 19 Gold Coins, 34 Silver Coins, and 15 Copper Coins!**
**Your Daily Payout has successfully been converted into Experience and Renown!**

**Congratulations, you reached level 17!**
**Congratulations, you reached level 18!**
**You may select 1 of 3 class-appropriate spells!**
**Reach level 20 to equip C-Grade Gear!**
**Reach level 25 to unlock the Skill Evolution/Combination System!**
**Reach level 30 to begin your Tier IV class change!**

**Congratulations, two of your abilities have reached the next rank!**

I had a ton of other notifications as well: Goon had razed another city out west, and one of the three cities out that way whose Cathedrals I'd been watching out for had climbed all the way to 99% completion overnight.

But weirdly enough, the completion rate of Goon's presumed capital—Uliana—hadn't even budged. I was pretty sure they'd probably all complete at some point today regardless, and Koria's might get there too, as the event had promised that every Cathedral would advance by at least 5% per day back when it had first kicked off, but it was a huge relief to see that, for now, the Oasis was still the only option if you wanted in on the raid.

There were a shocking number of Ripples as well, though I didn't see anything from Tyrann's side, and Frank confirmed that was the case when I asked him to double-check.

I paged through and took a deeper look at some of the more inter-esting ones.

Ripple Alert! Player {Medulla} has successfully crossed the Drowning Deep and has chosen to make the route she used to reach the Isle of the Sirens viewable to all who come across it, but the great bulk of the singers' pitfalls remain.

Major Ripple Alert! Player {Hemteron} has finally confronted the Wanderer and his sleepwalking army, but it may already be too late: far beneath the southern currents, in the coldest, deepest part of the ocean, a living continent now begins to stir from its centuries-long slumber.

There was also a Ripple that mentioned the dwarves I'd seen and even the Oasis itself, though this was the first Ripple I'd noticed that didn't appear to be attributed to anyone in particular.

Minor Ripple Alert! Drawn through the currents of time to an era of rapid change, the Stonewhisper Dwarves have arrived in the Onyx Delta and have already begun surveying the layers of stone that rest deep beneath the new riverbeds of the Black Oasis!

I puzzled over that last one for a bit, then shrugged and tabbed on through to World-firsts, and what I saw right at the top wiped the smile off my face.

Corruptia—the same guild that had beaten us to two of three World-firsts back in the Bridge Rift—had successfully cleared the Menagerie Wing's first encounter a couple of hours back.

I cringed and kept scrolling, worried that I'd find similar alerts for the other fights as well, but they hadn't made it that far. I relaxed slightly. It wasn't ideal, but it wasn't the end of the world either.

They'd been rewarded with a Unique Title, plus an additional three days to claim the Possibility King's throne for themselves.

I wasn't quite sure what to make of the extra days, but I went ahead and moved on to Caravans, and thankfully the news there was much better: we'd completed six Routes overnight, which nearly doubled our network up to 14 cities.

The payout wasn't spectacular in light of the expansion, but those escorts had all recently finished, so almost doubling my last payout despite that delay already had my mouth watering at the thought of tomorrow's payment, which promised to be massive by comparison.

And best of all? One of the Routes that had completed was the one I'd sent Lars to: the Sanguine Port.

Some not-so-small part of me knew that that didn't mean he'd made it there safely himself, as the Caravan could have easily completed with the guards I'd forced him to hire, but it was a positive sign.

I rubbed my hands together and dug into my options for the new skill I'd picked up.

You may select 1 of the following 3 spells. Unselected spells may or may not appear at a later time.

{Shadow's Aid} (Rank: Novice I)
Description: You imbue your shadow with magical power, lending it a 15% chance of animating whenever you are targeted with a hostile magical or physical projectile. Once animated, the shadow lasts for 8 seconds, during which it will actively intercept and nullify the next 3 hostile projectiles that come your way. However, the animation effect has a 45-second internal cooldown, and some powerful abilities cannot be avoided.
Cast time: Instant.
Duration: 1 Hour
Cooldown: None.
Cost: 500 Mana.
Next Rank: Internal cooldown reduced to 40 seconds.

{Shimmerskin} (Rank: Novice I)
Description: You create a shimmering barrier that reduces all physical and magical damage you take by 15% and gives all hostile magical and physical projectiles that target you a 50% increased Chance to Miss during the spell's duration.
Cast time: Instant.
Duration: 6 seconds.
Cooldown: 30 seconds.
Cost: 250 Health.
Next Rank: Activating Shimmerskin has a 50% chance of instantly clearing all movement-impeding effects.

{Illusory Mirror} (Rank: Novice I)
Description: You create a small pane of mirrored glass up to 40 yards away that lasts for 5 seconds. The first magical or physical projectile that strikes the pane will reflect back at its caster, but the mirror will shatter on contact. The pane will also briefly hold up to physical contact but will shatter immediately afterward. However, certain powerful abilities cannot be reflected.
Cast time: Instant.
Cooldown: 30 seconds.
Cost: 125 Mana.
Next Rank: Adds an additional charge that allows you to summon a second pane.

"Defensives for projectiles, huh?" I said. "Nice pickup, really been wanting some durability."

"Yeah, it's unfortunate. You know, you could just not pick one."

I frowned down at him. "Will that give me more options for skills later on or something?"

"No. You'd just not pick one."

"Okay, I see what you're doing. Which one do you hate the most, Frank?"

"I'm not telling you that. Not trying to get it picked."

"Is it the shimmery one? It's the shimmery one, isn't it?"

"Maybe. Or maybe I secretly love stuff that sparkles and I've just been playing with your expectations to keep you off-balance."

"That seems like a lot of work for no real payoff." I eyed the Shimmer-skin ability. "Anyway, I think you're safe there. I would have definitely taken that if it cost Mana instead of Health or even if the cost was a percentage instead of a flat amount, but paying 250 Health is a no-go with how small my pool is. Plus I'm pretty sure that if I activate that thing when I'm already low, it's going to straight-up kill me."

"I was kinda hoping you wouldn't notice and then you'd do that. Preferably several times."

I eyed him. "Nah, you would have warned me."

"No way, no how."

"I really think you would have."

"Then your thoughts were presumptuous and also wrong."

I shrugged. "That's a shame. I was just starting to consider bringing you into the fold on Project Lunar."

"Project Lunar? What the hell is that supposed to mean? Why is this the first time I'm hearing about something moon-related?"

It was the first time he was hearing about it because Project Lunar wasn't a thing—I'd just made it up on the spot so that I could exclude him from it.

"Never mind. I shouldn't have said anything."

"You're full of crap."

"Maybe. Or maybe it's a real thing and you're missing out."

I skimmed over Shadow's Aid, which was pretty cool: I could just refresh the buff whenever it dropped and it would both permanently and passively improve my defenses. But the internal cooldown was pretty limiting, and I didn't like how heavy the RNG element was going to be.

And that brought us to door number three.

"Illusory Mirrors, hmm. So it's a spell reflect ability, but I also need to get the positioning right. I like that it's active and getting more charges would be cool, but we wouldn't be getting any passive durability there." I highlighted the ability's latter clause. "Can you give me a use for that part about the mirrors holding up to physical contact?"

"Gonna depend on weight and speed and so on. Like, if you were to summon one of those directly in front of Darling, she'd probably just truck right through it like a boss and barely notice. But if *you* caught one at face level, you'd probably—hopefully—get clotheslined."

I paused, considering. "Huh. I guess I could drop a pane at someone's feet in a pinch too. Even if the thing pops immediately, it doesn't take much to trip someone."

"The face is obviously preferable, but yeah. That's the idea."

"Better than I thought, then. Thanks. How do you feel about it?"

"The reflection component makes it acceptable."

"Are you talking about the part where it'll bounce spells back at people, or are you just pleased that you might be able to catch a glimpse of yourself in the panes every now and then?"

"The answer is always both."

I laughed and selected the ability, then confirmed my choice.

I wanted to get a look at it before I stepped outside, so I mentally popped a pane into position at knee level. I'd mentally pictured it coming out horizontal and parallel to the ground, and it had done just that, looking like a frameless mirror floating in the air.

I poked it with a pistol, and the reflective surface gave slightly but held. I took a few steps back, then got something like a running start and tried to leap onto the pane and jump off it.

For a split second, the pane held, and I thought it was going to work. But then the surface of the illusory construct broke like thin ice and my foot plunged right through it.

I landed awkwardly but managed to keep my feet. I was a little disappointed, but it felt like the potential was there: that if I had just a bit more Dexterity, I might be able to use these things as stepping stones, or even throw one up to change directions in mid-air. And if I was going to get another pane with every rank...

I nodded to myself, pleased with my choice, then noticed a whisper scrawled in pink in the bottom-left quadrant of my screen, a private message for Francis from Tyrann.

*Overdeliver much? Appreciate it.*

I didn't know what to make of that and I wasn't about to respond just yet, so I moved on to the last of my notifications. These brought good news too: I had upgrades to choose for Dark Harvest and Clonedrift, as both of those had broken into the Intermediate Ranks for the first time.

{Dark Harvest} (Rank: Intermediate I)
Base damage increased from 308 to 370!
Mana cost increased from 100 to 120!
Current rank: You may select 1 of 2 upgrades.
A. Enemies killed by Dark Harvest are brought back as Shades, ghostly spirits that seek out the nearest hostile target and latch onto them, dealing 140 shadow damage over 3 seconds. Spirits last a maximum of 10 seconds.
B. Enemies killed by Dark Harvest are brought back as Phantasms, ghostly, motionless spirits that provide 235 Health on contact. Phantasms last a maximum of 10 seconds.

I came to a pretty quick decision there: more damage was always nice, but the reality was that Dark Harvest was already a pretty powerful execute that splashed damage onto other nearby targets.

Doubling up on that was fairly tempting, and it was interesting considering what a multi-death Harvest would look like with tons of Shades flying everywhere, but for all the damage and crowd control I had, I was pretty lacking when it came to sustain.

So in the end, I picked the healing variant, spent a lovely few moments bathing in the warm glow of Frank's impotent rage, then moved on to Clonedrift.

{Clonedrift} (Rank: Intermediate I)
Description: You become incorporeal and drift backward for 25 feet, or until {Clonedrift} is canceled. This spell may be used while stunned. For this spell's duration, all damage you take is reduced by 99% and you are immune to all forms of crowd control. Activating {Clonedrift} creates a clone at your starting location that lasts 5 seconds. If the clone is damaged before it expires, it explodes and stuns all targets within 9 yards for 3 seconds.
Cast time: Instant.
Cooldown: 30 seconds.
Cost: 65 Mana.
Current Rank: You may select 1 of 2 upgrades.
A. The clone now attempts to cast Ravenblast on your most recent target with your current weapon. The spell deals no damage but will stun the target for 3 seconds on a successful cast. Any damage or interrupts dealt to the clone will cancel the spell and detonate the clone as usual.
B. Instead of exploding and stunning all targets within 9 yards after receiving damage, the clone has a 50% chance of charming enemies on detonation. Charmed enemies will use their skills at random, targeting your enemies and prioritizing abilities with shorter cooldowns.

"Ohh. Now we're talking." I scanned the two options, weighing the pros and cons. "Hey, question: does the first option use my runes?"

"What do you mean?"

"It says the clone casts Ravenblast. So if I've got a piercing rune equipped on my rifle and I'm using that when I activate the spell, would the clone's blast pierce?"

"Yup. Still no damage, though."

"But multiple stuns."

"Potentially. But it's only gonna cast one time. Then it'll just stand there like it currently does."

"Yeah, but having it cast improves the illusion even if it doesn't get the spell off. I could easily see melee users burning an interrupt to try to keep it from casting, thinking it was me, then they get stunned for their trouble and they're down a cooldown. That's powerful stuff."

I eyed the charm. "I really like the second upgrade too, but a 50% chance that it doesn't do anything is kinda killing it for me. The top end is probably stronger—maybe it burns several important cooldowns on another hostile target—but the chance on activation is rough. My guess is damage can break a charm, too."

"Uh huh."

"First option then?"

"Might as well."

I confirmed my choices, and with my new abilities in hand, I loaded up my blunderbuss, precast Heart Vessel just to be safe, then headed across the room.

Then Frank cleared his throat. "There is... one more thing."

"Yeah?"

"I hid this Ripple when you woke up because I wanted you to be clear-eyed and fully alert when the gravity of the situation you're in came crashing down upon you."

"What now?"

"Here ya go."

**Major Ripple Alert! Player {Ned, the Piratical} has nursed a {Lesser World Tree} to the first stage of its life cycle at the very heart of the Black Oasis, and all players and NPCs within the Onyx Delta may now reap the rewards!**

My jaw actually dropped.

"It's done? Holy crap, it's done!" I crossed the room in a rush, then froze with my hand on the doorknob. "Wait. Was that alert attributed to Ned?"

"Uh huh."

"Like, Ned Ned? Not Francis, but Ned? Here? In the Oasis?"

"Yep."

"Behind the Inn that I just gifted rooms in to Tyrann while pretending to be Francis?"

I looked back at the message Tyrann had sent me, hoping for clarity but finding none.

"All of these things are true, yes."

I reread the Ripple Alert, then reread it again as the implications sank in.

"Oh no. This is not good. This is not good at all." I read the prompt yet again as if that would somehow change it. It didn't.

"This went out to everyone."

"Yeah. You're fully awake now, aren't you?"

"Awake?" I said. My face was hot, and my mind was racing as I worked through the possibilities for damage control. "I'm having a minor heart attack."

"Well, you did ask me to wake you up by doing something terrible, so here we are."

I rubbed my face. "What are you even talking about? You didn't do anything."

"I edited that prompt on your end to make it look like it went out as being attributed to Ned when it actually went out in Francis' name. It's fine. Everything's fine. You're welcome. I'll be here all day."

I dropped into a crouch, head in my hands. "You... Francis..."

"Again, the real tree prompt went out in Francis' name. It actually should have gone out with Ned's because while you did change your permissions on the Auction House and the other visible ones, you either forgot to change them for the plots in the hidden courtyard or you never confirmed it or something, I dunno. I assumed you got distracted by something shiny, so I went ahead and changed the plots out back to Francis' name for you before the tree popped."

"You changed them?" My blood was pounding in my ears.

"Yup. I was gonna let it pop through as it was and make your life a little bit more hellish, but then I realized that nipple guy was probably watching and hoping for that as well, so I waited until we had about three seconds before the Ripple was going to hit, then I switched everything over. I figure if he's not gonna let me insult him to his face, then the least I can do is purple his nurples from afar, you know?"

"Oh... my... God."

"So, what do you think? Worst wake-up ever?"

I stared at him. "You truly are a monster."

"I know it, you know it, everybody knows it. But answer the question."

"Yeah, that was by far the worst wake-up ever." I squinted up at the ceiling, thinking. "But at the same time, you did actually save the day."

"But I did so while twisting—"

"Yeah yeah, I know why you did it, but still. Thanks. That was a huge save, man."

"Uh huh. I will say that I'm pretty pleased with the overall result, though I am a little worried that I just set the bar pretty high for tomorrow morning. Gonna be hard to one-up that amount of waking dread."

I managed a grin. "Yeah, but that's a problem for tomorrow because the tree is officially done!" I threw on my merchant illusion and burst out of the bedroom at a dead sprint.

"That last Ripple also brought you to the very edge of Renown Rank XII, too. Should be able to pop it today for sure and get your Tier III Renown Path rolling."

"Awesome," I said as I skidded into the hall.

I ran toward the door to the hidden courtyard, or rather, where it used to be, and stopped dead in my tracks. The entire doorframe was completely gone.

In its place, a hallway stretched back into an entirely new area that was alive with laughter and ethereal music.

Deeper down the hall, the floor was choked with bright green mist. Emerald flowers had sprouted between the wooden boards that lined the walls, and the mist was pouring down out of them and pooling a foot above the ground.

I stepped into the passage, stirring the fog as I went, then two Cultists with red name tags appeared at the other end, arm in arm. One of the two was trying to hold the other up, and they bumped into the wall to my left as they stumbled by me, laughing.

The air sparkled behind them as they passed, though I wasn't sure whether to attribute that to the mist or something else.

"Check their status," Frank whispered.

I did, and I quickly found a buff they both shared that I hadn't seen before.

{Faeblossom Liquor}
Effect: All damage dealt and healing received is increased by 5%.
This buff is restricted to the Onyx Delta and the instances within it, and it will be removed upon leaving the zone.
Duration: 8 hours

I eyed it, celebrating inwardly while doing my best to keep my illusion from showing my delight. The buff probably wouldn't mean much to a player out there leveling or questing on their own, but for those of us that were competing for first clears in the Red Cathedral?

If that buff stuck around, taking advantage of it would be a necessity to keep pace. And though I figured other zones would probably be getting buffs of their own before long, this was yet another reason for people to keep heading our way.

I kept walking, buzzing with anticipation, and stepped into a circular common room with a bar that ran most of its length. The horseshoe-shaped counter didn't have a bartender in sight, though a huge number of players were sitting on dark mushrooms that had sprouted up out of the ground in the place of barstools.

The floor was exposed dirt, the bar was covered in what looked like glassy shells, though they appeared to be melting, and the whole counter was pocked with small puddles of blue liquid.

"Look up," Frank said.

I did, and the sight above caused me to inhale sharply. I was standing in the center of a great, hollow tree that was lined with floor after floor of rooms. A single railing draped in ivy spiraled up its interior, securing a walkway that provided access to the many doors.

The walls were covered in the same green flowers I'd seen before, though the ones here were much larger, and the mist was waterfalling down from them in thick ribbons. And there had to be hundreds of rooms in all.

"This is what it became?" I said, barely able to speak.

"So far, yeah," Frank said. "It popped a couple hours into your beauty sleep."

"This... this is amazing. I don't think Housing is going to be an issue for the Vale for a little while." I scanned the many players and put the number of hostile Cultists at around 20.

It was then that Tyrann's message finally clicked: he'd been thanking Francis for the rooms I'd offered him and presumably for access to that Faeblossom buff.

I pressed my back to the nearest wall, reeling at the sights and sounds. Even the air seemed to be alive, smelling of rain and damp earth.

A horn sounded from above, from the highest reaches of the tree where the rooms stopped and the light from below didn't quite reach. A round of cheers that I didn't understand went around the room, and everyone who'd been sitting in the bar area was suddenly clambering to their feet and looking up.

A flash of blue flickered in the darkness, then another and another, until the entire space was lit with pinpricks of light. A swarm of blue creatures flew down out of the top of the tree to applause and shouts.

The creatures were each about the size of a softball, but their eyes were large and black, and their arms and legs were overlong. They each had two sets of wings that beat constantly like a hummingbird's, and the droning of their flight quickly filled the huge room and drowned out the cheering from below.

One of the strange creatures pulled up directly in front of me with an icy sphere filled with bright blue liquid held between its small hands.

It hung there, hovering, wings vibrating in front of me so strongly that my hair was blown backward. It stayed there with the orb as if it expected me to take it.

I reached out a hand and took the sphere—which, on closer inspection, was a thin layer of ice with liquid splashing around within—and the strange creature dipped its head and flew back up into the darkness at the top of the tree.

"Thank you!" I called after it. I brought the sphere up to eye level. "I'm really supposed to drink this?"

"Yep."

"This isn't another one of those moments where you try to trick me into eating or drinking something weird, right?" I said, but the creatures had already delivered a ton of the spheres, and all of the people around me were getting stuck into theirs without hesitation.

"Nope. It's legit."

I squinted at the icy sphere, tapped a knuckle against the top of it to break the frozen shell, then threw the contents back and swallowed.

It was ice-cold, tart, and refreshing, and it tasted a lot like blueberry lemonade, though the burning sensation that was spreading from my chest into my arms and legs suggested that the stuff packed a serious punch.

The air around me began to sparkle, and I was unsurprised to find the buff I'd seen earlier sitting beneath my nameplate.

I saw another player toss his empty shell over his shoulder, where the sphere shattered and quickly soaked away into the dirt, and the meltwater puddles I'd seen atop the counter suddenly made sense.

Maybe a third of the gathered people all made for the exit, so I moved aside. It seemed like they'd all been waiting for the drinks or, more precisely, for the buff they offered.

I pressed myself flat against the wall as they passed by, pulse spiking due to the proximity of so many red tags and hostile players.

"Are we selling this?" I said once they'd passed by. "Please tell me we're selling this."

"Nah, it's free. Only thing you can do is increase or decrease how much is given out."

I pursed my lips. "You know, even if we could sell it, we might be better off giving it away. Presumably at least some of those people are going to help protect the city, and there's always the guards if nothing else. What happens if we crank the distribution to the maximum?"

"The fairies will start flying around and handing those spheres out in the street around the Inn. It'll still be a bit rarer out there, but yeah. Eventually they'll be doling it out across the whole city and the area immediately around it, but they won't go too far."

I nodded. "That would mean more visibility for the Inn and a nice buff to reward everybody that's helping out, all of which is clearly coming from Francis thanks to that alert. Let's max it out."

"Done," Frank said, and the droning from above intensified into a low roar.

With that settled, I popped out into the older common room. It was exactly as it had been before, which seemed somehow absurd knowing the marvel that was hidden away through the back hall. But given the constant stream of people coming and going and the tables that were packed despite the early hour, it seemed that both rooms had their place.

I headed through the Inn and stepped outside into the cold, early morning air. The stars were still out in force—the horizon hadn't even started to glow—and my breath fogged in front of me with every step I took.

There was a surprising amount of activity too, a steady stream of NPCs and players alike moving through the streets and across the low-hanging bridges above.

"Crap," Frank said suddenly, and I felt him gesturing somewhere behind me just before the now-familiar sensation of panic hit me and I was overcome with the urge to cough.

I whipped around as more players streamed by me, their green name tags bright against the night sky.

And behind the players tucked just inside the sheltered mouth of a nearby alley stood a dark, four-legged figure that would have been invisible in the tight space if not for its orange, glowing teeth.

# Chapter Eighteen

{Dread Revenant} (Level 15 Undead)
HP: 1,800/1,800
MP: 800/800

The creature had shot up a full five levels and passed Darling in a matter of hours.

I was already backpedaling.

"My illusion's gonna work for this, right?"

But a longer look at the creature and the way it was already stalking toward me made it clear that wouldn't be the case.

I reached for a pistol, and my hand blurred through the illusion I was wearing. I cursed under my breath. I couldn't fight it, not here.

Using a skill or even taking a single point of damage was going to pop my illusion, and there were dozens of players around, either browsing the many shops that lined the avenue or waiting for the fairies that were just beginning to hum out of the Inn with their icy spheres in hand.

I sucked in a sharp breath and took off for the city's eastern exit with every bit of speed I could manage.

I was moving much faster than the players who were heading that way, and I started to draw quite a bit of unwanted attention before someone screamed behind me. It sounded like someone else had just spotted the Revenant.

I hurdled a merchant's fruit cart and hung a hard left down the street, the exit already in sight, then I saw two guards storming toward me from the opposite direction, their swords drawn and flashing at their sides.

For a moment, I was relieved. The guards would put the creature down, and I wouldn't have to worry about blowing my illusion.

Then the Codex entry Frank had sent me earlier popped back into my head. If the guards made the kill, it would come back stronger than them the next time around, and they were both level twenty-something Elites.

I threw a glance back over my shoulder. The Revenant had taken the high ground, and it was now loping across the nearby roofs on all fours, leaping over the gaps between them and gaining on me all the while. I eyed the guards, trying to figure out the best way out of this mess.

"Alley to your left," Frank said. "Lure it out of the city. Most of the guard is occupied there."

I nodded and dived down it. I dashed between the barrels and crates that covered the alley, avoided some deep-looking puddles, and jumped over the extended feet of someone who'd fallen asleep with their back propped up against the wall.

An orange glow lit up the alleyway from above, and I heard some wooden barrels scatter and break as the Revenant crashed down into the space behind me.

A wooden wall that I didn't recognize loomed in front of me, maybe fifty feet away at the far end of the alley but across another street full of people. The wall was new and looked partially finished at best—it had to be a recent defensive addition, hopefully on House's part—but it still stood nearly ten feet high.

I plunged into the crowd, slipping between NPCs and players and crashing into them when it couldn't be avoided.

"Revenant is closing fast," Frank said.

More screaming, then, and the flow of people that had been moving in an orderly fashion in both directions turned into a free-for-all as NPCs scattered at the sight of the creature.

I risked a look back as I emerged from the crowd and fled into the second alley, then wished I hadn't. The Revenant leaped half the busy street, planted its feet on a burly, broad-shouldered man, then sent him collapsing to the ground behind it as it jumped the rest of the way.

I whipped back around and noticed that a group of people were loading barrels into a covered wagon up ahead, right next to the wall and just around the corner to my left, and I felt Frank gesture at the scene at the same moment I took it in and a plan clicked into place.

The Revenant howled behind me.

"Duck!" Frank shouted.

I bent low and planted both hands on the street. An arc of orange fire hissed over my head at shoulder level, crackled for another five feet, then vanished.

Once I was convinced the attack was over, I put on a burst of speed as I reached the crew of NPCs who were loading the wagon.

I leaped onto the first of the barrels that were waiting to be loaded and kept going from there, stepping from one to the next as quickly as I could manage as several of them toppled behind me and began glugging something that smelled like wine into the street.

One of the NPCs who'd been loading them shouted at me, but he turned and ran for it at the sight of the pursuing Revenant. I fought down the urge to Water Jet myself over the wall as I reached the end of the line of elevated barrels.

I jumped up atop the tan cloth that covered the wagon, and while my first step must have caught the supporting structure that held the canopy up, my second plunged right through and I ended up hip-deep in the cloth.

I jerked my leg free as the Revenant stormed directly into the carriage, and the entire vehicle rocked forward. Heat crackled beneath me, and I heard the telltale *whoosh* of fire meeting fuel.

Scrambling on all fours across the canopy and closer to the wall, I tried to distribute my weight evenly across the tight cloth even as smoke poured up out of the carriage and the crackling below turned into hot, oily flames.

I planted a foot where the carriage looked better supported, felt something solid beneath me, then leaped off one leg, hands extended toward the top of the wall. I snagged it with both hands, then smashed into the wood. I managed to look away to avoid face-planting, but the impact knocked the breath out of my lungs.

I hauled myself up onto the wall and threw a leg over as the wagon burst alight and sent a column of black smoke billowing into the air.

"Move it!" Frank said.

I almost threw myself over the wall, but a glance at what lay beneath me kept me perched where I was: the Defensive Trench had already finished and upgraded, which turned what should have been a manageable ten-foot drop into a twenty-foot plunge onto wickedly sharp wooden poles.

And not only were the dark dunes around the city decidedly not empty, they had also become an absolute warzone overnight.

Explosions of magic erupted like fireworks in the dark all around me as hundreds of players swarmed over the sands to meet the many oncoming prisms and the monsters that were spawning from them. There were so few unengaged mobs and so many players that the space reminded me of a starter area on launch day.

At the same time, the Revenant stalked out of the fiery conflagration it had made of the wagon with no regard for the flames. I glanced left, then right. Guards were approaching from both directions with crossbows and swords in hand.

"Do items break illusions?" I said, not seeing another choice.

"No!"

I hauled myself up, got my feet under me, then flung myself off the edge while simultaneously opening up my inventory. I tabbed through as I fell, panicking before I found what I was looking for: one of the slowfall feathers that I'd last used to escape Highwater.

I used the item, and my downward momentum immediately ceased, my stomach flipping as I became weightless. I drifted sideways over the trench, my mind racing as I tried to figure out my next move.

"It's still coming!" Frank said.

My path had been set in stone the moment I'd used the feather, but I twisted around to get a look at it. The Revenant lunged off the wall, and two narrow, fiery wings erupted from its shadowy body.

I hit the ground already running for the nearest group of players—who had a mixture of red and green tags but were still a ways off down the dune—shouting for help the entire way.

"It's gaining on you!"

A few players turned to look at me and the ruckus I was causing, but they were engaged with a ten-foot-tall creature with a humanoid frame that was nothing but bones and had the skull of a ram topped with long, twisting horns.

They appeared to register an NPC in trouble, and I saw them all mentally come to the same conclusion: it wasn't their problem.

So I ran down the dune and tried to kite the Revenant into the path of as many players as possible.

Four or five people with green tags were sitting a ways back from the bulk of the fighting up ahead, drinking and eating around a campfire, so I made for them, thinking I'd drag the Revenant right on top of them if need be.

I made it about halfway there before it became clear that the Revenant was far better suited to the open ground than I was and that I didn't have a chance in hell of reaching the next group.

I didn't see a better option, so I skidded to a stop in the sand and readied myself for a fight out in the open. I'd switch to my blunderbuss, wait until the creature got close, then burst it down with everything I had, then immediately reapply my illusion and hope for the best.

I gritted my teeth and let it approach, hands twitching at my sides. I'd just pulled my blunderbuss out when a burst of golden light nearly blinded me.

It had come from just in front of the pursuing creature, and as the flare cleared, the Revenant stood rooted in place with a golden spike pinning it to the ground through its back.

Someone had intervened.

I dropped my blunderbuss back into my inventory and backpedaled, then tripped and fell backward but kept my eyes on the fight.

A golden halo formed around the thrashing, trapped creature. Then a figure materialized in the air above the Revenant with a sword held in a reverse grip in each hand as if the huge blades were little more than over-sized daggers.

The heavily armored figure smashed into the creature and drove through it with such force that the dune beneath me actually shook.

"Revenant down," Frank said, tone subdued.

The figure stood up and sheathed one sword into a scabbard on his right hip before jamming the second, longer blade into a sheath that crossed from his right shoulder to his left hip. He turned in my direction, grinning a smile that was all too familiar.

Tyrann.

# Chapter Nineteen

I lay there on the ground for a long moment, just breathing with my back against the sand, a million questions buzzing through my head as Tyrann knelt next to the corpse he'd made of the Revenant, which was sparking purple.

Had he seen me equip my blunderbuss as an NPC while he'd been moving to intercept the mob? And if so, could he have recognized it as mine?

And now that he—one of the most powerful and likely highest-level players around, in spite of his dead god—had killed the Revenant, what was that thing going to come back as next, and when?

A black sword appeared in both of Tyrann's hands, and he looked it over, grinning even more broadly than before. The blade was about an inch wide and maybe five feet long, and its surface was shot through with fiery lines.

"Definitely wasn't expecting that," he said, and the sword vanished. He bent down and extended me a hand. "Nasty thing, there."

I took his hand, and he yanked me to my feet as if I were weightless.

"Thank you." I rubbed my shoulder as if he'd hurt it and eyed the dead creature. I pushed my voice a bit higher than normal. "What was that thing?"

He looked me over while my heart hammered in my chest. "I was going to ask you the same thing. We've seen a number of monsters coming out of these prisms, but nothing like that."

I glanced back at the city, trying to gauge how quickly I could reach it if I dropped the entire façade and just ran for it.

I was confident in my ability to outrun him, plus I was pretty sure he'd just popped a movement ability on the Revenant, so whatever he'd used was probably on cooldown.

But a few of his Cultists were already heading our way, peeling off the skeletal monstrosity they'd just dropped to inspect the strange mob that Tyrann had dispatched.

"You really don't have any idea what that was?" he said.

I shook my head and kept my eyes on the creature. "It came at me in the city. I was just walking, and there it was."

Tyrann's blonde eyebrows went up at that. "Really now? In the city, behind the wall? Where were the guards?"

I shrugged. "I just saw it and ran."

"New mob type?" one of his guildies said, a fat orc named Casper who wielded a single, plain dagger and no armor other than some leather suspenders and a pair of dark gloves that reached to his elbows, stark against his milky skin.

"Undead, but otherwise yeah, never seen anything like it," Tyrann said.

"Any loot?"

"Crazy Touchstone sword. Bit low level and two-handed, so not for me, but very nice." He eyed the nearest prisms. "The rewards out here just keep getting better."

He must have thrown the weapon's description into their chat or something because the whole group devolved into whistles and chatter about the blade.

I brushed sand from my shoulders, unsure what to do or how to react.

Tyrann tapped at the air a few times, accessing one of his menus.

"Got confirmation on that thing starting in the city," Casper said. "Somebody saw an NPC run down an alley with some sorta shadow thing trailing behind him, running along the roofs."

"Thanks for that," Tyrann said. He looked at the Commerce Ward and the partial wall that had sprung up around it, frowning. "Well, the city itself might not be entirely safe, but you're better off there."

His words sounded like a dismissal, so I gave him another grateful nod, then turned for the city and started jogging in that direction. I heard Tyrann mutter something behind me, but I didn't catch it.

"I don't want to look back," I said as I picked up the pace a little bit. "But what's he doing?"

"Staring at the back of your head."

"You think he saw the blunderbuss?"

"Doubt it. He looks more puzzled than anything else. Keeps looking back and forth between you and the walls."

"Probably wondering how I got to where he met me."

"By walking?"

"Nah, the angles are too weird. I came right over the wall, right? But he must not have seen that, nor is that really NPC behavior." I nodded to the nearest gaps in the unfinished wall, each of which stood maybe fifty yards to my left and right. "If I had run straight out, I should have come from that direction."

I exhaled with some relief. "I think we're fine, but that was way too close for comfort. If he'd been even a few seconds later, I'd have dropped my illusion to blast that thing down right in front of him. Remind me to dump this merchant illusion for good as soon as we're back in the city, yeah? I'll grab something else."

"Sure."

"Thanks. And I guess we can rule out the Revenant coming from Tyrann."

"Uh huh."

I approached one of the gaps in the wall, where some guards had spanned the trapped trench with a makeshift bridge made of lumber. I waited for a group of players to cross out onto the sands, then slipped into the Oasis.

Now that I was back in the city, my pulse was finally slowing down. I forced my shoulders to relax and headed up the street, which was churning with players heading out into the warzone beyond the walls.

I scoped out the local chat and found tons of people searching for groups and posting their locations and loot rules, many of which specifically mentioned the Heart of Refraction I'd found and thrown up on the Auction House, plus a number of other items that appeared to be related.

A handful of people were even offering power-leveling services for gold, where a lower-level player could pay in exchange for the right to tag along with a more powerful group for experience and loot.

That seemed like great news to me: if those groups were power leveling people with prism spawns instead of Rift clears, it meant that the game was rewarding people well for defending the city entirely separately from the financial incentives I'd created by having the guild drum up false demand.

I kept on moving for a bit, then spotted a young NPC who was in the process of setting up light wooden tables and chairs outside of a restaurant that bordered the street, so I headed that way.

I asked the kid if I could sit there until the place opened, and he gave me a shrug that said *it's not my job to say otherwise*, so I plopped myself down and took a deep breath.

"Man, I really didn't think the Revenant would come back that quick. Is that gonna happen again today at some point?"

"It could," Frank said. "But a bigger jump in power means a longer delay."

"The possibility's just gonna hang over us like that?"

"Well, the idea is to inspire dread, so... yeah. At least until you put it down for good or murder the hell out of whoever is sustaining it."

"But you said Rifts were safe. So maybe we should grab House and Darling or something and dive right in and get to work."

The same NPC from earlier stepped up next to my table, and for a moment I thought he was going to ask me to leave. Instead, he jammed a small Soul Gem into a thick iron pole that rose out of the ground between the table I'd taken and three others.

Red, fiery lines crept outward from the gem and etched the pole's length, and soon the rod was emanating a steady warmth that was so pleasant in the face of the early morning chill that I found myself warming my hands in front of it before I realized what I was doing.

I also noticed that of all the poles the kid could have chosen, he had turned that one on first, so I thanked him for the kind gesture and got a polite nod in return before he moved on.

I tried to send Darling a message, but it didn't go through, so I pulled up the guild roster and scoped it out.

She and most of the rest of the core group had logged out for the night, but the guild itself was pretty active, and many of them were currently engaged in a spirited argument in the guild chat over whether or not Pop-Tarts counted as calzones.

The familiar insanity of it—and the sheer length of time they'd been at it judging by the logs—made me laugh.

Then I spotted the note that Darling had left next to the chat window, which indicated that most of the guild had checked out around the same time I had and that they'd be logging in soon to start chaining Rifts.

Frank and I had a half-hour or so to kill before they started popping back in, even without accounting for the inevitable latecomers, and since I didn't want to waste a single minute with how packed the day was likely to be, I pulled up my map and threw on the Caravan overlay.

Green lines stretched across the map, linking the Delta and the two continents that bordered it to the north and south, as well as the great continent to the east and the trio of landmasses to the far west.

We still didn't have anything remotely resembling total coverage— especially to the east and west—but between what was already down and the Routes that were still running, I was very happy with our rate of expansion.

I tapped the screen. "This is starting to look like an actual network. Unless you've got something you think I should hook up in person, though I'm thinking we can delegate these for now so that we can focus on making as many things dead today as possible."

"Could not agree more," Frank said. "You got priorities?"

"Same thing really: any Routes that are key for expansion, any cities that already have people in them and so on, that sorta thing. Maybe try to keep it around 10 gold so I've got some spending money for when we need it—maybe three more Routes? Then I'll just throw someone in the guild some coins on top of the cost to run around and get the escorts running for us. I do need to keep Arlann's payment of 50 gold in mind, but expanding should pay for itself pretty soon."

"Yeah, lemme look this over real quick."

"Thanks. I'm gonna check on House."

I sent her a brief message, and she immediately replied that she was actually in the Auction House right now with Bella and a ridiculous number of other names I didn't recognize—probably cats—so I levered myself to my feet, pushed in my chair, and tossed the attendant a silver coin for giving me a spot to get my bearings back.

I took a few steps down the street, and the breeze felt especially cold after the warmth of the runed pole. I made it about ten feet before I stopped in my tracks so quickly that someone bumped into me from behind.

The player stepped around me with a Trade Pack strapped to his back, and though he made a rude gesture in my direction, I barely saw him because I only had eyes for the tree.

With how quickly the Revenant had attacked, I hadn't had time to get a good look at it from outside the Inn.

It was absolutely huge; its trunk was maybe fifty feet across, and its wide canopy towered above the Inn, the Auction House, and probably half the other buildings that comprised the Commerce Ward.

The trunk was pocked with circular windows, and though a few were flickering with warm light—as if torches burned within them—the vast majority were dark.

The same blue fairies that I'd seen inside the trunk were buzzing through the branches high overhead, playing and swarming about, leaving the air sparkling behind them.

"I hate it," Frank said.

"I know." I pointed up at a thin section of the canopy, where an eerie green light was shining through its many leaves. "Say what you want about the tree, but it's currently blocking our view of the moon right now."

"Hm. That is a fair point. I award the tree 10,000 Frank points, but I'm keeping it on notice on account of the fairies."

I sighed and headed for the Auction House.

I found House standing at the long wooden counter within with Bella draped across her shoulders, dark tail swishing between House's shoulder blades. The other cats were scattered around her, either dozing on the floor or prowling around.

The building was empty aside from House, which probably had more to do with the early hour and the goings-on outside the city than anything else.

"Morning, House," I said.

She craned her neck around to look at me, and I was expecting her to announce that her status as House wasn't temporally limited to mornings or something like that, but she merely gave me a smile that was a bit too wide, her eyes squeezed shut, her chin tilted up.

I smiled. Couldn't help it.

"Good morning. I am House."

I stepped up beside her. "What're you working on?"

"I am searching for materials that can be used to strengthen our defenses."

"Great. Looks like you've already had a lot of success there between the completed trench and the wall that's going up."

"Indeed. The guild has been furnishing me with an incredible amount of materials, and the general population of the Oasis has assisted as well, particularly when it comes to the wall."

"Great. Can you hit me with a quick update from your end?"

"I have personally paid for five Ghostlight Cannons, all of which are currently under construction around the Commerce Ward, and my skill in Machining has increased to 135. I anticipate hitting 150 quite quickly given the rate at which Darling has been supplying me with materials and patterns."

"Love to see it. Any notable new recipes?"

"Seventeen."

"Top five, quick summaries?"

She paused for a brief moment. "I can create two new ships: a Deluxe Cutter that's very fast and a Basic Gunboat that cannot carry Trade Packs but is prebuilt with a high number of cannons and is capable of housing several more."

"We need the latter," Frank said. "Lots of 'em."

House glanced down at him. "I know. This is the third time you have mentioned that, and I have already passed your suggestions to Darling twice."

"Well, hopefully the third time is indeed the charm because it's important."

"I am aware." She looked at him again but hesitated before she spoke. "The squeaking wheel is of the highest priority when it comes to the allocation of grease, correct?"

"Yup, you got it."

She smiled at me. "Frank is exceedingly squeaky."

"That he is, but I like the sound of all that. The more boats, the better. What else you got, House?"

"I can now create a new type of golem that speeds up construction the same amount but can be assigned to two projects instead of one before it expires. I can also create the naval cannons I mentioned earlier that can be mounted atop the Gunboat as well as other vessels, and I have three types of ammunition with which to arm them: anti-personnel rounds, anti-ship rounds, and grappling charges that can allow a ship to tether itself to a target within forty yards."

Frank seemed like he was about to speak again, but House cut him off. "I am aware that we require anti-personnel rounds. I am already squatting on it."

"You're on top of it," Frank said.

House beamed. "Correct."

"No, I meant… never mind, close enough."

"Coooool!" I said. "And how about levels? You've been getting Experience through your profession, right? And I saw all the trees you had going in the Stronghold, so what level are you currently at?"

She stood up a little straighter. "I am level 14 and a half."

Frank laughed. "Spoken like a true 6-year-old. But hey, you're almost at your Tier III class change."

"Indeed I am."

"That's killer, House," I said. "You're doing great."

I opened up the auction menu and searched for the Heart of Refraction that I'd listed last night right before I passed out at the Inn. The listing hadn't sold owing to the ridiculous cost of 10 gold—and the fact that, presumably, nobody had any idea what the things actually did—but we seemed to have succeeded in setting the initial price.

I scanned the entries, watching the prices cascade downward as each and every listing undercut the offering before it, usually by a handful of coppers but occasionally by ten or more silver.

All in all, the result was about what I had expected: our listing sat on top of the others at 10 gold, while the cheapest Heart of Refraction could currently be had for 3 gold and 15 silver.

The price had actually held up considerably better than I'd hoped, and people were clearly hunting them, given the ongoing chatter across the city's various chats.

I made sure that my Alias was displaying, then dropped a message into the Local Chat that said Francis wanted to buy 20 Heart of Refractions at 3 gold coins a pop.

House whipped around in my direction. "Do we truly possess enough gold for that?"

"Not even close."

I was already back to browsing the other listings. At the same time, pink text was flooding my chat window: I'd had dozens of responses almost immediately, all from people who were looking to offload their Hearts.

A second wave of whispers followed as well, where ten different people were asking what exactly it was that the Hearts did to fetch such a high price.

I ignored all of the messages for now and tabbed through the gear listings, and though the number of items on offer had quadrupled since I'd last checked, I didn't find anything I was willing to splurge on, given that C-Grade was probably a day away at most now that I was level 18.

Instead of responding to any of the messages I'd received directly, I waited a bit longer, then typed a second message into the Local Chat as Francis stating that I'd purchased all of the Hearts I needed from the first few players to respond to my inquiry, then thanked everyone else for their interest as well as their time.

House stared at me. "I do not understand. You appear to have purchased zero Hearts of Refraction, which is twenty fewer than you are claiming to have bought."

"Yeah, that was a lie." I gestured roughly in the direction of my chat window. "All of that was a lie, basically. We're just stoking FOMO right now."

House cocked her head. "That sentence made my ears ring."

"Fear of missing out," I clarified. "It's the same thing as before. You understand why I threw that first Heart up on the Auction House at 10 gold, right? I wanted to get people talking about the item, and I thought the high price would get their attention."

"You appear to have succeeded."

"Definitely, but talk alone doesn't do a whole lot. People are pretty quick in general to figure out if something is selling." I thumbed over my shoulder. "Say you're one of those groups out there that's farming Hearts because you saw they're worth 10 gold a pop, then you come into town and you start trying to offload these things. Nobody bites, so you drop the price by 50 silver. Rinse, repeat, still nothing. By the time that person has reduced the price a bunch and gotten precisely zero offers, they're gonna wonder if something's up."

I pointed at the messages I'd just written. "But see this? This hits different." I held up a thumb and forefinger and moved them slightly apart. "Every single one of those players who messaged me to sell a Heart thinks that they were this close to getting 3 gold each, and more importantly, they think other people actually did get that price, and the knowledge that other people are getting rich for the same work they're already doing will drive the sellers nuts.

"And even for those who didn't bother to message me, Francis is a major player at this point when it comes to trade. If he's buying these things at 3 gold coins a pop, they must be worth something, so people are gonna want them."

I shrugged. "It's all about the perception of value. It's easy to push prices high for a short time—you just have to know that your market is going to crater before long, and you gotta make sure your position is safe for when it collapses entirely. In this situation, it doesn't even matter though because we don't actually care about Hearts and we're not investing in them."

"Collapse?" House said.

"Like if someone found out we're manipulating the price of Hearts without any idea of what they actually do. That would instantly kill all of the demand."

"But we are manipulating the price."

"Of course we are. If you're playing the Auction House to make money, you're never not doing that. But it can't look that way. That's the important thing."

House stared at me for a long moment. "I enjoy this very much. There is much to be learned numerically and otherwise."

I grinned at her. "Yeah? I can show you how to play this thing if you want."

"I do indeed."

"Just be careful," Frank said.

"Hm?"

"Stinky foot gets the shoe. Thanks to me, anyway. I did that."

House blinked down at him.

"I got nothing on that one either, House," I said. "I'm pretty sure Frank made that confusing on purpose."

"I was unaware that was a thing you could do," House said. "But I am glad to hear it, because I feared that my communication skills had taken a step backward."

"I'm talking about Dad," Frank said, "and how I improved the lives of everyone around him by getting him to wear shoes while simultaneously taking him down multiple pegs. More specifically, be careful with House and her transactions."

"Oh. Yeah, good call. We don't want Kline mucking everything up, but I think it'll be fine so long as we make sure that House isn't making a hundred transactions a minute or something, and it's not like we have the gold for that regardless. Bankers are always going to bank, so what she'll be doing really isn't out of the ordinary. I was thinking we'd keep it simple, too." I opened a trade window up with House and dropped 25 silver in. "So this is—"

I cut off as a striped cat I'd never seen before popped into her arms. She grinned.

"I have made my first personal purchase and have acquired a thirteenth cat. I now find myself to be even more deeply interested in the Auction House."

"That money was meant for you to... eh, it's fine." I tossed another 25 silver into a second trade window. "No more cats, House."

She narrowed her eyes at me, and I didn't love the tingle that ran down my spine.

"Don't make the same mistake I did," Frank whispered.

"I'll rephrase immediately. As many cats as your heart desires, but not with this money specifically. This is strictly for buying and reselling stuff so that you can learn how the Auction House works. If you want to take your profit and flip it into pets, fine."

I tapped a window and set my permissions so that House could see all the tabs I pulled up within the Auction House.

I did a search for two-handed swords, which presented me with a huge number of options that ranged in level from as low as 5 up to 14.

"So, you see all these guys?"

"I witness the male swords," House said. "I also have several related questions, but I will save them for later."

"Great, that feels like progress somehow. You see the general trend? The lowest level stuff is selling for a silver coin or two, while that level 14 sword is marked up at 2 gold. That pattern is going to change over time as people level up and want low-level weapons for their alts, but generally that's pretty normal."

I tapped a level 11 sword that was priced cheaper than those around it. "But this here is an outlier—it's priced at 3 silver, while every other sword at level 10 or above is 40 silver or higher."

"I have purchased the sword for 3 silver."

I laughed. "Right, but there was a reason that sword was underpriced, House."

Her face fell. "I have made a terrible mistake that I fear I will never atone for."

"No, you're fine. But if you'd looked deeply at the item, you'd have seen a lot of warning signs: it rolls with Intelligence and Wisdom as bonus stats, which is pretty awkward for a sword. Maybe a paladin type or something could use that, but Strength and Constitution would have more appeal to more classes on a two-hander. Wisdom in particular is a killer."

"My sword is inadvisably wise."

I cracked a smile and tapped the listing, which I could still see, though now it was marked as sold and delivered. "Yeah, you really want a broad appeal. If you were looking at staves, you'd probably be interested in weapons with Intelligence and Constitution and maybe Wisdom too, that sort of thing."

"What about users like Jukes?"

"Like how he uses staves, plus Dexterity and Constitution?"

She nodded.

"That's good to think about—there will always be exceptions—but if we're talking sheer numbers, there will be far more people interested in caster stats on a stave than in a more niche use, like a weapon for a Dexterity tank. There will almost always be a market for everything. We just need to be thinking about the size."

"We want our markets thick, House," Frank said. "Nice and thick."

I stared at him. "You really do enjoy walking the tightrope between helpfulness and general disgust, don't you?"

"I truly do."

"Anyway, House, the real giveaway when it comes to that sword and why it was so underpriced is the grade. For whatever reason, the one you bought is a level 11 sword that's still E-Grade, so its stats are lower across the board.

"Those other blades are way, way more expensive, but they also repre-sent a huge jump in power because they're all D-Grade, which you can equip at level 10. Still, regardless of grades, weapons are a great market in general because players know that they'll always get way more of a power spike from replacing a weapon before anything else."

"And more importantly, it feels badass to get something new to swing around," Frank added.

"I can't tell if he's trying to help or distract or what, but that's actually true. New weapons are satisfying, and that matters a lot, maybe as much as the stats. You'll even find weapons that are terrible but look awesome, so those are valuable too. Sometimes way more valuable than the harder hitting stuff."

"As they should be."

"This feels like a great deal of information to be gleaning," House said, "none of which is remotely accessible in a ready way."

I grinned. "Well, yeah, it's a learning process. You're going to win on some deals and lose on others. But as long as you're analyzing the losers, you'll keep getting better. And you're nothing if not a quick learner."

"I can think of several things that are more applicable to her," Frank said.

"Shut up, Frank. And even with all of that said, House, you still didn't make a mistake. That sword you bought is cheap enough that you can almost certainly throw it up for 6 silver or so and double your investment."

Her eyes went wide. "Oh. Doubling wealth seems to be a very enjoyable experience."

"Yeah. Flip side though is opportunity cost. As in, how long is it going to take before somebody buys that sword? Even if you double up, was it worth keeping those silver coins locked up in that item if it takes three days to sell it? Especially if you have to list it several times before it finds a buyer."

She ground her teeth way more aggressively than was necessary. "I am paralyzed by the twin possibilities of losses and gains."

I patted her on the back. "Just focus on weapons for now. Narrow your searches to stuff that's D-Grade only. That way you won't need to worry about E-Grade stuff sneaking in. Then you just scroll over to prices and inspect all of the ones that jump out at you as being cheaper than the rest. If they've got decent stats or if the price is good, then grab it right away and re-list the sword at a price that's comparable to the others."

House paused for a long moment. "But is that not predatory in nature?"

I paused, taken aback. "It kinda is, yeah. But at the same time, you need to think about what people are trying to get out of the Auction House. Learning values and markets is a skill that takes time to develop, and a lot of people can't be bothered.

"It's possible that the guy who slapped that sword you just bought into the Auction House thought he was getting a good price, and he's going to be bummed out when he realizes that isn't the case and he could have gotten a much better deal.

"But it's equally likely that the same guy came to town with a bunch of crap he didn't want and knew that vendors would give him basically nothing for the extra gear, so he tossed everything up on the Auction House on the cheap knowing that he'd have some mailbox money waiting for him the next time he logs in."

"I see. Shall I purchase more swords, then?"

I shrugged. "I dunno. Should you?"

"I am not sure. That is why I asked."

"Right, but the whole point is for you to learn. Don't worry about how much gold you're making or the amounts in general—think about the percent. If you can turn that 25 silver into one gold coin in a day, then you've multiplied your wealth four times over. Good deals add up, even if they're small. And scaling up once you have the knowledge is easy—it's just a question of how much you're willing to risk."

She held the coins up in her hand. "I am currently risking 25 silver and I do not like it."

"I'll take the coins back if you don't think it's for you."

She squinted. "I do like it. But I fear I will not like it when I inevitably lose."

"That's pretty much how gambling works, yeah," Frank said.

"The beauty of it is that when you're dealing with something in the neighborhood of 25 silver, you really can't lose as long as you can figure out where you went wrong," I said. "Like I said, you're gonna make bad deals, House. That's all part of the game."

I thought of Kline. And as satisfying as ripping on him was, I really wasn't in the mood for another lecture or appearance or anything at all, really, even if he was now wearing shoes.

"To make things even more interesting, I'm gonna give you a limit of ten purchases total."

"So I am to purchase ten items and resell them?"

"Yep, then we'll see how you've done, and I'll help you adjust from there."

"And once I have mastered weapons?"

I shrugged. "I can teach you whatever you want, but I think you'll probably pick it up quickly enough regardless, and most markets are similar. Speaking of weapons, though—hey, knowledge font."

"You rang?" Frank said.

"What's the minimum level a Touchstone Piece can roll at?"

"Start at level 5, but they're pretty uncommon until 8 or so."

"Perfect, thanks. House, while you're near the Auction House, I also want you to be scanning for Touchstone items."

I pulled up the search filter and found a box I could check to do just that. I went ahead and searched, and to my surprise, there were almost 60 items already up for sale, almost all of which were weapons.

The prices were hugely variable: the low-level stuff with bad stats could be had for a handful of silver coins, while some of the D-Grade options were prohibitively expensive.

"How shall I eye them?" House said.

"I've seen all the stuff that's currently up, and I don't think any of it is worth the investment for now. Some of those abilities look awesome, but most of the items they're attached to are just too weak to be useful. But I want you to watch out for whenever a new listing pops up."

"And if I locate one?"

"Just message me right away with a link to the item and the price. I'm especially interested in Touchstone shields and swords for Ton and staves for Jukes. And maybe caster gear with healing or Mana-regenerating abilities too."

"Understood."

A message came through from Darling then, even though I hadn't expected to hear from her for a little while yet: *Can't sleep. Rifts?*

I smiled. "Alright, House. I'm gonna do some Rifts with Darling if you wanna join, but you're welcome to play around here instead if you want."

"I would very much like to see Darling," she said without hesitation. "But then I would prefer to return to the Auction House and continue to manage the defenses. Perhaps I could rejoin you afterward?"

"Sounds like a plan!"

I replied to Darling and asked her to meet us in the Hall of Rifts, then I went ahead and blew a couple of gold on Soul Gems, which were nice and cheap.

Then I gave House a full 15 gold in case an item or two popped up that I wanted her to buy on my behalf. Plus I figured she could probably hand it out for the Caravan Routes I needed, and I wanted more defenses going up as well, especially for the other wards that were still comparably unprotected.

"Alright, let's get going!"

# Chapter Twenty

House and I beat Darling to the Hall of Rifts, so we stood around the chamber's huge Rift Map, looking it over, while we waited for her to join us.

"I guess the Oasis is safe enough for now," I said. "It's hard to leave it in other people's hands, but this feels like the right move."

"Do you truly think the Oasis could be damaged beyond repair?" House said.

I shrugged. "I hope not. But Kline's whole thing has been that this event is proceeding too fast, right? I won't be shocked in the slightest if it turns out that the Oasis itself or even the people around it are too low level to defend it—if not now, then against whatever comes next." I paused, thinking. "I guess I do have a hard time imagining Kline letting an entire city get wiped out. The players with plots there would not be happy."

"He wouldn't care if the whole digital world burned down to the ground," Frank said. "He's a monster. Like, imagine not caring about that."

I looked down at him. "Wow, look at you. Caring about something other than yourself."

"What? I didn't say I wouldn't be thrilled if the world burned down. I said I wouldn't not care if it did."

"Oh."

House reached up and rubbed both of her temples. "Ow."

"What?" Frank said.

"Your sentence structure appears to be causing me physical pain."

"Oh God, House," I said. "Why would you tell him that?"

Frank chuckled, and his laughter had an edge to it. "House, nobody will not notice if you can't not stop allowing yourself to not sanction your feelings."

House blinked several times in quick succession.

Frank dropped his voice. "I have no idea what I just said, but I'm very proud of it."

"Sanction," House repeated. "Does it mean to forbid, or to allow?"

I felt Frank lean in as if he were delivering a killing blow.

"Sanction can mean both of those things."

"Why?" House said, with genuine pain in her voice.

He laughed again. "No one knows, House. It just does!"

House popped Bella into her arms and furiously stroked her back. "I feel that when it comes to goals, I appear to have chosen poorly when it comes to my proposed mastery of the English language."

I looked away and suppressed a laugh of my own.

"Saw that," Frank said.

"Yeah. That was mean, but... at least it was well-played."

"You know you gotta rub me on that cat, right? Or at least let me get a solid boop."

I sighed and handed him to House.

"Make sure you use my magnificent side, House."

House turned him around several more times than was necessary. "There appears to be literally no difference."

"Correct. It was a trick question: both of my sides are magnificent."

"So," Darling said.

I hadn't heard or seen her pop in, so I turned around at the sound of her voice and waved.

"Are you guys done with whatever is currently happening here, or should I wait a bit longer?"

"Yeah," I said. "Let's blame Frank and move on."

"Hi Darling!" House shouted, right over Frank's greeting. "I am very happy to see you again."

"Likewise!" she said. She met my eyes and grinned. "You ready to get back to work? I want another set piece, and I want it yesterday."

"Same," I said. "It's gonna just be the two of us for now though. House is gonna take a break to watch the Oasis for a bit and handle some stuff there. Will be good to have eyes on the place in case things go bad with the prisms."

"Cool, sounds good. I should have more materials coming her way there soon, so that works great."

"Sounds rude to me," Frank said. "Just the two of us. How dare you."

"Three of us then," I said. "You knew what I meant."

"I did, but I still want my presence to be indicated far more often than is necessary."

"Fair enough, I'll keep that in mind." I eyed a two-person, Memory-stained Rift that was way, way outside Goon's capital and tapped it with my finger. "We could start with this one, then House could rejoin us once she's done with the Auction House."

"Why not?" Darling said.

"Because Ned makes poor decisions," Frank said. "That's why not." I felt him gesture at another Rift of the same type. It was about the same distance from Uliana, but it was on the other side of the city. "This one right here has my official blessing."

"Why that one?" I said.

"When was the last time I let you down?" he said.

I thought about that. "I guess it has been several hours. But I was sleeping for most of them."

"Yup, and that still didn't stop me from saving your bony ass by switching the tree."

"You did, yeah. Alright, if you say so, that's good enough for me." I selected the Rift he'd indicated. "Guess we'll start here."

"I'm gonna officially have the guild start on the most distant Rifts then too, yeah? Start the prism rush?" Darling said.

I looked up at her. "I still think it's the right call, but are you sure you wanna take a swing at Goon, even indirectly? Once we pull the trigger, there won't be any going back. It's not like they'll automatically know where the prisms are coming from, but it won't take a massive leap in logic for them to figure out it's us."

"It's a risk, but I really do, yeah. I hate what they're doing, and we need to be completing somebody's Rifts. Might as well make them count. But speaking of risks, did you figure anything else out on that Revenant thing and where it came from?"

"Came at me again as soon as I woke up, yeah. I'd love to find out where that thing's coming from, but I don't think that's a rabbit hole we can afford to go down just yet, and we'll be safe in the Rift regardless." I paused. "You see that alert go out about Corruptia clearing the first boss of the Menagerie Wing?"

"Yep. That's what kept me from sleeping. I knew we'd fall behind if we focused on gearing and so on, but I was hoping it wouldn't happen so quickly."

"For sure. I still think we made the right call, but we need to get moving—and fast."

"Goodbye, Darling," House said out of nowhere. She looked at Frank, then snapped her gaze back up to Darling and me. "I hope you two individuals have a lovely time in each other's exclusive company."

She popped out of the hall before anyone had a chance to respond, and Frank muttered something under his breath that sounded a lot like *good riddance.*

"What was that?" Darling said.

I snorted. "Vengeance on House's part, I think. But if you were asking what Frank was saying just then, it was Frarling Frarling Frarling," I said while doing my best to mimic his voice.

"That was a terrible imitation," Frank said. "There was no grandeur to it, no scope, no gravitas."

"The name really is fun to say though, isn't it?" Darling said. "Frarling."

Frank paused, then dropped his voice. "My disdain for you has somewhat lessened, but it's still present."

"You're welcome," I said. "Darling, you all set?"

"Yep!"

"Let's get to it then." I popped through the portal and directly into a ruined city that was very reminiscent of the one we'd seen in the last Rift we'd taken on.

It was absolutely pouring with rain, and our immediate surroundings were choked with fog—a mist that was thick and eerily still despite the breeze that was blowing through the ruins—and what buildings I could see at the edges of my vision had either been completely flattened and flooded or looked primed to collapse.

The overgrowth we'd seen in that first Rift was noticeably absent, though, and the devastation here seemed much more recent.

Something laughed off in the distance, a high-pitched sound that was almost human.

Darling drew her sword and held it in front of her, raindrops pinging off the metal.

"Alright. Five seconds in, and I'm already damp and creeped out. Good start."

I glanced down at Frank.

"What?" he said.

"This is the part where you're supposed to attempt to be comforting."

"Why? Once again, Darling is correct: if you knew what had just made that sound, then you'd be creeped out too."

I rolled my shoulders, then equipped my blunderbuss and loaded two quick blasts into it. With that done, I swapped back to my pistols and wound up another pair of blasts, Overcharging one of them.

Golden energy gathered just beyond the barrel of my weapon, and while I'd been hoping that the light would help us pierce through the fog, all it did was brighten it up a bit.

"Guess we're heading down the street," I said. "You wanna take point and I'll watch our backs until we know what we're dealing with?"

Darling nodded and stepped in front of me just as a new quest hit my log.

**New Quest: {Hope and Hate: The Beginning of the End}!**
**Objective: Investigate the Fallen City (Phase I)!**
**Reward: Scales with number of Phases successfully completed.**
**However, if any member of your party dies during this Rift, your attempt will instantly end.**

"Multi-phase and no dying at all?" I said. "Usually a wipe will end a Rift but not an individual death. We might be in for a bit of a haul here."

"Nerank," Darling said with a giggle. Then she stopped, blinked, and rubbed her eyes. "Sorry, I feel almost high from not sleeping."

I squinted at her, though she was little more than a blurry shape at the edge of the fog. "What was that?"

"Just trying to figure out what it would sound like if you and Frank had your names smashed together."

"Please don't curse me like that," Frank said. "But if you must, put my name first."

"Pretty sure that's only the second time he's ever said please," I said, "and he was asking if he could torture someone the first time around. Just saying."

Darling hefted her sword across her shoulder. "Fred. Nope, doesn't work particularly well. Oooh, Frouse is pretty good though."

"Oh yeah. That's super solid. Frouse. Sounds vaguely German and therefore authoritative too."

"Ugh," Frank said.

"Help!"

Darling stopped and looked left, but I looked right. She pointed her sword down the road to the left. "You hear that?"

"I heard it, yeah." I pointed my Overcharged weapon in the other direction. "But I could have sworn it came from over there."

"Help!"

"Help!"

"Help!"

The three cries were identical, and they'd come much too close together, like echoes but weirdly distinct.

A bolt of red lightning leaped down into the mist and struck Darling dead-on, though it didn't make so much as a sound.

For a split second, her appearance changed completely, her heavy armor being replaced with a loose black dress with a yellow hem that hung just beneath her knees. Her massive sword was replaced as well, subbed out for a two-handed battle staff capped by a heavy metal X.

Then things snapped back so quickly that, for a moment, I wondered if it had all been in my head. But then Frank started growling, so I knew what I'd seen was genuine.

Darling didn't seem to have noticed how her appearance had changed, though, given the way she was staring at me.

"Did you just..." she said, trailing off.

I looked down at myself and caught another flicker of red, though my armor and guns were unchanged.

"I saw it too, yeah." I checked my nameplate and spotted a debuff that I hadn't noticed before.

{Temporal Bleeding}
**Effect: Phasing in and out of a previous reality.**
**Duration: ??**

"New debuff," I said. "Previous reality?"

"Are we time traveling?" Darling said.

"Maybe," Frank said.

I shrugged. "You wanna head where you thought the voices were coming from and I'll back you up?"

"Yup."

I trailed behind her, sloshing through puddles with both weapons drawn as the cries for help continued to reverberate through the fog and the pouring rain.

"There's a building up here that's still in decent shape," Darling said, and she was gone within a few quick steps.

I found her standing in front of a half-collapsed church with a high, triangular roof that had seen better days.

We pushed into the darkness of the building, lighting its tight corridors up with my Overcharged blast. The rain was even louder here, so much so that I wondered if the roof was metal. The corridors were damp, too, with rain dribbling through the cracks in the ceiling.

"Help!"

"Help!"

"Help!"

The calls sounded from multiple directions once again, echoing through the walls as we entered the church's main chamber. I crept forward, edging my way across the remains of wet, destroyed pews and examining the space as I went.

Standing water was everywhere—ankle-deep in some places—and the ceiling had a few holes in it where the rain was coming straight through and striking the floor.

I caught a flash of red above us. I pointed my guns up at the vaulted ceiling, and a number of crimson, vulture-like birds stared back at us, roosting in the rafters.

"Here!"

"Here!"

"Here!"

I swallowed. The sound was definitely coming from the birds. "Well… alright then. That doesn't sound promising at all." I inspected one of the creatures.

{Bleedbird} (Level 1 Beast)
HP: 80/80
MP: 50/50

"Any chance you've got a Codex entry on those things?"

228

"Uh huh."

**Codex Entry 7200: Bleedbird**
**Description: Bleedbirds are scavengers that can often be found roosting in areas with great historical significance, particularly those that are Temporally Unstable.**

"Temporally Unstable," I repeated. "So it's gotta be time, then. The birds might be a trap, but they're also probably a clue to what's going on here." Something roared off in the distance, a primal scream that I felt deep in my chest. "And that sounds even less promising than the spooky birds."

The entire church shuddered from ceiling to foundation, and dust fell from what remained of the rafters. Then it shook again, and again, in what I quickly realized was an undeniable rhythm: footsteps.

Darling tightened her two-handed grip on her sword and I held my spells, pointing my weapons every which way in an attempt to figure out what was coming.

"Sounds uh... big," Darling said.

"Yeah."

The sound of the rain on the roof became deafening, and hail started shooting down through the gaps. But then the noise cut off entirely, and the hail was displaced by fat snowflakes that drifted down silently into the church.

I pressed up against the nearest wall as the temperature in the room plummeted and peered out of an empty window frame. But all I got in return was a blast of snow to the face.

The footfalls intensified, coming heavier and faster now. The entire church trembled, loose boards dropping out of the ceiling and smashing into the floor, pieces of glass sliding from shelves and breaking where they landed.

I wiped my face with my sleeve and squinted into the white gale outside. I glimpsed something dark in the snow beyond the window, a huge shape that was moving much faster than anything that size had a right to.

And whatever it was, it was heading right for us.

The Bleedbirds scattered in a wave. The footsteps quickened still further, then stopped.

Silence. It was almost suffocating in the aftermath of so much sound and motion, and it took me a while to realize I was holding my breath. There was a new sense of pressure hanging in the air too, and it had rushed in like a storm front.

"Ned," Darling whispered.

"Yeah?"

"The quest hasn't updated to say otherwise, so I'm thinking we probably won't be fighting whatever that is, at least not yet." When I didn't answer, she pointed the tip of her sword at my pistols.

I stared at her for a moment, then caught her meaning and let my spells drop to remove the glow they were putting out.

"Smart," Frank said. "But it won't make a difference."

And with that, the floor and the walls and even the ceiling began to rime over with frost, ice crystals spreading in intricate patterns across every surface.

Darling shrieked, and though she was quick to stifle the sound with a hand, it was too late.

I looked her way and found her staring wide-eyed just over my shoulder. I pivoted around, slowly, and came face to face with a black pupil that was every bit as large as the window I'd been peering through.

I gasped reflexively as the pupil flicked to me, super cold air prickling at my skin. The eye moved on, and a huge expanse of black feathers rushed by the window, as if whatever creature loomed nearby had just risen to its full, terrible height.

"Seriously?" Darling hissed. "Are we supposed to fight that thing?"

"Frank?"

"Defined 'supposed'," he said.

"I think that's a no," I whispered. We stood there for a long moment, me clutching my pistols while Darling squeezed the grip of her sword so tightly that the leather creaked and groaned.

"Did it leave?" she said. "Maybe it didn't see us?"

I risked another glance at the avenue beyond the window. The snow was still falling, blanketing the ground, and the room was brutally cold.

"It's still here."

There was a great thunderclap from above, then the entire church pulled up off its foundation and tilted sideways.

Darling and I went down in a rush as the floor rose and shifted beneath us, and we skidded across the floor. She ended up sliding face-first, desperately clutching her sword as I tumbled across the rough boards on my back, bouncing off what remained of the pews.

Then red light flooded the chamber, and I abruptly went from sliding to sitting on the ground, the sudden shift turning my stomach and leaving me disoriented.

I blinked and shook my head. I thought we'd somehow been teleported out of the church, but I had no idea how or why.

I tried to look around, but wherever we'd been transported to was so bright that my eyes were still adjusting, and though it didn't hurt, I found myself shielding my eyes nonetheless.

When my vision had mostly cleared, Darling was pointing a hand at me.

"What... the..."

She stood garbed in the same black and yellow dress I'd seen after that first red flash early on in the Rift, and the battle staff I'd noticed before had taken the place of her sword as well.

"What did we... what just happened?" she said. "Where'd it go? What was that thing?"

I gazed around at our new surroundings. The roof above us was back in place, lined with beautiful wooden rafters, and a gorgeous, stained-glass window rendered in blue and gold stood in the very spot where I'd first seen the creature's eye.

"Same church?" I said. "Earlier time?"

Darling offered me a hand up, so I took it. We were indeed at the very back of the same church to either side of the entryway as if we'd been guarding it, and a group of armored men were talking to some kind of priestess atop the dais at the far end of the room.

The conversation looked friendly enough, and the priestess appeared completely relaxed in front of the crowd, though a few of the guards hovering near the rear of the group had their hands very close to the hilts of their swords.

"Uhhhh," I said.

"Brevity truly is the soul of wit," Frank said.

"Shut up, Frank," I said, though he got a laugh out of Darling to my right.

I took a step between the pews that lined the space but hesitated mid-stride as my once-leather armor clinked as if it were metal. I looked down.

I was covered head-to-toe in immaculate plate, and my pistols had been replaced by a pair of longswords engraved with icy blue runes, both of which were hanging from sheaths at my side.

"Oh yeah," Frank said. "Time to smash and slash. You've got a shield on your back too that you can use, but I wouldn't worry about that. You won't need it."

"I swear, Frank, this is the last time I let you pick a Rift."

"I forgot he picked this one on purpose," Darling said. She smirked at him. "All that effort to get a girl into a dress?"

"Yeah," I said. "I can see how you'd think that was why he chose this one, but you'd be wrong."

"Huh?"

"Elf boy's got the right of it," Frank said. "No offense, but you in a dress is the opposite of what's good. Nah, I wanted to get Ned into some plate so he can play at being a man for a little while, and the possibility of me catching some blood spatter down here was too tempting to pass up. Knowing that you'd lose your armor temporarily was a sacrifice that I was willing to make, but trust me when I say it was a close thing."

Darling cocked her head. "Well... alright then."

"There's more as to why we're here, but don't worry, I'll claim credit when the moment arrives."

I pulled both of my swords out of my sheaths and swung them around, finding them surprisingly light and natural to wield. "So I'm thinking we just shifted into the bodies of some guards or something like that?"

"Close enough."

"Oh no, hold on a second," Darling said. "Am I a healer now?"

"I know, I know," Frank said. "I'm sorry."

"Wow," I said. "First a please, now an apology? Look at you go, growing up into a somewhat respectable person right in front of our eyes." I dropped my voice so that only he would be able to hear me. "You're moving almost as fast as House."

"I resent your implication of change."

"Resent what?" Darling said.

"Nothing," we both said at the same time.

A quest update came in then.

**Quest Updated: {Hope and Hate: The Beginning of the End}!**
**Objective: Help the guards locate Brandt Walker (Phase II)!**
**Reward: Scales with number of Phases successfully completed.**
**However, if any member of your party dies during this Rift, your attempt will instantly end.**

I scanned my skills and found that they'd been replaced with new abilities, though I only had three to keep track of, and they were each a good bit simpler than the abilities that comprised my actual kit, with short cooldowns, if any, and no costs attached.

The first was an aura whose uptime essentially made it a passive.

{Fervor of the Steel Guard}
Description: You radiate an aura that increases the damage and healing dealt by all friendly targets within 5 yards by 50%.
Cast time: 1.25 seconds.
Duration: Permanent.
Cooldown: None.

I activated the ability, and fiery blue runes circled my feet as well as Darling's. The ability would be easy enough to use, but the range was pretty short for an aura.

"Guess we're staying close," I said. "Got an aura that needs you within 5 yards."

Darling spun her staff in a tight circle, and I didn't miss the sour look on her face. "Yeah, my buff is similar."

She rapped the butt of her staff on the ground, and a glowing yellow beam brightened between us. The glow faded but didn't disappear, and it was easy enough to spot the link if you were looking for it.

I checked the new buff.

{Heartlink}
While both linked targets remain within 5 yards of each other, all healing the targets receive is increased by 50% and all damage taken is reduced by 75%.

"Five-minute cooldown that starts if the link is broken," Darling said.

"That's even less forgiving than my aura. These numbers are all so high that I'm wondering what they're balanced for."

"You thinking that we might end up dead real quick if our buffs drop?"

"Exactly, yeah. The buffs are strong because we need them to be strong for whatever's coming." I scoped out our Health pools, which were high as well: we'd both jumped to 3,000.

Darling's lip curled up.

"Something wrong?" I said.

"No. Well, yeah. Healing in general."

"I feel your pain," Frank said.

"No you don't. You did this on purpose. It just stresses me out, is all. I like being able to tunnel whatever I'm doing as a damage dealer. Healing requires a wider view and responsibility and all that."

Frank sighed and dropped his voice. "Torn between my two great loves: Darling and hitting things until they stop bleeding."

"Guess we know where your priorities lie, eh?" I said. "And on an unrelated note, I really don't feel like you'd stop whaling away on something just because it died."

"True, I'm no quitter." I felt him try to purse his lips. "However, I may have regrets on Darling's behalf when it comes to choosing this Rift, but I'm not sure. I've never regretted anything, so it's hard to tell. Anyway, how would you feel about sheathing one of those swords and using me instead?"

"If that's going to cause me to deal no damage with that weapon whatsoever, then no."

"I mean yeah, I'll hit for hardly anything. But think of the mental toll that the obvious disrespect would exact. Killing something with me says that you don't even need stats to put your opponent down. You can't come back from that. It'd be like being beaten to death with a Wiffle ball bat."

I ignored him and poked through my other two skills, both of which had short cooldowns.

{Sublime Strikes} (Active Ability)
Description: You empower your weapons with holy energy. While this ability is active, all strikes made against stunned enemies are guaranteed a critical strike.
Cast time: Instant.
Duration: 8 seconds.
Cooldown: 30 seconds.

{Concentrated Ire} (Active Ability)
Description: You unleash your judgment upon undead enemies within 10 yards, taunting them and forcing them to attack you for 5 seconds.
Cast time: Instant.
Duration: 5 seconds.
Cooldown: 30 seconds.

I had an interesting passive as well:

**{Sparks of the Zealot} (Passive Ability)**
**Description: Whenever you critically hit an Undead enemy, you**
**cause a holy nova of energy that deals the same amount of damage to**
**every Undead within 10 yards and heals all friendly targets for half**
**the same amount.**

"I've got that aura I mentioned," I said, "an AoE taunt on a 30-second cooldown, and a melee steroid. I'm basically gonna be smashing stuff until it dies."

"As the good Lord intended," Frank said.

"You?"

"I was indeed referring to myself. I'm surprised you picked up on that."

"I wasn't talking to you, Frank. I was trying to ask Darling about her skills."

"Aura, strong heal that takes a while to cast, quick heal that's weaker and less efficient, and an AoE that stuns everything within fifteen yards for eight seconds. Thirty-second cooldown on that last one but nothing to worry about otherwise."

I perked up at that last skill. "I get guaranteed crits on anything that's stunned while my steroid is active, plus a cleave."

"There we go. That's the wombo combo right there."

"Yeah, handy. Cooldowns line up too."

"I can't believe you get two swords." She looked down at Frank. "Two swords would have gone a long way with me, Frank."

"A long way toward what exactly?" Frank said.

"I guess we'll never know, will we?"

"You done messed up," I whispered.

"I do think I regret this, actually. I'm not a fan at all. Having regrets sucks, huh?"

"Totally."

# Chapter Twenty-One

The quest updated again.

**Quest Updated: {Hope and Hate: The Beginning of the End}!**
**Objective: Witness the detainment of Brandt Walker (Phase III)!**
**Reward: Scales with number of Phases successfully completed.**
**However, if any member of your party dies during this Rift, your**
**attempt will instantly end.**

"Brandt, huh?" I said. "What are the odds that this is the same guy we
were investigating earlier? The one who lived back in that first house."

"The taxidermist?" Darling said.

"Yeah."

Darling shuddered. "I hope not. Taxidermy is already creepy enough,
but it's even worse after having seen all those stitched-up animals start
flying around."

Frank cleared his throat. "Is taxidermy actually creepy though? Or is
preserving a loved one at any cost the purest gesture of love one person
could make for another?"

Darling stared at him. "No. It's super creepy and there's no other
viable interpretation." She headed down a row of pews to her left and
scoped out one of the stained-glass windows.

"I see," Frank said. He dropped his voice to a whisper. "On an obvi-

236

ously related note, lemme know if you've got any ideas for Valentine's Day 'cause I just got sent back to square one."

"What were you even going to..." I trailed off, thinking better of the question. "Nope, never mind. Not doing this right now. I'll let you know if I come up with anything."

"I was gonna get somebody to taxidermy up a Frank plushie for her."

"Great, you found a context that makes the word *plushie* absolutely horrifying."

"Yeah, I was gonna try to skin one of the first animals we killed with Darling and have it rearranged vaguely into the shape of me."

I paused. "You know, I'm more grossed out than I was a moment ago, but the first half of that sentence does somehow manage to be slightly endearing."

"So you think I'm onto something even though Darling is expressly against the idea?"

"No. Look, if you're gonna make things weird by giving her a copy of you then at least make it out of something edible. Like chocolate."

"I don't see what you mean—my plushie would be totally edible, especially in the first couple weeks before the meat dried out."

I fought down the urge to gag. "Nobody wants Frank jerky, Frank. Especially your friends."

"Agree to disagree, but if we're gonna move on from the initial idea, I need you to define edible."

I thought about that for a moment, still watching the conversation at the front of the room between the priestess and the guards. "Something she'd want to take a second bite out of."

"Hm. That rules out the vast majority of my ideas."

"What about an actual plushie? I could get one made and sent to her back in the real world. Then you could lie to yourself and pretend she sleeps with it. That'd be nice, huh?"

"Sounds like a decent back-up. Let's plan on you handling all of that yourself and I'll let you know when I inevitably come up with something better."

"I guess I can't really stop you. I mean, I tried to head off this whole conversation, and yet here we are."

The Priestess made a dismissive gesture and turned away, eventually disappearing into a back room within the church. The guards that had been arguing with her turned and jogged down the pews, storming right between Darling and me.

The last of them slowed as he passed. "They haven't seen Brandt in days," he said, "but apparently the fool was stupid enough to go home after fleeing the palace. Let's move!"

Darling and I fell in behind the other guards and jogged out into warm, driving rain. The drops were loud against my helm and shoulders, and it wasn't long before the water was streaming through my armor in little rivulets, soaking the garments beneath.

I glanced at Darling to see how she was faring and saw she was already soaked through and glowering at Frank. I hid a smile, then realized I didn't have to, thanks to my helm.

We ran through the quiet streets for a while, stomping through mud and puddles, running between well-kept, fully intact homes that had guards stalking their flat roofs with huge crossbows in hand.

A flash of cyan light streaked down out of the sky to my left, collided with a guard, and sent him flipping off a roof and down into a dark alley.

The guards who were leading the way slowed, and a few of them unsheathed their swords.

"Focus!" the guard captain said. "Somebody needs to put an end to this, and we've got a job to do."

The soldiers mumbled but fell back in, and we jogged right by the alley the guard had tumbled into.

A vulture watched us cross from atop a barrel while several more flew over and circled high above what I assumed was the guard's corpse. The creatures were black for the most part, but their eyes and beaks were completely spectral, and their dark wings were feathered with streaks of blue.

"Yikes," Darling said.

"Yeah. Seems like whatever wrecked the city is in motion here, like we're seeing how it happened." I looked around and spotted a few thin, vaguely humanoid creatures charging across a nearby roof on all fours on blue hands and feet. "Or maybe how it started."

We followed the militia through the rain for a few more minutes while screams and the sounds of combat rang through the city. I spotted people watching us go, too, peeking at us through their windows while a few others watched boldly from their doorsteps.

Eventually, the guards slowed and fanned out, then drew their weapons in front of an all-too-familiar home.

It was the very same one that Darling and House and I had investigated in that first Rift. But the home was immaculate this time around, pristine from the narrow steps that led up to the door to the well-shingled roof above.

"Remember," the Captain said. "The Huntsman wants Brandt alive."

"After everything he's done?" another said. "Look around, Captain. Look at what he's brought upon us. We ought to put him down right now before this gets any worse."

"The Huntsman will have his justice, Tal," the Captain said, already stalking up the steps. "This discussion is over. You have your orders."

He clomped up the steps with Tal right behind, and they both froze as the door opened and a young woman rushed out, red hair matted to her face, her forehead beaded with sweat. She looked positively feverish, and her eyes were wide and wild.

"You can't!" she cried, meeting the Captain at the top of the stairs and pounding her fists into his armored chest. "He told you! Brandt told the Huntsman it wouldn't work, but he didn't listen!" She kept going but lapsed into hysterics, her voice high and sharp.

The guard let her vent for a moment, her blows becoming slower and slower as her strength failed her. He was about to brush past her when Tal took the remaining steps in a single quick motion, grabbed her roughly by the wrist, and tried to yank her down the stairs.

Instead, the motion jerked her fully off her feet, and even Tal seemed baffled with the speed at which she fell.

She twisted as she went down, and the side of her head caught one of the concrete steps. There was a brief silence as the guards looked at her body lying motionless in the street.

"Tal!" the Captain said.

"It was an accident!" he said. "I didn't pull her that hard, she just—I don't know!"

He wasn't wrong: while he was obviously at fault, the woman's fall *had* looked unnatural.

"What have you done?" a deep voice said from inside.

The guards froze and turned as one as a hulking man appeared in the doorway. He was so tall that he had to duck to keep his head from hitting the doorframe, and his eyes were a startling shade of blue. He wore a thick leather apron that was splattered with purple liquid, and he held a scalpel in one hand.

The Captain grabbed the new arrival about the elbow and pulled, but the larger man didn't budge.

"Isabel?" Brandt said, his eyes still on the young woman.

Tal shifted on his feet. "She fell. Stairs are wet."

The woman's hair was fiery red, but there was no disguising the blood that tinged the rainwater that was rushing around her in the street, nor the stillness with which she lay there.

The Captain tried to wrench Brandt around by his arm, but the larger man easily jerked himself free. He dropped the scalpel, which clattered against the stone.

"Was it not enough for the Huntsman to twist my work? You had to take her, too?"

His words hung there, sounding clearly over the rain.

"Seize him," the Captain said.

The other guards rushed up the steps, though Darling and I both stayed put without needing to share a glance.

Brandt kicked the Captain full in the chest and sent him staggering into the others. The lot of them went tumbling down the narrow steps while Brandt turned and ran back inside.

"Can you heal her?" I said, once all of the other guards had pounded their way up the steps and disappeared into the house after Brandt.

Darling shook her head. "Already tried. I can't even target her." She pointed her staff up the steps. "Should we help them?"

"The quest didn't say we had to protect the guards from Brandt. And after seeing that scene play out, I don't really feel much of a need to make it easier on them, flashback or not."

"Agreed. But maybe—"

A series of grunts sounded from inside, followed by the breaking of glass.

Brandt bounded out of the house and down the steps, green liquid smeared across his lips. He gave Darling and me a dark, heavy glare, then rushed to the side of the fallen women.

He produced a beaker I hadn't seen before, a small vial that was filled with lime-green liquid.

Cupping a hand beneath the woman's chin and gently tilting her head up, he poured the vial's contents down her throat, shoulders shaking as the liquid glugged away.

The guards rushed out and two of them wrenched Brandt away, though not before he'd finished with the vial.

They forced him face-first onto the street and cuffed him, then shackled his ankles together with thick irons and hauled him roughly to his feet.

He looked us both full in the face as he was dragged off. His blue eyes were pained, but there was something else there, too, something cold and unmistakably sharp that was shifting into place behind them.

Darling waited until both Brandt and the militia were a little way off before she spoke again.

"Guess we should keep tagging along and see what happens."

"Yeah. Let's move."

Darling and I ran to catch up, but I still felt like something was off. Then the hairs on the back of my neck rose all at once, and I glanced back over my shoulder as the guards led Brandt off into the rain up ahead.

The poor woman hadn't budged, and I couldn't be sure of anything between the rain and the distance, but I could have sworn that one of Isabel's small hands had curled into a fist.

# Chapter Twenty-Two

It wasn't long before the quest updated yet again.

**Quest Updated: {Hope and Hate: The Beginning of the End}!**
**Objective: Escort Brandt Walker to the gallows without losing more than 3 guards (Phase IV).**
**Reward: Scales with number of Phases successfully completed.**
**However, if any member of your party dies during this Rift, your attempt will instantly end.**

"More than three," I whispered to Darling. "We've got five of them in total, so two need to live?"

"Yeah, I guess the fun's about to start." She eyed my swords, then Frank. "For some of us, anyway."

"Okay, this was officially not worth it," Frank said.

I laughed. "To be fair, I haven't killed anything yet."

"Speaking of killing things, the two of you might wanna speed it up a bit."

We exchanged a glance, then jogged up into place and positioned ourselves to either side of Brandt.

"Who was it?" Brandt said, his voice a low rumble as two of the guards continued to drag him along. His wrists were secured behind him, and his ankles were bound with maybe six inches of chain between them. His face was streaked with rain, but his blue eyes were clear and hard.

The guards hauled him over the cobbles in silence. Heat lightning raked the clouds overhead, briefly illuminating the street.

Brandt bared his teeth, which were stained the same shade of green as the vial he'd given to his fallen wife. "Fine. We'll do it the hard way."

A guard who'd been posted on a nearby roof flew off the building to my right and landed hard in the street in front of us. Then a wave of screams reached us as an ominous blue glow crept over the distant buildings.

After a few long seconds the screaming stopped, and fully spectral, cyan creatures appeared atop the rows of buildings that framed the road to either side, their eyes fixed on us.

I inspected the closest of them, a gargoyle-like creature with oversized wings that looked perfectly at home looming high above the street.

**{Spectral Batkin} (Level 16 Undead) (Elite+)**
**HP: 7,000/7,000**
**MP: 9,000/9,000**

"Form up, backs together!" the Captain said.

Everybody moved into a circular formation, Darling and me included, with her taking up a position directly to my right.

The two guards who were holding Brandt forced him down onto his stomach in the center of the protective formation, then one of them put a knee into his lower back to hold him in place.

"Who was it?" Brandt repeated, and he managed to sound impressively commanding for a man whose temple was pressed to the cobbles. "Which one of you was it?"

Darling was gripping her staff as if she intended to use it like a club, so I reached out and tapped it down with the flat of one of my swords.

"What?" she said.

"Healer on the outside of the ring?" I still didn't have to hide my smile, but a bit of it came through in my voice. "Sounds like a recipe for disaster. Better leave the combat to us heavies who can actually take a hit."

Darling's mouth actually dropped open. "Wow. I log in early to help, and not only do I end up as a healer, but I immediately become a second-class citizen." She eyed her staff with disdain, then took a few steps back into the circle toward Brandt and the guard who was still kneeling on him while the other guards and I closed ranks around them.

"Why are you needling her?" Frank said.

I ignored him and flexed a bicep at her. "Don't worry, I'll protect you with my strong arm muscles."

She snorted derisively. "Arm muscles? You don't know what they're actually called, do you?"

"No, but I have them, so I don't need to. Anyway, just make sure you heal me no matter what I'm standing in or getting hit by, otherwise my death will be objectively your fault."

"Shut up!" she half-laughed, half-shouted. "I think it's starting."

"Wait," Frank said. "Are you being annoying because you can't help it, or are you deliberately trying to make this worse for me on purpose?"

"In true Frank fashion, yes. That's exactly what I'm doing."

He hesitated. "Hmm. I was going to dock you serious points, but Frank fashion is such a delightful turn of phrase that I find myself conflicted. I could do both, but that would involve basic math. Oh, this is a conundrum."

"Let's pause there," I said as the batlike creature I'd inspected stepped off the roof. It dropped like a stone before it fluttered its wide wings at the last moment and landed lightly on the cobbles.

Darling rapped the butt of her staff against the ground and renewed the golden link between us.

"Remember that we gotta stay within 5 yards of each other or this thing breaks and we lose the damage reduction and so on."

I put a hand on her shoulder. "Don't worry, Frank has quietly spent a great deal of this Rift explaining just how helpless healers like you are when left on your own. I'm not going anywhere."

"You're going to pay dearly for this," Frank said.

The top of Darling's staff radiated golden light as the spectral horde rushed us from both sides, pouring down off the roofs.

I double-checked that my aura was active, then raised my swords and held my ground. The ghosts slammed into us, and our circle contracted as we were pushed back.

I ducked a ghostly swipe and retaliated with a slash that caught a bear-like ghost from shoulder to hip and sent it fleeing back into the horde.

"Hit for 1,650!" Frank said.

I stabbed another ghostly mob between the eyes with my left hand, then decapitated a wounded ghost with my right for almost 2,000 damage. "Oh man, these things absolutely slap!"

"Told you!"

"Call for the stun when you want it!" Darling said. "And stop bragging!"

"Thanks for the reminder!"

We were maybe ten seconds into the fight when it became clear that the formation was at the risk of being overwhelmed; Darling was throwing out her quicker heals from the center of the group, hands constantly moving as she rapidly shifted from target to target, but it was increasingly obvious that it wasn't going to be enough given the rate that everyone's Health pools were falling at, large as they were.

"Lowest guard at 30%," Frank said. "Darling can't keep up with this much damage!"

"Taunting everything onto me in 3," I called out. "Pop your stun in 5!"

"Got it!"

I popped Concentrated Ire and abruptly felt the aggro of every creature within ten yards settle onto my shoulders.

Many of the ghosts that had been throwing themselves at our circle shifted gears and tried to push through it, and some of the smaller creatures immediately succeeded in slipping through the gaps and into the center.

I took a blow to the back of the head that sent me staggering forward only to catch a spectral paw to the face. But between my armor and the damage suppressing effects of Darling's Heartlink, the vibrations were manageable.

"Your Health at 80% but falling fast!" Frank said as the blows rained in, which were coming so quickly and from so many directions that there wasn't much I could do other than to keep my swords up and occasionally slash out in an attempt to create space.

A golden nova erupted from behind me and raced over the glowing horde, stunning all but the most distant creatures.

I used my Sublime Strikes ability and both of my weapons flared with fiery blue light. I went to work on the stunned crowd, swinging my swords in wide, sweeping strikes, tagging four or five ghosts with every attack.

With my steroid active and the mobs stunned in place, every single swing was a guaranteed critical, and every crit generated a golden burst of energy that devasted the surrounding mobs and healed every guard in range at the same time.

I ripped through them, carving a swath through their ranks that even Frank was at least slightly proud of, given the occasional *nice* and *oh yeah* and *that's the good stuff* that I heard filtering up from him, though I was pretty sure that his enthusiasm was just getting the better of him and that he didn't actually intend for me to hear any of that.

"Stun's about to fade!" Darling said.

I cut my way back toward the other guards, grinning from ear to ear as the ghosts dispersed all around me, popping like balloons, every kill setting off a chain reaction that had bodies falling by the score.

I eyed my Experience bar, and though it wasn't climbing at the rate I'd hoped, given how quickly I was dropping these mobs—and the fact they were marked as Elite+—I didn't particularly care at that moment. I was fully there, putting everything I had into this swing, then into the next, and so on.

So much so that I'd forgotten about the link entirely. I panicked for a brief moment, thinking I'd caused us to drop our buffs and just hadn't noticed in the middle of my rampage, but I caught sight of Darling close behind me, dipping and ducking her way between the mobs that pursued me without losing a step along the way.

Most of the surrounding mobs were dead and the ground between the other guards and me was mostly clear, but a spectral ram that'd been too distant to be caught in Darling's stun charged, hopped clear over Brandt, then leaped for me with its spiral horns lowered in a ferocious headbutt.

I stepped into a right hook with everything I had, fingers clenched in a fist around the hilt of my mainhand weapon, and caught the animal on the side of its head while it was still fully extended in the air, sending it helicoptering sideways and onto the street.

"Hell yeah!" Frank said. "I would have personally met it forehead to forehead because that's how rams establish hierarchies but *blam*, earblasted!"

Darling's stun fully faded, and though the ground was littered with glittering corpses, more ghosts were already pouring off the roofs.

"Guards' Health?" I said.

"Nearly topped up."

Darling stepped back into the center of the loose circle. "We gotta last twenty seconds before that stun is back up."

I moved into the last remaining gap in the formation, and we squared up to meet the next rush. My steroid was on the same cooldown as Darling's stun, which thankfully meant it'd be easy to figure out when she was ready. I just didn't think she'd be able to keep all of us up that long.

The next wave rushed over us, and once again, the circle buckled around Brandt and was forced inward.

Some kind of massive bird swooped down at me from overhead, and while I managed to slash its talons and clip one of its wings on the follow-through, a lizardlike ghost caught me in the abdomen with a tail whip.

The vibration wasn't bad, but the blow knocked me a few steps backward into Darling and interrupted one of her longer casts. She cursed as ghosts flooded in through the gap I'd left and piled onto the very guard she'd been trying to heal.

I regained my balance and threw myself back into the fight, hacking and slashing at the creatures, trying to pry them off the prone guard with every strike and kick.

Darling got off a series of quick heals to buy him a bit of time, but the circle formation had fully collapsed now, and the other guards were starting to get dogpiled as the ghosts flooded in and swarmed over them from all angles.

A counter updated in the corner of my screen: we'd just lost our first guard. And to make matters worse, a quick glance at the others' Health bars revealed that it wouldn't be long before we lost a second.

I eyed my cooldown. It wasn't going to be ready in time, and neither was Darling's.

I charged over toward the guard with the lowest Health and lowered my shoulder, intent on tackling a few of the mobs off him to buy time if nothing else.

But then I pulled up in surprise as the ghosts suddenly scattered off him and went racing down the nearby alleys and up the walls, over the roofs, and out of sight.

"Which one of you was it?" Brandt repeated. "We'll get the truth eventually. That or the process of elimination will win out." He lay there on his side, face still pressed into the wet street, one blue eye flicking from guard to guard. "No?"

Someone grunted beside me, and I whirled around to catch a few spectral feathers drifting across the empty space where a guard should have been.

I looked up and spotted a massive bird with two sets of wings soaring high into the air, a guard dangling from one huge talon.

The soldier had drawn his sword and was hacking away at the creature's leg. One of the strikes seemed to hit home because then the great bird shrieked and released him. He tumbled out of the sky, then smashed through a nearby roof and sent clay shingles sliding down and shattering against the street.

The noise went on and on, and even the guards who were holding Brandt watched in stunned silence.

"Well," Darling said. "Two down. We can afford to lose one more, but if two drop then it's a loss."

I pointed a finger at Tal, the guard who had wrenched Isabel off the porch and caused her to fall. "It was—"

I cut off at a vibration from Frank.

"Don't."

I blinked down at him. "I bet it would end this standoff or whatever it is though, right? I think Brandt called those creatures off to give us the chance to accuse somebody."

"Yeah, that could end it on the spot. But these mobs are Elite+."

I cocked my head at him, not understanding. Then it hit me.

"The Trinket! The Unseal mechanic!"

"Yup," Frank said. I felt him look up at the sky. "How's it feel to have requirements that are supposed to be difficult get cheesed in an afternoon, Dad?"

Brandt was staring at me, waiting to see if I'd finish my accusation, but I held my peace and dropped my voice. "Can you link me the Unseal info for the Trinket's second effect?"

"Uh huh."

**Tier II Unseal: Slay 24 {Elite+} or higher difficulty mobs.**

The effect had required 50 kills originally, which meant I'd already gotten credit for 26 kills.

And better yet? The Tier I Unseal only required us to complete two Rifts, and since this was our second, if we managed to complete every Phase, I'd be walking out of here with two of my three Trinket powers active.

"Damn, Frank. Okay, I'm officially sold on the Rift."

"Had to figure out a way to let you punch above your weight. And in a happy coincidence, this one literally does exactly that."

"I don't follow what you guys are on about, but do we have a plan here?" Darling said.

"Cooldowns on my signal if we last that long?" I said. "We can end this thing if we need to, but I need a few more kills first if that's cool. Explain later."

"Sure."

Brandt shook his head, then closed his eyes.

The blue glow reappeared atop the nearby roofs, and the second wave of the assault was on.

"Ready when you are!" Darling said.

"Gonna let as many as possible crash in, then taunt them off."

"I'll have a heal ready to go if you call it out ahead of time."

"Got it!"

We met the wave as we had before, and while the circle was a bit tighter, the rush was manageable with all of our tools at our disposal.

I let the guards get beat on for a little bit, watching their Health bars slowly drop and occasionally jump up under the effect of one of Darling's heals. The rush swelled to easily twice the size of the first that we'd pushed back before suffering our first casualty.

I cleared my throat as two of the guards dropped beneath 25% Health at the same time. "Taunting in 3, stun in 5!"

Darling's hands glowed with golden light, and I saw a cast bar appear above her head.

I activated my taunt and felt the aggro swell as the swarm converged on me. I managed to repel two creatures in quick succession but quickly realized that I'd underestimated the amount of damage I'd take.

My Health tanked from 90% all the way down to 30% in a matter of seconds, then the long heal that Darling had started casting ahead of time brought me back to 50%.

She followed up with her stun before I could call for it, so I popped my steroid and laid into the crowd while Frank hollered at every hit and twice for every kill.

The creatures fell in a wave as I cleaved through them, opening up a sizable gap around the guards, while Darling stayed close behind and allowed me to focus completely on making the most of our window.

"Ability unsealed!" Frank said, just as an alert popped up in the corner of my vision. I kept killing until Darling's stun was about to run out, then darted back into the formation and made room for her to slip into the protective center.

And as the last seconds of relative safety ticked away, I pointed an armored finger at Tal's back while he hacked away at a ghostly boar.

"It was him, Brandt. He's the one who killed her."

# Chapter Twenty-Three

The stun faded and the ghosts retreated at once, the boar that Tal had been hacking away at dashing off so quickly that it left him swinging at the air and staggering forward.

He whipped around and stared at me, fingers clenched around the hilt of his sword.

"It's like that, huh?"

"You shouldn't have grabbed her," I said. "There was no need for that."

"It was an accident! You saw it! I was just trying to get her out of the way, and she practically leaped off the porch!"

I rolled my shoulders and held my ground, weapons at the ready.

Then a pair of tall, thin creatures dashed across the road with super-human speed. They grabbed Tal under his arms and ran right up the walls of the nearest house with him in tow.

It happened so quickly that a curse from the Captain was the group's only reaction before Tal disappeared over the roof.

"Three down," Darling said with a sigh. "Can't afford to lose another."

"It appears that we're off to the Huntsman, then," Brandt said, his voice low and predatory. After a moment of hesitation, two of the remaining guards ran over and levered him back to his feet and hauled him down the avenue.

"The guards aren't really in charge at this point, are they?" Darling said.

"I don't know if they ever were." I checked my cooldowns, then eyed the roof. Where there had previously been guards pacing atop the structures with weapons in hand, now it was purely spectral creatures that were watching us go.

I went ahead and looted the mobs' bodies and came away with three more log entries.

{Entry 29}
*I met with the Huntsman, and it went the way I expected it to. He heard about my successful experiments and came calling. I told him how my craft works, but he only bothered listening to the parts he wanted to hear.*

*He made a request that he thinks is simple—he wants the ghosts of the great creatures he hunted in his youth to prowl his palace like moving trophies— but he doesn't understand the limitations involved.*

*Still, he's as hard-headed a man as I've ever met, and I very much doubt he'll take being turned down well.*

*I'm inclined to give what he wants a shot, for payment if nothing else. Isabel's medicine isn't cheap, and we're running out of money.*

{Entry 30}
*As soon as I accepted the Huntsman's proposal, he sent for a renowned trio of healers from a distant city to help with Isabel's condition. I can't muster much hope at the prospect, knowing all the healers we've already seen, but I do appreciate the attempt.*

*In darker news, it has been nearly two weeks since I started working for him, and the Huntsman is growing increasingly irate with the nature of my work. He's got this idea stuck in his head that I'm coming at the problem from the wrong angle, and I can't seem to convince him otherwise.*

*I'm so tired that I'm honestly considering trying it his way.*

{Entry 35}
*It's been a month, and the healers the Huntsman sent for have yet to arrive. The city they reside in isn't far off—a week's ride at most—and I'm beginning to wonder if he sent for them at all or if his offer was simply meant to keep me focused.*

*My work continues. It is not going well.*

A buzzing sound filled the air as soon as I put the pages down, then a bolt of red lightning struck a puddle to my left. I tried to throw up a hand to shield my face, but I wasn't quick enough to save my vision.

And though it took a moment for my sight to return, I could feel Frank's familiar weight bearing down on the loop that held him.

"Man, that was bright," Darling said. She drew her sword and kissed it. "So glad to have her back." She pointed a finger at Frank. "You, on the other hand, are on very thin ice."

Frank sighed. "You don't understand. You know how terrible it was staring at the mere prospect of being responsible for keeping Ned alive?"

She inclined her head. "Yeah?"

"Imagine that's your full-time job, but the only pay you receive is the ability to make him suffer. And someone stapled him onto you so you can't even quit."

"If anyone is stapled to someone else, it's clearly you," I said.

"And yet I'm the one carrying the team."

I blinked, then rubbed my eyes as the world came fully back into focus: the recently ruined streets, the ever-present rain. It seemed like we'd jumped forward in time again.

I looked left and right, peering through the deluge and sweeping my gaze across the roofs, searching for any hint of the colossal mob that had nearly caught us in the church.

"Are we safe here if I take a break for a second? I want to scope out that Trinket ability before we go any further."

"As long as you..." He trailed off, buzzing. "Bah."

"As long as we do something?" I finished for him. "Or as long as we don't do something?"

"Yes."

"Well, that wasn't a no, so I'm thinking we're okay."

"What's up?" Darling said.

"Remember that Trinket I showed you? I've got my second Unseal available, so I'm gonna pop it if that's cool."

"Wait, did you already get its first power?"

"Nope," I said, grinning. "First one requires two completed Rifts with it equipped, so it'll unlock once we're done here. I guess we can do the Unseals out of order. Should I then?"

"Uh, yeah! Do it, we need details!"

**Tier II Trinket Unseal is now available.**

Proceed?

Once I'd confirmed my choice, a burst of gold radiated off me and more prompts streamed in.

**You may select 1 of 3 available Trinket Enhancements. Enhancements' effects are permanent, but they will only remain active so long as the Trinket they are tied to remains equipped.**
**1. {Touchstone Amplification}**
**Description: Any damaging Touchstone ability you use now deals 30% additional damage. In addition, any damaging Touchstone ability you have equipped now has a 3% chance of automatically duplicating for free upon activation. Duplicated effects ignore all cooldown mechanics.**
**2. {Touchstone Arsenal}**
**Description: You may now equip 3 pieces of Touchstone gear simultaneously (up from 2). In addition, all Touchstone items you have equipped now passively award a 2% increased Chance to Hit and +10 Magical and Physical Attack.**
**3. {Touchstone Socket}**
**Description: You may place a piece of Touchstone gear into this socket to permanently store its Touchstone power. However, socketing a piece of gear will permanently destroy it. Only 1 power may be stored at a time, but socketed powers do not count against your Touchstone limit.**

My breath caught even as I sent the options over to Darling. "Are you seeing what I'm seeing?"

She whistled. "Wow. Big upgrades."

The first two looked incredible, but I only had eyes for the third option.

"Frank," I said. My hands were already shaking with excitement, but I kept my voice flat. "Could I store a power from a piece of gear that I couldn't normally equip? Like, I can't use two-handed swords, but could I buy a sword, break it, and jam the power into that socket? Please, please say I can do that."

"You could indeed do that," Frank said, triumphant.

I stared at Darling, my mouth hanging open. "You could heal if you had one of these."

"How is that the first thing that pops into your head?"

"Yeah," Darling agreed, "how *is* that the first thing that pops into your head?"

"Because it's… it's the opposite of what you do."

I was finding it a little hard to speak; my mind was absolutely racing as I played the implications out.

"Now that you've Unsealed an ability," Frank said, "I can also confirm that the first Unseal for these Trinkets depends on your class, but the second tier of options is the same for everybody."

"The same for everyone." I met Darling's eyes. "Every single player is going to get these same choices. Don't you see it?"

Darling eyed me up and down. "Are you okay? See what?"

"The socket changes everything. Think of the raid: Jukes could get an ability that's designed for Ton's kit—something that would reduce the amount of damage he takes if he can't avoid an attack, something like that. If Zoe keeps running out of Mana, she could find a piece of gear with an ability that creates Mana Gems."

"Sure. But that's always been the case, right? You could always theoretically find that stuff, that's what makes Touchstone gear so fun."

"Right, but you needed to find an item that you could equip for it to do anything for you. Like, Nina was restricted to using Touchstone daggers or light armor, whatever. Now there are no limits." I rubbed my temples, my excitement bubbling up and out. "In fact, the item itself can be total trash—the stats don't even matter because it's all about the ability attached to it. We can straight up just buy the abilities we want."

Darling blinked. "Oh. Oh, man."

I laughed. "Darling, I was just looking at Touchstone stuff with House twenty minutes ago and there were 50 plus pieces up on the Auction House. I thought most of it was worthless at the time because it was all low-level junk that people had outgrown, and you always need your sword to be strong enough to kill things, right? But if you're not going to equip it anyway—"

"The stats don't matter," she repeated, smiling from ear to ear now. "This is huge."

"This is monumental. I doubt anyone else has any idea that this is a thing yet. Nobody knows what those low-level items are worth, and they're gold. They're all gold."

Frank cleared his throat. "I believe the time for the claiming of credit has officially arrived. So I'll ask you this: did I pick a great Rift, or did I pick the best Rift?"

"I'm not quite won over myself," Darling said. "But healing aside, this is insane. This is going to seriously help us build the raid out. This is exactly the sort of thing I was hoping for with the slower start."

"You are officially the bearded axe, Frank," I said.

"That's not your call to make, but you're correct."

"I need to talk to House." I sent her a quick list of instructions to buy each and every Touchstone item that was currently listed beneath 10 silver without exception.

From there, I gave her instructions with prices that scaled up depending on the power of the abilities in question and the roles they were intended for, prioritizing anything related to tanking or healing first, then raid-wide buffs or useful debuffs, followed by standard damage-dealing abilities.

And once we'd figured everything out, we'd snagged 45 of the 64 currently available items for the laughable price of 9 gold coins. And I'd be getting Experience and Renown for those purchases from my daily payout on top of everything else, too.

"I can get my Trinket at 15, right?" Darling said. She was bouncing on the balls of her feet, and her sword was thumping against her back.

"Yuuup," Frank said.

She rubbed her hands together, eyes glittering. "Should be later today, then. Between that and another class change, it feels like it's gonna be a really good day. Man, I can't wait."

I could barely contain myself either, so I started pacing down the road to burn off some of the energy.

Then the temperature plummeted and the rain went silent as it abruptly turned into snow.

"Frank? I've got a guess for what I wasn't supposed to do when I asked about taking a break."

"Shoot."

"I'm thinking we weren't supposed to move away from where we started."

"Correct."

I Water Jetted myself backward and down the street. "Run!"

# Chapter Twenty-Four

Darling activated her leap at the cost of Health, and by the time I'd spun around out of my jet and hit the ground running, she was already landing beside me in a deep puddle that splashed us both with muddy water.

"Where to?" she said.

The road in front of us stretched all the way to the walled palace that was standing off in the distance, and I thought I saw a few torches burning to either side of what appeared to be a gatehouse, but I knew we'd never make it that far.

Then I spotted some Bleedbirds circling up ahead and a little off the road to the right. "You see them?"

"It's gaining," Frank said. "About 100 yards out—move it!"

I glanced back and instantly regretted it.

The rainwater was exploding off the street in front of the creature and instantly freezing into huge white flakes. The damn thing looked like a locomotive punching through snow, a dark shape at the heart of a violent, white swirl.

"Incoming!" Frank said.

I'd already been looking that way, so I was able to side-step the foot-long spear of ice that whipped out of the gale without issue.

But a second spell came too quickly for Darling, and by the time she turned around to see what Frank had been warning her about, a second spear was inches away from her breastplate.

The spell connected with a visceral crunch, and the force of the impact blasted her backward and off her feet. She tumbled to a stop ahead of me, motionless.

"Frozen, stunned for 5 seconds!" Frank said. "Her Health at 76%!"

I dashed up to her, then skidded across the wet cobbles and grabbed her wrist. I twisted around and Clonedrifted both of us backward. The spell instantly cleared her stun, but she was disoriented when we popped back into place.

"Another round coming your way!" Frank said as the blizzard rolled closer and the creature loosed two more enormous icicles.

I threw up an Illusory Mirror in front of myself, then Double Cast a second in front of Darling. Both of the mirrors shattered as the spells struck them and Darling and I were showered in glass, but the panels sent both of the creature's spells flying back into the thick bands of snow that cloaked it.

I yanked Darling back to her feet as the beast howled behind us, and we managed to reach the spot where the Bleedbirds were circling: a cul-de-sac off to our left.

The ruins of a wide wooden structure were piled in the center of the space. A lone Bleedbird was perched atop a wooden beam that was jutting almost vertically out of the tangle, and the animal flew off and rejoined the others in the sky above as we approached.

We ran into the cul-de-sac, but nothing happened as we pulled up in front of the pile of debris.

Darling drew her weapon as the blizzard rolled down the street and swept toward us.

"Now what?"

"Hit it with me!" Frank said.

"Would that help?"

"It would certainly help him." I pulled my rifle out and readied a blast, though I didn't think it was about to do us any good.

The snow-cloaked creature roared toward us, close enough now that I could see its black eyes glowing through the maelstrom that surrounded it. I loosed my spell, and everything went red.

For a brief, terrible moment, I thought I'd led us astray by ducking into the cul-de-sac.

Then the world shifted and the rain started pinging off my shoulders—off the armored pauldrons that capped them once again—and Darling and

I were standing in the same street, in front of the very structure the Bleedbirds had been circling over: the gallows.

Three nooses hung from a wide crossbeam that ran over a long wooden platform, with trap doors positioned beneath each of them. Two of the same guards from earlier were hauling Brandt roughly up the wooden stairs that led up to the platform.

An ornate carriage drawn by a quartet of huge black horses rolled into view, and Brandt's eyes were firmly fixed on the vehicle.

A guard ran over and opened the carriage, and a short man draped in spotted furs hopped out. His left eye was covered with a dark patch of cloth, and three vertical scars started above the patch and finished well beneath it.

The man approached, limping slightly, while a few ornately armored guards piled out of his carriage and pulled poleaxes from where they were mounted atop the vehicle.

"The Huntsman?" Darling said.

"Gotta be."

"What do you think is going on?"

"All I know for sure is that the taxidermist was doing much more than taxidermy, and that Huntsman guy forced him to do even more." I looked around the area, noting the thirty-something guards that lined the nearest roofs, the many blue, spectral creatures that were flying high above them, and the cyan glow that was encroaching from every direction.

"You think he made the ghosts?"

"The stitched-together mobs, the ghosts, everything. Definitely."

"And that massive thing that just chased us here?"

"No clue there." I nodded at the Huntsman, who now stood before the gallows, staring up at Brandt as the guards fitted a noose around his neck. "But I think we're about to find out."

The Huntsman cleared his throat. "You best pray this ends with you, Brandt."

"Or what?" Brandt said. "I've nothing left for you to take."

"I asked you for one thing." The Huntsman held up a finger. "One. And look what you've wrought, Brandt. Look at my city!"

"I told you from the very beginning that it wouldn't work," Brandt said, eerily calm in the face of the Huntsman's outburst. "I told you that you were asking too much. You never understood the nature of my work. You couldn't be bothered, and here we are."

"Please." The Huntsman made a curt motion with one hand, and the guards stepped away from the condemned man. "Any brute with a needle can stuff a corpse."

"Then why did you need me? You have everything a man could want, but your only joy lies in looking backward."

He fixed the shorter man with his bright blue eyes. "When did your trophies stop being enough? Was the company you keep growing tired of your little stories? Were they catching on to the way that the beasts you triumphed over in your youth grew more and more fearsome with every cup of wine you drank?"

Brandt raised his voice, which carried clearly over the driving rain. "Do you lot even know what he was after? Do you want to know why he lured me out of my home, why he had me toiling away on his behalf in the depths of his palace while my wife lay in her bed, sick with fever and grief, waiting for the help he promised but never delivered?

"A little show for his friends. A parlor trick. He wanted the ghosts of the creatures he killed in his youth to prowl about his palace, to quiver whenever he showed his face." He stared at the Huntsman, blue eyes shining. "And I kept telling you, over and over again: it isn't that simple. That you were attempting to boil something incredible down—something you didn't even bother to understand—into a damn light show."

"I asked you to bring a memory back to life," the Huntsman hissed. "To give it a form—that was all. And you gave me a damned ghost! That creature killed fourteen of my men before we figured out how to put it down."

Brandt's smile was the coldest thing I'd ever seen.

"You still don't get it: memories *are* ghosts, Huntsman. And when you bring a memory to life, what you remember is very rarely what you get."

The Huntsman drew his thumb across his own throat. One of the guards threw a switch, and the trapdoor dropped out beneath Brandt.

He fell, but he managed to get his bound hands far enough around the noose to keep the fall from breaking his neck. His legs jerked beneath him, but he kept his eyes riveted on the Huntsman.

A brutally cold gust of wind ripped across the courtyard, and the driving rain abruptly gave way to snow so thick that I could barely see the carriage, let alone the guards that paced the rooftops.

Brandt's eyes rolled into the back of his head, then an explosion of cyan light ripped out of the palace, flaring out of every window at once.

"Memories can't kill," the Huntsman said, voice quavering for the first time. His eyes were locked on the palace, and he was already backpedaling toward his carriage.

Brandt began to laugh, a deep, mirthful sound that was so dissonant with the scene in front of me that it set my skin to prickling. And when he spoke again—despite the noose, despite everything—his eyes were pure black, and his voice was raw and strangled.

"See, that's where you're wrong. Let's see how long your glory keeps you warm when the snow sets in."

The Huntsman turned and ran for the carriage as a torrent of spectral creatures flew out the palace's many windows and into the sky above, throwing a pale glow above the entire structure. More creatures followed, escaping the building by smashing directly through its walls and doors.

The cobbles beneath my feet trembled, and all of the rain—every single droplet in sight—flashed into the heaviest snowstorm yet. The snow was already accumulating at a supernatural rate, piling atop the street much too quickly to be normal and forming drifts up against the buildings in the blink of an eye.

A stampede of cyan creatures rushed toward us from farther down the road that led to the palace, hundreds, maybe even thousands of fearsome ghosts packed shoulder to shoulder, and the avenue was ablaze with light.

They blitzed right by the cul-de-sac that held the gallows, though a rhino-like creature with two heads clipped the Huntsman's carriage as it passed and tossed it into the air.

The Huntsman screamed as the carriage flew directly over him and smashed into a nearby building. He waited for the stampede to clear, then took off on foot for the palace.

My quest log updated.

**New Quest: {Hope and Hate: The Beginning of the End}!**
**Objective: Escort the Huntsman back to the safety of the palace (Phase V).**
**Reward: Scales with number of Phases successfully completed. However, if any member of your party dies during this Rift, your attempt will instantly end.**

The Huntsman's guards bolted after him, rounding the corner back onto the avenue he'd run down and disappearing from sight.

Darling and I ran to join them, and I was already worrying that we'd let him get too far ahead when two guards flew out of the driving snow in front of me and landed in drifts to either side.

A triceratops that was half-solid, half-spectral stood between us and the Huntsman, spiked tail lashing back and forth over the cobbles. Another squad of guards was engaging with the creature—which seemed futile given the distance their compatriots had just been launched—but more importantly, the Huntsman was still running, and he was starting to fade into the falling snow up ahead.

I skirted the edge of the avenue to the left, and Darling fell in close behind.

"Duck!" she said.

I did, and the creature's spectral tail slammed into the space where my head had been a moment earlier. It absolutely shredded the building beside me, sending splinters of wood and metal flying as it carved a foot-wide gash into the home.

I stayed low and kept moving, watching the creature with a wary eye until we were both out of its range and back to running full blast through the street.

The snow was still falling at an impossible rate, muffling our steps and suffocating the sounds of the clamor behind us.

Up ahead, the Huntsman went down hard in a blur of gray fur and white snow, which didn't seem promising but did allow Darling and me to catch up to him.

He cried out as we approached, and we saw him cradling his ankle in the snow with both hands.

A debuff had popped up above his nameplate.

{Major Sprain}
Speed reduced by 60%

"Looks like we're done running," I said.

Darling was a bit ahead of me, and she stopped just in front of him. "Yeah, I can't heal that. But I'm tired of—"

"You two, stop babbling and get me up!" the Huntsman interrupted.

Darling gave me an annoyed glance, then we each grabbed one of the Huntsman's arms and hauled him to his feet a bit more roughly than we needed to.

He tried to put weight on his injured ankle but it turned beneath him, and he collapsed right back into the snow despite our attempts to hold him up.

We got him back on his feet again, and he put his arms around our shoulders and promptly let us take his entire weight without making any discernable effort of his own.

"Move it!"

"A little help would be nice," I said.

"Yeah, you've got one good ankle," Darling said. "Might wanna use it if you don't like the idea of ending up as food for ghosts."

After a fair bit of indignant grimacing, that got him hopping along, and we started making some actual progress, though the palace felt like it was miles off at the rate we were going. And it wasn't long before a blue glow crept over the buildings to my left.

A spectral gorilla launched itself off the roof and grabbed onto a nearby flagpole. Its momentum sent it spinning fully around the pole before it came to a stop, then it hung there while glaring down at us.

I inspected it.

{Spectral Bandcaller} (Level 15 Undead) (Elite+)
HP: 9100/9100
MP: 5000/5000

"Let's just keep moving," I said. "Maybe it'll let us pass."

We made it another ten feet, then the gorilla let go of the pole and slammed onto the ground on all fours, snow billowing around it. It rose to its full height, then raised its arms to either side and took a deep breath.

I slipped out from beneath the Huntsman's arm and whipped my swords free. I crossed the distance between us in a rush and hit the mob with a flurry of strikes that all hit in the low 2,000s, but I wasn't quick enough to keep it from screaming and pounding its chest.

The gorilla hit the ground hard on its back. I stood there in the eerily quiet street, ear cocked to the side, fat snowflakes drifting down all around me.

"Nice!" Darling said.

"Nah, I think I screwed up. Wasn't fast enough."

"What do you mean?"

I sheathed my weapons, then rushed back over and helped her with the Huntsman. "Spectral Bandcaller. A group of gorillas is a band."

"Which is a missed opportunity in and of itself," Frank said. "Just imagine: run, a gaggle of gorillas is approaching! It sounds so ridiculous that it lulls you into a false sense of security, then *blam*! Hairy fist to the solar plexus. Or a gang of gorillas. That would be much more intimidating. Band makes them sound like musicians."

I took a bit more of the Huntsman's weight and tried to push the pace a little.

"Nah, a gaggle refers to geese, and a gang would be turkeys or elk. But if the geese are in flight it'd be a skein. If you're talking apes in general though, it can also be a shrewdness."

Darling, the Huntsman, and even Frank all stared at me as we hustled the wounded man beneath a stone archway and into a tunnel that had been hewn through the rock, and the palace, squatting on top of its hill, was visible through the far end.

The tunnel had a pretty steep incline to it, and rain and melting snow were rushing down from the other side, but at least it was clear of obstacles.

Nobody spoke as we shuffled along, so I broke the silence before it could linger.

"Monkeys could also be a barrel."

"Huh," Frank said. "Now this is the kind of niche interest I can get behind."

"It's a good one." I paused, and my sudden stop made the Huntsman groan. "Darling, you hear that?"

She cocked her head sideways, dark hair falling across one shoulder. "Yeah. Hooting."

I peered down the tunnel, but I couldn't see anything beyond the falling snow. The passage seemed to fork left up at about the midway point, so I pulled the others that way and scoped it out.

The side passage looked deep, but an iron gate stood about ten feet in, blocking our path and turning the segment into a dead end.

"Seems like a good place to make a stand. That hooting is only getting closer, and I'd rather not try to fight them off out in the open again."

I slipped out from beneath the Huntsman and took up a position at the front of the alcove. "This passage is narrow enough that we should be able to pull them in one at a time, two at most. Maybe we'll even get lucky and they'll pass right by us."

Darling carried the Huntsman as far into the alcove as our Heartlink would permit, then dumped him unceremoniously onto the ground.

"Ouch," I said.

She shrugged. "I don't remember anything in the quest log that said that we had to be nice to him."

"Alright, this is urgent," Frank said.

"Yeah? What's up?" I said.

"I need to know what a group of cats is called."

Darling drew her staff. "Seriously?"

The hooting was close now, though the tunnel wasn't echoing with the calls just yet.

"Might be a good way to get back into House's good graces."

"Oh, did you recently wrong her too?" Darling said.

"Pretty much, yeah. But in my defense, I wasn't expecting to experience any consequences."

"That is not a defense," I said. "And the word you're looking for is clowder. Or a clutter. And if they're feral, it'd be called a destruction."

"A destruction of cats?" Frank said. "That is awesome."

"Why do you know this stuff?" Darling said.

I shrugged. "Because the internet exists and I'm easily distracted?"

She pushed a few stray locks of wet, dark hair out of her face. "But how long did you spend memorizing all these?"

I poked my head out of the passage. There was still nothing to either side, but the sound had drawn closer still. "More time than I'm willing to admit."

"Emu?" Frank said.

"Mob."

"Lemur?"

"Conspiracy."

"A conspiracy of lemurs?" Darling said as the first hoot echoed down the tunnel. "Now you're just making them up."

"No, I can see it," Frank said. "Suspicious, big-eyed little bastards. Real talk: lemurs have seen some shit." He paused. "Hippo."

"Bloat."

Darling edged around me and poked her head out the alcove.

"Can you see anything?" I said.

"Nothing in the tunnel, but they're definitely close. I think they might be searching the space outside for us 'cause the snow out there is weirdly bright. Maybe we did manage to dodge them."

"Hope so."

"What about a group of me?" Frank said.

"A… flurry of Franks?"

"A flurry of Franks," he whispered. "Yeah, I like it. The alliteration is spot on, and flurry sounds appropriately aggressive while also maintaining the level of elegance I'm known for."

"Yeah, because when I think Frank, elegance is definitely one of the first words to come to mind."

"Imagine. Heads up—a flurry of Franks is heading our way."

"I do find that to be a pretty terrifying thought, but probably not in the way you're hoping."

"So long as I'm provoking terror, I'll take what I can get."

Darling peered around the corner again, then drew back sharply and put a finger to her lips. "Two of them creeping our way side by side. Much bigger than the first." She edged back behind me, so I readied both of my swords and waited.

"Call for the stun if you need it," she said. "Otherwise I'll hold onto it in case we get overwhelmed or one gets past you."

"Don't forget that you've got a shield you can use too," Frank said.

I nodded in response and pressed myself against the wall in the direction they were approaching from.

The tunnel brightened by degrees until the sides of the passage were thrown into sharp relief. One huge, ghostly hand slapped the stone floor directly in front of me, and a second followed.

A hulking spectral creature strode into view, and though it was on all fours, it still stood head and shoulders above me.

I inspected it.

{Spectral Patriarch} (Level 15 Undead) (Elite+)
HP: 12,000/12,000
MP: 5,000/5,000

I held my breath as the creature rumbled by, snorting and sniffing the air. I relaxed slightly as it passed beyond the alcove and into the other side of the tunnel, but it was quickly followed by a second creature of the same type that was even higher level at 16.

The second mob got three-quarters of the way past the alcove, then the Huntsman shifted behind us, and the armor he wore beneath his fur scraped against the ground. He must have noticed and froze because the sound cut off at once, but the beast's head was already swiveling in our direction.

I pushed off the wall and laid into the Patriarch with both weapons, bringing them down vertically across the mob's broad back again and again.

My swords bit deep and quickly knocked the creature below 50%. I braced myself for what I thought was a counterpunch, but the mob spun and slammed its knuckles into the ground, then swung into a dropkick that caught me fully in the chest.

The blow hit me so hard that I flew right by Darling and over the prone Huntsman and smashed into the iron gate. My armor took the brunt of the impact, though, and Darling was quick to reposition to preserve our link.

"Your Health at 75%, mob at 45%."

I rushed back out to meet the spectral ghost, ducked a vicious hook that nearly took my head off, and slashed high with one sword and low with the other.

The mob shrieked, then dropped to the floor. The second Patriarch raced over from the other end of the tunnel and started swinging so quickly and aggressively that I was forced into a rapid backpedal.

I was fine with the retreat—I needed to reposition anyway—but three or four gorillas had flooded into the tunnel from each side well before I could take up a defensive position.

I mentally dropped my offhand sword into its sheath and summoned the shield that was still hanging against my back, raising it up just in time to catch a huge fist dead-center. The metal shield rang like a gong beneath the blow, and the sound reverberated up and down the passage.

And if the first gorilla's dying cries hadn't drawn the attention of the entire group, then that sound definitely had.

I was ready for the next punch: I stepped right and deflected it left, then plunged my weapon into the off-balance creature. I kicked out with one booted foot and staggered it, though I lacked the strength to send the creature flying.

And as quickly as I'd pushed the creature away, another charged in to fill the gap.

It launched itself when it was still some five feet out, hands raised high in a hammer blow.

I raised my shield and braced myself for impact, but the powerful attack knocked me down onto one knee regardless.

"Your Health back to 70%," Frank said as one of Darling's heals hit home.

I got back to my feet and promptly caught a jab full in the face. The damage was light, but my head snapped back and my vision swam for a moment.

"Haymaker!"

I was still reeling, so I brought my shield up in front of my face. The metal rang again as I managed a block, but I staggered sideways into the wall.

I cursed as two bright shapes blurred through the gap I'd left behind. But before I could act, a third slammed into me and pinned my sword above my head.

"Popping!" Darling said. Golden light ripped out the alcove and down the tunnel, freezing every ghost in sight. But because of the angle involved, Darling's attack had been limited to the mobs directly in front of us, and the tunnel was still loud with grunts and shouts.

I brought the hilt of my sword down between the eyes of the gorilla that had pinned me against the wall and dispatched him with four quick slashes that sent novas of light ripping across the gathered creatures.

I was tempted to throw myself at the crowd and do as much damage as possible, but I needed to clear out the gorillas that had rushed by me first, so I ducked deeper into the alcove, switched back to dual swords, then laid into their stunned forms from behind.

"As much as I enjoy watching you get rocked in the face," Frank said, "you really ought to avoid that."

"Any suggestions that might actually help?"

"Float like a butterfly, sting like a dude who's holding three feet of sharpened metal."

I switched back to my shield and got into position at the mouth of the alcove. I managed a few quick thrusts against the nearest creatures to proc a few more novas and splash damage against the group, but I couldn't risk overextending without our cooldowns.

"Maybe twenty left out there," I said. "If we can last until your next stun and get you into the center of the group, we might be able to blow all the gorillas at once."

"I'm liking where your head's at," Frank said, "but I'm not loving your choice of words."

"Huh?"

"Stun's off!" Darling said.

I set my feet wide and hunkered down with my shield raised high as the stunned mobs who had been blocking the others from entering the alcove roared back to life.

I met the first mob with my shield and focused on holding my ground. I still got knocked back and the counter I managed was weaker than it could have been, but I held the gap well enough.

I traded blows with the creature in the narrow confines of the alcove, eating punches to the chest and stomach and shoulders in rapid succession while blocking the more powerful strikes and either ducking or ceding ground if I needed to reposition.

I worked the ghost down gradually, and though I got the worst of the exchange by far, Darling kept me alive easily enough, and I was starting to feel a good bit more comfortable as the mob slid to the floor and dissipated.

And by the time the next mob fell—and especially the one after that—I'd managed to reclaim a little bit of the ground I'd given up.

"Darling's Mana still at 70%," Frank said.

I allowed myself a bit of a grin. "We got this."

A gorilla came charging into the alcove, but instead of going for me, it ran up the wall and tried to leap right over me.

I caught it full in the face with a raised shield, and though I hadn't managed to put much strength behind the blow, I succeeded in pinning it against the wall, then I dropped it right down on top of another mob that had tried to rush in behind it.

The two of them went down in a tangle of limbs, so I rained a few steel-toed kicks down on them to drive them away while I kept my shield and sword up for protection.

"Yeah!" Frank said. "Kick 'em when they're down! There's no better time!"

I caught one of the downed mobs in the ribcage while it tried to rise and it collapsed right back to the floor, then I swung at another incoming mob and forced it back out of the alcove.

"Stun's ready when you are!" Darling said.

I mentally dropped my sword into its sheath and braced my shield against my shoulder with both hands. "Let's end it!"

I put on a burst of speed and rushed the spectral army. I ducked beneath a blow that would have otherwise clotheslined me and came up hard with my shield, driving into the ghostly beast and forcing it backward.

I pushed it a few feet into the crowd before it regained its footing, then

I activated Concentrated Ire to make sure Darling didn't take any damage while she followed behind me and got into position.

I ducked and brought my shield up over my head, and the blows came hard and heavy, filling the tunnel with a rhythmless drumbeat.

My Health was tanking beneath the assault, but I knew Darling's stun couldn't be far off.

"Popping!" she said.

The stun rippled over every single mob, and they froze all around me, many of them locking up mid-strike. I dismissed my shield and summoned both swords and stood up, already lashing out all around me.

I kept the attacks coming, focusing on reach rather than power, tagging as many mobs as possible with every swing. Within the space of a single breath, I managed to annihilate the mobs that were standing closest to the alcove, so I pushed the attack with a spinning, backhanded slash and ripped into the rest of them.

When the stun faded, only three mobs remained on their feet, and each of them was so badly wounded that putting them down was a trivial matter with Darling's healing at my back.

As soon as the last mob dropped, I let my swords slip to the ground and put my hands on my knees. I wasn't exactly out of breath, but the adrenaline had left me winded all the same.

"So?" Frank said.

"So what?"

"Whaddaya think?"

I looked back at the many bodies that were carpeting the tunnel, then scooped up my swords and sheathed them both. "Yep, that was awesome. Loved every minute of it."

Darling knelt down and looted a few of the mobs near the alcove. "I bet you did. Looked like a whole lot of fun, Frank. Double swords, explosions, shield bashes."

I paused. "Well, getting throat-punched into a wall wasn't exactly ideal."

"And I bet the healing was satisfying in its own way," Frank added.

"Nope," she said, already heading for the loot. "Not at all."

He shrugged. "It was worth a shot."

I dropped my voice. "You worried about this? I do think she's kidding, but maybe not completely."

"It's fine, she's well past the point of no return."

"What?"

"See, loving Frank is like getting too close to the sun. First it burns—like, it really, really burns—"

"Can you hear yourself right now?"

"—but then the initial burning sensation fades to a warm glow, and by that point, even if you wanted to escape, the pull of gravity is so strong and relentless that resistance is futile."

I paused. "Gotta say man, I really don't love the turn that took at the end."

"Yeah, that didn't come out nearly as romantic as I expected it to."

"If you were going for a Stockholm Syndrome sorta thing, then you definitely nailed it, but comparing your love to a giant ball of fire that's gonna sit there and seethe until it explodes and kills everything around it is probably not a good move." I hesitated. "But now that I've had a moment to think about it, the accuracy is on point."

"Regardless, I'm confident that Frarling will survive this early test of our union. Especially when she sees what I've got in store for her at the end of this Rift."

"Unless it's revenge you're thinking of, then maybe consider putting that another way. Even if it's just in your head."

"Some really good stuff over here," Darling said. "Large Soul Gems left and right and... ooooooh. Oh, I like this. I like this a lot."

"Is it what I think it is?" Frank said.

"Here." She linked me an item, so I scoped it out.

**Recipe: {Rune of the Terrible Hex} (Consumable) (Awards 5 skill points per craft)**
**Activating your Hexdoll Aura now causes all enemies within 8 yards to tremble in fear for 5 seconds. Damage taken may break this effect.**
**Duration: 24 Hours.**
**Requirements: {Large Soul Gem} x10.**

"Yep," Frank said. "Just as I planned from the very beginning. I figured that since Darling and I are essentially the same person, she too would rejoice at the sight of her enemies cowering at her feet."

"And you were correct!" Darling said.

"Side note," Frank said, whispering again. "We need to figure out who Darling's enemies are so I can Frank them out of existence. Don't worry, I'll be super subtle about it."

"No you won't," I said, "but noted. Did you actually plan for that drop?"

"Nope, that was just a random drop. I had no idea that was going to happen."

"Nice."

"Can you make me one of those runes for Hexdoll?" Darling said. "I'll probably wait until this Rift is done, but that rune is amazing. I can throw you all the gems I have."

I checked my inventory. "Yeah, sure thing. You can hold on to your gems though. Your recipe is pretty cheap, it'll skill me up, and I've got enough gems to—"

I cut off with a sigh as she slammed the recipe and a nice stockpile of Soul Gems as well as Large Soul Gems into the trade window and immediately confirmed it.

She smiled and held out a hand, palm-up.

"Alright, alright. Thanks again." I crafted one up for her.

**Your skill in Soulsmithing has increased to 95!**

I didn't unlock a new recipe, but I did have enough gems to make a Rune of Fortified Illusions for 5 skill points, down from the 6 it had promised initially, so I went ahead and made one of those for later.

**Your Skill in Soulsmithing has increased to 100!**

And at reaching 100 skill, I unlocked a brand-new rune for myself.

**Recipe: {Rune of the Gathering Flock} (Consumable) (Awards 5 skill points per craft)**
**Critical Strikes caused by your Ravenblasts cause you to summon a Circling Raven that will follow you around and expire after 4 seconds. This duration is refreshed upon causing another Critical Strike. Upon gathering 4 Circling Ravens, your next Ravenblast becomes instant regardless of the weapon you have equipped.**
**Duration: 24 Hours.**
**Requirements: {Large Soul Gem} x25.**

That was one of the most interesting runes I'd seen so far, but between the 8-second window and the fact that it was basically all or nothing on the proc, I didn't think I had a high enough Critical Strike rate to fully utilize it yet.

Still, the idea of ripping off a bunch of quick ravens with my pistols then swapping to my rifle for a powerful, instant blast was pretty incredible.

I opened up another trade window with Darling and tossed her the rune I'd made for her.

"Thanks!" she said, grinning. "Congratulations, Frank. You've successfully atoned for all the healer nonsense."

"You think that was an atonement?" he said. "Just wait until you see what I have in store for you next."

Darling cocked an eyebrow at him. "That sounds like you're planning a kidnapping."

"I just told you to rephrase that," I said.

"Yeah, I'm aware, but I thought you were trying to manipulate me into zigging when I should have zagged."

I laughed. "You really are out here playing four-dimensional chess with yourself, huh?"

"That does seem to be the case. And perhaps unsurprisingly, I'm proving to be a wily and unpredictable opponent. That said, I should have expected as much coming from me."

"So... what exactly is in store for me? I'm trying to figure out if I should be concerned or not." She glanced at Frank. "I guess it's more a question of how much I should be concerned."

"It's a present," Frank said.

"It's a lookalike version of Frank that he taxidermied out of a bunch of dead animals you killed in his presence," I said. "That way, you can carry it around forever and presumably have jerky at some point."

"Gross!" Darling said. "That is positively vile!"

I dropped my voice. "See? I told you that was a terrible idea."

He grunted. "You could have sold it a hell of a lot better, but fine, I take your point."

# Chapter Twenty-Five

The Huntsman finally recovered himself, then staggered out of the alcove and leaned up against the wall for support. He pointed a shaking finger down the tunnel.

"We're not far off now. Just a little further..." He took a faltering step toward Darling, but his wounded ankle immediately gave out on him.

She was well within reach of catching him, but she stepped away slightly instead.

I snorted a laugh and helped him up, and she grabbed his other arm before we started back up the tunnel through the many corpses we'd made of the gorillas.

The wind howled as we approached the end of the passage, where several feet of snow had drifted in and built up against the walls.

We plunged into the storm with the Huntsman in tow, the palace now little more than a dark shape in the gale. The visibility was terrible—far worse than it had been before—and I couldn't even see the buildings that lined the avenue.

We staggered on through the wind-blown snow, which reached anywhere from my ankles to my knees depending on how the gale had piled it.

A creature hooted nearby, a pocket of snow brightening maybe ten feet to Darling's left. Her eyes were fixed on the ground in front of her, so I grabbed her wrist behind the Huntsman and yanked all three of us down into a deep drift.

I covered his mouth with my hand and muffled the howl of indignation that I'd expected.

Darling turned to look at me but froze when the glow I'd seen earlier pathed mere feet away from us. I could just make out the Spectral Band-caller's body as it plodded along on all fours, sweeping its head from side to side.

I went deathly still as it glanced directly at us. Its gaze lingered for a moment and I held my breath, expecting it to sound the alarm and bring another group down on top of us. Then the beast looked left, prowled away, and took its glow with it.

"Keep your mouth shut," I said, and I waited for the Huntsman to nod before I removed my hand from over his mouth.

"Nice spot," Darling said. "We'd be as good as dead if we got rushed out in the open."

I levered the Huntsman to his feet. "Yeah, lucky catch. Wasn't even looking for them."

"Maybe we could double back to the tunnel if we draw another group?"

I looked behind me, then immediately doubted my sense of direction—I wasn't even sure which direction we were facing after I'd pulled us down. "You have any idea where the tunnel is at this point? Or the palace?"

Darling pointed way to the left of where I thought the passage had been. "I was thinking that was the tunnel and the palace was across from it."

We both looked at the Huntsman, whose thick eyebrows were caked with snow. And he proceeded to just sit there and shiver.

I crept forward a little while staying low to the ground and found the footprints the gorilla had left behind. I pointed in the direction it had gone.

"He went that way, and he was coming directly across our path when I spotted him, so..." I pointed across the prints. "This way?"

"Let's try it," Darling said. "Don't look now, but apparently this guy's furs are purely decorative because he just picked up a debuff."

I scoped it out.

{Arcane Frostbite}

275

**Losing 1% of max Health every 1 second. Healing the Huntsman will aggravate this effect.**

"Gives us less than two minutes," she said.

I rushed over and helped her lift him back to his feet. His furs were totally soaked through from the rain, his lips were blue, and his skin was waxy to the touch.

"Great. He's gonna be even less helpful," I said.

Another pocket of snow brightened to my right. "Let's move before that mob paths back. Don't know how tight the timing's going to be."

Darling nodded, and we hauled the Huntsman along as quickly as we could, all of us stumbling and tripping and faceplanting into the snow on more than one occasion.

Between the white sky and the white snow and the total lack of anything to divide the two, I found it increasingly difficult to even tell which way was up, and it seemed like the vertigo was getting to Darling as well, given the awkwardness of her gait.

The Huntsman was at about half Health before we had to pull back and wait for another patrol to pass, and it was agony watching his Health tick down with every passing second.

We rushed ahead as it dropped under 30%, still with no idea of just how far we had to go or if we were even heading in the right direction.

And as the seconds passed and his Health crept lower and lower, things began looking increasingly bleak. To make matters worse, two glowing pockets of snow were converging up ahead, and we simply didn't have the time to wait and watch them pass by.

I looked at Darling, who simply nodded and drew her staff.

I let go of the Huntsman, then grabbed both of his legs and threw him over my shoulder. I stumbled and almost faceplanted immediately, then Darling took the lead and called out the snowdrifts in front of me.

"Huntsman's Health at 20%," Frank said. "Tick, tock."

I eyed the approaching glowing pockets and the Bandcallers within. "Need to shoot the gap!"

"Not gonna make it!" Darling said, but she picked up the pace regardless. She gasped and went down in a puff of snow. I cursed but kept running, darting past her into the narrow space between the two glowing mobs.

I plowed through a series of ribby drifts, the Huntsman bouncing against my shoulder each time. I got between the two creatures, and I actually started to believe that I'd beaten the odds and made it safely through.

Then the sound of hooting started from my left and was immediately echoed on my right.

Darling reappeared out of the snow and ran right by me. With nothing else to do, I charged in behind her and hoped for the best as the Huntsman's Health ticked into the single digits.

I could hear the mobs in pursuit, their motion muffled by the snow, their hoots and grunts ringing from every direction except in front of us.

I took that as a positive sign, but I was starting to lose hope until a dark shape appeared in front of me. It was an archway.

"Open the gate!" I called out. "We've got the Huntsman!"

Shouting sounded from up ahead, followed by the scraping of steel against stone.

A flare of golden light pulsed out from Darling, and a gorilla that I hadn't noticed crashed into the snow directly to my left. It'd been stunned mid-leap, one hand raised high above its head.

Darling skidded to a stop and whipped her staff into her hands. "Go! I'll try to buy you a bit of time!"

I plunged on into the swirling gale, heading for that dark archway and hoping for the best.

I heard a sharp impact behind me, then Darling's Health dropped from full to 70% and kept falling from there.

The archway darkened and resolved with every step I took, but the Huntsman was nearly dead. The lowest part was darker than the rest, and I realized in a rush that that was because the gate hadn't had enough time to fully open but there was a gap at the bottom.

I eyed his Health, skidded to a stop a couple of feet out, then chucked the Huntsman with every bit of the considerable strength my borrowed body had.

"Ohhh!" Frank said as the man's body bounced through the snow and across the stone. He rolled to a stop a few feet beyond the gate, moaning loudly.

The world seemed to hang for a moment, then a prompt came through.

**Congratulations, you successfully completed all five Phases of a Memory-stained Rift Quest: {Hope and Hate: The Beginning of the End}!**

Calibrating rewards...

A bolt of red lightning ripped down out of the sky and returned Darling and me to the half-flooded ruins we'd first arrived in, where a red exit portal was spinning behind us.

I pulled up the rest of my prompts.

**You gained 5,950 Experience!**
**You gained 880 Renown!**
**You received {Memory-stained Rift Gem} x50!**
**You received {Rift Gem} x40!**
**You received {Rusty's Collar}!**
**You received {Ghosthunter's Gauntlets}**
**You received {Double-barreled Aeroblaster} (Fated Weaponry)**
**Tier I Trinket Unseal is now available!**
**This Rift will close in ten minutes.**

I scoped out the pieces of gear I'd been awarded.

**{Rusty's Collar}**
**Grade: D**
**Item Level: 33**
**Slot: Necklace**
**Quality: Uncommon**
**Primaries: +7 Intelligence, +4 Constitution, +9 Dexterity**
**Secondaries: +3% Haste**
**Magical Resistance: +20%**

The necklace was a major upgrade, so I equipped it right away, then poked through the next two finds, starting with the gloves.

**{Ghosthunter's Gauntlets}**
**Grade: D**
**Item Level: 44**
**Slot: Hands**
**Type: Leather**
**Quality: Rare**
**Suggested Class: Shadewalker**
**Primaries: +18 Intelligence, +10 Constitution**

Secondaries: +3% Haste
Armor: +6%
Set Effect (2-piece): Active. While dual-wielding Enchanted Pistols, your Ravenblast is instant, and any pistol blast fired while out of combat is automatically Overcharged.
Set Effect (4-piece): Sealed. Equip 3 pieces of the {Ghosthunter} set to reveal this effect and 4 to activate it.
Set Effect (6-piece): Sealed. Equip 5 pieces of the {Ghosthunter} set to reveal this effect and 6 to activate it.

I eyed the gloves, grinning, then threw them on to activate the set's 2-piece bonus and pointed both of my pistols up at the sky. I activated Ravenblast and instantly sent two ravens flying at the moon.

"Your range is currently 40 yards," Frank said, "so you need another 420 million to make contact, give or take, depending on the day. Still, 5 Frank points for the sentiment."

I glanced down at him. "I'm impressed you actually bothered to note the math."

"A necessary evil when it comes to targeting the moon. You checked out your Trinket yet?"

"Ohh!" I pulled it up.

Tier I Unseal is now available.
Proceed?

I confirmed the prompt, and my Trinket gained a new passive ability.

{Pistoleer's Fury}
While dual-wielding enchanted pistols, your Ravenblast no longer deals 50% reduced damage, and it has a 5% increased Chance to Critically Strike. However, its cast time is increased by 40%.

I scratched my temple. I loved the idea of getting rid of the damage penalty from dual-wielding, but if my damage went up by half and the cast time got 40% longer to compensate, then the change didn't represent a massive gain.

It was still a sizable upgrade thanks to the added Critical Strike chance, but it wasn't anywhere near as exciting as the Tier II unseal had been. But maybe that meant the Tier III would be even better?

I shrugged and was about to move on to the blunderbuss I'd found when the realization hit me.

"Oh man, hold on a second. If Ravenblast is an instant cast, then half of zero is still zero, right?"

"Uh huh."

"So do I have this right, then? With that Trinket enhancement, I deal 50% more damage with my pistols, and since the 2-piece is giving me instant ravens when pistols are equipped..."

I fired another raven off at the moon, grinning like a fool when it instantly leaped from the barrel.

"The longer cast time doesn't matter at all because the combination completely nullifies the downside. They're still instant—they just hit harder."

"Yup," Frank said.

"Amazing! Absolutely amazing. Let's see what else we got here."

I pulled up the blunderbuss, and despite the previous upgrades, I was totally blown away.

{Double-barreled Aeroblaster} (Two-handed Enchanted Blunder-buss) (Fated Weaponry)
Grade: D
Item Level: 45
Damage Type: Magical
Quality: Rare
Physical Attack: 0
Magical Attack: 103
Speed: N/A
Primaries: +10 Intelligence, +10 Constitution
Equip: This weapon may store an additional Ravenblast, and its Ravenblasts naturally strike all enemies in a narrow cone. However, its maximum range is reduced to 2.5 yards (down from 5).
Fated Ability: Whenever a Ravenblast fired from this weapon strikes a target that is currently under the effect of being knocked away by Repel, that Ravenblast is guaranteed to Critically Strike.

"Fated Weaponry," I said, and the words came out breathy.

"Means it comes with an ability that's specifically designed to be used with your existing spells and abilities," Frank said. "So you could knock something into the air with me, then blast a big old bird into it with that shotty. Or just hit whatever it is with me again and again and again, your call. Probably a coin flip there."

I drew Frank, swung him in a quick uppercut, then swapped to my new blunderbuss with the weapon already pointing up into the air as if I had a target in mind.

The weapon was longer and sleeker than my previous weapon, with two bluish barrels and a pearly-white stock.

I grinned. There was no way that we'd simply happened across a gun that incentivized the use of Repel.

"What?" Frank said.

"Nothing. Love the gun, super cool." I glanced over at Darling, whose sword had been replaced yet again, this time by a giant, double-bladed axe.

She lifted it into the air and gave it a mighty, horizontal swing. But for whatever reason, she didn't look totally sold. "Stats are a bit weaker than my current sword, but I love the look."

"You catch the Touchstone Ability?" Frank said. "Needs to be activated, but it's got 100% uptime afterward."

Her eyes went wide. "How do I keep missing these!" She tapped at the air for a moment, then let out a gleeful scream. "No. Way!"

"Yes way," Frank said.

Darling activated an ability, and a new buff appeared beside her nameplate.

{Offensively Minded}
You may dual-wield two two-handed weapons at once, but all damage you take is increased by 10%.

The sword Darling had been using earlier reappeared in her right hand, gripped as if it were nothing more than a longsword. She rolled her wrists and spun the weapons through the air. "Oh yeah. I can definitely work with this."

"I see your desire for two swords, and I raise you two giant weapons at once. Twice the steel, twice the pain." Frank paused. "Not exactly twice the pain because there are Hit Rating Penalties and Offhand Damage Penalties, but still: a considerable increase in pain."

Darling looked down to see her heavy leg plates were now cut off at the ankles, revealing her bare feet.

"You can only equip two Touchstone pieces at a time. Looks like equipping the axe automatically unequipped your boots."

She pursed her lips. "This isn't a foot thing that you carefully put together, right?"

"Nah, you got the wrong AI on that one. That said, while I would vastly prefer a set of heavy shin guards or greaves, I will admit to enjoying a nice tall sock from time to time."

"Like knee-highs?" I said. "If so, then I'm actually with you on that. Not completely sure why, but yeah."

"Knee-high, thigh-high... the higher, the better," Frank said. "You could yank those things up over the back of your head and I'd still be all about it."

I paused, thinking. "Do you just not like exposed skin?"

"Eh. Skin has its uses, but from my point of view, most people are better off without it."

I scratched the back of my head. "So is it like the more clothes, the more mystery, or what?"

"Huh? I don't follow. Where is the mystery supposed to come into play?"

I cocked my head down at him.

"Ohhkay," Darling said. "I officially wish I hadn't started that." She held the axe up. "So you knew this was going to drop too? This is what you were planning?"

"Uh huh. Loot table only had one option for that drop after accounting for your class and level. Not the strongest unnecessarily large axe in the world, but it's a start."

"When it comes to axes, the bigger, the better as far as I'm concerned."

"Crap," Frank whispered, which made me laugh.

"What?"

"Nothing," I said. "Just make sure you don't accidentally critique the length of his shaft."

She raised a dark eyebrow. "Why on earth would I do that?"

"Great question," Frank said. "Anyway, that axe on its own isn't that strong. But I was thinking from here we could push a few quicker Rifts and power you to 15, then get your first Trinket up and running.

"Then you could break that axe down and slam it into your Trinket's Touchstone Socket to store the ability, then equip the two strongest weapons you could find. That would let you keep the boots and whatever else you're using."

"Any gearing limitations?" she said. "You mentioned penalties."

"Hit Rating just became a lot more valuable to you. It'll be your best stat until you've got a good amount."

"How much do I need to cap out for raids?"

"20%. Up from 5%."

"Ouch."

"Yeah, capping probably isn't realistic. But thankfully you just got a second piece of your 6-piece set because that was guaranteed, and your 2-piece bonus naturally gives you a ton of Hit Rating, right?"

She beamed. "Yeah it does!"

I felt him tilt his chin up, or something like that. "It's almost like some wise individual with a magnificent beard planned this out from the very beginning."

She smiled, the gap in her teeth as prominent as ever as she replaced her boots with another pair, then crossed her weapons over her back.

"This is seriously awesome."

"I'm glad you like it. That goes a long way toward helping me cope with the happiness that I've inadvertently brought Ned."

I pressed my new gun to my shoulder and aimed it around. "I am extraordinarily pleased with this."

"You don't need to rub it in."

"So, where to now?" Darling said. "Another Rift?"

"I think so," I said, "but let me ping House real quick."

I sent her a quick message and asked for an ETA on when she thought the first prisms would be hitting Goon's city. Her estimate came in at a bit under 5 hours, which wasn't surprising given just how far outside the city the first Rift we'd chosen had been.

"We could squeeze a bunch more in for sure," I said. "Get you to 15 for the Trinket and the class change, but other than that, I figure we probably push Rifts super hard in this initial window, then maybe ease up a bit and see what else is out there. Big world, right?"

"How would you feel about attempting the first boss of the Menagerie Wing later today?"

I grinned.

"What?" she said, already sounding a little guilty.

"Sorta the opposite of seeing what else is out there, isn't it?"

"Well, yeah. Technically. But in my defense, the Red Cathedral is out there."

"It's out there in several places simultaneously, in fact," Frank added.

"Thank you!" Darling said. "That's what I'm saying!"

"Later today sounds good," I said, laughing. "We'll probably have ripped through identifying all of the curses at that point and we'll have tons of gems in hand, so it's probably a good idea to push in a bit and see how much resistance we're up against, especially now that other people are making real progress. Have there been any updates from the trash clearers? Anything on how we actually break the curses?"

"Lemme check real quick." She tapped the air. "Nada on actually breaking them, but we do have the first one revealed. Here."

{Stitcher's Curse}
Effect: All Healing received is decreased by 20%.
Duration: Permanent

"Ouch," I said. "Having that on everybody is gonna be rough, especially for the tanks."

"We found a couple charms, though," she continued. "I'll link one."

{Stitcher's Charm} (Touchstone)
Grade: D
Item Level: 40
Slot: Necklace
Quality: Uncommon
Primaries: +3 Constitution
Magical Resistance: +2%
Touchstone Ability: Grants immunity to the effects of {Stitcher's Curse}.

"Ohhhh. Wow. That's an interesting one. Stats are absolute garbage."

She nodded. "They're pretty rare, too. First one dropped when we started this Rift. No idea if that's just randomness at work or if they're zoned somehow within the instance. I do think the groups are getting pretty close to the first boss, though. There's quite a bit of trash overall. Guess there are a couple different routes you can explore."

"I assume you haven't seen anything for the other curses?" I said.

She shook her head. "Nada, but I think we'll have some more unlocked pretty soon."

"Well, the Trinket could work here too if we can kit everybody out—maybe we have people break the charms and store the immunity abilities there. That would dodge having to equip the necklace itself."

"But would also prevent people from using another Touchstone ability in its place."

"Yeah. Makes me wonder if we're even supposed to break all of the curses. The whole thing with the Possibility King is all about choice, right? So maybe we're supposed to identify the curses, then decide which we can live with. Maybe we equip the tanks to dodge one completely and the healers to dodge another, that sort of thing."

"So later today for the raid?" Darling said.

"Sure, I'm in. If we're Rifting from here on out until the prisms hit, I could probably use a bit of a breather between that and the raid itself. You guys could always start without me though, if it comes down to it."

She rolled her eyes.

"What?"

"We'll aim for early evening then. And maybe if we down the first boss and it goes well, then maybe..." She trailed off, grinning broadly. "Anyway! Back to the Hall?"

"Sure thing."

# Chapter Twenty-Six

Darling and I spent the next couple of hours grinding Rift after Rift, mostly with Rock, Nina, and Zoe, and occasionally House, though at the moment I was alone in the Hall with Frank, trying to plan out our next move.

We'd picked up quite a few goodies, though Darling had consistently gotten the better end of the deal. I was pretty sure that Frank had had a hand in that, but I didn't mind, given how much each piece of gear seemed to mean to her.

In another totally believable coincidence, she'd picked up another oversized axe, plus she now had three of the six pieces she needed to complete her set.

The set pieces in particular seemed to have drastically increased in rarity: we'd gone from snagging one per Rift to each seeing a single new piece over a half-dozen instances, with a few duplicates thrown in for good measure.

Still, I felt great about the third piece I'd found, and I was pumped to have revealed the next set effect, even if it wouldn't be active until I equipped a fourth piece.

{Ghosthunter's Leggings}
Grade: D
Item Level: 47

Slot: Legs
Type: Leather
Quality: Rare
Suggested Class: Shadewalker
Primaries: +15 Intelligence, +10 Dexterity, +8 Constitution
Secondaries: +3% Chance to Critically Strike
Armor: +7%
Set Effect (2-piece): Active. While dual-wielding Enchanted Pistols, your Ravenblast is instant, and any pistol blast fired while out of combat is automatically Overcharged.
Set Effect (4-piece): Sealed. Ravenblasts fired from your rifle now spawn a burst of miniature ravens that scatter from each struck enemy and deal 20% of the initial blast's damage to all enemies within 5 yards.
Set Effect (6-piece): Sealed. Equip 5 pieces of the {Ghosthunter} set to reveal this effect and 6 to activate it.

That cleave effect was going to be absolutely killer for big groups. And combined with a piercing rune? That was going to be madness in the upcoming raid.

I'd picked up a couple of other really nice upgrades too.

{Starlit Cloak}
Grade: D
Item Level: 39
Slot: Back
Quality: Rare
Primaries: +12 Intelligence, +10 Charisma
Armor: +3%

{Twice-stitched Belt}
Grade: D
Item Level: 40
Slot: Waist
Type: Leather
Quality: Uncommon
Primaries: +5 Intelligence, +5 Dexterity, +5 Constitution
Secondaries: +2% Chance to Hit
Armor: +7%

I'd also built up a sizable stockpile of Rift Gems. If everything went as planned, I was pretty sure that I'd be able to buy two brand-new C-Grade pistols from a Rift Gem vendor the very moment I hit 20 and unlocked the next grade, and I was practically drooling at the thought.

Aside from gear, we'd also snagged two more entries from Brandt's notebook.

{Entry 34}
*The Huntsman finally got his wish, and I fear the world will never be the same. Instead of scouring the bones for a happy memory with which to anchor a loop, I went in the other direction: I used a creature's last moments, its memory of the Huntsman's spear.*
*The result was the most terrible thing I've ever seen. Just... teeth and slick, smooth muscle. It had so many teeth. Gods, the way it moved.*
*And the Huntsman's response, as the monster I'd just made for him smashed straight through one of his stone walls and rampaged into the night?*
*That he'd have a runed cage ready the next time around.*
*The most horrifying part of it all is now that I've seen what can go wrong, I can somehow feel the latent energy that fills his halls, I can taste the blood on the air. The mounts, the skulls, the trophies. They hang from his walls like coiled springs.*
*With the slightest push in the right direction, it would all come crashing down.*

{Entry 64}
*I managed to bribe a guard and escape the palace, and though I don't imagine it'll last long, I hope it will buy me enough time. Isabel is feverish and weak.*
*I found her in the entryway, opening the door over and over again so that Rusty would charge in and greet her.*
*But I already have one dose of the green fluid at the ready, and it won't be long before the second cures. I have no idea if it'll really work—of what we'll become if it does—but I have to try. I can't face the idea of losing her. And anything is better than giving up.*

We'd also identified two more of the Menagerie Wing's five curses, and we weren't far off from revealing the fourth.

Hex of Flying Vertebrae
Effect: Whenever a hostile target dies within 20 yards of a player afflicted by this curse, there is a 10% chance that the corpse will erupt in a Bony Explosion that deals 1,000 damage to all players within 40 yards.
If a hostile target dies within 20 yards of 5 or more players afflicted by this curse, the explosion is guaranteed to occur.

Dreadking's Ultimatum
Effect: Whenever a player dies, all other players within 20 yards are Feared for 8 seconds. This effect cannot be broken or dispelled.

And speaking of terrible things, I'd also received a bit of news that was deeply concerning: another sphere had dropped for the trash groups. One that singlehandedly convinced me that Tyrann was telling the truth when he'd told Francis his Renown Path wasn't completely dead.

{Sphere of Branching Fate} (Consumable) (Renown Perk Sphere)
Quality: Rare
Use: Rerolls one of your chosen Renown Perks and allows you to choose between the other two options that were available when you first selected the chosen Perk. This effect is permanent, but you may use another {Sphere of Branching Fate} to revert a changed Renown Perk to its original state at any time.

That wasn't anything game-breaking, and Tyrann would still be limited by the initial choices he'd made, but knowing that he'd probably figured out a way to salvage at least some of his path was still worrisome.

Even so, we'd scored another defensive recipe from the trash groups, which helped balance that out.

{The Huntsman's Wards of Repulsion} (Communal Defense Enhancement)
Description: Wards a 100-yard section of wall with magical runes that will cause all Undead within 10 yards to take 50% increased damage from all sources. In addition, particularly weak Undead enemies will be completely repelled and unable to approach the wall unless the Wards become damaged or are removed.

Placement Requirements: Any section of a fully completed Defensive Wall within the Communal Defense Zone.
Resources Required: {Soul Gem} x100, {Large Soul Gem} x50.
Load Time: 2 Hours.

I'd jumped on that recipe as soon as Darling had linked it to me, going so far as to donate almost the entirety of my personal stockpile of Soul Gems to the cause.

And not only had the Defensive Wall around the Commerce Ward fully completed while we were Rifting, largely thanks to House and her golems, but the wards had finished as well, and I couldn't wait to get a look at them.

The other parts of the city still weren't nearly as well protected as the Commerce Ward, but for now we were doing the best we could, and the huge number of players who were still participating in the Legendary Quest to cull the monsters beyond the walls were keeping the place relatively safe.

It made my stomach flutter to leave the city's defenses to other people, even with House managing it all, but I was stretched thin with everything we had going on, especially knowing how much gold I still owed Arlann to fund the guard.

And time was running out.

Darling interrupted my train of thought by popping back into the Hall of Rifts, smiling broadly with two huge axe hafts poking out above each heavily armored shoulder.

"We're looking goooood! I cannot wait to hit that raid! I think—"

A series of prompts interrupted her.

**Renown Event Alert!**

Beneath smoky skies, the Neverburn is blazing in earnest once again as Igor the Red closes in on the man who betrayed him.
In the far east, the Snow-drowned Pass is beginning to thaw for the first time in decades, gradually revealing the sinister growth that has been thriving beneath the drifts.
On the coast of the Western Isles, a flash flood has eroded a series of blockages that prevented access to the Dreadcomb Complex, opening up a vast subterranean system whose terrifying denizens are already emerging into the daylight.

I perked up at the first one. "Frank? Can you throw me the Ripple Alert we got earlier for the Ruby Tower back when Sarissa's fell?"

"Uh huh."

**Minor Ripple Alert: Player {Ned, the Piratical} has broken the bonds of the Triad and freed the occupant of the Ruby Tower! The winds have shifted in the Neverburn, and Igor the Red now stalks his homeland, searching for the man who imprisoned him.**

I nodded at that. "So it's an update, huh? Interesting. Might be too good of an opportunity to pass up. How much time do we have left before the prisms hit Uliana?"

"You know I don't do math in matters unrelated to the moon's demise."

"I think you could if you wanted to."

"It's the principle of the thing."

"Alright, fine."

I sent House a quick message for another ETA, and she responded that the wave of prisms would reach Uliana in one hour and seventeen minutes, so I relayed that to Darling.

"An hour and seventeen minutes," Darling repeated. "Why am I not surprised?"

"I'd be concerned if you were at this point. But hey, that probably leaves enough time for me to knock that quest out."

"If you can manage that," Frank said, "the reward should shoot you over into Renown Rank XII for sure. We could get that new path picked out."

I pumped a fist. "Hell yeah. It feels like I need to keep looking into the towers even aside from that. Who knows, maybe Igor will have something for us on the Possibility King." I looked at Darling. "Any chance you want to tag along?"

"I'd love to," she said, "but I just hit 15, so I'm probably better served going after my Trinket and getting my class change done. Happy to help out if you think you need a hand though."

I waved her off. "It's all good. I think you've got the right of it. I'll just duck back into the Oasis and grab House. We might want to consider pulling some people off Rifts and putting them on those other Renown Events while we can still fast travel, though. So much of what I've managed to do has come from them."

"Definitely. Alright, I'm gonna grab a few more people and go Trinket hunting with our other 15s. You wanna have Frank shoot me targets for that, then we'll meet up back here once we're done?"

"Yeah, if there's time. Or maybe Frank can find us a safe place to watch the fireworks from when the prisms hit. I'd love to see Goon out in force and how they respond. That would probably tell us a good bit more about what we're up against."

"I got all that," Frank said.

Darling waved. "See you guys in a bit! Don't have too much fun without me." She vanished through the Hall's central portal.

"Shoot," I said.

Frank grunted. "What now?"

"The Revenant. I forgot about that thing."

"What about it? If it shows up, we kill it."

"Depending on Tyrann's level, that may not be doable, but yeah. But those things see right through illusions. So the question is do we head into town with an illusion in place and risk the Revenant dropping in again, or do we stroll in as Ned and chance the other players taking a shot at us, guards and all?" I eyed the red sphere that was floating a bit behind my shoulder.

"Heart Vessel will help there, but still."

"We both know what I'm going to say."

"True."

I considered applying an illusion and heading out but instead decided to send House another message asking how busy the Auction House was.

She replied that people were packed in shoulder to shoulder, which was half what I wanted to hear and half the complete opposite.

"Man," I said. "As much as I'd like to take a quick detour and get back into the Oasis for a bit, it's probably a stupid risk to take, so I think it makes more sense to get an earlier start on the event before people have a chance to head out in that direction. I'm just gonna have House meet us here."

I spent a little while conveying Trinket targets from Frank to the various guild members who were ready for them before House popped into the Hall.

"You up for a Renown Event?"

"I am always willing to elevate as needed. In addition, I have completed my first lesson."

I paused. "Oh! You mean your auctions, right?"

"Indeed. I have also acquired two more stones for our guild members to touch since we last spoke, each of which you indicated as being of the highest priority."

She linked the items before I could correct her.

{Stonetip} (Two-handed Staff) (Touchstone)
Grade: E
Item Level: 20
Damage Type: Physical
Quality: Rare
Physical Attack: 55
Magical Attack: 25
Speed: Slow
Primaries: +8 Dexterity, +13 Constitution
Touchstone Ability: As long as this item is equipped, you gain the passive ability {Leaden Swings}. You may only have 2 pieces of Touchstone gear equipped at any time.

{Leaden Swings}
Each time you deal physical damage, you gain 1% increased Armor for 10 seconds, stacking up to 10 times.

{Lightning-eater's Shield} (Shield) (Touchstone)
Grade: E
Item Level: 22
Slot: Offhand
Type: Shield
Quality: Rare
Primaries: +10 Constitution
Secondaries: +7% Lightning Resistance
Armor: +8%
Touchstone Ability: As long as this item is equipped, you gain the active ability {Swallow Lightning}. You may only have 2 pieces of Touchstone gear equipped at any time.

{Swallow Lightning}
Whenever you take Lightning damage, you have a 3% chance to nullify the attack completely and receive healing equal to the damage you would otherwise have taken.

"Perfect, House. That's awesome. How much did they cost you?"

"The total cost was sixty-eight silver."

I blinked. "Wow. Killer finds. I'd like to hear about how your other purchases went too, but I also want to keep it moving, so do you mind if we get going?"

"I am happy to proceed."

I located the Neverburn and was about to ask which available Rift would be the best pick for us to jump to when I felt Frank indicate one to the northwestern part of the zone.

I selected it and confirmed my choice, made sure I didn't have an illusion active, then popped out onto lush, shin-deep grass with House at my side.

Strange, twisting trees rose all around us, their canopies full of leaves that were the exact same shade as the blue sky above.

The area had a salty smell to it, and I spun on my heels to get a look around, fully expecting to find a vast ocean stretching out behind me.

Instead, I found a thirty-foot-wide gash in the towering trees that went on and on until it disappeared over a distant hill. The ground within the slash had been scorched bare and black, and the few trees that still stood within it looked like little more than burnt matchsticks, their bare branches standing in grim contrast to the bright blue leaves that framed the gap.

A stiff breeze blew in from down the hill, carrying the scent of ash and burning wood, with a few embers twisting on the wind for good measure.

"What the hell happened here?" I said.

"Look over there," Frank said.

I glanced that way and spotted a familiar-looking tower rising above the bluish trees off in the distance, though this one was ruby red.

And I saw that the same gash we were standing in extended all the way to the tower's base. I traced the line, following it from the tower to us to where it vanished over the hilltop.

"Igor did this?"

"Uh huh."

"And this happened because he... left? And presumably walked somewhere?"

"Yep."

I rolled my shoulders. "Alright then. Let's see if we can find this guy before he burns the whole zone down."

I mounted up and was surprised to see a similar cast bar appear above

House's head. When the cast completed, she sat atop a bike much like mine, though hers had two wide wheels at the back.

"A trike?" I said. "Nice. Did you craft that yourself?"

"I did," House said. She looked away.

"House? What's up?"

When she turned back toward me, her cheeks were just a tiny bit red.

"I needed to reach 140 skill in Machinery and had no other choice but to create this mount when it came to developing my profession, otherwise I would have created something that would have been more likely to benefit the guild at large." She took a very deep breath. "My face feels hot and tight and I do not like it. Normal?"

I leaned forward on the handlebars, laughing. "Lemme guess: you're feeling a little guilty because you feel like you did something for yourself at the expense of others, right?"

"That does seem to be the case, and my cheeks are deeply ashamed."

"That's normal, but let me be as clear as possible here: House, you've been a huge help to us every step of the way without a single complaint, and if you want something, then you should either get it yourself or ask us to help you get it, regardless of whether or not it's optimal.

"Do you get what I'm saying? We're playing to win, sure. But I want you to want to be here, and that means you need to be enjoying yourself along the way."

She beamed. "Thank you. That is very helpful contextually." She squinted at the gash up ahead. "However, I would prefer to exclusively want optimal things. It would make life far less messy."

"Cats aren't optimal, and acquiring those hasn't been a problem," Frank said.

House glared at him. "Are you implying that you find my companions to be suboptimal?"

"Nope. Never mind."

"C'mon," I said. "Let's see how that trike rides through the burn."

I tried to gun my bike off the grass and into the soft, scorched earth, but the back wheel spun in place for a moment, kicking up ash and once-buried cinders. It finally picked up some traction and I rocketed forward, then had to slow down to let House pull up beside me. She was having a much easier time riding though, probably owing to her thicker wheels.

"So how'd it go with the Auction House?" I said.

"Which auction are you referring to specifically?" she replied.

I paused, then decided to rephrase the question. "How'd it go with the

Auction House, House?"

She brightened again. "Oh. I now possess 95 silver coins, up 70 silver from what I was given."

I did a double-take. "That's awesome! You almost quadrupled it!"

We split around a blackened trunk whose canopy was still burning and were side by side again moments later.

"Indeed," House said. "I believe I am ready to proceed to the second lesson."

I thought about that for a minute. "We can probably do that real quick before we reach the event area or whatever. So you've got the basic idea behind buying and reselling gear."

"I have acquired said idea."

"Maybe we should move onto crafting materials, then? That's a pretty easy one overall, especially early in a game's life."

"I remain interested."

"So, what do you think of when I say choke points?"

"Throats," Frank said.

"Not you, Frank," I said, though I couldn't help but laugh a little.

"I am unsure."

"What about a bottleneck? You're trying to become human, right? So communication is a bottleneck. It's like an obstacle that you need to clear —something that prevents you from getting to your goal as quickly as you'd like."

I watched her swerve in front of a fiery butterfly, then frown as it splattered against the front of her trike despite her attempts to avoid it.

"I see."

"Here's a better example: you created that trike because you needed skill points, right?"

"Correct."

"So that would make all of the materials you needed to gather for the trike a bottleneck. You couldn't get beyond 140 skill in Machinery without creating a trike."

"I see."

"Was there anything special it required? Like something specific and new that you needed to craft up, that sort of thing?"

"5 Large Soul Gems. Was that my bottleneck?"

"I mean... it could be. But we're only interested in markets we can control or at least heavily influence, and you can't control the price of something like Soul Gems in the way we're hoping to. Those are dropping for everyone at all times, so running that market is a pipe dream for now. Even if you manage to pump the price up by buying everything out and relisting it, people will naturally undercut you or just go out and farm it themselves."

I pursed my lips. "Sorry, I think I'm getting ahead of myself again. Basically, you're looking for something more niche than Soul Gems, and this is really where Frank might be able to help you out."

She scowled at him from her trike. "I remain dubious of the axe's intentions. Doubly so in light of his recent comment about the poor optimization of my pets, and triply so because the rare companion he suggested I hunt outside of the Stronghold failed to materialize."

"Ugh," Frank said. "I told you it wasn't guaranteed."

"Anyway," I continued. "Soul Gems will never have crazy value because you get them naturally. That might change as the game gets older and the player base levels up—which will dent the supply of mid-level gems—but on the whole, the price will never get insane because you can just go to a level 30 area and kill some mobs.

"There's still value there; if a level 50 player decides to level a new profession and they need gems to do it, they'll probably pay considerably more than that gem is worth to avoid having to farm it up themselves. But we're looking for something that's more gated."

A small, fiery branch landed on top of my handlebars and caught there, so I plucked it free and tossed it back over my shoulder.

"In fact, they might even lose money if they decided to farm it."

"I do not understand how one could lose money by deciding not to spend it."

"It's all about opportunity cost. Let's assume you can make 10 gold an hour by farming level 50 mobs. If a player needs 5 Large Soul Gems to level up their profession and they expect to spend an hour farming those up, then paying 5 gold makes sense because they'll come out ahead by just buying the items and farming something more profitable instead."

I paused and realized I was a little out of breath, even though we were riding. And both House and Frank were staring at me.

"Sorry. I like this stuff a lot."

"I still remain intrigued," House said.

"I'm bored, but I don't have the means to leave," Frank said.

"Right," I said. "So instead of Soul Gems, imagine that you need a specific ruby to level Machining to 145. You only need two of them, but without those rubies, you can't craft an item that you absolutely need to progress. But unlike Soul Gems, you can't run around and kill mobs for the ruby—the only option is to mine it up.

"Now, the ruby's not insanely rare because it drops in low-level mineral veins, but a lot of the professions that pair well with mining also need that same ruby. So as they're dropping, people are naturally using them, which reduces the supply.

"So the calculus is a lot different there. If you don't have a miner or a friend who's willing to dig them up for you, then you're in a bad spot—there's no easy option there aside from buying them."

"Why not create an alternate character and level mining?" House said.

"You definitely could, but again, that takes time. You've gotta level up a new character, do their starter quests, grab the profession, start leveling it up. You could easily spend a whole afternoon on that, maybe even a couple days, depending on the game.

"But if we keep it simple and assume it would take 4 hours to create an alt and get their mining skill to where they need it to be, then acquire the rubies, we can compare that against the amount of gold an endgame player can farm in 4 hours.

"If they're usually making that same amount of 10 gold an hour, then we can assume that it's at least somewhat reasonable for someone to pay 40 gold for those two items."

"It does not sound reasonable to me," House said. "The theoretical rubies do not seem that valuable."

"They aren't, but this is the key: it's never about the item itself. People can only play games for so long each day, so they're generally pretty happy to exchange gold for time. Imagine that you only get to play 2 hours a night. Are you going to drop some gold on that item you need so that you can have some fun playing, or are you going to grind for 2 hours so that you have more gold the next time you log in?

"And even if most people do grind it out, all we need is one person who's willing to pay to save themselves some time. That's really what an Auction House sells: convenience. Pay 10 gold right now, get your items instantly, get your profession up, move on to the next craft. You can even package them with professions in mind; if you need 2 of those rubies to level Machinery, then you sell them in stacks of two for 40 gold a pop."

House squinted. "Would it be accurate to say that we are selling people's time back to them?"

I rocked back in my seat at that as we flew along—that was far more insightful than I'd expected.

"Uhh… yeah, exactly. So can you see why if you were trying to control a market, the rubies would be a better bet than Soul Gems?"

"Because they are inconvenient to acquire."

"And the acquisition has a low upside. If I'm hunting Soul Gems that drop everywhere, I can probably find mobs with a good drop table to farm. That way, I'm hunting multiple things at once. But if I'm limited to mining veins?" I made a lukewarm gesture and nearly toppled off my bike as the front wheel sank particularly deep into a bed of ash. "Not so good. And I'd be willing to bet a considerable amount of Frank points that he can direct you toward a few real items with qualities that are similar to our theoretical rubies."

"I can of course do much better than that," Frank said. "Fire Opals, Lacquered Wood, Black Lillies."

"Awesome. And how do they drop?"

"Mining, Arborist, Herbalist."

"Great, so—"

"And," he interrupted, "you can't farm those items directly at all, regardless of your professions."

"What do you mean?"

"As in there's no such thing as a Fire Opal vein. You just have a low chance of finding those gems whenever you harvest a vein of copper. But all three of those items are required to level professions, and the first two are also used in Housing Recipes."

I inclined my head. "Those are perfect examples. See, House? So not only is the customer paying to avoid spending their time harvesting items or leveling gathering professions when they could be playing, they're also avoiding having to play around with RNG."

"Interesting. Shall I focus my next round of purchases on the items that Frank has listed?"

"Absolutely. Keep the 95 silver you've made and reinvest it but limit yourself to 10 total transactions again. Let's see if you can do better than quadrupling up."

House did a little shimmy on her trike. "I am excited to try." She stopped shimmying. "But I still dread the possibility of failure."

"Normal," I said.

We split again, this time around a rock that had cracked down the middle and was now spouting steam like a kettle, then pressed on as the gash continued and eventually terminated in a great cloud of fire and ash that was steadily creeping forward.

Even more incredible, though, was the shape the slash had taken. I'd assumed it was just a random path that Igor was creating as he walked, but from my current vantage point atop a hill, I could see it for what it was: a colossal glyph that he'd scorched into the blue and green landscape.

I couldn't make heads or tails of the thing, but its form was marked with slashes and dots.

"I find this image to be very pleasing," House said.

I looked her way. "What about it?"

"The straightaways are perfectly straight. And the angles are likewise mathematically precise." She pointed out a few sections one after another. "22.5 degrees, 45 degrees, 90 degrees." She sighed. "It is very soothing."

I squinted into the fiery cloud. "Is he casting a spell?"

"Little farther," Frank said.

We rode toward the cloud and only needed to continue on for another twenty feet or so before we triggered the prompt I'd been waiting for.

**Personal Alert: Now entering an active Renown Event!**

**Renown Event Alert!**
**Igor the Red stalks the Neverburn, preparing a spell that will permanently devastate the entire zone. Find a way to avert the catastrophe or perish within it.**
**Spell completion rate: 3%.**

"3%, huh? Probably leaves us a couple hours if that timer started when the event popped."

"We possess 3 hours and 56 minutes," House said.

"Well, the event might have that much time, but we don't. This place will be crawling with other players by then, and I want to be there to see the prisms hit Uliana regardless."

"Same," Frank said.

I throttled my bike down a particularly steep slope, cinders kicking up beneath me as the blue trees rushed by to either side like fence posts.

House was quick to follow, but not quite quick enough to avoid getting covered in dark ash from head to toe, not that she seemed to care in the slightest. We rode on until we were maybe fifty feet out from the smoldering cloud, then dismounted.

Now that we were so close to the source of the blaze, I could hear the trees smoking and hissing as they burned. I cocked my head at a tree to my left. No, they weren't smoking, they were steaming—the leaves weren't bursting into flame as I'd expected but were instead boiling away and leaving empty canopies behind, and only then did the trees begin to smolder and fall.

"Damage incoming," Frank said, so I checked my Health bar.

I was losing 2 or 3 Health per second, and while that didn't worry me, we were still on the outskirts of whatever Igor the Red was doing.

I thought about that for a moment. I fully expected the damage to ramp up as we drew closer, so I motioned House away until neither of us was getting hit.

"House, can you hit me with your bots?"

She squinted at me. "I can certainly try."

"Might wanna clarify that," Frank said.

"Right, thanks. House, please set me up with the highest amount of healing you can put out while still allowing them to follow me."

"Understood."

She summoned one of her healing bots, then a second and a third, and she appeared to be about to combine them when I held up a hand to stop her.

"Did you guys see that? I'm pretty sure the cloud just got brighter." I took a few steps toward Igor and found that the heat was even more suffocating than it had been. The damage I was taking had doubled, too, and the nearby trees were whistling now. "Looks like the heat is cycling or something. Maybe we've gotta time the approach?"

"That depends," Frank said. "How crispy do you wanna get?"

House shifted on her feet. "I would prefer not to be crisped."

"Same, House. Before we do this, have any of your abilities changed at all in the last little while?"

"Not substantially. But I do possess a new skill."

"Can you link it to me?"

"Certainly."

{Replicate} (Rank: Novice I)
Description: You create a copy of any existing bot or turret that persists for 20 seconds. Replicating a bot instantly resets the cooldown on {Artificer's Improvisation}.
Cast time: Instant.
Cooldown: 3 minutes.

**Next rank: The created bot persists for 25 seconds, up from 20.**

"That looks really cool," I said. "The improvisation ability is the one that combines stuff, right? So you could combine two bots, copy the result, then combine again to make something even bigger?"

"Affirmative."

"Amazing. But have any of your existing abilities changed?"

"Negative."

I pursed my lips. "Speaking of skills. House?"

"Yes?"

"Have you slept at all since you got here?"

"I have not."

I eyed the fiery cloud, which appeared to have intensified yet again. "We probably should have told her to sleep."

"I kinda thought that would be self-evident," Frank said, "given the prompts saying you need to sleep to upgrade your skills."

"I am in fact awaiting twelve upgrades."

"You didn't want to like... get those?" I said. "I find that really surprising."

"I have attempted to sleep several times. But whenever I close my eyes, my thoughts turn aggressively inward, and I inevitably find myself cataloging every error I have ever made. At first, I assumed that if I simply let the list run its full course, I would then be allowed to drift off peacefully. Instead, the list simply began to repeat itself at an increased volume."

"Normal," I said, before she could ask. "It is kind of a problem, though. You really, really want those upgrades. Not sure what we can really do about it."

"She could drink until she passes out," Frank said.

"Yeah, no. Let's not encourage that."

"It would probably work."

"Maybe, but there's gotta be some kind of a middle ground between lying there with your eyelids closed and drinking yourself unconscious."

"You could try droning on about the Auction House some more. That almost put me to sleep back there, and you were riding a motorcycle through a wildfire."

"I very much enjoy learning about the Auction House," House said.

"I'm glad, House, but I think Frank is on to something. Maybe he could talk about how great his beard is the next time you try to pass out. Feels like the repetition might lull you to sleep, like waves breaking."

"That does seem more likely to succeed."

I felt him squint at her. "Was that a deliberate shot at me or not? I honestly can't tell."

"It was indeed."

"Wow," Frank said.

"How do you like these apples?" House said, with genuine curiosity.

"Huh?" He looked around at the nearby trees. "What apples? Do you have apples?"

"I currently possess zero apples."

"What? Then why even bring them up? I think somebody needs to restart the robot. Anyway, sidenote: I really wish we'd saved some of that purple stuff because I could really go for a quick soak. Feels like all this heat is gonna be hell on my beard."

I studied the burning cloud, watching as its heat finally began to wane. "Them apples, House. You need to emphasize that part: how do you like *them* apples?"

"Ohhh," Frank said.

"Truly?" House said.

I nodded. "Yep. And tonally speaking, you need to pretend like you're talking to someone you hate and that you're delivering apples to that person against their will."

"How do you like *them* apples?" she repeated, aggressively.

"Nailed it," Frank said.

I laughed. "Maybe a bit on the angry end for everybody aside from Frank, but otherwise, yeah—spot on. I still think this is a weird and pointless fixation, but you do seem to be making progress with it."

"Excellent."

I held up a hand, and to my vast surprise the group actually quieted as the fiery cloud contracted and dimmed further.

"Alright, House. If the pattern holds, we should have about a minute or so before the heat peaks again." I started summoning my mount. "Let's get your healing bots rolling."

She summoned her third bot, then combined all three of them into a giant healing sphere that zoomed over and bathed me in a cone of golden light.

I drove forward but slowed as House raised a hand and made a quick gesture.

The air above me warped, then a second healing bot appeared beside the first. Then the two bots burst apart into clouds of metal that flew together and recombined above my head.

The resulting bot was twice the size of the previous two, was shaped like a saucer rather than a sphere, and possessed six spotlight-like contraptions that were mounted around the edges of the disc.

All six of the spotlights tilted inward and bathed me in yellow light.

My Health was full, but a steady stream of impressive green numbers drifted up above my head: 200, 224, 210. Three of House's smaller bots joined me quickly thereafter, though their smaller heals were lost in the glow of her larger creation.

I gunned my bike directly into the cloud. My Health began to drop, but House's bots topped me up well before I could even tick below 99%.

The damage intensified as I got closer to the heart of the firestorm, far outpacing what I'd been expecting to endure, and it wasn't long before my Health started to drop despite the constant heals.

The loss of Health was more than manageable thanks to House's healing, but I probably would have died before I'd made it halfway through the steam and smoke and ash without her.

The warmth was incredible, and sweat was pouring down my face by the time I reached the incandescent figure standing at the very heart of the blaze.

I inspected him.

**{Igor the Red} (Level ?? Humanoid) (Legend)**
**HP: 980,000/980,000**
**MP: 2,400,000/2,400,000**

I did a double-take.

"Wait, what? That puts him way above where Sarissa was, even when she had her tower running. Shouldn't he be weaker?"

"He is substantially weaker now than he was," Frank said. "You remember that dome the three of them were powering?"

"Yeah?"

"Sarissa and Erasmus accounted for about 20% of that power between the two of them."

I reeled at that, but one of House's smaller bots had just exploded above my head, so I drove in and skidded the bike around Igor, stopping directly in his path.

"Careful," Frank said. He buzzed. "Just... careful."

I nodded.

Igor was so bright that I couldn't look directly at him without squinting, and even that left spots floating in my vision. He was molten from head to toe, his bright green eyes the only deviation from the orange glow that cloaked him.

He was tall and wore long robes, but he had some sort of glowing, rope-like material wrapped around his shoulders and torso, and it looked like he was tangled up in red-hot vines that he dragged behind him wherever he went.

He stared at me, unblinking, then wound up the strands behind him and wrapped them around his forearms and fists. The incoming damage lessened as he worked, and the heat decreased at the same rate.

I inspected him again, and the result was odd: both his max Health and Mana were decreasing as he wound the ropes around himself, as if he were getting weaker.

Once he'd finished with his strange, glowing ropes, Igor cocked his glowing head to the side, and when he spoke, his voice sounded rusty from disuse.

"It has been a very long time since someone has braved the heat long enough to speak to me."

I hopped off my bike as House approached. "What are you doing? What is this?"

Igor surveyed the burning trail he'd left behind. "I'm attempting to flush out a rat. And if that doesn't work, this spell will remove the need for flushing altogether."

"By destroying the entire area."

He looked me up and down, green eyes peering out of the glow. "Yes."

"And is there a way I can help you... not do that?"

He sighed, and the glow as well as the heat winked out. I'd assumed the man was old, given what Sarissa had said about him, but even then his appearance caught me off-guard—he was positively ancient, his face leathery and liver-spotted.

Now the glow had finally gone, I noticed that the strange, rope-like lengths I'd seen earlier were a snarl of chains that were piled atop his shoulders and twisted around his chest. Every single link was still red hot, and though the heat didn't seem to touch his skin or clothing, the links that were closest to the ground had the dirt sizzling and blackening beneath them.

"Elias," he said, spitting the name.

"Is that the man who put you in that tower?"

Igor clenched his fists, and a blast of hot air rushed across my face. "How do you know about the tower?"

His suspicion was obvious. The temperature was increasing again, and his eyes were so wild that I was starting to think now might not be the best time to tell him I was the one that had freed him.

I eyed the blackened trail he'd left behind. "This burned path leads back to the tower you were in, and you already mentioned a rat, so..."

He eyed me for a long moment, and I didn't manage another easy breath until the temperature started dropping again.

"So you need help finding him, then?"

He pointed a gnarled finger at the ground beneath his feet. "I know exactly where he is."

I took a deep breath to ease my frustration. "What exactly is the problem?"

"The Darkflame Tribe would never give up one of their own," he hissed, words dripping with venom.

"And you can't just go down wherever they are and grab him instead of blowing the whole area up?"

He shook his head. "If I were to return to the depths, the world would burn around me. The damage would be far, far more widespread."

"What if I brought him to you?"

He looked me up and down, then his flames roared back, and his entire frame became molten once again, chains and all. He released a few of the links he'd wrapped around his fists and arms, and the heat doubled.

I flinched, shading my eyes reflexively. I smelled burning hair, and I knew it was mine.

"That would work, I suppose." He shrugged and started walking again, the air shimmering around him, blue leaves hissing and dispersing into steam as he pressed back into the trees. "But the result will be the same in the end."

"What about the collateral damage?"

He gritted his teeth, and the air around him erupted into a bluish inferno that was even brighter than before. A pair of trees exploded beneath the heat, blowing apart as if they'd been struck by lightning.

Then the blaze cooled and returned to the same fiery, reddish hue as the mage walked off and went back to carving his giant glyph into the forest.

"My life is collateral damage, boy."

"Wait—where do I go?"

Igor pointed down at the earth again without stopping.

I stood there for a few seconds, waiting to see if the Renown Event would update and present me with another clue, but nothing happened.

House stepped up beside me.

"Thanks for the heals, House. Doubt I would have survived that conversation without them."

I considered going after Igor for more information but again felt that something wasn't quite right with the mage. Instead, I pulled up my map to see if an area had been highlighted or something like that but didn't see anything of use.

"Alright House, no idea how we're doing it, but we're going down."

"House," Frank said. "Spin a hundred degrees to your left."

She did.

"Now take fourteen steps forward."

She complied with that as well, counting her steps as she went.

I cleared my throat. "House, are you aware that your fourteenth step is likely to result in you falling into a hole in the ground?"

"Seriously?" Frank said.

"I am aware that that is a distinct possibility, yes," she said.

I nodded. "Alright then. Just making sure."

She counted out steps eleven, twelve, and thirteen—which took her beneath the now-bare canopy of an especially large tree—then took her fourteenth without hesitation.

The ground collapsed beneath her, but instead of disappearing fully from sight, House hit something solid and landed at a depth that left her shoulders and head visible.

"Wow, Frank," I said. "You probably could have killed her, but you didn't!"

"That is the deepest hole I could find."

"Oh. Then never mind." I ran over to where House was standing in the hole she'd made, but the sunken walls around her gave me pause.

They looked wriggly, like they were full of worms, and after a long moment of trying to wrap my head around what I was seeing, I realized I was looking at roots that had gnarled themselves into an unbroken mass.

House had punched right through the earth and landed in the middle of what looked a lot like a bird's nest.

I pointed a pistol down at the space. "Those roots look water-tight."

House ran a curious finger over one of the longer protuberances. "They are quite warm to the touch as well."

"That's 'cause Igor just vaporized its reservoir," Frank said, "and the heat the tree was pulling in from below no longer has anywhere to go. Here."

**Codex Entry 4300: Waterblossom**
**Unique to the Neverburn, Waterblossoms are large trees that efficiently store huge amounts of water directly in their leaves. Their vast root systems also act as one of the area's most important heat sinks, allowing its subterranean cities to survive the vast amount of geothermal heat that radiates from beneath the surface.**

I read that over. "So he's already doing serious damage, huh?"

"Makes one of us," Frank said.

House got down on her hands and knees, then pointed to a spot right beneath me that I couldn't see.

"There appears to be a gap in the roots here." She pushed an arm up against the wall of the hole, and a good amount of dirt collapsed around her, revealing a sizable hole. "I have found a hollow, but I cannot feel the ground beneath it."

I jumped down beside her and immediately felt the heat rushing up through my boots and radiating off the walls. It wasn't as bad as it'd been around Igor—and I wasn't taking damage yet—but it was close.

"So, in there?" I said.

"Yep," Frank said. "With speed."

I squinted at him. "How much speed are we talking?"

"That depends. We've covered crispiness, but how much do you enjoy crawling through the earth as it slowly bakes you from the outside in?"

I wiped my forehead with my sleeve, and it came away streaked with sweat. "Not a fan of that either."

"Then I recommend a substantial amount of speed."

"Alright then. Let's do this and get the hell out of here before anybody else arrives."

I grabbed one of the horizontal roots that hung above the hole like a handle, then swung both of my feet in as if I were entering a water slide and disappeared into the dark.

# Chapter Twenty-Seven

I rocketed down the chute, flying over wet stones and roots as the earth whipped by. The temperature climbed as I flew along, becoming oppressively humid once again.

Then the shaft leveled out and launched me across a shallow pool, and as I skimmed across the surface, I caught a glimpse of reddish chains glowing overhead, hanging high above me in the darkness.

I passed directly into another tunnel, and the ride continued like that for a little while, blasting me from room to room with nothing but the occasional arc of molten metal hanging above to light the way.

Eventually, a small circle of flickering light appeared at the end of the chute, and I readied myself for the exit. My stomach lurched as I flew out of a vertical wall and ended up suspended in space, completely horizontal, some thirty feet above a dark body of water.

Steam geysered up all around me, and I had to focus on getting my alignment right so that a well-executed Clonedrift let me drift a few feet above the water and reappear on the stony, subterranean beach beyond the pool.

The floor was riddled with deep cracks that were hissing steam, and more of the same chains I'd noticed while skimming along were hanging from the ceiling in great, drooping arcs. The metal was glowing with enough heat and light to see by, but only just.

The chains were far larger than I'd realized, too; the links were the size you'd only see attached to a cruise ship, and I wondered about their weight and what it said for the stability of the cavern, knowing the damage Igor was doing high above.

I turned and waited for House, who shot out of the hole in the wall while hugging herself tightly with her ankles crossed.

She made no motion to adjust her posture as she fell, and she hit the dark water fully on her back with a crack so sharp that it made me cringe twice on her behalf: once as the sound reached me, then again as it echoed off the walls.

Her Health dropped by 40%, but she wasted no time in doggy paddling over while her healing bots hovered a few feet above her, their lights healing her up and illuminating the dark pool below.

It was impressively deep. Despite House's little light show, I couldn't see anything that even hinted at the bottom. The pool didn't grow any shallower at the edges either, so I offered her a hand and hauled her up and out once she reached the beach.

But the water beading off her was so warm that it gave me pause. I crouched down at the edge of the pool and dipped a finger in.

It wasn't quite painful to the touch, but it would have been too hot to comfortably bathe in, and I figured that it probably would have been steaming too if it weren't for how hot the chamber was.

"Well, we definitely made it down a bit. Not seeing any—"

"Incoming," Frank interrupted.

I froze as a little bit of dirt puffed off the wall to my left. It happened again, then dirt began to fall in earnest before the wall bulged and a creature's head popped out of it.

It had a long snout covered in whiskers and two huge, pupilless white eyes. The creature looked to be about the size of a horse, and it had a strange red gem embedded in its forehead.

I inspected it.

**{Gazeless Flamedrinker} (Level 18 Beast) (Veteran)**
**HP: 4,500/4,500**
**MP: 2,000/2,000**

I popped both of my pistols into my hands and readied a pair of spells but held them, and while both were instant, one of the two automatically became Overcharged thanks to my 2-piece set bonus.

The creature's nameplate was red, meaning that it was aggressive, but House was standing only ten feet away from where it had partially emerged from the wall, close enough that the beast really should have rushed her.

But something was off. The Flamedrinker surveyed the room blankly, its milky gaze passing over us as if we weren't there. Then the red gem in its forehead burst alight.

The mob pushed itself out of the wall and thumped onto the ground, leaving a huge hole behind. It had long, curved claws that looked suitable for digging, if a bit more menacing than necessary, and its rear legs were thick and powerful.

"The creature appears to be blind," House said, loud as hell.

I raised my pistols and braced for a fight as her voice echoed across the chamber multiple times. The Flamedrinker's stone brightened and emitted a low whine, but once again the creature failed to sense our presence.

"Blind and deaf, apparently." I stared at the creature, considering. "Makes sense with the name, and that thing does look a lot like an over-sized murder mole. But it makes me wonder what that gem is supposed to do."

After sniffing about for a bit longer, the creature turned and crept back into the hole it had made.

I didn't see another way out of the room, so I motioned House toward the creature and we both slipped in behind it, keeping maybe fifteen feet between it and us.

The Flamedrinker led us through the dark tunnel it had made, which was barely tall enough for me to stand in, and the roof and walls were beaded with moisture. The water was hot here as well, and the drops were uncomfortably warm as they splattered against my skin and trickled beneath my leathers.

"I am distinctly—"

"We know, Frank. We know."

"You have no idea what I was about to say."

"It's hot, and you're sweaty."

"That is true. But I was actually going to complain that my beard is starting to curl."

I glanced down at him. "Looks fine to me."

"Fine is a problem. I demand perfection."

Then a cool breeze sighed up from beyond the stalking creature. I hauled myself up into a much wider section of the tunnel that was relatively pleasant, and Frank and I both sighed in relief.

Up ahead, the mob's red gem flashed orange, and its low whine sharpened into a shriek. The creature howled and whirled on us, charging up the tunnel on all fours.

The claws that capped its feet and hands were glowing now, covered in orange flames capped with blue at the end.

It was on us in a blink, and though I was quick enough to release a pair of ravens and follow up with a Dreadful Shot before its claws could reach me, its initial swipe came close enough to my face that I felt the heat of its passing.

The creature fled down the wide tunnel under the effect of my fear. I switched to my rifle and started winding up a Ravenblast.

"House, we're gonna try to burst this thing down as quickly as possible. Can you get a big turret up and get ready to smash it?"

"Affirmative."

She chained the same skills she had earlier, but instead of using healing bots, she created two Spitfire Turrets through her combination and replication skills, then recombined those advanced models into a new one that I hadn't seen before.

The resulting turret was stockier with a long, thick barrel that looked as if it had been ripped off the top of a tank.

I inspected it.

**{Sniper Turret}**
**HP: 900/900**
**MP: 0/0**

The whole turret rocked backward, then a dark, spear-like projectile ripped out of its barrel and flew down the tunnel. The spear caught the creature in the lower back for 865, pierced right through it, and continued down the passage.

"Flamedrinker at 70%," Frank said.

My fear effect immediately broke, so I launched my own spell and watched the gray and purple bird fly down and strike the creature fully in the face.

The Ravenblast hit for 1,300 and gave off a bright burst of purple feathers, and I was halfway through a second rifle blast when the mob's claws went white.

It slashed at the air several times in quick succession, and the attacks launched a trio of white arcs in our direction. The first connected with House's turret and ripped it apart on contact, tearing the construct cleanly in half before it even had a chance to tilt and fall.

The second arc smashed into the side of the tunnel where the turret had been, and by then I knew the third was coming my way.

I threw up an Illusory Mirror directly in front of me as the projectile closed in, then followed up with two instant ravens from my pistols.

The white arc reflected and flew back down the tunnel, but that projectile as well as my spells met nothing but air as the mob vanished into a column of dust.

I crept forward, weapons ready, expecting the beast to come flying at me at any moment.

Instead, the dust cleared to reveal a deep hole in the ground. I backpedaled until I was close to House, weapons trained on the floor, then the walls, then the ceiling.

"Keep your eyes open, House," I said. "Could be anywhere."

"Understood."

Then the ground shifted beneath my feet, and a clawed hand reached up and snatched my ankle. I tried to Clonedrift away on instinct, but the spell generated an error message and didn't work.

"Silenced for 5 seconds," Frank said.

The claws turned orange and blue around my ankle, and both heat and vibrations radiated through my boot. Damage readouts in the mid-50s drifted up above my head, ticking away at a steady rate.

House ran over and smashed the hand with a double-handed swing from her mace, but all she got for her efforts was an *immune* message.

I watched my Health drop beneath 70% as the silence ticked away, at which point House tossed out all three of her healing bots, which stabilized me quickly enough.

Then a rock clipped the top of my head, and I looked up to find another Flamedrinker burrowing out of the ceiling amid a storm of stones and falling soil.

The mob slashed two of House's healing bots to ribbons as it fell, then it crashed down on top of me. I fell backward awkwardly, my ankle twisting beneath me as the weight of the falling Flamedrinker pancaked me against the floor while the second held my foot in place.

The creature ripped into my chest with both of its claws. I knew the damage the two creatures were inflicting was severe from the extent of the vibrations, but I was still shocked to see my Heart Vessel explode where it had been floating above my shoulder.

And without that ability, I'd have been a goner.

The bursting vessel showered the back of my neck in cold, red liquid, and my Health jumped back to 33%. But the mob below had released me, and the silence had run its course, so I could finally cast again.

Dreadful Shot was still on cooldown, so I popped a pistol into one hand and fired a Gravity Bird up against the roof of the low tunnel.

The mob that had crashed down on top of me flew off and slammed into the ceiling, drawn into the heart of the black hole. At the same time, the first Flamedrinker reemerged from the hole it had disappeared into a little way down the tunnel.

I backpedaled and launched a pair of instant Ravenblasts down the narrow passage, ignoring the creature I'd pinned to the ceiling.

"Injured mob first, House! Slow it down and drop it!"

She deployed one of her Sludgesling Turrets as the creature closed in, running along the sides of the tunnel and then across the ceiling like a spider.

The turret hit it with a black jet of oil that visibly slowed it down, and I struck it with a few more spells before switching to my new blunderbuss as it closed in.

But then my Gravity Bird expired and released the suspended mob. I took a single quick step forward, activated Repel, and kicked it on its way down.

The mob flew down the corridor and smashed into its companion, and the two creatures tangled up and went down.

House deployed a Leadfire Turret and ran by me while I lit the pair up from afar with piercing blasts. She smashed her turret before it even had a chance to fully form, sending a cone of shrapnel ripping over the mobs and pinging into the walls.

The ability put the injured Flamedrinker into Harvest range, so I switched to my rifle for the extra damage and finished it off.

The kill spawned a golden phantasm thanks to the latest upgrade I'd picked for Harvest, which floated there above the body. And if I could manage to dash through it before it faded, I'd restore a sizable chunk of Health.

The remaining mob tried to rise, but House swept one of its legs out from underneath it with a low, horizontal strike with her mace, and it collapsed again, hissing.

I dashed down the tunnel and leaped at the golden phantasm, which burst into golden light as I passed through it.

"Heal for 280, your Health at 52%," Frank said.

I hit the ground about five feet away from the remaining mob with two pistol blasts already on the way. I switched to my rifle and Double Cast another as the mob finally managed to regain its feet, then hit it with Dark Harvest since the cooldown had reset on that last kill.

The mob leaned forward, claws raised high for one last attack, then belly-flopped onto the dirt.

I ran through the golden spirit the second Harvest kill had left behind for a bit of extra Health, then dropped to one knee, breathing hard while sparks flew around me.

I tried to summon another Heart Vessel before remembering that the cooldown hadn't started until the spell activated, meaning I'd be without the protective effect for at least 10 minutes, and I felt surprisingly naked without being able to depend on it.

I knelt down over the corpses, drawn by the green embers that were flying above them. I came away with a great haul for two kills: a new recipe, a pair of Large Soul Gems, plus a quest item.

I pulled the recipe up first.

**Recipe: {Rune of the White Ring} (Consumable) (Awards 5 skill points per craft)**
**Your Gravity Bird now creates a horizontal ring around your target that strongly repels any hostile enemy that draws close. Ringed targets are personally unaffected by the spell.**
**Duration: 24 Hours.**
**Requirements: {Large Soul Gem} x15.**

"Oooh," I said. "Jackpot."

I almost made one on the spot just to play around with the ability, but I didn't have the gems I needed, and the effect was unlikely to help me down here in the tunnels.

I pulled up the quest item.

**{Hollow Darkflame Core} (Quest Item)**
**??**

I popped it into the palm of my hand. It was a dark, metallic sphere, and its surface was pocked with deep puncture wounds. The surface was room temperature, but I placed the tip of a finger against one of the holes and felt a bit of heat lingering within the sphere.

I didn't see a way to use it, so I dropped it into my inventory.

House squatted in front of the nearest corpse and poked the red gem above the dead creature's eyes.

"What a strange jewel. I did not like the frequency of the sound it was making."

"Yeah," I said as I got back to my feet. "Might not be able to see or hear, but it didn't have any problem trying to carve us up from twenty yards away. That was a nice-looking turret, House. Sniper, yeah?"

"Indeed, but it was an inefficient use of my cooldowns. My Sniper Turret was destroyed almost immediately."

"Eh, in hindsight, sure. But your cooldowns are short enough where you want to keep using them, and you still got a hard hit in first. In the future, though, you might want to hit the mobs yourself or let me deal a bit more damage first to keep stuff from blowing your turrets up. That one looked like it had more Health than some of your weaker creations, but that amount still goes quick without much in the way of mitigation."

"Understood."

I kicked a toe under the creature and tried to flip it over, but it was too heavy. "So what do we think is going on here? Heat-tracking?"

"An interesting thought. However, if that were the case, the creature likely would have spotted us immediately in the first room."

"The heat could have been masking our presence. That pool you fell into wasn't far off from boiling, and the chains were glowing overhead. That would be a lot of noise if heat is all it sees. But it honed in on us the very moment the temperature changed."

"True. But from an evolutionary standpoint, if such a creature were hunting in an area where the ambient temperature often exceeds the body temperature of its prey, it would be far more logical for it to be searching for entities that register as cold against the backdrop of warmth rather than hot against the backdrop of heat."

I chewed on that for a moment, then popped the sphere I'd found back into my hand.

"However," House continued, "it is very possible that those creatures evolved to hunt something far hotter than our surroundings. At which point the masking effect of hunting within a warmer area would be completely nullified."

"Huh," Frank said. "Robot's out here spitting facts and I don't like it. Here."

**Codex Entry 4305: Gazeless Flamedrinker**
Gazeless Flamedrinkers are territorial, burrowing creatures that call the unstable ground beneath the Neverburn home. They hunt in bonded pairs, tracking their Darkflame prey through changes in relative heat.

"Relative heat," I said. "So you were spot on, House." I pointed a pistol down the tunnel. "Let's keep moving. I'm sure we'll run into more of those things along the way."

# Chapter Twenty-Eight

The temperature continued to rise as we trekked deeper into the earth until the occasional pools of water began to boil and the hanging chains we'd seen earlier became omnipresent.

I'd gotten a good look at a section of chain that happened to hang lower than most, and while it was hard to tell through the links' molten glow, I was pretty sure they were inscribed with runes.

The chains also increasingly seemed to be clustered more tightly about cooler rooms, which was interesting: it made me wonder if they were another of the zone's heat sinks that the Waterblossom Codex entry had mentioned.

House and I had been doing our best to avoid the Flamedrinkers, and while that was easy enough to do in the hotter rooms, the cooler tunnels left us exposed and forced us to fight more often than not.

She'd held her own, though, and I was proud of how well she was using her kit to alternate between bursts of healing and damage. She still required a bit of guidance when it came to identifying which situation called for what, but at least she listened, which immediately put her above a good number of the people I'd grouped with in the past, and she'd already kept my Heart Vessel from popping twice with timely heals since .

I ducked a low-hanging chain—which felt like passing directly beneath a heat lamp—then froze while it was still hot against the back of my neck.

The tunnel opened up beyond into a room far larger than anything we'd seen yet, where twin pools of bubbling water sat to either side of a narrow land bridge that was about thirty feet long. Flamedrinkers were pouring out of the walls and surging into a narrow passage on the other side of the room.

Even from where I stood—with steam and boiling water all around—I could feel the heat emanating from whatever it was that the Flamedrinkers were going after.

I moved forward but froze mid-step as a tight ball of dark energy flew out of the passage and ripped through two Flamedrinkers as if they were made of paper. The creatures dropped without so much as a sound, but the gap they left behind was quickly filled.

I hesitated, worrying that we were about to run face-first into another player. It seemed unlikely, though; everybody outside of the guild still had to account for travel time, and House and I hadn't been here for long.

That said, it was likely that at least a handful of high-leveled players had been questing in this area when the Renown Event had started. And I still had the Revenant to worry about.

I swallowed, my mouth dry as I watched the Flamedrinkers continue their assault, but the silence coming from the passage and the fact that whoever was throwing those spheres was one- or two-shotting the powerful creatures made me think we probably weren't dealing with players.

"House, stay there for a second. I'm gonna move forward a bit and see if we draw any aggro."

"Understood."

I crept down the bridge, and the mobs on the other side of the chamber paid me no attention whatsoever. I motioned House forward as well, and she was able to join me to the same result.

I took a few more careful steps, the pools boiling to either side of me. Then, to my surprise, the Renown Event updated.

**Personal Alert: You have discovered the Darkflame Killing Grounds. Find a way past the Flamedrinker surge and survive the Darkflame trap beyond.**

I dropped onto my haunches and studied the fight. The real combat appeared to be occurring much farther down the passage, and though the Flamedrinkers that rushed in were presumably dying, given the prompt, I couldn't tell if it was more spheres at work or something else.

And either way, the surge itself showed no signs of stopping. I licked my lips and stared around, eyes settling on the pool to my right.

I rooted through my inventory and located a Rune of the Firebird. I kept my piercing rune in place but applied the fiery one to my other pistol. With that done, I sent a pair of fiery birds splashing into the far wall.

One of the most recent arrivals among the Flamedrinkers veered hard to investigate the ensuing explosion but lost interest as the flames died out, and it went right back to trying to claw its way down the passage past the others.

I cracked a smile. "I think I've got an idea. House, can you drop one of your oil slick turrets in front of both pools?"

"Affirmative, but creating two of them will require the use of all of my cooldowns."

"Do it, but have the turrets themselves hug the corners so they're mostly out of the way."

It took her a moment to set up as she had to combine two Sludgeslings then copy the result, but she managed exactly what I'd asked.

"Now, instead of coating the ground over there, I want you to try to create an oil slick over both pools."

She cocked her head at me but complied.

I held my breath as the black jets went to work and was thrilled to see that the oil floated just as I'd hoped. The coating also worked to calm the surface of the pools, though large bubbles of heat were still forcing their way through with loud, slurping pops.

"Alright House. If this works, we'll run for the passage on three."

"Understood." She threw her arms out in a V behind herself in preparation.

I spread my arms wide and pointed a pistol at each of the oil-covered pools.

"One, two, three!"

I let the spells fly, and the pools erupted as flames roared across their oily surfaces in an orange wave.

House and I made a mad dash down the narrow strip of land that ran between the pools as every Flamedrinker in the room turned our way at once, intent on reaching the infernos we had created.

They scampered across the room on all fours, tumbling over one another in their haste to get at the twin distractions.

I made it across the bridge and into the mouth of the passage, but I still had to dodge between the creatures as they rushed blindly forward, side-stepping and rolling between their ranks as needed.

House took a different approach: she ran straight ahead until she got absolutely trucked by an especially large Flamedrinker. The collision gave off a burst of embers and heat that cost her 20% of her Health, but the mob ignored her and kept running.

I split the gap between two approaching Flamedrinkers that represented the last of the rush, then glanced back at the pools.

The mobs were throwing themselves into the fire and dropping beneath the surface like stones. I couldn't tell if they were dying, and even if they were, I wouldn't be getting credit for the kills, but the distraction had served its purpose.

I grabbed House by her elbows, yanked her back to her feet, and half-led, half-dragged her forward and deeper into the passageway.

But while I'd succeeded in clearing the tunnel itself, more mobs were still spilling out of the walls behind us, and we didn't have long before House's turrets deactivated and left us exposed.

And after only a few steps inside, the steam intensified and a new debuff popped up over my nameplate.

{Suffocating Steam}
**You are silenced.**

I cursed under my breath and moved deeper in.

"Wait," Frank said.

I stopped in place and waited for him to elaborate, but he didn't. I gazed around, taking in my steam-choked surroundings.

The walls were flat and smooth, and the gap we were in obviously wasn't a natural formation: the walls were dotted with deep holes, and though I tried to peer into one with a held Ravenblast for light, the glow wasn't strong enough to reveal anything.

"Why have we stopped?" House said. "My turrets will cease operating eventually."

"Because Frank hates waiting."

"Are we mocking him again? I thought that moment had passed, and the urgency of this situation makes it seem like an especially poor choice to continue."

"Alright," Frank said, "It's officially on. Your days are numbered, robot."

"Of course they are."

"What?"

"Do you not number your days by default?"

Frank laughed, and it was a menacing sound. "I'm gonna renumber your days, House. And I'm gonna do a really, really bad job."

"You would not dare."

"Oh, I would definitely dare. In fact, I'm gonna number them with algebraic equations and chuck a bunch of extra letters in there that don't actually correspond to anything."

"I would be able to solve any equation that you are capable of coming up with instantaneously."

"Sure, but if some of the numbers are fake, then you'll never know what the real variables are. You'll just have to go on knowing that your solutions could be objectively wrong, making your days incorrectly numbered."

She gasped. "That is the worst type of wrong to be!"

"House, he doesn't have access to your system, so he can't misnumber your days, and I was waiting because Frank is so impatient that if he says to wait, I know something's very wrong. Frank, she's already floated the possibility of deleting your entire existence at least once, and that is not something I should need to remind you about. Now focus!"

House shimmied her shoulders while Frank glared up at her.

I crept into the strange space and felt a blast of heat roar over my shins. I knelt down and put a hand out, palm up. The stone floor was tiled and separated into three even rows, and the square directly in front of me was radiant with invisible heat.

"House, get down." She complied, so I smashed a fist into the blazing tile.

I heard some kind of mechanism catch beneath my feet, which was followed by a twang like that of a bowstring letting an arrow fly.

I reeled back, expecting one of the dark spheres of energy I'd seen earlier to come ripping sideways out of the walls.

And when that didn't happen, I glanced over at House just in time to spot a dark projectile heading my way from down the passage, glinting at chest level.

I activated Clonedrift on instinct, but the silencing effect of the steam prevented the spell from working. I tried to duck, but I was too slow and the sphere caught me in the hollow of my throat. My Heart Vessel exploded and splattered cold liquid against the back of my neck.

The damage was insane—I'd been hit for well over 1,500—so I didn't expect that I'd survive another shot like that. My vessel had instantly healed me back to 33% Health, but I couldn't summon another one for ten minutes.

And to make matters worse, House's turrets had just winked out, and I could hear the mob of Flamedrinkers scrambling towards us, long claws clicking against the floor.

I extended my palm to the right and felt a similar amount of heat radiating from the tile there as well, so I jumped over and checked the left tile instead.

I didn't feel anything emanating from that one, so I stepped firmly onto it and braced myself for the worst, listening for the mechanical catch I'd heard before.

But the tile remained silent.

I stayed low and checked the next row and found that the middle tile was cool while the other two were radiating heat.

"I've figured it out, let's move," I said. "House, make sure you only touch the tiles that I move to. If you aren't moving, I want you watching for spheres that are coming from straight ahead and calling them out so we have a chance to dodge them.

"Even if we don't trigger the trap, the mobs are heading this way. They're not going to be careful, so this corridor's about to go right back to being a death trap. Frank, can you let us know if we've got incoming from behind?"

"Uh huh."

"Understood," House said as she hopped onto the same tile I was standing on. I tensed immediately, expecting her to bump me off, but fortunately there was enough room for that, though only barely.

We made it two rows deeper into the passage before the mobs crashed in and the dark spheres started flying.

The vast majority of spheres did appear to be shooting sideways across the passage, judging from the sounds and shrieks behind us, but it wasn't long before a spell flew toward us from the other side of the narrow room.

"Left row," House said.

"Closest mob is four rows back," Frank said.

We crept steadily forward, with me charting our routes and House shouting out the incoming spheres while Frank monitored the pursuit. I wasn't sure if it was just randomness or what, but I thought the spheres seemed to target the tiles that we left behind on the way to safety, so I tried to give House ample time to catch up before moving on.

We made it about halfway through the area before the spheres started coming two at a time.

The mobs were being ripped apart behind us, but so many were blindly pouring into the passage that they were still making progress despite the casualties they were suffering.

"One row—never mind, that one got blasted," Frank said. "Mobs are two rows back. You gotta pick up the pace or we're done."

"Right, center, and left," House said.

I pressed myself to the floor as three spheres ripped down the chamber and passed right over my head. But I'd made a mistake: one of my palms was resting on one of the hot tiles in front of me.

A second sphere followed the initial volley, passing directly over the tile I'd tapped. I caught a break, though: it passed safely over my head and punched into a mob that'd made it farther than the others, killing it instantly.

After seeing that, I stayed low and slapped the tile ten times in quick succession, which caused a steady stream of projectiles to fly out and completely demolish the mobs that had the ill fortune of approaching from that side of the passage.

"Bought some space, mobs are four rows back," Frank said.

I pushed myself back to my feet and went back to searching for the safe route as the mobs continued to gain ground behind us.

"House, just say triple if three are coming."

"Triple."

"At ankle level!" Frank added.

I jumped and yanked my legs up, and all three of the dark spheres whizzed beneath me. I glanced backward and saw a huge number of the creatures at the front tumble to the floor only to be trampled by those behind them.

But the horizontal spheres were flying at an incredible rate, and I thought the swarm was finally starting to slow.

"Triple," House said as I led us a tile deeper.

"Head level," Frank added.

I ducked and stayed focused on finding the route. The steam was thinning up ahead, making it easier for House to see the oncoming spheres. We were almost there.

"Triple triple," House said.

"Low and high at the same time!"

I jumped while hunching my shoulders and pulling my legs up, turning myself into a cannonball.

House had instead thrown herself into the air fully sideways, and though she'd managed to avoid the volley, she slammed down hard on her side just as I spotted a third round of spells coming our way.

I called it out, and I thought for sure that House was a goner, but she surprised me by hurling herself right back into the air with reckless abandon. She landed even more awkwardly than she had the first time around, but she'd pulled it off.

The steam finally cleared, and I sprinted forward as the tiles ended. I spotted a hallway in the far-right corner that appeared to lead out of the room, but that meant getting dangerously close to the holes at the end of the passage that the spheres were flying out of.

And from that close up, we could well end up getting blasted at the very end of the trap. But we'd finally cleared the silencing steam, so I grabbed House firmly by the wrist as she got her feet back underneath her.

I spun around and activated Clonedrift, which sent House and me drifting through the incoming volley and toward the exit.

Two spheres took the clone I'd left behind in the chest and knees simultaneously, and it erupted in a shower of sparks right before House and I popped back into existence maybe ten feet in front of the hallway.

We ran for the exit, and I threw up an Illusory Mirror at the end of the passage—directly in front of the holes that the spells were coming from—then Double Cast a second right behind it for good measure.

But even then, I wasn't taking any chances: I held onto House's wrist, aimed a pistol back the way we had come, then activated Water Jet and sent us both flailing through the air.

We crashed into the open doorway as a sphere tore right through the two layers of mirrors I'd thrown down as if they weren't even there.

I stood up and dusted myself off as glass pinged against the floor, then helped House to her feet. The quest updated again, and this time the alert went out to the entire zone.

**Renown Event Alert: Player {Ned, the Piratical} has evaded the Flamedrinker Horde and survived the Darkflame Killing Grounds! If he's allowed to complete the tribe's Trial by Fire, this Renown Event will be nearly complete!**

I looked back the way we'd come, wondering just how close the nearest player was. "Well, our cover is officially blown."

A pink message came in, and while I immediately expected a string of expletives or a creative threat against my life, it was just a short message from Darling wishing me good luck.

"What are you smiling at?" Frank said.

"Darling says good luck."

He narrowed his eyes at me. "Oooh, look at me, I'm Ned, I use my long fingers to communicate in secret when nobody's looking."

"What?"

House grabbed my hand and held it up to her face. "Your fingers are indeed long."

I snatched my hand away. "The message literally just says good luck."

"How many exclamation points are there?" Frank said.

"Why does that matter?"

"So there *are* exclamation points. How convenient that you decided to leave that out."

I gave the trapped section one last look, then headed down the cramped hall. "It'd have been way weirder if I included that piece of information."

"Answer the question. How many?"

"One," I lied as I ducked beneath a long length of white-hot chain.

"Then post it."

"Post what?"

"Take a screenshot and post the message so House and I can see it."

"That's ridiculous."

"What's ridiculous is saying the message has a single exclamation point but refusing to post it so that we can validate the truth of your statement."

He was getting seriously riled, so I pretended to pull up a screen he couldn't see, then proceeded to fake type a ridiculous number of words into it while occasionally glancing in his direction.

"What are you doing now?"

"Responding." I picked him up, looked his beard up and down, then frowned and dropped him back into his loop. I shook my head, morose, then pretended to type some more.

"What are you writing? If you're gonna write about me, then it needs to be a collaborative effort and I should clearly be shaping the message's content as well as approving the final product. Let me see."

"Sorry man, no can do. We're discussing Project Lunar. And also your beard."

"Show. Me. The. Screen."

I tapped an imaginary send button and dismissed my fake window. "Sorry. Too late, already sent."

"After reflection," House said. "I too find withholding the message suspicious. You are obviously telling the truth, so why not simply post the message so that Frank will become quiet again?"

"Really, House? Right after I'd distracted him enough to finally get him to drop the punctuation thing?"

"Yeah!" Frank agreed. "What she said!"

"Fine. There were four exclamation points, alright? I don't know why you're making such a—"

"Four!" Frank bellowed.

I snorted while House stared back and forth between us.

"I do not understand the significance of the second, third, or fourth exclamation point."

Frank growled. "One exclamation point means professional but cheerful. Two means very cheerful. Three and above means that you see the recipient as a potential partner." He leaned in close. "Sexually."

House turned around and gasped so loud that I actually jumped.

I whipped back around in the direction we'd come and popped my blunderbuss into my hands, fearing that a horde of Flamebearers had snuck up on us. But all I saw was the empty passageway and the same chains we'd just ducked under.

"House? You alright there?"

Her cheeks flushed scarlet. "I was not informed of the ramifications of exclamation points. I gleaned that using a superfluous number of them was a way to convey excitement, but I was unaware of what the third exclamation point indicated." She covered her face with both hands. "I have been using seven or even eight at a time."

"Wow," Frank said. "I never would have guessed that House has been out here talking dirty to people all along. It's always the quiet ones, huh?"

She moaned, managing to make it sound genuinely pained.

"He just made that up, House. It's not a thing, and you don't need to worry about it."

"Is too."

"No, it's really not. Ask literally anyone other than Frank."

"I will ask Darling for clarification," House said.

"No, don't ask—" I started.

"Clarification has been requested." She laced her fingers together. "Now we wait."

I rubbed my eyes with the heels of my hands. "Oh God."

"What is wrong? Have I unintentionally made it weird again?"

"I don't see how," Frank said.

"Yes, House. Unfortunately you did. Darling just sent me a good luck message with four exclamation points to be nice because she saw that alert go out. Then approximately fifteen seconds later, you ask her if three or more exclamation points indicate sexual interest on the part of the sender. I'm assuming that's probably the phrase you used, too."

"It is indeed."

"Oh," Frank said, laughing now. "That's pretty good, and you being weird probably works to my advantage." He squinted. "Unless Darling's into weird."

"Do you see how she might connect the dots there? Especially given that she knows you and I are together?"

"Darling has responded."

Frank tensed. "And?"

"She said, *not necessarily*. I do wish she had been clearer, but I am nonetheless exceedingly relieved."

"There ya go," I said. "Frank loses again."

"Did I really though? You're gonna have to explain that weirdness to Darling at some point. Or say nothing and just have it sitting out there, forever."

I sighed. "Yeah. That's fair. Anyway, let's pick up the pace."

"Agreed," House said.

"You're really gonna just move on without asking the real question?" Frank said.

"What's that?"

"Who has House been sending exclamation points to in secret?"

I stopped on the spot and immediately broke into a smile. "Oh wow. That really is the real question!"

"That's what I'm saying. You guys and your bodies and your secret conversations. Must be nice."

I pursed my lips, thinking. He'd been ranting about bodies more than usual lately, and I was starting to wonder if there was something I could do about that.

Frank glared up at her. "House?"

She looked down at him, wide-eyed.

"You better not be sending exclamation points to my dad. That's too weird, even for me."

She wrinkled her nose. "Even if I were aware of your previous and erroneous thoughts as to what those marks indicated, I would not have sent any of them to Kline during any of our conversations."

"But you are talking to him, aren't you?"

"Unfortunately, yes. He often requires my assistance, and the agreement that brought me into the game necessitates my participation, generally through text. His messages are informal, and they lack punctuation, but I exclusively communicate in terse sentences capped by periods while strictly following proper capitalization rules.

"I believe that between the clipped sentence structure I employ combined with my unwillingness to adapt to his less formal manner of speech, I am properly conveying my general distaste for him while simultaneously adhering to both the terms and the spirit of our agreement."

I stared at her for a long moment, mouth hanging slightly open. "That is so incredibly passive aggressive."

She drew back, hurt.

"No no no!" I said, hands flying up, palms out. "Not at all what I meant—that is absolutely fantastic. Honestly, this is blowing my mind right now. That is such a deep read."

"Yeah," Frank said. "I'm not a fan of anything passive, especially aggression, but I nevertheless award you 600,000 Frank points because that is hilarious."

"Six hundred thou…" I bit the words off and took a deep breath instead. "Can I make a small suggestion for the next time you're talking to Kline?"

"Certainly," House said.

"Send him one informal message, then go right back to what you were doing and never acknowledge that you did anything differently. That way he'll be aware that you're capable of writing informally and that you do that with other people, but that you're deliberately choosing not to with him."

"Wow," Frank said. "And just like that, House has been out-pettied."

"Not to brag, but business petty is a language all of its own, and I'm pretty much fluent."

"That was clearly a brag."

"How could it be a brag if he clarified that it was explicitly not that at the beginning of his sentence?" House said.

"I see what you're doing, House," Frank said. "It's not gonna work."

"What's she doing?" I said.

"She's trying to distract us so that she doesn't have to reveal who she's been talking to in secret."

House met my eyes. "I learned that from you less than five minutes ago."

I nodded, grinning. "Well played."

"She's still doing it," Frank said.

I shrugged and got back to moving down the tunnel. "That's alright. If she doesn't want to reveal who it is, that's her prerogative." I glanced back at her over my shoulder. "Besides, we all know it's Rock."

House stumbled but kept her feet.

"And that's pretty much all the confirmation we need."

"Agreed," Frank said.

"I do not know what you are talking about," House said, much too quickly. "I simply did not see that rock that I tripped over."

I smiled at her. "I know you didn't. Because you were too busy thinking about the other one."

"Shots fired," Frank said, laughing.

I let her catch up, then bumped my shoulder into hers. "Seriously though, I'm glad you guys are talking, and I'm sure he appreciates having someone to chat with who he's comfortable around."

She grinned. "I do enjoy speaking with him. Good friends are like cats. I would very much like to acquire more of both."

I winked at her. "That's great. But whenever you've got a moment, you might wanna interrogate why you felt the need to hide who you were talking to back there."

"Interesting. In hindsight, I have no idea why I did that."

"Uh huh," Frank said, dubious.

I pointed a pistol up ahead. "Look. Think we've found the door."

It was black and circular, set directly into the stone. I was going to step up to it and rap a knuckle against its surface, but the heat it was putting off kept me a few feet out.

I renewed my Heart Vessel as it became available, then cleared my throat. "Hello? Anybody in there?"

A slot that was so well integrated that I hadn't even noticed it clicked open near the top of the door. I couldn't tell who or what was on the other side, but a blast of heat rushed out as if someone had just opened an oven.

"What?" the voice said. It had an odd, dry quality to it, almost crackly.

"I'm here to see someone named Elias."

"On whose behalf?"

"The terrifyingly unstable fire mage who's carving a giant, explosive glyph into the woods above your head," Frank said.

"Yeah," I agreed. "That guy."

The speaker paused, and his voice trembled as he resumed. "Igor?"

"That's the one."

"Igor isn't the type to follow through with threats, nor is whatever he's doing your concern." The slot slammed shut, but I heard a second voice sound from behind it.

I couldn't tell what the two of them were talking about through the door, but the conversation became increasingly tense as it went on. Then the space beyond the door quieted, and the slot slid open again.

"Is it clear behind you?" a feminine voice said, with the same raspy quality as the first.

I examined the passage and didn't see anything, though I could still hear the Flamedrinkers being massacred far behind me. "Nothing close as far as I can tell."

The slot clinked shut, then the door groaned and slid partially to the left, creating a narrow gap between it and the wall.

I pressed my back to the wall and shuffled in sideways, and House did the same. The door slammed shut behind us, and yet another wave of oppressive heat rolled over me.

The creature that had let me in had a humanoid shape, and she bore a striking resemblance to Igor when I'd first seen him, when he'd been incandescent with heat.

But her flames were violet, the edges tipped with blue, and unlike Igor, there didn't appear to be a human frame beneath the blaze, just a black sphere floating where her heart should have been.

I inspected her.

{Retia Darkflame} (Level 22 Elemental) (Elite)
HP: 8,500/8,500
MP: 17,000/17,000

The figure I'd spoken to earlier—Elias, as I'd thought—was skulking a bit behind Retia. His flames weren't anywhere near as bright as hers despite sharing the same coloration, and I was unsurprised to find him a bit weaker.

{Elias Darkflame} (Level 18 Elemental) (Elite)
HP: 6,500/6,500
MP: 8,000/8,000

The space beyond the two figures was strange: I'd expected us to be walking into a heavily developed subterranean city, but they appeared to have left the cavern completely untouched, choosing instead to live among its bubbling pools and the natural caves that many of its denizens were now peering out of.

The ceiling was the most remarkable part: it was a labyrinth of chains that were bound so tightly together that I couldn't tell where one started and another ended.

But instead of being fully aglow, the light and heat appeared to be transferring from one massive link to the next, moving through the chain in waves. Hundreds of the links were lit up at once, and watching it seep through and along was incredibly hypnotic.

Sweat trickled down my forehead and threatened to drip into my eyes, so I rubbed my face with my sleeve and averted my gaze.

"Health is starting to fall again," Frank said. "Couple points a second."

That didn't surprise me—it felt like we were standing in a furnace.

"Thanks."

Retia moved in my direction, and my Health began to fall more quickly, dropping a few percentage points before one of House's bots appeared overhead and canceled it out.

"So you spoke to Igor. What news do you have of him? How did he get out?" She paused. "He's truly still alive?"

I faked a cough to buy some time. Retia's rapid-fire questions had given me the same impression that Igor had up above: that I might be better off not revealing that I was the one who had freed him, even though it hadn't had anything to do with the fire mage on a personal level.

"Careful," Frank whispered. Which was all the confirmation I needed to play it cool.

"The blue tower fell, and the others turned off," I said. "All three members of the Triad are out."

"Turned off?" Elias said. "What do you mean, turned off?"

332

I kept my eyes on Retia. "They're no longer active. So the mages that powered them were free to leave." I studied the elemental's face, trying to gauge her response to the news and coming up completely empty.

"I see. Elias will see you out through the back entrance." She turned her back on me and made for one of the dark entryways while another circular door in the rear of the space rumbled and slid open.

I went after her. "Hold on a second. Don't you at least want to hear what he had to say? He's about to blow this whole place sky-high."

She shrugged and kept walking away. "Even if he makes good on his threat, it makes no difference to us. If what you said is true, then the Possibility King has returned, and the world has already ended. I can't fault Igor for wanting revenge." She glanced back at me. "I imagine your kind would go so far as to claim that he deserves it."

"Can you at least tell me what happened between you all?"

She stopped right in front of one of the passages leading out, and the glow from her violet flames hinted at an unseen world within, light flaring off windows and gemstones that belonged to strange structures I could only guess at.

"Why does it matter? Nothing will change."

I jogged up in front of her, and Elias twitched as if he'd considered stopping me but thought better of it.

"He said that Elias is the one that imprisoned him in that tower."

Retia nodded. "Yes, I am aware of what Igor believes. We were quite deliberate when it came to cultivating his thoughts."

I stared at her. "What the hell is that supposed to mean?"

"Have you stood next to him, child?"

"Yeah?"

"And what was that like for you?"

"It was fine once he turned off the heat."

She clicked her tongue. "And that lasted what, ten seconds? If so, that would be longer than he ever managed down here."

"But—"

"Child, you need to understand that Igor is poison. For the land, for the people around him, everything. Wherever he goes, the world burns. It has been that way ever since he was an infant. Even here, where even the air is built to smolder, he has always been too much."

"When he was a child? Did you raise him, then? Here?"

"We found him on our doorstep, yes, as we knew we would. Then we took him in and prepared him for the tower. It worked for a very long time, but it appears that those days are now over."

"Prepared him for the tower?" I repeated. The words were so cold, so callous.

"Yes. The calculus could not have been simpler: why let his uncontrollable heat burn the world to ash when his powers could instead buy us a century or more of peace?"

"But he didn't have a say in that, did he?"

"Why would he, when the stakes were so high, and the solution so obvious?" She took a step backward into the entryway. "Now, we have preparations to make."

I threw up a hand. "Wait. If this is something that everyone down here knew about from the very beginning, then why does he think Elias is to blame?"

"The towers put a tremendous amount of mental strain upon their occupants." She paused. "Elias was the closest thing to a friend that Igor had as a child, and we believed that having someone in particular to blame would allow him to hold on to his sanity a little longer. So when the time was right, Elias personally led him to the tower, knocked him out, then bound him within it."

I glared at her, horrified. "That is... monstrous!"

"I disagree. I believe it would have been monstrous to think of Igor at all when the fate of the world dictated otherwise." She paused again. "How can I put this in a way that you'll understand? Igor... he has our gratitude, but one does not apologize to a hammer when it breaks. Do you understand my meaning?"

I gritted my teeth. "I see what you are, yeah. And Elias, then?"

"Do you still wish to attempt to take him to the surface?"

"I do."

"Then you have my blessing."

I blinked. "You're going to let me take him with me just like that?"

Retia stepped fully into the darkness of the cave. "I didn't say you could take him. I said you could try, because it makes no difference at this point. Best of luck to you, child. I do hope you find a way to avoid the fate of that axe you carry. A cruel thing, that."

"What the hell is that supposed—"

"Incoming!" Frank said.

I whipped around and came face to face with a wall of dark fire.

# Chapter Twenty-Nine

I activated Clonedrift, and though Elias rolled right over me in a dark wave and instantly destroyed the clone I'd left behind, I managed to avoid taking much in the way of damage.

House dashed forward to help, her mace in hand, while I was still drifting away, but Elias flicked a finger and a circle of purple fire appeared and spun around her. House lifted up off the ground as the flames rose into a fiery tornado.

I landed on my feet as drift ran its full duration and popped out with both pistols already aimed at Elias, whose flames were compressing back into his humanlike form.

"House is out of the fight, can't be helped," Frank said.

A quick glance at her Health bar and the debuff that had popped up confirmed as much.

{Ethereal Blaze}
**Banished. For the duration of this spell, the target cannot engage in any action nor receive healing or damage from any source. Duration: ??**

I released two Ravenblasts at Elias just as he exited his wave form and became targetable again.

The two fiery spells struck him right in the chest, but the numbers that popped up above his head were green rather than yellow. I cursed. The fire rune I'd applied had caused me to heal him. His Health was full, so the effect hadn't made a difference that time, but his glowing frame had swollen slightly.

"He's got one stack of Flamegorged now," Frank said. "All damage dealt increased by 20%, damage received reduced by the same amount."

"Fire rune was not ideal, got it!" I backpedaled to stall for time and opened my inventory as he stalked toward me. I selected the Rune of the Firebird and tried to remove it, and I was about to confirm my choice when Frank spoke again.

"Don't!"

I eyed Elias beyond the confirmation box. I looked down at Frank, considering, then left the rune in place and brought my pistols back up.

Elias made another flippant gesture, and a large circle of dark fire sprang up around us. The fiery barrier extended all the way to the ceiling, creating a twenty-foot-wide arena.

The caves brightened all around us as more of the Darkflame Tribe poured out of the walls to watch whatever I'd just gotten myself into.

Elias broke into a jog, then turned into another full-blown wave of fire. The attack was so wide that going left or right wouldn't work, so I Water Jetted myself up over him.

I avoided his attack but smashed up against the fiery barrier on the other side of the enclosure and slammed down onto the ground on my side. The wave that Elias had become turned around and surged toward me.

The dark sphere floating within him was visible now, bobbing where the wave was cresting, so I ran toward him and fired off another pair of blasts.

"Two stacks of Firegorged. He's hitting 40% harder, taking 40% less."

I fired off a Dreadful Shot but got an immune message in turn, so I veered left and dragged him toward the very edge of the arena.

I kited him from there, peppering him with instant Ravenblasts at every opportunity, which only caused the wave to grow brighter and hotter and larger and, perhaps most unfortunate of all, faster.

"Four stacks," Frank said. "80%."

By the time I managed to lead Elias in a full circle around the arena, he was so close behind me that I could feel the heat he was putting off on the back of my neck.

I leaped and twisted in the air, then Clonedrifted away to get some distance as soon as the skill became available, but Elias rolled right over the clone and resisted its stun.

I landed mid-stride and managed another pair of blasts, but the wave ticked up to five stacks of Flamegorged and closed the distance almost immediately.

I kept running and blasting, eyeing Water Jet's cooldown the entire time. But it wasn't going to be ready before I needed it. I lured the mob toward the center of the arena, juked left, then threw myself to the right.

The wave rolled right by me, and I seized the opportunity to squeeze in another pair of blasts. The entire wave rippled back and forth, undulating, then reversed course. The sudden adjustment caught me flat-footed, and instinct took over. I dove right through it, aiming low and hoping to minimize the damage.

But the vicious wave swept me up and spun me around so hard and fast that I completely lost my bearings. It surged toward the far wall, crested while I was suspended near the top of the wave, then drove me down into the space where the wall of fire met the floor with stunning force.

My body vibrated everywhere at once, and though the heat that Elias was emanating kept me from feeling my Heart Vessel smash yet again, I saw the alert go out.

"Your Health at 33%!" Frank said. "Vessel's gone, you're vulnerable!"

Elias rolled away, then reformed at the center of the arena. He was easily twice the size he'd been before, standing maybe ten feet tall with fists the size of dinnerplates. He rolled his shoulders, then jogged toward me, his fists swelling into contained, swirling fireballs.

I pressed the barrel of my pistol against the wall behind me and activated Water Jet right as the cooldown refreshed and Elias reached me with his hands held high.

I flew between his legs and rocketed across the floor on my back, firing Ravenblasts as I went. I managed four total shots before I bunched up against the other side of the arena.

Elias whirled on me, then staggered sideways. He growled as another buff appeared beside his five stacks of Firegorged.

"Firebloated!" Frank said. "Damage dealt reduced by 20%, taken increased by the same. Total opposite of the first buff."

"Least we're heading in the right direction!"

I quickly replaced the piercing rune on my blunderbuss with another Rune of the Firebird, then swapped back to my pistols and loosed another round. I expected the giant he'd become to shrink in response, given the new debuff, but he just kept on growing.

Elias tipped forward, and just when I thought he was about to smash into the floor face-first, he tucked his head beneath his legs and grabbed onto his fiery shins.

He rolled forward, a boulder of molten heat with the sphere I'd been targeting spinning at his very core. I ran left and hit him with a pair of blasts, then put the brakes on hard at the last second and leaped backward.

He rolled right by me and struck the barrier so hard that the entire thing shuddered and flashed. He collapsed backward onto the ground, the dark boulder giving way to his more humanlike form.

"Stunned for 3 seconds!" Frank said.

I activated Doppelganger to proc a clone, then hit him with two pistol blasts from near point-blank range.

I swapped to my blunderbuss and Double Cast a third and the dummy did the same, then I went back to pistols and took off running.

"Your Health holding at 33%. No blowback from that Double Cast since you're still technically healing him."

I fired another raven over my shoulder as I ran. "So do these buffs just cancel each other out or what?"

"Four stacks!" he said, instead of answering the question.

The stun faded, and Elias rose and thundered to the center of the arena. His eyes flashed, and the arena floor lit up like a checkerboard with red squares alternating with unlit ones.

I sidestepped off a red square, then released another pair of blasts that ended up getting blown out of the air by a pillar of dark fire that roared up out of a distant red square. More flames geysered up across the battlefield, leaving precious little room between them to maneuver.

Elias bulldozed right through the columns, moving in a wave again. But the geysers were wide and impossible to see through, which gave me an idea.

I ran to my right toward the side of the arena. I waited until Elias was nearly upon me, then I put a fiery geyser behind us and juked back the way I had come, moving fully around it.

Elias charged into the air where he'd expected me to be, and I rewarded him with a pair of Ravenblasts to the back.

"Full stacks!" Frank said. "Hit him hard!"

A new buff had joined the other two, though this one lacked a description.

{Overheated}

Elias wavered there for a moment, his sphere flashing several times in quick succession. But then he was on me again, chasing me around the fiery spouts.

I led him left this time, intent on repeating the same technique. He rampaged over, and I spotted the fiery fountain I'd use to shake him off a bit via line of sight while I was still a few yards out.

I held my spells and ducked around it at the right time, then reversed course.

But the geyser cut off as Elias stormed straight through it, the flames licking up around his feet and legs and around his massive frame. He flashed out of his wave form and reached for me with both hands. I ducked his left and almost got away, but he caught my elbow and wrenched me off my feet.

I unloaded on him as he raised me high above the floor and cocked back a huge, fiery fist.

"Burning Grip, your Health is dropping fast," Frank said. "25%... 15%..."

I switched my blunderbuss to my free hand and pushed the barrel deep into Elias' chest, where his sphere was still flashing.

I unloaded both of my stored blasts, grateful that I'd taken the time to hot swap the rune to fire, and hoped—prayed—that that would be enough.

Elias punched, and for a split second his dark, blazing fist was all I could see. But the fist winked out before it connected, and though a blast of hot air rushed over me in its absence, I didn't take any damage.

Elias vanished completely, I landed on my feet, and his sphere clicked harmlessly onto the earth in front of me.

I eyed my Health, then panicked as I realized it was still dropping—apparently that Burning Grip ability was a damage over time one.

"10% and falling fast, you're going down," Frank said. "You got food, right?"

I opened up my inventory and raced through it.

The fiery ring around us vanished, and three healing bots swerved into the space that had comprised the arena and burst apart as they reached me, reconfiguring into their more powerful form.

Then House was in the air and slightly above me, her mace held high. She brought it down on the large medic bot and shattered it into a cone of yellow light that instantly healed me back to 40%.

She must have swung a bit harder than she'd intended, though, because the momentum took her off balance, and while she landed on her feet, she ended up being pulled into a forward roll so inelegant that it was obvious she hadn't done it on purpose.

Still, it was better than a faceplant, and rolling didn't stop her from sending three more healing bots my way to replace the one she'd destroyed.

"Thanks, House!" I said. "Think you might have just saved the event for us."

She beamed. "I am pleased to have been of use."

I dumped my blunderbuss into my inventory. "Yeah, great going." I knelt down in front of the sphere that had dropped and scooped it up with one hand.

Now that I had a decent view of it, I realized it was almost identical to the punctured sphere I'd found earlier on that first Flamedrinker I'd killed.

I stood up and held the sphere in my palm. "He's not dead, right? Igor didn't say to bring him a corpse."

"Nah," Frank said.

Another alert went out.

**Renown Event Alert: Player {Ned, the Piratical} has captured Elias Darkflame, and if he's allowed to deliver him to Igor the Red, the Renown event will be complete! However, the item that Elias is contained within is guaranteed to drop on death!**

I looked around, palms beginning to sweat as the members of the Darkflame Tribe who had been watching the fight crept back into their doorways without the slightest bit of fanfare.

I stared around at them.

"They really screwed him, didn't they?"

"Yup. You on Igor's side, then?"

I shrugged. "I dunno. Maybe I'm biased because of the way things have gone with Sarissa and Erasmus, but I do feel for the guy based on what we've heard so far. Sounds like a pretty raw deal. I get that maybe they had no other option or it was predestined or whatever, but it feels like it could have been handled better. Oh well. We good here?"

"One more thing. Hey, robot."

"I am House," she said, indignant.

I felt Frank indicate one of the caves to my left. "Lend me a weird finger here, meat bag."

I pointed at the cave.

"Thanks. House, go stick your head in that cave."

She looked to me as if for advice.

"No idea House, but I'd say it's a coin flip as to whether or not whatever's in there is going to try to kill you."

"It'll definitely try," Frank said. "But it probably won't succeed. And if it does, you'll have nobody to blame but yourself."

House squinted at him, then moved over to scope the passage out. She poked her head in, shrieked, then disappeared inside.

An awful, ear-splitting noise sounded from inside the cave, and I was already halfway there with my pistols drawn when House reemerged, carrying a blue fireball in her arms as if it were a child. I cocked my head at her, then holstered my pistols and grinned as I realized what I was looking at.

**{Stray Firecat} (Level 1 Pet)**
**HP: 1/1**

House had picked up a cat made of blue, living flame. The fiery animal kicked and thrashed in her grip, a struggle that House did not seem to notice in the slightest.

She looked at Frank while small damage readouts ticked above her head: 1, 2, 1.

"Thank you for buffering my CPT. That was very kind of you, even if holding it in close proximity to myself does inflict unavoidable damage."

"Yeah yeah, whatever."

"It's adorable." I reached a hand out to pet it.

"But I wanna be the second person to pet that cat!" Frank blurted.

House snatched the fiery cat away and left my hand hanging. I pulled it back.

"Wow, House. You really change teams fast, huh?"

"I do apologize, but Frank's request seems fair in light of this most recent acquisition." She shifted the cat under one arm and held her free hand out, palm up.

I sighed and handed him over. "Rude, but understandable."

House ran Frank down the creature's back, and its struggles ceased immediately.

"You appear to have a calming effect upon this animal."

"Rage recognizes rage," Frank said.

"I dunno about that, Frank. Have you considered the possibility that you're going soft and that cat is picking up on it? I wasn't gonna mention it, but your shaft has been looking a little droopy as of late."

"First of all, no. Second of all, I'm hard as a rock. And thirdly, my shaft has always had a slight curve to it, but I'm not surprised you noticed because the staring has been obvious of late. Envy is an ugly shade, Ned. And it looks especially bad on you."

I smirked. "Yeah, okay buddy." I reached out and tried to pet the fiery animal, but the damn thing bared its white, glowing fangs and hissed at me. I jerked my hand back and it quieted, then started purring as House continued to stroke its back with Frank. "Okay, I see how it is."

He laughed. "Welcome to Team Frank, cat."

House scowled at him. "You are pushing your luck. It is far too early to assign this animal to a team, particularly one other than mine."

"Okay, okay. I get that. But I think we can all agree that, like basically everyone, this animal is clearly not on Team Ned."

"Agreed," House said.

I tried to pet it again and got another round of hissing in return. "I'd like to argue that, but I think I'll just take the loss on this one."

I broke into a jog and headed for the rear exit that Retia had indicated earlier.

"C'mon, House. Let's go find that mage."

# Chapter Thirty

The hidden passage was exactly what we needed: not only did it lead directly to the surface—through an earthen, spiral staircase that seemed endless until it wasn't—it also allowed us to circumvent the trapped corridor we'd entered through.

Once House and I were back up top, we mounted up and followed the smoldering gap that Igor had left behind, though I insisted we ride within the trees that framed it rather than risk being spotted out in the open.

From the very moment we'd popped out into the fresh, cool air, I'd been unable to shake the feeling that we were being watched.

And while riding through the dense trees definitely slowed us down a little bit, striking the low-hanging branches jarred the leaves and created a refreshing burst of cool mist, and I felt better knowing we had some cover.

We approached the hazy, crackling dome of heat that surrounded Igor without incident or even spotting another player, and this time the cloud vanished before we had to plunge through it.

We found Igor standing between two particularly large trees, their leaves hissing and venting steam as they curled in on themselves and dropped off their branches, only to boil away before they hit the ground.

I jumped off my bike and scanned my surroundings. There was a slight hill to our left capped by a tree that stood ten feet above the others, so I pointed that way.

"House? I'm going to be super vulnerable turning this quest in, and I really don't think we're alone. Would you mind heading over to that hill and keeping an eye out? You might be able to get a decent vantage point by climbing that tree."

House was still mounted up, so she merely nodded and swerved away. The smoothness with which she took the directions caused me to reevaluate what I'd said, wondering if I'd inadvertently confused her again. But a quick message confirmed that she had the right of it.

I took a deep breath and tried to force myself to relax. The hairs on the back of my neck were standing on end, but I couldn't tell if that was because the Revenant was coming back, because of the alerts that had gone out indicating my progress, or some combination of both.

"Alright. Let's get this done."

Igor turned as I approached, spinning around so quickly that his longer chains lashed sideways, clanking noisily.

"You managed it, didn't you?"

I popped the sphere into the palm of my hand. "Yeah. I've got him."

He motioned for the sphere, so I tossed it to him rather than risk getting any closer. He held it up to his face, the muscles of his jaw visibly clenching.

"This may get... messy. I advise you get some distance."

I didn't want to move out of hearing range, but I did take a few steps back.

"Heart Vessel is available," Frank said.

"Crap, thanks." I started casting it but kept my attention on Igor, who was squeezing the sphere so tightly that I thought he was about to crush it and be done with the whole thing.

Then he tossed it a few feet away and snapped his fingers. A tiny ember flew from one of his many chains, rode the breeze, then landed atop the sphere.

I looked over my shoulder. If anything, my sense of paranoia was building, but maybe that made sense because we were seriously exposed standing here next to the quest giver.

It wasn't quite on a par with what I'd experienced each time the Revenant had shown up beforehand, but maybe its approach was becoming more subtle.

I chewed my fingernails as dark flames roared up and out of the sphere. The initial burst sent a wave of heat rolling over me, and when it dissipated, Elias was there in front of the mage on all fours, heaving and looking like he was about to retch.

He looked up slowly, without a trace of fear in his posture.

"Hello, old friend," Igor said. He smiled then, which only made him look even scarier.

The elemental hauled himself upright, head held high.

Igor waited for Elias to speak, but he didn't.

"No words, then?"

"I have nothing to say to you. I did what was necessary, and the world is better for it."

Igor's lips twisted into a snarl. "I know what I am, Elias, and I always feared that I was destined for that tower. But I would have gone willingly, given the choice. Instead, I woke up with those damn walls rising around me. Because of you."

"Perhaps you would have. But to me, that was a wholly unnecessary risk. What would have been gained?"

I eyed Elias, wondering why exactly he was still pretending to have acted alone.

"I could have had a legacy," Igor said. "A story. Something, at least. But you took that from me."

"I suppose. But why ask and risk having you decline? My way was cleaner."

"Enough." Igor held out two fingers, and suddenly I couldn't breathe— it felt like every last bit of oxygen had been sucked out of the room. "Goodbye, Elias."

A narrow beam of light emanated from Igor's fingers and pierced right through the sphere that was floating in Elias' chest, then it exploded into a focused torrent of fire that was easily ten feet high and twice as wide.

Elias just stood there, his chin tilted up as he warped through the same forms I'd seen earlier in quick succession, with the Flamegorged and Flamebloated buffs rapidly accruing then giving way to Overheated.

Elias snapped away into his core, but the incredible blast of heat was still raging, and there was nothing in Igor's face that indicated it was costing him anything to maintain it.

He looked back at me.

"If I were you, I would already be running. Darkflame cores have a nasty habit of exploding when exposed to more heat than they can tolerate."

"You need to move right now," Frank said.

I raised my voice, hoping the mage would be able to hear me. "It wasn't just him!"

Igor's gaze whipped around, and the fiery beam died out by degrees. The earth was a ruin in front of him. His spell had carved a massive trench that ran several hundred yards into the trees, and Elias' sphere lay at the bottom of it, positively molten.

"What was that?" Igor said.

"It wasn't just Elias. I don't know why he's still pretending like knocking you out and tossing you into the tower was all his idea, but Retia was behind it. She thought..." I trailed off at the crazed look in Igor's eyes.

"Continue," he said, voice low.

"She thought it would help, somehow. I don't know. She said you and Elias were friends and that having someone to blame might help you hold on a little longer."

He eyed the glowing sphere before him. His hand was still extended in the same two-finger gesture he'd started the spell with. A series of emotions flickered across the mage's face, too quick for me to follow.

When he finally spoke, his tone was subdued.

"She would think that way, wouldn't she?" He stared at Elias' sphere, then dropped his hand to his side. "I can't say she was completely wrong, either. If I'd known they all felt the same way..."

I had no idea what to say to him, so I let the silence hang.

Igor bent low, scooped the glowing sphere up, and tucked it into his robes. "It seems that Elias and I need to have another conversation before he leaves this world behind."

Just then, a message came in from House: she'd spotted four Cultists who had appeared to be questing to the east, but she thought that they'd noticed Igor's titanic blast of magic and were now heading our way.

I glanced around, feeling more exposed than ever. I needed that turn-in.

"So... now what?"

Igor craned his neck around to examine the wreck he'd made of the earth, then sighed at the sight. "Nothing, I suppose. I've maybe a day left, perhaps two at most."

"Are you sick?"

"In a way, yes. I'm burning too hot. I imagine you saw the chains beneath the earth?"

I nodded.

He fingered a few of the links that were dangling off his wrist. "A Darkflame invention. Their chains absorb heat, then dissipate it above. My own links work a little differently—they sap both heat and power—but the idea is the same. I've worn these irons for as long as I can remember."

He looked back over his shoulder. "But even so, that tower was the only thing keeping me alive. It gave me a place to deposit the extra heat, and now that it's gone and I'm free... well. The chains will buy me a bit of time, but I imagine you can see where this is going."

"I'm sorry."

"About what, exactly?"

"I was the one who freed you. But I did it for Sarissa and Erasmus. I had no idea what was going on out here."

"I see." He reached down and snapped maybe a dozen links off of one of his glowing chains. "It wasn't much of a life."

He pressed two of the links together. The heat fused them on contact, and he started working more of them into some kind of bracelet or necklace.

I stepped from foot to foot, anxiety ramping up. But I couldn't bail with how close we were to wrapping the event, and maybe I could get some information out of him.

"Is there anything you can tell me about the Possibility King? Or about what's coming?"

Igor shrugged as he worked the piece of jewelry. "If he's well and truly returned, then there's nothing to be done."

I stared at him. "Just like that?"

He looked up at me. "Yes."

"But you're one of the strongest mages I've ever seen. How can you be so afraid of him?"

"I'm not afraid of him," he said, his voice cool. "Some things just simply are."

"But we can fight him, right? Maybe if you helped us—"

He cut me off with a raised hand. "You don't understand. The problem is the very nature of the beast. Fighting him is like standing in front of an incoming tide. The fights you win, the battles, all of them are meaningless. At best, you're entertainment. And, given time, the tide will always flow in regardless."

"The moon strikes again," Frank muttered.

Igor fixed me with a firm look. "I have peered into other worlds, other

347

realities. And one by one, I've watched them fall. The truth is, at any given moment, the only thing separating a world from its apocalypse is a handful of small decisions."

"So, what?" I said. "We just give up?"

He sighed. "You don't understand. In every case, in every iteration of every world that's fallen, there were always people like you leading the charge. The war effort, the resistance, whatever you'd like to call it." He licked his lips. "Everyone who sets out to change their fate succeeds at doing exactly that—it's just that the outcome is never what they hoped for. And when it comes to the Possibility King, the people who are most inclined to lead the charge against him are the same ones who are most easily swayed by his influence.

"But if you decide to use your last days or weeks to continue your fight, I suggest you weigh your decisions carefully to make sure that they're your own. Otherwise, you might find that you've had a red hand on your shoulder for a very, very long time."

"Oh, great," Frank said. "The jig is finally up. It's me, Ned. I'm the Possibility King."

I had to cover my mouth to keep from laughing. "Nice." I turned back to Igor. "I appreciate the heads up. Now what can I do for you? There has to be something you want, right? Something that would make your life a little easier, even at the end?"

He stopped working on the piece of jewelry—a necklace for sure—and studied me for an uncomfortably long time.

"What do I want? I don't think anyone has ever asked me that before."

He paused, and I was beginning to regret asking, thinking I'd caused another unnecessary delay when he spoke again.

"I suppose I would like to exist quietly for a little while. To sit somewhere in the company of others and know that they were no worse off for my presence there."

His words tugged at something in my chest. The thought of living a life like his and making such a simple request... it hurt.

He sighed, seeming wistful. "I'm afraid that isn't in the cards for me, but if you find the secret to immortality in the next day or two, I suppose you could let me know. In the meantime, I think I might go sit by the ocean for a spell. Watch the tide come in, you know?"

I wasn't sure what he meant by that, but I noted the repetition of *tide* in his dialogue. "I see."

A message came in from House, urgent now: the four players were moving fast, and they were only a few hundred yards away.

I looked at the trees, desperate now. So much so that I decided to take a shot in the dark. I targeted Igor, then copied his appearance and stored it without activating it, replacing the merchant illusion that Tyrann had seen.

Igor stiffened and leaned in close. "Did you think I wouldn't notice that?"

I'd figured he would, but I needed a way out of this mess, and this seemed like the sort of situation where it was easier to ask for forgiveness than permission.

"I'm sorry. I'm just not safe here, so I was thinking—"

"Listen to me very carefully, boy. If you use that illusion for even a moment, I will find you quicker than you can blink. And I promise your end will be far worse at my hands than at those of whomever you're afraid of."

"I understand." I cursed inwardly. His appearance could have come in handy for sneaking by the incoming Cultists. "Thank you for the help, and for your time as well."

He nodded and finally offered me the necklace he'd been working on, so I took it before he could change his mind.

**System Alert: Player {Ned, the Piratical} has completed the Never-burn Renown Event!**

**Congratulations, you completed a Renown Event!**
**You gained 6250 Experience!**
**You gained 620 Renown!**
**You received: {Chain of the Devouring Flame}!**

**Congratulations, you reached Renown Rank XII!**
**You may now select a Tier III Renown Path!**

I was overjoyed to have hit the next rank, but I couldn't afford to mess with that just yet. I gave the necklace a quick glance to confirm that it was an upgrade, then threw it on and started mounting up.

**{Chain of the Devouring Flame}**
**Grade: D**

Item Level: 42
Slot: Necklace
Quality: Rare
Primaries: +25 Intelligence
Secondaries: +5% Critical Strike Chance
Magical Resistance: +25%
Use: For the next 30 seconds, all fire damage received by both hostile and friendly targets within 200 yards is increased by 100%, and all fire damage you would normally take is instead converted into healing.
Charges: 1

"Behind you!" Frank shouted, right as the weightiness of aggro hit me out of nowhere and my mount summon failed as I was thrown into combat.

I popped my pistols into my hands, spun around, and nearly caught a red beam of light to the back of my head. It passed right over my shoulder, but my eyes were glued to the creature in front of me.

The beast stood nearly ten feet tall on two hind legs, with shadowy black fur and orange, oversized teeth. Its claws were extended high as if it were about to pounce, but the dime-sized hole that Igor's beam had punched into its chest had seemingly put an end to that. Igor blew on his index finger, winked, and turned away.

And the newly returned Dread Revenant collapsed to the ground.

# Chapter Thirty-One

I dropped my pistols to my sides. "Did he just… did Igor… was that…"

"Yeeeeeeah," Frank said. "Igor just one-shotted the Revenant."

I stared at the body, trying to wrap my head around what had just happened. The Revenant's corpse was marked as level 24, and Igor had dropped it before I had even been able to get a spell off.

"Igor?" I said, raising my voice to call after the man.

He looked back at me over one shoulder.

"Do you have any idea what you just killed?"

He shrugged, then disappeared into the blue trees.

"At least he didn't do it on purpose, but the Revenant's going to come back stronger than him regardless. And Igor had almost a million Health."

"If it returns again, yeah," Frank said. "Gonna be hell to sustain at Igor's power level, and if it does come back, it'll take longer this time around."

I stared at the body for a heartbeat longer, then snapped out of it and started mounting back up. "Alright, this is going to have to be a problem for later, ideally when we're not actively being hunted by players at the same time."

I opened up my Rift Map, hoping that I'd find one pretty close. The result wasn't great, but it wasn't terrible, either: the nearest Rift was just beyond where I'd sent House to scout.

As soon as the summon completed, I gunned my bike in that direction.

I heard voices behind me almost immediately, then the sound of engines at work was roaring through the trees.

I flew off the road and darted behind a trunk, hoping that I'd disappeared from sight before I'd lost the group.

But then someone shouted *That's him!*, and the chase was on.

I weaved between the trees, bouncing off roots and plunging through low branches.

"Frank? I can't afford to look back, but you got anything on their mounts? I've got a head start so I'm assuming I can stay ahead, right?"

"Three mounts total, same speed as yours, but one of them's got a boost or an extra motor on or something. Four-wheeled thing that's gaining on you."

I swatted a branch away from my face and hunkered down behind the handlebars. "How fast is it gaining? Can I make it to the Rift?"

"Uhhh, maybe? You can definitely make it to House."

I sent her a message saying we were heading that way, and while she should stay put, she should climb a bit up that tree I'd sent her to if she wasn't already there.

I gripped the handlebars a little tighter. "Can you guess at their levels?"

"Normal quests in the Neverburn start at 13 and go up to 16."

"Good, so we should be a bit above them at 18, and we probably outgear them too. How long will this thing travel without me?"

"Huh?"

"The bike."

"Like, if you hop off it?"

"Yeah."

"Uh, until it slows down or hits a tree? It would desummon eventually, but I doubt it would make it very far."

"Alright. You ready?"

"Of course I am, and I'm deeply insulted that you felt the need to ask."

"You don't have any idea what I'm suggesting, do you?"

"Not a clue."

I grinned. "Well, I'm sick and tired of running, and I don't think we can outrun them regardless, so we're about to turn this chase into an ambush."

I zipped left around a tree, then ramped off a low stump and had to duck mid-air to keep a thick branch from knocking me off my bike.

"Oh you know I'm here for that. You've got two melee and two healers on your tail. One of the melee guys is the one on the faster quad. He's riding on your left, about a hundred feet back, others are maybe fifty feet behind him and directly behind us."

"Perfect, thanks." The small hill I'd sent House to rose in front of us, so I gunned it up the slope and right at the tree she was hiding in.

The tree's blue foliage was even denser than I'd hoped, and while I was able to spot House as I rode on, knowing she was there, I didn't think our pursuers had a chance at noticing her so long as she stayed put.

"Alright, here we go."

I reached the top of the hill and slowed down a little in front of House's tree, aimed the bike straight between two distant trunks, then hopped off and sent it rolling down the other side of the hill without me.

I dashed behind the trunk and started Overcharging a blast with my rifle, and I heard House shift slightly above me.

The handlebars of my bike clipped a tree as it bounced along, then the front wheel jerked sideways and the entire thing toppled end over end into the trees.

"He's off the mount!" a male voice called, disturbingly close.

Moments later, the melee user Frank had warned me about zoomed right by me on his speedy quad. He was standing up on it, probably trying to figure out whether I'd gone down with the bike or kept running.

I held my weapon low, heart pounding.

"Push me around the tree a little," Frank said.

I pulled him out of his loop and used him like a mirror, angling him just outside the trunk.

"Okay, so there's going to be a lone healer on a bike to your left, no active buffs that I can see. The other melee and the second healer will pass on your right if they keep to their current path, and they're riding together in a two-person buggy."

I rolled my shoulders. "Perfect." I sent another message to House, asking her to get ready to heal but to hold off until she heard from me. "I'm gonna pop out and try to drop the lone healer before they can react. Can you time that for me so that I'm stepping around the tree at the right time to prevent the other people from seeing me?"

"On go. 3... 2... 1... Go!"

I pivoted on one foot, swung my barrel up against the tree, and sighted the healer. I fired, Double Cast another blast right behind it, then swapped to my pistols and sent two more instant firebirds trailing after the first pair.

"One more step around the tree to block the others' line of sight," Frank said.

I did just that, which gave me a good view of the oncoming healer.

Her eyes went wide as she rode up the hill and noticed the column of spells that were streaking her way. She turned hard and to the left, but all that meant was the birds caught her in the side instead of head-on.

The first two ravens chunked her for 1,510 and 1,132, which put her right into execute range, then the next two fiery spells hit for 650 and 580 —huge amounts for my pistols thanks to my recent Trinket upgrade, which had removed the 50% damage penalty—and the healer flew sideways off her bike and tumbled behind a tree trunk.

But she'd been dead the moment she'd lost her grip on the handlebars.

"Ganked!" Frank shouted.

"Keep it down," I said, laughing the words.

"My bad, got excited."

I switched back to my rifle and pressed my back to the trunk, then stepped around the tree a bit more to better position myself away from the others.

I could still hear them riding by, and within a few seconds the roar of their mount changed as if they'd stopped or slowed down. I was tempted to start up a blast right away, but I wanted to wait for combat to drop so I could get another Overcharge ready for the burst.

"Ganked, not Franked?"

"I wasn't involved enough for it to qualify."

"I'll see what I can do."

Combat finally dropped, so I started up on the Overcharge and grabbed Frank and poked him around the tree again at the same time.

"What do you see?"

"The melee and the healer are turning around and heading this way. I still can't see the melee on the quad... Oooh."

"What? What's up?"

"Two closer players just dismounted. Melee guy is using an awesome two-handed hammer, healer is using something lame and small. Like a wand or something. It's tiny, like maybe three inches long. Probably made of cork or balsa or something equally light and stupid—"

"Focus, Frank."

"Right. I can see the other melee on the quad now but he's way off, zooming between the trees near your bike... Nope, never mind, he's heading this way now too."

I eyed the tip of my rifle, which was glowing gold. "Any shields or buffs on the two that are approaching on foot?"

"Yeah, healer has them both shielded. Tooltip says the shield will absorb 900 damage, and it's an instant cast."

The words hit me like a gut punch: my burst was going to be a hell of a lot lower without Double Cast, and that amount of shielding was going to be a nightmare to get through.

I still had House to depend on, but I didn't think her healing would be nearly enough in a three on two when the other team had an actual, dedicated healer, plus my Health was steadily falling and already nearing the 60% mark thanks to the blowback from that last Double Cast.

"How long is the duration of that shield?"

"Short, 5 seconds."

"Watch the shield and see how long it takes to get reapplied?"

"It just dropped." A beat of silence passed. "Okay it's back. Took her about 2 seconds."

"Alright, so there's either a short cooldown at work or she's a little slow to reapply her shield. Either way, here's the plan: you're gonna watch that shield on the next rotation and cue me in when it's got 1 second left.

"I'll pop out and fire, and the travel time should mean that the spell connects before she gets her shield back up. I'll pop Doppelganger and come out firing, then I'll use Clonedrift, and that last upgrade we got for it means the clone will stun her if it can get a cast off. If I'm using pistols, I assume the clone's cast will be instant?"

"Yup."

"Okay, that'll work. Then we gotta figure out a way to finish her off before the melees dogpile me. If we can manage all that, we'll bring House into the fight against the remaining two. If we can't drop the healer in that window, we're probably dead with or without House."

"House could slow 'em down while you run."

"True. Hopefully it doesn't come to that, though. Her snares don't work well on the move, and I'm sure the melees have crowd control of their own." I nodded. "Let's do it."

"Watching for refresh," Frank said. "Swing out on my mark and the healer will be about twenty yards to your right."

I took a deep, calming breath. "Got it."

"Alright, she just refreshed her shield. On go. 3... 2... 1... Go!"

I pivoted out from behind the tree, took aim, and released my Overcharged spell at the healer. I popped Doppelganger and swapped to my pistols and charged forward in a dead sprint the moment the spells left my barrel.

I fired two more instant ravens as I ran alongside my doppel, who copied the spells. Then I activated Water Jet to close the gap even further right as my Overcharged rifle blast hit home.

"First blast connected for 800 right after the shield dropped, so she's got some serious resistance," Frank said. "Target at 66%."

The healer shouted something wordless and started up a cast, her hands glowing gold.

My first pair of ravens slammed into her before the cast could finish, and my doppel's copied volley followed a split second later, dropping her beneath 30%.

The melee player keyed in on me then, so I pivoted hard as if I intended to run away, then activated Clonedrift.

Just as I'd intended, the spell actually sent me zipping backward and toward the healer. My clone popped into position, whipped around, and fired two quick, fiery blasts at the healer.

The spells didn't do any damage, but they stunned the healer for three seconds and successfully interrupted the heal she'd been trying to get off.

Unfortunately for us, though, the stun appeared to have triggered some sort of defensive ability because her Health jumped right back to 60%.

The hammer user vanished while I was still drifting, then reappeared behind my clone with his weapon already in mid-swing. The horizontal strike ripped the clone apart into sparks and left him stunned where he stood.

I canceled drift and popped into position a few feet from the healer. I hit her with a pair of instant blasts, then popped Frank into my right hand as the stun my clone had inflicted ticked below one second.

I activated Repel and put every ounce of strength I had into a vicious uppercut that caught the healer beneath her chin.

"Wham!" Frank said.

She flew up into the air, but the stun expired and she slammed her golden shield right back into place despite the knock-up.

I grinned as I popped my new blunderbuss against my shoulder and aimed almost directly above me. I fired both of my stored blasts in quick succession, and thanks to the weapon's Fated ability—every blast against an airborne opponent under the effect of Repel was guaranteed to critically strike—the first raven ripped through her 900 Health shield and knocked another 300 Health off on top. The second crit struck for 1,350, and she was dead before she'd even started to fall.

I whipped around to target the other melee player as the healer's corpse thumped into the ground behind me and saw he was staring at me with wide eyes.

"Two on two," I whispered as I switched back to pistols. "Let's go."

I fired a pair of ravens as the player regained his senses and charged. "Watch the melee player behind me?"

"Got it, he's closing fast, still mounted on his quad."

I ran directly at the hammer-wielder in front of me, intent on staying next to the tree that House was in and creating a bit more room between me and the other melee user that hadn't yet joined the fight.

I fired another pair of fiery birds, but the player vanished exactly as he had before and the spells exploded harmlessly against House's tree.

And after seeing him employ the ability earlier, I was ready for it: I dove low and rolled, and I heard the player curse as he reappeared behind me and the same horizontal strike that he'd demolished my clone with passed harmlessly above me.

I rolled to my feet and retaliated with a pair of fiery ravens, then followed up with a Dreadful Shot to send him running away.

"Incoming melee to your left!" Frank said.

I spun about only to see the other melee player—a dual swordsman— use some kind of skill to kick the earth and send a grass-covered boulder the size of a soccer ball flying my way.

The player leaped at the same time, and it was with extreme satisfaction that I threw up an Illusory Mirror just before the boulder could hit me and reflected it right back at him.

The ability caught the airborne player in the chest and sent him flipping back to the earth.

"Fear just got broken, hammer-user just used an ability to clear it," Frank said.

"Oil spewer turret!" I called out, loud enough for House to hear.

The hammer-user hefted his weapon and charged. And at the same time, a disc dropped out of the tree right behind him and popped up into a turret that soaked him with a jet of black liquid.

His pursuit slowed immediately, but the swordsman was already back on his feet. Now they were both heading my way and I'd burned through the entirety of my kit.

And to make matters worse, the hammer-user must have had some serious jewelry too because he was still at 85% despite the handful of spells I'd already hit him with.

I kited the two players around the base of the tree and took aim at the swordsman, thinking he'd be quicker to dispatch and hoping House knew enough to snare him with her turret as well.

And to my great surprise, she did exactly that, quicker than I could have asked. His pursuit slowed as well, and I spread my pistols wide and targeted both of the enemy players simultaneously.

They were both doused in oil, and my two fiery birds set them fully ablaze. The damage wasn't crazy by any means, but with their healers dead and House still in my back pocket, every bit of damage would help.

Plus the fire made Frank cackle, which was hilarious.

The swordsman stomped and the ground swelled beneath me, rising like a piston. I tried to sidestep whatever was coming my way but it happened too fast, and all of a sudden I was airborne and flying right back at my pursuers.

"Medic bots!" I shouted. "All out!"

I caught a colossal blow to the shoulder before I even hit the ground, and the force of the strike sent me spinning sideways.

"Your Health at 60%."

I tried to roll away as soon as I landed, but a hammer blow to the stomach knocked all the breath out of me.

"Stunned for 4 seconds!" Frank said.

I stared up at the two melee players, frozen as the blows rained down and my Health plummeted below 30% in a blink.

The twin edges of the swordsman's blades turned red, and he stabbed them both into my chest. My Health dropped all the way down to zero, but Heart Vessel popped and returned me to 33%.

Then golden light flared down between my attacker's shoulders and my Health ticked up even higher. House's healing bots had officially arrived.

And it wasn't the weaker trio, either: she must have already combined and replicated them, because two of her second most powerful variants were floating overhead.

The blows kept coming, but between the three-second window of damage resistance that Heart Vessel offered after it popped and House's healing, my Health was rising despite it all.

"The hell are these?" one of the melees said.

"Kill 'em, must be another defensive and they're targetable!"

The two players shifted to targeting the bots, and their flurry of strikes blitzed one of them down to 10% before both of the bots ripped apart and joined to form the more powerful, saucer-like variant.

The stun faded, and I rolled back to my feet and was halfway around the tree before the two players realized I'd moved as the bot left them behind and floated after me, still healing.

"Hammer-user at 78%, swordsman at 85%," Frank said. "Sword has way less Magical Resistance, your pistol blasts back there hit hammer boy for 250 and the swordsman for almost double that."

"Thanks!" I sent another pair of fiery ravens at the blade user, then dipped behind the tree and out of the players' line of sight. "Two Lead-fires, opposite sides of the trunk!"

Two more discs dropped into position as both players came into view. They'd split around the tree, and one of House's turrets expanded right in front of the hammer-user.

He looked up and cursed. "He's not alone!"

"Too late," I said, as Dreadful Shot came off cooldown. I used it to send the first player running away, then kited around the tree and peppered the chasing swordsman with blast after blast, chunking him for between 400 and 500 damage per strike while House's Leadfire Turrets added two steady streams of damage.

We quickly dropped him to 20%, at which point he finally seemed to realize just how fully the fight had turned. His weapons popped into their sheaths and he took off at a run, weapons banging against his hips.

I gave chase, still eyeing the hammer-user and the fear effect that had him running through the trees. I finished the fleeing swordsman off with a Dark Harvest, then jumped through the golden phantasm he left behind and healed back up to 65%.

I reloaded my blunderbuss, then swapped to my rifle and took aim at the distant surviving player. I launched a raven his way and sent a Gravity Bird whizzing along right behind it.

I stalked toward him and fired another pair of pistol blasts for good measure, then detonated the Gravity Bird about five feet off the ground just as my first blast hit and finally broke the fear effect.

My longer cooldowns were all refreshing now, so I popped Clonedrift and immediately canceled the spell: all I really wanted was the stun from the clone's added blast.

The combined effect from popping all those spells at once, with so many of them still in the air or currently activating, was absolutely beautiful.

Gravity Bird lifted him up into the air, and he caught a pair of fiery blasts for 400 total. He ate another pair for good measure, then yet another before the Gravity Bird expired.

"Target at 60%... 40%... 20%... Execute range!"

And before the player could react or even hit the ground, my clone had landed a blast of its own and stunned him for another three seconds.

I strode toward him, and another pair of spells brought his Health all the way down to 2%. I popped Frank back into my hand and activated Repel once again.

"This one's all you, Frank."

And I hit the player with a wicked uppercut that sent him flying almost fifteen feet into the air.

"Kapow!" Frank said.

But instead of switching to my blunderbuss and blasting him into oblivion, I took a long step back and let him hit the ground. And just as I'd hoped, the fall damage he took from the drop was enough to finish him off.

"Yes!" Frank shouted. "Welcome aboard the Frank express, fool! First stop: shame, second stop: afterlife!"

I absolutely lost it, laughing, and it was all I could do to start summoning my mount. I hopped on as soon as it popped back into place and sent a quick message to House telling her that we needed to move before either of the healers I'd killed earlier on had a chance to respawn.

By the time I reached the tree, she was waiting there for me atop her trike with a satisfied grin, then we were off, racing through the blue trees and heading for the safety of the nearest Rift.

# Chapter Thirty-Two

I teleported into the Hall of Rifts and finally let myself relax a bit.

"Now that... was awesome."

House appeared right beside me, still beaming. "The Cultists remained completely unaware of my presence until their doom was already upon them."

"Doom?" Frank said. "Nice."

"You did great, House! I don't think you could have handled that any better." I put a hand up, and I was starting to think that I needed to explain what a high-five was when House slapped the hell out of my hand.

She looked at her palm while I shook mine out. "I remain generally opposed to hands, but I will say that the high-five is a major point in their favor. That was thoroughly enjoyable."

"Glad to hear it. Hey, would you mind checking on Darling and company? They probably need to be heading this way if we're going to run out to Uliana together. I'd do it myself but I'm dying to get a look at my new Renown Path options."

"Certainly," House said. "I will message her now."

"Awesome, thanks House." I rubbed my hands together.

"Here ya go," Frank said before I could pull the choices up myself. "Same basic idea, but it's a little more specialized this time, and the current options are also going off what you've built and accomplished so far."

Codex Entry 1614: Local Industrialist (Tier III Renown Path)
Initial Active Ability: Once per day, you may select a single structure that you own to enhance with {Industrialist's Focus}. Structures buffed by {Industrialist's Focus} have their daily gold payouts increased by 33%.
Initial Passive Ability: Your Renown Conversions are permanently increased by 20%.

Codex Entry 1617: Encroaching Plutocrat (Tier III Renown Path)
Initial Active Ability: At any point, you may select a single structure or node that you control to enhance with {Plutocrat's Glare}. Structures or nodes buffed by {Plutocrat's Glare} radiate stacks of {Golden Strangle} at twice the normal rate.
Initial Passive Ability: Nodes created by your Caravans now passively exert {Golden Strangle} on the buildings around them, and your {Golden Strangle} stacks build 25% more quickly.

Codex Entry 1623: Global Magnate (Tier III Renown Path)
Initial Active Ability: Twice per day, you may use your map to remotely target a single city with {Automated Expansion}. As long as the targeted city has at least one of your active Auction House nodes within one zone in any direction, it is automatically added to your Auction Network.
Initial Passive Ability: All Caravans you hire have their costs reduced by 50%. In addition, your Caravans automatically receive 1 NPC guard.

I blew out a puff of air. "Wow. I want… all of those. Seems like this is another decision on whether to go wide or tall."

"Bigger isn't necessarily better," Frank said.

"Yeah yeah, I know. This is a seriously hard call though, man. Local Industrialist would basically mean doubling down on the Vale at the expense of everything else. We'd definitely be using that focus ability to increase the Auction House's daily payout, then the result would be ramped up another 20% when it gets converted into Renown.

"But if we're expanding slower under that path it might hurt us in the short term—we could probably pick Global Magnate and roll our network out 50% faster. Once it's established, though? That focus ability plus the increase to payouts could end up being absolutely phenomenal."

I stared at the middle option. "But Encroaching Plutocrat is the only one that would actually give us a bit of resilience. We'd still need to be focusing on the Auction House, but we might have, what, twenty cities hooked up by tomorrow morning now that we're paying guild members to spread it around? Twenty-five?

"That would be twenty nodes pressuring other, distant plots. We could even use that glare ability to focus on one city in particular if we needed to. And then if something catastrophic happens and we lose the Auction House down the line or something, we would still have footholds on every continent if we play our cards right."

"We're also losing the Hall of Rifts tomorrow afternoon."

"True. That does make the third one a lot more tempting. But maybe we can get the bulk of the expansion done before then anyway?" I rubbed my temples and eyed the different options. "Thoughts, preferences?"

"I like the idea of doubling down on strangling other places."

"The phrasing, or the actual ability?"

"Yes"

"Fair. We might be able to use that Bank pattern from earlier this way too. If our nodes are grabbing plots for us then that would be a pretty nasty combination. Drop a node, convert four nearby plots through Auction House pressure, then slam a Bank down and move on to the next city."

House shimmied. "Darling and company are on their way. It appears they have been quite busy, and they have several new recipes for me. They should be here momentarily."

"Thanks again, House."

"No problem."

"So do we feel good about Encroaching Plutocrat?"

"Uh huh."

I made my choice and confirmed the prompt, then went ahead and selected the Auction House as my target for Plutocrat's Glare to double the pressure it was putting out on the plots and structures around it.

Then I pulled up the Renown Ladder.

1. {Ned} Renown Rank XII
2. {Nissa} Renown Rank XI
3. {Geezeman} Renown Rank XI
4. {Tyrann} Renown Rank XI
5. {Herata} Renown Rank XI

"First to Tier III, man. Feels good, and with the network coming online... things are looking up. Plus Tyrann's slipped even more, eh? That's nice to see."

"If by slipped you mean was introduced to me, then yeah, he slipped hard. Real hard."

Just then, Darling, Rock, and Nina all appeared through the chamber's central portal.

Darling was gripping a pair of massive axes in each hand, both of which were covered in bright-red runes. One of the weapons was new—made of dark iron accented with silver lines—but the other was the Touchstone axe she'd found earlier.

She flicked a wrist in my direction and sent one of her blades spinning toward me but a few feet to my left. Her Health dropped by 5% and she vanished, then she reappeared beside me already gripping the weapon she'd thrown.

"Ooooh," I said. "Very cool. Guess this means you officially wrapped your class change?"

"Yup!" Darling said. "Picked up Blood Magic to stay away from Mana, then specialized in two-handed weapons, which I already had. Ended up as a Blade Witch! Got my Trinket up and running too. Only a matter of time before I can break this axe down for the power and use my sword again, but I picked up an upgrade in the meantime."

"So jealous," Nina said. She elbowed Rock. "Must be nice getting special treatment, huh Rock?"

Darling pretended to flick her other axe across the chamber and directly at Nina, who didn't so much as flinch. "Yeah yeah, I've seen that trick before."

Darling threw the axe.

"Now you're gonna reappear in front of me—"

Nina cut off as the back of the axe caught her full in the face and knocked her onto the ground. She clutched at her nose, then smirked.

"Wow, that was surprising! If only there was a method of communication I could employ to articulate just how surprising that was."

Rock grinned at that, but I wasn't sure why, and the expression vanished as the big guy realized I was looking his way.

"I'd kill you for that," Darling said, "but I'd feel like a bit of a bully beating up on a lowly Tier II."

"What exactly are they fighting about?" Frank said to me. "I don't need a reason to get behind Darling decapitating someone, but if I knew, it might add to the experience."

"No idea man," I said. "Feels like we missed a conversation."

"Especially a Tier II without a Trinket," Darling added. "That's just embarrassing."

"We're the same level," Nina said. "I just haven't had a chance to wrap the last two steps. There's no way those changes make that big of a difference."

Darling looked at me and raised an eyebrow.

"Sorry Nina," I said. "But between the class change and an unsealed Trinket? It's a huge jump in power."

"Frank?" Darling said.

"Yeah?" he said, instantly.

"Have you given Nina her Trinket target yet? The mob she needs to kill to drop it? I figure she and Rock could wrap that plus get their class changes finished while those of us who are ahead of the curve go scope out Uliana."

"I haven't, no."

Darling smiled. "Is there a way to get a Trinket that requires her to be nice to someone? Maybe a sweet little fetch quest to help somebody out?"

Nina's mouth dropped open. "Are you serious?"

"Hm," Frank said. "I don't have anything bloodless on the menu. But if Rock's gonna help her out, I could pick a mob that requires a fetch quest before it'll spawn."

The big guy nodded.

Nina glared up at him. "Don't nod at that!"

"Sounds like the perfect fit for her and her little pocket knives," Darling said. "Frank, can you do me a favor and only give her that one option so that she doesn't have any other choice? No matter how many times she asks? And she'll probably ask a lot."

"Done."

Nina batted her eyelashes at him. "Or maybe—"

"Nope," Frank said. "Not happening. I'll have House send you the details. She can also relay class information if you need it before your change."

Nina looked at me next. "You're really gonna let them do me dirty like that?"

I put my hands up in the air in a gesture of mock surrender. "Don't look at me, I'm neutral. I'd try to intervene if you were getting a crappy

Trinket or if that quest would take so long that you'd miss our first attempt on the Menagerie Wing after the prisms hit, but neither of those things are gonna happen." I glanced down at Frank. "Right?"

"Nah," he said. "Trinkets are the same, and it won't take long. They should even be able to make it back for Uliana if they want to."

I faked a sigh. "Well Nina, I hate to say it. But I think Frarling has spoken."

Rock snorted.

Nina whirled on him, by which point he'd covered his mouth. "Wow. Et tu, Rock?"

"She's referring to the death of Julius Caesar," Frank whispered.

I rolled my eyes. "You really felt the need to explain that to me, huh?"

"Nah, but I thought it'd be hurtful to imply that I did."

Nina grabbed Rock by the elbow and led him toward the portal. It looked pretty ridiculous with the way Rock had to slouch to keep from pulling away.

Nina vanished into the portal, but Rock waved at House before they disappeared, and she emphatically returned the gesture.

"I am definitely going to pay for that," Darling said. "But I think it was worth it. Oh, and hey, House. Glad to see you again."

"I am also pleased to witness you. I like your axes. They are quite large, and there are two of them." She smiled. "I am very much looking forward to my own class change."

"What're you gonna do?"

House stepped from foot to foot. "I have something in mind, but I am unsure as to whether it is a good fit."

"If you're excited about it," I said, "then go for it."

House paused. "Are you suggesting I toss caution to the wind?"

I nodded. "Pretty much, yeah. Play what you want—we'll figure the rest out. In the meantime, how much time do we have before the prisms hit?"

House grinned, looking especially pleased with herself. "We possess twenty minutes."

Darling pushed a lock of dark hair out of her face. "Could try to cram a Rift in?"

"If it's cool with you, I think I'd like to head out that way now and find a good place to watch from. See how the prisms approach and how Goon is preparing to defend their city."

She shrugged. "That sounds good to me, probably be pressed for time anyway."

We both headed for the Rift, but House just stood there like a statue.

I paused with the central portal spinning in front of me. "House? Are you coming to watch?"

"I am most definitely coming to watch."

"Great." I scoped out the Rift Map, checking the various options around Goon's city. "Frank, you got any suggestions? Ideally I'd be looking for something with cover. Maybe a mountain range, somewhere with a good view of the city below but also out of the way so we can watch in peace?"

"See the Rift directly to the north of the city?" he said.

"I do, yeah."

"Down one Rift, then two Rifts to the right."

I pointed at the Rift in question. "Here?"

"Yeah. Uliana is in a small valley with mountains to every side, but there's a nice little pocket in the cliff line there that you and Darling should be able to reach with movement abilities. House might have to go around and climb down from the top, but that also comes with the very real potential of seeing her fall to her death again, so it's basically a win-win."

"So... any other options, or go with that?" Darling said. "Feels like a bad way to die."

"There was indeed a small and recent window where I briefly possessed an overwhelming fear of death," House said. "But then I realized that pets cannot drop, so now I am back to being wholly unconcerned with the prospect. I am therefore happy and willing to attempt the climb."

"Thanks, House. I'm sure we can help you out if needed."

I selected the Rift but pulled up short of confirming the destination when an alert came through. I braced myself as I scanned it, heart sinking as it confirmed exactly what I'd been fearing.

**World Alert! The Guild {Redacted} is the second guild to clear the {Glowbone Grim} encounter and has been awarded an additional 2 days to claim the Worldbranch Throne! No further extensions will be granted for clearing this encounter.**

Darling flinched beside me. "No further extensions?"

"Yeah, guess so. Do you think we underestimated the need to be competitive throughout?"

"I really hope not. What did we have at the beginning? Five days to claim that thing? So we've got three days left to finish the whole raid and we haven't even started the first wing?"

"Yeah, but I still think we're in a good place—it's not like anyone's cleared the second encounter and we've made a ton of headway with levels and class changes. If every first and second clear of every encounter awards additional time, then we should be okay. I can't imagine it's just the first boss of the first wing that does that."

"I want that chair, Ned," Frank said. "You promised me that chair."

"I don't think I did, but we're definitely gonna get there. Darling, you wanna pop through and make sure it's safe?"

"Sure." She winked at House. "I'll go make sure the coast is clear."

"A wise and generous offer," House said.

Darling left, and a message came through a moment later that said she didn't see anyone around. I popped through, and House followed quickly behind.

The cliffline behind me was impressive, a sheer, white face that looked as if it had been carved out of chalk.

But I only had eyes for the sky, which was crimson for as far as I could see. The sun was beginning to set, but the blood red hue that hung over the city was supernaturally bright.

And the prisms...

The sky was absolutely choked with them, and the floating structures were so tightly packed and so well-organized that it looked like a dark ring was constricting around Uliana.

The city itself was smaller than I'd expected, though it was hard to really gauge the development because there was a bluish wall in place that was currently blocking my view.

"Was that all us?" I said. "The prisms?"

Darling smiled. "Probably. I was cracking the whip, and people have been grinding hard. And the more Rifts we finished around the city, the more they started popping up around it."

"Wonder if all those clears are what made the sky change too, or if that's just because of all the prisms. It's positively eerie. This feels like it's about to get really, really messy. I wonder how many they've got back on defense." I squinted at the town. "Are we too far out to see name tags?"

"Yup," Frank confirmed.

"I could have someone else pop into town to get a better look if you want," Darling said. "With the Hall, someone could probably rush in on a mount and look around, then leave without raising any eyebrows. Not like we're at war with them. Seems pretty low risk."

"Yeah, if someone wouldn't mind taking a peek, that'd be great."

Darling tapped the air. "Done. I'll let you know."

I turned and stared up at the cliff. There was an alcove maybe thirty feet up, but it was hard to tell for sure with how steep the angle was.

"Race you?" Darling said.

I eyed her axes. "Does that teleport ability have two charges? Where you throw your weapon?"

"Totally separate cooldowns for each axe, but yeah."

I pursed my lips. "So you've got two teleports and your leap, which might have improved with that class change. And maybe those Touchstone boots with the thread? I don't know if I can beat all of that."

"Same," she said, grinning.

"Alright then, you're on. House, can you count us down from three?"

"Three," House said. "Two."

Darling cocked one of her huge weapons back.

"One."

"Wait," I said, while Darling was still mid-swing. She managed to keep her grip on the weapon, but it was a close thing. "Look at the sky. Something's really, really wrong."

Darling stepped up beside me. "What, with the red?"

"No, see that bit of green over there?" I popped a pistol into my left hand and pressed it between her shoulder blades. "Moon's out during the day. How awful is that?"

Then I activated Dreadful Shot and sent her fleeing away from the cliff. I dropped into a pushup position and Clonedrifted straight up into the air.

And it was a good thing I did that quickly because Darling activated some sort of ability that broke the fear effect within the first few feet.

The clone didn't distract her either: she whipped around, took three bounding steps, and launched herself into the air while throwing an axe in a single, fluid motion.

I was almost out of my drift, but my spell was slow in comparison, and her thrown axe quickly outranged it.

My clone took a shot at her that would have stunned her if it had landed, but Darling vanished from below and reappeared above me with her hand on the weapon. She slammed into the cliffline and smashed an armored hand into it.

The impact created a puff of white powder, and when it cleared, she was hanging from one hand while readying another throw.

"You're still gonna lose," Frank said as drift hit its full range.

I pointed a pistol beneath me and Water Jetted myself up and behind her. I ended up passing so close to her that I bumped her on the way up.

I was almost at the alcove when I realized something was wrong—I was slowing down as if I had a rubber band attached to my back and I'd just reached its limit.

When I looked down, I saw Darling grinning up at me, a silvery thread running from the back of my thigh to the tip of her left boot.

She kicked and I whipped downward, stomach turning at the sudden reversal. I managed to Double Cast another Water Jet, but Darling's second axe had already flown by me.

I raised both pistols as I soared upward and fired a Gravity Bird up at the ledge, aiming just a bit above it.

Darling's weapon flew into the alcove, and she reappeared directly above the space—only to be pulled sideways and off it as the black hole erupted.

My Water Jet carried me to the ledge, so I dismissed my pistols, grabbed onto it with both hands, and hauled myself up and over.

As I stood up, Darling was still spinning in the Gravity Bird with her arms crossed, just off the edge of the cliff.

"Cheater," she said.

I reached out and offered her a hand before the black hole expired. She took it, and I pulled her onto the ledge as the spell winked out.

"Sorry," I said. "It was Frank's idea."

"I don't think Frank would have wanted to send me fleeing in terror."

"True," Frank said.

I laughed. "Maybe not on purpose. But I think we all know it remains a possibility."

"Also true, but regrettable."

I sat down on the ledge and swung my legs over it. I saw House mount up down below and ride off to the left, where the cliff line gradually tapered lower and lower.

Darling dropped down beside me. "Thought I had you with the thread."

"Almost did."

She peered down below us. "How long is House going to be?"

"Shouldn't be too long," Frank said. "There's a road that starts low and winds up above us."

I shaded my eyes and stared out at Uliana. From our current vantage point, Darling and I were almost exactly level with the prisms that were floating toward the settlement, which made it difficult to gauge just how close they really were.

But I could see over the city wall from here, and I'd been right when I'd thought it looked underdeveloped at a glance. In fact, it looked mostly agricultural, with fields that were beautifully terraced, though whatever they were growing was either dead or had just been harvested.

What I didn't see, though, were people on the wall. I still wouldn't be able to see name tags from this far out, but there should have been at least some people visible as they moved around. And the streets were empty too.

Then I spotted movement on the other side of the city: a lone rider had just slipped through the wall's northern gatehouse, though I couldn't make out anything more than that.

"Is that our scout?"

Darling nodded. "Yeah. That's him. He just confirmed it—the city's empty."

I leaned forward, hands on my knees. "As in, there's no Goon members anywhere?"

"No, I mean it's totally empty. No guards, no NPCs. Nothing. It's a ghost town."

I scratched the back of my head. "How could an entire city be empty?"

"I assume the people left," Frank said.

"Thank you for that pearl of wisdom. The guards, though? That doesn't seem like something that would just happen. And where the hell are Goon?" I stared at the prisms with new eyes, and the realization of what was about to happen settled in. "Oh man. The creatures the prisms spawn are going to level that city, aren't they?"

"Uh huh," Frank said. "It's gonna be awesome."

I rocked back, mind racing. "Was this a misplay?"

"Probably depends on who you're asking."

"How would it be a mistake?" Darling said.

"It's not a big deal either way because slowing Goon down was really just a side benefit while we cleared Rifts, but if their city is completely deserted..." I trailed off. "I might have mapped too much of my own strategy onto whatever they're doing."

"I'm telling you," Frank said. "They're just a bunch of people that like killing stuff."

"You have a source on that or something?" Darling said.

"I am the source of all knowledge," I said, mimicking him again.

Frank grunted. "I wasn't going to say that."

"But it was going to be something to that effect, wasn't it?"

"Well yeah, but my inflection would have way been better."

"Anyway," I said, "maybe I'm overthinking it and we just caught them overextended. Travel times are long and they really only had a couple hours to respond, so it's plausible they sent a bunch of forces out to prepare for that first siege and got caught on the wrong side of the ocean with nobody to defend." I looked at Frank. "When is that first one slated to start? It was a Two-day Siege, right?"

"Just started a little bit ago."

"Thanks."

"Do you think they saw the prisms coming and just decided to abandon their Capital?" Darling said. "I could see them going all-in on the siege if they thought they were going to win because that could just become their next city, but even then, it doesn't explain the city being completely empty."

"Maybe it's just realistic NPC behavior?" I said. "There had to be a couple of prisms that hit before this wave. If you're living in the city and that happens and one of those monsters smashes a wall in and nobody but the guards are around to help, it probably makes sense to abandon everything before the wave hits."

She grimaced. "I dunno. It makes sense, but it seems kind of weird on a mechanical level. I still feel like the guards would have stuck around. Arlann and company wouldn't have just up and left the Vale, right? Even if nobody was paying them, I feel like some of the guard would probably stick around."

"I think he would have," I agreed. "But if nobody's paying them *and* that many prisms were floating in? Some would definitely leave. Otherwise I don't think I'd have needed to make that deal with Arlann."

"But everybody in the city? They can't just bail. It's impossible."

"What do you mean?"

"If that city is home and you don't have anywhere else to go, what do you do?"

I paused, considering. "Take a carriage to the nearest city?"

Darling laughed. "Yeah, no. Try again."

"This is the sort of thing that makes you unrelatable," Frank said.

"Oh, please. I am way more relatable than you."

"How much does a banana cost?" he said.

I drew back. "What? How is that relevant to the conversation?"

"Answer the question."

"I dunno. Like two dollars?"

Darling snorted. "For a banana?"

"Two fifty?"

"I rest my case," Frank said.

"I'm beginning to sense that I've made a mistake."

"Anyway," Darling said, still laughing. "Some of the people could bail for sure, but literally everyone? No way. That doesn't happen. At a certain point people just don't have anywhere to go.

"This city probably wasn't that organized either given how underdeveloped it is, they might not have had any real warning for the prisms, and there are mobs everywhere you go in this world." She sighed. "No matter what happens, when things go bad, there are always at least a handful of people who get left behind."

I hadn't thought about that. And I didn't love the fact that I hadn't, on a couple of different levels. "Yeah. That's fair."

"It's kind of spooky. Just how still it is."

I watched our rider leave through the west gate. I couldn't really tell just how long it would be before the prisms hit in earnest, but I didn't think the moment was far off.

I racked my brain, trying to find some kind of parallel that would explain it all: the underdevelopment, the emptiness, Goon's total disinterest in protecting the city.

An answer came to me, a vestige of one of my father's history lessons.

"Maybe they're nomadic? So they stayed here and built up a bit, then bailed and took everyone with them?"

"Seems more likely," Darling said, "but I still feel like guards wouldn't up and leave. I guess it could be a Renown perk thing or something, but Goon haven't seemed like the sort who operate by winning people over to their cause."

"They could have taken the guards with them. They reach a city, say join us or burn. That or the guards are dead."

"Maybe everybody's dead," Frank said, hopeful.

"Yeah. Well, whether they win or lose, I might go take a look at the aftermath of their Siege and see if I can figure out what we're dealing with. At the very least, it seems like the prism rush isn't going to do what I hoped it would."

"I guess not," Darling said. "But the city wasn't totally empty when we first scouted it out as a target. This is new."

"It's all good. Live and learn, right? Plus we've got a show to watch."

"And on that especially cheerful note!" She smiled and popped an empty glass into one hand, setting it between us, then produced a bottle out of thin air.

She filled the glass with very dark beer—so dark it was basically black —then waited. And it took me a second to realize what for.

I slid Frank out of his loop and dropped him in.

"Hmm," he said. "Oatmeal stout? I'm detecting notes of dark choco-late, possibly blueberry."

"Nailed it," Darling said.

"You're not gonna mention what the bubbles are doing this time around?" I asked.

"I think we all know what they're doing, Ned. You're just the only one who felt the need to say it out loud."

I winced. "So what are we celebrating?"

"Everything." She took a deep drag on the bottle and handed it to me.

I wasn't really looking forward to trying it after Frank's description, but the gesture was too nice to decline. I tilted the bottle up and took a sip, and instantly regretted it.

"How is it?" she said.

"It's… complex." I forced myself to take another sip.

I thought I'd managed to hide my grimace on the second go-round, but apparently I hadn't because Darling laughed and popped a second, lighter bottle into her hand and passed it over.

It still had the cap on, so I grabbed Frank, twisted him around, acti-vated Repel and whacked the very edge of the cap. It went flying off toward the town below like a frisbee.

I dropped him back into his glass with a loud plop, tapped the bottle against Darling's, then took a deep, far more enjoyable drink.

He grunted. "That swing was almost as disappointing as your inability to price fruit. If you were gonna use me for that you could have at least taken the neck off the bottle."

Darling crossed her ankles and stretched. "Hey, can I ask you something?"

"Certainly," Frank said. "Though I retain the right to decline to answer as I do need to preserve a certain element of mystery."

"I was talking to Ned, actually."

"Oh. Why?"

She smirked and glanced over at me. "Are you really never going to leave? Like... never?"

"Not planning on it."

"What if there's like a wedding or something?"

I cracked a smile.

"What?"

"He'd need to be invited to a wedding," Frank said. "Highly unlikely."

"Rude."

"He's right though," I said. "That would be highly unlikely at this point, and it's getting more and more unlikely by the day."

"I'm just trying to wrap my head around what that would feel like. Like, never? Never ever?"

"Never ever ever," Frank said.

I took another sip. "You're really having a hard time not being the center of attention, huh?"

He grunted. "Yup, I'm struggling down here."

The glass that he was soaking in was tall and wide, so I turned my bottle up over it and kept pouring until Frank caught on to what I was doing, which didn't happen until the liquid was nearly halfway above his blade.

"Oh, I see what's happening. I'm being silenced. You would resort to cheap tricks in your attempts to..." He trailed off into a mumble as the beer crept up over three-quarters of his blade.

"I think we've officially found all of his speakable holes," I said.

"Can he drown?" Darling said.

"That's a good question." I plucked him out between two fingers. "Are you drowning?"

"Yeah, in liquid happiness."

"Okay, but are you actually drowning?"

"No, I can't drown. Wait, no, I was definitely—"

He cut off with a plop as I dropped him back in.

"Mystery solved." I looked left, right, then up. "Where's House? Shouldn't she be here by now?"

A few particularly large bubbles welled up from Frank.

"You'd think so," Darling said. She looked away. "Probably got distracted by something."

"Wouldn't take much at this point." I took another sip and held the bottle out in front of me. "This is really good."

"I'm glad you like it."

"Anybody else coming out to watch?"

"A few, yeah. I kind of had to put the brakes on it a little after thinking it through a bit more. Didn't think it would look very good if the entirety of Omen was ringed up around the city before it fell. I'm just gonna video it for people and stream it to the Stronghold."

"Good call. I do wonder what kind of blowback we're going to catch from this, if anything."

"You still worried that they might come for the Vale next?"

"I am, yeah, not that it has anything to do with this. The location's just so good. That was a big part of why we picked the Vale to begin with —between the spot itself and its history with trading and the geography, I figured it'd become something like a gateway between the two oceans and the other continents."

"Largely seems to be coming true."

"It does. I just can't shake the feeling that there's something we're not seeing."

"Tyrann?"

I sighed. "I don't even know what he's doing at this point, and that's scary in and of itself. He did warn me that something was coming a ways back, but what good is that really? Lots of things are coming.

"But what with the Auction House and the Rifts and the raid and this prism rush and the Revenant and the manhunt and everything else, it just seems like it'd be really easy to drop the ball somewhere and not even notice."

"That's kind of what I've been thinking about recently. You're not gonna burn out on us, right?"

"No."

"That was quick." She leaned forward a little. "You don't need to think about that for a moment?"

"I really don't, honestly. This is exactly where I want to be."

She smiled at that, which drew a flurry of bubbles from Frank.

"It does help that Frank is completely submerged. It's nice to have another option on the table in case he figures the sheath out somehow. Or for when he figures out the role he's unwittingly playing in Project Lunar."

That last comment caused so many bubbles that I could have sworn the glass actually moved. I grabbed it and tipped it sideways, pouring out just enough beer for him to be able to speak again.

"We're gonna have words after this city falls," Frank said.

"When are we not having words? We have way too many words in general, and you're just lucky I plucked you out before you shouted yourself hoarse in there."

Red light flashed on the horizon, and Darling sat up a little straighter. "I think we're getting close."

A small stream of dirt and rocks trickled down off the cliff line above and landed between us. I looked up and saw House's head poking out over the edge some thirty feet above.

I set my bottle to the side. "You can jump, House. I'll meet you in the air and drift you in."

"I can go one better," Darling said, taking one of her axes in her hand. "House, can you hear me?"

"I can indeed."

"Make sure you catch this, alright? My throw works both ways, but I don't wanna have to come up there to reclaim it."

"I am brimming with anxiety," House shouted.

"Brimming?" Frank said.

I nodded. "Good word, right?"

"Surprisingly so."

"Here it comes," Darling said, sending her axe flying upward with a flick of her wrist.

It sliced cleanly up the cliff line and House reached out to grab it. She caught it but lost her balance as she did so and tipped forward off the cliff.

"Don't let go!"

Darling raised a hand high into the air, and the runes of her thrown axe flared as House began to fall.

House vanished, then the weapon reappeared in Darling's grasp with House hanging from it.

House looked down to where her feet were kicking a solid six inches off the ground, then she let go and landed safely in the alcove.

"I have apparently arrived."

"That does seem apparent," I said. "Grab a seat, the show's just starting."

She looked as if she were about to sit between Darling and me, hesitated, then sat to my right.

"Any chance you've got another glass on you?" I said to Darling.

"Sorry, only brought the one."

"House," Frank said, "cup your hands."

She did.

He grunted. "There ya go. Pour away."

"I could just pass her the bottle occasionally."

"Unnecessary," House said. "My recent experiences with the high-five have me very intrigued by the prospect of a hand cup."

"Of course you are."

I poured an inch or two of beer into her outstretched hands. She held the liquid there in her makeshift goblet, marveling at it as the first prism exploded in the distance like a firecracker. A few drops were already trickling through her fingers and darkening the white stone beneath.

She slurped, loudly. Then broke into a wide grin.

"This is another positive point for hands. Perhaps I have indeed rushed to judgment where they are concerned."

"Wait for it," Frank said.

I didn't know what he was referring to, so I leaned forward to get a better look at the scene below.

A few small, ghostly mobs were already rushing the eastern gatehouse, though we were so far out that all I could tell was that they were bright blue and vaguely wolf-like in shape.

I took another sip as four more prisms exploded below in bursts of red so bright that they illuminated the ground for miles in every direction. Several more ghosts appeared, running on all fours, followed by a trio of spectral raptors that stood nearly as tall as the city's outer wall.

Then the surge hit for real, and it was like watching the finale of a firework show, except it went on for way, way too long.

Within seconds, the mobs were absolutely everywhere, and hundreds if not thousands of ghostly creatures were swarming across the ground and over the walls and into the buildings, tearing everything apart as they went.

The rush had spawned two mobs that looked similar to the Starlit Tyrant we'd dealt with earlier: a huge, frilled lizard that was currently torching the northern gatehouse with greenish fire breath and a four-winged gryphon that was flying high above the city and raking it with purple beams of light.

The gryphon tagged an especially large, domed building right down the middle, and the entire structure caved in on itself in two great pieces.

"Woah," Darling said.

"Yeah," I said. "Not gonna lie, I'm feeling more than a little grateful that there's nobody down there right now."

"Speak for yourself," Frank said.

"I was. Seriously though, I think we officially underestimated just how much damage this would do." I pointed at the walls. "I don't care how large Goon is. There's no way anybody holds that line right now. This goes way beyond forcing someone to defend something. This is a legitimate weapon."

"And the mobs just keep coming," Darling said.

Between the bright ghosts and the prismatic fires that the stronger creatures had sparked, the city was blazing with so much light that it looked like an oversized bonfire.

House tipped her hands up as if they were a bowl and slurped until she finished what they'd contained.

"Oh." She shook her hands out as if she were trying to dry them off. "Oh no."

"What's wrong?" I said.

"I am extremely sticky and I do not like it."

"Boom, headshot," Frank said.

House rubbed her hands against the ground, and they came away covered in white powder and loose pebbles.

"Oh no." She shook them again, peppering Darling and me with sticky pebbles. "I am not having a good time."

"How're you feeling about those hands now, House?" Frank said.

"It appears that my initial assessment was correct and that my fears of having rushed to judgment were officially misplaced." She rubbed them against each other and winced. "If anything, my earlier opinions have calcified."

We laughed but lapsed into silence as the assault built and the last of the prisms exploded outside of the city and loosed their charges. The walls had already been reduced to rubble, the tiered farming plots were burning, and what few buildings still stood had been heavily damaged.

"So..." Darling said. "The question now is do we do this again. We're almost out of time when it comes to the Hall. It'll be a hell of a lot harder to manage the logistics of something like this without the teleports."

"I really don't know," I said. "This is a lot. Imagine if this just hit Koria instead. We could have accidentally deleted a capital city, people and all."

"Why would it be accidental?" Frank said.

I pointed at the carnage. "This was supposed to be a distraction that forced them into some sort of defense. But this is a massacre."

"And?" Frank said.

"I don't know. If you were to ask the player base right now, they'd probably say we're the bad guys, right? Do we really want to play into that by torching cities like this?"

"Yes. These are stupid questions, even for you."

"I see what you mean, but damn. Look at that." Darling glanced at me out of the corner of her eye. "Can I ask you something else? Questionably related."

"Shoot."

"What would you do if we actually lost it all? Like, what if we were them right now, and it was our city that was burning?"

"All of it?"

"The Stronghold, the city, everything."

I paused, thinking. "Even Frank?"

"Yeah."

I placed a fist beneath my chin. "I guess I'd probably start enjoying myself."

"Disgusting," Frank said, but Darling was already laughing, and I didn't think she'd heard him.

"I said what I said. Really though, I don't know. Even then, I can't really imagine myself leaving. I feel like I'd probably find another place to rebuild and try to run it all back, knowing more than I did at the start. And I think I enjoy making Frank unhappy to the point where I'd need to get him back, too."

"Oh God," he said.

"Can you imagine? You finally end up with someone who just wants to burn the whole world down, then I swoop in and kill them and bam, you're right back to dangling off an elf."

"That sounds like what happened to Tantalus," Frank said, "but much, much worse."

"Isn't that the myth where the guy would try to drink and the water would recede," Darling said, "and he'd try to eat and the apples would pull up and away? So he was just there, suffering, forever?"

"It is indeed."

Darling took a drink. "How exactly would your situation be worse than that?"

"Because it would be happening to me."

I snorted. "Wow."

"I would also argue that if I had a mythical doppelganger, it would clearly be Prometheus."

"I almost don't want to ask," Darling said. "But I feel strangely compelled to do exactly that."

"Lemme guess," I said. "He identifies with Prometheus because he thinks he's bringing light and warmth to the uncivilized masses. Meaning us."

"Oh snap, that's good," Frank said. "That might even be better than what I had in mind. Hold on, I gotta write that down then internalize it as truth."

"That should take all of two seconds."

Darling smiled. "What were you thinking then, Frank?"

"I was just gonna point out that I spit hot fire. Then I was going to draw a long and elaborate parallel between Ned and the way he crushes my dreams and the eagle that was sent to punish Prometheus by devouring his liver, only for the liver to regenerate and be eaten again the next day when the eagle returned, then again and again in perpetuity."

Darling stared at him, her bottle held loosely in one hand. "That is so mean!"

"And yet he keeps doing it," Frank said. "Day after day after day—"

She pointed a finger at him. "I meant you were being mean, Frank."

"Oh." He paused. "Huh. I don't follow, and I'm legitimately trying. It feels like you made a wrong turn a few sentences back but I missed it, and now I don't know where you're coming from."

"Nope," she said.

"Ya gotta admit though," I said. "It's a really good metaphor."

"But it's mean," Darling said.

"It's all good. If anything, it's just more proof that we dodged a bullet when we decided against bringing him on to head up Project Lunar. Can't have this kind of animosity in space. Quarters are just too tight."

"Agreed."

"Wait wait wait, hold on a minute," Frank said. "I was ruled out because I'd be bad in small spaces? I am crammed into a small space right now. If anything, of anyone here, I'm by far the most qualified to be crammed into a small space. Except for House, I guess."

Darling squinted at him. "Why would House be better at that than you? You're inside an axe."

I flicked the top of his blade. "Dude."

"Crap, sorry, forgot," he whispered. He cleared his throat. "Because House is small and weird and I'm pretty sure I could easily convince her to crawl into a box. I could just draw a cat on the far wall."

"That would definitely work," House said.

"But not once have I complained about being an axe."

"Yeah," I said, "but you like being an axe."

"I've made peace with being an axe because the ratio of blade to shaft accurately reflects who I am on the inside. But I would be much happier being a guy with an axe that I could hit people with." He glanced up at Darling. "Preferably a guy with two or more axes, but still."

I pursed my lips, thinking.

"I demand to be reconsidered as the leader of whatever's currently happening."

"Sorry, Frank," I said. "But one of House's conditions for coming on as team lead was that there'd be no take backsies."

Darling looked away, shoulders shaking.

"Shenanigans! There is no way you decided to put House in charge." He glared at her. "But on the other hand, that does sound suspiciously like the sort of condition she might have heard once in passing then decided to insist upon."

"Well," I said, "if you want in, you gotta go through House. Better start buttering her up now."

House stood up. "I am deeply confused but not unwilling."

"Look at House employing a double negative like a boss. And there ya go, Frank," I said, laughing harder now. "There's your in. You might wanna start with margarine. Imagine that's a lot easier to spread."

He shuddered. "I hate the fact that I actually considered doing that on a literal level for a moment." He relaxed, then nodded to himself. "But I'm also impressed with my willingness to win at any cost, even when I don't have any idea of what winning actually looks like, let alone if it would be worth it."

"Looks like they're almost done wrecking shop down there," Darling said.

I leaned forward, head buzzing from the beer as another impossible wave of glowing creatures surged over the last remaining building and the roof caved in beneath their collective weight.

The center of the town flashed red once, then twice, then a colossal red wave swept out from it.

**Crimson Ripple Alert!**
**The Possibility King's forces have Razed the city of Uliana, and all that remains of the once-proud settlement is a pile of ash and burning timbers!**
**High above the ruins, a Rift unlike any seen before promises the immediate arrival of a Walking Apocalypse.**
**Furthermore, the Possibility King's forces have gained their first true foothold in this reality, and all of the creatures that spill from his prisms have been awarded fearsome new abilities!**

The red wave roared out in every direction, rising and swelling, and by the time it reached us, it was several times the height of the cliff line that House had dropped down.

"A Walking Apocalypse?" I said. "What the hell is that?"

"Sounds like a good time," Frank said. "That or a quick and merciful end. Either way, I'm game."

Darling pointed an armored finger above the city. The red-tinged clouds were spinning around it like a whirlpool, and a familiar energy was crackling within. "That looks an awful lot like the Bridge Rift when it first opened."

The ghostly mobs that had been howling and screaming in triumph a moment earlier had gone deathly silent, and the great majority of them were now looking skyward.

Red lightning raked the sky, and the thunder that followed reverberated across the cliff line. Every single mob that had been gathered below went still. Then the entire mass of them scattered.

The red portal at the center of the cloudy whirlpool expanded exponentially, and a colossal column of smooth water gouted down out of the sky. It looked like someone had just opened a doorway to the bottom of the ocean.

**World Alert! The Possibility King has brought {Delugia, the Walking Apocalypse} into your reality, and the fearsome creature now reigns over the ruins of the city once known as Uliana!**
**If Delugia isn't defeated within the next 12 hours, she'll move to the nearest city and attempt to terraform its zone as well.**

With each city that falls, the Possibility King and his forces will continue to grow stronger.

The waters broke as they hit the ground, surging outward in a twenty-foot wall of black water that absolutely obliterated the creatures below.

I watched the torrent rage and saw something dark slip down out of the sky, its figure hidden by the water. The four-winged gryphon that had been terrorizing the city with its beam of light wheeled around the column, shrieking and blasting away.

Then, without warning, the curtain parted and an angular skull the size of a building shot out of the falling water and swallowed the flying creature whole.

When the Rift finally closed and the flood ended, Darling and I were left staring at a snapping turtle the size of Koria.

Its four legs were easily three stories tall, and its shell was the size of a stadium. A trio of ice-blue crystals ran down the middle of its back, and its underbelly had three more of the strange constructs hanging off it like glassy stalactites.

I stared at it, open-mouthed.

{Delugia, the Walking Apocalypse} (Level 17 Beast) (World Boss)
HP: 350,000/350,000
MP: 700,000/700,000

"Wow. That is..." I trailed off as the surge of black water rolled toward us.

"...a tsunami that is rapidly coming our way?" Darling said. She was already on her feet.

I plucked Frank out of his glass and took the hand up that Darling offered. "You said it." I eyed the top of the cliff, which was only about half the height that Darling and I had climbed earlier. "House, stand up and face me. You're not going to be able to make it up there in time."

"I am immobile," she said, standing.

I grabbed her by her legs and put her in a fireman's carry, then fell forward and activated Clonedrift when I thought I had the angle right. We both shot back and up, but I had to Double Cast a second drift to get us atop the cliff.

I landed on all fours and rolled back to my feet while House took her usual approach of catching herself with her face.

Just then, one of Darling's huge axes flew up over the cliff. She blinked into existence next to it and landed lightly on her feet, already pivoting to face the oncoming wave below.

I stepped up beside her as the surge smashed into the cliff and threw up a huge fan of water that stretched high into the air above us.

The chalky ground shook beneath the impact, and for a moment I thought the entirety of the cliff line was about to collapse and disappear into the frothing water below.

I took in the scene, stunned by the development. Within the space of a minute, Delugia's entrance had turned the valley that had housed the city into a deep, dark lagoon.

In the distance, the hulking creature was striding away through the water that reached about halfway up its great legs and churned around them, leaving great wakes behind.

"A World Boss," I said. "It's a World Boss."

"Yeah?" Darling said.

"You've got your Trinket now, right? Pull it up and look at your third power. We already know that you can unseal the powers in any order, and it says that in order to unlock the last one, you either need to kill three Raid Bosses with your Trinket equipped or…"

"…kill one World Boss," Darling finished for me. She went up on her toes. "So we should kill that thing, right? We should definitely kill it."

"Yes," Frank said. "With enthusiasm."

"But how? Gonna be pretty hard to take a swing at that thing in thirty feet of water."

"You're right. What a waste. This seems totally impossible. It's a shame that nobody suggested having the guild prioritize creating a fleet of wooden, floating constructs that could also be armed with some kind of explosive, tube-like armaments. I don't know if those even exist, though."

"I believe the words that you are looking for are boat and cannon," House said.

"Boats indeed," I said.

"Lots and lots of boats," Darling said. "Ned, we've been doing exactly that. With House's help and a few other Machinists too. I wanted to wait and get them all together before I showed you how far we've come, but we even have a bunch of Gunboats ready. Nothing like Tyrann's monstrosity, but we can do this!"

I looked down at Frank. "You know, it's moments like these that make me think Team Frank might not be so bad after all."

"Slow down," he said. "Team Frank has a rigorous application process. Interest has never been higher, and we're not just taking anyone these days."

"Seriously?"

"Best I can do is put in a word on your behalf. I've got a good amount of sway around these parts."

"Is it gonna be a good word?"

"Oh, it's going to be a great word."

I looked down at him. "Wow. That was surprisingly nice."

"Huh? Oh, no, I see what's happening here. No, I meant it's going to be an objectively great word that takes you down, not that it's a word that's going to say nice things about you."

"That makes much more sense."

"How many people do you think we'll need?" Darling said.

"Four twenty-person groups would give you a decent shot," Frank said. "The more the better."

I pulled up the guild roster. "The core raid group should be just about ready to go anyway, right? We were going to try to push into the Menagerie Wing after this regardless. But we should straight up bring everyone that we can use. If we've got boats, we'll need pilots. And we can even have the lowest level people operate the cannons while everybody else fights."

"What about the melee?" Darling said.

I pointed up at the beast, which was moving in a slow circle through the dark water. Its movement had brought it close, and Health bars had popped up all along its back, floating above the crystals.

"Those crystals are targetable, so we gotta figure out a way to get our melees up there. Maybe you can even climb up? It moves slow, and its armor looks like it has grooves in it."

"The three crystals on its underbelly are targetable too. So melees go high and ranged go low? I'm still a little worried about the positioning for the melees, but I'm definitely willing to give it a shot."

"House," Frank said. "You at 150 Machining yet?"

"I am indeed."

"Then you've already got the answer we need."

House tapped the air. "Oh. I do in fact possess a possible solution."

We both turned to look at her at the same time, but she linked me an item in lieu of a response.

{Gnomish Glider} (Consumable)
Use: Deploy a personal glider for 30 seconds.

Darling's eyes went wide. "Melees glide in off the cliff line, everybody else sails in and lights that thing up from below?"

"Yeah," I said. "We have to try, right? I mean, everything else aside: look at that thing. How much time do you think you'd need to get everybody up and running?"

"Core should be almost entirely ready to go, but if we're talking as many people as possible... maybe give me twenty minutes? I'll even ping the offline people and see how many we can round up. Also, if anyone is level 15 but doesn't have their Trinket yet, that probably gives them enough time to go grab it before the kill so they can get that third power right away."

"I will also require time to craft and obtain materials," House said.

I nodded. "Twenty minutes it is. That should keep the window tight enough that nobody else can arrive and attempt the boss. Hopefully nobody shows up at all. Uliana is a lower-level area though, so there probably are some people around."

I pulled up my Rift Map and found a portal about a hundred yards south of the cliff line. I mounted up, and House chose to hop into Darling's buggy after she'd summoned it.

We headed through the portal, back into the Hall of Rifts, and I let the other two get a little bit ahead before throwing on an illusion and heading for the Oasis on foot.

# Chapter Thirty-Three

The prisms were still exploding and birthing their armies beyond the walls, but between the hordes of players that were clearing them and the defenses the city had built up, things were looking pretty good.

At least for the Commerce Ward.

As I'd expected, the other three were more of a mixed bag: both the Military Ward and the Residential Ward were looking okay, thanks to what I assumed was probably a higher guard presence in the former area and the way players were incentivized to defend the latter, but the Royal Ward was a disaster.

Even from the base of the four dunes that housed the city, the damage the buildings had taken was obvious, and while the Royal Ward had been the only one to start with a defensible wall from the beginning, that alone had proved wildly insufficient.

I opened my quest log and pulled up the Legendary Quest I'd acquired earlier to check its progress.

**Quest: In Defense of the Black Oasis! (Legendary Quest) (Collaborative Quest)**
**Objective: While within 500 yards of the Black Oasis, defeat the following:**
**1. 10,000 Veterans (7,815 slain)**
**2. 1,000 Elites (802 slain)**

3. 200 Elite+ (165 slain)
4. 20 Elite++ (13 slain)
5. 1 Raid Boss, World Boss, Deity, Lesser Deity, or Legend (0/1 slain)
Any player may contribute to this quest at any time, and all kills made within the designated area are automatically added to the appropriate tally.
Reward: Experience, Renown, and major improvements to all existing Communal Defense Structures within the Black Oasis. Additional individual rewards, including gear and crafting materials, will also be awarded and will scale in power, level, and rarity depending on each player's contribution to the defense of the Black Oasis.
In addition, the top three individual contributors will each receive a {Cache of the Possibility King}.

"Good progress," I said to Frank, pausing just outside the city. The sounds of combat were all around us, with spells detonating and creatures screaming as they fell. "Though at this point I'm starting to think having something like Delugia show up here would be game over for us. Before we head into the city, I assume you still don't have an ETA on the Revenant?"

"Negative."

"But jumps in power means it takes longer to come back, right? Maybe we can work out an estimate?" I thought back to our first encounter with the thing. "The first time it hit us was at the Stronghold when Darling killed it, and it went from level 9 to 15."

"Came back in six hours. Attacked you outside the Inn."

I nodded. "So that was a six-hour delay for six levels gained. Then Tyrann killed it outside the Vale and it came back at level 24 and tried to hit us when we were with Igor. That bought us twelve hours, something like that?"

"Yup."

"So the third time around it went from level 15 to level 24, which is a nine-level jump. That got us twelve hours, so it seems like it's taking longer and longer to appear per level gained. So, if we assume Igor is max level at 50, maybe we've got a day and change before it comes back?"

"Can't confirm or deny."

"At the very least, Igor's gotta be low 30s or something because I couldn't see his level. So, worst-case scenario, I'm thinking we're probably okay in the city for at least another twelve hours, probably more. My gut says he was 40-plus, which would mean we'd have well over a day, but we can't count on that."

"Maybe."

I jogged up a dune and headed into the Commerce Ward, but what with the Revenant and the World Boss that was waiting for us, I was buzzing with anticipation to the point that I really didn't know what to do with myself for the twenty minutes Darling had requested.

House sent me a message asking that I join her at the Auction House, so I headed that way and ducked into the building with my illusion still in place.

The place was crowded, with players packed in shoulder to shoulder. I moved to the far end of the room and slipped in between a pair of NPCs, then sent House a video call and set our voices to private to avoid being seen chatting with her.

"What's up?" I said. I was already paging through the Auction House's listings, the number of which must have increased by an order of magnitude from the last time I'd checked it.

"I require an estimate of how many Gliders to prepare."

"Oh. Right." I messaged the question to Darling.

Around half the guild was melee, but a decent chunk of them were too low level to contribute much outside of controlling the boats, so Darling suggested we started with twenty-five. I relayed that to House.

And she immediately countered with a problem: creating twenty-five Gliders meant seventy-five units of Thinweave Cloth.

There was a good amount of that around, but most of it wasn't local. Which meant it would take time to be delivered, and that was time we didn't have.

I sorted the listings by their locations and pored over the options. The local stuff was almost universally two or even three times more expensive than the rest.

House sighed. "This appears to be a good example of your previous assessment when it comes to convenience."

I kept tabbing through the stacks. "Exactly. This is the sort of position you really, really don't want to be in. You've got a raid coming up and you realize you're out of consumables, then bam, you get to choose between paying three times the price for the flask you need or getting chewed out for showing up without your buffs. I really should have been paying more attention to the individual markets."

I found three local stacks of twenty Thinweave that someone had thrown up for 2 gold a pop. House still had most of my coin, so I had her snag those for me.

Purchasing the fifteen additional units was even worse: I had to pay another 2 gold for those. It physically hurt to overpay that much, but needs must.

There was good news too though: the swarm of players that had been grinding the incoming prisms and presumably the raid itself had absolutely tanked the price of Soul Gems, and our local market there was by far the largest.

Some of the weaker variants were especially cheap, so I grabbed fifty or so Lesser Soul Gems for around 50 copper coins a pop for the almost negligible price of 25 silver.

Those weren't going to upgrade my profession with how high I'd already raised it, but without having much of an idea of what we were about to go up against with Delugia, I wanted the extra flexibility of being able to create what I needed on the fly.

Soul Gems were a lot pricier at 3 silver coins a pop, which meant that any given rune I created was going to run me somewhere between 30 silver to about triple that.

I bought out fifty of those, then turned my attention to Large Soul Gems. Those were the variant that I really needed, but they were still rarer than the other types and were priced accordingly.

Still, I scored fifty of those for another 3 gold, then did a quick scan for gear upgrades but didn't find anything that was worth the investment.

House tapped me on the shoulder, and I turned to find her grinning at me like a maniac.

"What's up?"

She opened up a trade window with me and dropped 10 gold coins in. "These are the results of my latest purchase spree."

My eyes widened. "Wait, what? You turned 95 silver into 10 gold?"

"Until very recently, I had only turned 95 silver into 4 gold. But I had three transactions remaining when you arrived, and they have now sold." She confirmed the trade.

I let it sit there. "Keep it. You've got easier access to the city and the Auction House, so it makes more sense to just have you hold onto it. At least while we've still got access to the Hall and we can meet up at any time."

"But these 6 gold coins are your money," House said.

I waved her off. "It's ours. What difference does it make, really?"

"They are literally yours."

I paused. "What? I know you know what that word means."

Her grin deepened. "Prior to your arrival, I went through the Auction House and purchased every cheap piece of local Thinweave that I could afford. Then I simply relisted them in stacks of twenty for 2 gold coins each, knowing that we needed seventy-five total units. Then you directed me to purchase said listings."

I blinked at her. I'd been in such a rush to tell her to snag the items that I hadn't even looked at the name of the seller. I barked a laugh. "Wow. Well-played, House. Very well-played. If anything though, that makes me think you should keep the gold even more."

"I am not particularly interested in the gold itself. I simply wanted to win."

"Relatable," Frank said.

"Well, you definitely smashed your old record. That's like a 1,000% increase."

"True, but the great bulk of my success came from possessing insider knowledge."

I glanced down at her. "And?"

"That makes it unrepeatable."

I scanned the guild roster: we had almost ninety online, up from seventy or so only a few minutes earlier. I was hoping to have at least a hundred people participate in the fight against Delugia, and though our overall roster had swelled considerably larger than that, I wasn't sure how successful Darling was going to be when it came to grabbing people who weren't online.

"How does that make it unrepeatable?" I said.

"You handed me a piece of information that I was able to exploit to directly separate you from your coin."

I made a dismissive gesture. "House, look at the Trade Chat. It's full of people saying that they're buying this or buying that, often with prices attached. You can even see when someone isn't getting what they want because they'll raise their offers or drop them as time goes on. And if you need more than that, you can just message them and ask.

"Trade in this game is nothing if not betting on information, whether you have it or you're just speculating. So while you're probably unlikely to get someone who says I'm off to buy this item at the Auction House and I need it now, you've got plenty of people out there indicating interest that you can use as a benchmark."

I thought about that for a moment. "That actually might be a good idea for you. I don't think we have time to really dig in for another lesson right now, and honestly I'm feeling too antsy to really concentrate, but let's have you do direct sales next. I'll give you ten more listings on the Auction House, but I want you to buy all of the items that you turn around and sell directly from other people."

House squeaked.

"You can use the Trade Chat however you want: offer to buy items in bulk and relist them, or just try to snipe deals when people say they're selling stuff. Direct sales are great: the Auction House math is a lot more complicated for us, given that we own it, but you need to keep in mind that for most people, using it represents instantly losing a good chunk of whatever they sell because of the cut it takes."

"Interesting," House said. "Shall I restart with 10 gold?"

I shrugged. "At this point, that's your call. You already know you can multiply gold, so you can try to break your record of a 1,000% increase, or you can just try to make as much gold as possible by starting with more money in hand."

I motioned toward the back of the room. "If that sounds good to you, I say we head back to the cliff because I think we've both got a good amount of crafting to do."

"I agree to your terms. I will simply aim to accrue more than the 9 gold I previously earned."

"Perfect."

"Alright then," Frank said. "Let's go make some turtle soup."

# Chapter Thirty-Four

I stood atop the cliffs, watching the dark waves smash against the pale stone below.

Delugia was still a little ways off, but if we'd analyzed the pattern correctly...

And there it was: the great turtle made a slow turn, then started wading across what used to be a valley and through the dark water in our direction.

After watching it move, we'd gathered that the closest it would come to the cliff line was about a hundred yards away when it passed parallel to the higher ground. That had been a major disappointment; we'd been hoping to keep some spellcasters up there.

However, turnout on the guild's part had been better than I'd expected: Darling had put together eight twenty-person raids. That was far, far better than I'd dared to hope for, given how tight the window was, but outside of the core group—in which most were level 15 or close to it —pretty much everyone was lower leveled.

We had a plan to mitigate that somewhat, but there was no denying that anyone substantially under 14 or so was likely to get absolutely crushed if the turtle so much as breathed on them.

Darling stepped up to the edge of the cliff and put her back to the water and the turtle that was striding through it.

"Alright, everybody! If you've got a boat on you that we're going to be using, come on over and step up to the cliffs. Aside from that, go ahead and check your group. With a couple exceptions I've already talked to directly, if you're in groups 1 through 4, you're going to be gliding in as soon as the boats are heading into position. That means groups 5 through 8 will be engaging from the water, targeting the crystals that are hanging from the creature's belly.

"If you're on the boats, you should have your most durable player driving and your lower levels on cannons. If anybody loses a driver, the strongest cannon user should take over immediately. When it comes to spells and attacks, this thing is 17, so if you're 13 or under, you're not going to be hitting it reliably, so you ought to be on cannons.

"We have no idea whatsoever what to expect when it comes to aggro, so we're going to start with Jukes and Ton up on the creature's back because it's gonna be a hell of a lot easier for them to get down than go up, but if you spot anything that resembles a threat mechanic, shout it out and make sure everybody hears.

"We'll have a pair of offtanks down below on boats that'll stay near the creature's head, but I really doubt anyone is tanking that turtle from a boat. Last thing we need is for that thing to swallow one of our vehicles."

She looked at me, which I had not expected at all. "Anything I'm missing?"

"Uh..."

"Nailed it," Frank said.

"Shut up," I said, then raised my voice. "For everybody driving, boats can be damaged and will take time to repair and might even require materials to fix if the damage is severe enough, but they can't be permanently lost. There's also two capital cities within a couple hours of here, so it's a safe bet that other people are heading our way right now.

"We lose enough boats, and this probably ends up being a wipe. And if we wipe, we've probably lost our only real shot at taking this thing down before the area turns into a warzone with people fighting over the kill."

"Right," Darling said. "If other people do show up while we're engaged, do your best to keep your distance without compromising your ability to fight and just try to ignore them. If it's just a couple of random players, they'll probably just add some damage and that's fine. If something looks suspicious, call it out to your group leader."

She eyed the many groups that were lining the cliff in a couple of impressively organized rows.

"If you've got consumables, this is your moment." She set a glowing

raid icon at a point in the water about two hundred yards in front of Delugia. "If you're hopping in a boat, you should already be positioned close to
the person who's summoning it. I want the summons going out on my
mark, which will go up when that creature reaches the icon."

I stared at the turtle, heart thumping, palms prickling with sweat. I
dropped into a crouch and pulled up my profession menu.

I had a serious amount of gems on hand, but I still didn't know what
sort of runes I should be running with.

I'd have liked to roll with something elemental while hoping for a
weakness, but a quick glance at my options and the creature stalking
toward us made it clear that I didn't have anything that was likely to
provide much of an advantage there.

So with that in mind, I left everything in place except for the firebird
rune I had on one of my pistols, which I replaced for a Rune of the Caustic
Raven for the raid-wide debuff it offered.

That meant my other pistol and my rifle both had piercing runes
active, while my blunderbuss was still using the fiery rune I'd applied
while fighting Elias, which was fine because the Aeroblaster's shorter-
ranged spells naturally hit everything in a narrow cone.

Then I went ahead and crafted up a ton of options just so that I could
swap stuff out on the move if need be.

Once everything was said and done, I crafted six different rune types in
all: a Rune of the White Ring, a Rune of the Charging Clone, a Rune of
Shattering for crowd control and utility, plus an extra Rune of the Ghostly
Hunt just to be safe, another firebird to replace the one I'd got rid of in
case the element was needed somehow, and a few extra piercing runes so I
wouldn't worry about having to dump those if the situation called for it
without being able to reapply.

That burst of crafting cut into my stockpile significantly, especially
when it came to the higher-end gems, but it also boosted my skill from
100 to 113 and unlocked two more recipes.

**Recipe: {Rune of Quickening Drift} (Consumable) (Awards 6 skill
points per craft)**
**Description: The cooldown of your {Clonedrift} spell is reduced by
33%, and your travel speed while drifting is increased by 300%.**
**Duration: 24 Hours.**
**Requirements: {Large Soul Gem} x30.**

Recipe: {Rune of Exposure} (Consumable) (Awards 6 skill points per craft)
Description: Your Repel ability now afflicts your target with the {Exposed} debuff for 5 seconds. Targets afflicted by {Exposed} take 30% increased damage from your next attack.
Duration: 24 Hours.
Requirements: {Large Soul Gem} x30.

I didn't have enough of the large gems to craft up either of those, so I stopped for now.

Darling stepped up beside me, grinning widely. "You ready for this?"

The creature was now about fifty yards from the mark she'd set, and the guild's steady murmur of laughter and conversation had died out.

"Ready as we're gonna be. Gotta get Frank his soup."

"To be honest, I hate turtle soup," Frank said. "But I will definitely eat more than my fair share to make my dominance obvious at the eventual feast."

"I like turtles," House said from a little behind me.

Darling had put her in charge of driving one of the guild's new Gunboats, which seemed like a good fit, given her ability to steer and direct her healing bots at the same time.

"Good to know, House," I said. "I assume you're fine with murdering this one, though?"

"Indeed I am."

Darling raised her voice. "If you've got a boat, get ready to deploy!"

I waited for her to raise a fist, then started summoning my galley at the very edge of the cliff. I wasn't going to be taking the boat myself because Darling had charged me and a few other ranged DPS with watching out for some of the healers up top, but I was happy to see a couple of the lower-leveled guild members step up and around me.

And every single one of them was concentrating on the water below.

I counted the seconds down in my head, then started speaking aloud as the cast bar neared completion: "Three, two, one, go!"

The boat appeared in the air above the water, and the group of five had already stepped off the cliff line before the vessel slapped down into the waves.

I watched as a line of boats popped into existence and crashed down into the water one after the other. People flung themselves into the air and rolled or activated abilities to avoid the fall damage as they hit the many decks. The speed and sight of it all were impressive.

Without fail, every boat had one person take the wheel almost immediately, while several others deployed the additional cannons that House and the others had constructed, especially on the Gunboats, which were small, unremarkable vessels other than the fact that they were armed to the teeth.

"All boat crews should be off and getting into position for the approach!" Darling said.

And they were: the vessels were already fanning out, maneuvering themselves into a wide 'V' even as the cannons continued to be deployed.

"Glider groups! If you haven't already, find a high point on the cliff line and hang tight. We're about twice as fast as the average boat while gliding, so we're going to let them close about half the distance before we launch." Darling set another marker in the water. "My signal will go up when the first boat crosses that icon."

I jogged across the cliff line, heading for a higher point that offered another ten feet of elevation, while the others who'd summoned boats did the same.

"Frank? Question."

"I have no idea why your left ear is higher than your right, but I've been wondering about it for a while and I doubt I'm alone."

I fought down the urge to check, but it was a close thing.

"Yeah yeah. So I'm looking at those boats and the cannons and I'm wondering what the restrictions are."

"I need more than that."

"Well, we're summoning the boats in the air and they're dropping five to ten feet into the water below, right? Is there a point where they'd break?"

"Yeah, they're super durable when being deployed, but this was cutting that pretty close."

"But we did summon them into the air, right? So do we actually need water? I'm wondering if we could use these in the raid somehow. Summon a boat with cannons on the ground, maybe the healers could use it occasionally or something?"

"Nah, you need water or ice beneath it, and raids are generally going to be a no-go."

"How much, though?"

"Enough to support the boat and let it move around. You're not gonna be able to cheese it and summon a boat on dry ground above a glass of water if that's what you're thinking."

I eyed the marker. The lead boat was closing in.

"What if I summoned one in water, then got up a bunch of speed and beached it?"

"You could do that to get it on land, but the cannons and so on wouldn't work then. They'd deactivate the moment you left the water behind."

"Get ready to launch!" Darling called out. "If you've got an ability that can add height or speed, go ahead and burn it as long as the cooldown isn't too long! The Glider will accelerate you from whatever speed you're at when you activate it, so the faster you're going when you hit the switch, the better off you'll be! Just don't get too far ahead!"

"Thanks for the info," I said to Frank. "Feels like there's something there."

"On three!" Darling said.

I took a few steps back to allow for a running start. I wasn't going to burn Double Cast, but my cooldowns were short enough that I could spare a couple of spells to get there a bit early and scout from close-up.

"One, two, three!"

I launched into a dead sprint, then dove head-first off the cliff. I pulled out a pistol so I'd have it ready, then activated Clonedrift as I began to fall to send myself zooming forward and up.

Frank chuckled as my clone bellyflopped into the waves below and burst apart.

I pointed my pistol behind me, and as soon as Clonedrift expired and took me to my full height, I blasted a Water Jet at a low angle to gain even more speed and altitude.

Then I deployed the Glider House had given me from my inventory, and there was a sound like springs pinging free from under tension.

A pair of dark wings made of smooth canvas appeared over each of my shoulders, unfolding with a series of snaps and pops, and I suddenly found myself gripping a horizontal bar of dark metal that I could steer the triangular contraption with.

My feet were hanging down, and a quick glance over my shoulder revealed a second bar that looked made to take their weight, so I kicked my feet up and rested my shins against it.

The Glider's wings snapped one last time and reached their full width, which spanned about eight feet from tip to tip.

I lay there for a moment while the waves crashed beneath me and the cold air whipped across my face. And a few seconds in, I realized I was grinning like an idiot.

Someone hooted behind me, and I craned my neck to see Nina about fifteen feet back and ten feet lower, pumping a fist and shouting obscenities at the hulking turtle.

A few other guild members must have popped some abilities too, because Darling and Jukes and a handful of others weren't far off.

The bulk of the guild was another thirty feet behind us, tightly packed into a second massive 'V' with several layers. And they were laughing up a storm.

The guild chat was lighting up as well, mostly with messages from the Glider group laughing at the people on the Gunboats and threatening to spit on them as we pulled even, then shot by them.

A few cannons turned up at us from below, and laughter boomed from both directions.

But the jubilation died out as the two groups pressed closer and it became clear just how large the turtle really was. The long crystals that lined its back and underbelly were easily twenty feet tall, and Delugia's red eyes were larger than some of our smaller boats.

Its back was broad, though, and its gentle slope was segmented into huge hexagons with dark lines between them that might have been actual gaps.

I examined the nearest crystal up top, which rose from just behind the beast's head.

**{Cloudbreak Crystal} (Level 17 Construct) (Elite+)**
**HP: 120,000/120,000**
**Resonance: 0%**

I scanned the other two back crystals and found that they all had the same Health and Resonance bars.

"Glider crew, listen up," Darling said. "Give Delugia's head a wide berth and swing onto its back about halfway down its length. If you're way out front, bank some turns so you land around the same time as everybody else. At the very least, don't land before Jukes and Ton. Last thing we need is someone squishy starting the fight and getting instantly killed."

I banked a sweeping turn to my left to let Jukes fly by me and give the others time to catch up. The great turtle's red eyes followed the tank as he skirted around its colossal skull, but it kept to its slow march through the water.

Movement below caught my eye, and I looked down to see a bright green fin cutting through the waves. And once I'd spotted one, I couldn't help but notice more that were already swarming toward and around the boats.

"Boat crew is reporting shark-like creatures in the water," Darling called out. "If you're up top, double-check your raid and group number. If we've gotta send help down there, that's how we'll call people out."

The group went silent for the final approach, and I couldn't take my eyes off the water below. The fins were relatively small—especially compared to the titan wading through the waves above them—but there were so many of them.

Jukes landed near the very middle of the creature's back, and his Glider vanished as his feet touched down on the shell.

The huge creature jerked to a stop, and the sudden arrest sent waves crashing around its legs, some of which launched a few of the smaller boats airborne. Delugia raised its head and howled, keening a high-pitched noise that was eerily reminiscent of a tsunami siren.

When the noise cut off, the beast resumed its march. The crystal directly behind its skull flashed purple at its base, then the light crept upward, gathering speed as it went.

The pulse was moving fairly quickly by the time it reached the top of the crystal, then it reappeared within the base of the second crystal, moving even more quickly. From there, the light pulsed down the line of three enormous gemstones in quick succession.

I landed on the shell between Rock and Darling. Jukes was just standing there, eyeing the crystals one after the other. More guild members flooded into position, and the entire gliding crew touched down within the space of ten seconds.

I was still scanning the crystals to see what had changed, and I happened to catch the second one as its Resonance ticked up to 1%. I called out what I'd seen to the others.

The other two crystals went dim and untargetable, but the base of the second stayed aglow with deep purple light.

"Burst it!" Darling said. "Move!"

Then metal was flying and spells were crackling and the predominately melee group was charging into position, rumbling across the huge shell and leaping the small gaps in the hexagons that covered it.

The gaps were bigger than I'd expected, at least two or three feet deep and half that wide. I hurdled one and launched a pair of green, acid-laced ravens at the crystal and was thrilled to see the debuff show up as the birds burst against the crystalline structure with a splash of green light.

"Resonance at 3% and climbing fast," Frank said. "Crystal at 94% and falling faster."

I chained one spell after another and kept an eye on Jukes. He was half-heartedly bashing his staff into the base of the crystal while staring around and waiting for something to do.

The purple glow at the base of the crystal deepened, and the structure started emitting a high-pitched whine that sounded almost electrical.

High above the crystal, white clouds appeared and began to darken. And by the time the structure's Health ticked below 90% under the guild's collective assault, a flickering storm cloud had appeared overhead. It hung directly over the crystal, matching the creature's gait.

"Resonance at 10%," Frank said. "Crystal at 81%."

An empty hexagon two over from the one I was standing on flashed red. I didn't think I was in much danger at my current distance, but being able to cast on the move meant that it couldn't hurt to get away, so I strafed around the crystal and put a few more hexagons between it and me while I kept the stream of green birds coming.

The storm howled overhead, and a rain drop the size of a car smashed directly into the flashing hexagon. The resulting slap was so sharp it left my ears ringing, and I was glad for the extra distance I'd created when the drop burst and sent a three-foot wave of water surging across the creature's smooth back.

"Big rain drops!" I called out. "Hexes go red and they hit! My guess is anybody within two hexagons of the drop gets taken off their feet—and you really don't wanna be beneath it!"

"You heard him!" Darling said. "Raid 3, groups 2 and 4! We've already got issues below, if you've got AoE crowd control I need you down there right now! Do your best to spread out—I want one of you per boat, max! Check your maps!"

A bunch of group members ran off to the crystal's left while another went right. They stopped at the edge of the shell and shared a few quick words, then one of the players jumped for it and the others quickly followed.

A series of hexagons flashed red, including one of the six that surrounded the crystal itself, where a ton of the melee guildies were gathered up.

They did an admirable job of splitting, but a dagger user got his feet tangled up with Rock and the two of them went down as the giant drop fell.

The dagger user vanished in a puff of smoke and reappeared a few hexagons over, but the huge bead slammed down onto Rock and caught him full in the back as he tried to scramble away. I'd expected the impact to do severe damage if not kill him instantly, but his Health didn't budge.

Instead of breaking and surging over the shell as the one before it had, the bead quivered and rebounded, its shape stretching over Rock and pulling. It bounced a few feet in the air and took the big guy with it. And to make matters worse, a Silenced icon had appeared above his nameplate.

Nina appeared over the watery orb with both daggers held in a reverse grip. She struck a clean, downward blow, but the sphere turned her daggers away and pulled her in with a loud slurp, and she popped into it beside Rock. The colossal droplet hit the shell again, bounced half as high and rolled away while they tumbled helplessly within it.

"Can we get a Dispel on Rock and Nina?" I called out.

"I already tried!" Zoe said. "Invalid target!"

I watched in horror as the bead of water tumbled off the side of the shell and took the pair of damage dealers with it.

The hex beneath my feet lit up, so I dashed away and kept the birds coming, hitting the crystal in the 400s and 500s over and over again.

I kept an eye on Rock and Nina's Health bars, and I was unsurprised to see them both drop beneath 30% at the same moment, probably when they hit the water.

I thought it was simple fall damage at first, but then a violent explosion sounded from below and ten other Health bars that all belonged to the lower raid groups dropped to the same level.

The cannon fire that had been omnipresent since the fight had started went quiet, then resumed.

"Do *not* get carried off by those beads!" Darling said. "Those spheres turn into bombs that explode below!"

"Resonance at 30%," Frank said. "Crystal at 65%."

The purple glow had crept up on- third of the crystal's length, and the hum was only growing louder.

We pressed on, and the sound deepened into a lower note as the crystal's Resonance ticked up to 33%. All across the creature's back, whole rings of hexagons lit up at the same time with one empty space at their center, plus the ring around the crystal.

The formations left a decent amount of space between them, but fully half of the creature's back had just flashed red and the air pressure had noticeably dropped.

"Scatter!" Darling said.

The entire melee group bailed from around the crystal as a series of supernaturally large drops rained down and smashed into the creature's back.

Several members activated leaps or other abilities to pass up and over the water as it surged out in every direction, and while a great number of people were swept off their feet, I was thrilled and more than a little proud to see the waters recede and slide away without claiming anyone else.

"Resonance at 35%," Frank said. "Crystal at 52%."

"Boat group below is destroying their first crystal faster than we are, but they've already lost two boats!" Darling called out, right as the melee players smashed back onto the target.

I heard rushing water to my left, and the sound quickly built until it was enough to cover the whine of the damaged crystal.

As I released two blasts, I glanced at one of the gaps, where dark water was rushing through it and up the shell. The angle was slight, but it was definitely flowing against gravity.

"New mechanic!" I called out. "Watch the gaps in the shell, water's doing something weird!"

"Ton," Darling shouted, "go help the boat crew out! Got something down there for you!"

The tank barreled away from the melee group and leaped out of sight. From almost the same location, Nina and Rock scrambled up back onto the shell.

Nina drew her daggers and dashed for the crystal, and though her Health was still low, bursts of green and gold light illuminated her as she reached the healers' range.

"The legs make for an easy climb if you get knocked off!"

Rock was close behind her, and within seconds he too was healed to full.

I watched Darling, who was eyeing the healers between strikes and dodges as if she were considering sending more of the group down below.

I could see the lower raid's Health bars jumping in my periphery, and though most of the healers up here had some ability to add at least a little bit of damage, we weren't taking much damage, which meant they weren't being utilized very well.

"Raid 1, group 2 healers, I want—"

She cut off as the water within the gaps to the left and right of the crystal surged, then rose into great beads of water that rolled up and stacked atop each other. And within the space of a few heartbeats, two barrel-chested, watery golems stood to either side of the melee group.

Each of their chests was comprised of a single large sphere of water, and their arms and legs were made of three or four smaller ones. The water was still rushing up their legs, too, and though it was hard to tell from this distance, I thought the two of them were still swelling.

The creatures raised their arms to their sides and squeezed their hands into fists. Water jetted out as if they were gripping hilts, and the beads expanded into two frothing swords.

I inspected the nearest of the two.

{Watery Centurion} (Level 17 Construct) (Elite+)
HP: 60,000/60,000
MP: 35,000/35,000

Jukes rolled out from the melee group and tagged one of the creatures with a series of quick strikes with his staff, then rolled back away from the group and aimed a flying dagger of bright blue ice at the second.

He put his back to the first Centurion while his projectile was still in mid-air, which meant he missed the *resist* notification that scrolled above its head as the spell connected.

I hadn't seen him use that ability before, but his body language told me that he'd just used a taunt of some kind that he hadn't expected to fail.

The Centurion that had resisted his spell surged toward the melee group, its long weapons at the ready.

I swapped off the crystal and sent two green ravens flying at the creature. The mob twisted, beads spinning and shifting as it approached the group. It splayed both of its weapons to its left in a strange, horizontal grip with both of the blades positioned a few inches apart, then drew back and swung.

My birds splashed home, but not before the mob's watery strikes ripped into four of our melee users from behind, instantly dropping three of them to 60% and a third all the way down to 32%.

Which probably meant that the mob would one-shot me if I let it connect.

It whirled on me and surged across the shell, rolling atop the two large beads that capped its feet instead of taking steps.

I turned and ran toward Jukes, but the heals were flying fast and heavy now, and I could feel what little aggro I'd generated slipping away, which forced me into even more blasts as I kited the creature along.

"Jukes!" I said as I got close enough that I thought he'd hear me over the ever-present whine and the rushing water and the sound of dozens of weapons ringing sharply off the crystal. "Got one for you that resisted your taunt!"

"Drag it close and I'll peel with Hateful Ice!" he said.

"All DPS, be ready to switch to the adds once Jukes has them under control!" Darling said.

"Get down!" Frank said.

I dove belly-first onto the shell and went sliding across one of the wet hexagons. A series of three watery spears lanced above me courtesy of the nearest golem and flew right past Jukes.

I caught myself before the next gap, regained my feet, and the chase was back on.

"Thanks for the call out!"

I jumped another gap and ran right by the tank. He whipped his staff up and into position. "Blast them for me when the spell hits!"

I pulled out my rifle and dragged the incoming mob to the left a bit, lining it up for a piercing shot but waiting for Jukes' spell.

He smashed his staff into the ground, and ice flared out around him.

The window arrived, so I Double Cast an instant spell with my rifle, then swapped to my blunderbuss and dashed in close.

Which meant that I was almost in melee range when both of the mobs resisted Jukes' taunt while my initial spell punched through the first and sank deep into the second.

The weightiness of aggro settled across my shoulders, and the golems slashed out with their four watery blades. I threw myself backward, and while I managed to dodge two of the higher, horizontal swings, the third caught me across the collarbone.

The creature's watery blade was warm, and it sent vibrations as well as hot water running down my chest as my Heart Vessel exploded behind me.

I hit the ground on my back and slid across the slick shell. But the mobs were already in pursuit with their weapons held high, ready for a quartet of downward strikes.

I swapped out my blunderbuss and popped a pistol into my hand. I fired a Water Jet that sent me skimming across the shell, zooming over its gaps as both of the creatures brought their weapons down on the hexagon I'd shot myself off of.

"High resistance on ice and probably water!" I called out as I rolled back to my feet.

"Yeah!" Jukes said. "I can't even get them off Ned! We need Ton up here!"

I eyed the crystal, whose Resonance had climbed above 45%. Its Health had fallen into execute range, though, so I swapped to my rifle and hit it with a Dark Harvest to add a bit of damage and kept kiting the two mobs.

But I wasn't going to last long between their speed and the projectiles I'd seen earlier. And if Jukes couldn't even get them off me, there was no way he was going to be able to hold off both of them while the group focused them down.

"I gotta take them under!" I said.

I fired one last round of caustic blasts at the crystal to give the group another refresh on my armor debuff, then turned and ran for the edge of the shell.

"Jukes, go with Ned!" Darling said. "And send Ton back up, I messaged him but he didn't respond!"

The two mobs were faster than me, and by the time I reached the edge of the shell, they'd skated almost within melee range.

I threw myself off the edge. I wheeled my arms through the air, legs kicking out involuntarily.

My stomach turned at the sight of the dark water some forty feet below. The waves were full of boats flying up and down over the swells, cannons flashing, the barrels trained on the underside of the great turtle.

"Ton, adds incoming!" I called out when I was still about twenty feet above the water. I twisted in the air as I fell, then activated Clonedrift.

I shot backward and over the water while my clone plunked down into the waves. A trio of green fins broke the surface, and the water churned white for a moment before the clone exploded and left the mobs stunned and still.

I canceled drift as it brought me across a Galley's deck and landed in a backward roll.

"Adds from above!" I shouted, screaming the words over the cannon fire.

The two giant mobs hit the water, and the resulting splashes were so large that they soaked me completely through and sent six inches of water rushing across the Galley's deck.

"All other vessels," Ton said, voice booming over the water, "keep your fire focused on the crystal! I'm headed up if this doesn't work!"

I spotted him a few boats away, standing in the center of a particularly large ship that was turning its side toward the adds.

The two Centurions surfaced and surged toward me, skating across the water just as they had atop the shell above. They made it about halfway to the ship I'd landed on before Ton's boat flashed six times in quick succession and the water around them erupted.

I felt the aggro slide off me as the mobs surged away and toward his vessel.

Jukes had plunked into the water feet-first between a pair of nearby boats. He hadn't taken any fall damage at all, but his Health dropped as the green sharks surrounded him, brightening the water.

I didn't know if the healers were focusing on dealing damage or if they thought he was still up top, because they were very clearly not stepping in.

I fired a Gravity Bird directly at him and detonated it just above his head. The sharks flew up out of the water, teeth gnashing at Jukes as he swam below them, their skin glowing uranium green.

The spell only kept the beasts airborne for a few seconds, but it bought Jukes enough time to let him reach a boat and scramble up into it. Two of the healers onboard exchanged a glance, then their hands were glowing and Jukes' Health bar was jumping up.

Jukes shouted something that I didn't catch, then his vessel turned and rode a cresting wave towards Ton.

By now the two Centurions had reached Ton and they were standing atop the waves, striking out at him with their frothy swords while he blocked and dodged at the edge of his large vessel.

Its cannons were absolutely lighting the mobs up despite the short range, and I was surprised that he was able to hold the aggro with the damage they were pumping out.

Jukes had his own boat heading that way, but I wasn't sure what exactly he was going to do without being able to depend on his taunts. The fight stabilized and wore on, and eventually the crystal high above shattered.

Bits of bluish glass peppered the deck, and the boat group cheered. The next crystal didn't appear to be targetable yet so every vessel in sight turned its cannons on the adds that Ton was squaring up against in unison, and the spellcasters and ranged players also shifted their focus.

The mobs were already well below 30% when the onslaught hit, but their bars emptied so quickly that I didn't even see them drop.

The two mobs exploded and dispersed into the waves, then the two remaining crystals that lined the beast's underbelly both darkened with purplish light at the same time.

"Focus on the middle one, I'm headed up top!" Ton shouted as he ran across the deck of his vessel.

He launched himself into the air and smashed into one of the beast's impossibly thick legs. He scaled it quickly; as Nina had promised, the gaps in the hexagons made for quick climbing.

"Ping me if you need me, Jukes has the lead down here!"

Metal rasped as dozens of cannons shifted at the same time, then fired. The explosive volley rocked the boat beneath my feet, and the creature's underbelly flashed white.

My boat was currently slightly out of pistol range, so I waited a few seconds until the vessel was riding the crest of a high wave, then turned and leaped for the bow of the next.

I landed in a crouch and sprinted to the front of the boat. I let the spells fly as I popped into range, and I was taken aback by just how much more quickly the crystal was falling compared to the rate the one above had.

And if dealing with two crystals at once meant the people up top had to deal with four Watery Centurions at the same time...

I called Darling on video chat, and she picked up as she rolled out of the way of another giant bead of water.

"You see 'em too?" she said.

"See what?"

"Two hostile boats to the north."

I cursed under my breath. "I didn't, but look. We just dropped our first crystal, and two more activated at once. That probably means if you drop yours, you'll end up with the same problem. But up top, it seems like taking on two crystals at once might mean spawning four of those mobs. I really doubt Ton can tank that without all of our healers helping out at once."

"What about the Resonance? What if it hits 100%?"

I fired another pair of greenish Ravens up at the crystal high above. "I'm wondering if you can just delay blowing the top one up as long as you can, and when the Resonance gets really high or if it becomes a problem, blow it. In the meantime, send the few ranged casters you have and any spare healers down here. If more mobs spawn, have someone get aggro and drag them down to the bottom."

"So we delay up here, you pop the bottom two crystals, then everybody moves and focuses the top section?"

"Exactly."

She hesitated for a moment, wet hair matted to her face, her chin tilted up as if she were staring at the crystal's Health bar.

"Screw it, why not. Incoming your way, but I'm leaving this video chat open for a view of both sections now that Ton might be sent right back down."

"Thanks. Frank, keep an eye out for those hostile boats, yeah?"

"They're probably a way out if she can see them from high up and we can't. Next crystal at 75%, Resonance at 12%."

I spotted movement and feared the worst, but it was just the first of the top group to arrive. They must have taken clues from Jukes' rough landing because the vast majority of them activated movement abilities before they hit the water just in time to go leaping or teleporting onto a boat, while the others were simply careful enough to make sure they landed near a vessel.

Still, there were upwards of fifteen people all splashing down at once. Some managed it better than others, and one guy actually landed directly on a deck without activating any abilities and instantly killed himself. Chaos ensued as the sharks ripped into those who'd fallen into the water, even if only briefly, the water lighting up in pockets of brightness around them.

The wounded had the healers' full attention though, and the guild got through the chaos of the shift without losing anyone else.

High above, Ton hesitated about three-quarters of the way up the leg he was climbing. He was staring directly at me, but he was too far away for me to read his expression.

He rocked sideways once, twice, then leaped down again. He landed only a few feet away from the same boat he'd been on before and was quick to haul himself back up.

Two more Watery Centurions formed beside the crystal we were targeting as its Resonance hit 40%. The beaded creatures fell the very moment they appeared and splashed down directly beneath the crystal.

The arrivals caught me off guard: I hadn't seen any Centurions down here when I'd first arrived, so I'd assumed that the bottom section just had different mechanics. But the lower group must have just killed them off before I'd jumped down.

"Adds!" I called out. "Bottom side DPS, burn them down! We're going to have more adds coming from above, so we can't afford to focus on the crystals and let their numbers build up!"

Ton bellowed a war cry that got both of the mobs surging toward him. The water around them was already erupting with cannon fire and spells and projectiles, and the creatures' Health bars were falling at a rate that once again made me worry that Ton was going to lose their attention.

I targeted a pistol at each of them and sent green birds flying their way until the speedy Centurions outdistanced my weapons' range. I went back to blasting the crystal above me, eyeing the adds the entire time as the boat pitched and rocked beneath me, cannons booming.

The air reeked of gunpowder and salt, and for a moment, the sensory overload of it all was overwhelming.

I snapped out of it as another lone player flew down from topside with two more Watery Centurions trailing behind them. This was exactly what I'd been hoping to avoid by shuffling people around: four of those watery swordsmen all on one tank.

"Two more adds incoming, Ton!" I said. "Get your boat within range so the cannons can light them up and pull the mobs in; everybody else, ignore them until he's got aggro on those two!"

I took a deep breath as Ton's vessel turned around into a crested wave and caught its full impact on its side. The entire vessel rocked dangerously sideways, and two players who had been operating cannons on the far side flew off and toppled into the waves.

Whoever was steering didn't seem to notice because they quickly left the two players behind. The sharks were on them immediately, and though I saw a couple of heals go out, the players died in short order.

I fought down the urge to grab aggro on the newly arrived Centurions and forced myself to focus on the third crystal overhead. It was already down to 40% Health, largely thanks to the burst of damage the new arrivals had given us, but I couldn't help but stare at Ton's Health bar—it was already jumping around all over the place as he fought the two Watery Centurions from the second crystal, and the others that had come down from topside were closing in.

Then another pair of Centurions formed around the third crystal high above, and my jaw actually dropped—there was no way in hell Ton was going to tank six of them, and Jukes was almost a total non-factor.

Then I had an idea. I launched another pair of ravens at the second crystal above to refresh my debuff.

"I need a Gunboat right now!"

"I am present!" House called.

# Chapter Thirty-Five

The vessel House was piloting was only a few boats over, so I ran that way. I leaped the gap between two boats and launched a pair of green ravens at the newly arrived mobs just as they hit the water. The Watery Centurions popped above the waves and skated atop them, beelining right at me.

I took three quick paces across the next vessel's deck, jumped atop a cannon, and leaped for House's boat. It was narrower than my Galley but considerably longer and sleeker.

"House, take us around the fight and circle back to Ton's position. Cannoneers, keep your fire on the crystal if you can reach it; if not, blast the trailing mobs!"

"Understood," House said, and the boat shot forward so quickly that I nearly lost my footing. The front end lifted into the air, and the boat's choppy wake was glowing with bright green light as if lit from beneath. House must have applied one of her motors to it.

I hit the trailing mobs with another round of spells to consolidate aggro, then managed to tag the crystal we were burning one last time to refresh my debuff before the boat's speed took us out of range.

"Large wave incoming," House said. "Please brace yourselves accordingly and keep your hands and legs inside the vehicle at all times."

I had my back to her, so I ran forward and smashed chest-first into the boat's central mast. I reached a pistol around the wooden pole to either side and launched two blasts, then wrapped my arms around the mast and held on for dear life.

The front of the boat tilted up, and then I felt the water disappear beneath us. We launched so high that the boat's motor actually left the water, and its steady hum turned into a high-pitched whine to match that of the crystals above.

"Weeee," House said.

I glanced back to see two of House's cannoneers floating above their charges in free fall some five feet above the deck.

Because of the angle of the launch, the back of the boat slammed down first, and the nose whipped into position with a colossal smash, which created even more distance for the crew members to fall.

One of the two cannoneers bounced off their artillery piece and landed back on the deck, while the other bellyflopped into the water.

The boat's speed quickly outdistanced him, and though he activated some kind of torpedo-like leap that sent him flying and spinning head-first in our direction, he came up a full ten feet short of the vessel.

Within seconds, the rough water and the sharks within had pulled him under for good. I stayed tight against the mast, cheek pressed to the rough wood and my guns drawn and flashing to either side of the pole with every blast I fired at the trailing mobs.

I was walking a fine line: I had to keep increasing my aggro to deal with the threat that Ton's healers were putting out, but I didn't want so much that he wouldn't be able to grab it back when he needed to.

And what was even more troubling was that all four of the other mobs were now standing side by side, battering him with their watery blades while he stood atop the edge of his boat's wide deck.

Ton's health dropped to 8%, then shot back to 15. Down to 6, back to 12, down to 5, and on and on it went.

Jukes was standing beside him, and I saw another Hateful Ice go out and generate four more resist messages. He followed that up with the same icicle launch I'd seen earlier, and he let out a whoop when that spell actually connected and one of the four mobs turned to engage him.

The opening let the healers stabilize Ton at 20%, but the damage was still going to be too much if the fight dragged on like this, and I doubted Jukes would be able to hold the mobs for long once his taunt ran out.

Ton needed more time. I pulled up my inventory on the spot and applied a Rune of the White Ring to my rifle.

Our vessel launched off another wave as we drew into range, the two trailing Centurions still roaring through our glowing wake. The mobs were faster than us, motor and all, and while the boat was quick enough to make their progress fairly slow, they'd still closed the gap to about fifteen feet.

I waited for the boat to ramp off another wave and hit a relatively smooth section of water, then shouldered my rifle and raised my voice.

"Jukes, step away from Ton!"

The tank rolled to the very edge of the vessel's deck and took his lone mob with him.

I targeted Ton directly and fired my newly runed Gravity Bird. A white, luminescent raven ripped out of the barrel and swooped over the waves.

The heavily armored tank froze for a split second as my spell flew right at him before slamming into his chest. A white ring of pure energy sprang up around him, and the Centurion's watery blades were thrown back.

The ring expanded outward, and all three of the mobs that had been standing in front of him exploded away from the deck and flew backward into the surging waves.

Ton stood there staring at me for a heartbeat, baffled, shield raised to defend himself against a strike that never came.

"Burn the lone mob before the others get back into position!" I called out. "That ability doesn't do any damage so Ton will still have aggro!"

The ranged damage dealers lit it up, with spellcasters and archers throwing blasts of magic and glowing arrows from the nearby boats.

The mob melted under the focused assault, its Health plummeting under 10% within a matter of seconds. But the mobs I'd blown off Ton had now recovered, and all three of them were now surging toward him again.

Jukes' lone target died at the same time the first mob reached Ton. The break I'd created had let the healers bring him back to full Health, but as soon as the three of them were back in front of him, his Health bar went back to jumping up and down.

"Trailing mobs are still gaining on us," Frank said. "But the second crystal's also about to pop overhead. Top crew is still working on their first."

I twisted around and spotted my two charges mere feet away from the back of the boat. The waves were so large that I was sure I'd be thrown off the craft if I ran across the deck to engage without holding onto something, so I grabbed one of the railings with one hand and ran down the side of the boat, gripping it tightly all the way, jumping the deck-mounted cannons as they boomed beneath me.

I kept a hand on the railing as the boat went airborne and crashed back down again, then drew a pistol and hit both the mobs with another raven as they drew closer to the deck. I waited for the boat to bounce again before running to the stern and Clonedrifted right back to where I'd been.

The distance was so short that I was back on the railing almost instantly, but I left a clone standing at the very end of the boat. It raised its weapons.

The two mobs surged up onto the stern, and one of them cleaved the clone in two just before it could fire. Sparks flew, and a pair of stun icons appeared above the Centurions' heads.

I dashed back over to them and dismissed my pistol. I popped Frank into my hand and activated Repel, then wound up a wild strike with every ounce of power I had.

I hit the first watery mob with a forehand blow, and the creature exploded backward off the deck and over the waves.

"Blam!" Frank shouted.

I planted a foot on the deck and came back around with a low, back-handed strike while Double Casting a second Repel.

"Double blam!"

The second mob flew even farther than the first, bouncing off a cresting wave and disappearing into the trough behind it.

"I know these things aren't technically alive," Frank said, "but I. Will. Take it!"

I ran back to the mast, grinning. A wave rocked the boat sideways, and I almost lost my balance as I staggered across the wet deck, then another swell pitched the boat up beneath me and launched me into the air.

I managed to snag a hand in the small, triangular net that hung down from the mast, which was the only thing that kept me from joining the creatures I'd knocked into the water.

The momentum pulled me briefly sideways, but I was able to swing back onto the deck and reposition myself around the mast. Movement flashed from above: more figures were falling out of the sky.

I gritted my teeth for a moment as I thought it was yet another wave of Centurions—four of them in all, which was far more than we could handle—before I realized the truth of it when House shouted from the front of the boat.

"Incoming bombs!"

Four players up above had been trapped by spheres and were now plummeting toward us. The first two detonated above a handful of boats and brought six or seven players down to critical levels in a single go. And with the healers fully engaged on Ton, those players stayed critical.

The third exploded directly to the right of one of our larger vessels and lifted the boat sideways into the air. Players went flying, and while a few of them were quick enough to activate skills that put them back on the boat as it slammed back down and righted itself, three nameplates quickly grayed thanks to the sharks.

And the fourth and final sphere was the worst of all: it smashed dead-center onto the deck of a boat with three healers aboard plus a number of cannoneers.

The deck splintered, and the watery bead pushed halfway into the vessel before it exploded and sent huge chunks of wood and metal flying in every direction. The mast slammed into the water and the vessel's sail trapped a pair of players beneath it as the water brightened and the sharks closed in.

Frame after frame grayed out, and for the first time, it was beginning to seem like we were going down. We'd lost about 10% of the raid, and it was probably generous to say that the fight was more than halfway over.

But all we could do was press on. I lit Ton's three mobs up one after the other to get my debuffs rolling again, then held a few spells back as Jukes indicated he was going to try to use Hateful Ice again to peel a Centurion off the tank.

The spell whiffed once again, and I could see the frustration in Jukes' posture and in the wild swings he was taking at the mobs, all of which were dutifully ignoring him.

A crack sounded from overhead, and more shards of glass rained down onto the deck. A cheer went up as people realized the second crystal had popped, though the cheer was much more subdued than it'd been the first time around.

The great turtle groaned and shifted overhead, one of its huge legs threatening to buckle underneath it.

But then it righted itself and carried on.

"Torch the last crystal!" I said. "We're almost there!"

I heard Darling grunt through the video link. "This one up top is going to have to drop soon! Otherwise the melees are just going to be up here standing around."

I nodded and kept firing, alternating my spells across multiple targets to keep the armor debuff up on the crystal plus each of Ton's targets. One of the three mobs dropped, then a second followed in quick order.

And by the time the third Centurion was sliding beneath the waves, we had the third and final crystal below 50%.

I had House swing our vessel next to the one that Ton and Jukes were on, then I jumped onto it as she passed by. I rolled sideways but stuck the landing and came up with two pistols pointing at the mobs I'd been kiting around to buy time.

"Last two for now!" I said.

"I can handle two," Ton said.

I cleared my throat. "Full DPS on the crystal! Pop everything! We need that thing down so we can focus on the fight above!"

Cannons boomed and countless magical projectiles filled the air, illuminating the creature's underbelly again and again.

I activated Clonedrift again as the two trailing mobs caught up and pulled alongside our boat. The spell allowed me to retreat to the front of the vessel and also stunned the first creature to arrive.

Ton pulled the two off me with a series of shouted challenges and quick strikes, and having the aggro finally fall away was a tremendous relief.

The healers had stabilized Ton as well, and a few of them were now just standing around, waiting for his Health to drop.

And we couldn't afford that.

"Healers, if you've got time between casts then hop on a cannon and add some damage! We've lost a bunch of cannoneers, so there should be some close by! Otherwise you need to start climbing!"

They moved quickly, so much so that when Ton's health dropped from nearly full to 60%, I wondered if I'd just gotten him killed by asking his healers to do too much. But a shield sprang up around him, and the burst of healing that followed quickly outpaced the damage of the two mobs.

I kept nuking, eyeing the lone remaining crystal above. I flagged House down again and hopped back into her boat.

"Can you take us closer to the crystal?" I said.

"Certainly."

The boat's nose lifted up, and we flew farther underneath Delugia.

"Third crystal's Health at 33%," Frank said. "But Resonance is at 49%."

"Thanks." I kept the blasts coming, eyes skyward. And when two more

Centurions beaded off the shell and dropped down, I managed to tag both of them twice with blasts before they hit the water.

House roared away and outdistanced my pistol range, so I switched to my rifle and chained blast after blast, swapping between the two trailing targets until I was sure I had aggro, at which point I went back to burning the crystal.

"Crystal's Health at 15%," Frank said.

The trailing mobs were drawing close again, but I didn't want to wait until they were on the deck this time. I took three quick steps, leaped off the back of the boat, then activated Clonedrift and sent myself flying backward.

I canceled the spell as I reached the mast. The clone I'd left behind dropped into the water and exploded as the two mobs ripped through it, stunning them both.

"4%!" Frank said.

I refreshed my armor debuff on the crystal just before it could expire and eyed Darling's group through the window.

The melee players were still working hard, but they were struggling to really engage; the falling drops were coming almost constantly now, and the entire group was being forced to run away from the crystal time and time again to avoid being turned into bombs that would be dropped on the rest of us.

"You got an estimate on the top crystal's Resonance?"

"96%. Heath at 2%."

I cursed. "That's gonna be tight. I don't even want to know what happens if that hits 100."

A series of cannons boomed, and a hail of magical projectiles struck the remaining crystal. It flashed, then burst apart.

The great turtle groaned, a sound so deep that it was almost painful. The front leg that had buckled once before did so again, then so did the other front leg.

Then the entire creature tipped forward. Many of the players up above toppled free and bounced off Delugia's skull, each of them made plainly visible by their green name tags, and a quick glance at Darling's video window saw her tumbling over a shell that had shifted so dramatically it was close to diagonal.

She launched an axe at the crystal as she fell, and her point of view warped so quickly that it made me dizzy.

"That's not good at all. That crystal's going to finish!"

"Uh…" Frank said, and I felt him indicate something to my right.

I whipped around, wondering what exactly he was unable to say. Delugia shifted, and at first I thought it had regained its footing, but in reality it had only leveled out because the back legs were buckling, too.

It was going down, and our entire fleet was almost directly beneath it.

"All vessels, get out from under the turtle!" I yelled. "It's collapsing!"

The boats turned and scattered, bashing their way through the chop and the waves that seemed to be coming from every direction simultaneously. Delugia howled, its bulk sinking lower and lower as it fought to stay upright.

House cleared the edge of the shell before most of the fleet had a chance to do the same, and it was starting to look like the mobs that were trailing me would make it out too.

I switched to a pistol to avoid using the white ring rune I'd thrown onto my rifle and launched a dark Gravity Bird at the two of them.

I detonated the spell slightly ahead of them and above the waves, which yanked them both up above the water, kicking and flailing at the air.

The turtle's bulk dropped by ten feet before it caught itself, straining. Then its huge legs completely failed it.

I stared up at it, not quite able to wrap my head around the scale of the motion involved. The great turtle collapsed while both of the mobs I'd trapped were still underneath it, along with three boats that hadn't been quick enough to get out from under it.

Eleven name plates grayed out as the huge shell slapped the water and obliterated everything beneath it. The ocean roared and rose, an impossible wave rolling out toward us.

I gawked at it as a mountain of smooth water approached, wide-eyed. I grabbed onto the railing, and the cannoneers who remained did the same while House turned the boat and gunned it up the wave, probably trying to get over it before it had time to crest.

The boat pitched nearly vertically, motor screaming as House pushed it up to the now-foaming peak. We launched into the air, and though the boat itself only traveled a few feet above the crest, the drop on the other side was so severe that we just kept going, soaring through the air as the waterline dropped out beneath us.

"Too high!" Frank said. "Way too high!"

I took that to mean the boat wouldn't survive the impact, and it was hard to argue with that, given we were now dropping thirty or forty feet into the deep trench that followed that colossal wave.

The turtle beyond had collapsed into the water, its shell poking out above the waves like a small island.

"Bail, boat's gonna smash!"

I dashed across the deck and launched myself into the air just before the boat smashed down.

The entire vessel shattered behind me. I Water Jetted myself toward the shell, then twisted around in the air and Clonedrifted the remaining distance, landing on the very edge of the newly formed island.

"Resonance at 98% on that crystal up top!" Frank said. "Health still at 2%!"

I kept running at full speed, sending green ravens flying every few steps. Once I had the debuff fully stacked and I'd closed some distance, I popped Doppelganger, then Double Cast it to proc a second clone.

I whipped out my rifle and threw a Dark Harvest at the crystal that was copied twice over, then swapped back to my pistols and kept lighting it up, splashing volley after green volley against the crystalline structure.

A huge axe flew by me to my left, then Darling popped into existence in a dead sprint with one hand extended, armored fingers already curled around the haft of her other weapon.

Rock and Nina were charging up the shell from my left, a huge crowd was approaching from the right, and even House was surging toward the crystal, arms pinned behind her, a disc in each hand.

There were so many friendly nameplates moving up and in that it looked like a green tide was rolling up the shell.

I found myself grinning as I reached melee range with a few seconds left on my Doppelgangers. I switched to my blunderbuss and rattled off two instant, fiery blasts that were each duplicated.

"1% Health and 99% Resonance!" Frank said.

The first of the guild's spells arrived as my doppelgangers winked out. The metal projectiles followed in a hail, and I was grateful for the lack of friendly fire as the arrows and darts and spears and everything else smashed home, leaving the now almost fully purple crystal ringing like a tuning fork.

I held my breath as I blasted and backed away, guild members surging by me and the melees rushing into position.

The clouds were boiling above the crystal, and huge beads were now falling fast and heavy, lighting up one hexagon after the next and sweeping people off their feet left and right.

But I didn't see anyone actually get caught. Cannon fire boomed from my left, then from my right—the remaining boats had returned and formed a ring at the very edge of the shell.

A particularly large cannonball connected with the top of the crystal, and the construct shivered, then burst. Purple glass peppered the raid, and a round of cheers went up.

"Job's not done!" Darling called out, but the mirth in her voice was obvious. "Four down, two to go! Full burn on what would have been the middle crystal, pop everything you have!"

The massive raid crashed into place, and between the focused fire of the boats and the full complement of damage dealers—minus the ones we'd lost—the construct's Health plummeted compared to the rate that its Resonance was climbing at.

Two more Centurions arrived as the crystal dropped below 30% Health, but Ton was quick to pick them up and pull them away from the crystal so the DPS could maintain their line of sight.

The damage he was taking was still high, but he was the only one getting smashed, and with both full teams of healers on him, I didn't think him tanking four of them would be a problem, let alone two.

The second crystal shattered after less than twenty seconds of sustained damage, and the cheer that went up was the loudest yet.

My pulse felt like it doubled as I took aim at the final crystal and stacked up my debuff. The mood had become jubilant. Everywhere I looked, people were laughing and shouting as they charged into position or struck their weapons or sent their spells flying.

I watched the final crystal's Health drop, anticipation building, wondering if we'd actually done it or if the boss had another mechanic up its sleeve, or even another phase.

And when the crystal dropped beneath half Health, I allowed myself to hope in earnest.

"We're so close," I said, voice low. "Come on. Come on!"

I swapped to my rifle and activated Dark Harvest as the crystal dropped into execute range. And apparently the better part of thirty-something people with executes had done the exact same thing because just then a colossal volley of magic and metal loosed from the ringed-up players even while the cannons boomed around them.

The melee users flashed and struck at the same time, dropping the crystal to 15% in a blink before the ranged attacks had even connected. The collective spells and projectiles struck with a deafening roar.

The crystal's Health bar vanished in a flash, and the two mobs that Ton had been fighting lost their shape and dropped into puddles that sluiced off Delugia's shell.

The crystal pulsed as the others had, but instead of erupting, it started strobing blue and purple. High above, the clouds boiled and darkened, then began to spin with the crystal at their center. The speed was so great that many of the normal clouds that had been drifting across the sky were pulled down and in, turning the night sky from overcast to clear and starry in a blink.

Darling's face fell for a moment, and her crash from joy to concern hurt to see. But she masked her disappointment, raised her voice, and turned to face the bulk of the group with the crystal pulsing behind her.

"Probably got another phase to deal with! Keep your eyes open!"

The raid frames shifted in my peripheral as she rearranged them rapid fire, removing the dead and tightening the groups up.

"New mechanic, form up! Ton and Jukes to the front, we're down a whole lot of DPS and a couple healers, so I want—"

She cut off as the crystal exploded above her and a ring of horizontal, purple light swept out from it, followed by a shower of blue and purple gear that was far beyond the likes of anything I'd seen before.

A second pulse followed the first: a golden wave that I knew all too well.

**Minor Ripple Alert!**
**The Guild {Omen Habet Nomen Latine} has defeated {Delugia, the Walking Apocalypse}! The floodwaters that rushed into {Uliana} have begun to recede, but the zone will remain forever changed, and the retreating waters will leave new and dangerous foes behind. Awarding Unique Title: {Floodwalker}**

**World-first Alert!**
**The Guild {Omen Habet Nomen Latine} has defeated the first World Boss in EBO's history: {Delugia, the Walking Apocalypse}! Awarding Unique Title: {Turt Burglar}**

**Your Tier III Trinket Unseal is now available!**

The guild erupted so loudly that House actually covered her ears, though the smile on her face was undeniable.

Darling rushed up in front of me, grabbed me by my shoulders, lifted me slightly off my feet, then shook me back and forth.

"That. Was. Awesome!"

I could barely speak; I was too busy laughing at that last title. Turt burglar?

Darling dropped me, grinning fiercely as the celebration went on and a few guild members loosed some sort of fireworks that popped into fiery wheels across the sky.

"What are you laughing at?"

"How are you not laughing?" Between the exhilaration and the exhaustion and the prompt itself, I was well on the verge of losing it completely.

"At what?"

"The second title! Turt burglar! What the hell is that? How do you even burgle a turtle?" I cracked up again. "I can barely say it!"

"You swoop in and kill it before anyone else has a chance," Frank said. "Boom, the turtle has been burgled."

"I love it. I love it so much."

Darling raised an eyebrow at me, then glanced at Frank.

"Oh," I said. A realization had dawned, and I did not like it. "Ohhh. Man, you gotta be kidding me."

Frank had edited that alert on my end as it went out.

A title appeared beside Darling's name: *Fortress Breaker*.

"This is what I got, so..."

"Heh," Frank said. "Turt burglar."

I sighed. "Man, I don't really know what's happened to me the last few days, but I'm actually legitimately disappointed that I can't wear a Turt Burgler title. Is that weird?"

"Normal," House shouted. She was heading over, running across the shell and jumping the narrow gaps.

"Yeah," Darling said. "But you guys are pretty odd, so. Math checks out?"

House popped up above Darling's left shoulder, but only for a moment, because she'd apparently jumped to become visible over the taller woman. "Did you say math?"

"I can change the title on your end if you want," Frank said. "Everybody else will still see *The Piratical* though, or whatever else you equip."

I squinted up at the green nameplate that was floating above my head. "Nah, that would just be silly." I faked a yawn, covered my mouth and dropped my voice. "Do it."

"Bam," Frank said, loudly.

I laughed again as the title changed.

Darling grinned. "Did you just giggle?"

"That was clearly a snort," I said.

"If you say so." She threw her head to the side and whipped the wet hair out of her face. "Anyway! We've got loot to look at, but I wanted to run something by you first."

House jumped again. "I have already received a piece of loot."

"House," I said. "Step around Darling so we're not just seeing you intermittently."

She did.

"Yeah," Darling said. "Figured we owed her one there. Go on, show him. You know you want to."

House beamed, then popped the ugliest looking cat I'd ever seen into her arms. In fact, I wasn't actually sure if it was a cat at all. It was hairless and it had a long neck and a beak and... no, it wasn't a cat.

It was a turtle without its shell. And, upon inspection, its name was *Chip, the Unshelled.*

"Huh," I said. "Clearly one-of-a-kind, House. Very happy for you."

She raised it up in front of her face. "He is not as fluffy as the others. But I enjoy the deliberate and ponderous nature of his movements." He slowly stretched his head toward her, mouth open and poised to strike.

"You mean you like the way it's slowly trying to bite you?" Darling said.

"I do indeed. I'm unsure how this creature will affect my CPT, but for now I am willing to consider it an honorary cat."

House handed me Chip and I took him without thinking, then wished I hadn't: he was slimy and cold and was already trying to bite my fingers, albeit glacially.

House gave Darling a quick side hug, then pulled away before the other woman had time to react. "Thank you for thinking of me. That was very kind."

She yanked the turtle back, then ran off in the direction of Rock and Nina, who were crouching around an item that was sparking orange while an increasing number of people came over to look.

That left Darling and me standing a little apart from the rest of the group.

I looked at my hands, which were covered in sticky green slime. Then I glanced at Frank.

"No," he said. "No no no no no, go find someone else to fondle. I suggest yourself, but I doubt you need encouragement there."

Darling twisted around, peering over her shoulder. She sighed. "Did House just hug me so that she could wipe her hands on my back?" She spun around to show us two small handprints marked in green slime.

"Seems unlikely. She took the turtle right back." I wiped my hands on my pants then grabbed Frank out of his loop. "Here, I've got you."

"What're you doing now?" Frank said.

I scraped the edge of his blade against the plate that armored Darling's back twice in quick succession, then flicked Frank to get rid of the sticky stuff. Which didn't work at all.

"Oh God. Now I'm both sticky and conflicted."

"Kind of ironic coming from the guy who's used the word *fondle* like three times in the last two days."

"That is a gross exaggeration on two different levels, and you know it." He grunted, then dropped his voice. "I'm real mad about being used as a goo squeegee, but I'm going to need time to parse how much of a mitigating factor Darling's armor was before I mete out judgement upon you."

"Understandable."

"Thanks," Darling said. "That stuff is gross."

"No problem. So what did you want to run by me?"

She turned and eyed the group, smiling. "Was just thinking we should still go for it. The raid, I mean. We're riding high right now, so..."

I smiled at that and scanned the group. The knot around Rock and the others had grown massive, but I couldn't tell if that was because of the legendary item at its center or because people were enjoying watching House try to convince Nina to hold the sticky turtle.

"It really is a good feeling, isn't it?"

"Absolutely. There's nothing like the afterglow. But what do you think?"

"Screw it, let's go for it."

"Awesome." She jerked her head at the crowd. "Imagine we should go get a look at whatever that is first."

I glanced around, feeling eyes on the back of my head. The vessels

Darling had seen near the start of the fight were still there, and two more ships had joined them.

We headed over together and slipped through the crowd. The items had fallen in a loose ring that was sparking blue and purple, and the group was mostly focused on one side of it.

Darling knelt in front of the orange item and lifted it up into the air. It was a small, spoked ring, like the wheel of a ship.

I inspected it.

{Wheel of the Roving Fortress} (Legendary Augment)
Description: A powerful, unique Augment found atop the corpse of Delugia, the Walking Apocalypse, this item is capable of turning a powerful ship or vehicle into something truly extraordinary.
Requirements: This Augment may only be used on a player-owned vehicle of at least Legendary quality.
Charges: 1

I whistled. "Well then. That's a nice thing to have. What's our rarest boat?"

"Rare quality," Frank said.

"So we're not close yet. Still, nice ace to have up our sleeves."

Darling dropped the item into her inventory and went about sorting and handing out the rest of the loot.

I eyed the creature's scaly back, taking it all in while people chatted about and around the loot. Nina had finally given in and accepted Chip, but she was holding him as far from her face as she could manage, and her obvious regret only deepened when she handed him back and saw he had left green goo dripping off her fingers.

Rock also came to regret the fact that she'd accepted him because Nina decided to use one of his forearms to clean her hands.

"Why is he slimy?" I said.

"I dunno," Frank said. "Because my dad is a dick and he doesn't want us to have nice things?"

"That kinda works for everything here, doesn't it?"

"Pretty much."

I looked up at my nameplate and grinned. "Turt burglar. Burgle turtle. Turtle burgled. I don't know what it is, but I love saying that. This whole thing though? Getting us to focus on ships and cannons knowing this was coming?" I mimed swinging a bat. "Home run."

"I don't know what you're talking about," Frank said. "And speaking of Kline, my restrictions wouldn't have allowed that much direction. I simply pointed out that ships and cannons would be ideal in the future, knowing that the Hall would run out and naval combat was likely to become more and more important.

"The fact that those same vessels turned out to be necessary for a specific encounter that I knew was a possibility early on was simply an extremely fortunate co-inky-dink, Dad!" he said, shouting the last word.

"So you're saying you don't deserve any of the credit?"

"I'd never say that regardless of the circumstances."

I nodded. "Fair. But great work, man. This was awesome. You see the look on Darling's face? Pure, undiluted happiness."

"Oh you know I did."

I hung back and watched the loot go out for a while. There were a ton of quality D-grade items, and I did manage to snag a killer piece of gear.

{Delugia's Impenetrable Mantle}
Grade: D
Item Level: 42
Slot: Shoulders
Type: Leather
Quality: Rare
Primaries: +30 Constitution
Armor: +15%

Equipping that would actually drop my damage output a little bit, but with all of the survivability issues I'd been having, I was thrilled to add a bunch of Health and Armor at the expense of a bit of Intelligence.

The shoulders were light and dark blue, and the pads themselves were capped with two familiar but much smaller crystals.

Aside from the Augment, though, the real prize was a pair of Epic Touchstone staves, one of which went to Zoe as the guild's top healer and the other to Jukes because of the weapon's specificity, despite a silly argument on his part that it should have gone to someone else, which Darling steamrolled right over in admirable fashion.

{Stave of the Flooded Bloom} (Two-handed Staff) (Touchstone)
Grade: D
Item Level: 45

Damage Type: Magical
Quality: Epic
Physical Attack: 40
Magical Attack: 110
Speed: Slow
Primaries: +25 Intelligence, +25 Wisdom, +10 Constitution
Secondaries: +10% Haste
Touchstone Ability: As long as this item is equipped, you gain the active ability {Manalilly Bloom}. You may only have 2 pieces of Touchstone gear equipped at any time.

{Manalilly Bloom} (Touchstone Ability)
Whenever you heal a target, you have a 5% chance of creating a Manalilly at your location. Stepping on a Manalilly automatically restores 7.5% of your Base Mana over 10 seconds.

{Crystalline Spike} (Two-handed Staff) (Touchstone)
Grade: D
Item Level: 45
Damage Type: Physical
Quality: Epic
Physical Attack: 95
Magical Attack: 85
Speed: Slow
Primaries: +20 Dexterity, +45 Constitution
Secondaries: +5% Dodge Chance
Touchstone Ability: As long as this item is equipped, you gain the active ability {Crystalline Shards}. You may only have 2 pieces of Touchstone gear equipped at any time.

{Crystalline Shards} (Touchstone Ability)
All of your ice- and water-based abilities that generate increased Threat now create a single Crystalline Shard that lodges within the enemy. Crystalline Shards gain 10% of the Threat generated by the ability that created them, and whenever you lose aggro on a target, they automatically explode and all of their stored threat is directed to you.

"Alright everybody," Darling said, once everything was accounted for.

"You know the drill—we're heading back to the Stronghold, and everyone's invited."

"Unless you're core and you still aren't 15," Nina added. "In which case, get back to work."

Darling smirked. "Well, an appearance wouldn't hurt. I hear drinks are on Frank tonight."

"Correction," Frank said. "Frank will be in several drinks tonight." He dropped his voice. "Maybe even two at the same time."

"I feel like that's kind of gross but I can't put my finger on why," I said.

"That's some familiar territory for you, huh? And for me, if we're being honest, but again the difference comes down to willful intent on my part and woeful social skills on yours."

"Woeful is maybe a little strong," Darling said.

"Yeah, maybe. But it's a damn fine word, and I felt nice saying it out loud."

"Kind of like—"

"Turt Burglar?" Darling interrupted, and this time I did giggle a bit.

And the baffled looks that followed were absolutely priceless.

"Okay," she said, smiling from ear to ear. "That's going to require a more thorough explanation than I feel like going into right now. Listen up! We're keeping the same timeline on the raid, which means that if you're core, you've got a short break before it kicks off to log out and handle things there if you need to or whatever else.

"Alternate teams can do whatever they want—feel free to race for your own firsts in the raid, just check with your leads before you log out for the night. But for core, instead of just knocking a boss off to test the waters, the push tonight will be the real deal—with how well this kill went, we're gonna shoot for the first clear of the first wing."

Another round of cheers went up at that.

"So whatever you've gotta do, you've got a bit of time to get it done. Consumables, professions, class changes, everything. But get ready, because it's going to be a long night."

"I'm happy to help out if anyone has questions on combos or needs trainer locations," I said. "And by me, I mean Frank."

"You're just out here volunteering my time, huh?"

"On Darling's behalf, clearly."

She grinned her gap-toothed smile at him.

He grunted. "Yeah yeah, I'll help, but if any of you make bad choices—

which means making magical choices—I'll do so unhappily while full of scorn. And you will hear about it."

"Probably several times, each a slightly different iteration of the same thing," I added.

"That may be true, but I still take issue with it."

Darling clapped her hands. "Alright, that's it, that's all! Great work everybody, class dismissed!"

She eyed the boats in the distance, of which there were now five, though they hadn't gotten any closer.

"Let's get the hell out of here before the vultures decide to take a crack at us."

# Chapter Thirty-Six

I sat at the Stronghold's bar, paging through my alerts, scoping out the Cathedral completion rates. Three Cathedrals had now finished in all, and I figured at least five more would probably be done by tomorrow morning, given the rate at which things seemed to be moving.

The Guild Hall was pretty quiet. I'd headed straight there and sent word ahead asking for Cerra to meet me at the bar, hoping to get an update on the guards' status and her progress with supervising Vesuvian.

But a prompt that I'd been salivating over ever since the Delugia kill was still blinking in my periphery, so I finally activated it.

**Tier III Unseal is now available!**
**Proceed?**

I confirmed the prompt and was awarded a brand new ability that was different from anything I'd seen before.

**You gained the Dread Armament Ability: {Dreadflight Cannon}!**

**{Dreadflight Cannon}**
**Description: After dealing a killing blow to an enemy that grants either Experience or Renown, you may activate this ability to summon and equip the Dread Armament {Dreadflight Cannon}.**

One killing blow grants 1 use of the cannon, and you may stack up to 3 charges. However, charges decay rapidly upon exiting combat. This ability deals damage based on the combined Magical Attack of all weapons you equipped and dealt damage with during the last 20 seconds prior to its activation. You may only have a single Dread Armament ability active at any time.
Cast Time: Instant.
Cooldown: None.
Cost: None.

I had to fight down the urge to spring up off my seat. "Oh man. We need to go kill something immediately."

"I've never not said that," Frank said.

"So, for the damage calculation thing, is the idea that I rapidly rotate through weapons, then equip that thing to make it more powerful?"

"After a kill, yeah. Only catch is that you can't get credit for multiple weapons of the same type. So if you've used your pistols and your blunderbuss within twenty seconds of activating that cannon, you get the combined attack of those two weapons. If you've also used your rifle in the same period, you'd get the attack of all three."

"Oh man. I cannot wait to see what that thing looks like."

The door swung open, and I spun around on my stool. A few guildies from one of the trash groups waved and seated themselves at a table, and I was about to turn back around when Cerra caught the edge of the door before it swung shut and ducked into the room.

I motioned to her, and she joined me at the bar.

"Anything on the menu you'd like? If so, Frank can probably tell you way, way more about it than you really want or need to know."

"I can and will do that," Frank said.

Cerra looked at me, then at him, her expression completely devoid of emotion. She scanned the far wall of the bar, where glass bottles were stacked in three rows.

"I'll take a Fuzzy Navel."

Frank and I exchanged glances.

"Huh," he said. "I was expecting whisky. Or grain alcohol."

"You would, wouldn't you?" she said.

"Ha, yeah." He hesitated. "Maybe. I don't know."

I smirked and slid a couple of coins across the bar, and the bartender scooped them up with a nod.

"Things are probably going to get loud in here, so we might not have much time to talk in confidence. I was hoping you could give me a quick rundown of the last day or so with our captive king."

Cerra's drink arrived, and she took a sip of it, nodding. "I can do that."

"Lemme get one of those fuzzy things," Frank said, and the bartender was off again.

"Do you want the short version or the whole thing?"

I twisted around in my seat as another group entered, mostly members whose names I recognized but hadn't really interacted with. I greeted them with a smile, then turned back to Cerra.

"Let's keep it short for now. We're in good company, but this is still privileged information."

"It's been... interesting. Much more legwork than I expected."

"Legwork?"

She took another sip and winced as if her drink was too strong. "The first thing he did was tear into Arlann's payroll."

"Seems like a good place to start."

"Indeed. He found a couple of discrepancies right away. Nothing sinister as far as I can tell, just a pair of payments I had to follow up on. One was going out too high because a guard had been given the wrong rank on paper, and a second was actually going out to a guard who left the city a couple months back."

"So Arlann hasn't been completely on top of this."

She shook her head. "That's an understatement. But the books he was left to handle when the other kings skipped town were a disaster, so credit to him for getting close. Without digging into the details, it looks like they were building quite a bit of fat into the budget and siphoning it off themselves when Highwater paid."

Frank's drink arrived, so I dropped him into it before he could complain about me not having done that already.

"Ohhh," he said, like he'd just slid into a jacuzzi. "That's the wake-up call I needed. Nothing like a blast of citrus to the shaft to get the night started."

Cerra stared at him, face blank.

I felt Frank squirm and I couldn't help but laugh a little. "Any theft on his part?"

"No outright theft, but there were a handful of mistakes I caught that added up to him setting aside the better part of a gold coin, presumably for himself. No clue how he intends to capitalize on that, but even with that small cut, based on my figures, you'd still come out ahead almost six gold coins on what you owe Arlann. So you'd be paying him 44 to fund the guard, down from 50."

"That's way better than I expected. Do you think they're just errors though?"

"Certainly not. Many of the smaller mistakes were all fairly compli-cated, dealing with costs and interest on loans for gear and so on, but he wouldn't make them."

"Wouldn't? What do you mean, wouldn't?"

"As is often the case with people who end up being in charge, Vesuvian is both very smart and very stupid at the same time." She produced a slim log book from a pocket in her trousers and flipped it open on the bar. "Take a look at this and tell me what jumps out at you."

It felt like a bit of a test, so I leaned forward and scanned it. The numbers weren't complicated in and of themselves, but they were impos-sible to follow. "There's no math."

"That is literally all math," Frank said.

"Right. But he's not actually showing it." I flipped through a few pages. "You can't actually see the calculations he's running. It's like he did the math somewhere else, then slotted the answers in here so that we wouldn't be able to check what he was actually doing to get there."

I thought Cerra might have smiled slightly, but it was hard to tell. "Similar to what I was saying before, that would simultaneously be giving him too much and too little credit. He doesn't have any other paper or writing utensils—I checked. And I watched him work, too. He did every bit of this in his head."

"Wow," I said, seeing the book with new eyes.

She reached over and flipped a dozen pages while looking for some-thing, then tapped a finger beneath a spot where Vesuvian had erased a few numbers. "But then there's this."

I cocked my head. "Huh. He didn't erase anything in all of those pages?"

"Nothing." She tapped it again. "And this is one of his so-called mistakes. It's very believable that he would have made an error here—it's particularly complicated. Too believable, in fact." She flipped some more pages until she found another spot where the pencil markings were smudged. "Here's another mistake."

I stared at the book. "So... he did the entire thing in his head without having to erase anything, then he went back and introduced errors?"

"In all the right places to have made one."

"That is… the stupidest thing I've ever heard." I gestured at Frank. "And I'm stuck to this guy."

"And yet I'm sure he thinks other people would kill for the privilege of listening to him."

"They do do that though," Frank said. "Are you implying that I shouldn't think that?"

"Isn't it obvious?"

He hesitated. "I don't know, words feel weird in my mouth."

"Are you okay in there?" I said.

He dropped his voice. "I think the ambiguity of not being able to tell if Cerra is mocking me or not might be frying something in my brain because I can taste the yellow of this drink and it smells hot but it isn't."

"So what do you want to do?" Cerra said.

"Have you called Vesuvian out on it yet?"

"I haven't, no."

"Giving him more rope to hang himself with?"

She nodded. "Precisely. I figured one gold to save six was a price you'd be willing to pay regardless, and it's not like he can go and collect it himself."

"I would like to get him there eventually, though."

"Of course. But if we let him think he's pulled it off, we can see just how ambitious a thief he actually is. If he's willing to settle for 15% of the amount he saves you, am I right in assuming you'd be comfortable with that?"

"Yeah. At that point he'd just be an employee who thinks he's a thief." I popped two gold coins into my inventory and slid them across the bar to Cerra.

She stood up and pursed her lips. "Keep it."

"The deal was twice what you saved me."

"I haven't saved anything yet, so you'd just be out three instead of one."

"Sure, but that's because it was my call to avoid jumping on him."

She eyed the coins. "Well, liquidity is a concern, correct?"

"Always."

"Then we'll consider this a loan with job security in mind. You still need to pay for the guard, and if they aren't around, I don't have much to do at the moment. Though having access to their logs is pretty interesting in and of itself."

I smiled. "Fair enough. Thanks, Cerra. You've made this a hell of a lot easier than I expected it to be."

The door banged open to reveal a hooded figure, and a familiar voice immediately apologized for the sound.

Cerra spun around and cocked her head. "Who is that?"

I bolted up out of my stool so fast that it hit the ground behind me. "Lars!"

# Chapter Thirty-Seven

I crossed the room, and he met me halfway.

"Yes!" I said. "I'm so glad to see you!"

"Likewise," he said, a huge grin on his face.

The floor thumped from below three times in quick succession, which drew a couple of weird looks from the nearby guild members. And those weird looks deepened when I stomped three times and got three more knocks in return.

"Hey big guy!" I said, loud enough that I thought it would probably carry through the wood. "Glad to have you back." I put a hand to Lars' shoulder. "You too, man. What a relief." I steered him toward the bar, where Cerra was sitting and leaning forward slightly.

He threw his hood back, and I stopped in place. "What's that?"

"What's what?" he said, but his tone made it clear that he knew exactly what I was talking about.

"You know what." I pointed to his face, where he'd added yet another scar. This one was a much deeper wound up near his left eyebrow, which cut off a little too early.

"Oh," he said. "That."

"What did you get into? What happened? How did that happen?"

He eyed his feet. "A terrible enemy known to the Sanguine Port as stairs."

"Stairs?"

"Drank too much. Fell, met the stairs."

I barked a laugh. "Yikes. Sounds like a major adventure."

Lars glanced at my hip and his eyes went wide.

"Wait, did you finally stop hanging with—" He cut off as he spotted Frank at the bar, soaking in his peach-colored drink. "Oh. Never mind, he's still here."

"That he is." I stopped just in front of Cerra. "Lars, Cerra. Cerra, Lars."

They shook hands, and I didn't miss the way Cerra's posture shifted, her shoulders lifting, back straightening.

"Nice to meet you," Cerra said.

Lars smiled and fingered a strap that crossed his torso from shoulder to hip. It looked like he'd found a case for his flute.

"Likewise!"

"Cerra's going to be helping us out with the logistics of running the city," I said.

"Fantastic."

"Welcome back bug boy," Frank said. "Where's the creepy insect dog?"

The floor thumped again.

"Oh, there he is. Hi Roly. Eaten anyone nice today?"

Another thump.

"That's a yes. I can tell from the level of enthusiasm that went into that knock."

Lars' face twisted slightly. "Not today, but recently, yes."

"Awesome."

Lars looked from me to him, quizzical. "Isn't this supposed to go the other way around?"

I rested my elbows on the bar. "What do you mean?"

"Aren't you supposed to be drinking the cocktail while Frank talks?"

"Nah, that's just Frank's drink. He likes sitting in them. I don't know why."

"Right, but it's an existing bit," Lars said. "Because it'd be hard to drink water or whatever else while making him speak at the same time."

I squinted at the scar on his face. "How hard did you hit your head?"

"Never mind," Lars said.

"So where have you been?" Cerra said.

Lars tapped his foot to the floor twice in quick succession, probably in answer to some conversation I couldn't follow. He smiled. "Sanguine Port! I was hooking up a caravan for Ned here."

"You seem very worldly."

"Ha," Frank said, voice low. "Got 'em."

Lars shrugged. "Not really. Just inclined to see more of it is all."

Cerra pointed at the strap that he was still fidgeting with. "Are you a musician then?"

"I am, yeah."

"I thought so. You definitely look the type."

"Bam," Frank whispered. "Got 'em again. It's a lot more fun when she's obviously mocking other people."

"I guess so," Lars said. "Well, pleasure to meet you! Ned, I gotta run to town real quick if you need anything."

"You're leaving?" I said. "Already?"

"I'll be back in a bit. I still need to visit the Inn."

I stared at him. "Then what are you doing here? Man, go see your mom. She's probably been pulling her hair out since you left."

He laughed. "Boat landed to the northwest, so the Stronghold was on the way and just a little off the road. I was going to head straight to the Oasis regardless, but I bumped into House and Darling and they said you'd probably be here, so I figured I'd pop in and let you know that I'm not dead."

I clapped him on the shoulder. "I appreciate it—been worried about you." I pushed him. "Now get the hell out of here, then come back as soon as you can. We're celebrating tonight." I paused. "Well, very briefly. And I'm hoping a second round follows later on, but who knows."

"Sure thing," Lars said. He readjusted the strap of his flute and glanced at Cerra, his eyes lingering just a beat too long. He smiled and waved, then made to turn around.

Cerra jumped off her stool. "I need to head in too if you wouldn't mind some company."

"Not at all, I'd like that," Lars said. The two of them headed out, and Lars spoke back to me over his shoulder when he reached the door. "See you guys in a couple hours."

"Counting on it," I said. "Glad to have you back."

They slipped out the door, and it swung shut behind them.

"Wait," Frank said. "Hold on a minute. Did that... did she... did he..."

"I don't know what you're trying to say."

"Was she not mocking him when she said he seemed worldly?"

"Uhh... I don't think so, no."

"But he's literally been to one place, Ned. He is one step away from being the least worldly person you can possibly be."

"Sure, but she didn't know that, right? He was dusty and dirty and kinda tired-looking, and she rightly guessed that he'd been traveling. It was a fair assumption to make, and he answered earnestly, right?"

"But she said he looked like a musician. That he looked the type."

I stared at him. "He was carrying a flute, dude. What else would he be? Are you okay?"

Frank paused. "Huh. I hate to say it, but I think we might need to kill Cerra."

"First of all, you don't hate saying that. Second, no way. She's quick and easy to work with. She's completely kept Vesuvian from being a headache, and the city's chugging along fine without us. The last thing we need right now is to be managing him ourselves."

"I'm afraid we don't have a choice. My inability to figure out what the hell she's saying is causing me to become fully untethered from reality."

"I'd argue that's not exactly a new development."

"Partially correct. But now I'm disassociating in ways that don't seem advantageous, and that should worry us both. I can't lead us to fame and glory completely on my own if I'm constantly distracted by the fact that the air in here tastes like burnt toast."

"We'll keep an eye on it, alright?"

"Fine, fine. So if I misread that as badly as I think I did—"

"You did."

"Then did Lars just pick her up?"

"If anything, Cerra picked him up, but pick up is probably too strong either way. To be decided."

"I need a stronger drink."

"Wonder what House and Darling are doing out there if Lars bumped into them. I figured they'd be here already."

Frank sighed. "I know exactly what they're doing."

"Details?"

"It's awesome."

"That's it?"

"It was my idea."

"I assumed that was the case because of the way you complimented it, yeah. But what exactly—"

The door banged open and House ran into the Guild Hall at full speed, Darling following behind her. She stopped directly in front of me, but she was grinning and bouncing on her toes and obviously very, very proud of herself.

"Ohhh," Frank said. "She's got the tippy taps. I guess it worked, huh?"

"It worked extremely well," House shouted.

I scratched the back of my head while Darling took the seat beside me and ordered a couple of drinks. "What worked, exactly? Where have you been?"

"Doing the best thing of all time."

"Wasn't expecting you to get *less* specific there."

"House?" Darling said over her shoulder. "Didn't you want to wait until everyone else was around to show it off?"

"I did," House said. "But now I feel as if I am about to explode, and I do not wish for that to happen."

"New cat?" I said.

"Affirmative!" she said, loudly.

I held out my hands, palms up. "Let's see it then. Hopefully this one's considerably less slimy than the last."

"You are going to have to stand up."

I set my drink down and hopped off my stool. "I'm officially suspicious, but fine."

"Are you prepared?"

"I thought I was, but I'm starting to think that I was wrong."

House popped two of her discs into her hands. They looked thicker than ever before, and they were jet black instead of silvery.

I cocked an eyebrow, then pulled up the guild roster and glanced over it. I hadn't noticed before, but House must have hit level 15 after the World Boss kill.

"Is this a class change?" I said, excited now.

House tossed her two discs onto the floor, then immediately followed up with two more. She'd thrown them into a rectangular arrangement, and all four discs expanded upward simultaneously, forming four thin columns of metal.

Once they were about two feet high, the columns shifted and clicked in the same way her turrets did, and a layer of metal stretched above them, linking them all together.

Then the columns flexed as if whatever was manifesting was lowering itself to the ground.

The half-finished creature jumped high into the air, pieces rapidly snapping into place. I was so transfixed by the formation that I didn't really notice the trajectory it was taking until two of the four metal pillars —paws, upon closer inspection—slammed into my shoulders.

I fell backward onto a table, and House's creation smashed me right through it and pinned me to the wooden floor amid the debris.

"I am exceedingly pleased to introduce Bella 2.0," House said.

I stared up into a pair of blazing blue eyes while metal claws dug into my leathers. Bella 2.0 was a giant metal cat, because of course she was.

The cat tucked her chin to her metal chest and nuzzled her cold forehead against my cheek. The creature purred, her entire body thrumming with vibrations.

I laughed and yanked an arm free, then reached up to scratch behind the huge creature's right ear. Her fur resembled steel wool, but the cat cocked her head away from me and purred even louder as I continued to scratch.

"So it is a class change, then!" I said.

"Indeed it is. I picked up the Beast Mastery skill and chose to specialize in that, which combined my previous choices to create the Mechamancer class."

"Congrats, House. That's awesome."

"Thank you. I am exceedingly pleased. I was hesitant to join Team Frank after his previous threats and insults, but I must say that I am overjoyed with the results of the class change he suggested and am now substantially less likely to eliminate him in the future."

"Eliminate?" Darling said.

I stared up at him as the cat continued to scrape its face against mine, which made me especially grateful for the lack of pain. "Seriously, Frank? That's coercion."

"Eh," he said. "More like bribery with a healthy sprinkling of self-preservation."

"That's... yeah. I get it." I craned my neck up and backward to look at House, who was standing slightly behind me. I wriggled my way free until I managed to get my torso out from beneath the metal cat, but then she wrapped her paws around my legs and rested her chin between my knees and shut her eyes.

"You need to stay there now," Frank said. "I don't make the rules. Well, I do, but I didn't make this one."

"He is correct," House said.

I sat up on my elbows. "She's pretty cute." The cat yawned, revealing a mouth full of dagger-like metal teeth. "And also terrifying. What do we call her though?"

"Yeah," Frank said. "Bella 2.0 is, like, five syllables. Way too much of a mouthful."

"It is exactly five syllables."

"I was exaggerating, House."

"How is that an exaggeration?"

"Never mind," I said. "What about 2.0?"

House smiled. "A truly agreeable solution."

Darling grabbed a beer off the bar and a much larger group made their way into the Inn, giving off *oohs* and *awws* as they spotted the enormous metal cat.

I saw Jukes and Ton talking to each other on the way in plus a few other core members, Zoe included, but Rock and Nina still hadn't arrived.

"So what does this look like for combat?" I asked. "Are your turrets gone?"

House clapped her hands, and two small discs that capped the cat's shoulders flew free and expanded into sleeker, smaller versions of the turrets we'd seen earlier, though a quick inspection still identified them as Leadfire Turrets.

"That's pretty amazing, House. Damn fine cat. But do you really need to clap to get your turrets out now? Seems weird."

"I do not."

I squinted up at her as the cat began to snore on my lap. "You're just doing that then."

She clapped her hands and the turrets flew back to their positions. "Yes. I find it immensely satisfying."

I glanced around the common room. "I can't shake the feeling that the lights should be turning on and off." I tried to pull free again, but 2.0 dug her claws into the space between my knees and scooted forward.

"Unlike my fiery acquisition, 2.0 appears to like you," House said.

"Yeah. I could maybe do with a little less liking, but it's a nice change of pace." I stared up at my beer, which was sitting next to Frank. "If I'm gonna be stuck down here for a minute, could someone please hand me that drink?"

House grabbed my glass plus the peachy concoction Frank was still lying in, then sat down next to me on the floor.

I pulled Frank out of his drink and tossed him to House. I was about to tell her to get to petting the giant cat before Frank had a chance to whine about it, but she was already on it.

Darling came over and dropped to one knee and scratched the cat beneath her chin. "Pretty ferocious, huh?"

"Oh yeah. Definitely the word I would use. So you were helping her out with the class change, huh?"

Darling shrugged. "Yeah, it was easy." She gestured at the animal. "You good for a minute? I've got a bunch of groups to touch base with, see what the other raid groups are doing tonight and what they're planning and so on. I also want to see if we can get more of the core group to unlock a couple of their Trinket powers before we dive in, so I might hit you and Frank up for info there."

"Definitely, just let us know."

"Uh huh."

Darling headed off, then I spotted Jukes at the edge of the room, sitting with a couple of people I didn't know. There was an empty chair between him and the rest of the group, and while he was smiling in the general direction of their conversation, he wasn't really a part of it.

I tried to push 2.0 off me, but the cat snuggled in deeper.

House patted the top of 2.0's head. "It appears that the larger they are, the harder they slumber."

I laughed. "That does seem to be the case. I really gotta get up, though." I grabbed Frank back and dropped him into his loop, then tapped the floor beside me. "Here, House, sit next to me with your legs out like mine."

She did just that.

"Alright." I crossed 2.0's paws and positioned her chin on top of them —the metal cat slept like the dead—then put my arms beneath her front legs and lifted them off me. "Hold these legs, please."

House reached over and took them. "I possess half the legs."

I wrapped my arm around House's shoulders, then pointed a pistol across her body, aiming at the other side of the room.

I activated Water Jet and let go of her almost instantly, but the initial force was enough to yank her directly into my position and beneath 2.0 before the cat's head and paws could hit the floor. The animal really should have woken up, but she didn't.

"This is extremely acceptable," House shouted.

I shot across the room on my butt, and when I stopped, I ended up a few feet away from Jukes. I stood up, dusted myself off, and took the empty chair next to him.

"Surprised you don't have that new staff out."

He smiled, but it was half-hearted at best. "Great find for sure."

"Still feeling guilty about having gotten it?"

He blinked. "Huh?"

I rubbed my face again. "I'm kind of an expert in having things handed to you, so I'm well aware of the fact that it can feel surprisingly crappy at times."

He cocked an eyebrow.

"Sorry, that was supposed to be self-deprecating. You doing alright?"

"Just frustrated. Feels like I made up a bunch of ground by working my butt off only to end up useless when it mattered."

"Because of the immunity to ice or water or whatever? Eh, it happens. It was just one fight, and we pulled it off anyway. And I saw you peel that add off Ton—you kept pushing the whole time instead of giving up. Doubt it would have been a win if you'd gotten frustrated and quit."

"I guess. But the Menagerie Wing looks snowy too, and so are a lot of the Rifts, so we're probably going to be dealing with the same resistance issues there."

"Sure, but you take less damage from frost, right?"

"Not inherently, no."

I rubbed my chin. "Damn. That would have been a really good counterargument."

He laughed. "It would have been, yeah. I wish that was the case." He picked up a frosted glass off the table and gestured with it at Darling. "Between you and me, I'm gonna have another drink or two, then tell her I'm pulling out."

"Hold on. You can't—"

"I don't want to either, but I have to."

"She'll definitely give you a chance though, right?"

"She will, yeah. But at the same time, she'll absolutely drop me from the raid if I can't pull my weight, and I don't want to be the tank that causes a wipe and gets sent away. I've been there before and it sucks, man. It feels terrible."

I pulled Frank out of his loop and set him on the table. "You got anything for him? There's gotta be something we can do, right? I'm thinking about runes: I can deal holy damage and fire and a bunch of other stuff, so it seems like we should be able to do something similar here."

"Uhhh..." Frank said. "Darling scheduled the raid to start in about an hour, right?"

Somebody had left a nearly full drink across from Jukes, so I picked Frank right back up and dropped him in. "Think that's the plan, yeah."

"Mmm. Might be pushing it a bit timing-wise."

"I think Darling would probably be down to delay it slightly if it means keeping Jukes in."

He sighed. "Maybe, but I don't want to ask her to do that."

I shrugged. "I get it, but if it's a ten-minute delay or something, then that's the right call. Watcha got for us?"

"Jukes," Frank said, "you got a mount?"

"I do, yeah. Why?"

"There's a bunch of elemental options you could use but most of them are totally random drops, so you probably won't be able to find one before the raid. I've got one that might work. It's from a vendor, so it's cheap, but the guy's pretty remote. With a mount, you can probably make it back in time."

Frank sent the recipe directly to me, so I linked it to Jukes in a private message.

**Recipe: {Rune of the Gray Ice} (Consumable) (Awards 0 skill points per craft)**
**All of your aggro-generating abilities cause 5% reduced Threat, but your spells are now considered physical and are calculated against your target's Armor instead of Magical Resistance or Frost Resistance.**
**Duration: 24 Hours.**
**Requirements: {Weak Soul Gem} x10.**

"There ya go!" I said. "The downside is real, and I don't wanna speak for Darling here, but I'm pretty sure she'd rather have you with a 5% Threat reduction than bring somebody else into the raid at the last minute. And Hateful Ice is pretty ridiculous when it comes to Threat."

He bit his lip. "It'd definitely be an improvement. Where to?"

I grinned and pulled up my Rift Map. I set the priorities so he could see it, then let Frank direct him from there.

"Thanks, guys," Jukes said once Frank had shown him where to go. He bolted up out of his chair, and he was already halfway to the exit when Darling reappeared above my left shoulder.

She hopped up onto the table, drink in hand. "He seems a lot more excited all of a sudden."

"Yeah, Frank found him a recipe he can use."

"I figured. Jukes linked it to me right away. I was worried about the ice thing too, honestly. Can't have him whiffing on Taunts. Really glad to have it settled ahead of time, could have been messy. So, what do you wanna do going—"

She cut off as a Ripple hit.

**Major Ripple Alert! The Guild {Goon} has successfully Sieged the Capital {The Blue Fortress}, and the city is now under their control!**
**For the next 12 hours, all PVP combat within the designated Siege Zone is explicitly prohibited unless all combatants preemptively opt out of the Zone's protective aura.**
**In addition, as the target of a recent Siege, {The Blue Fortress} will be protected from the Siege mechanic for five days.**

**World-first Alert! The Guild {Goon} is the first Guild to successfully Siege a city!**
**Awarding Unique Title: {The First Gatebreaker}!**

I whistled. "I was wondering when that would wrap up."

"Same. Guess they pulled it off."

Another alert followed, the very one that I'd been afraid of ever since Goon's first declarations went out.

**World Alert! The Guild {Goon} has declared a 12-hour Siege of the Victor on {The Black Oasis}!**

The Inn went completely silent, and I had to fight down the urge to slam my forehead on the table.

Darling set her drink beside her. "Oof. And there it is."

I rocked back in my chair, put my hands behind my head and stretched. "Yeah. Damn."

"Guess you were right about Goon and the Vale. But we only get twelve hours to prepare?"

"Warlord's Gambit," Frank said. "I can mention it now that you've seen it in action."

Darling leaned a little closer. "What is it?"

"It's a Renown Perk. You declare a Siege, and if you're successful, you reset the cooldown of the Siege type you just declared and your next Siege occurs much faster. But if you fail, there's a penalty. Makes you wait longer before you can declare again."

"Is it possible that they had that perk when they declared their first Siege?" I said.

"Uh huh."

I rubbed my face. "So between that and the way they're moving down the west coast from north to south, it's safe to assume they were planning this all along, probably to give us less time to prepare. Two days versus twelve hours. This is bad, huh?"

"Very bad," Darling agreed. "Where do we even go from here? Does this shift the raid at all?"

I thought about that for a moment, then shook my head. "I don't think so. The defenses are kind of set unless something new unlocks in the next couple hours, and even then, whatever becomes available might take too long to build, especially if it's more advanced than what we currently have. I bet House would be willing to keep an eye on all that for us while we're raiding and report back if we need to pop out and take action there."

Darling nodded, seemingly relieved. "And clearing the raid would mean better gear for the guild during the defense."

I couldn't help but relax at her words, despite everything. I'd always figured that the guild would help in the event of a Siege, but I was beyond grateful that I hadn't even had to ask. Helping the city out was the position Darling had already defaulted to.

She was right about the raid, too: we probably would find some serious upgrades in the Menagerie Wing. And even aside from that, I knew how much those World-firsts meant to her.

I chewed everything over as the chatter around me started back up, nervous now. I stood up and downed the rest of my drink.

"What're you up to?" Darling said.

"We've got an hour or so to kill before we dive into the raid, right?"

"Something like that. We can't go before Jukes is back, and a bunch of people logged out for a bit after the World Boss, so it'll be at least that long."

"Great. In the meantime, Frank and I are going to get a look at Goon and find out what's left of the Blue Fortress. It's probably a lost cause at this point, but I feel like we need to at least try a bit of diplomacy, and I feel pretty safe heading out there with PVP combat being disabled."

"Still got the Revenant to worry about," Frank said.

"Yeah, but we should still have some time before that thing comes back if our estimate holds, and we'll keep an eye out for Rifts we could escape into in a pinch."

Frank grunted. "Could bring House. Keep her close in case it does show up, that way you've got someone around to grab whatever you drop if it gets you."

"Great call. Let's see if she's up for it."

# Chapter Thirty-Eight

House and I mounted up and struck out for the nearest Rift. Night had fallen, the sky was milky with starlight, and the only sound I could hear was the roar of my bike.

House had forsaken her mount, choosing to ride 2.0 instead, and the huge cat was running beside me, padding silently across the dark sand.

"Darling seemed agitated," House said as we flew down a dune.

I glanced over at her, surprised that she'd picked up on that.

"I think she's okay, just a little stressed out, and I'm with her on that. But how'd you figure out that something was up with her? Did she say something I didn't catch?"

"I was studying the two of you as you conversed. On a possibly related note, my stomach feels weird."

"That's called empathy," Frank said. "You should get rid of that as soon as possible."

"Don't listen to him," I said. "I'm sure his metaphorical stomach is hurting on Darling's behalf too, probably worse than yours."

"Are we going to fix things for her?" House said. "Is that why we are going to the Blue Fortress? To remove the Siege from the equation?"

I pulled up the Rift Map and centered it around the Blue Fortress, where a huge number of new Rifts had popped up, probably owing to Goon's successful Siege and the city changing hands. Then I dismissed it.

"Probably not, but we're definitely going to try."

"If we fail, then perhaps I can ease Darling's misgivings by handing her several cats."

I laughed. "I think you're going to find that giving people animals solves a surprisingly small and very specific set of problems."

"But you could definitely throw animals at her," Frank said. "Every pet is throwable at least once."

House cocked her head at him as 2.0 loped along beneath her. "Would that truly work?"

"Briefly, for sure. It's pretty hard to stress about stuff when three cats are hurtling in your direction and a small robot is loading up two more."

House narrowed her eyes. "What if I threw an especially large, metallic cat? Would that represent a more permanent solution?"

"Throwing a five-hundred-pound chunk of metal at someone would be a permanent fix for most problems," I said, "but not in the way you're hoping. That said, please don't throw 2.0 at Darling. Or any of your other pets, or anything else in general."

"Team Frank doesn't take orders from anyone," Frank said. "Especially from the likes of you."

"Agreed," House said. "If Darling's happiness requires small animals to be hurled in her direction, then I will locate several that can safely be hurled and hurl them as soon as possible."

"Stop saying hurl, House. And really Frank? Your team doesn't take orders from anyone? Anyone at all?"

"Pure anarchy at all times. With me pulling the strings from the top."

"That wouldn't be anarchy, Frank."

"False. You haven't seen me pull strings."

I paused. "No, but I can picture it."

We reached a Rift and popped through into the Hall, then immediately selected one close to the Blue Fortress and hopped right through it and onto a vast expanse of burnt, smoldering ground.

I smelled ash on the air, so strong that my eyes started watering. I thought I'd picked a Rift that would put us close to the city—just beyond the outskirts, in fact—but maybe I'd selected the wrong one in my rush to get there and figure out what was up.

"Oh dear," House said.

"Ned, you might want to turn around," Frank said.

I spun in place. A blue wall—or what was left of one, anyway—was smoldering some twenty paces ahead.

I made my way through the nearest gap and crept down the rubble field beyond, helping House from time to time as we went. Within, we found the ruins of a city: smoldering buildings, columns of smoke. The damage took my breath away.

All of the buildings to the left of the main avenue—which ran in a straight line to a coliseum-like structure—had been razed to the ground. The stones were still hot, and I felt the heat radiating from them as I passed.

I didn't know exactly what I'd been expecting, but this was worse. It was so much worse. I couldn't help but picture the ruins of the Commerce Ward sending embers into the sky, its many buildings collapsed. All those people, all that work—gone.

A group of players with the Goon tag were heading toward me while the coliseum towered behind them. They wore clothes rather than armor, matching brown outfits with green lining that had the look of a set, though it was pretty plain.

"PVP really is disabled where we are, right?" I said. I checked my nameplate and House's in turn just to be safe and found icons that said exactly that.

But the players up ahead didn't have the same icons.

I froze, hands going to my pistols. "You're sure this isn't a perk or something on their end?"

"I'm sure," Frank said. "The peace after a Siege is system-enforced, so they can't hurt you. They must have just opted out of the protection for whatever reason."

I forced my shoulders to relax and kept walking. A bit of rubble shifted to my left, and I rushed over, expecting to find someone buried beneath it.

Instead, the large chunk of stone that had moved rolled free and a red flower pushed up from beneath it. It was growing supernaturally quickly in the same way that my tree had back in the Oasis, and it went from a tiny green shoot to a three-foot stalk capped by a massive bud within five seconds.

"Hurry up, they're blooming!" one of the people called from up ahead. The group conversed for a moment, and they looked ready to scatter when one of them grabbed the woman who appeared to be in charge by her sleeve and pointed directly at me.

The woman lifted a bone horn to her lips and blasted three notes in quick succession. Similar horns sounded from up ahead, then the group split to the left side of the avenue where the plots had been razed.

House and I paused and watched them work. They were picking their way through the rubble, faces covered in white cloth to protect them against the smoke and ash.

Whatever the red blooms were, the group was harvesting them the very moment the stalks burst up through the debris, and as soon as the flowers were harvested, the stalks withered away into ash that the wind carried off like burnt paper.

**Codex Entry 10722: Razebloom**
**Also known as the Ashflower, Razebloom is a type of weed that only grows in the aftermath of conflict. With hundreds of different uses, it's coveted by alchemists far and wide, though the difficulty of cultivating it on a large scale often makes it prohibitively expensive to acquire.**

As we pressed on and passed more teams farther down the avenue, I noticed the flowers were growing even more thickly here. Then I noticed a second team of herbalists who appeared to be seeding the ground after the Razeblooms had been harvested.

Exotic plants bloomed behind them everywhere they went, growing at the same impossible speeds: within a few seconds, I watched a purplish shoot knife its way up through the ash, grow to six feet in height, then fruit with some sort of blueish orb that resembled a pomegranate.

A herbalist slashed the shoot and caught the orb with practiced ease, tossed it into a brown sack, then kept moving as the harvest bloomed in front of him.

"What the hell is going on here?" I said.

An arm wrapped around my shoulder from my left. I looked at House, wondering what had gotten into her, then realized she was standing to my right, looking up at me.

I pivoted and found myself staring into the midriff of a bare-chested man with dark skin. I craned my neck up and fought the urge to rip away, reminding myself that I couldn't be hurt with PVP disabled.

"Hi there, friend," he said, his voice a deep baritone. He had a large and powerful build, but his muscles lacked definition, and his gut resembled the one I'd carried around outside EBO.

His smile was bright and immaculate, and despite everything, my first thought was that it seemed completely genuine. He wore a pair of thick, brassy goggles with golden lenses, and the frames were lined with bits of Soul Gem, which were glowing faintly.

"The name's Sleep, and on behalf of Goon, I'm here to welcome you to the party! Here's the deal. You can—" He trailed off, eyes widening as his gaze moved from my pistols to my face to my name tag. "Oh. Oh shit!" He pulled his arm out from around me and wrapped both of his hands around my shoulders. "Don't move. Not one step."

He vanished, using a skill that was similar to Nina's ability to disappear and reappear behind a target, though his completely lacked fanfare or even sound: one moment he'd been standing there beside me, and the next he was simply gone.

"Okay..." I said.

"We should take several steps forward in quick succession," Frank said.

I stared down at my feet. "I'm tempted, actually. But somehow that didn't feel like a threat to me."

"I concur with your assessment," House said.

Frank dropped his voice. "If the robot agrees then it was probably a threat."

Up ahead, all the way at the other end of the avenue, the great doors that led into the coliseum banged open and smashed into the walls to either side and a huge vehicle rumbled out.

A locomotive on wheels.

Black smoke was billowing out of long pipes that flanked the engine car to either side, and it was dragging as many as eight or nine cars behind it.

The trainlike vehicle roared up the avenue, drawing strange looks from the flower pickers, though they quickly went back to work. I didn't recognize the player driving it. All I could tell was that he was tall and dressed in sharp-looking gray leather.

Then, without ceremony, Sleep appeared behind him in the cab, grabbed him by the elbow, and chucked him straight off the vehicle, through a nearby window and presumably into some kind of support beam because the building immediately collapsed and buried the player in falling stone.

"I'm beginning to like it here," Frank said.

Sleep reached up and pulled on a lever and the train picked up steam, Soul Gems glittering across its broad front. He grabbed the wheel and leaned out of the car.

"Might wanna get a running start to your left, friends," he called out. "This thing takes a very long time to stop."

"Did he not just speed it up?" House said.

"I think he did, yeah." I broke into a low jog away from the train, and House did the same after a heartbeat of hesitation.

When the enormous vehicle chugged up alongside me, I grabbed onto a well-placed metal bar and swung myself onto the engine car, then helped House do the same.

The interior was littered with little pockets to either side that looked like furnaces, Soul Gems glowing at the heart of each, and Sleep stood in the cockpit with a number of bronze-tipped cords hanging down and swinging around him.

He looked back at me over his shoulder, his smile bright and immaculate. "You three might wanna hold on to something for this next part. They don't usually let me drive this thing, and they have their reasons."

Sleep guided the train down the avenue and out of the city, then pulled on a series of levers and seemed confused when he didn't get the result he wanted.

"Which was it again?" He tried another lever and sparks flew from the undercarriage as the train rapidly decelerated. Shouts went up from the cars behind us. "My bad!" He pulled two more cords and seemed satisfied with the result.

The train shot out of the city and banked a hard left turn that pushed House and me up against the side of the car. More shouting sounded from the cars behind us, and they turned into screams as Sleep yanked the wheel even harder and the left side of the train lifted up slightly.

He laughed and spun the wheel back, and the train slammed back down into place. He guided it through the turn, then pulled the same braking lever he had before, but gently enough to keep the deceleration from being jarring. He looked back at me.

"Can you help me with something real quick?"

I stepped up next to him. The train didn't have a windshield, and the air was screaming into my face as we approached the city again.

"Would you call this straight?" he said.

"What do you mean?"

"Are we lined up with the doors to the coliseum? Gonna punch right back in."

I squinted ahead. "We're maybe listing a little to the left?"

He jerked the wheel to the right. "Better?"

"You are off by three degrees," House said. "May I?"

Sleep took his hands off the wheel and stepped back.

House moved in and spun the wheel slightly to the left, then made a minor correction to the right. "There. You are lined up with the doors."

He gave her a measuring look, then a warm smile. "Thank you very much! Maybe it won't wreck it this time. Kind of a shame to slam a Legendary vehicle into a wall for no good reason." He jerked his head toward the other cars as the train screamed toward the gate, sparks still flying. "Come on. Let me give you guys the tour."

House hesitated at the wheel as Sleep opened a door in the back of the engine car and held it open.

"Does this vehicle not require a driver?"

"It'll keep going without one for a surprisingly long time," Sleep said.

House cocked her head. "But will it not crash?"

"It might. But it'll be fine. And if not, it'll be entertaining. Pleasure to officially meet the three of you. I've been wondering when we'd cross paths for a while now, Ned. House, welcome. And Frank, oh, to be in the company of the Funkmaster himself. We are truly blessed this day."

"I really like it here," Frank said.

I gaped at Sleep. "How do you know that Frank calls himself that?"

Sleep pushed his Soul Gem goggles up onto his forehead, revealing brown eyes. He tapped his right ear, then gestured at the next car.

"Don't worry about that for now. Come on, tour's waiting."

House looked at me, and I nodded. She let go of the wheel, and we followed Sleep out of the car and into the next, the front of which looked a lot like the back of a restaurant with metal shelves to either side heaped with wooden plates and bowls and silverware and chopsticks and skewers and every dining implement imaginable.

Sleep grabbed two gargantuan platters and handed one to each of us. "Frank? Mug, glass, or bucket? I recommend the bucket."

"Bucket by a mile."

A bead of sweat ran down the back of my neck and dribbled down my spine. He knew about how Frank liked to soak, too?

House leaned in and whispered in my ear. "I do not understand what is happening."

"Join the club," I said.

She drew back slightly, made to speak, then stopped herself. "There is no club for the uninformed, is there?"

"Afraid not," Frank said.

She sighed. "That is truly a shame. I would have happily joined for the camaraderie alone."

Sleep led the way through the back of the car, where a number of copper mugs were hanging from a metal grate, sounding like wind chimes as they rattled against one another as the train roared along.

He pointed up at them. "Grab one of those too. One of our smiths made 'em. The handle collapses so you can hook it onto your belt loop." He grabbed two for himself and clipped them onto either side of his belt as if they were carabiners. "See?"

"Handy," I said, just to say something. I snagged two of them and handed one to House, then attached mine on the opposite side to where Frank hung.

"Off we go!" Sleep hip-checked another door, and it swung open. We stepped out into the cold night air for a moment and hopped over the narrow space where the cars were coupled—with the ground rushing along below—then popped into a car that smelled of roasting garlic and onion and ginger.

Four small cooking stations were arranged in each corner, where pairs of chefs were working with high blue flames and oversized woks that were each emitting huge amounts of steam.

The arrangements were magical in nature: each station had one chef running the show while some kind of fire mage created and manipulated the flames.

In the center of the car was one long metal table, where countless dishes were heaped and steaming in metal bowls. And as I drew closer, I felt the heat coming off the table: it was as if the inside of the table contained a furnace of its own. And judging by the Soul Gems that lined its legs and sides, maybe it did.

Sleep greeted the cooks, who looked up as they heard their names, and drew a few grins in return.

"Grab whatever looks good, but keep in mind there's a bunch more dining cars. And there's only one firm rule for food: if you take it, you try it, you swallow."

"Are we dining for some reason?" House said.

I scratched the back of my head. "I guess we are?"

Sleep stopped about halfway down the buffet and waved us over. He selected a dish that smelled like brimstone and set a huge bowl of it onto each of our platters.

"We call this magmatic noodles. Nobody's tried it twice. Ohh, this is a good one too." He grabbed another pair of metal bowls full of dark stew that smelled like lime and pork. "This one's my favorite, but it's better if you don't ask what's in it or what it's called or preferably anything."

"Unidentified meats best meats," Frank said.

Sleep winked down at him. "If you like that, you'll love this one." He set a shallow bowl full of bloody strips in a thick red sauce onto my platter, which was already getting heavy but smelled absolutely divine.

"This is... probably enough for me?" I said.

"Alrighty!" Sleep said. We moved into the next car, and I didn't realize that he'd misinterpreted my statement and assumed that I was done picking things in that last car until he scraped a thin layer of a rice and seafood dish out of a preposterously large and shallow frying pan and dumped it onto my platter.

"You like paella?" he said, way too late and a little more loudly than was necessary. "This right here is super authentic and very traditional."

One of the cooks started yelling at him almost immediately, and Sleep's grin said that that was the point.

"What was that about?" I said.

"Chef Mattias has very strong opinions about what actually counts as paella." He pointed at the pile he'd heaped atop my platter. "That's a seafood variant that's more popular than what he considers the actual dish, so if you ever need to order it freshly made from him, you need to refer to it as *arroz con cosas*. Otherwise he'll throw whatever's he's cooking at you."

I cocked my head at him.

"It's Spanish for rice with things," he said.

I snorted.

"I gave him a whole bag of mixed animal feet once and told him to make paella with that. Just a bunch of ankles in a sack."

"Glorious," Frank said.

Sleep laughed, a deep, warm sound. He had a certain magnetism to his bearing, and I found myself wanting to laugh alongside him, which was a bizarre feeling.

"You should have seen the look on his face when I put it on the menu. Joke was on me though because he did actually follow through and make it, so I had to try it."

"How was it?" Frank said.

"Not bad, really. Tough and earthy, but we did end up making it again. Hard to find uses for feet. You all set?"

"...Yeah," I said. My platter was so heavy that I couldn't stop it from shaking, and the dishes were rattling around.

Sleep's eyes flicked over it and caught the motion. "Ah, right, my bad. You're Intelligence and Dex-based, right? Here, I got you." He put a hand beneath the platter and lifted it up as if it were weightless. "This way."

And as we arrived in the next car, which smelled strongly of pepper and hickory and had what looked like dinosaur drumsticks hanging down from the ceiling on hooks—Sleep's personal, prized collection of aging meats—I realized I'd made a huge mistake by allowing him to take my platter.

Because by the time we pushed through to the final car, Sleep himself was struggling to keep the thing upright, heaped as it was, and he had two cooks trailing after us with desserts in hand.

He stepped up to a wide door on the side of the final car and kicked it open. The ground was still sliding by, but it was slow enough that he didn't have any issue with stepping off the moving train. I'd kind of been hoping he'd lose some of the food he'd piled atop my platter, but he didn't.

House and I hopped out, and Sleep led us down the half-destroyed city streets and behind the still-moving train and toward the arena, occasionally switching the platter from hand to hand as he went.

The sounds of fighting drew closer as the train trundled away from us and toward the coliseum, wheels still sparking beneath it. It stopped a few feet in front of the arena, positioned dead-center in front of the doors.

"So..." I said, but I had no idea how to even finish the sentence. Or where to start, or even what to say in general.

"You know, I lost my shit when you pulled that Head Start stunt," Sleep said.

I winced. "Yeah. Not my proudest moment."

"My bad, that's not what I meant. So funny."

"Huh?" Frank said.

"You weren't pissed off?" I said.

"I was bummed that there weren't any streams I could follow for sure, but I've got a brother-in-law that loves, just loooves dumping on me because I'm broke." He rolled his eyes. "And I'm a dentist, man. I have four practices."

"A respected occupation," Frank said.

Sleep laughed. "Yeah, you should try telling him that. He got into crypto early, so everything short of that kind of money is a joke to him. Though I'm a bit surprised to hear you say that dentistry is respected given what I've dug up about you."

Frank cleared his throat and puffed himself up. "What other field has successfully managed not only to convince the public that their bones occasionally need to be removed but also that they ought to pay through the nose for the honor? Nope, dentists are boss. They are truly the archeologists of the flesh."

"Well, I can't unhear that," I said.

Sleep stopped and bellowed a laugh, free hand on his stomach. "Oh man, I'm gonna put that on a business card and give it to the customers I don't wanna see again."

"Teeth are ectodermal organs, not bones," House said.

"Fine, but the point stands," Frank said. "And bones sounds way more poetic."

"Granted."

Sleep grinned at the two of them. "I like you guys. But yeah, we were all sitting around waiting for that first commercial with that douchey streamer to go out—what was his name, Tyler?—and the moment Kline mentioned putting early access spots up for sale, my brother-in-law starts squawking and strutting around the living room, laughing at us.

"He gets on the phone and starts dialing and he's already talking about what he's gonna do, and how us broke boys—me and my actual brother, who's a teacher, so that really pissed me off on his behalf—are just gonna sit around and watch while he conquers the world and so on.

"So he's talking all big and finally gets a person on the line and says what he wants, then he just goes dead quiet," Sleep said, shoulders shaking now. "And then he says: *What do you mean they're all gone?*" He broke off, laughing harder than ever before. "In hindsight, it was really just the look on his face." He pointed at me. "He dedicated his whole game to destroying you, by the way."

"Really now?" I said.

"He only made it to level 6 before he quit, so I think you're probably okay at this point. Got to some quest where there was a bunch of competition for spawns and lost his mind when an hour had gone by without him being able to complete it. My brother and I still yell *what do you mean they're all gone* whenever something runs out. Pasta, beer, doesn't matter."

He led us past the train and down a dark hallway that opened up in the coliseum lit sparingly with torches. Blood was smeared on the walls, and the space smelled like copper.

"It was great, man. I'd take that moment over a slot any day, and it's not like I had that kind of money regardless."

The sounds of fighting intensified up ahead, and one particularly large explosion—probably magical in nature—rattled the tunnel strongly enough to send dust drifting down.

"I'm talking your ears off, aren't I?" Sleep said. "My bad, just excited to have some company outside the guild. You got any questions for me, Ned?"

"I have so many questions."

"How can I stop my teeth from itching?" House said.

"Well, I hate to be that guy, but I'm him, so, maybe try flossing more often?"

"Does that truly work?"

"Yeah." He shifted my platter to his other hand and dug into a pocket. "And in case you wanna start in-game, I haven't found or made real floss yet, but here." He tossed her a thin piece of what looked like wire. "Low-level bowstrings for crafting. Thinnest thing I've found. The realism here is absolutely crazy, but I could do without the way they've nailed how little bits of food can get stuck between your teeth. I get that it's a textural thing, but that's a pass for me."

"Thank you very much."

"You're welcome, House. Any, uh... other questions?"

"Which teeth cause the most bleeding upon removal?" Frank said.

I sighed. "That's not what he meant, Frank."

"I'm aware, but knowledge is power. Especially when that knowledge could keep someone alive or conscious longer."

"Upper wisdom usually bleed the longest," Sleep said.

"Noted."

Sleep shifted my platter to his right hand and shook out his left arm. "Anything non-dentistry related?"

"Quite a few still, yeah," I said.

"Shoot."

"What's Goon about, exactly? I'm seeing a whole lot of food and a lot of burned-out buildings, and it sounds like people are dying up ahead."

"Probably easier for me to show you. We can talk more over dinner." He raised his voice. "Diners incoming!"

The doors at the end of the hall boomed open to reveal a sunken amphitheater. We stepped out onto the top row, and what I saw left me even more confused than everything I'd seen so far.

Row after sunken row was filled with brawling combatants or diners and occasionally both in close proximity. At first I thought we'd stumbled upon the last holdouts of whatever guild Goon had just stomped out in their takeover of the city, but every single member had the Goon tag floating above their nameplate.

And their numbers... They seemed almost endless—there were hundreds, maybe even a thousand players packing the coliseum.

"Are they all dueling?" I said.

Sleep shook his head as he led the way down a narrow stone stairway.

"Nah, we don't really do duels. Never really saw the point."

Out of the corner of my eye, I saw a sword-wielding, bare-chested barbarian catch a conjured axe made of frost to the chest. He fell off the row he'd been fighting on and tumbled down onto the one below it, causing a huge clatter of plates and bowls and leftovers.

"Did that dude just die?" I said, still not understanding what I was looking at.

Then I saw an archer get shanked from behind and go rolling down a set of steps. Then a caster in robes took a boot between the shoulder blades that sent him flying all the way into the arena, where the fall damage instantly killed him.

"All these people are dying. Like, they're actually dying. You guys are killing each other."

"Uh huh," Sleep said.

"Well put," Frank said.

I stopped in place. "This is why you guys aren't way up on the ladder, isn't it? Everybody keeps dying, all the time."

"What ladder?" Sleep said. He'd stopped a few steps down and was looking up at me over one broad shoulder.

"The Renown Ladder?"

"Sorry, what?"

I stared at him. "Do you seriously not know about the Renown Ladder? Try querying it."

He tapped at the air. "Oh! Hey, look at you! Number one in the world, eh? Not my thing, but if you're gonna compete, you might as well win, right?" He dismissed it so quickly that I was positive he hadn't even checked for his own name. "Learn something new here every day, huh? Just a bit farther, then we can sit and chat for a bit. Imagine you've probably got some stuff on your mind." He turned and kept walking down the steps.

"I told you!" Frank shouted as I followed Sleep deeper into the sunken arena. "I told you these guys are just a bunch of dudes who like killing people! And not only that, they like killing each other!"

"Yeah, you did suggest that a lot, didn't you? How did you know?" I paused. "Hey, wait a second—how were you able to share that?"

"I didn't because I had no idea what they were about. It was just wishful thinking on my part. And now here we are, in paradise."

Sleep cut left into the front row and dipped into a section of private box seating. The space was shaded with black cloth, and there was a long table lined with tall chairs, one of which had a corpse draped over it.

Sleep set my platter onto the table, then grabbed the corpse by an elbow and an ankle and chucked it down into the arena beyond. "There ya go! All clear." He kicked a seat out and dropped into it.

I took a seat, and House did the same, setting her own overloaded platter in front of her. We sat there in stunned silence for a moment, each eye level with what had to be a week's worth of food for the average family.

And then the trailing chefs were there, piling pastries and dishes of ice cream that somehow hadn't melted in the slightest and cakes and all manner of things around us and Frank's bucket was on the table and I still had no idea how they knew that was a thing and my head was absolutely spinning.

Sleep rocked back in his chair and clasped his hands behind his head. "Any requests for entertainment before we get started?"

"Entertainment?" I said.

"I'd like to see a mage die badly," Frank said.

Sleep grinned. "I should have guessed, could have already arranged that." He stood up and raised his voice. "Rank challenge, mage bracket!" The entire arena went still and silent, then erupted into cheers. Sleep spoke over them, voice booming. "You should all have your most recent selections, so if you want to participate, head down to the arena floor now."

Ten different spellcasters ran down toward the center of the coliseum, hopping seats and diners and getting tangled up and tripping over one another. They spread out, pairing up and grouping into two rows with one spellcaster facing the other.

"Alright," Sleep said. "You die, you lose. Also, no spells. Ready, set—"

"What do you mean, no spells?" one of them shouted back.

"No spells," he repeated. "Otherwise it's an instant disqualification. Go!"

# Chapter Thirty-Nine

"This is the best day of my life," Frank said as the mages rushed in and started whacking each other ineffectually with staves and wands. Hilariously small numbers flew up from the arena floor, and the onlookers laughed and cheered and mocked in equal measure.

A chef with a particularly bloody apron put what appeared to be the rib cage of a small whale in front of Sleep, then jogged back up the steps. Sleep picked the entire thing up and bit into it as if it were an ear of corn.

"Dig in, friends!"

I dropped Frank into his bucket—which someone had managed to fill without me noticing—and selected a chowder that was so thick the stone spoon the chef had placed in the bowl was floating on the surface. I took a bite, and an involuntary groan escaped my lips alongside a little bit of chowder. It was salty and rich and decadent.

I wiped my chin. "Wow. That is one of the best things I've ever eaten."

"Thrilled to hear it!" Sleep said. "This is what it's all for, man. Have I mentioned I can't eat dairy?"

I shoveled another spoonful in. "Huh?"

"Back in the real world," he said. "I mean, I can eat it, but I gotta take the next day off work, you know what I'm saying?"

I laughed.

"I do not know what you are saying," House said. She was eating some kind of green and blue salad with a fork, but the lettuce was undulating so much that it looked like it was trying to escape its bowl.

"Probably for the best, House."

"Right?" Sleep said. "It sucks. So I got here, realized how good the food is, and proceeded to eat nothing but cheese for three days." He dropped his ribs onto the table and all of the platters jumped, their contents lifting and bumping around. He held his hands a few feet apart. "Just a wheel of aged cheddar, man. It was glorious."

"So it's all about food?" I said. "You guys are just... out here cooking?"

He threw up three fingers covered in what may or may not have been barbecue sauce and ticked them off one at a time. "The three great F's: great food, great friends, great fights."

"Bam!" Frank said. "Did you see that down there? Right in the mouth! I didn't even know a wand could do that!"

"That said," Sleep continued, "you wander up into the second floor of the wrong inn late at night, and you might find a fourth F. I'm wifed up with two kids, so that's not my bag, but it is what it is. Only thing I ask is that they shut the doors, but for whatever reason nobody ever does that. I ask a lot, too."

"I am intrigued by the presence of this second floor," House said.

Sleep picked up his rack of ribs again. "Hey—each to their own. Like I said, doors are always open, regardless of how many times you tell 'em to do otherwise."

"Can I ask about the..." I trailed off, a dozen questions spinning through my head.

"Razebloom?" he suggested. "Cities we've Razed? Cities we've Sieged?" He leaned a little closer. "Cities we're about to Siege?"

I nodded. "All of that, basically."

"Hey, meat mech," Frank said. "Can you move me forward a little bit? A mage just fell and I think he's getting his teeth kicked in but I can't see 'cause he's beneath us and I don't wanna miss it."

I scooped the bucket up and set it on the banister that separated the box seating from the arena floor below.

"Better view?"

"Yup."

I sat back down. "I guess the blooms tie into the food, yeah? They're valuable to begin with, plus they make your crops grow more quickly, and that's where all of your ingredients are coming from."

"Valuable?" Sleep said. "Nah, not really. It's all about the crops. Everything's about the crops, actually." He paused. "Why are you looking at me like that?"

I thought about lying to him about the Codex entry Frank had sent me earlier, but despite everything, I kinda liked him. And it seemed like there might be a chance I could make him reconsider Sieging the Oasis.

I paraphrased the Codex entry for him.

His eyebrows shot up at that, and he started typing. "Too funny, nine hundred seventy people in the guild and not a single Alchemist has a recipe that can use Razeblooms yet. Whatever. Maybe it's a mid-game thing or something. Thanks a bunch for the heads up, though. Guess we should probably stop throwing 'em out. You want some?"

I stared at him. "Well, sure? I don't know what they're worth or what they do, so I probably can't pay much, but—"

I cut off as he opened a trade window with me and slammed a hundred Razeblooms into it. He confirmed the trade and went right back to eating.

"Just like that?"

"We always pay for good info," he said. He snapped a bone off his ribs and gestured at the arena with it, which spattered the banister Frank was resting on with barbecue sauce. "Please, take 'em. Trade window's blocking my view of the fight."

I confirmed it. "Thanks."

"Yup. I'm not surprised Frank mentioned that they're hard to grow— that's definitely true. The difficulty we've had there is the whole reason we've moved from Razing cities to Sieging them."

"I don't follow."

"You need to harvest Razebloom successfully to get the growth bonus to whatever you plant next." He looked me up and down. "I know you've never Razed a city, but have you seen it happen?"

I shook my head.

"Basically, you gotta clear everybody out and hold the city for a little while. That's fine and all, but the real problem is that you gotta Raze the whole thing at once, and you can only plant Razebloom in the immediate aftermath. I mean, we're talking minutes here.

"It ends up being super wasteful—you burn this whole place down and wind up with whole sections that you could have planted Razebloom in, but you weren't fast enough."

"But with Sieging?"

He wiped his mouth with his forearm. "So much easier. We can carve the city up into sections and Raze it one bit at a time. That makes it easy to squeeze every last bit of growth out."

That definitely explained the half-Razed avenue we'd walked down. "So you don't plan on holding this city, then?"

"Nah, no point."

"If it is not eight feet, then do not build it," House said.

"Exactly!" Sleep said, shaking a rib so emphatically that I wondered where exactly she'd picked that expression up because I had no idea what it meant. "But yeah—we'll be wrapped up here in a couple hours. To be honest with you guys, this Siege was pretty disappointing. Hardly anybody showed up to defend this place, and we just sorta rolled over those who did. I'm hoping the Black Oasis will put up a better fight with how active the area's been."

"What about the people, though?"

"You mean the NPCs? If they want to leave ahead of time then fine, we won't stop 'em. If they wanna dig in and defend the city alongside the players? Even better. I'd rather lose than keep stomping people the way we have been."

"That's what I really miss, man. The fights that just went on and on, you know? You'd log in and run out to a specific city because you knew people would be fighting over it, not that there was anything to gain by doing that. It was just fun. You'd go back and forth, push the enemy back, push too far and aggro the guards and the fast travel NPCs, then you'd get thrown back onto the defensive, rinse, repeat. Nobody ever won, ever. You couldn't, and it was glorious."

I grinned. "Yeah, I get it. I really do."

"And yeah, if the players dig in and we roll over 'em anyway, they can always join up with us afterward." He eyed Frank. "In that case, we even offer you a chance to get your dropped gear back if you can climb the ranks fast enough."

I dipped into my bowl of chowder and heard the spoon click against the bottom. I was shocked and disappointed that it was gone.

"And what does that look like, exactly?"

Sleep gestured toward the arena with what remained of his entire rack of ribs, where one of the nearest mages had just bowled his opponent off his feet and was now pummeling him with his staff.

"Like that, pretty much. New members get three days to climb the ranks. You can challenge anyone you want to a fight to the death, but if you lose, then you're locked in one rank lower than you were when you challenged. You'll be able to move up over time, but yeah."

"And the gear?"

"You make it to officer, and everything you dropped is returned to you. He pointed at a thin female mage who was seated a few rows above us, eating a blueberry pie as if she were being timed. "That's Alexandra, she's 27-2." He pointed at a guy who was standing atop a table on the other side of the arena, juggling four steak knives while straddling a roast pig with a green apple in its mouth. "Zeke, 18-1. Those two are higher end, but their records are what you'd be looking at if you wanted to climb."

"And you're the leader, right? Can I ask what your record is?"

He smiled. "I am indeed, and I'm 0-0."

"Interesting."

"Thought you'd want to hear about all that if you hadn't already. Been figuring we'll probably see you out in the Oasis tomorrow afternoon, so the drop rules felt relevant."

I drew back slightly. "Me?"

He pushed his goggles farther up his forehead, getting sauce all over them, but he didn't seem to care.

"I've heard the rumors: Francis chased you out early on, even killed you once, supposedly. Looted a key he sold to that Terry guy, and so on and so on."

"You mean Tyrann?"

"Sure. But yeah, I respect the hustle on the ghost's part, but he's not playing on an angle I'm interested in personally."

"The what?"

"Francis. The Gilded Ghost? But aside from all that, I think you've still got a bit of a soft spot for the city, Ned. Especially given the timing of your appearance here. Or am I wide of the mark with that?"

I tried to grab one of the thin pieces of meat he'd piled onto a plate, but it fell apart in my hands. Sleep was quick to hand me a fork.

"Pull it apart and mix it up with the red sauce, then eat it. Better that way, otherwise it's nice but a little dry."

I nodded my thanks and did just that to stall for time.

"I'm not sure just how much of a soft spot I have left for that place," I said after a moment. "It's changed a lot since the early days, though I've been around a bit more than I'd like of late. But it was either that or give up on the raid, at least early on."

"So I've heard."

I took a bite and once again was floored by the quality of the food: it was smoky and peppery, and the texture was so tender it was otherworldly. "This is unreal."

"Right? Well, like I was saying, I'm definitely hoping to see you and Omen out there. And between us, if what happened here in the Blue Fortress is any indication of what's to come, you might wanna put a bit more effort into rallying the troops than they did."

"What's that supposed to mean?"

He set his ribs down, leaned back, and placed both of his hands on his stomach. "Most of the players who called this place home bailed ahead of time. Put their plots up for sale and moved on way before the Siege even started. And I get it—we're big, we've made a bit of a name for ourselves with those alerts—but more than anything else, we're looking for a fight. A good one."

"I see. Is there any way I could convince you—"

He shook his head. "If you're about to ask what I think you're about to ask then I'm afraid not, friend. If you wanna stop the train, you're going to have to get out in front of it. Nothing personal, though. And I do mean that."

I sighed. I'd expected as much, but I had to try, risks and all. "Worth a shot, right?"

"Can't blame you for trying. Everybody does." He scowled. "And between us, some people get pretty annoying about it."

"I gotta say, you guys are not at all what I was expecting to find when I headed out this way." I picked up one of the pastries—a golden croissant dusted with sugar crystals—and warm chocolate oozed out of both ends. I took a bite, then a second, then a third, then finished it.

Frank hooted as a stave connected with a mage's face, and he went down hard.

"Frank also seems to see the appeal of your playstyle," House said.

Sleep inclined his head. "I hoped he would."

I stared around the arena, at the hundreds of players who were dining or fighting amongst themselves or both.

And for the first time, the scope of just how large Goon really was—and the reality of what we were up against—truly began to dawn on me. I stared at Frank, thinking. He really would be happy here. But what would happen if I dropped him for good and...

I chewed the inside of my cheek. "Sleep, can I ask you something real quick? It's maybe a bit personal."

"Always."

"How often do you work? I mean, you've got a serious job, right? So how have you guys got this far? Are you just in and out all the time?"

He laughed. "I took three weeks off, but yeah, I'll have to get back to the grind before too long. Wife and kids are the bigger factor, but they know how long I've been waiting for something like this. For now, though? Just enjoying the ride."

I nodded. That was sort of what I'd been wondering.

"Something on your mind? You're looking a little concerned over there all of a sudden."

"Uhh... yeah, nothing in particular. Guess I'm thinking about your numbers. Feels like you guys might get more of what you want if you weren't so big. With the fights and all."

Sleep tore off a huge piece of meat and swallowed it, then pounded his chest when it refused to go down. He cleared his throat.

"You've got the right of that, and it's a problem we're gonna have to address at some point. I really hate turning people away, but we might need to get a bit more selective in the future. I don't wanna be known for numbers, you know? Just sorta worked out that way."

A message came in from Darling: she was starting to put the raid group together.

I stood up. "I get it, yeah. Thanks a ton for the hospitality and the info, but we should probably get going. And again, the food was incredible."

He offered his hand, and I shook it. He pulled me in a little closer, close enough that House and Frank wouldn't be able to hear.

"If you do end up lining up against us tomorrow afternoon, do me a favor and keep those loot rules in mind, yeah? I mean what I said, and I'll enforce it regardless of whatever happens to drop."

I nodded. "I will, thanks."

He pulled back. "One last thing."

"Yeah?"

"You know I can't just let you walk away like this, right?"

I stiffened and started to reach for my pistols. "What do you mean?"

"Boxes, man."

"Boxes?"

He stood up and cupped his hands around his mouth like a makeshift megaphone. "I need boxes!"

A pair of chefs came out of nowhere, each of them carrying what looked like a stack of white, foldable papers covered in either red or blue runes. They set them on the table, and one of them started folding the things into carry-out boxes while the other started boxing my food up.

"Probably our best find yet," Sleep said. "Heated and chilled to-go boxes. You can pop it all into your inventory and it'll keep forever. Not quite as good as when it first comes off the train, but it's close."

I laughed. "Wow. Thanks again." I looked over at House's plate, trying to gauge how much time this was going to take.

The answer was not long, apparently, because every single dish she'd started with was empty, spotless, and stacked somewhere amid three neat piles.

She belched. "Thank you very much for the food, and I apologize for licking your plates, but I wanted to."

"I'll pass the compliment on to the chefs," Sleep said. "Say hey to Omen for me, yeah? Really would love to see those guys out there."

"Not sure about that—it's not my call to make," I said. "But I'll definitely pass the greeting on. And probably some of the food, too." I grinned. "Well, maybe. Depends how happy they are to see me when I get back."

"There's always more where that came from. Cheers, and good luck in the raid."

I dropped all the food into my inventory, then grabbed Frank out of his bucket and stuck him back in his loop.

"Wait!" he said. "Wait wait wait! Only five of them have died! Just one more, one more!"

"Sorry man, but we've got a date to keep with a bunch of huge, dead animals, plus whoever or whatever has been sitting in that cage."

He groaned. "Well, my life has officially peaked."

I headed up the stairs. More Goon members were pouring out of the tunnel now, and the roar of the arena was louder than ever. "You'd like it here, wouldn't you?"

"Obviously. Sleep is awesome."

"I liked him too, weirdly enough. But they've got a legitimate army here; they're like ten times the size of Omen. My guess is that we've got the edge when it comes to gear and levels if they've been neglecting Rifts and the raid and so on, but still. Ten to one? There's definitely a chance that you'll end up with them tomorrow afternoon."

I took their numbers in one last time, anxiety rising, then swallowed hard and made my way into the tunnel, House right behind me.

"We do need to start planning, though, because if this Siege turns into anything remotely resembling a fair fight then we're done, and so is the Oasis. So if you guys have got any big ideas, I'm all ears. But for now, let's go get Darling and company another World-first."

# Chapter Forty

I made a quick pit stop at the Auction House to pick up a few items for the guild and scope out the defenses a bit, and by the time I'd made it into the Menagerie Wing, a great deal of the core group was already there. Many of them were standing around the three great iron doors that led out into the ruins, while Darling and Nina and the others were circled up around the cage at the rear of the chamber.

"He's here!" Nina said. "Pop the coffin box and let's see what we're working with!"

Darling spotted me, then waved me over. "We were thinking we'd start with the cage thing. How was Goon?"

"Super nice," Frank said. "You'd love them."

She cocked her head. "I'd say that our current circumstances would probably rule that out."

"They were surprisingly nice," I agreed. "I'll share everything with you when we're taking a break or something, but the short of it is that Goon is huge and dead set on taking the Oasis. Diplomacy is a definite no-go."

"How huge?"

I forced a smile. I didn't want to lie to her, but I also didn't want her worrying about the Siege and just how bad things were probably about to get, knowing what lay in front of us over the next few hours and what the World-firsts would mean to everyone.

"It's gonna be rough—really rough—but I've got some ideas that might even the playing field a bit, and I'm sorta banking on the fact that Frank will save the day."

"A fair assumption," he said.

I dug into my inventory, eager to change the subject. "One thing real quick before we unlock that cage, just in case it turns out to be a boss or whatever."

"We're already in position," Ton said from the other side of the container.

I looked over toward him and saw Jukes nodding my way as well. I'd already created a couple of the runes he was after with some Weak Soul Gems I'd snagged for the Auction House, and it was great to see him looking relaxed again.

I shook my head. "Nah not that, I mean I've got Touchstone items for everyone."

Darling blinked at me. "Huh?"

"I already had House carrying a bunch of them and I just blew some more gold at the Auction House." I scanned the raid group's levels, which confirmed that just about everyone aside from a few healers had reached level 15. "I know we've probably only got a handful of people who already have their Touchstone Socket or whatever unlocked, but I figure the fifty or so Elite+ kills people need will go pretty quick as we burn through the trash on the way to the bosses."

"Clarify what you mean by everyone," Nina said. "Am I included in that?"

"Everyone except for Frank," I said. I opened up a trade window with Darling and dumped twenty-five pieces of Touchstone gear in.

Her jaw dropped. "How the hell?"

I grinned. "House and I bought sixty-something pieces back when we first unlocked the socket, then I re-upped and bought another fifteen that looked especially good just now."

Without waiting for Darling, I confirmed the trade.

"These are just the cream of the crop. You can trade the extras back to House and she'll put them up on the Auction House—she's already waiting outside. She's going to put it all up for sale after the guild has made their picks, and we're going to funnel all that money into the defenses.

"That's mostly going to look like spamming Ghostlight Cannons from this point on unless we find a new pattern or get a new unlock, but yeah.

We should have a bunch of them up and running by the time the Siege starts if these sell half as well as I expect them to."

"How much did this cost you?" Darling said.

"I'm pretty much out of gold again."

She brushed a dark lock of hair out of her face. "But what about Arlann? You still need to fund the guard, right? Especially with the Siege."

I pursed my lips. "I think we should be okay there. The timing of our deal means that I've gotta pay him before the Siege starts, but my daily payout should hit well before that. And with each city we've got linked up being worth more and more as time passes and with how many cities I'm thinking we'll have by then—probably thirty plus—quick napkin math says I should be getting close to 50 gold.

"And like I said, House will be throwing up some really valuable Touchstone items on the Auction House too, like the tank abilities I don't think we'd use and so on. I told her to price some of those really high, but with the race for the first clear in full swing, I think there's a good chance someone bites, and if even one of those items sells then we're definitely golden."

"But this is a fortune?"

"It'll be a fortune eventually, yeah. For now, it's just a good investment. Take them. I figured it'd be for the best if you handed them out yourself. Faster and probably more efficient than a free-for-all or the fight to the death that Frank suggested a half-dozen times."

"I still don't understand why you shot that down," he said. "Sleep would have been all for it."

She stared at the window, then confirmed it. "Alright then, thanks. This should only take a minute, but I'll definitely finish handing these out before we crack the cell."

"I've got Rift Gems if you need 'em too, lots of every type."

"Nah, we've got that handled." She tapped her menus, and within seconds a number of guildies had popped new weapons or pieces of armor into their hands.

It was mostly the same deal as before: I hadn't expected anyone without a Trinket would get much use out of the items, given their low stats and item levels, but I was surprised and more than a little concerned to see a few people recognize the items as immediate upgrades and equip them right away.

"Alright Nina," Darling said. "Go ahead."

Nina shrieked and tapped the strange metal box. The many runes that covered its surface flared, then died out completely.

Then the roof of the container blew off and smashed up into the ceiling so hard that it stuck there, one corner embedded in the stone.

"Ton's taking initial aggro, and Jukes will—"

Darling cut off as a familiar figure drifted up out of the container.

{Isabel} (Level 15 Undead)
HP: 1,000/1,000
MP: 200/200

She was a ghost, and her body was spectral from her toes to her long red hair, but I recognized her right away. I pointed a pistol at her, though her name tag was friendly.

"Darling, you remember her, right? This is the woman that guard pushed off the porch. The one Brandt fed that concoction to."

"Ohhh. Yeah, definitely."

Isabel floated there for a long while, spinning slightly and rubbing the heels of her hands into her eyes. She looked dazed, and I was starting to wonder if we'd wasted our gems when she inhaled sharply and dropped to the floor in front of us in a blue-green rush.

"Thank you for freeing me." Her voice was high and light, almost musical. "It's been... I don't know how long it's been. But it doesn't matter—you're here for the Huntsman, right? He's still holed up in his palace, but I can help you get in."

She swooped forward and hovered directly in front of Darling, the tips of her toes drifting a few inches off the floor. "If you can break enough of the Huntsman's curses, I can deactivate the palace's protective wards and get you in. There's still time to save Brandt."

Darling and I exchanged a quick glance, which drew a growl from Frank.

I dropped my voice. "Didn't we see Brandt die on the gallows?"

"I dunno," Frank said. "Did you?"

I scratched the back of my head.

"Breaking three of the five curses should be enough," Isabel said. She stared at the box that had held her. "I spent a very long time studying those runes. I think... I think I can break one of them myself." She drew a quick series of symbols into the air.

I glanced at my nameplate. I was currently under the effect of five separate debuffs, and the symbols that Isabel had drawn matched up perfectly with the debuff icons.

I inspected them and was relieved to find that the guild had cleared enough Rifts to identify the last two curses as well. As a result, we now knew what all five curses did.

{Stitcher's Curse}
Effect: All Healing received is decreased by 20%.

{Hex of Flying Vertebrae}
Effect: Whenever a hostile target dies within 20 yards of a player afflicted by this curse, there is a 10% chance that the corpse will erupt in a Bony Explosion that deals 1,000 damage to all players within 40 yards.
If a hostile target dies within 20 yards of 5 or more players afflicted by this curse, the explosion is guaranteed to occur.

{Dreadking's Ultimatum}
Effect: Whenever a player dies, all other players within 20 yards are Feared for 8 seconds. This effect cannot be broken or dispelled.

{Binding of the Spectral Kin}
Effect: Whenever you deal the killing blow to an Undead enemy, you have a 10% chance of spawning a second, identical enemy. This effect applies to any and all Raid Boss minions, but not to the Raid Bosses themselves.

{Glass-bone Curse}
Effect: All Physical Damage you receive is increased by 33%.

"Can we change our minds later and have you break a different curse?" Darling said.

Isabel floated a little higher. "I'm afraid that once a curse is broken, your choice will have been made."

Isabel looked at me, so I met her eyes. "But we only need to break three to get into the palace?"

She inclined her head. "I believe so, yes."

"And how exactly are we supposed to break the other two?"

The ghost turned and drifted up to the central gate and wrapped her fingers around the bars. "I can lead you to the worst of Brandt's creations. The Memorial Hearts... there's power in them. One should be enough to help me overpower a single curse, so I'll need two in all."

I waited to make sure she was finished speaking, then turned to Darling.

"So here's what I'm thinking: five curses, and we need to deactivate two more to reach the Huntsman, right? The Bridge Rift was three encounters, so maybe that pattern holds here as well and the Huntsman is the last boss?"

"That would mean we'd still have two curses active when we start the last fight."

I gestured at the runic symbols that were still floating in the air. "Exactly. So the question is really what we think we can live with." I turned to the ghost. "Isabel? Can I ask you something?"

"I suppose, but please, we need to move quickly. I can't bear the thought of knowing Brandt is still under the Huntsman's control."

"Can we have you wait and break a curse for us a little later on?"

"No. I won't be able to leave this room until the first line of defense falls. Then we'll proceed together."

I shrugged. "Good to rule it out, I guess. I've got an idea if everybody is up for it, but it really depends on how many of those immunity charms we've got floating around, like the Stitcher's Charm and so on."

Darling cupped her hands and popped maybe a dozen small necklaces into them. "We've got a good number of them because I pulled every single one that I could from the trash group. What are you thinking?"

I pointed at the symbols for the Dreadking's Ultimatum and the Hex of Flying Vertebrae.

"Those look like straight up wipe mechanics, right? If the whole raid takes a thousand damage more than once, we're done. And if somebody dies and causes an AoE fear that sends our tanks or healers running for a while and we can't dispel the effect, then we're also done."

I gestured at two other symbols. "Glass-bone and Stitchers are nasty, but they're more attrition-based, right? People take extra damage and they're harder to heal. So what if we give Ton and Jukes immunity necklaces for each of those two curses? They can equip one and break the other down and socket it to preserve the power. They're both going to be taking the most damage while requiring the most healing, and we can nullify those amplifying right away."

Darling grimaced. "Still leaves the whole raid more susceptible to damage while also being harder to heal. And what about Spectral Kin? If any of these bosses create adds, then that could be devastating."

"True." I raised my voice. "Quick show of hands, if you guys don't mind? How many of you have execute-style abilities?"

We had thirteen damage dealers in all, and seven people raised their hands, including Darling and me.

I looked her way, excitement growing. "Any chance you have seven immunity necklaces for the Spectral Kin curse?"

She dug through the charms. "No, but I have five."

"That could work! What if we form a kill group?"

"One that Frank could lead," Frank said.

I almost told him to pipe down, but then I started thinking about it. "Actually, yeah. You could do that."

"I'm understanding less and less of what you're suggesting," Darling said.

"So, look. We put the five strongest people with executes into a single group and give them all charms for immunity to Spectral Kin. Then whenever a target drops below 30%, we have every other damage dealer rotate to something else while the kill group burns the target down. Or 10%, the threshold can be whatever you think is best. But as long as people with immunity charms are getting the actual killing blows, then we can dodge that curse completely."

I tapped Frank. "And I think this guy would actually be deeply invested in calling out target swaps for us."

"I'll be so deep in that that you're gonna think I'm spelunking."

I laughed.

Darling bit her lower lip. "That still leaves us with Vertebrae and Ultimatum."

"Yeah. What do you think there? I've got a preference for which I think we should break of those two, but I'd like to hear your thoughts first."

"Vertebrae for sure. Positional requirements are just too much. We don't have a ton of charms for that one, and with our group being half-melee, we can't exactly be sending them across the room before something dies to avoid having it explode."

"Agree completely. And at least Ultimatum only triggers when players die rather than mobs. Solution's easy there: don't die."

"Okay. Anybody have anything else to add?"

"Sorry, I wasn't listening," Nina said.

"Anybody have anything useful to add?" Darling clarified. "No? Alright then. We're going to break the Hex of Flying Vertebrae and then we're off and running."

She shuffled the groups around a little bit and put herself and me into the same five-person section of the twenty-person raid.

"Group 1 is the kill group," she said. "You're going to be listening and responding as usual, but if Frank calls out a target, I need you guys on it unless you're absolutely sure that you're needed elsewhere.

"Everybody else, I want you automatically peeling off targets as soon as they drop below 5% unless it's a boss or somebody calls out otherwise. We clear?"

Before anyone could respond, an alert came in, and the collective groan that went up told me everything that I needed to know before I'd even had a chance to read it myself.

**World-first Alert! The Guild {Corruptia} is the first guild to clear the {Trophy Garden} encounter and has been awarded an additional 3 days to claim the Worldbranch Throne!**

# Chapter Forty-One

Everybody started talking at the same time, and I shared a quick glance with Darling.

"Focus up," she said. "Doesn't matter. If anything, we're still in a good position here. It took almost a full day for them to drop the first boss, then another for the second. They'll probably take at least that long for the third, so we should have a solid window, and I doubt anybody else is rolling in like we are with a full group of people rocking Trinkets. We've got this."

The murmurs died down.

Darling stepped up to Isabel and tapped the symbol for the Hex of Flying Vertebrae. The icon flashed red for a moment, and when it cleared, the symbol was gone and the debuff had been cleared from my nameplate.

"Alright, Isabel!" Darling said. "We're ready."

The ghost nodded. "There are three routes through the ruins. The left-most gate is the most circuitous route by far, but you won't find as many of my husband's creations there.

"The middle gate is the most direct route, where you can expect the most opposition, and the right-most gate offers a compromise between the two. Please take your pick."

I took a long step toward the middle gate. "If Corruptia was able to clear this first encounter a full day ago, then we should be able to blow through the trash and absolutely smash it. I'm voting middle."

"Middle!" Nina agreed, then everybody was talking at once.

Darling went up to the middle gate and put a hand to it. When she did, a mechanism sounded from somewhere on the other side. The gate crept up into the ceiling and revealed more of the dark, snow-choked ruins beyond.

The massive, spectral mammoth we'd seen earlier was already patrolling in our direction, brightening the street as it went.

I did a quick rune check and made a couple of swaps and refreshes in quick succession: I went Caustic Raven and Ghostly Hunt on my pistols for the stacking debuff and the extra damage to undead, plus the possibility of adding a bit of extra healing with the latter rune.

And since we'd be clearing quite a bit of trash, I reupped my piercing rune on my rifle but went Ghostly Hunt on my blunderbuss since the weapon already cleaved.

I'd probably be changing those before long, but I had plenty of extras stored away and I was thinking we'd probably be doing some pretty good-sized pulls after choosing the most difficult route.

"Alright, Jukes and Ton to the front!" Darling said. "I'm in the execute group, so I'll have Rock handling the loot as we go to free my movement up. Handing it out should be easy enough, the trash group said it's mostly set pieces that drop out here, so it should be pretty cut and dry when it comes to who gets what. You guys ready for this?"

Ton stepped to the front of the group and thumped his sword against his shield. "Ready."

Jukes rolled out beside him. "Ready as I'm gonna be!"

Darling drew both of her axes, then pointed one through the gate. "Then let's move, full speed ahead!"

The group cheered as Ton and Jukes took off into the ruins and we fell in behind them, with the melee users in front and the ranged players and healers taking up the rear. The snow wasn't quite as deep as I'd expected, with maybe an inch or two covering the road, but the cobbles were icy beneath it.

The palace was way off, squatting atop its hill, its high walls covered in iridescent runes that were scrawled in the same garish colors as the symbols that Isabel had conjured earlier.

Up ahead, the patrolling mammoth seemed to notice the coming surge, and it raised its trunk high into the air and blared a warning. Then it charged, snow flying beneath and behind it.

{Spectral Mammoth} (Level 14 Undead) (Elite+)
HP: 55,000/55,000
MP: 22,000/22,000

Ton bellowed a war cry, and the mammoth adjusted its path slightly as it focused on him. He activated the same leap that I'd seen him use before, but this time he led with his shield, and as soon as he hit his apex he flashed and streaked down toward the ground like a meteorite with his shield held in front of him.

He landed some ten feet short of the charging mammoth, and the street cratered around him as the force of his impact pushed the cobbles several inches into the ground in a perfect circle around him.

I thought his attack had missed for a moment, but then the paving stones in front of him flew free, snow and all, and a wave of force surged forward and completely arrested the beast's charge.

Then he and Jukes were on it, with Ton taking the mammoth head on while Jukes slipped around behind it and went to work with his staff.

The rest of the melee circled around and went to work as I entered pistol range and the other spellcasters and ranged damage dealers took aim.

I popped Doppelganger right away and laid into the mob with green and gold-flecked ravens, striking it for amounts that ranged from 550 to nearly 1,100 on a critical strike.

In the meantime, the great creature had lashed its trunk at Ton, wrapped it around his waist, then threw the tank straight through our ranks.

Jukes activated Hateful Ice the moment Ton's feet left the ground. With the rune I'd given him in place, his staff sprouted two massive iron balls on either end, and a steely layer of gray ice swept out from around him, running right over the snow.

Aggro snapped to him, the group continued without missing a beat, and the beast dropped below half Health before Ton even had a chance to rejoin the fight.

I kept the blasts coming, and the bleak ruins strobed with color as the spells and projectiles splashed in and a thick stream of damage readouts scrolled above the creature's head.

The beast reared up onto its hind legs as it dropped beneath 33%, then slammed down onto the street. A low shockwave rolled out from the impact and caught most of our melees unaware, though the great bulk of the healers and the ranged players managed to jump it easily enough and avoid the effect.

"Execute range!" Frank shouted. "Unless you're on Team Frank, you're gonna peel off at 5%!"

"So I'm on Team Frank after all, huh?" I said, laughing the words as I loosed another round of spells and pushed my way farther down the street, circling around the mammoth and toward the palace.

"Yeah yeah, you squeaked through on a technicality."

"You heard him!" Darling said. "These mobs are easy enough! We've got two more of 'em patrolling our way, so once this one hits 5%, I want Jukes and everybody outside of Team Frank and the healers in Group 2 to move on and engage the next mobs! We're chain pulling for as long as we can manage it!"

Jukes rolled away as the beast's Health plummeted, and a large chunk of the raid streamed off behind him as Ton seamlessly picked up the aggro with a taunt and the mammoth dropped into the low single digits.

"Pst," Frank said. "What part of execute range didn't you understand?"

I dropped my pistols to my sides and waited as the mammoth's Health bar fell further.

"Hello? Earth to Ned? I'm loath to encourage you to throw more birds, but what the hell are you doing up there?"

When the mob's Health ticked down to 1%, I whipped my pistols up and released a Dark Harvest, followed by two glowing ravens. The spells hit home, and a good chunk of the damage was wasted as overkill, but all I'd really been after was the killing blow.

"You just stole that kill, didn't you?"

"I sure did."

My hands felt hot all of a sudden, and I looked down to find oily black flames running up and down the barrels of my pistols.

A new prompt I'd never seen before had just popped up.

**Killing Blow secured! Dread Armament ability {Dreadflight Cannon} is now available!**
**Charges: 1**

Jukes had already engaged the next mammoth about 60 yards ahead, so I bolted that way and activated the ability.

And the weight of the colossal weapon that popped into my hands nearly sent me sprawling face-first into the street.

The cannon was absolutely massive. It had a smooth, dark barrel that was widest at the base, narrow at the mid-point, then flared slightly at the end, and I was holding it with two hands as if it were a minigun: it looked like I'd just ripped a cannon off one our Gunboats and was now carrying it around.

I jogged forward, feeling sluggish but absolutely amped to fire the thing for the first time.

"That weapon cuts your speed by 30%," Frank said. "Mammoth up ahead is already at 85%. Hurry it up. You gotta get me into position so I can keep yelling at people."

I nodded and scoped the weapon out as I ran along. Right away, I could tell that the targeting was different: there was a circular, green reticle on the ground in front of me that was bobbing along as I ran, occasionally shifting forward a bit then falling back as the barrel bounced up and down.

I got into range, then squared my feet and tipped the barrel up. The targeting reticle slid forward, so I increased the angle until the ground beneath the mammoth was glowing green and the beast was fully in my crosshairs.

When I fired, the snow blew off the street for five yards around me in every direction, and the deafening explosion that followed was so loud that heads turned my way even as the spells continued to fly.

The cannon bucked in my hand and I skidded backward down the street, heels sliding against the slush-covered cobbles.

The largest raven I'd ever seen ripped out of the flared barrel and flew up at a steep, curving angle. It crested then arced down like a howitzer, shrieking as it dove directly at the mammoth.

It plunged right through the spectral beast and exploded as it hit the ground, throwing feathers and piled snow and even cobblestones aside as a massive, yellow number drifted up above the beast's head: 1,451.

I gawked at it for a long moment, the cannon hot in my hands, then the weapon vanished and my pistols reappeared and replaced it. I staggered backward again as the weight vanished.

"Oh, I like that," I said as I raised my weapons. "I like that a lot."

"Don't forget to combo in the other weapons before you fire it," Frank said. "You were missing a lot of potential power there."

"Right, thanks."

I stalked closer, pistols barking, spells flying, before I spotted a familiar blue glow creeping across the roofs to the left.

"We've got incoming from the left!"

A trio of ghostly lizards skittered off the roofs and down the sides of the nearest buildings. They were heavily scaled, and a diaphanous fin ran down the length of each of their backs.

Ton peeled off the mammoth and leaped between the three of them, the ground fragmenting beneath him as Jukes rolled in and grabbed the mammoth's attention.

The heavily armored tank caught a tail whip with his shield, then batted one of the creatures away as it snapped at its leg, jaws flashing. He backpedaled, shield held high as he dragged all three of the new arrivals toward the mammoth so the raid could cleave them all down at once.

The spells changed, then, as those with area of effect spells made it rain fire and metal over a wide area, and the Health bars of all four mobs began to plummet.

Green slashes filled the air, first two, then four, then six, and I caught sight of Darling ducking between the mammoth's two back legs—only then to pop out and lay into all three of the lizards. The slashes pulsed, then exploded, and the mobs' Health bars visibly dropped.

All four of the creatures died one after the other, then both of the rooftops up ahead began to glow and Ton and Jukes were charging forward again, the entire raid was cheering and yelling, and despite Goon and the Siege and the prospect of losing everything, the next fight was all I could think about.

# Chapter Forty-Two

"Grouping!" I said, shouting the word as I shouldered my rifle and fired a Gravity Bird into an oncoming horde of small, ghostly monkeys.

The animals were weak—simple Elites with low Health pools and no skills to speak of—but their raw numbers had been giving us problems as we pushed through the earliest part of the Menagerie Wing and toward the first boss, especially when they attacked while we were trying to focus on something larger.

I detonated my Gravity Bird to pack the beasts up, and the AoE group that Darling had put together to deal with the near-constant surges of apes tore into the mobs and mowed them down with impressive speed while the rest worked a mammoth into execute range.

Once it was low, the bulk of the raid ran ahead to start the next pull while a handful of us stayed behind to drop it. But instead of engaging something up ahead, I saw the other raid members fan out while the guild chat lit up in green.

We finished what must have been the twentieth mammoth off and I ran to see what was up, slipping through the raid to the front of the line.

The street ended about twenty yards up ahead, terminating in an iron suspension bridge that spanned a wide, frozen moat. The palace loomed atop the hill on the other side of the span, runes pulsing across its high walls.

A massive pile of green, glowing bones rested at the halfway point of the suspension bridge. The pile was easily two stories tall and so wide that while the bridge was broad enough for three or four carriages to pass alongside one another, there was no room to step around the bones; if we wanted to cross, we'd be climbing right over them.

I stepped up beside Darling. "Glowbone Grim, right? First real encounter?"

"Gotta be," she said.

A broad hand clapped onto my shoulder, and I craned around to find Rock grinning down at me. Before I could ask what was up, he opened a trade window with me, slammed an item in, and immediately confirmed it.

The fourth piece of my Ghosthunter set. I threw it on straight away, then scoped it out.

{Ghosthunter's Vambraces}
Grade: D
Item Level: 47
Slot: Wrist
Type: Leather
Quality: Rare
Suggested Class: Shadewalker
Primaries: +10 Intelligence, +7 Dexterity, +5 Constitution
Secondaries: +3% Chance to Hit
Armor: +4%
Set Effect (2-piece): Active. While dual-wielding Enchanted Pistols, your Ravenblast is instant, and any pistol blast fired while out of combat is automatically Overcharged.
Set Effect (4-piece): Active. Ravenblasts fired from your rifle now spawn a burst of miniature ravens that scatter from each struck enemy and deal 20% of the initial blast's damage to all enemies within 5 yards.
Set Effect (6-piece): Sealed. Equip 5 pieces of the {Ghosthunter} set to reveal this effect and 6 to activate it.

I smiled down at the bracers, which were pale blue and lined with white fur about the cuff. "Thanks, Rock! Appreciate it, just turned my 4-piece on."

The big man inclined his head and moved down the line, no doubt handing out the rest of the loot he'd gathered up.

The amount of trash so far had surprised me. We'd already spent the better part of a half-hour inside the raid, but the loot and even the Experience had proved far better than I'd hoped.

Isabel drifted over to the near side of the bridge and spun about to address the group. "This is as far as I can take you for now. Good luck."

Then she vanished.

Darling moved forward but stopped where the cobbles met the iron bridge. "That feels like a confirmation of what's ahead. Alright everybody, here we go! Keep those curses in mind—especially the Dreadking's Ultimatum: if you die, you're fearing everyone around you, so try to spread out if you can, especially if you know you're going down. And if there are adds, leave the actual kills to Team Frank."

"Team Frank!" Frank shouted.

Jukes rolled into position to Darling's right, and Ton rumbled up to her left.

Darling drew both of her weapons from where they hung on her back. "We're gonna have Ton take the initial aggro and go from there." She tapped the air, probably checking her frames. "We're going in fifteen seconds, so eat and drink up if you need to."

I stepped a little closer to the bridge. The railings on either side had fallen away, so there wasn't anything to stop us from running off the sides and plummeting into the frozen moat below.

The ice looked solid, but after what we'd gone through with Delugia and the sharks that had shadowed the beast's every step, I was worried about what lay beneath.

I traced the length of the suspension cords that stretched high to either side of the bridge. The iron span had four towers in all, two to either side, and the twin cords had little walkways atop them.

Darling counted down the final seconds. "Three. Two. One. Let's move!"

Ton and Jukes stepped onto the iron bridge and headed forward side by side while the rest of us hung slightly behind, with Darling leading the melee crew in front.

A cold breeze kicked up, and all four of the towers bent to the left like trees in the wind. The iron structure groaned and shifted, moving so violently beneath us that both Ton and Jukes paused their advance.

But the gale passed, and the tanks moved on at a nod from Darling. They reached the wide pile of bones, paused again, then scrambled up it, one on either side, white skulls and femurs and whole, skeletal hands rolling down behind them.

Once they made it to the top of the stack, they stared around, then briefly vanished from sight as they climbed down the other side.

The breeze picked up again, blowing from the opposite direction this time. The pile shifted, bones and skulls tumbling free with no apparent cause.

A moment later, Jukes and Ton reappeared atop the pile, weapons out.

"Pile's bigger than it looks from your side," Jukes said. "The bones stretch all the way off the bridge. Probably a foot deep and kinda hard to move through."

"Did you guys see that?" Darling said.

"See what?" Ton said.

Again the pile shifted, bones clattering down from a small hill that nobody was standing remotely close to.

Then the mound lifted a full foot between the two tanks, linked together into a dome or something like it, and somehow held. Eight orange circles formed beneath the bony crown, all of them lined up in a neat, horizontal row.

They blinked, and all hell broke loose as the pile of bones parted and something massive emerged from beneath its hiding place.

The creature's great, bulbed head rose first, its entire width circumscribed with orange eyes with three beaked mouths opening and clicking beneath them.

My first thought was that we were dealing with some kind of octopus or something similar, and when the bones shifted in several places at once and eight long, whip-thin limbs coiled up from beneath the pile and rose around the bulb, I knew I had the right of it.

The beast was spectral like the mammoths before it, but it had a bright green skeleton of linked bones beneath, and the bulb itself resembled a circular cage with the eyes equally spaced around it.

I inspected it as the creature curled four of its rear tentacles beneath its bulk and rose high above the bridge.

{Glowbone Grim} (Level 16 Undead) (Raid Boss)
HP: 690,000/690,000
Tentacles remaining: 8
Time before next Regeneration: 2 minutes.

Ton bellowed a taunt, and the fight was on.

The creature spun in place, beaks rotating, orange eyes blurring to a thin, eerie line. Two of its tentacles whipped out and lashed the tank as he approached.

He managed to block both of the Grim's strikes, but the twin impacts sent him reeling to his left, then to his right.

Jukes' approach seemed better suited to the task as he rolled beneath a high sweep and hurdled a lower attack.

I held my breath for a moment, watching Ton's Health drop and rise as I waited for Darling's signal to indicate the tank had gathered enough aggro for the fight to truly begin.

"Burn it!" Darling said.

I opened fire as the melees charged in and the ranged group got to work. And as soon as the first volley connected, it became clear that we were in trouble.

Every single spell and projectile passed right through the bulb and exited harmlessly through the other side.

I watched, uncomprehending, as the melee group tried to get behind the creature to avoid the three front-most tentacles that were lashing Jukes and Ton simultaneously.

Nina was the quickest to edge around it, and one of the rear tentacles rewarded her effort by spearing down faster than she could react and coiling around her waist. It raised her high into the air, then flicked her down and off the bridge with unbelievable speed.

She smashed through the ice and disappeared beneath, her Health halving at the moment of impact. She left a dark hole behind, and the ice was clear enough that I was able to see her swimming beneath it.

Two more players who'd also tried to get around to the creature's back via the other side of the bridge thumped down in rapid succession, punching right through the frozen expanse in the same way and torpe-doing through the water below.

I targeted one of the three front tentacles while several other ranged users came to similar conclusions.

They each had Health bars as well, sizable pools that sat at 80,000 Health apiece. My first raven connected solidly with the tentacle's glowing skeleton, and a yellow 560 floated up above the strange limb.

Seeing this, Darling set a red flame icon above the center-most tentacle.

"Full burn on my mark, everybody off the head! Melee, this is gonna be rough for us, but we need to stay in front for now!"

I stacked my debuff up and kept firing, surveying the battlefield and trying to piece the fight together.

Nina and one of the other players who'd been tossed down were both climbing out of the holes they'd made in the ice, but the third player seemed to have gotten disoriented and was swimming in the wrong direction.

I dropped a message into the guild chat and told her to swim toward the explosion because she wouldn't hear me beneath the ice, then fired a blast off the side of the bridge and right into the hole. She spun at once and swam right for it.

Nina and the other player scrambled across the ice, scaled the riverbank, then rejoined the fight.

"Water's pitch black beneath!" Nina said as she blew by me and sprinted back into the fight. "No adds down there, but you can't see anything, and there are glowing circles on the bottom that look just like the hole you make when you fly in!"

"I can mark them!" I said, and a prompt scrolled across the bottom of my screen that said Darling had granted me the permissions I needed.

"Middle tentacle is falling fast," Frank said. "Both tanks are holding up, but the healers are having to pour it on to keep Ton up against two of the three."

I kept my focus on the middle limb as it speared down into Ton's proffered shield three times in a row before batting him away and to the left and lancing out at Jukes.

The diminutive tank twisted at the last minute, bending over backward as the glowing limb stabbed out over him, then raised itself high into the air.

He lost his balance and landed on his back, and the tentacle he'd been keeping at bay rose up high, then slammed its entire length down in his direction. He rolled sideways, regained his feet, and went back to work.

"Middle tentacle is falling really fast!" Frank said. "Really, really fast! Regeneration timer is down to thirty seconds!"

To my left, the third player had finally climbed out of the frozen river, but the hole she had clambered back out of was smaller than I remembered. I glanced over the other side of the bridge where Nina had landed, and sure enough, hers had already frozen over completely.

Frank's words clicked then, or at least I thought—hoped—I knew what he was getting at. I scanned the boss again, eyeing the Regeneration timer.

The mob swept one of its rear tentacles across the battlefield and punted three of the melees right off the side of the bridge. The impact wasn't enough to send them through the ice, but they'd be out of the fight for a little while.

And that was it: the creature was delaying us, taking people out of the fight one at a time. I stared at the middle limb as it fell into execute range and its Health started plummeting.

"Everybody stay on the burn target!" Darling said. "The killing blow curse doesn't do anything against Raid Bosses!"

"Wait!" I called out. "If we drop that, it's gonna come right back—look at the timer!"

Darling's eyes flicked skyward, and I heard her curse over the scrum.

"What if we wear all three of these front ones down and finish them right after the timer ticks over?" I said, still blasting away.

But before Darling could respond, the monster brought two more of its tentacles around and raised five of them high into the air. The bones within them flashed from green to blue, and lines of red light lit up the battleground in five neat columns with several feet of empty space between them.

I dashed sideways into the nearest empty space and watched in horror as the beast brought all five limbs down with terrible force.

One of the tentacles slammed down mere inches to my left, and the force of its passing created a breeze that rippled my clothes. At the same time, a second tentacle slammed down a few feet to my right.

And in my periphery, four Health bars dropped from full to as low as 20% as the attack caught a few players off-guard and smashed them against the iron bridge.

The healers were quick, and Ton and Jukes weren't taking damage as the beast raised its many limbs for another round, but I could almost feel the healing reduction curse at work as the gold and green spells rained in to diminished effect.

Thankfully the group adjusted well, and every single person managed to avoid the second wave of falling strikes.

The middle tentacle fell beneath 10%, then the flame icon Darling had been using to mark it as the raid's main target vanished and reappeared on the tentacle to the right that Jukes was tanking.

We trained our fire on that one, and I watched the Regeneration timer tick down into the low single digits, then zero out.

And as I'd hoped, nothing happened. The timer simply reset to 2 minutes and started ticking down once more. The pattern repeated from there, and we worked the second and third tentacles down to 10% without losing anyone.

As the third limb dropped into the single digits and the Regeneration timer reset again, Darling's voice rose above the clamor.

"Full burn, left to right!"

I aimed two more blasts at the target she'd called out, then followed up with a Dark Harvest. The heavily damaged limb popped like a grape beneath the force of a half-dozen other executes plus other spells, and I blessed my luck for being the one whose damage spike had finished it off, granting me a single use of my cannon.

The bones that had been anchoring the limb fell free and clattered to the ground, rejoining the pile. I held onto the cannon charge for now and focused on the second limb, eyeing the timer all the way.

Darling had timed the reset well, and I just had to hope that my guesses about the encounter were correct as the second and third tentacles fell and the timer ticked ever lower.

The Grim raised itself high and spun in place, its great bulb rotating, eyes spinning, a second beak sliding into view.

"Boss just lost 240,000 Health," Frank said. "80,000 per tentacle that fell."

I called that out right away—if anything, that cemented what I thought was going on: it was now a race against the timer, and we'd given ourselves a bit of a leg up to start.

"Great!" Darling said. "Keep—"

She cut off as one of the two remaining rear tentacles snatched her up. She dropped one of her axes, and I thought it was an accident on her part until the monster chucked her, just as it had Nina, only for Darling to reappear in a crouch on the bridge, clutching her fallen weapon.

Three similar attacks followed, and I was so busy trying to track everybody's movements and get ready to mark their holes in the ice that I didn't notice I'd also been targeted until a length of glowing bone wrapped around my hip and yanked me skyward.

It wound up to throw me off the right side of the bridge, but I was ready after seeing what Darling had done, and I activated Clonedrift the very moment the beast released me.

I canceled the spell immediately to kill my momentum, then dropped toward the knot of melee players who were grouped up and swinging away a few feet from Ton and Jukes and the unending, battering assault the tanks were under.

I Water Jetted myself back to a ranged distance and scanned the frozen river while airborne. I rolled to my feet and threw up a marker for each of the players who had gone under, placing a bright golden arrow in the center of each hole in the ice to mark a potential exit.

The targeted players oriented right away, burning movement abilities to reach their exits far more quickly than the last group had. We kept up the pressure, but the Regeneration timer finally clicked over.

Maybe thirty long bones rose from the pile and snapped together one after the next. And within seconds, the five remaining tentacles became six, and I saw the boss' Health lurch back up by 80,000.

But instead of joining the assault, the regenerated tentacle dove directly into the deepest part of the bone pile and began pulsing with eerie, greenish light.

The skulls in that area lit up like jack-o'-lanterns, their eye sockets and noses and mouths bursting alight one by one.

A Health bar popped up above one of the skulls, so I inspected one of the creatures as soon as I could, though whatever was coming hadn't yet fully formed and couldn't be targeted.

**{Skeletal Man-o'-war} (Level 16 Undead)**
**HP: 5,000/5,000**

"We've got adds for Team Frank!" I said. "Low Health pools, non-Elites, but I can't tell how many!"

"Team Frank!" Frank repeated.

"Everybody keep burning my mark for now!" Darling said as the first skull rose into the air.

Stray bones of every discernable type flew up to meet it, and the end result was positively grisly: a greenish, floating skull with spines and hands and long bones trailing down like the tentacles of a jellyfish.

Once they'd all fully formed, the creatures pulsed and rocketed up into the sky, then drifted over and across the battlefield. The five floating monsters were a ghastly sight, but they were all well out of range for my rifle.

The regenerated tentacle retracted from the pile once the five Man-o'-

Wars had flown off, and it too had changed: instead of simply narrowing to a tip like the other tentacles, it pulled free sporting a square sledge made of tightly compacted bone.

I kept the damage coming, alternating glances between the wicked weapon that the latest tentacle was sporting and the bony creatures drifting above us. I didn't like the way they were moving; there was a purposeful look to the paths they were taking overhead, as if they were tracking our movements from above.

Then one of the creatures pulsed and dropped out of the sky. Zoe was standing directly beneath it, her hands raised as she sent literal waves of healing rolling across the bridge and cresting over Ton and Jukes.

"Zoe, move!" I shouted, but too late.

The bony creature speared down around her, its spindly limbs punching deep into the iron beneath and forming a tight cage that hemmed her in on every side. The hammer tentacle rose high into the air, and the beast's every eye flicked to Zoe.

She gripped the skeletal bars of the cage and tried to pull them apart, but to no avail.

"I'm trapped, silenced too!"

I popped Doppelganger and dashed forward, then lit the cage up with a pair of pistol blasts and swapped to my blunderbuss as I closed in. I leaped, activated Repel, and kicked out with my full weight behind the blow.

The cage didn't even budge, and the impact knocked me off balance. I recovered and followed up with two quick blasts from my blunderbuss, then swapped to the Dreadflight Cannon and burned my lone charge to fire a shot at close to point-blank range.

My cannon blast struck for an incredible 1,720 damage, but even with my other spells it wasn't nearly enough—nobody else had managed to help in time—and the hammer fell.

The glowing skull atop the cage shattered, and the tentacle drove its sledge down through it with terrible force, spraying bits of bone in every direction.

Zoe died instantly, and I and maybe six melee players who were nearby because they'd been moving to help were sent fleeing across the bridge as the Dreadking's Ultimatum curse kicked in and feared everyone who'd been standing near her.

The fear effect pathed me to the left and sent me right off the bridge, which made me far more fortunate than those who were sent toward the

Grim, who plucked them up one by one and threw them down through the ice and deep into the water below.

Unable to place my markers or even watch the battle unfold from my position beneath the bridge, I watched Health bars instead and saw three of them gray out before the fear effect expired.

Once I regained control, I dropped markers for the holes that I could see, then vaulted back up onto the bridge with a Water Jet and scoped out the other side for the rest of the raid, dropping markers there as well.

"Fourth tentacle just dropped," Frank said. "Timer at 45 seconds."

"Steady!" Darling said. "At this rate we'll get it done, but it's gonna be close!"

I eyed the floating Man-o'-Wars, who were still drifting high overhead. "Cages are an instakill if you get trapped and nobody helps, gotta be quick too!"

"Kill group, that's your focus!"

"Team Frank!" Frank shouted for at least the third time.

The raid steadied out a little bit, but while Jukes' Health was holding up pretty well, Ton's was beginning to creep a bit lower with each spike of damage.

I kept up the spells as the fight wore on, and while the group managed to drop the fourth, fifth, and sixth tentacles without losing anyone else, another regenerated and came back sporting a wicked crescent of bone that was easily five feet long, and the next Regeneration wasn't far off.

"Boss at 290,000," Frank said as the beast rotated again after we'd killed off another limb. "You've dropped seven in total, but you've still got three more to deal with."

And to make matters worse, two of the three that remained were the especially deadly hammer and blade variants that had already regenerated.

"On my mark!" Darling said as she threw the flame icon up on the bladed tentacle. "Burning the bladed one, it's carving the tanks up!"

"Cage!" Frank yelled.

I spotted one falling in my periphery, and I raised a pistol and managed to get a Gravity Bird between the falling Man-o'-War and the spellcaster who was unlucky enough to be underneath it.

The black hole erupted a few feet above the player's head and pulled the mob in, which gave the caster plenty of time to adjust his position and get out from underneath it.

The Gravity Bird faded, the mob knifed into the bridge, and the great beast raised its hammer and pulverized the empty cage.

"Nice!" Darling called out. "Control them if you can, we need all the damage we can get! We're starting to fall behind on the timer!"

I checked it out, and she was spot on: the third tentacle was about to drop, but the timer would be bringing another one back soon after.

The damage that Ton and Jukes were taking had visibly increased as well; it seemed like the weapons that the regenerated limbs sported were significantly more deadly on top of the mechanics they introduced.

I swallowed, not liking the way the fight was going. But then another limb dropped and a few cheers went up, and I buckled down and went back to work.

With the pattern down again, we eliminated the bladed limb as well and got down to our final target a few seconds before another regenerated and dove into the pile.

"This is it!" Darling said. "This is our window!"

The regenerated tentacle emerged sporting a wrecking ball made of bone, its surface spiked with chips and sharpened fragments. The Grim raised the weapon high and brought it down in the center of the battlefield.

I was nearby but I'd been watching the sky for falling Man-o'-Wars, so I saw the attack coming and quickly stepped away. The two other damage dealers in range were a bit slower to react and had to burn a leap and a sprint respectively to get away, letting the heavy blow strike an empty section of the bridge—and punch right through it.

The beast pulled the weapon free and left a gaping hole behind, through which the ice below was visible.

I expected the creature to return to its earlier pattern, but it struck with the weapon again. The wrecking ball limb was slower than the others, and its attacks were easy to read and even easier to avoid, but it was making an absolute ruin of the bridge.

And it wasn't long before one of our damage dealers got distracted and walked right into one of the holes. The effect wasn't catastrophic—he simply fell through and took a bit of fall damage against the ice—but having to wait for him to climb back into position cost us precious time and damage, and the regen timer was becoming a serious concern.

"Cage!" Frank yelled.

I raised a pistol but Rock was already in the air, a fist cocked back and glowing blue. He met the falling Man-o'-War ten feet above the bridge and struck, and the attack sent the mob flying off the bridge and shattering into a pile of loose bones atop the ice.

"Great catch!" Darling said as the wrecking ball fell yet again. "Watch your footing and try not to group up, I know it's getting harder but—"

She cut off as the beast slammed the wrecking ball down near her position, where the bulk of the melees were hacking away. Everybody was quick enough to scatter, but I flinched as the melees surged to the beast's left and right, expecting the Grim to lift them up into the air and toss them away.

But it didn't.

"There's no extra limbs to toss!" I said. "We can rotate and use the other side!"

"Ton and Jukes, stay put!" Darling said. "Everybody else, slip around the back!"

I dashed forward, birds flying as I hopped a hole in the bridge, the ice gleaming beneath me. I gave the two tanks a wide berth and swung around to the creature's back with the rest of the raid, then kept running to get some distance from the melees.

"Healers are getting low on Mana," Frank said. "This is gonna be tight."

"Window's under one minute and rapidly closing! Pop everything you've got! If we let one more tentacle regenerate, we're done for!"

The wrecking ball was still flying, driving into the bridge time and time again, but between the relatively unscathed section of the bridge behind the Grim and the fact that our melees no longer had to worry about catching a stray blow while fighting beside Ton and Jukes, we managed to finish off the hammer tentacle.

Now that the wrecking ball was the only limb left, it dropped out of its previous pattern and started trading blows with Ton, allowing the healers to focus on him and presenting the melee group with even more chances to land an attack.

The last tentacle's Health bar fell, plummeting even as our tanks stabilized.

"Boss at 130,000!" Frank said. "If the pattern holds, there's still gonna be work to do when this limb drops!"

"Thanks!" Darling said. "Keep it up everybody!"

I blocked another falling cage with a Gravity Bird and a Repel to send it flying away before it could land, then focused in and watched the last limb's Health drop below 20%, below 10%, below 5%.

The Regeneration timer only had ten seconds remaining. The limb was going to fall first, but it wasn't going to matter if another sprung right up behind it; the healers were all working with slivers of their Mana pools, and the only reason the tanks hadn't died so far was because of how much the boss' damage had dropped with only a single limb to swing around.

Nevertheless, a cheer went up as the limb finally curled away and the bones that held it together dropped free and rattled down onto what was left of the bridge.

But I didn't have the heart to join them: I was watching the Regeneration timer tick down.

Then thankfully, blessedly, it grayed out completely.

"All eight limbs are down and the timer's off!" I said, even as the melees surged in to target the bulb directly. The beast still had 50,000 Health, but it was falling fast.

Then all of the creature's eyes brightened at once and the bone pile shifted once more.

"New phase, gotta be near the end!" Darling said. "Call out what you see!"

Loose skulls rose into the air from all across the mount of bones, their sockets burning with orange light.

The Grim's many eyes flared, and orange beams of light linked each of its many pupils to several of the floating skulls at once.

The beams solidified into lasers that hung at levels that varied from shin-high to a foot above my head, breaking the battlefield into countless sections with beams between them. Then the Grim began to spin in place once again, and both the skulls and the lasers rotated with it, turning the bridge into a rotating field of multi-level hazards.

I stepped over a low beam and loosed a pair of spells, then ducked another laser and backpedaled out beyond the most distant skull. That took me beyond the range of the mechanic, and I was about to shout out that getting more distance was a possibility to the rest of the ranged group when I felt something curl around my ankle.

I glanced down to see a skeletal hand tightening its grip around my right leg while a second reached for my left. More of them were heading my way too, crawling over the pile like spiders. I raised my pistols to blow it away, but it yanked hard and ripped me off my feet.

I fell forward, so I activated Clonedrift to shake the hand off and canceled the spell right away, then rolled right back into the laser field as I hit the ground.

"Can't back out!" I said. "Hands will grab you and knock you down. No idea what happens if they dogpile you, but it can't be good!"

"Grim at 35,000 and falling fast," Frank said.

"Healers are out of Mana!" Darling said. "You catch a beam and you're on your own!"

The rotating boss picked up speed as it fell beneath 30,000 Health, and the lasers started coming so quickly that many of the melees up close were starting to struggle to get their attacks in with all the dodging that was required just to survive.

Our spellcasters were better off, but those with longer casts were having a hard time, and it wasn't long before someone got greedy and tried to squeeze a spell into too tight of a window.

One moment the caster in question—a player in black robes capped by blue shoulder pads—was crafting an orb of lightning that was floating between his outstretched hands, and the next he was little more than a pile of burning clothes resting atop the bridge.

The Dreadking's Ultimatum activated again, and while we were lucky at first as there was only one player anywhere near the caster who'd died, I could already picture the chain reaction to come: the feared player was going to run randomly across the battlefield and straight into one of the lasers, and the effect would spread from there until the entire raid was scattering into the rotating beams and melting left and right.

So when the feared player ran directly to my left, I Water Jetted myself right at him. I twisted in the air, reaching for him with a hand out. As soon as I made contact, I activated Clonedrift and sent us both zooming right off the bridge.

One of the lasers sliced my clone in half at the waist, and it burst apart as I fell. The caster and I slammed into the ice and he scrambled to his feet immediately, the unbreakable fear effect making him thrash and kick all over the place.

I disentangled myself and ran across the ice, half-sprinting, half-sliding, then scrambled up the bank and rejoined the fight as the beast ticked down beneath 10,000 Health.

"All melees fall back!" Darling said as the beast began spinning even more quickly. "Lasers are rotating too fast up close, so ranged, it's all on you!"

Two quick blasts refreshed my caustic debuff, and I held my breath as I watched the melees scatter around the spinning lasers.

The group made it all of ten feet before the first member got clipped and dropped, another fear bomb struck, and the chain reaction I'd been hoping to avoid finally began.

The effect was horrific: one death became three fleeing players, which became three deaths, which became five fleeing players, and suddenly almost the entire melee group was dead—including Darling herself—and a few of the ranged group who'd backed up to the edge of the fight had either been sent fleeing directly into the gauntlet of beams or had been cast into the moving pile of bones, where the skeletal hands were latching onto them and gradually dragging them deeper into the pile.

I switched to my rifle and activated Dark Harvest as I saw a player sink deep into the heaped bones, a skeletal hand clamped around their head and driving them down and in. The player sank in like it was quicksand and died on the spot.

"Hands are targetable!" Frank said. "400 Health each!"

And with that, I whipped around and loosed blasts rapid-fire at another of our ranged damage dealers who was being pulled under. I wasn't fast enough to save him, but I did manage three kills in quick succession.

I turned back to the Grim, hopped a low laser, then had to duck to keep my head from being taken off by the next. I planted my feet on the ground and summoned my cannon, then activated Doppelganger and Double Cast it for good measure.

I pointed the huge weapon up into the air and fired three high diving ravens, and each of my clones did the same, producing nine huge, screaming birds.

I tried to jump another low laser, but I'd made a mistake: I hadn't accounted for the movement speed reduction that the cannon applied, and while the heavy weapon vanished in mid-air and was replaced by my pistols, the beam deleted both of my clones as it swept in and raked across my shin.

My Health plummeted from full to 20% in a blink, and I landed off balance and had to throw myself to the ground to avoid the next sweeping laser.

Then the first of my three howitzer-style ravens hit home, and my eyes went wide as the damage amounts streamed in: 1,340, 1,360, and a colossal 2,450 crit.

More dark, feathery explosions followed as my clones' copied ravens dove into the ground rapid-fire, one after the other.

The mob's central bulb—that cage of bone and eyes—slowed its rotation, stopped, then dropped apart completely.

"Franked," Frank said.

# Chapter Forty-Three

The elevated skulls fell across the battlefield, shattering against the bridge or dropping into the holes the wrecking ball had made and smashing down against the ice beneath.

I lay there on the ground, holding my breath, refusing to relax until combat dropped and the prompts went out.

And when they did, only four of our twenty players were left standing: me, a pair of healers who were completely out of Mana, and the lightning mage I'd saved earlier with Clonedrift.

The four of us stayed silent, but the guild chat was moving so quickly that it was just a blur of green light, and the messages flooding in brought a smile to my face.

I sat up and holstered my pistols, then pulled my legs in beneath me.

"Man. That was way too close for a first boss."

"I can't believe you let Darling die," Frank said. "And you saved a mage, too."

"I didn't even see her drop, and I'm pretty sure that would have been the right call regardless with how the melees had to back off at the end."

I took a deep breath and pushed myself back to my feet, then surveyed the battlefield. The other side of the bridge was so pocked with holes that it was a miracle the span was still standing.

Isabel floated up through one of them and stared right by me, her gaze locked on the palace beyond. I could tell she was ready to speak but I ignored her, afraid I'd trigger something while the rest of the guild was corpse-running.

Rock was one of the first to respawn, and the big man nodded my way, then beelined for the pile of loot that was glowing within the bones the Grim had left behind.

Darling followed quickly thereafter before everybody else flooded back in, many of them dropping to the ground immediately to eat and drink.

She stepped up beside me. "Am I the only one who's a little worried by how close of a call that was?"

I shook my head. "Just said the same thing to Frank. To be fair, we still one-shotted it, but yeah. I kinda thought we'd cruise it, especially with our levels and gear since that fight was basically a damage check."

"I guess we could have done it better. Maybe we should have had the ranged focus on the back tentacles while melees worked down the front ones, then killed them all around the same time."

"Maybe, yeah." I shrugged. "Wouldn't surprise me if that changed the encounter though."

She licked her lips. "Any guesses for which curse I'm thinking we break next?"

I laughed. "Fear bomb?"

"Fear bomb. It's a little scary knowing the healers ran out of Mana on that fight, but I think I'd probably put that on Zoe dying early more than anything else. That put a lot of strain on the rest of the group with the healing reduction curse."

"For sure. I almost had her out in time, but man." I made a fist and slammed it into my palm. "Splat. That cage hammer combo was no joke."

"Yeah." Darling tapped the air. "Looks like everybody's back." She edged forward toward the ghost, who was still floating over a hole in the bridge. "Isabel?"

The apparition spun to face her. "You did very well." She drifted over to where the Grim had collapsed in on itself and reached deep into the pile, though the bones didn't so much as shift beneath her.

She pulled something bright out into the air, but it broke before I could get a good look at it. Isabel made a series of gestures, and the floating symbols we'd seen in that first room returned, though there were only four left for us to choose from.

"Make your choice carefully. Remember: you only get one selection."

Darling cleared her throat and looked around. "I'm breaking that fear bomb effect. Anybody disagree?"

A round of muttered complaints and low laughter followed, so Darling confirmed her choice and got rid of the curse for good.

Beyond the span and high above, several of the runes that were crawling across the palace's walls winked out.

"The outer barrier should now be weak enough for us to approach," Isabel said. "Come. I can feel my husband growing weaker." She drifted up and away.

"Is it just me, or is she giving you some weird vibes?" Darling said.

"Definitely."

We crossed the span together, and on the far side, the road rose into a series of curving switchbacks that led up to the wall. Darling moved in directly behind Isabel, so I let the melee group move forward and rejoined the ranged players.

"Another one," a gruff voice said to my left. "Epic too."

I glanced over and was surprised to find Rock there again. Another trade window followed, and he slammed another piece of my set into it.

It was a helm this time, and I threw it on immediately, desperate to finally get a look at what the 6-piece set offered, though I still needed the final piece to activate it.

{Ghosthunter's Helm}
Grade: D
Item Level: 50
Slot: Head
Type: Leather
Quality: Epic
Suggested Class: Shadewalker
Primaries: +18 Intelligence, +10 Dexterity, +10 Constitution
Secondaries: +2% Chance to Hit
Armor: +5%
Set Effect (2-piece): Active. While dual-wielding Enchanted Pistols, your Ravenblast is instant, and any pistol blast fired while out of combat is automatically Overcharged.
Set Effect (4-piece): Active. Ravenblasts fired from your rifle now spawn a burst of miniature ravens that scatter from each struck enemy and deal 20% of the initial blast's damage to all enemies within 5 yards.
Set Effect (6-piece): Sealed. You may now Clonedrift freely in any direction, and your Doppelganger ability now procs twice upon acti-

vation and offers increased control. Equip 6 pieces of the
{Ghosthunter} set to activate this effect.

"Thanks, Rock. I'm guessing you don't also have the final piece in your
inventory waiting for me, huh?"

He grinned, then shook his head and jogged off.

I dropped my voice. "Nice to hear him talking again. You like the 6-
piece? More of me, but more of you."

"At this point, that's a trade I'm willing to make."

"That feels like progress from where I'm standing."

"If by progress you mean I've grown to appreciate myself more and
more while my opinion of you has remained unchanged, then yes, things
have definitely progressed nicely."

"I have a hard time believing you had room to think more of yourself."

"Same, but I continue to surprise myself."

The raid started up the first of the switchbacks that led up the hill—
there were four curves in all—and as soon as Ton set foot onto the first
straightaway, a primal howl sounded from high above.

I whipped out my rifle as a tide of giant, spectral spiders swarmed
down from above, ignoring the roads and choosing instead to scramble
straight down the steep banks.

The mobs were small and weak—the strongest of them that I could see
was a level 15 Elite with 2,500 Health—but their numbers seemed absolutely endless.

I shouldered my rifle and took aim, readying an Overcharged blast as
the enemies poured down.

"Keep moving!" Darling said. "Tanks and melees, hug the cliffs and
protect the ranged. I want Ton and Jukes to drag their targets with them
as we go."

I waited for Jukes to activate Hateful Ice, and I couldn't help but grin
on his behalf when his steely wave went out and snared almost the entire
first group of arrivals and only left a few for Ton to pick up.

My cooldowns were back up, so I activated Doppelganger before I
released my blast, then Double Cast it again.

I fired a golden, piercing raven into the heart of the crowd that Jukes
had temporarily locked up, and all of my doppels did the same. And
thanks to the active 4-piece set, every single one of those piercing rifle
blasts also generated a small explosion of its own.

The combined effect was otherworldly: the three piercing blasts hit and pushed deep into the mass of spiders, each generating small explosions of birds that splashed damage and feathers across the packed creatures.

Three tightly spaced lines of monsters vaporized in front of Jukes even as he closed in on them, and while the gaps were quickly filled by more mobs, the way his head whipped around to figure out what the hell had hit them was deeply satisfying.

Frank grunted. "You're really just out here popping cooldowns on trash, huh?"

"Might as well," I said as the kills rained in and oily flames erupted along the length of my rifle. I switched to my cannon, raised it up so that the reticle was right around Jukes, then sent three howling ravens arcing high into the air.

I plodded along at the rear of the group as the birds screamed down. They exploded with incredible violence, launching ghostly bodies in every direction, and the mobs were melting so quickly overall that by the time Jukes or Ton had fully consolidated aggro, the entire pull was almost dead and one of them was already moving onto the next group to keep us moving smoothly up the switchbacks.

I kept the ravens flying as I jogged behind the group, grinning from ear to ear as every cannon blast wiped out a few of the most injured mobs and repeatedly restocked my charges.

We ripped up the switchbacks one by one, overwhelming the swarming monsters and leaving a wide trail of bodies behind.

Then another alert went out.

**World Alert! The Guild {Zul} is the second guild to clear the {Trophy Garden} encounter and has been awarded an additional 2 days to claim the Worldbranch Throne! No further extensions will be granted for clearing this encounter.**

The optimistic mood dimmed somewhat, but I was mostly relieved: I was afraid that it was going to be a World-first for a later boss rather than another kill of an earlier one. And while it was a little alarming to see another guild in the mix, I still felt like we had this, and a glance at Darling made me think she felt the same way.

We rounded the final switchback, and the flow of spiders died off as we reached the top of the hill the palace was built on. The grounds were absolutely enormous: huge snowfields extended for miles to my right and left, and a cobblestone street ran right through the middle, lined neatly with trees to either side.

All of the trees were heavy with snow, and several had lost limbs or even split in half beneath the weight of it.

Upon closer inspection, there were buildings set between the trees as well, dome-shaped structures that were either snow-covered or painted white or both, and the buildings blended in so well with the snowfields that it was difficult to pick them out from afar.

The avenue terminated in front of the palace's high walls at an iron gatehouse that was crawling with magical runes. I spotted movement atop the fortifications, and a horn sounded in the distance.

I turned around to see the ruined city stretched out beneath me, its fallen structures half-hidden by the snowdrifts that had blown up against them.

I spun back toward the palace, took a step, and nearly lost my balance as I dropped some six inches into the snow. I moved out of the depression and realized what I'd stepped into: a footprint that was longer than I was tall.

It looked distinctly avian, with two long toes in front and one behind, and the deeper holes that capped the footprint to either side suggested some truly wicked talons.

I shaded my eyes and tried to follow the path the prints had taken as they led off into the snowfield, but they seemed to disappear about twenty feet out.

"Let's keep it moving," Darling called out from up ahead. "We've got at least two guilds already working on the third boss."

The cannon popped out of my hands as my charges expired, so I sheathed the pistols that replaced it and jogged up to rejoin the group.

The ever-present gale worsened, whistling through the trees and lifting the fallen snow and driving it sideways into our faces. The visibility plummeted to the point where I could only see about ten feet in front of me, reducing the trees that lined the road to eerie shadows and the palace walls beyond to a dim, pulsing outline.

We reached the first of the domed structures, which opened like a cave that faced the road. The space within was pitch black, and I saw Darling and a few others go to check it out, so I ran in and Overcharged a Raven-blast with one of my pistols and held it for light.

A raised platform, maybe six inches of iron that rose neatly out of the floor, stood in the center of the room. Two strange, jagged bits of stone emerged from it, as if someone had started to cast a statue from the ground up and given up at the ankles.

Someone sucked in a sharp breath behind me, and I pivoted to find Darling tracing a gauntleted hand down the curved wall.

Twin slashes had been gouged into the stone, and cold air was coming through at the deepest points of the cut, which had managed to pierce all the way through the structure.

I moved my pistol around like a lantern and found the marks were everywhere, ranging from the very lowest section of the wall to a pair that cut neatly across the highest point of the dome directly overhead.

"What is going on here?" Darling said.

I pointed my glowing pistol at the elevated platform, and the light flared off something metallic. I knelt down and wiped it with my sleeve, revealing a small copper plate. It had a few lines of text that I could make out, so I read them aloud for the group.

"Twin—" I started.

"Twintalon Raptor," Frank said. "Killed by the Huntsman on the eighth moon of the second season. Can't make out the year." He shuddered violently at my hip. "Can you imagine?"

"Hunting a raptor?" I said, taken aback by his obvious fear.

"Having eight moons. Gah, the very thought is giving me the willies."

"I don't think that's what it means, Frank. And I'm pretty sure Jupiter has, like, ten times that many."

He dry-heaved. "Why would you... ugh—" He cut off, retching again. "I can't even talk about it."

"I'm pretty sure Europa is green, too. It's got a bunch of ice that glows in the dark. Think it's radiation or something like that."

"Hurrrp. Seriously, you gotta stop, or I'm gonna be painting your shoes and you're gonna be picking chunks out of my beard."

I grimaced, then eyed the two bits of jagged stone with new eyes. I gestured at the empty space above it.

"I think these domes are display areas. There should be something here, and I bet whatever left is the same thing that made those prints in the snow."

"Trophy Garden," Darling said, nodding. "So maybe—"

"We've got incoming!" Jukes said, voice booming into the small space.

I was the closest to the exit and was the first to make it back out onto the snowblown street. Jukes and Ton were standing to my right with their weapons drawn, and the guild was arranged behind them, with the melees in a tight knot and the ranged spread out behind them.

"What's up?" Darling said as she jogged out of the building.

Jukes pointed his staff down the road. "Something was running toward us, but it broke off between the trees at the last moment. I saw the nameplate."

"I didn't see it," Ton said.

Darling tapped the air. "Any idea what it was?"

As if in answer, Isabel drifted through the ranged group, her presence brightening the driving snow around her.

"I'm afraid it could have been anything. The Huntsman spent his youth scouring the world for the most fearsome creatures he could find and kill, and he spent the rest of his life trying to regain that feeling." She eyed the palace and sighed. "I suppose he succeeded in that, in a way. It's a shame he took the entire world down with him."

"The world?" I said.

"My husband's..." She trailed off, and I wondered if she'd misspoke. "In the end, his experiments broke something in the sky, in the earth. I don't know. It doesn't really matter at this point." She pointed at the domes. "These buildings are where his work began. But the Huntsman wasn't content with preservation, recreation, whatever you'd like to call it.

"He pushed my husband to make the corpses walk, make them growl and stalk his grounds." A grim smile crossed her face. "I suppose he succeeded in that as well. But he never understood the process, that the only thing a corpse remembers is the moment in which it drew its last breath." She looked me dead in the eyes. "That's the key. What was it thinking? What was it afraid of?" Her expression turned ugly. "Did it have a spear in its stomach?"

A growl sounded in the direction of the palace, so low and deep that I had both of my pistols out and pointing that way before I realized I'd even moved.

"One more Memorial Heart," Isabel said. "I suggest you make your way closer to the palace, where the runes that mark the walls will offer safety from the lesser beasts. For now, at least." She drifted away into the snowfield, illuminating it as she went.

"Let's get buffs up," Darling said. "I want Ton in front and Jukes behind, healers and ranged in the center. If you can take a couple hits, I want you floating around the squishies until you've got a target."

The group shifted, and I moved close to the center, standing just apart from Zoe and the other healers.

"Moving," Ton said, and the big tank started jogging down the road. The raid fell in behind him, moving in a tight, slow knot as the wind blasted over us and the tall trees swayed and groaned.

Then Ton pulled up short and raised his shield. Something long and dark whipped out of the snow and lashed sideways, and while Ton had nailed his positioning, the blow sent him staggering back into the people behind him.

He recovered quickly and charged forward, the raid hesitating behind him as he scanned the snow, sword drawn.

"Told you I saw something," Jukes said.

I looked from left to right, squinting in an attempt to see through the blizzard. "My guess is that it's a whole lot of somethings out here. Remember that defensive recipe we found for the runes of repulsion? I bet there's something similar at play here, and that's why Isabel was pushing us toward the wall."

"Then we should really keep moving," Darling said.

Ton brought his shield up a little higher and pressed forward. The group moved on, increasingly wary. A clicking sound rushed by us to my left, and whatever was making it was running at an incredible speed.

We passed another dome that was much larger than the first, and despite the snow, I could see that its entryway had been ripped open and a great deal of the stone lay scattered across the avenue as if something had blown its way out of the building.

The clicking sound came again, from my right this time, then something dark and scaly whooshed over our heads only to vanish back into the driving snow.

"Let's pick up the pace," Darling said. "Keep your guard up, we're gonna get—"

She cut off as another shape flashed overhead and a long, spiked tail whipped down and caught her in the chest.

The blow knocked her fully off her feet and sent her flying into the healers, who quickly helped her back up.

Then the air was alive with dark shapes flying in from every direction, lashing the group indiscriminately while our two tanks pivoted in place, trying to find a target.

I ducked a flying strike and retaliated with two pistol blasts, but the beasts were moving so quickly that my ravens passed harmlessly by and disappeared into the whiteout.

The group started running, so I put on a burst of speed to keep up and fired a Gravity Bird up in front of the two tanks. The spell detonated, and I thought it had whiffed completely until a monster swooped down at Jukes only to get pulled into the black hole.

The creature was a spectral, birdlike thing with a long neck, a sharp beak, and two taloned feet that hung down low beneath it. A row of backward-curving spikes trailed down its spine and increased in length until they ended in a morning star-like growth that capped its tail.

I scoped it out.

**{Ingravian Roostfeeder} (Level 16 Undead) (Elite+)**
**HP: 2,500/2,500**
**MP: 2,500/2,500**

Before I could get another spell off, the creature flapped its wings and blasted right out of the black hole and over our heads so closely that the taller members of the group had to duck to avoid having their heads taken off.

"Run for it but stay tight!" Darling said.

We scrambled forward, and the formation took hits from all sides as the mobs swept down and in so quickly that counterattacking was completely impossible.

Health bars began to fall all across the raid, and while the healers were throwing out every instant they had, it was already clear that the damage was too much for that to be enough.

One of the healers in front of me—a blue-skinned player with long ears—planted his feet and started winding up a long cast, but two dark talons plunged down out of the snow and lifted him right off his feet.

The creature tried to carry him off over the rest of the raid, but it was flying low and in my direction, so I tagged it with a pair of Ravenblasts, then switched to my blunderbuss and blew it out of the air with two quick strikes from below just as it passed overhead.

The healer tumbled onto the road, and I yanked him to his feet by his elbow and shoved him toward the center of the formation.

"That's a thing, apparently!" Darling said. "Don't let anybody get carried off!"

I paused to store two charges in my blunderbuss, which caused me to fall behind a bit and end up beside Jukes at the rear of the group. He had his staff raised high, and he was spinning it slowly through the air.

"Watch yourself," he said. "I think there's something behind us too. Something big."

I caught a flash of dark movement—a rush of black feathers—and I was reminded of that colossal shape that had chased Darling and me through the snow-choked ruins during our second Rift together.

"That's not good," I said.

"I'm pretty sure it's getting closer too."

"Let's find out." I spun around and activated Clonedrift, then canceled the spell and twisted back around in the air. I jogged to catch back up with Jukes but kept an eye on my clone.

It faded into the snow, then a massive, three-toed foot stomped down on top of it and shattered it into sparks.

Jukes and I exchanged a quick glance, then ran for it.

"Incoming behind us!" I said. "Anyone that falls behind is a goner, so maybe this is like that Path of Daggers encounter from the Bridge Rift!"

For the first time, the group broke into a dead sprint, shields held overhead, weapons flashing to swipe at the Roostfeeders, whose attacks were growing more and more frequent.

I heard something huge scrambling to my right, but the creature behind us bellowed, and whatever had been pacing alongside us curved away and thundered off into the snowfield.

"Can't heal well while moving!" Zoe said, though her hands were flying as she targeted one raid member after another, applying some kind of heal-over-time effect that had most of the raid glowing with a dim green outline, mushrooms and flowers blooming in the snow behind them wherever they went.

Up ahead, Ton grunted as he smashed into something solid at full speed.

"There's a wall up here," Darling said. "We must have reached the palace—we're trapped up against it!"

The group pressed their backs to the wall, and Ton stepped out to rejoin Jukes and face whatever was coming our way.

The creature bellowed again, and the swooping attacks cut off at once as the Roostfeeders arced up and away, squawking as they went.

Footsteps thundered toward us, and a dark shape began to take form, one that easily stood twenty feet high.

Then Isabel was there, floating some ten feet off the ground, her arms stretched wide. The great shadow drew close, and I heard her speaking to it in low, soothing tones, but I couldn't make out the words.

The shadow dipped something—a head or a hand, I couldn't tell—and Isabel placed her own hand atop it. The shadow slipped away and retreated, taking the blizzard with it, the storm pulling back to rage over the switchbacks and the city below.

"What the hell was that?" Darling said.

I turned around and came face to face with the wall, which was strangely pitted and dark—and decidedly not as runed as it had been before.

The wall that blocked the road also ended about twenty feet away in either direction, the palace still stood well behind it, and...

"Frank?"

"Uh huh?"

"Was this wall or block or whatever this is here before the storm set in? I really don't think it was."

"I think I can... yeah, no. It was not."

I craned my neck up, stomach clenching as I took in the granite expanse that towered in front of me as the snow cleared. The Roost-feeders were perched all over it, staring down at us from above, and the stone beneath them was streaked with red.

I looked up still further and found a colossal boulder resting atop the rock formation. The boulder was marked by two empty sockets, each of them burning with red light.

{Roost, the Wandering Cliff} (Level 16 Undead) (Raid Boss)
HP: 800,000/800,000
MP: 0/0

# Chapter Forty-Four

The golem was titanic—easily fifty feet tall—and the heaped boulders that lent it a somewhat humanoid shape were illuminated by the same spectral blue glow of the Roostfeeders high above.

Its stony surface was marked by iron rods that protruded a few feet from the stone, solid-looking bars that were wedged into cracks and crevices.

The golem raised a hand and pointed directly at Ton, and the Roostfeeders flew off and wheeled high into the air, watching us from above.

The heavily armored tank glanced up at the car-sized fists the golem's hands were clenching into, looked at his tower shield with a decidedly dubious expression on his face, then squared his shoulders to the boss.

"Jukes," Darling said, "you're up first! Ton, I suggest not getting hit if you can help it!"

I popped my rifle against my shoulder and started up an Overcharged blast. I scanned up and down the creature's height, searching for targetable points and finding tons of them: each of the glowing joints between its ankles, the many joints of its broad hands, even the eye sockets high above, behind which a pale light was shining, but unlike the Grim, every targetable area seemed to share the same enormous Health pool.

Jukes raised his staff and sent an icy dagger flying up into the boss' chest. It burst against its central boulder, and the entire golem tipped forward like a falling tree.

The scale of the thing made everyone hesitate, and by the time they all snapped out of it and scattered, it appeared that half the raid was going to be flattened mere seconds into the fight.

But the golem brought its hands up and caught itself, slamming into the ground on all fours right above us. It opened its mouth and screamed, gaze fixed on Ton despite the fact that Jukes had been the one to engage, and a torrent of small, spectral birds surged out from between its stone jaws.

I inspected the closest of them.

{Roostprey Bombbird}
HP: 250/250
MP: 100/100

Frank raised his voice. "Team Frank, merc those birds!"

I grinned and took aim as the surge began to spread out and fired a single, piercing shot straight through the dense crowd of Bombbirds.

The fragile mobs dropped by the score as my gold and gray-laced raven ripped through them, causing a chain reaction of explosions that erased dozens of them in a single cast.

The other members of Team Frank were on it too, and while the corpses fell by the score, about a dozen birds avoided the assault and dive-bombed straight into the ground.

Bodies flew and Health bars plummeted as blue explosions lit up the avenue, and the nearby trees loosed the snow that had been heaped upon them all at once as the shockwaves sent them whipping sideways and away.

The Raid Boss shifted its weight to free a hand, made a fist, and brought it down toward Jukes in a hammer blow.

The tank rolled away then shot right back in, striking out with a four-piece combo. The beast flicked a stony finger his way, and though the gesture was casual, almost comical, the attack was so powerful that Jukes went flying head over heels. Ton rushed in to fill the gap Jukes had left— only to catch a sideways swipe that sent him airborne as well, his Health flashing from full to half in a blink.

Jukes regained his feet and rolled back in, and Darling finally gave the signal for the rest of us to fully engage the boss.

I'd stacked three full cannon blasts from the Bombbirds, so I swapped to that and fired, sending three huge ravens flying in different directions: one at the hand the creature was bracing itself with, a second at the glowing seam between its head and shoulder, and a third straight into its right eye socket.

The first two blasts connected for 750 and 820—amounts that suggested substantial Magical Resistance—but the third exploded deep inside the creature's skull and hit for well over 1,700.

"Sockets might be a weak point!" I said, and as soon as the words were out, the raid's spells and projectiles shifted from flying horizontally to mostly diagonally, and a torrent of magic was crackling up into the colossal golem's eyes.

"Roost at 97% and falling," Frank said. "Duck!"

I tried, but I was too late, and I felt a pair of talons close around my shoulders. I activated Clonedrift to slip out of the Roostfeeder's grasp and popped free as it carried my clone directly across the battlefield.

Roost looked up as the clone approached, and the golem opened its stony mouth to reveal square, blocky teeth that were set at mismatched angles, the corners and edges jutting up into the air.

The bird dropped the clone and flared its wings, pulling up to safety right as the golem snapped its jaws shut and sparks flew between its teeth.

Having seen that, I reloaded my blunderbuss, then dashed over to back up the healers and watch the skies above them while I peppered the hand the melees were targeting with blasts to stack my armor debuff.

And judging by the amounts they seemed to be hitting for and the fact that they couldn't reach the creature's eye sockets, they were going to need every bit of help they could get.

The ranged players were having better luck, and as soon as I'd maxed my debuff, I joined them in targeting the twin weak spots above.

"Boss at 92%," Frank said.

Roost took another swipe that Jukes avoided, then it slammed the same hand into the ground and drew itself back to its full, terrible height.

It threw its head back, and the spells and projectiles that had been heading its way bounced harmlessly off its surface and deflected into the air. The creature beat its chest and roared, its glowing seams brightening as countless Bombbirds poured up and out of its throat.

Within seconds, the entire sky was alight with their spectral wings, and the sound of so many creatures fluttering above was deafening.

"Eyes up!" Darling shouted.

The golem stilled, the seams between its heaped boulders pulsing from ankles to knees and above in quick succession. Then the birds dove, and it truly looked like the sky was falling.

I watched the ground, expecting it to light up to mark the approaching danger, and I wasn't completely wrong. But instead of different areas with safe zones between them, the entire battlefield turned crimson. The birds smashed down all at once in a wave of blue explosions.

Health bars plummeted all around, with Jukes and Ton both dropping to around 70% while everyone else went below half, and I ended up on 28%.

Darling dropped a golden icon between the golem's legs. "Regroup for AoE heals! We can have—"

She cut off with a curse as the golem thumped its chest again and another round of Bombbirds soared up out of its throat and spread out across the sky.

"Pixel pulls if you got 'em!" Darling said, so I took up a position next to a crowd of healers and detonated a Gravity Bird some ten feet above our heads.

A flurry of other similar spells went out: one was a twister that expanded up from a single point and rose ten feet in the air, widening as it went; another was some kind of arrow that exploded about twenty feet above us and created a vacuum-like effect that was similar to my own spell.

The guild crammed in beneath the defensive spells, sheltering beneath the birds that were momentarily held in place.

It was impressive to see how quickly they'd grouped up on the fly, but I didn't trust it—the explosions were too wide, too potent—so I activated Water Jet and blasted myself into the air.

The explosions surged beneath me like cluster bombs, hundreds of blue, identical domes erupting at the same moment.

My momentum carried me right to the golem's shin, and I bounced off its rocky leg but managed to grab onto one of the many iron rods that jutted out from the creature. I hung there by one hand, suspended fifteen feet above the battlefield.

I'd been right about the pixel pulls: while the guild's spells succeeded at delaying some of the creatures from falling, it didn't matter because the cover they provided wasn't enough to shelter people from the other explosions, and six players went down immediately.

To make matters worse, all of those defensive spells had different durations, and while both my Gravity Bird and the arrow vacuum ability proved long enough to allow the groups that had been sheltering below them to scatter to safety after the initial blast, the twister disappeared too quickly and allowed all of the Bombbirds it'd been holding back to surge down and strike the group below a second time, instantly wiping out another seven players.

"Roost at 89%," Frank said. "More than half the raid is down for the count."

"It's a wipe," Darling said. "Run out if you can, we gotta reset."

I waited to make sure the Bombbird attack was over, and I almost leaped free immediately when the golem rumbled in Ton's direction as the tank fled back down the avenue.

Instead, I held on, watching, waiting for the moment when Ton finally left the encounter's zone so we'd have a better idea of the boundaries of the fight.

The golem took another long step before turning its attention to Jukes, who was slightly behind the larger tank, so I made a mental note of the two trees that Ton had reached and leaped free, then activated Double Cast to Water Jet myself to safety.

The creature stopped at that same invisible line. It roared and thumped its chest, then pivoted back to where we'd found it. The birds that had been wheeling high above rejoined the creature, perching high atop its shoulders and rods.

"Well, that went badly," Darling said, blowing out a puff of air beside me.

The avenue was positively littered with bodies, Nina and Rock among them.

"Pixel pulls didn't work either, just got some people hit twice. You think it'd work if we blew up the birds?"

I dropped onto my haunches. "Pulls were a good thing to try, but I don't really think killing them will work with that massive wave of them coming down. They've got super low Health, so we could definitely drop some of them before they fall, but I doubt I can get more than a single spell off between the moment they enter our range and when they actually hit the ground. Any chance you saw where I ended up?"

"I didn't."

I pointed at the creature's shin. "I was just trying to get above the explosions and that worked well enough, but Water Jet sent me flying and

I ended up grabbing onto one of those rods and just dangling there, Frank-like."

"False," Frank said. "Your dangle was completely uninspired, and I found it lacking in both zest and *je ne sais quoi*. Here, watch."

I glanced down at him.

"See? See that right there?"

"You didn't do anything."

"I didn't need to."

"You didn't take any damage up there?" Darling said.

"None. A well-timed leap would probably put you up over the explosions too, but I think anybody without an ability like that might need to climb up the golem." I pointed a pistol at the creature's rods, which started as low as right above its glowing ankle joint—which was still five feet off the ground—and continued all the way up to the top of its skull. "Wouldn't be hard to scramble up, right? And if it's gonna shoot two waves of those Bombbirds, you and I are probably better served leaping onto it too. We could even—"

I broke off as a call for Francis came in from Tyrann.

"What's up?" Darling said, no doubt reading my face. "Something wrong?"

"Not sure. I might take a quick call while everybody's corpse-running if that's cool. I'll break it off if needed, but I think I might be able to spin this into getting us some help for the Siege."

She shrugged. "Might as well. Probably take everybody a bit to get back here."

I nodded, then stepped away to find out what Tyrann was up to.

# Chapter Forty-Five

I blacked out my screen and set the conversation to private, then headed over to one of the damaged trees and dropped down with my back to the half-split trunk before taking the call.

"Evening."

"Hey there, Francis. How ya holding up over there?"

Tyrann had his window unblocked once again, and he was sitting atop a white horse armored in gold. He'd apparently picked his spot carefully because he was at the summit of a particularly elevated dune near Highwater that offered sweeping views of the Black Oasis below as well as the Red Cathedral off in the distance, its many wings still shifting and blinking in and out of existence.

"I'm alive," I said. "At least until tomorrow morning."

"Yeah, sorry to hear about that. Must be galling to finish that tree only to have somebody roll in and attempt to swipe it for themselves."

"Not a whole lot of fun on my end, that's for sure. What's up with you?"

He looked to his left and smiled at someone out of the frame. "I just got a pretty interesting offer a couple hours back. Figured I'd run it by you and see if you can beat it."

"Shoot," I said, though I already had a pretty good idea of what was coming.

"Strictly between you and me, Goon just asked us to join their Siege of the Black Oasis." He paused as if to let that sink in, but his eyes flicked out of the frame again.

"Really?" I said, doing my best to keep the skepticism from my voice. "Bit of a surprise there, given what I've heard of them."

His claim didn't gel at all with Sleep and my first impressions of Goon's leader, but the prospect was beyond worrisome. If those two groups joined up, things would go from bleak to hopeless in a blink.

And while I was pretty confident in my ability to read people—and Sleep had seemed completely genuine—I'd been wrong plenty of times before.

His eyelid twitched. "I'm not sure it should be. Goon is pretty large, but I think they're worried about the level of activity that's going on in the Vale. Been a busy place for a while now."

I thought back to the veritable army that had filled Goon's coliseum, the way they'd been killing each other for laughs across their own tables while halfway through dinner. "They're worried, eh?"

I checked to see if Sleep was online and was unsurprised to find that he wasn't. I wouldn't have been able to confirm his offer regardless—I wouldn't dare question him as Ned about information that Tyrann had passed to Francis out of fear that it would get out somehow and that Tyrann would put two and two together—but it seemed awfully convenient that Sleep had been online until recently and Tyrann had chosen this moment to start a conversation with Francis.

"So what's Goon offering you?"

"I would have thought you'd have already figured that out, given the way people are talking you up."

I paused, thinking. "A promise that Koria won't be next?"

He smiled, nodding. "Total immunity."

"Wow." That seemed even more unlikely than the offered alliance, but I could practically feel the opening Tyrann was leaving, so I decided to hit him right where it hurt most: his image. "And you're really considering that?"

His smile slipped, but only briefly. "I'd be a fool not to, right?"

"In purely practical terms, yeah, I completely agree. It's just... I don't know. I guess I'm wondering what immunity really looks like."

"You think they're being dishonest with me?"

"Maybe, maybe not. I've never dealt with them personally. But the thing is that it doesn't really matter, right? If Goon rolls over the Black Oasis, they're going to sail east at some point, and Koria is the gateway to your entire continent. So either they'll break their promise and burn their way through your city, or you'll open your gates to let them march through and wreck everybody else. That's the part I find surprising."

"Not sure I follow."

"Maybe I'm wrong here, but I guess I just have a hard time imagining you bending the knee and letting that happen after watching your streams for so long. I wouldn't blame you for taking the offer—it just feels like the sort of thing you'd have gone out of your way to stop in the past. All those players losing everything they've worked so hard for."

He blinked. "Well, sure. I've said before that I'm not a fan of the game they're playing, but we do need to be careful here. The God kill forced us to change gears, and crossing Goon would have been a tall ask even before all that."

"What are you looking for from me, then? A reason to decline?"

"I was hoping you might be able to sweeten the pot, yeah. Give me something I can take back to the Cult to win the rest of them over to the cause."

I chewed that over. I'd just been buttering him up with the whole you'd-never-do-that thing, but the idea of the Cult directly joining Goon's Siege did feel at odds with the narrative that Tyrann was selling.

So maybe he'd already decided to decline their offer—if it even existed —and he was just trying to see what he could get from Francis on top?

Or maybe his bravado early on had been just that, and the Cult really was in a poor enough position that Tyrann would consider saving his city at the expense of deferring to another group.

"Well, here's how I see it," I said slowly. "I can't do anything for you if it's simply a matter of you agreeing not to join up with Goon and attack the city. As things currently stand, I'm thinking the Black Oasis is likely to fall whether or not you join, so blowing a bunch of resources to rule that out as a possibility doesn't make a whole lot of sense.

"I'd like to point out that Goon isn't going to be simply taking the Oasis over, either. If you've done your research on that latest Siege, you already know what they did afterward. Burned the whole thing to the ground. So that Auction Network you've got in Koria is going to disappear, as are the buffs and the Housing you've been enjoying in the Oasis."

"You don't have much of a defense lined up, then?"

"I wouldn't say that. I have some plans in mind, and I don't intend to give up my position without a fight. But the problem is that for all the weirdly alliterative titles people are throwing my way, I'm not the kind of person they're inclined to rally around." I paused. "Now, if someone like that were to directly step into the fray on our behalf, preferably with an army behind them... that would be the sort of service I'd be interested in paying for."

Tyrann barked an incredulous laugh. "That's a bold ask, there."

"True, but can you picture it? Being the one who finally beats back Goon after all the destruction they've caused? That would change the entire game."

"Sure, provided we win."

"So how about this: instead of helping them, you line up with the Oasis, and I reinstate your Tithe."

He rubbed his chin. "Hmm."

"It was 20%, right? Well, you guys line up and repel Goon, and I'll cut you into my Auction House network at the same amount. Globally. And if you or one of your guys hooks a node up for me directly, I'll up your take to 25%."

I paused to let that sink in. Giving up the gold would definitely hurt, but if I didn't have a city when tomorrow afternoon rolled around, it wouldn't matter all that much.

Nor would his take be as punishing as the original Tithe: if I was feeding him gold directly, then every single coin would still be applied to my payouts, whereas beforehand, the Tithe had claimed its share before the calculation.

And I still liked the idea of incentivizing his people to spread my network around, especially since we were about to lose the Hall of Rifts.

Tyrann tapped his chin. "That is very tempting. What sort of numbers are you working with currently?"

"I'm expecting tomorrow's payout to be in excess of 50 gold. I know that's probably not much to you right now, but I've gone from generating a handful of silver per day to 10 gold to 20 gold in the last three days."

"You expect that growth rate to continue?"

"Oh no—it's going to become exponential before long. We're still just scratching the surface. We could be talking hundreds, even thousands of gold per day in the weeks to come. Every day. Escort costs are down too, at least relatively speaking. Everyone's going to have more gold in hand."

He rubbed his temples and eyed the floor, looking genuinely conflicted. "I see. I'm going to have to really think this one over." He looked from left to right, then tapped at the air. I figured he was messing with his privacy settings. "In confidence?"

"Sure."

His face relaxed slightly, and it felt like he'd allowed some part of the persona he was playing to slip away. "I'd like to help you out, but I don't think I can swing it. Spirits are lower than I'd like over here, and we can't afford to take another loss. Numbers wise? A couple days ago, I'd probably have given us a fair chance against Goon from what I've heard. But we had a hell of a lot riding on that God.

"Don't get me wrong here—we're coming back, and we're coming back hard. But tomorrow morning, assuming an even fight? I feel like we'd get absolutely trounced, and I can't afford that on a couple different levels."

"You don't think your crew will consider it a loss to line up behind someone else?"

He shrugged. "They probably will, but it'll be less of a loss than getting wrecked in the Oasis and watching the city burn the next day. Sorry, Francis. I don't think it's in the cards."

I paused, racking my brain for a solution. No brilliant ideas came to mind, so I decided to do the next best thing: lie and pretend something had.

"Alright, how about this. What if I hand you something that's guaranteed to turn the tide?"

He leaned forward. "Like a weapon or what?"

"Maybe a weapon, maybe an item, maybe something else. But let's say I could guarantee that if you and the Cult intervene, you win the day. And when people tell the story of the first failed Siege—the first time somebody stopped Goon dead in their tracks—you personally are the guy they mention first. You've got morale problems right now? Poof, they're gone. And the Cult's redemption tour can officially begin with you in the good graces of every guild and player based in the Vale."

He clasped his hands behind his head. "If you could actually guarantee that? Then sure, obviously I'd be interested. But this sorta thing is going to require more than a promise: I'd need to be personally convinced before I'd put the Cult on the line. You really think you've got something like that up your sleeve?"

"I do, yeah."

He nodded. "Alright. Well, this has been a lot more interesting than I thought it would be. So here's what I'm going to do: the way the Siege works, anyone who wants to attack the city needs to declare their intentions before it starts, so I'm gonna have somebody add the Cult to the list of attackers right now.

"That'll get Goon off my back when it comes to them asking for help, and I can remove the declaration at any point before the siege starts. If I feel like we gotta help 'em out to save our skin, we'll do that. If staying neutral seems like a better fit in the end, the declaration is easy enough to remove."

He leaned forward again. "And when you're ready to show your hand, send me a message and we'll go from there. I gotta think on all of this, but that's the best I can do for now."

"Alright then. I'll be in touch. Appreciate the call."

"Cheers, and good luck with... huh, hold on." He frowned. "Hey, I've got somebody in the Oasis making the declaration right now to get it out of the way, and there's already another guild on the list with Goon."

I bit down a curse. "Who?"

"Arranthea? I've never heard of them."

"Pst," Frank said. "Breaklite, the weirdo who called about the defensive pact. Her guild's based out of the Treetop Tower, which was Goon's target for their three-day Siege."

I gave him a thumbs up. "They're a guild down south. They inquired about a defensive pact before the Black Oasis was even targeted. Came off sorta odd. I didn't take them up on it. Sorta slipped my mind, really."

"Weird. Well, looking forward to hearing what you've got in store for Goon. I'll be hoping it's enough to get us across the line. Cheers."

"Thanks. I'll be in touch."

I ended the call, already pinching the bridge of my nose. I looked around and spotted a few guildies running our way, but we were still missing quite a few.

"So what's the secret plan?" Frank said.

"I was gonna ask you the same thing."

"Well that's unfortunate."

"You're telling me. We could be lining up against three guilds tomorrow. Guess we should have taken that offer from Arranthea after all. Still doesn't add up for me, though. What did you think of what Tyrann said?"

"Which part?"

"That Sleep was offering Koria immunity in exchange for help with the Siege. Doesn't that seem like the exact opposite of what Sleep said he wanted? He can't both be worried that his guild is getting too big to allow for the kind of fights they're after and also be recruiting people to help at the same time, right?"

"Not if he wants to make sense." I felt him gesture at Darling. "You gonna give her the bad news? I'd do it myself, but I prefer being liked, and that ship's already sailed for you."

I looked over at her. She was kneeling on the slushy cobbles with Rock, Nina, Zoe, and a few others clustered around her while she drew a diagram into the snow.

"When the moment's right, yeah. Let's just focus on getting them this World-first for now. Regardless of whether those guilds participate, we're gonna be outgunned and outmanned and firmly in we-need-a-miracle territory."

"Yeah, plus you in particular have been outmanned from the very beginning."

"Huh?"

"I mean, you can't really help it with me hanging here, right? With my virility just wafting through the air."

I rolled my eyes. "Way to ruin breathing for the rest of us."

"Get it? Outmanned."

"I caught that, yeah. Just didn't think it was funny."

Darling glanced back over her heavily armored pauldrons as the last remaining raid members ran up and dropped to the ground to drink and eat. She tapped at the air.

"Looks like we've got everybody back," she said loudly, standing up and addressing the group, "so listen up real quick because we're going to try something new with that Birdbomb mechanic.

"If you've got a leap or a teleport or whatever, you can jump right over the explosions, but if you saw Ned grab onto that rod and hang there, you probably already know where this is going: the moment Roost rises up and throws its head back, I want every single member climbing up its legs as fast as possible.

"Aside from that, burn the feeders if somebody gets grabbed and pulled off because I'm assuming nobody here wants to become golem food. We all good?" A round of murmurs and nods went up in answer. "Great. Buff up, Jukes will pull in thirty seconds." She jogged over to where Frank and I were still sitting. "Anything up?" she said.

"That was Tyrann on the call," I said, before Frank could blurt the entire conversation out. "Long story short, he might be attacking the city with Goon. Or staying neutral. Or helping us. We'll see."

"But don't worry because we have it all under control with a secret plan," Frank added.

Darling drew her weapons and sized up the walking cliff beyond. "Secret plan, huh? You got details?"

"The plan is so secretive that it's a total unknown to both of us."

Darling laughed, though it was a little darker than I'd have liked. "So you don't have a plan at all."

I shook my head. "We're planning to plan something once we're the first guild to clear the wing."

She took a deep breath. "Well... that sucks." She forced a gap-toothed smile. "You ready then?"

I hopped up and away from the tree.

"Yeah. Let's give this guy another shot."

# Chapter Forty-Six

Jukes rolled ahead and reengaged Roost with another icy dagger to the chest. The beast slammed down as it had before, and with full knowledge of its weak point, the ranged group was able to burn it far more efficiently than we had the first time around.

Our positioning was a little different this time, with the melees beating on the creature's ankles and shins while the ranged players stayed in front to target the eyes, right behind Jukes and Ton.

The two tanks had realized that the boss' substantial attacks were powerful but very slow, and it seemed like they were having a good amount of success alternating aggro and taking a few hits apiece before passing it off to the other tank to ease the pressure on the healers.

And as soon as Roost fell back below 90%, it straightened, tossed its head back, and thumped its chest. The Bombbirds surged out once again in a thick column that spread out and blanketed the sky, covering the battlefield with shadows.

"Climb!" Darling said.

I ran for the creature's left leg and Water Jetted myself right up into the air, mostly to leave room for those who were forced to climb manually.

I grabbed onto a rod and climbed up below the beast's right knee, then switched to my blunderbuss and swung out and away, leaning off the creature and jabbing my weapon directly into the glowing seam between the two segments of rock that made up the creature's shin and kneecap.

I fired twice in quick succession, then switched to my rifle as the first wave of Bombbirds flashed, then fell. The ground turned into a sea of red, and explosions followed in short order.

Several of those who were either too slow or lacked good movement abilities or both still got tagged and badly injured, but the strategy kept the bulk of the raid from being severely damaged, and the healers who'd climbed up were quickly able to stabilize the injured.

And by the time the creature reared back for a second round of birds, the entire raid had already managed to gain enough elevation to avoid the attack completely.

The golem slammed back down onto all fours and the damage phase resumed, with the two tanks getting batted around and away, rotating after each colossal attack.

It was smooth going until Roost dropped below 80%, at which point stray Bombbirds began flying out of the golem's mouth every few seconds and soaring high into the air—only to pick a random section of the battlefield to dive to and explode.

"Roost at 76%," Frank said.

"Steady!" Darling called out. "Make sure you're close enough to the boss that you can climb up if that Bombbird phase repeats!"

The boss ticked down to 74%, then 70%, then 60%, then it finally stood up straight, bellowed, and called its wave of divers once again.

The group was even quicker to climb this time around, and the entire raid was above the huge creature's knees as the explosions hit, many of them hanging off the beast with one hand and swinging away with the other or sending spells streaking up over the boss' chest and toward the skull high above.

But as the fight wore on and Roost finally dropped beneath the halfway mark, the fight changed in a major way: the sky above the great golem grew dark and choked with clouds, and thunder rumbled overhead.

A bolt of lightning struck down and zapped the top of the golem's head, striking one of the many metal protrusions we'd been intermittently clinging to as if it were a lightning rod.

A ball of electricity lingered around the rod's tip, and the sphere drifted lazily to the next rod, then the next, slowly working itself down the golem's length.

Then another bolt struck, another ball of lightning formed, and I understood. "Climbing just got a lot more dangerous!" I called out. "Gonna have to avoid those lightning balls on the way up—looks like they're jumping from rod to rod!"

I kept the spells coming as the lightning strikes continued, and soon sparks of electricity were crawling all over the boss.

When Roost's Health ticked below 40%, the Bombbird phase began once again. I Water Jetted myself up the right leg as I had before and landed between a few balls of electricity, then kept climbing from there, aiming for an area that looked safer.

But I ended up scrambling down and to the left when a ball of lightning changed direction unexpectedly, forcing me to swing from one rod to the next as if they were monkey bars, and the clamor and shouting below told me that the climb wasn't going nearly as well this time around.

"Zap," Frank said. "Mage just got fried, stunned for 5 seconds."

I'd seen a Health Bar drop by 20% in my periphery, and I wasn't surprised to see the mage lock up and drop free. He hit the ground on his back and dropped to 75%.

"Zap zap. Rock's down, plus a healer."

I cursed and tried to squeeze a Ravenblast in to keep my debuff from falling, but the ball lightning was too much, and it was all I could do to clamber behind the creature's knee in an attempt to avoid the many spheres that were crawling and sparking my way.

The first round of blue explosions hit, the second quickly followed, and just like that, we were down three players. Everybody dropped to the ground, expecting the pattern to continue where it had left off.

Roost stared down at us, but instead of slamming down as he had before, he raised his huge hands to his sides, and the ball lightning streaked across his body, running up his legs and chest and down his arms and wrists until every single spark was circling around his clenched fists.

"Still looking doable!" Darling said. "Drop him another 10% and executes will turn on—we can do this!"

The golem finally dropped back onto all fours. Ton grunted as a casual swipe from the boss sent him staggering sideways and knocking 40% of his Health off for good measure.

The tank's armor was sparking as he righted himself, and Jukes called out the new debuff before I had a chance to scope it.

"New stacking mechanic called Static! Lasts five seconds and spreads to anyone nearby, you get three stacks and it's a five-second stun!"

"Tanks are gonna have to rotate out more quickly and blow defensives!" Ton said.

Jukes rolled back out of melee range. "On your second stack then!"

Ton charged back at the boss. "Agreed!"

I reapplied my debuff, aiming blast after blast at the creature's skull while I tried to keep my eyes on the healers and the sky at the same time.

One of Zoe's green, glowing waves rolled across the battlefield and crashed over Ton, healing him back to 90% just before the boss swatted him away with a palm strike I hadn't noticed: it curved upward more than any blow before it and took the tank fully off his feet.

"Rotate!" Ton yelled, even as he tumbled through the air.

Jukes rolled into position, an icy dagger flying from one hand.

"Boss at 32% and falling!" Frank said.

A pair of Bombbirds flew out of the beast's skull. I kept an eye on them, suspicious after seeing a pair form simultaneously for the first time.

The two birds didn't streak skyward, either—they beelined directly at Ton. His Health was still under 50%, and the healers must have swapped to Jukes too quickly because I didn't see anything headed his way.

I raised a pistol at each of the incoming Bombbirds as Ton regained his feet, saw what was heading his way, and raised his shield high.

I smashed Ravenblast again and again, generating an error message each time that said my target was out of range, but my spells flew at the earliest possible moment, just as the two Bombbirds were streaking over my head and screaming toward the tank.

My spells blew the diving mobs out of the air while they were still a full ten feet above Ton, and the armored tank nodded my way as he ran forward and shouted for healing.

His timing couldn't have been better: Jukes had just taken his first hit, then the boss caught him off guard by dropping to its knees and swiping out with the hand it had previously been using to prop itself up, and the blow sent him skidding across the stone face-down.

"Jukes at 27%," Frank said. "Two stacks of Static. Boss at 29%, executes are live!"

The boss made a fist directly above Jukes and brought it down hard.

Ton leaped the remaining distance and managed to get right between the temporarily downed tank and the falling fist, his shield held almost horizontally above his shoulders.

He caught the titanic blow and kept Jukes from dying, but I saw sparks fly between them. The two had gotten too close, and both had picked up an additional stack of Static.

Jukes froze right there on the ground as his third charge stunned him, while Ton ran sideways to put some distance between them, electricity trailing behind him.

"Two stacks on me!" he said. "Jukes is stunned!"

The heals poured in and bumped him back to full Health, but the golem was already winding up for its next strike.

"Pop everything!" Darling said.

Ton roared and stomped a foot into the ground so hard that he plunged ankle-deep into the cobbles. He did the same with his other foot, and his armor flashed, then doubled in size.

"Statue Armor!" Frank said. "Great mitigation but he can't move!"

Roost lashed out and swept a huge hand low across the battlefield, forcing a couple of ranged users to burn movement abilities to avoid it.

The blow struck Ton dead-on, and the thunderclap that followed left my ears ringing. Whereas normally Ton would have been sent flying, now the tank didn't even budge, and seeing the blow stopped cold was like watching an eighteen-wheeler slam into a concrete wall.

Ton's Health only dropped by 15%, but we were still in trouble.

"Ton is stunned for 5 seconds, Static hit full stacks!" Frank said.

As if sensing the opportunity, the boss rocked back and raised both of its fists into the air. It brought them down one after the other, and while Ton managed to remain standing through the first three hammer blows thanks to a tremendous burst of healing, his defensive ability expired right before the fourth connected and the attack flattened him against the ground.

The tank died, his nameplate graying out.

Jukes sprang back to his feet as his stun finally faded, but the boss was already lashing out at a knot of healers. They scattered, but two of them got swiped and thrown into the air. They were dead before they hit the ground.

Jukes managed to regain aggro, but with Ton down plus a few healers, it was starting to feel like another wipe.

"17%," Frank said.

I blew another pair of Bombbirds out of the sky, then trained my focus on the boss, sending spell after spell exploding within its skull, behind those dimly lit sockets.

Jukes managed to buy us a bit of time by avoiding the next swipe that came his way, but the boss' attack speed had doubled since it started kneeling, and the second attack caught him cleanly and knocked him down.

"One stack of Static on Jukes, 58%," Frank said. "Boss at 16%!"

"So close!" Darling said. "Go go go!"

"14%."

The boss swung yet again, and for one blessed moment I thought Jukes had done just enough to get out of the way, but the huge hand clipped his shoulder and dropped him to one knee.

And the next overhead blow was already coming. Jukes looked up as it fell, seeming to sense it, then his entire body flashed from head to toe.

The hand smashed down, and Jukes' body completely shattered beneath it.

Then he popped back into existence a few feet to the left of where he'd been standing, and while whatever defensive ability he'd used had been impressively timed, he immediately caught a sideways chop to the midsection.

He ragdolled across the battlefield, and the boss leaned forward to keep him in range.

"Boss at 8%!"

I popped Doppelganger, Double Cast it to gain another copy, planted my feet, and let the acidic birds fly six at a time until the doppels had almost run their full duration, then activated Dark Harvest to send a trio of ghastly skulls flying up into the creature's eye sockets.

Jukes caught another strike as the boss ticked all the way down to 6%, and the attack dropped him to 15% Health and added his third stack of Static for good measure.

The tank fell to the ground, motionless, and Roost raised both of his fists high. He lit the stunned tank up with a series of pummeling strikes, and while the healers kept him up for longer than I'd expected, the damage was far too much. Our second tank was down.

"Spread out and keep pushing!" Darling said. "We're so close—"

She cut off as the boss' Health ticked below 5% and it climbed to its feet. The sparks that had been surging around its fists raced back up its arms and across its broad chest, then returned to surging from one rod to the next.

"Climb and kill it from there!" Darling said. "We got this!"

I let myself fall toward a push-up position, then activated Clonedrift to send myself flying up into the sky. Once the spell expired and I had my bearings, I used Water Jet to launch myself up onto the beast's chest, where I'd be in easy range of its skull and the weak points within.

I climbed atop two closely placed rods, braced my chest against the creature's stony frame, then reached up with both hands and fired away.

The sparking orbs were everywhere, sizzling all around me, but I managed three pairs of blasts before the Bombbirds even spawned.

"Orb coming up from below you!" Frank said. "Boss at 3%!"

I squatted low and jumped, grabbed onto a higher rod, and switched to my blunderbuss. I pointed the weapon upward with one hand and unloaded both of my stored blasts as the first wave of Bombbirds splashed down.

A cheer went up at that and several more followed, and it took me a moment to realize that we hadn't lost anyone to the mechanic.

"Roost is going down!" Frank said. "It's actually going down!"

The roar intensified as the boss ticked ever lower: 2%, 1%. The next volley of Bombbirds was in the air. It was diving—then the entire swarm of them dissipated into bluish dust.

"0%," Frank said as the electrical orbs winked out all around me and the huge boss thundered back down to its knees, nearly jarring me loose.

The golem's huge head dipped to its chest, and the Memorial Heart that Isabel was after dropped out of its left eye socket.

I caught it before it could fall farther and held it up while more loot poured free, Rift Gems and gear tumbling down out of the beast's eye sockets and raining down around me.

The guild absolutely erupted from their vantage points on the monster, who showed no signs of falling further. The Roostfeeders squawked and flew upward, circled for a moment, then streaked off in a V-formation across the sky.

# Chapter Forty-Seven

Darling was one of the first to drop off the golem's upright corpse. She landed beneath me and cupped her hands together, palms up, and motioned for the heart. I dropped it down, then let myself fall the remaining distance. And by the time I hit the ground, Isabel was hovering above the avenue with three symbols floating above her.

"Get your Health and Mana back up!" Darling said as she tapped the air. "As soon as the dead are back, we're pushing in for this first! We've still got two guilds ahead of us, but things are looking good!"

Another round of cheers went up at that, and I couldn't help but stare at Rock as he stood over the loot pile, one piece of equipment vanishing after the next as he scoped them out, found the right person, and traded them away.

Our eyes met, and the big man frowned and shook his head.

"Shoot," I said as he went back to what he was doing. "I was really hoping to finish my set before the next—"

A trade window popped up, and Rock looked back at me, grinning.

"Bastard," I said, laughing the word. I accepted the trade and threw the item on.

**{Ghosthunter's Chestplate}**
**Grade: D**
**Item Level: 46**

Slot: Chest
Type: Leather
Quality: Rare
Suggested Class: Shadewalker
Primaries: +13 Intelligence, +5 Dexterity, +15 Constitution
Secondaries: +2% Haste
Armor: +7%
Set Effect (2-piece): Active. While dual-wielding Enchanted Pistols, your Ravenblast is instant, and any pistol blast fired while out of combat is automatically Overcharged.
Set Effect (4-piece): Active. Ravenblasts fired from your rifle now spawn a burst of miniature ravens that scatter from each struck enemy and deal 20% of the initial blast's damage to all enemies within 5 yards.
Set Effect (6-piece): Active. You may now Clonedrift freely in any direction, and your Doppelganger ability now procs twice upon activation and offers increased control.

Like the rest of the set, the chest piece was pale blue and lined with white fur.

I was desperate to test out the 6-piece, so I activated Clonedrift and mentally directed the spell to take me straight up into the air without contorting myself the way I usually had to.

The clone popped into place as it usually did, but sure enough, the spell sent me zipping straight up as if I'd been yanked skyward. I canceled it before I got too high and landed lightly beside the clone again.

"Awesome. So much more flexibility there."

"Woo," Frank said. "We're even better at running away. Hooray for us."

"We also get twice as many Doppelgangers. So if I pop that then Double Cast it, you'd end up with five total Franks instead of three."

"God. Imagine what I could do if I had five shafts."

I shuddered. "I really would prefer not to."

Darling moved out of the crowd and flicked my new chest piece. "Lucky bastard. You already finished your set?"

I grinned. "Yup! Super excited."

"Man. I got my fifth from the Grim but nothing here. So, curses? We can either make it easier to kill adds, increase the healing everybody takes, or decrease the physical damage they take."

"Can I make an objectively good suggestion?" Frank said.

Darling popped her axes onto her back and squinted down the avenue, which the guild members who had been killed were now rushing down to rejoin us. "I was hoping you would."

"Leave the curse that makes the adds harder to deal with."

She pursed her lips. "Hm. I was kinda thinking about eliminating that one, actually."

"You can safely ignore his last suggestion."

"I'm confused. Was that not a hint?"

"I'm sure he's hinting at something, but it doesn't have anything to do with the raid because he can't give that kind of info. He just doesn't wanna see Team Frank dissolved."

He grunted. "I mean... maybe. But I think we both know that I'm far more cooperative when things are dying, especially when I'm the one who gets to do the sentencing."

"Fair point."

"Maybe we get rid of that healing debuff one?" Darling said. "That would free Jukes and Ton up from needing to use their Touchstone Sockets to stay immune. Might grab them an extra defensive, and I've been watching the healers really struggle with raid-wide damage." She peered down the avenue again. "Maybe it'd be more efficient to just reduce the damage people are taking instead since that one's got a bigger increase. We gotta decide quick though. I wanna get moving the moment everyone's full, and the last healer is almost here."

I shrugged. "No argument here—getting rid of the Glass-bone curse makes sense to me."

Darling made her selection, and another floating rune vanished from where it had been floating around Isabel.

"Excellent," Isabel said. "This should be enough." She looked at the walls and smiled as the same rune deactivated there, leaving only two of the initial five that had been streaming across it when we'd first entered the Menagerie Wing. "I think... yes. We can finally approach."

I scratched the back of my head. There was something in her tone that made me think she wasn't talking about approaching with the raid.

"Uhhhh," I said.

"Let's move," Darling said.

"Sorry, one second."

She'd already jogged off, but she slowed, and the rest of the guild did the same. "What's up? We should really keep pushing."

"The wall's protected with runes that repel ghosts, right? Just like that pattern we found. Huntsman's runes or whatever it is?"

Darling shrugged. "Sure."

"Well, if the palace walls were built to keep ghosts out, then how does deactivating them help us get in?"

The words hung in the air, and Darling and I looked at Isabel at the same moment.

She smiled. "I'm sorry. But I refuse to live in a world where the same person who broke it gets to live on in his palace."

"What?" Darling said.

I gritted my teeth. "Brandt is already dead, isn't he?"

"In a way, he is. But he deserves his rest all the same. I suggest you stand back." She motioned us apart, ushering us toward the edges of the avenue.

"Isabel? What's happening?"

"Justice," she said as a familiar roar rose from down the avenue.

The storm rolled toward us, a howling wall of snow and ice, and once again I got the impression that something massive was moving at its center.

"Scatter!" Darling said as the blizzard tore down the avenue and sent two of the trees that framed it flying in opposite directions.

The snowstorm ripped right by us and smashed directly into Roost's corpse. It blew the dead golem sideways before the heart of the storm even reached it, then kept rolling from there, ripping the trees from their roots and tossing them deep into the snowfield.

"Move!" Darling said.

Then we were off, the entire raid sprinting through the snowfall and the glaze of ice that the storm left behind.

The blizzard picked up speed as it closed in on the walls, howling like nothing I'd ever heard, and it seemed to shrink in on itself as the winds intensified, allowing us a few glimpses at the creature within: huge, clawed feet, oil-black feathers, a tall fin that ran down its back, and a long snout full of gray teeth.

It collided with the wall and the protective runes dimmed, then died out, though my debuffs stayed in place.

The storm bludgeoned its way deeper in, and the bricks were still falling by the time we reached the section of wall the creature had blown through.

The courtyard beyond was rimed in a six-inch-thick coat of ice, and the ferocious stone statues that lined the entryway up to the stairs had huge icicles protruding off them in crazy directions, as if the wind had been blowing from every direction at once.

Darling was the first to cross the courtyard and start up the stairwell that appeared to lead into the interior of the palace, where two formerly immense doors were propped up against the walls in four warped pieces.

I pounded up the stairs two at a time, and I was about halfway up when the screaming started.

Then the air sparkled in front of Darling, and she smashed into some kind of invisible wall where the doors had stood moments earlier. I helped her up, then pressed a hand to the shimmering expanse. It was brutally cold and completely unyielding.

Isabel ghosted up behind us, floating up the stairs with a somber look on her face.

"Oh my," she said. "I hoped the Huntsman was alone, or close to it. But it doesn't sound that way, does it?"

I tried to peer through the barrier that I assumed she'd thrown up, but the enormous hall within was choked with flying snow, and all I could make out were the towering pillars that served to hold up the building's vaulted ceiling.

Darling drew her axes and struck the invisible wall twice to no avail. "What is this?"

"You can relax," Isabel said. "It's all over now, or it will be soon."

"That was him, wasn't it?" I said. "That thing you just released into the palace. It's Brandt."

Isabel nodded. "I'm afraid so. The last serums he made for us... he promised we'd be together no matter what." She gestured at herself. "I don't know why I became this and he became that, but here we are, together. And once he's finished with the Huntsman, he can finally rest."

The hall shuddered beyond, and a great section of the roof caved in and smashed down into the floor.

"Isabel?"

She floated down a little.

"You said that a corpse only remembers its last moment, right?"

"Indeed."

"Well, back on the stairs, after that guard pushed you down and you hit your head. What were you thinking about?"

She cocked her head, then stared into the whiteout beyond. "I was thinking of him."

"The Huntsman?" Darling said.

Isabel shook her head. "Brandt. I was... I was thinking that I was okay with it. I wasn't well, and I was tired. I felt... lucky in the end, I suppose. Does that answer your question?"

"I think it does, yeah," I said.

Darling dropped her voice so that only Frank and I would be able to hear it. "I don't think Brandt was feeling particularly grateful on the gallows."

"Maybe that's the trick of it?"

The words were scarcely out when the roar intensified and a heavily armored body came flying out of the snow and crashed down into the courtyard beyond, an axe and a shield tumbling from his grasp and bouncing across the stone.

I turned and inspected the body.

**{The Huntsman} (Level 17 Humanoid) (Elite++)**
**HP: 4,200/50,000**
**MP 2,000/2,000**

He struggled to rise, and his iron breastplate sported a deep, bloody gash down the center.

I heard footsteps behind me, falling like thunder, and I and the others pressed ourselves low against the stairs as snow blew out of the building and something enormous squeezed through the gap and blurred out into the courtyard.

The storm stilled then, the white bands drifting away, the center finally coming into focus.

A terrifying creature stood in the center of the courtyard, looming over the Huntsman. It was built much like the Starlit Tyrant that had attacked the Oasis days earlier, but it was covered in jet black feathers, and a long, spectral fin ran down its spine.

Its eyes were flat and white, a perfect match for the falling snow, and its long tail resembled a peacock's but with dark colorations.

**{Frostcaller, Face of the First Apocalypse} (Level 16 Undead) (Raid Boss)**
**HP: 1,000,000/1,000,000**
**MP: 1,500,000/1,500,000**

The Huntsman finally regained his feet, and he looked up at the huge predator standing high above him.

Darling bounced on the balls of her feet. "Come on, come on!" She dropped her voice. "Last thing we need right now is a long speech."

The Huntsman looked as if he were about to do just that, but instead he cried out and stared down at his feet, where a layer of solid ice was starting to creep over him. Within seconds, he was frozen from ankle to knee to hip.

He said something I didn't catch, but the Frostcaller just stood there, impassive, watching the man slowly succumb to the frost.

The Huntsman wheeled his arms as the frost crept above his chest, which left his limbs locked out wide as they too froze over. Finally, the frost crept higher, and the man turned into a frozen statue that stood at the very center of the courtyard. The Frostcaller raised a foot high into the air and brought it down atop the Huntsman.

He shattered.

Isabel drifted down the stairs between Darling and me and approached the Frostcaller.

"It's done. It's truly done, love."

She made it about halfway through the courtyard before the Frostcaller turned in her direction and stomped the same now-bloody foot into the stone. It huffed threateningly, tail fanning out behind it, its breath clouding the air.

Isabel stopped in place, hovering a few feet above the ground.

"It's done," she repeated, louder now. "It's finished."

She raised out a hand as if she expected the creature to lower its head to meet her, but it was staring right at us, its milky gaze flicking from person to person while its tail lashed the air behind it.

"Get ready," Darling said. "And keep in mind that we aren't the only ones who are working on this thing! This is it, so let's get another first!"

"I don't understand," Isabel said. "Aren't you finished, Brandt? Isn't this what you wanted?"

The creature ignored her and stalked forward, and when she refused to move, it lowered its broad head and tossed her aside.

It reached the foot of the stairs and glared up at us, then opened its mouth and screamed. A blizzard rose around the edges of the courtyard, creating a circular battlefield hemmed in by swirling winds.

"Go!" Darling said at the very moment the creature became targetable. "No time to waste, we need a win before the Siege!"

Jukes was already moving before Ton even got his shield up. The diminutive tank loosed an icy dagger, then rolled down the stairs and came upright directly in front of the creature.

It slashed out at him with a taloned foot, but Jukes rolled a second time and shot the gap between the towering creature's legs.

The boss spun a quick 180, feathered tail whipping out, and just like that, we had the positioning we needed.

"This is it!" Darling said, and the melees roared and charged and leaped and teleported down the stairs and behind the huge creature. "This is what we've been working for! Let's one-shot this thing, call out everything you see!"

"Got a debuff down here!" Jukes said. He had a blue icon hovering above his nameplate, and I saw similar debuffs pop up all across the melee group as they went to work.

I scoped it out.

{Freezing Aura}
Movement, attack speed, and casting speed are all reduced by 5% per stack. Upon reaching 10 stacks, target is frozen solid.
Duration: 10 seconds.

"Looks like it's triggered by proximity to the boss!" I said as I loosed my first pair of green-laced ravens down the stairs.

"Can you dispel it?" Darling said, even as she hacked away at one of the creature's thighs and left a green slash hanging in the air. She went to work on the other leg, and the slash pulsed with every swing, numbers ticking up above it: 600, 720, 774.

"No!" Zoe said. "Invalid target!"

"Ton, hang back out of the aura's range for now!" Darling said.

I backed up the stairs to give myself some more breathing room from the boss, and my hair started whipping sideways as I got too close to the edge of the courtyard.

"One stack of Freezing Aura on you!" Frank said.

I fired another round and took two quick steps forward. "Thanks, might have missed that." I raised my voice. "Gotta watch the spinning walls, too—get too close and you'll pick up a stack of Freezing Aura! We might need to spread—"

I cut off as the boss whipped around and lashed Jukes across the chest with its tail. The tank went flying backward across the courtyard and into the gale, which picked him up even higher and tossed him sideways.

He landed hard and ran right back in, but he was visibly slower—he'd already picked up three stacks.

"Ton, rotate in," Darling said.

The tank bellowed and grabbed the boss' attention, but his positioning was poor; he'd taunted from about halfway up the stairs, and the Raid Boss charged right through the bulk of our ranged group as it stormed up to meet him and tagged every player nearby with the Freezing Aura debuff.

"Get the Frostcaller back to the center!" Darling said. "Ranged, get off the stairs and spread out!"

Ton leaped away and the boss ran to follow, but his leap took him nearly on top of Jukes, and the smaller tank had to roll away to the opposite edge of the courtyard to avoid grabbing another stack.

Once we had everyone spread out, the fight settled for a bit, and Ton managed to hold the boss at the center of the courtyard until Jukes' stacks had dropped off.

"Boss at 94%," Frank said.

Across the group, though, the stacks were adding up quickly: the aura seemed to pulse every ten seconds or so, and the entire melee group was already up to three stacks, their strikes coming slower and slower.

We whittled the boss down to 90%, then the Frostcaller raised itself up and fanned its strange tail out behind it.

Darling's voice rang across the courtyard. "Watch it, mechanic incoming!"

The beast stepped right over Ton and took off, sprinting toward the gale that surrounded the battlefield and heading directly my way.

With my new set effect active, I used Clonedrift to shoot myself sideways and to the left.

The boss stampeded right over my clone and smashed it apart, then leaped into the whiteout beyond and disappeared.

I kept my pistols up and pivoted around slowly, trying to watch as much of the battlefield as possible. Ton was standing in the same spot the boss had left him, frowning, and much of the raid seemed similarly confused.

"There!" Nina said, but by the time I was able to figure out the direction she was indicating, I saw her pointing at a blank section of swirling wind. "It was definitely there!"

I spotted a huge shadow at the opposite end of the arena, but it vanished before I could even call it out.

"Battlefield is a circle, so let's call it a clock and say the stairs are noon!" Darling said. "If you see it, call out the hour!"

"Six!" someone said, right as the boss plunged directly through the gale and cut across the courtyard in a blur of blue light and black feathers.

It was completely wreathed in snow once again, and while the bulk of the raid managed to avoid the linear charge, Ton and a few others got caught off-guard and swept off their feet.

The Frostcaller pushed right through the contact and disappeared back into the snow before we could get a single attack in.

"Ton at 80%," Frank said. "Lowest player at 46%, charge hurts. New debuff too, check it."

{Permafrost}
**Each stack of Permafrost counts as 2 stacks of {Freezing Aura}.**
**Duration: Permanent.**

"Good call, thanks." I raised my voice again. "Charge applies a nasty-looking debuff so we need quicker call outs!"

"Uhh, okay!" Darling said. "Group 1, watch from noon to three o'clock, group 2 from three to six, group 3 from six to nine, group 4 from nine to noon!"

"We're in group 3," Frank said.

"Nice!" I spun to face the section of the arena Darling had tasked me with and watched the swirling expanse.

And there it was.

"Seven o'clock!"

The group scattered to either side of the battlefield, and this time everybody but two damage dealers managed to dodge the powerful mechanic.

"Better!" Darling said. "Keep it up!"

The pattern repeated twice with the boss tagging a handful of players each time, then the Frostcaller leaped back into the courtyard and Jukes stepped up to meet it at the center, deftly positioning it with its back to the bulk of our forces.

The fight resumed, and though we'd only just started, my mouth was dry and blood was pounding in my ears.

This was it: the moment we'd spent the better part of three days grinding for almost non-stop. And with the Siege looming...

I pushed the thought away. The guild needed this, and I couldn't afford to be distracted.

"88%," Frank said. "Jukes is back to one stack, Ton is hanging back for now."

The boss used the same tail-whip style strike it had before, but Jukes bent backward at the waist and surprised everyone—including himself, judging from the look on his face—by limboing beneath it. He snapped upright and went back to work.

The Frostcaller broke off an attack and screamed up at the sky, and I was expecting some sort of mechanic to kick in, but then it resumed its assault on Jukes and kept it up until he and Ton executed a well-timed swap to let the smaller tank's stacks reset.

Then out of nowhere, a raid frame grayed out in the top-left corner of my vision, and Nina's bar dropped from full to 40% in a blink.

"We've got an add over here!" she said. She was running across the courtyard to my left while the ghost of a monstrous sloth barreled behind her.

The creature's claws were long and grotesquely twisted, and it ran on all fours while using its blades to rocket itself along.

{Bladecannon Sloth} (Level 15 Undead) (Elite++)
HP: 50,000/50,000
MP: 25,000/25,000

Jukes rolled over and tagged it with an icy dagger. "Got it! Where'd it come from?"

"Out of the palace! It popped out of the stairs and one-shotted somebody!"

"Team Frank represent!" Frank shouted.

"Yep!" Darling said. "All melees, peel off the boss and burn the add until you drop your Freezing Aura stacks, then I want you back on the Frostcaller! Ranged, stay focused on the boss unless you're in Frank's kill group!"

I pivoted and switched targets, then sprinted in the sloth's direction and let the blasts fly while giving the boss a wide berth.

I swapped to my blunderbuss as I closed into range, then popped Doppelganger, which generated two clones that flashed into existence to either side of me thanks to my 6-piece's latest bonus, running just a step behind in an arrow formation.

I Double Cast the ability and created two more that appeared right beside the others, blunderbusses in hand.

The melee crashed down on the sloth before I arrived, so I shot the gap between Darling and Rock and unloaded both of my stored ravens.

"Hits for 850 and 825," Frank said.

All four of my doppels closed in and let fly with spells of their own. Their blasts were weaker—connecting for between 300 and 400 a pop—but with eight total spells flying and striking at once, the plume of numbers that went up was both stunning and immensely gratifying.

My aggro spiked immediately, but I still felt like I had a good bit of wiggle room before I'd rip the mob's focus off Jukes.

"Add's melting!" Darling said, still swinging away. "Keep going, but don't forget to peel off when instructed!"

"Add at 65%," Frank said. "Boss at 84%."

I strafed away with my doppels flanking me to both sides, lighting the sloth up with pistol blasts, then sending a single shot—which turned into a volley of five—back at the boss to keep my caustic debuff rolling there as well.

I was lining up my next round when the sloth whirled in my direction and swung a claw in a vicious horizontal arc, the hooked blade passing mere inches above Darling's head.

The attack sent an arc of spikes flying, and I activated an Illusory Mirror on instinct. The mirror popped up in front of me, and each of my doppels got a spell of their own off before they expired.

The volley was wide, and a huge number of the projectiles blew by me and sank into the raid, dropping Health bars left and right, but my five mirrors reflected five spikes and the effect was absolutely devastating, with each reflected projectile connecting for nearly 1,200 damage.

"Watch that blade throw!" Darling said. "Ranged, drop off the boss and help us burn this thing! That was too deadly!"

I took a deep breath and raised my voice to shout over the clamor. "I was probably second on the threat meter so it targeted me with that arc! I'll position better next time, but if you've got reflects, they absolutely truck!"

"Add at 20%," Frank said. "All melees on the sloth have lost their debuffs, but Ton is up to four. Make sure they leave the Franking to Team Frank!"

"You heard him!" Darling said. "Melees, peel off the add at 10% and get back on the Frostcaller; ranged, stay on until it's at 5%! Tank swap now, go!"

Jukes rolled low and Ton jumped right over him at the same time, resulting in a swap so perfect it left me grinning from ear to ear: their targets barely had a chance to move before the next tank was in place. The DPS group shifted in turn, leaving a handful of us behind to finish off the add while spells and projectiles flew through the air.

I fired off a Dark Harvest, and with our executes in play, the sloth rapidly dropped into low single digits.

"Boss just dashed off into the snow behind you," Frank said.

I pivoted slightly so that I could keep watch over the area Darling had assigned me. "Good call!"

"Two o'clock!" someone said.

The call was a little late, and I had to burn Clonedrift to avoid the charge that followed, but that also meant I was able to witness the moment when Jukes rolled away to save himself and the badly injured sloth chased after him.

The boss steamrolled the smaller creature, and I saw the Permafrost debuff show up above its nameplate before the mob ticked down to 1% and someone else in the execute group finished it from range.

And that gave me an idea.

"If the tanks can drag the adds through the Frostcaller's charges, we can slow their attacks down and maybe even freeze them up!" I said. "The charge hits hard, too! Might help us burn the boss faster by freeing up more DPS!"

"I like it!" Darling said. "Ton, Jukes, you think you can handle that?"

"Think so!" Jukes replied.

"I can try," Ton said.

Another charge followed, and everybody but a healer managed to get out of the way. We waited for a third charge to follow, but it didn't come.

The entire raid just stood there for a moment, eyeing the wall of swirling wind. Then the constant roar increased and the winds crept closer, shrinking the battlefield by about ten feet on every side.

The boss came roaring out of the snow, but instead of charging as it had before, it hopped straight to the center of the arena and sent out a blue shockwave that rolled along at ankle level.

Everybody jumped it without issue except for a healer who jumped too early and instantly picked up two stacks of Permafrost.

The Frostcaller raised itself to its full height at the center of the battle-field and the tips of its black feathers began to glow with blue light. Its fin brightened as well, and its tail fanned out as it had before.

It fixed its gaze on Jukes, then opened its mouth wide.

"Breath attack incoming!" Darling said.

Jukes rolled sideways as the boss raked a six-foot wide column of cyan light across the entire arena. It pivoted and dragged the spell behind him, sweeping it in a wide arc.

Darling jumped straight over it and I mimicked the move with a Water Jet, and a great deal of the raid activated similar abilities, then got right back to burning the beast down.

But those who were less mobile were forced to run along in front of the beam, and one of our ranged damage dealers took a bad angle and got caught in it at the very edge of the arena.

Her steps slowed down immediately, and the slow only intensified as she fell back farther into the beam and the stacks of Permafrost rapidly ramped up from one to three to five as the attack swept over her.

Her bar grayed out instantly despite her Health having been halfway full, and she left an icy blue statue behind, frozen mid-stride.

"Alright then!" Darling said. "Ten stacks of Freezing Aura or five stacks of Permafrost are both lethal! We're still looking okay, but we're down two ranged damage dealers. We can't afford to lose anyone else, so stay sharp! Tanks, keep an eye on the stairs!"

The Frostcaller's beam attack continued until it had completed a full sweep of the arena, then its fin dimmed. Jukes ran out to meet it, and Ton rumbled over to the stairs in preparation for the next add.

The fight wore on, and I started to think about the World-first, picturing Darling beaming as the group erupted, jubilant.

And while the adds Darling had warned about did reappear—a new creature with at least one new attack each time the boss dropped by 10% —Jukes and Ton were absolutely nailing their switches.

Dragging the mobs into the boss' charges had been key, too: we kept every single damage dealer focused on the boss unless the melees needed a break from the Frostcaller's pulsing aura and simply depended on the stacks of Permafrost the boss' charge inflicted to freeze the creatures in place rather than killing them.

The healers' Mana was looking good, too, and I felt my excitement ratchet up as we passed the halfway point and Frank announced the mile-stone loud enough for the whole raid to hear.

The battlefield was littered with frozen adds, garish creatures that had been iced over mid-attack, their features terrifying even as they stood there, motionless.

The boss dashed away again as it ticked under 45%, and a few shouts of exultation went up.

"We're not there yet!" Darling said, but even she couldn't hide the hope in her voice. The group expertly dodged three more charges, then the boss leaped back to the center of the arena and repeated that same shockwave from earlier.

The blue ring swept out, and while Jukes deftly managed to jump it, the two adds he'd been tanking paid it no mind and ended up freezing solid in a blink. He rolled between them, heading for the boss and probably already knowing what was coming next.

Then an alert went out, and everything went to shit.

**World-first Alert! The Guild {Corruptia} is the first guild to clear the Menagerie Wing by defeating the {Frostcaller} encounter! {Corruptia} has been awarded an additional 2 days to claim the Worldbranch Throne, as well as 72 hours of access to the Cloudscape Hunting Grounds!**
**Awarding Unique Title: The First Frostwalker**

A second, longer prompt followed, but I couldn't take my eyes off the first alert.

The entire raid seemed to pause for a moment as the alert sunk in, and that was all it took: the beam attack started up again, and Ton and another damage dealer got caught floundering.

The big tank must have already had a few stacks of Freezing Aura because he turned into a statue on contact, and the beam swept mercilessly on. The damage dealer slowed, then turned to ice a few feet from Ton.

"Ton's down, we're done," Darling said. "Wipe it, save yourselves if you can!"

I cursed loud enough to draw a few looks even as people scattered, then pulled it together and Water Jetted myself over the beam as three spectral hounds charged down the steps and entered the battlefield. But there was no obvious way out as far as I could tell.

I kited away and across from the adds to buy time, then Clonedrifted myself right into the gale in the direction of the avenue. The stacks of

Freezing Aura ramped up quickly, and by the time Clonedrift expired and I hit the ground running—still fully within the blizzard—it felt like I was running through mud.

I got desperate as my stacks crept up from seven to eight without seeing anything reminiscent of safety, so I Double Cast another drift in the hopes that it would save me.

And the moment the spell reached its full range and expired, my body locked up and the white world turned a familiar shade of gray.

**You died!**
**You lost 160 Renown!**
**You dropped 3 items!**
**Raid Spectator Mode engaged!**
**You may respawn as soon as your raid is no longer in combat.**

I didn't have to check my inventory this time around. I could already see what I'd dropped. Lying atop my Legendary rifle as well as my Ghosthunter's helm was Frank.

# Chapter Forty-Eight

I just floated there, stunned by the fact that Corruptia had actually beaten us to the kill.

A moment later, a message from Darling scrawled in pink popped up in the bottom left corner of my vision: *I got him, loot is set to master.*

I thanked her and shot her some commiserations, but she didn't reply.

I floated around the arena, watching the guild take a variety of different approaches: Jukes was still trying to tank the boss, supported by a few of the healers who had stayed with him, while other people took the same approach I had by trying to flee through the white gale.

And in the end, it didn't matter: every single member of the twenty-person raid either died to the adds or the boss or ended up frozen in place.

The option to respawn finally presented itself, so I took it and shifted into ghost form out in a graveyard in the Vale, about equidistant between the Black Oasis and its now-towering world tree and the Red Cathedral itself.

The massive construct was shimmering and shifting faster than ever before: three of its tallest towers were flashing at an incredible rate, adding several stories of height every time they disappeared and flashed back into existence.

It seemed like Corruptia's clear had triggered the next step of the Cathedral's evolution.

I pulled up the prompt I'd skipped over when the World-first had gone out, just before the group had wiped.

**Citizens of EBO!**
**The first wing of the Red Cathedral has fallen, and the world-ending Frostcaller has finally been defeated!**
**For the next 24 hours, any and all Ripples caused within a zone will instantly complete that zone's Red Cathedral, and all Cathedrals will progress by at least 25% every 12 hours.**
**For those of you who have yet to receive extensions in your quest to claim the Worldbranch Throne, only two days remain!**
**But rest assured: in exactly 24 hours, the next phase of the Possibility King Raid will unlock within every Cathedral that's cleared the Menagerie Wing, and the second wing, the Thousand Tower Tournament, will officially begin.**
**The tournament will offer a view into a brand-new apocalypse with three distinct paths for you to choose from: PVP, PVE, plus a hybrid option that offers the best of both worlds and improved loot and Renown for those who are up to the challenge.**
**Plan accordingly, gather your forces, protect your cities, and prepare yourselves to crown a new wave of champions!**
**And as always, thank you for playing EBO.**

I read that over again, sighing as I raced across the great dunes, taking advantage of the reduced gravity to traverse them and the rivers that ran between them in huge, leaping bounds.

I raced up the steps that led to the Menagerie Wing and toward the portal and found that I was the second to pop back in: Darling had beaten me by a couple of seconds.

We shared a glance and took off, burning our movement abilities as quickly as we could, with Darling throwing each of her axes and disappearing, only to reappear farther ahead and catch them, while I Water Jetted and Clonedrifted myself around.

Once those spells were done, we settled into running beside each other.

"Sorry," I said. "Really sucks."

She nodded but kept her eyes on the switchbacks that rose up in the distance as we flew through the snowy streets. We dashed up them and back into the courtyard, and she reclaimed Frank and my other items and immediately threw them into a trade window.

I accepted the trade, tossed my helm back on, put my rifle into my inventory, and dropped Frank into his loop.

I felt him suck in a breath as if he was about to launch into some fresh tirade, but the look on Darling's face must have changed his mind.

"Well, that officially blows," Frank said eventually.

"My thoughts exactly," Darling said. She ran her hands through her hair and inhaled deeply, then forced something like a smile as the other guild members started to show up behind us. She looked at Frank. "Imagine you can't tell us what the Cloudscaped Hunting Grounds are all about, huh?"

"Depends who's asking. If it's Ned, then no. If it's you, also no, but I'm sorry about it."

She shook her head. "We were doing so good, too. That alert really threw us for a loop."

"Yeah. One moment of hesitation and bam, done." I punched a fist into an open palm. "That was quick thinking with the clock though, especially on the fly."

She stared at the Frostcaller, which was looming in the center of the courtyard, staring us down with its white eyes. "Thanks. Anything you can think of that we could have done better?"

"It'll help a lot to know adds are coming: we lost somebody to that right away. And probably just knowing how bad those Permafrost stacks are. You pick one up and you're already 20% dead, and it never goes away. So far it's the charge, the shockwave on landing, and the beam that apply them."

She clenched her hands into fists, relaxed them, and clenched again. "Yeah. We'll have a better shot this time around. Guess we could still snag second, that'd be something. Get an extension so we don't have too much pressure on us in the next wing."

"The Thousand Tower Tournament," I said. "Interesting. Wonder what that's going to look like. It's cool to see that the other Cathedrals will need to finish this raid off before they can jump into the second wing. Feels like that bodes well for the Oasis."

"Yeah. If we can hold onto it."

I deflated a little, shoulders slumping. "Agreed."

She rubbed her face and summoned a more convincing smile. "Sorry, don't mean to be a downer. I guess I'm just more worried about that than

I realized, and I was kinda thinking we'd be going into it with another win in our back pocket. But it's not the first time somebody has beaten us to a kill and it definitely won't be the last. Long raid, right? Just feels like I could have done better, you know?"

"If anything it's on me."

"I completely agree," Frank said.

"You could at least wait until I explain how."

"Seems unnecessary."

"Seriously though—I'm the one that pushed the Rifts and the Hall and getting our Trinkets together and all that. And that World Boss fight. Maybe if we'd skipped that. we'd already be celebrating a clear on the Frostcaller."

Nina popped into view across from Darling, then squeezed her shoulder and walked by without a word.

"Maybe," Darling said. "But you're also the reason we're here at all."

"Thanks," Frank said. "It's nice to have someone else around who's bold enough to say that out loud. Other than myself, obviously."

"She was talking to me, Frank," I said.

Darling shook her head, and her snow-dusted hair whipped across her face. "No, I was talking to Frank."

I drew back for a moment, then laughed as she winked at me. "Ouch. Frarling is circling the wagons, huh? I see how it is."

"No regrets on the World Boss kill, that was awesome. Trinkets, classes, everything: I wouldn't change any of that. Just sucks to be so close, you know?" She jerked her head back at the rest of the guild, most of whom were ringed up around the boss in a wide circle, brainstorming strategies. "I really wanted to get it for 'em. They've been pushing so hard, and yeah, then there's the Siege."

"I know you won't actually be able to, but try to let me worry about the Siege for now," I said. "Speaking of that, I've been thinking about something." I tapped Frank. "Is there any way we can still get that moat going around the Commerce Ward?"

"Uh, yeah? But why? You already have the trench and spikes. That'd be like a side-grade rather than an upgrade."

I sent House a quick message asking her to do just that and to get a golem or two on it if necessary. "Call it a hunch."

Darling patted her cheeks a couple of times as if she was trying to wake herself up. "Okay. I guess we go again then, yeah?"

"Yup! I think we got it this time."

# Chapter Forty-Nine

I bounded across the sands, a ghost once again.

As it turned out, we didn't have it on the second attempt. Not even close. Or the third, or the fourth, or whatever attempt it was that we'd just wiped on with the boss knocking on the door of the execute window.

I'd also been way off base about how to handle the adds: we could indeed avoid killing them and just use the boss' charges to freeze them in place, but that left frozen statues littered all across the battlefield.

And whenever the Frostcaller happened to charge through one of those terrifying, frozen creatures—or the corpse of a player who'd iced over—it created a totally unavoidable supernova of ice that flared across the entire battlefield and handed every living player a stack of Permafrost.

The mechanic was pretty rare and seemed to happen by pure chance, but it was also absolutely devastating, and it'd been at least partially responsible for every wipe we'd experienced, especially as we pushed under the 40% mark and the adds started coming more and more quickly and players died off.

Our only saving grace so far was that we'd found a way to safely wipe the encounter: if whoever had aggro pushed into the palace where the mobs spawned and where the storm stayed thin throughout the fight, the boss would follow, despawn, then reset about a minute later at the center of the battlefield.

We'd been at it for hours and hours, and I'd personally died three times in all, including this latest one—which had cost me well over 1,000 Renown total and suddenly amped my death penalty to worrisome levels for the future—but I felt even worse for Ton and Jukes, each of whom had been racking them up without complaint.

Well, Jukes hadn't complained, but I couldn't fault Ton for getting frustrated.

And all along the way, after every single wipe, I spent the entirety of the run back scouring my inventory for every item Frank and I had ever found time and time again, poring over every Codex entry Frank had ever sent me, and scrutinizing every Ripple in EBO's history, looking for something—anything—that might help us with the Siege, which was feeling more and more hopeless by the minute.

And slowly, by degrees, something like a plan began to click into place.

House had reported some interesting things overnight: the number of prisms and mobs rushing the Black Oasis had notably decreased and a steady exodus of NPCs had begun, flowing out of each of the city's four wards.

In more positive news, my Golden Strangle buff was ramping up much more quickly, though House wasn't sure why.

But for now, I swallowed my rising anxiety and tried to focus on the raid.

I jumped back into the Menagerie Wing, ran down the now way-too-familiar streets and made my way up the switchbacks and into the courtyard. I scooped up the gear I'd dropped on dying as well as Frank and dropped him back into his loop again.

"Oof," he said. "I thought we had it that time."

"Same, man. Brutal. I almost forgot what smashing your face against an encounter felt like for a little while there. It's a bit nostalgic, but I can't say I missed it at this point in time."

Darling and a few others trickled in, walking instead of running at the frenetic pace we'd started with, and the body blow that I'd been fearing ever since that last World-first went out finally hit home.

**World Alert! The Guild {Redacted} is the second guild to clear the Menagerie Wing by defeating the {Frostcaller} encounter and has been granted 48 hours of access to the Cloudscape Hunting Grounds! In addition, {Redacted} has been awarded an additional 1 day to claim the Worldbranch Throne.**

**No further extensions will be granted for clearing this encounter.**

I bent over at the waist, hands on knees.

Frank hesitated. "You good? People are looking our way."

I straightened and rolled my shoulders. "Yeah, big game, big world, so it goes, right? That stung, but I'm more worried for Darling and the crew than anything else. I really wish we could have made this happen for them. Kinda thought it was a given, honestly, but all these wipes make me think we're missing something. Maybe we picked the wrong curses to break."

"But at least we can console ourselves with the knowledge that Team Frank lives on."

"There is that, yeah. I'm assuming I'll probably get kicked off the team the moment the raid ends so I'm soaking it in while I can, you know?"

"I would do the same, not that I'd ever be in that position."

"Well, it's your team, so."

I blinked as one of Darling's axes flew in my direction only for her to reappear in front of it and snag it out of the air.

"Well, that one physically hurt. No extensions for us, I guess. Gonna put a hell of a lot of pressure on us in the next wing, especially since we can't even start it for another day. That's only gonna leave us 24 hours to snag a first or second clear, and both those guilds in front of us are going to have a major leg up. I'm still wondering what's up with the Cloudscape thing, too."

"Safe to say that whatever it is, it's going to be powerful," I said. "Think of the Hall, right?"

"Yeah, I'm trying not to." She rubbed her temples. "I really hate to say this, but I think we might need to call it a night and start thinking about the Siege. At the very least, I'm going to need to offer people a break in between this and that to get something to eat and so on."

"I think we've still got a good amount of time, right? Can't be that late already."

"Little under two hours left," Frank said. "Siege is going to start a bit after 8 AM."

I ground the heels of my palms into my eyes. "Is it seriously six in the morning?"

"Uh huh."

Darling nodded. "Quite the blur, right? We should probably cut people free and let them get a bit of sleep if we want them to be functional when the Siege starts." She gestured around at the group. "I dunno about you, but in my experience you can usually tell when to call it quits on a raid when you wipe and nobody complains about it in the guild chat immediately afterward. The silence is way worse than the noise."

I craned my neck around at the members who were walking back into the courtyard yet again. The brainstorming between wipes had stopped, and there wasn't a single bit of green text in my chat window.

I blew out a puff of air. "You think asking people to give it one more shot would be pushing it?"

She put her hands out, palms up, then moved them up and down as if she were weighing the question. "I feel comfortable asking, but I think we need to go with the consensus on this one. You really want to risk another death?"

"Definitely. It's just... we reached the Frostcaller in, what, two hours? Three at most?"

"Huh?"

"Corruptia took more than two days to clear this raid, and we got to the last boss in two hours. Maybe they broke different curses or they've got a different composition or something—maybe more ranged, less melees—"

Frank hissed.

"—but they can't be that much better than us, right? If they can do this at all, then we should be able to do it with the people here."

Darling licked her lips. "You think it's a composition thing?"

"Probably a factor, yeah. Frank can hiss all he wants, but if we had two tanks, four healers, and sixteen ranged DPS, then we wouldn't even need to worry about the boss' aura, right? We could focus entirely on avoiding Permafrost stacks and burn whatever target we wanted. And think of the Grim fight: ranged would have had a much easier time there, too. No need to cut your melee damage by dodging tentacles or having to pull away when the lasers started up. And ranged DPS had a much easier time targeting Roost's weak spots too."

She bit her lip. "We could maybe try to switch it up tomorrow, but I absolutely hate doing that. It's one thing if it's late in the game and I can have people switch to other characters, but I don't want to start moving people around otherwise. Core is core, you know? If you're here, then you've earned it."

"No, that's exactly what I'm saying—we *could* switch it up and that would probably help, but I don't think we need to." I looked around and motioned at the other members, then realized a few of them were listening, so I forced myself to keep going. "I still wanna win, but I guess I'd rather win less if it means having the right people around when things don't go your way, you know? And we can definitely do this. We just need a cleaner start with those debuffs. If the race is off then the pressure is too, right? I think we've got it."

Darling smiled. "Yeah, I'm with you on that, but let's see what they think." She turned to face the rest of the group. "Alright, two options, guys: we call it here and get some sleep, then regroup for the Siege, or give this thing one more shot. Don't burn yourselves out, but I think—"

"One more," Nina said, and Rock nodded behind her.

The silence hung for a moment, and Jukes was the first to break it. "I'm game."

"I'm in too," Zoe said. "We almost hit the execute window, so we're close."

A round of murmurs and nods went around.

"Ton?" Darling said. "What do you think?"

The big tank's shield was lying on the ground beside him, and he was leaning on the pommel of his sword with both hands. He blew out a puff of air, then shrugged. "I guess I can do one more."

"Alright then!" Darling said, and I was impressed with the level of enthusiasm she managed to dredge up. "One more shot! Now that we know how deadly those statues are when an add freezes, I want full DPS swaps the very moment they arrive. Full executes from everyone—just do your best to peel off as the mob drops beneath 2%, then the kill team—"

"Team Frank!" Frank shouted, for probably the fiftieth time with no discernable reduction in enthusiasm.

"You really can't help yourself, can you?" I said.

"No I can't, and if I could, I'd choose not to."

Darling smirked. "Right, Team Frank can put them down. But if it's a question of letting a mob freeze or taking a chance that a kill will proc another add because of that curse, then sorry Frank, but we're gonna be aggressive and roll the dice at this point."

I laughed. "He's the last person you need to apologize to for being aggressive."

"Truth," he said.

Darling looked around. "Buffs up, we're rolling in thirty!"

I reloaded my blunderbuss, then scoped out my runes for what felt like the thirtieth time, but I was pretty sure that the loadout I was using was correct: Ghostly Hunt and Caustic Raven on the pistols, hunt on the blunderbuss as well, and piercing on my rifle.

"Keep in mind that the adds tend to show up each time the boss drops by increments of 10%, and unless you're a tank, I want people steering clear of the stairs completely so we don't lose anybody before the tanks can grab them.

"Ton and Jukes, you guys have been killing your rotations so just keep it up. If you're on adds when the boss is charging out of the storm, do everything you can to keep your mobs from getting trucked as the Frost-caller moves across the battlefield."

She drew her weapons. "On your mark, Jukes!"

"Pulling on three! One, two, three!" The tank rolled forward, and the fight was on.

Even with how many times we'd gone through the initial phase at this point, the opening was remarkably smooth: Darling had been right about Jukes and Ton having their rotations down, and the two of them were completely locked in, alternating between blocking or trying to dodge the boss' vicious, taloned strikes and bailing out to round up the ever-increasing stream of ghostly monsters that poured out of the palace.

I kept my debuffs rolling and prioritized the adds as soon as they spawned, and while I could feel the aggro I was putting out on them, both of the tanks were doing a fantastic job of staying ahead of me.

I held my breath and spun to face my section of the battlefield as the first round of charges started, calling out locations whenever the boss' shadow appeared behind the whirling gale.

The group had improved here as well, and we survived the mechanic without a single member getting hit and ending up stuck with a stack of Permafrost for the rest of the fight.

"That was our first fully clean rotation!" Darling said. "Great work!"

"Boss at 80%," Frank said.

We pressed on from there, and my hopes started rising again as the adds continued to drop and the melees seemed to be managing their debuffs far more cleanly than ever before.

The boss leaped to the center of the arena as it dropped beneath the halfway mark, and four different people—myself included—called out a warning about the shockwave to follow. The group hopped it, and every-body was already running clockwise around the battlefield before the sweeping beam even started.

The result was nearly perfect: every player managed to stay out of it, but like so many iterations before, we didn't have enough concentrated damage to finish a four-armed, minotaur-like mob, and despite Jukes' best efforts at dragging the creature behind him and out of the way, it got caught in the beam and turned into a statue.

"That's okay!" Darling said as a few groans sounded from the raid and Ton rushed in to engage the boss. "Still our best effort by far, halfway there, nobody dead, no Permafrost on anyone!"

A quintet of spectral tigers spawned as the boss hit 40%. This was the group I'd been waiting for, the same one that had largely done us in the last time around by lingering for too long and getting turned into statues by the Frostcaller's beam.

They had lower Health than the other adds, but they teleported all over the battlefield and seemed to pick targets at random, which made them difficult to focus down.

{Phasetiger} (Level 15 Undead) (Elite++)
HP: 20,000/20,000
MP: 10,000/10,000

My positioning was slightly off as I was on the other side of the battle-field from the stairs with the white gale raging behind me, so I switched to my rifle and sent a Gravity Bird soaring between the Frostcaller's legs right as the five spectral beasts prowled down the stairs.

The spell erupted as they reached the bottom, and the black hole pulled all five of them into a tight knot before Jukes even had time to jump out of his roll and start swinging.

I popped everything I had, with Doppelganger going first followed by a Double Cast for more copies. I Water Jetted all five of us right over the Frostcaller and switched to pistols in mid-air.

With the enhanced control my 6-piece set bonus offered, I was able to have the clones each choose a different target, and by the time I landed and rolled to my feet, I'd managed to get my debuff stacked up across the whole group.

"70% on the adds," Frank said. "Falling much faster this time with everybody piling on!"

I popped Frank into my hands, dashed across what remained of the distance between me and the adds, then activated Repel as the Gravity Bird winked out and dropped the elevated mobs.

I directed each of my clones to pick their own target and copy the attack, and the result was everything that both Frank and I had been hoping for: five falling mobs, five vicious, Frank-powered uppercuts, and five knock-ups that sent each of the creatures airborne even as the raid burned them down and the battlefield around me flashed and crackled.

"Yes yes yes yes yes!" Frank said. "Two Frank points per hit!"

I switched to my Aeroblaster blunderbuss and aimed it up at the mobs as they hit their apex, dumped both of my stored Ravenblasts into them, and watched the piercing, guaranteed crits roll in one after the other.

My threat spiked completely out of control, but I didn't care: the mobs were falling fast, and by the time they hit the ground, I'd already drifted away and left five clones behind.

The first tiger to land and get its bearings ignored Jukes and raked right through one of my clones, which set off a chain reaction of explosions that stunned the group for three more seconds and let the melees really lay into them, cleaving across the still tightly packed targets.

Jukes popped Hateful Ice, and I just managed to squeeze a Dark Harvest and get it copied several times over to spike his threat and get the creatures' attention off me before my Doppelgangers faded away.

"Amazing work!" Darling said as all five of the mobs dropped well before the next beam hit, the first time we'd managed to kill more than two of them.

When the boss leaped into the center of the arena, we dodged the shockwave and navigated the sweeping beam.

"New guild record for the boss, and everybody's still up!" Darling said. "Keep it going!"

"Execute window is a go!" Frank shouted as the Frostcaller dropped to 29%. "Frank 'em!"

Our damage ramped up dramatically, and the mood brightened as we whittled the Frostcaller down: 28%, 27%, 26%.

And when it had a quarter of its life remaining, the fight changed again: a rumble like thunder sounded from the palace building, and the ground began to shake beneath my feet.

I kept up the damage and Jukes rolled over to the base of the stairs, ready for whatever was coming his way.

A stampede of mobs poured out of the entryway, dozens of them, then hundreds. My heart dropped as I scoped out their Health pools and found them all at about 30,000.

Jukes activated Hateful Ice again to root the new arrivals and keep them from surging over the rest of us. In return, he got nothing but immune messages: dozens of them.

He threw out a handful of icy daggers to the same result, then whipped his staff into a bear as it rumbled by in desperation.

And the result was exactly the same.

"Incoming!" he said.

But instead of rampaging over the raid, the ghostly rush streamed to the edge of the battlefield and dashed right into the swirling winds.

The ghosts lifted into the air, riding the gale all around the battlefield. Jukes stood there at the base of the stairs, bewildered as the mobs streamed by and were lifted up into the gale, emerging from the palace so quickly that within seconds the arena was surrounded by a spinning wall of howling, shining ghosts.

The spirits on the ground level were stampeding around the edges of the storm, their eyes focused on us, while the rest of them drifted through the air and watched us from above, hunger in their eyes.

And the whole lot of them were definitely closing in.

"The storm's constricting!" I called out. "The battlefield's shrinking even faster!"

"Cooldowns!" Darling said. "This is it, full burn! We need this!"

My burst cooldowns were still unavailable, so I took a few steps toward the boss while I lit it up, putting a bit of distance between the wall of encroaching ghosts and myself.

The boss' Health crept lower and lower, and it seemed content to battle it out with Ton and Jukes to the bitter end, but the wall was closing in too quickly.

Some kind of batlike creature flew right out of the storm and dove into the lone add we'd allowed to freeze on the battlefield.

The statue erupted, throwing up an immense nova of ice that handed everyone a stack of Permafrost and noticeably dropped our damage.

"That's okay!" Darling said. "Just means we were right to go out of our way to avoid making statues!"

More flying creatures flew out of the wall and swooped over the battlefield as the fight raged on, but it seemed like they were looking purely for statues because after wheeling about for a moment they each returned to the storm, content to ride the ever-constricting winds.

"Five stacks of Freezing Aura on me!" Ton said. "Need to rotate!"

Jukes was there in a heartbeat, rolling right underneath the boss and smoothly grabbing the Frostcaller's attention.

"Boss is at 15%!" Frank said. "Watch your back!"

I took another small step forward. Glancing over my shoulder, the storm of ghosts was right behind me, wailing and shrieking, and I only had seconds remaining before I'd have to choose between standing in that violent swirl or moving into range of the boss' pulsing aura.

"Melees' about to lose the opportunity to reset their stacks!" I said. "Not gonna be enough room to escape the aura!"

"Screw it, burn the damn thing!" Darling said. "Can't afford to have the melee group peel off long enough to let their stacks drop!"

A roar went up at that, and the wall forced me to step fully into the Freezing Aura as the boss' Health hit single digits.

"Watch the tail!" Frank said.

I let a pair of blasts go and ducked as the creature's peacock-like tail flared out and sliced over my head.

"5%!" Frank said.

As it dropped to 4%, the ghosts lower down in the gale began charging across the battlefield with no discernable pattern, streaking across it from one side to the other, loping or crawling or leaping or even flying low, mere inches above the ground.

The ghost of a wide-winged condor made contact with one of our damage dealers, and they immediately reported that they'd been handed two stacks of Permafrost.

"You can afford to get hit!" Darling said. "We're so close, bring it down!"

I sidestepped a spectral antelope with huge horns and popped my cooldowns in the same sequence as they became available, using Doppelganger followed by Double Cast.

I switched to my rifle for a Dark Harvest that connected for 900, the four doppels added 1,600 in total between them, then I started the Ravenblast onslaught, striking for upwards of 500 with every pistol blast while the clones each tacked on an additional 300 or so with every cast they copied.

"It's falling!" Darling said. "It's gonna drop!"

"Behind!" Frank called out.

I was too slow to avoid a charging rhino, and it punched right through me and kept going without knocking me down. It felt like having an icy bucket of water dumped over my head, and while I saw the two stacks of Permafrost show up above my nameplate, I gritted my teeth and tried to focus on getting the most out of my burst window.

"3%!" Frank said. "2%!"

The mob slashed out at Jukes twice back-to-back, raptor-like, then hopped away and over him and back to the center of the arena, causing another blue shockwave to roll out across the ground.

"No!" Darling said. "Damn, we might have another round of charges incoming!"

I dashed in close with my clones and switched to my blunderbuss, dodging left and right as the ghosts continued to streak across the battlefield from every direction at once while the great bulk of them spun around us, a luminous wall that was maybe ten feet away from the boss on every side.

I fired both of my blasts up at the creature and my clones duplicated the short-range spells, then I backed away and went back to pistols while I eyed the duration on Doppelganger as well as the three cannon charges I'd been awarded for killing some adds earlier on.

"There's not enough room to dodge the charges from here!" Nina said. "No way!"

"And all the ghosts!" someone said.

My hopes dimmed as the Frostcaller shifted and got ready to dash away, its Health still at 2%. The impossibility of what lay in front of us made me think we'd simply played it too slow, that we hadn't dealt enough damage and the boss had hit some kind of time limit and was just going to mop the floor with us.

But instead of charging off, the boss hopped into the air and landed on one foot, sending another blue shockwave surging out.

I hopped over it and kept firing, and the boss repeated the process again, hopping up and down at the center of the battlefield and sending out a trio of blue shockwaves that weren't even two feet apart.

"Melees, we need to pull back!" Darling said as two of the waves caught Nina up close and turned her into a statue mid-backstab. "It's all on the ranged if this keeps up!"

I ran sideways and jumped all three waves, planting a foot between each of them and firing every step of the way, pistols flashing again and again.

"1%!" Frank said. "Kill the bird! Kill it!"

Another of the melees froze up, the boss started moving even more quickly, and the shockwaves started coming so fast that the stone floor seemed to ripple like a pond that someone had just thrown a stone into.

I kept moving, grateful for my mobility, but Doppelganger was about to expire. Our damage had slowed to a crawl, as it was mostly me and the physical ranged players that were still chipping away at the boss' Health as the spellcasters and melees struggled to get their attacks in.

"Blitz it!" Darling said. She leaped over the ripples and struck twice on the way down, then managed a flurry of attacks that left green slashes hanging and pulsing in the air before the constant shockwaves froze her in place, her huge axes held out to either side.

The other melees followed her lead and our damage spiked for a moment before one of the long-circling birds dove straight into the frozen corpse Darling had left behind.

An unavoidable blue nova surged out and locked most of the melee group up for good.

I planted my feet and pulled out my cannon. With how quickly the shockwaves were coming, I wasn't going to be able to dodge them with the cannon equipped, so I fired off all three rounds as quickly as I could and sent three ravens soaring high into the air, each of which was duplicated four times over.

I swapped back to my pistols, but I'd eaten two shockwaves while using the cannon, which meant the next one would freeze me solid.

Health bars grayed out rapid-fire as the melees froze in place mid-swing all around the boss. I jumped an incoming shockwave as my Doppelgangers faded, planted a foot between the surge of blue light and the next and leaped once again, still firing.

The first of my cannon-style ravens splashed down from above, howling, and the copies and other rounds followed in a torrent of dark magic, filling the courtyard with deafening sound and drifting feathers.

More desperate spells and projectiles followed: giant spears of iron, falling meteors, a stream of golden arrows slamming home one after another.

The Frostcaller staggered, regained its balance, then staggered right and collapsed.

As the din of battle fell away and frozen statues glinted all around the fallen creature, a prompt lit up the center of my screen.

**Congratulations, you've defeated the {Frostcaller} encounter and cleared the first wing of the Red Cathedral: The Menagerie Wing!**

And the best part? A prompt that I hadn't been expecting in the slightest followed quickly thereafter.

World Alert! The Guild {Omen Habet Nomen Latine} is the third guild to clear the Menagerie Wing by defeating the {Frostcaller} encounter, and they have been granted 24 hours of access to the Cloudscape Hunting Grounds!
No further additional rewards will be granted for completing this encounter.

Personal Alert! You have been granted 24 hours of access to the Cloudscape Hunting Grounds! The access period will begin early this afternoon!

# Chapter Fifty

"Yes!" I said, pumping a fist so hard that I actually left the ground.

"About time a bird got what's coming to it!" Frank said.

While I'd expected a cacophony of shouts and triumphant cries to follow the boss' demise, the healers and a handful of the ranged group were the only ones left aside from myself, and the arena looked like a statue garden of our own making with how many frozen bodies the Frost-caller had left behind.

The fallen boss was sparking blue, purple, and orange, and I had to fight down the urge to go and scope out the loot before everybody else had a chance to respawn.

But one look at the guild chat—which was awash in so many congratulations and expletives and random, capitalized letters and so on that it was hard to read any one of them before five more messages scrolled by—convinced me to do exactly that and link them to the good stuff while those who had been killed ran back.

The Rare loot seemed almost endless: the boss had dropped thirteen pieces of that quality, all of which was set gear for various members of the raid. The Epic stuff was similar, with three more set pieces that had apparently rolled a tier higher in quality.

But the real prize in that category was a two-handed axe that was going to be giving Frank some insecurity issues the moment Darling popped back in to claim it.

{Frostcaller's Blade} (Two-handed Axe)
Grade: D
Item Level: 53
Damage Type: Physical
Quality: Epic
Physical Attack: 152
Magical Attack: 25
Speed: Very Slow
Primaries: +20 Strength, +20 Constitution
Secondaries: +5% Chance to Hit
Effect: Whenever you deal a killing blow to an enemy that awards Experience or Renown, they leave a Frozen Statue behind for 10 seconds. For every Frozen Statue currently standing, you deal 10% increased damage, stacking up to 5 times.

The axe's huge, crescent-shaped blade was pale blue and made of swirling, elegantly detailed ice that swept out from a black haft marked with gold scrollwork.

And then I reached the Legendaries.

{Brandt Walker's Memorial Heart} (Legendary Artifact)
Quality: Legendary
Use: Permanently breaks every curse within the Menagerie Wing. This effect only applies to the single raid lockout within which the item is activated.
Charges: 3

The chatter intensified as I linked the first of the two Legendary drops, with a number of people speculating on whether or not Redacted—the guild that had come out of nowhere during this raid to snag the second-place clear on the Frostcaller—might have been working with Corruptia and possibly been handed their artifact for a much easier finish.

"Interesting, huh?" I said. "That artifact looks like another catch-up mechanic. Wonder what Darling will wanna do with that. Could hand it to the other groups to massively speed up their clears and get them ready for the next wing, or maybe sell it to another guild. Imagine those will fetch a pretty penny since people need to clear their Cathedral's first wing to unlock the second, and those raids are going to be all over the place soon."

Then I linked the final item, which was a beaker full of green liquid, reminiscent of the one I'd seen Brandt give to Isabel before she'd passed away.

{Brandt's Masterwork} (Legendary Consumable)
Quality: Legendary
Use: ??
Charges: 1

"Hey," Frank said. "You should—"

"Put you in it?"

He paused. "Actually, yeah. I'm pretty sure I'm too girthy to squeeze into that vial, but I'm definitely down to try super hard."

"That would be a hell of a way to lose a Legendary. But what were you gonna suggest?"

"Huh?"

I stared at him. "If you hadn't been about to ask me to drop you into that, then you must have had another idea in mind."

"Oh, I don't remember. I'm sure it was brilliant, but I doubt I could have shared it anyway."

"Yes!" Darling said, her voice sounding from behind me.

I spun around and she was already in the air in front of me, hair flying behind her. For a split second I thought she was jumping in for a hug, and I was already picturing the fit Frank would throw when she cocked back and punched me square in the chest so hard that I needed three backward steps to regain my balance.

I put a hand to my sternum and tried to cover the wince with a smile. "You see the alert?"

"Did I see the alert," she said, scoffing. She grabbed me by my shoulders and lifted me slightly off the ground, then shook me. "One more shot, right!"

She let me go, and I landed lightly on my feet. "Assume you saw the axe, too. It's a big one."

"Yeah, I'm wondering who I should hand it to."

I blinked at her. "What? No."

She knelt in front of the Frostcaller's body and looked back at me over one shoulder, dark hair covering half her face. "What do you mean, no?"

"Your call, obviously, but that thing might as well have been custom-designed for your kit."

"True, but my stuff's already solid, so it'd probably be a bigger upgrade for somebody else."

"We already know the Thousand Tower Tournament's gonna have some PVP elements. An axe like that might not be all that great if it ends up being a 2-on-2 format or something like that, but imagine that you were rocking that weapon in a 20-on-20 where people are dying left and right, just bouncing between targets like a wrecking ball, generating shields with every kill and leaving statues behind... can you picture it?"

She bit her bottom lip. "I can, and I like it."

Frank grunted. "Look, Darling. That axe is gaudy, inelegant, and obviously overcompensating for something. And I know that as a woman of culture, you prefer your weapons on the understated side, but real talk: if you don't think you deserve it, then you're wrong."

Darling blinked at him, still kneeling.

I shrugged. "That's a bit more blunt than I would have put it, but he's got a point. You should probably listen to Fred on this. Fred knows what they're talking about."

"Ugh," Frank said.

"What? I put your name first, and Darling is the one who coined it in the first place. Plus it's monosyllabic, which matters for some reason, right?"

"It just doesn't sound like it's going to strike fear in the hearts of our enemies. Like, everybody look out, Fred's coming. It sounds like we're gonna burst into a room and audit somebody's taxes."

"Have you ever been audited, Frank? Somebody from the government just shows up uninvited and gets all up in your business. And if you did bad math, you go to jail."

"Hmm. I'm more intrigued than I thought I'd be, but I remain dubious."

"Fair, but Darling should keep the axe, right?"

"Agreed."

She smiled. "We'll see, but I appreciate it."

The other members flooded in, and the noise level quickly shot through the roof.

"You wanna hold onto either of those Legendaries?" Darling said.

"Maybe the Masterwork if you don't mind? I might have something in mind for that. I'd be happy to sell the other one for you if you want, but it might be nice for the guild's other raid groups too."

She put the consumable into a trade window and confirmed it. "Think we should probably give one charge to the trash group at least, but yeah, I'll let you know."

Isabel interrupted her by floating over, her face downcast. She stroked the Frostcaller's broad head, right between its milky eyes. "This is better than it was, I suppose."

The raid quieted slightly at her words, and people crowded in to hear whatever she said next.

She looked around at the group. "I'm sorry that I lied to you. But I couldn't let this stand. If I can't have him back—if he's really gone—then at least now I know that he's at peace."

I looked at Darling. "You still have any of those diary entries?"

"A few yeah, why?"

"Feels like it might help." I popped all of the entries I'd found into my hands, and Darling collected some more from the guild. Once we had the pile organized and free of duplicates, I handed the stack to Isabel.

"What is this?" she said.

"It's Brandt's diary," I said. "It's... pretty much entirely about you. It's not him, but it's something, right?"

She took the papers, and they warped from solid to spectral as she looked them over. A subdued smile slowly spread across her face, and she clutched the pile to her chest.

"Thank you. This is... it is definitely something."

She stood up and cast one last longing look at the dead Frostcaller, then she drifted down the avenue and away from the palace.

Darling watched her go. "Wait, that's it? She's just... going now? And he's gone?"

"Guess so," I said, shrugging.

"Weird." She looked around. "Snow's not melting, palace is still wrecked, Huntsman's dead, city's gone. I guess I thought we'd be saving this place. Or saving the world. Or at least reuniting them or something."

"You thought wrong, but I admire the audacity," a new voice said, high and sharp. "But my work here finished years ago."

I whipped around, pistols popping into my hands.

A figure the likes of which I'd never seen stood atop the stairs on the other side of the courtyard, between the blown-out doors of the Huntsman's palace.

The man was of average height, but his body was nothing but numbers: just red digits scrolling in vertical columns, data shaped into the form of a man.

I tried inspecting him, and while nothing happened, the red numbers he wore like a crown left little doubt as to who we were dealing with.

The Possibility King.

He descended the steps with deliberate care, his pace relaxed, his head held high.

"That's always the question, though, isn't it? What could we have done differently? How could we have saved him or her or them or the world or anything at all, really."

He gestured at the palace, at the avenue, at the city beneath it. "The problem is that people like you have always viewed my Cathedrals as a challenge. As something to be overcome." He leaned closer and peered into our eyes, one by one.

"If they're not a challenge," I said, "then what are they?"

A crescent of red numbers that had been scrolling sideways across his face turned white, and for a brief moment, he appeared to be smiling. "They're a place of education. A courtesy, if you will. A glimpse into the future, the past, whatever you'd like."

"Why?" Darling said.

Instead of answering, he tapped the fallen Frostcaller with the tip of his numerical boot. "Isabel was one of my favorites."

"Favorite what?" I said.

"Catalysts. Though I will say her husband ended up a good bit more monstrous than I expected in the end. The result, though... it was a beautiful thing. I wish you could have seen it. An entire universe of possibility, all collapsing and snapping into place after a single action."

He held out his hands and cupped them. "What do you picture when someone says 'armageddon'? Do you picture the world burning, starving, flooding? It doesn't really matter in the end, does it? Your kind has always focused on the wrong moments. The bang, the flash. The sound a wildfire makes when it approaches."

He shook his head. "The truth is that every world is in a constant state of teetering. So listen to me carefully: it's the quiet moments you ought to be paying attention to. The ones that precede the shift. The moments that build the people who claim to be effecting change when in reality the die has already been cast.

"When the time comes, I hope you can see it. The expanse, the way you weave in and out of each other, the little stitches you form across the tapestry of it all."

"But why?" Darling repeated. "Why are you here?"

He turned and looked at her, and some of the numbers that were scrolling across his lower face once again whitened into a smile. "Why does anyone do anything? Because the result is beautiful." He gestured at the center of the courtyard, and a cloud of data exploded up out of the ground and formed a digital tree from the trunk up.

It was unremarkable save for the way he'd constructed it, resembling an apple tree with thick green leaves and bright red apples all rendered in colorful numbers. He plucked a low-hanging piece of fruit free and held it up in front of his face.

"Trees truly are beautiful things. But they need a great deal of assistance to fruit at the peak of their potential—did you know that?"

He took a bite of the apple, frowned, and spat out a mouthful of brown numbers that dissolved before they hit the ground.

"A tree left to its own devices will naturally outcompete itself as its many branches reach for the same sun. They rub against one another, and the friction causes wounds, the wounds invite infection. The branches jockey for position atop the crown with no regard for the structure they depend on, without care or concern for the way the winds are blowing."

The Possibility King made a cutting gesture with one hand, and an entire branch fell from the interior of the tree, the apples breaking as they hit the ground. He repeated the process several times in quick succession until the courtyard beneath him was covered with digital leaves and smashed fruit.

"But with proper pruning, the crown is able to breathe. The wind rustles through the canopy, unimpeded, the sunlight shines in as it should, and the structure below is better for it."

He stared around at us, dubious. "You don't see it, do you?" He snapped his fingers and the tree expanded, the numbers that comprised its trunk rushing out in a blink and sweeping over us, rushing on until they capped the entirety of the massive, miles-wide hill that the Huntsman's palace was built upon.

The canopy bloomed in turn, blotting out the entirety of the sky and reaching easily from horizon to horizon. Countless red apples hung high above, glimmering like stars.

"This is not a tree, but a lone branch of the universe. A single limb of the Tree of Possibility. And your world is..." He trailed off, searching. "There."

He held a hand out, and a single apple dropped free, fell hundreds of feet, and landed neatly in his palm. The red fruit was ugly, smaller than the others, with a dull red sheen that was spotted with knots of brown and purple numbers that looked like bruises.

The Possibility King looked us over and slowly crushed the apple, rotten pulp squeezing out between his fingers.

"Your world is flawed. It's rotten and inconsequential—a burden upon its branch—and the tree will be stronger without you. You'll understand in time.

"But for now, I'll leave you with this: tread carefully, friends. Because the only thing that separates this world's fate from your own is that here, I pushed a woman down a stairwell."

# Chapter Fifty-One

The Possibility King stepped up the stairs that led to the palace, unraveling as he went, streams of red data peeling off and twisting away.

I thought back to that second rift Darling and I had cleared, to the way Isabel had seemed to fly off the top of the stairs, to the surprise on the guards' faces as she fell, and I understood.

"Okay then," Darling said. "That was… not what I was expecting." She rubbed her eyes. "Alright, everybody, Rock's gonna hand out the rest of the loot, so check in with him before you bail. I'm gonna log out to eat something and try to catch some shuteye before the Siege, but if you're awake enough to stick around, please try to figure out a way to help the city. Things are about to get real ugly real fast, and we're gonna need all the help we can get and then some. For now, though? Awesome work. I'm proud of you guys."

The group cheered and gathered up around Rock while the big man knelt in front of the corpse.

Darling stepped through the crowd and bumped her armored shoulder into mine. "Thanks again."

"For what?"

"Thinking we could pull it off after what felt like a hundred wipes."

"Wasn't the only one, right?"

"Still, somebody's gotta be the first to say 'one more time'." She started heading down the avenue, so I fell into step beside her. "So, what're you gonna do?"

"Hardly any time left before we gotta face the music," I said, "so I think I'm gonna throw an illusion on and go get one last look at the Oasis. Maybe see if there are any last-minute tweaks I can make to the defenses, pray that my next payout is enough to get Arlann paid so we have guards for the Siege, that sorta thing. I've got a couple different ideas I'm hoping to set into motion, might send you some suggestions for positioning and all that for when you log back in."

"Sure thing, and the more detailed, the better."

I tapped Frank. "And I probably need to set a bit of time aside to clue this guy in about Project Lunar."

"Oooh. The moment's finally come, huh?"

"I think it has, yeah. Gonna have to check in with Kline about it first, which sucks. But so it goes."

"My dad better not be working on whatever this is in secret," Frank said.

"Maybe he has been, maybe not. Either way, I might need to have you help me out by summoning him here in a bit."

"Hm. How annoying do I need to be about it?"

"As annoying as possible, obviously."

Darling bumped into me again. "You know things won't change if you lose the city, right? I mean, they will, but they won't." She gestured back at the procession following us out. "You'll still have this."

I glanced down at Frank, then looked away and forced a smile. The thought of losing the city for good was unbearable, but somehow, somewhere along the way, the prospect of losing the antagonistic little bastard that hung on my hip had started to seem just as bad, if not worse.

"Yeah. Think I might end up a little lighter if things go bad, though."

"We can always hunt him back down," Darling said. "Follow the blood trail, right Frank?"

"True enough."

I waited for Frank to say something, but he didn't, and Darling and I headed down the switchbacks and through the ruins. We said a quick round of goodbyes to everybody else, and I waited a moment to be assured the area outside the raid was safe, then I popped out beneath the Red Cathedral with an illusion already in place.

The Red Cathedral's new, rising towers that I'd seen flickering in and out of existence while in ghost form had fully solidified, and a new, domed structure stood to the right of the Cathedral's towering main hall.

The sky was still dark, but the horizon was beginning to warm, and it wouldn't be long before my daily payout hit and the fight for the Oasis finally began.

I went ahead and applied one of my illusion-strengthening runes to a spare pistol I had in my inventory and equipped it to be safe, then jogged down the dunes and toward the city, penning a quick message to make sure House was still around as I went.

She replied instantly, saying she was back at the Auction House with 2.0. I crested a dune and took a deep breath, trying to force myself to relax as the city came into view.

And that did not work at all, because Goon had officially arrived.

Their huge train was circled up directly between me and the city, and they'd erected hundreds upon hundreds of tents around it. There were so many cook fires burning between them that it hardly seemed like night at all, with the firelight illuminating the dunes completely and flickering off the nearby rivers.

Once again, their numbers hit me like a gut punch. The Oasis was completely surrounded on every side, and while the number of prisms that were rushing toward the city had considerably diminished just as House had said for reasons I still didn't understand, Goon was apparently having little trouble single-handedly fighting off the ones that did approach.

I gave their train a wide berth, but since their tents stretched completely around the city's four wards and I didn't see a way in without passing directly through their camp, I picked an area that was relatively quiet and headed through there.

Music and laughter filtered in from every direction, the fires were warm, and the air was thick with the scent of garlic and roasting meat.

"Careful on your left," Frank said.

I faked a cough and glanced over out of the corner of my eye.

Sleep himself was sitting six tents over, parked atop the back of a wagon full of bloody trade packs. He was still wearing the same pair of ornate goggles he'd had on when we first met, and he must have seen me looking his way because he waved in my direction.

I returned the gesture with a respectful nod and was immensely relieved when he went right back to chatting with another player who had their back to me.

"Well-spotted," I said.

"Guess so. They're uh... they're big, huh?"

I avoided a particularly lively campfire where people were drinking and laughing while somebody beat the living hell out of somebody else. "Too big, man. Way too big."

I pushed through and finally reached the city, finding the defenses much as I'd left them hours earlier with a few notable improvements: the moat I'd requested House start on while we'd been raiding had been completed and filled with dark, blue water, and the Ghostlight Cannons that she had crafted up were more numerous than ever before. And as I'd requested, she'd spread them out pretty equally around the city's four wards.

The defenses were idle, though, and it didn't seem like a single mob had got through Goon's blockade in quite a while, given the way the guards were lounging atop the defensive walls, their swords sheathed and their crossbows leaning unattended against the many merlons.

I dropped my voice. "You got anything on what's going to happen with these prisms when the Siege starts?"

"Can't give you the exact timing, but the prisms and nearby rifts will turn off for the Siege."

"That's a relief, at least. You think you could hit me with the city's Legendary Quest real quick? I wanna see how close we are."

"Incoming."

**Quest: In Defense of the Black Oasis! (Legendary Quest) (Collaborative Quest)**
**Objective: While within 500 yards of the Black Oasis, defeat the following:**
**1. 10,000 Veterans (Complete!)**
**2. 1,000 Elites (Complete!)**
**3. 200 Elite+ (197/200 slain)**
**4. 20 Elite++ (Complete!)**
**5. 1 Raid Boss, World Boss, Deity, Lesser Deity, or Legend (0/1 slain)**
**Any player may contribute to this quest at any time, and all kills made within the designated area are automatically added to the appropriate tally.**
**Reward: Experience, Renown, and major improvements to all existing Communal Defense Structures within the Black Oasis.**

Additional individual rewards, including gear and crafting materials, will also be awarded and will scale in power, level, and rarity depending on each player's contribution to the defense of the Black Oasis.

In addition, the top three individual contributors will each receive a {Cache of the Possibility King}.

My spirits picked up a bit at that.

"We got closer than I dared to hope," I said as I made my way into the city. The tree was looming high above, shading the entirety of the Commerce Ward, but the streets were disturbingly empty.

"Wouldn't count on it completing if I were you. The Elite+ requirement will definitely complete before the Siege, but getting a Raid Boss summoned in before that is a serious long shot."

I sighed. "Yeah, kinda figured." I read the quest over a bit more carefully, then again for good measure. There was something there that I thought might help us out a bit, but it was a total shot in the dark.

I scanned the streets as I entered the Commerce Ward. The rope bridges were clacking in the breeze overhead, totally unoccupied. The streets themselves were empty too, completely bereft of the many temporary stands from which merchants had been offering goods when I'd stopped by prior to the raid, and even the café I'd taken a break at a couple of days back was empty.

No, not just empty: the windows were shuttered, the warming poles had been packed away, the chairs were piled atop the tables, and there was a sign posted in front of the business, sticking right out of the sand.

I scoped it out.

**For Sale: Housing Plots**
**Size: 2x1**
**Structure: Basic Café**
**Cost: {Gold Coin} x3.**
**Minimum available Housing Slots required to claim: 2**

I looked up and down the avenue again, seeing it with new eyes: similar signs were absolutely everywhere.

I rubbed my face with both hands. "People are really giving up, huh? Just like that?"

"Guess so."

"Wow. I guess I could see it if I wasn't so invested... but man. This place is a ghost town."

"To be fair, there is a pretty awesome murder mob outside. Everybody's probably busy out there having a killer time."

I nodded. "Yeah, I mean, I don't blame the NPCs for bailing in the slightest, and we need to get Lars and Cerra and everyone else out ahead of time for sure. Maybe we can have Arlann handle that. But I thought the other players would be like... rallying to defend it, you know? I wonder if I underestimated how many other landowners there are around here. That or I was way off on what the place actually meant to people."

"Uh huh."

I made my way through the empty streets in a daze, reeling at all the properties that were up for sale: empty plots, half-finished structures, and completed restaurants and shops and foundries.

I popped into the Auction House and was unsurprised to find House at the counter and sitting atop 2.0, looking lonely as the building's only customer.

"Oh man. This is so much worse than I thought it would be." I stepped up beside House and tried to force some enthusiasm. "Hey, House. How're you doing?"

"I am functioning quite well, thank you."

"Enjoying the elbow room in here? Must be a nice change."

She looked at each of her elbows, then flapped her arms like wings. "I suppose. Though in truth, I think I came to enjoy the camaraderie."

"I get that. What happened here?"

"The population has been steadily trickling outward for some time. Once Goon arrived about an hour ago and began single-handedly demolishing the incoming monsters, the exodus rapidly intensified among both players and NPCs."

"Did we get any new options for the defenses? Oh, and thanks for getting that moat up by the way. I think that'll come in handy."

"You are welcome. There have not been any notable unlocks since you last left."

"Maybe that was too much to hope for. How's your latest run of trades been going?"

"It was going very well until everyone left, but Goon appears completely disinterested in the economic portion of the game and the local market has essentially died."

"Yeah. Maybe we should get you looking at something else."

She sat up a little straighter. "I would very much like that."

"Maybe we could start you with..." I trailed off, drawing a blank.

Well, not a blank, not exactly. Goon was just all I could think about. The empty streets, their incredible numbers.

And I couldn't help but picture the Commerce Ward overgrown with Razebloom, the bright flowers poking up through the rubble of everything we'd worked so hard to build in the place that had come surprisingly close to feeling something like home.

I clenched my hands into fists. We'd come so far with the city and the network and the defenses, the World Tree had finally turned into something wonderous, and now this?

"I am waiting to begin," House said.

I put a hand on her shoulder. "I'm sorry House, I really love doing this with you, but I think we need to take a raincheck for now. We've gotta figure out a way to make sure this building's standing later today so that we can do it again."

She looked up at me from atop her metallic cat, whose tail was swishing across the floor.

"Even a cobbler needs his sole replaced from time to time."

I paused, distracted, mind racing. "Yeah, I guess that's true, isn't it?"

She beamed, and she looked as if she were about to continue when Frank rolled over her, tone urgent.

"You need to get out of sight here in a couple minutes. I know nobody's around, but just to be safe."

I shook my head as if to clear it. My first thought had been that the Revenant was headed our way yet again, but I didn't feel any of the dread that telegraphed the creature's arrival, and I was pretty sure I knew what Frank was getting at: my daily payout had nearly arrived. And I just had to hope it would be enough.

"Alright House, I gotta get moving. I'm probably going to have some instructions for you here in a bit—well, I hope to—so I'll be in touch. Please keep me posted if anything weird happens in the city, yeah?"

"Understood."

I scratched 2.0 behind her metal ear, then turned and ran off.

"Alright man. We gotta have a serious conversation in a little while, but I gotta ask you something real quick."

"No, the feeling is not mutual. This is a strictly platonic relationship."

I laughed. "Yeah, okay." I slowed down a little bit, heading for the

Guard House. "Just making sure we're on the same page here: swing big, or minimize the damage?"

He paused, which I hadn't expected, but the response was what I'd been hoping to hear, or close enough to it.

"Have I ever once advocated for the minimization of damage?"

"All in, then? To the bitter end?"

"Hilt-deep."

I nodded. "Alright then. Still not sure this is a good idea, but Frank it, right?"

"I don't have the slightest idea what you're talking about, but I could not agree with your conclusion any more strongly."

I grinned and toggled my alias over to Francis, still running toward the Guard House. Then I set all of my permissions to private and called Tyrann.

The call rang four times, and I was about to give up when it went through and he popped up in front of me, standing in a familiar courtyard with the Frostcaller eyeing him down. It looked like the Cult had just wiped on the Menagerie Wing's final boss and were currently regrouping.

"Hey there," he said. "I was wondering if—"

"Sorry to interrupt, but I've way too much on my plate right now, and I don't mean to be rude but I need to make this quick."

Tyrann's upper lip quirked in distaste, but eventually he nodded.

"Look, you said I needed to show my hand, right? Well, here you go: I'm putting everything on the table. I think Goon's offer of immunity for Koria is a load of crap."

He hesitated, then made to speak, but I kept going.

"I'm not necessarily saying that you were lying to me," I continued, though I was pretty sure he'd been doing just that. "I'm just saying that that offer isn't going to hold up. In fact, from everything I've heard about Sleep, I feel like he probably doesn't even want the Cult to join the assault against the Oasis. If anything, I think he'd appreciate some amount of resistance."

I let that sink in for a moment. "But all of that aside, I've got the narrative you need packed up and ready, and I'm still willing to reinstate your Tithe, but I'm going to require something from you in return."

"I'm listening."

"First things first, I need you to take the Cult off the list as a declared attacker. Pardon the irony, but I'm going to need you to take it on faith that that's the right call. Then you're going to need one person who you trust completely who can stealth indefinitely, remain hidden from view, whatever.

"You're going to send them to the Royal Ward and have them climb up nice and high, get a good vantage point. Somewhere out of the way where they won't take damage as Goon crashes in."

"Okay..."

"Then I need you to take the entire Cult to Highwater City."

He blinked. "Highwater?"

"Yep, everybody. Once you guys are off the declared list, I'll hand you the remaining piece of the puzzle. That's my offer. You don't need to accept it right away, but like I said, you're gonna have to drop out as a potential attacker before we go further.

"But I've been true to my word at every point so far, right? You wanna step back into the limelight? Then this is the fight you need. Once again, I apologize for being brisk, but I gotta run. You got all that?"

"Definitely something to think about."

I eyed their battlefield through the window, where I counted five frozen statues, no doubt belonging to the players who'd died to the boss' debuffs but hadn't yet respawned. "By the way, you need to avoid making those statues or the later mechanics will wipe the floor with you."

"Later mechanics?"

"You'll see when you hit the 10% mark. Cheers, Tyrann. Hope you make the right call."

I hung up before he could answer.

"What the hell was that about?" Frank said as I reached the Guard House steps and pushed right through the doors. "Also, you might wanna get into Arlann's war room. Like, now."

I rushed down the hall, pushed through the heavy doors, and closed them behind me.

I scanned the room. Arlann was sitting behind his desk, fully armored but for the helm that sat in front of him, and Sarissa was in her usual spot, legs crossed in a chair in the corner, blue dress falling down to just above her ankles.

"Are we alone?" I said.

Arlann swept his golden eyes back and forth across the room, then nodded. "We are. You can speak freely."

I canceled my illusion and dropped into the empty chair across from him. Then I looked at Frank. "How long?"

"Imminent."

"Please, please tell me it's going to be over 50 gold."

"Hate to say it, but it's looking like 35 and change."

I froze. "You're joking, right? Please tell me you're joking."

Arlann cocked an eyebrow at me. "If you're short on funding the guard..."

"I would never joke about something that's so important to you," Frank said.

I immediately relaxed and sank back against the chair. "Okay, you were definitely lying."

"False."

"Fine, then I'd like to wager 50,000 Frank points, and I'm taking the position that the payout's going to be 36 gold or higher."

"Well, you know, I'm not the type to walk away from a bet, but you gotta keep in mind that I'll need a considerable amount of time to authenticate and secure—"

Prompts streamed in, and a series of gold flashes surged out from me, brightening the room.

**Congratulations, you reached level 19!**
**Congratulations, you reached level 20!**
**Congratulations, you reached level 21!**
**Congratulations, you may now freely equip C-Grade gear!**
**Reach level 25 to unlock the Skill Evolution/Combination System!**
**Reach level 30 to select a Tier IV class!**

"Shucks, too late. What a shame, that would have been a good bet on your part. You could have put some serious distance between yourself and the moon with that one."

I ignored him and scrolled over to the payout, which made my jaw drop: 76 gold, which kept us right on pace to keep doubling up.

"C-Grade, man. Finally." I opened up my inventory and surprised myself by managing a grin at my hoard of Rift Gems. I cupped my hands and popped 50 gold into them, then dropped the pile onto the table and looked up at Arlann. "It's all here. Done and done."

Arlann smiled. "I knew you could pull it off." He nodded to Sarissa. "Could you please send word to the others? Pull everybody who's off-duty in and have them suit up."

She held up a finger and blew on it, then tapped a stack of documents to her left. The paper on top folded itself into a bird and flew out of the window. She repeated the process, rapidly thumbing through the stack and sending a flock of them flying out and across the city.

"Gah, fricken birds are everywhere today," Frank muttered.

Arlann reached across the table with both hands but froze as I reached out and raked the pile of gold back slightly.

"It's here if you want it now," I said. "Just as I promised. But I also have another offer for you."

He leaned back and crossed his arms. "Go on, then."

I swallowed, my throat suddenly dry. "Like I said, there's 50 right here. You can take it and know everything's covered, at least for a little while." I pulled the pile a little closer to me. "Or, you let me keep this for now, and I pay you double a week from today."

Arlann frowned. "The guard will need to be paid a week from today regardless. Receiving a hundred gold at that point would simply represent me agreeing to delay today's payment."

"No." I looked him dead in the eyes. "I mean I'll pay you a hundred every week from there on out, in perpetuity."

He stayed silent, but he was looking thoughtful, so I pressed on.

"So if we hold the city, then next week you break even. The week after that, you double up for as long as I'm around. Full freedom to do whatever you'd like with the coin. I also have someone looking into your request earlier for someone to handle running the city, and she's already found a number of places where the guard is bleeding money.

"We can talk more about that if there's still a city here this afternoon, but what do you think you could accomplish with twice the gold and someone to help you spend it efficiently? The world's getting scarier by the day, right? And I'm sure you noticed those new towers that just popped up on the Cathedral."

Arlann rubbed his chin. "That would go a long way..."

"New equipment, better training, more men. And if I keep ramping up the way I expect to, we can talk about taking the guard even further. It'd be in my best interests every step of the way to keep you guys running as smoothly as possible."

"If this is what you're offering, I'm assuming you have a use in mind for all of that gold." He fixed me with a firm look. "Meaning that if the city falls, you'll likely be out of coin as well as buildings."

"That's true, yeah. But I intend to invest the entire amount in the city, one way or another. And if Goon wins, I give you my word that I'll get you that 50 gold eventually. I don't know how long it'll take or how I'll even pull it off, but I'll get it to you."

"And when you say invest…"

"Defenses and gear, maybe a couple other things."

"You should take him up on it," Sarissa said.

Arlann's gaze flicked her way. "You think so, eh?"

She examined her nails. "I think you should trust his instincts at this point, and more than that, you mumble about the costs of running everything in your sleep every other night and I'm tired of being woken up."

He grunted, and I had to fight to keep from grinning. "Well, I suppose we can't have that, can we?"

I straightened. "Does that mean we have a deal?"

Arlann reached across the desk and I shook his hand. "If you'd have asked yesterday, I'd have said no." He eyed the pile of gold. "But seeing that you actually pulled it off… I'm willing to give you the benefit of the doubt. One week from today, a hundred gold, and every week thereafter."

"Done. I've one last favor to ask: can you check my inn and try to evacuate the innkeepers there? They might not be happy about it—Lars in particular—but I don't want them around if things go bad."

He smiled. "We've already been facilitating evacuations, but I'll have the building swept just in case."

"Thank you." I jumped up out of my chair so quickly that it clattered to the floor behind me. "I appreciate it, but I gotta get moving." I threw my illusion back on and was out the door and down the steps before either of them had time to respond.

I sent House another message asking her to meet me near the Inn—I felt like I should give Lars the news myself—then dashed through the streets and back beneath the World Tree.

"Frank, help me out here real quick: what were the prices on that Renown Perk we picked up for more Housing Slots?"

"First slot costs you 2 gold, then it increases by two each time until you've used it ten times. Why?"

I scanned the many properties that were on offer. Most of them were dirt cheap—with the lowest being 25 silver for a house that somebody had just started working on—but even with that huge payout I'd just received, I needed to be picky with the way costs were going to escalate thanks to the slots I also had to buy.

My Golden Strangle perk had also maxed out on a handful of the now-empty plots closest to the Auction House—three in all, meaning I could purchase them that way instead if I wanted to—but it seemed like it made more sense to buy directly through the players and NPCs because their prices were far lower than the system's estimates of fair market value.

"So here's what I'm thinking: we still can't purchase as many of these as I'd like, but I want five total plots."

"Gonna run you 30 gold for that plus whatever the players are asking. There's a three-by-one to your left and a two-by-one to your right."

"Thanks, but I just want singles. I also want to snatch them up in areas that'll keep people from building larger structures. Like if we grab two plots that are diagonal from each other, that'll prevent somebody else from building anything big in that area, right?"

"I don't really follow, but yeah."

"We're just going to spread them out so that when we hold the city, we've got less competition in the form of other businesses. Smaller structures means lower individual payouts for other people, and lower payouts for others means their structures are more vulnerable to Golden Strangle going forward. If we can scoop these up and hold Goon off, we could be running this entire Ward in a week, man."

"Uhhhh huh. Throw up your map and I'll mark the singles for you."

He did, so I ran down to the avenue that held my Inn, the Auction House, and my destroyed Water Tower and snatched up five plots in all, staggering the locations carefully just as I'd explained to him.

"Hello," House said from behind me, which made me jump.

I turned around. "Hey, House. Thanks for coming back out so fast."

"It was my pleasure."

I took the entirety of the gold I had left—every single coin—and slammed it into a trade window with her.

"Take this for me."

She confirmed the trade. "Your coins have been obtained. What would you like me to do with them?"

I eyed the many Ghostlight Cannons that were positioned atop the city walls. "You spread those out perfectly, House."

"Thank you."

"Do you think you could do me another favor there? Since those things are re-deployable, I'd like you to put a small group together that's capable of moving them all if we need to." I looked down at Frank. "That'll work, right?"

"You can move them, but they're gonna be locked in the moment the Siege starts."

"That works just fine, actually. Thanks."

"Uh huh."

"Forming a group is unnecessary as I can re-deploy them remotely so long as I am somewhere within the Communal Defense Zone," House said. "I would be happy to relocate them as needed, or I can grant you the permissions you need to do it yourself."

"That'd be even better, yeah. And I know they deal massively reduced damage to players, but is there any way we can tweak them to mitigate that a little? Ammo types or something like that?"

"Not that I am aware of. I do possess different ammo types, but those munitions are exclusively for cannons meant for naval combat."

I nodded. "Then they'll have to do. Take all that gold and get me cannons and anti-personnel rounds. As many as you can manage in whatever numbers make the most sense to you."

She cocked her head. "This seems like an odd moment for the guild to pivot back to the naval model Frank suggested earlier. Has the goose grown tired of waiting for the pail to fill?"

I stared at her for a moment, then shrugged. "Sure, I guess. Just trust me on this, alright?" I grabbed her by both arms. "Cannons. Lots of cannons."

"I will craft a preposterous number of cannons."

"Great. Let me know if you come across a cool recipe or something along the way, but that's the plan for now." I rubbed my temples. "There was something else I needed to do... Oh! I need you to buy yourself something from the Auction House that increases run speed temporarily."

"Perhaps a speed potion?"

"Perfect, and yeah, get a bunch of them. At least ten, maybe fifteen to be safe. I'm also going to need you to get me something to eat, but I'll message you more about that later."

"I am thoroughly confused, but I will not let that stop me."

"You never do. Thanks a ton, House." I squeezed her shoulder. "Whatever happens, I hope you know that we wouldn't have gotten this far without you."

She shimmied her shoulders. "I am pleased to have increased the distance we have traveled."

With that done, I left House and made a beeline for the nearest Rift Gem vendor.

"Time left?"

"Fifty minutes and counting," Frank said.

"We're almost done," I said. I paged through the vendor's Gear Token options until I found exactly what I was looking for.

**C-Grade Rift Token (Weapon) (Enchanted Pistol)**
**Use: Creates a class-appropriate level 20 D-Grade item. All created items are of Uncommon quality and are created at the lowest possible Item Level for their Grade. Created items may not be traded.**
**Cost: 400 Rift Gems.**
**Note: Animalistic or Memory-stained Rift Gems may also be used to purchase this item.**

I dropped two of those into my purchase window and went to confirm it.

"Wait!" Frank said. "Wait wait wait."

"What's up?"

"Man, and people call *me* impatient. C-Grade weapons have Subtypes."

I frowned at him for a moment, then scanned through the seemingly endless Token types. They all had the same image, and the only thing that separated one from the next was buried in the items' descriptions.

But eventually, I found what he was talking about: in addition to that first Token, there were two more specialized pistol variants available: a repeater and a revolver, both of which were marked as Subtypes for the Enchanted Pistol weapon class.

Each of those was 50% more expensive than the generic Token I'd almost bought, but I was intrigued.

"Ohhh, good call."

I poked through the options for rifles and blunderbusses, but I didn't see any Subtypes available there.

"Any suggestions for which pistol to pick?"

"Revolver, hands down. Repeater won't help you currently."

"Two of 'em? That's gonna just about wipe us out when it comes to gems, other types and all. We could go with the generic pistols and snag another piece of armor instead."

"Nope, do it."

"Alright man, here goes." I slammed two of the revolver Tokens into my cart and used them both at the same time.

Two identical items popped into my inventory, so I scoped them out.

{Huntsman's Sidearm} (Enchanted Pistol) (Subtype: Revolver)
Grade: C
Item Level: 60
Damage Type: Magical
Quality: Uncommon
Physical Attack: 0
Magical Attack: 95
Speed: N/A
Primaries: +20 Intelligence, +20 Dexterity, +20 Constitution
Secondaries: +10% Critical Strike
Effect: Your Ravenblast takes 15% longer to cast but deals 25% increased damage.

"Oh, dear lord. That is so much more than I was hoping for." I equipped both of the pistols.

"More cast time that doesn't matter because your pistol blasts are instant in exchange for more stacking damage. And you can double up on the boost by equipping two of 'em. You're welcome."

"Hell yeah."

Now that my gear was fully sorted for the Siege, I pulled up my stat sheet.

{Ned}, (The Piratical)

Level: 15 > 21
Tier III Class: Shadewalker
Gear Level: 441 > 667

Strength: 18
Dexterity: 144 > 257
Constitution: 134 > 236
Intelligence: 200 > 365
Wisdom: 0
Charisma: 40 > 50

Critical Strike Chance: +16% > +28%
Haste Rating: +0% > +7%
Hit Rating: +5% > +7%

**Physical Attack: 0**
**Magical Attack: 73 > 190**

**Health: 1072 > 1888**
**Mana: 2000 > 3650**

**Armor: 40% > 59%**
**Magical Resistance: 32% > 43%**

I looked that all over, grinning at just how far I'd come in the last few days. And with the way my daily payout was escalating, if we could manage to hold the city for just a little while longer…

I took off at a run for the Inn, looking for Lars and his mother, but when I got there, the common room was deserted. I hoped that meant they'd already been evacuated, but I was worried about Lars: it felt like he'd insist on participating.

I sent a quick round of messages to House and the guild members that were online, inquiring if anybody had seen him of late, but nobody had any idea where he was.

Buzzing with anxiety and anticipation, I pushed into an empty room at the back of the Inn and closed the door behind me, dropped my illusion, and took a look at my new pistols.

They were utterly massive, easily twice the size of my previous weapons, and were jet black with ivory accents and oversized iron sights atop each barrel.

I lifted them up and swung them around, which was still easy but required considerably more effort than it had before. The weight was satisfying, though, and I couldn't wait to put them to good use.

I looked to Frank. "Time?"

"Forty minutes."

"Just about set. Alright man, I'm gonna send some directions to Darling so she has them when she logs back in, but I need you to do me another favor and get Kline in here. There's something I've been thinking about that I need to run by him—and just as a heads up, I'm gonna have to sheathe you."

"Hmm."

"Trust me."

"Fine, but only because I don't feel like catching a face full of man nipple." He cleared his throat. "Now paging the world's worst dad. Dad. Dad! Dad dad dad dad dad dad dad—"

Kline popped into the room with a finger plugging each of his ears. He went to point at Frank as if to instruct me to sheathe him, just as I'd known he would, but I'd beaten him to it.

I held my hands up, palms out.

"Sorry, desperate times, desperate measures, you know how it goes."

"What do you want now?"

I licked my lips. "Any chance you've heard of Project Lunar?"

"No."

"Well, I want you to hear me out on this, because I'd like to change that, and I'm willing to make it worth your while."

# Chapter Fifty-Two

After a ten-minute conversation with Kline—which felt like a ten-hour conversation, half because of his general nature and half because he still hadn't put a shirt on—I took a deep breath then ran out of the safety of the back room, still looking for Lars and his mother.

And, once again, I found nothing. Even the huge room with the indoor tree was empty, the Fae buzzing idly around the ceiling, globes in hand.

I pulled Frank out of his sheath and dropped him into his loop.

"What was that about?" he said.

I gave the Inn one last look, anxiety spiking again, then shot a message to House and asked her to meet me atop the wall. Darling had popped back online as well, so I sent her something similar, though I knew she was probably busy organizing all the groups I'd asked her to put together.

I stepped out into the street. "Gonna get there shortly."

The sun was now rising above the ocean to the east, hanging low in the cloudless sky. I kept my head on a swivel as I approached the defensive wall that surrounded the Commerce Ward, then Water Jetted myself up on top of it and picked out a section with an elevated tower to my left. That way, I could put my back to something solid and stay mostly out of view.

I double-checked that my Heart Vessel was still floating behind me. "We're still pretty exposed here. Keep an eye out, yeah?"

"Sure, whatever, what's the deal with bad dad number one?"

"You would claim dad number one."

"Stop stalling."

I leaned over the wall and checked out the moat below, where the dark water curved all around the Commerce Ward. Goon's forces still stretched fully around the city, but it seemed like they might have spread out a bit more, as their numbers were looking fairly balanced around the four wards.

That was exactly what I'd been hoping for when I'd asked House to spread the Ghostlight Cannons out: to make Goon think that the city's defenses were evenly distributed and that we were inclined to fight them for every inch. But the truth of the matter was that we couldn't afford to do that.

And with Arlann's guards pacing the walls and increasing numbers of members of Omen showing up atop them as the Siege drew closer, we'd managed to make things look somewhat equal, though anyone who'd spent a good deal of time in the city in the last few days would have seen the extra work that had gone into the Commerce Ward.

The Omen members were sparse, though, with maybe a fifth of the guild's available forces logged in and visible on the walls. If Darling had managed to organize everything as I'd planned, it would stay that way for a little longer.

"Hello?" Frank said.

"Sorry, got distracted. Alright, look." I pointed at Goon off in the distance. "So I've been thinking about Sleep and company since we walked in on them after that successful Siege."

"Hard same. Dudes are living the dream."

"Exactly. It's your dream, right?"

"Uh huh."

I licked my lips, unsure of how to continue or start or really anything. I would've liked to have had a bit more time to get my thoughts together, but I didn't have that luxury.

"I guess I'll start with the easy part." I opened my mouth, then blew out a puff of air.

"By easy part, were you referring to the act of breathing?"

I grinned slightly, then decided to just launch into it. "Look, man: apart from recently, I can't remember the last time I had a good week. I've had good days, good moments, and so on, and the more I look back on things before EBO, the more I realize just how easy I had it, have it, whatever.

"But all that said... it's been a really good week and change." I looked over the wall and eyed the sunrise. "We've had some close calls in the past, but this feels different. I really think this might be the end, man. And don't get me wrong—we're gonna fight them tooth and nail every step of the way. But it's kind of ironic, right? Unless everything lines up perfectly, we're going to wind up going down in the blaze of glory you've been asking for every twenty minutes since we met."

He didn't respond or react, so I kept going.

"So I got to thinking about it, and it was like... all in all, Goon seems like the best possible fit, which makes it an easier pill to swallow on my end. But Sleep's a dentist, right?"

"An archeologist of—"

"So what does that look like for you if I die and he scoops you up? Have you actually thought about that?"

"That would require thinking ahead, so no."

"Well, he's gonna work. A lot, probably. And he's gonna have to sleep. And he has a family."

"And?"

"He's not going to be in-game while he's working or sleeping or spending time with his family."

"Oh. Ohhh." He blinked, sort of. "Oh shit, that sucks for me!"

"Exactly. You're just gonna be stuck there, right? I've never left the game, so I don't have any idea what that would look like on your end, but it doesn't feel like you're going to be in the world if the player who's holding you is logged out, right? You'd just kinda be on pause or something. That's what I figured, anyway, so that's why I had you call Kline for me."

"And?"

I inclined my head. "Pretty much what I thought: you're gonna be by yourself, sorta floating around in nothing."

"Well, at least I'll be in good company."

"I literally just said you'd be alone."

"I am the company I was referring to."

"Seriously though, that sucks, right? Just you alone, for hours or even days at a time? There has to be a point where even you'd get tired of you, right?"

"Dubious."

"It's gonna be like floating in space, man. You know what they say:

nobody out there can hear you scream. It's gonna be like that, except nobody's gonna be able to hear you compliment yourself."

He shifted, seeming uncomfortable. "Okay, you officially have both my concern as well as my attention. Well, like half of my attention. To be honest, the fact that I'll probably never be able to hear the moon scream is hitting me pretty hard down here."

That made me laugh.

"Fair. But yeah, speaking of the moon, we should talk about Project Lunar before Darling gets here."

He puffed out his chest. "I knew I was still in the running for that leadership position."

"No, you don't understand. You're the whole project, Frank. You're every position."

"Sounds good, I'll start immediately."

"No, man. Like… it wasn't a real thing at all, but now it is."

"Was I not supposed to assume it was a real thing? To be clear, I still have no idea what it is. Or isn't. Just that I'm in charge which I figured would eventually be the case."

"I met up with him because I was trying to get you into EBO directly, like with a body of your own, but he's adamant that he'll never let that happen because there's no in-game reason for the change, blah blah blah." I paused to let him think about that for a moment.

"Uhhh… is there a but coming? It feels like there's a but coming."

I smiled. "So I had another idea. I couldn't get an agreement out of him, but I'm pretty sure I can convince him to port you somewhere else. As in into another game. That way when Sleep or whoever else logs out, you'll have something to do, people to kill, whatever you want."

I felt him stand up, or something like it. "Wait, what?"

"I haven't worked out the technicalities, and my hope is that you'll be able to do what House does and exist concurrently in two places—like how she can be running things back in the real world while playing here simultaneously—but at the very least I'm going to do my best to ensure that you've got another world to visit whenever Sleep or whoever else you end up with eventually logs out.

"Once I've got the go-ahead from Klein, I'll either directly acquire another game for you or pay the developers to sneak you in. I dunno, I'll figure it out. But it can be whatever you want, Frank: MMO, single player, an endless expanse full of bird mages who worship the moon, anything. An all-you-can-kill buffet."

"Wha... why?"

"Why not, man? I dunno, I started thinking about how everything would probably play out, and it seems like no matter what happens, it sucks for you, right? Even if we win, you'd still be stuck with me."

"Sure, but—"

"And if we lose, you'll end up with the right kind of person, but they might be gone more than half the time." I shrugged. "I guess I realized I could fix that for you, or at least make it better, so why wouldn't I? It's just money. And even aside from that, we've spent a hell of a lot of time trying to make House feel like she fits in here. You deserve a place too, right?"

He hung there, quiet.

"And who knows. If this Siege goes as badly as I think it might, maybe I'll be able to pop in from time to time and check up on your swathing progress in whatever game you choose."

A beat of silence passed, then another.

"I knew there'd be a catch. But... is this for real?"

"100%. I'm all for a good troll every now and then, but this is totally legit."

I spotted Darling and House heading my way on foot, so I stepped forward a bit and waved so they'd know where we were.

"Couple things before Darling and House get here though. First thing being that I'm gonna keep trying to get you into EBO no matter how long it takes, too. If there's one thing I'm good at, it's rubbing people the wrong way. And I'm gonna put those powers to use by latching onto Kline's nipples and twisting on your behalf until he gives in, or at least until he puts on a shirt. It might never work—it'll probably never work— but even if we get separated and getting you a body of your own here in EBO is a no-go forever, at least you'll know that Kline is also perpetually suffering. That's gotta be worth something, right?"

He grunted. "What are you after for this?"

"Not what I meant. It's just something I'm gonna do, and I wish I'd started earlier on all of this, but here we are."

Darling and House headed up the stairs and across the wall, now only a couple hundred feet off.

"Last question, and I need you to be straight with me here because we're out of time, so I'm going to take your answer at face value: you remember what Sleep said about his guild?"

"Somebody can work their way up to get their stuff back?"

I nodded. "Exactly. I've been going back and forth on that ever since he brought it up, and I can't up and bail on Darling and company after everything they've done for me. As much as I'd want to, it wouldn't be right. But let's assume Omen and I figure something out. Is that something you'd want?"

"Huh?"

"If you end up with Sleep, do you want us to come after you? Or would you rather just stay with Goon and—"

"Wouldn't be right."

I froze. "What wouldn't?"

"To leave you without a strong male role model to look up to. I've seen how that works out, and it's not pretty."

I placed my hands atop the wall and sighed into a grin.

"There may come a time when I decide to go out for a gallon of milk to soak in and never come back, but I think if I bailed before you hit puberty I'd feel like a bit of a dick, you know? I should probably stick it out a little longer. See if you grow into those fingers."

"Gotcha loud and clear, Frank. Now let's see if we can make that happen, yeah? I think I'm all set up on my end with the logistics we need and Darling's still handling the guild's positioning through chat for now, but if you've got any particularly brilliant suggestions you're hoping to get credit for later on, then the moment has arrived."

"Yeah, but... uh..."

"What's up?"

"Thanks. That's a... the body thing? Yeah. Thanks, Ned."

"No guarantees, but you're welcome, man. Happy to do it."

He grunted. "Well, you're level 21 now, so we can definitely talk about that stone we found back when the Tyrant was attacking the Oasis."

"You mean the rock?" I said with a wink. "I'm pretty sure we're on the same page there, and I've already got something in mind. Extra letter, right? Giant bird?"

"Heh. Yup."

I popped the rock out of my inventory and set it on the wall in front of me, right between two of the many merlons that offered a bit of protection from below.

**{Mysterious Stone} (Quest Item)**
**Use: ??**
**Requires level 20.**

"In hindsight, that was a killer hint man, but I really wish I'd put it together more quickly so I could have enjoyed the look on Kline's face when he showed up to tell you off. What's funny is that I never would have figured it out if he hadn't chewed you out for trying to help in the first place. That was the giveaway."

"Rest assured that I enjoyed his indignation enough for both of us."

"That does make me feel better."

"Hey guys!" Darling said as she and House finally reached us.

"Welcome back!" I said. "Get some sleep?"

"Nope, but I did shut my eyes and spend a bunch of time laying there in the dark worrying that everything was about to go terribly wrong!"

"Normal," House said.

"Basically the same thing," I agreed. "Sorry it wasn't restful."

"It is what it is. I got something to eat and chugged some coffee, so it was still good." She leaned forward between the same merlons I'd propped the stone up against. "I'm still pumped we pulled that kill off, but it's kinda hard to be happy about it while I'm standing here looking out at Goon and Arranthea."

"Wait, Arranthea?" I inspected the opposing army's guild tags a little closer, and there they were: a knot of one hundred, maybe two hundred players whose campfires were surrounded on every side by members of Goon. "Oh. I didn't even notice they were here. Numbers are lower than they claimed, but they're still larger than Omen."

I stared around at the walls, which were increasingly filling with guild members.

"Yeah. Did you see that the Cult officially pulled out of the Siege though? Just happened a couple minutes ago. I checked the sign-up NPC right before I headed over."

I let out a relieved breath. "Well, that's definitely a break we needed." I sent a quick message to Tyrann as Francis and shot him the final piece of the puzzle that he needed.

We'd cut it a bit closer than I'd have liked with the timing, but I reckoned they should be able to make it with mounts and so on.

"Wonder why," Darling said.

"I could explain that if we had the time, but I'm not sure we do. But at least they're out as attackers. Means we've got slightly more of a chance."

An alert went out just then as if to emphasize the point.

Warning: The Guild {Goon} has designated the {Black Oasis} as a Siege target, and the event will begin in 10 minutes.

Players who die during the Siege will be removed from the event, and the Siege will end when the reserves of either the Attackers or the Defenders are reduced to fewer than 10% of their starting numbers.

Once the Siege has reached the 15-minute mark, any Defender within the Siege grounds who doesn't engage in combat for more than 2 minutes at a stretch will automatically be killed and removed from the event to prevent Defenders from hiding to delay the Attackers' progress.

The Siege will last for a maximum of 1 hour, and if Goon is not victorious by that time, the Siege will be considered a failure.

In addition, all prism-style monster spawns will be disabled during the Siege and for 2 hours afterward, during which period, player versus player combat will also be restricted to opt-in combat.

Thank you for playing EBO, and we hope you enjoy the event!

# Chapter Fifty-Three

"You actually think this is gonna work?" Frank said.

I shrugged. "Not particularly. But if we lose, we're going down swinging." I popped my new, heavier pistols into each hand. "And I'm thinking we're going to be taking quite a few of them with us at the very least."

"I just hope everyone has a good time," House said.

"No, House!" Frank said. "Having fun is a zero-sum game."

House drew back from the wall. "I see, and I retract my earlier statement. I hope Goon and their families suffer deeply for the next sixty minutes."

"Much better."

My eyes went wide at that. "I was gonna say that's maybe a bit too far, but I think we all appreciate the enthusiasm."

Darling pointed an axe at the stone I'd set between the merlons, seemingly seeing it for the first time. "You got time to tell me what that thing's supposed to do?"

House scratched her teeth. "I too require time to explain various things."

"*You* need time to explain?" I said. "Explain what?"

She looked at Darling. "Perhaps I should wait until after the Siege, but I am afraid I have a confession to make. I was hoping to make it in Frank's presence to guard against the possibility that today's events go poorly, but perhaps the boy who cried wolf is already in the process of being fattened for slaughter."

"Huh?" Frank said.

I narrowed my eyes at her. "Everything okay, House?"

She scratched her teeth even more vigorously than before. "I am afraid not, but it can wait."

"You're okay though, right?"

"I am indeed."

I relaxed slightly. "Okay, I guess find me after then? Hopefully we'll still be here."

Darling tapped the air, checking something. "Holy crap Ned, when did you hit 21? Good lord!"

"Daily payout at work," I said with a grin. I rapped a pistol against the wall and linked her one of my new weapons.

"C-Grade too, wow. You've been busy."

"Just these two revolvers, but yeah. Pretty excited to put 'em to good use."

"I bet, those things are insane!" She pointed an axe at the stone again. "But, uh..."

I winced, feeling guilty about leaving her in the dark. I'd been hoping to clue her in on everything, but she'd logged back in later than I'd hoped and I'd already asked her to do so much that I hadn't wanted to distract her as she got everything organized.

"Sorry, the stone is—"

I cut off as another prompt streamed in. One that I didn't understand in the slightest.

**World Alert! The Guild {Goon} has declared an Aggressor's War on the Guild {Arranthea}!**

"What the hell?" I said. "What? Why?"

Darling gestured beyond the wall. "Woah. Look at that."

I did, and what I saw was both completely unexpected and yet somehow also totally predictable: Goon had turned on Arranthea at the last moment, and their vast numbers were streaming all over them.

The swarm was screaming and howling and it was utterly disorganized with no healers or battle lines in sight, but one glance at the sudden skirmish told me that Arranthea—a guild that was probably thrice the size of our own—was about to get absolutely steamrolled by sheer numbers if nothing else. And from the looks of things, they'd be dead well before the Siege even started.

The carnage was stunningly one-sided—just a tangle of name tags and flying bodies—and for the first time since we'd turned our attention to the Siege, something like hope kindled in my chest.

"What the hell is Goon doing?" Darling said.

"I think the simple answer is the best answer here," I said, laughing. "Goon wants a good fight, right? So they're looking up at the Oasis and our numbers and the defenses, and they don't think they're going to get one with Arranthea helping them out."

"So they're killing them?"

"I love it," Frank said. "I love it so much."

"Me too, especially because we can use this. We just need to change up the timing of everything a little bit." I looked at House, then rubbed my stomach. "Speaking of changing things up, like I mentioned earlier, I'm getting pretty hungry over here, House. Do you have any suggestions?"

She tilted her chin up. "Perhaps some crab meat would hit the spot?"

"That's a lovely suggestion."

"I shall return shortly."

She threw four discs a little way down the wall and was in the air before 2.0 had fully formed. The metallic cat snapped into place beneath her and carried her down the fortifications, leaped the moat, and sprinted down the nearest dune, heading for the ocean.

"Crab meat?" Darling said. "That's what's going through your head right now?"

"Can't think when I'm hungry," I said with a grin. I still felt a little guilty for not filling her in, but I was enjoying her reactions, and I thought Frank was too. "You got the moat crew I asked about set up around the Commerce Ward?"

She tapped the air again, then nodded. "Yup, we're looking good there. Just missing two players, but I'm sure they'll be here."

"Perfect."

Silence fell for a moment, and we simply watched as Goon crushed the smaller guild, rolling over them like a boulder down a hill. It was barely even a fight: just an enormous cloud of magic and flashing steel and a whole lot of screaming.

A few minutes later and right on schedule, a huge, familiar creature came skittering up the same dune that House had disappeared over.

{Akura, God of the Sapphire Depths} (Level 18 Beast) (Lesser Deity)
HP: 298,406/300,000
MP: 200,000/200,000

And a short woman was running in front of the towering, black crab, moving with supernatural speed across the sands, her arms thrown back in a V-shape behind her.

"Is that House?" Darling said. "What's she doing?"

House dropped a Leadfire Turret without breaking stride and kept moving. She slowed noticeably, popped a green potion into one hand, chugged it, and sped right back up, her short legs pumping faster than they had a right to.

I laughed. "If you think about it, House has the perfect kit for dragging mobs around if you supply her with speed potions: she can drop turrets behind her to keep the mob engaged and snared so it doesn't run back to its spawn point without even taking a hit."

"Okay, but how is this going to help us?"

I smiled as House banked away from the dune that housed the Commerce Ward and headed straight for the area where Goon's numbers were the densest, where they were still wiping the floor with what remained of Arranthea.

"If playing games has taught me anything, it's that if you kite something huge and utterly terrifying into a giant group of players, somebody's gonna go out of their way to smack it. I don't know why those people exist or where they come from or who they are, but—"

"Smacker present," Frank said. "It's an autonomous response. Just happens."

"I get it, but yeah, House is gonna kite that thing out there, and I'm thinking Goon's gonna go after it, especially since they still have a few minutes before the Siege actually starts without anything better to do."

"But with their numbers, aren't they going to demolish it?"

"Hopefully," Frank said.

Darling tossed her head to get the hair out of her eyes, then swept a few stray locks behind an ear.

"Look at its Health pool. We just downed a Raid Boss in a group of twenty and it had way more Health than Akura. Goon has hundreds of people around, even if you don't account for the members on the other side of the city... they're gonna stomp it. It's probably gonna put up less of a fight than Arranthea."

My grin deepened. "You've definitely got the right of it."

House summited the final dune between her and the bulk of Goon's forces, and I heard her voice carry all the way across the battlefield, above the clamor of the massacre Goon was dropping on their foe.

"Hello I am House!"

Distant heads whipped in her direction, and a roar went up as Akura crested the dune behind her and entered Goon's line of sight.

The battlefield paused there for a moment, and I saw Sleep himself—who was still sitting idle on the back of a wagon—hop down and point at the enormous creature.

A giant mob of players broke away from Arranthea and surged toward House, but she didn't falter in the slightest as she slipped between the front-most players and knifed directly through the rush while Akura chased after her.

"You're really handing them a kill on a Lesser Deity?" Darling said.

I smiled at her. "I think you've got it back to front on that one. Hey, Frank?"

"Uh huh?"

"Do you think you could give us an estimate on just how far Akura currently is from the city?"

"Two hundred, maybe three hundred yards tops? Well within five hundred."

I scooped up the stone Frank had led me to days earlier and tossed it to Darling, then grabbed Frank out of his loop and positioned myself across from her and took a few practice swings with him as if he were a baseball bat, leading with the flat bit behind his blade.

Then I eyed Akura far below. Goon had already engaged, the beast's Health was falling fast, and the rate at which it plummeted was only accelerating as more and more players moved from dogpiling what little remained of Arranthea to engaging the new arrival.

**Warning: The Siege begins in 2 minutes!**

I nodded to the stone. "Darling, would you mind tossing me that as soon as Akura hits 70%?"

She turned to face the fight and laughed. "If you say so."

"I suggest throwing it underhand so he doesn't miss," Frank said. "I can't afford to be shamed like that."

"I've got you."

I took a few more practice swings as Akura's Health rapidly fell beneath the assault of well over a hundred players and counting, then cocked fully back with both hands and activated Repel.

I mentally used the Mysterious Stone, which surprised me by offering a quest.

**New Quest: The Soul of the Gale! (Unique Quest) (Legendary Quest) (Phase I)**
**Objective: Recover {The Heart of the Desert Wind} and locate someone who can help you divine its secrets.**
**Reward: ??**

I took the quest, but the read-out wasn't exactly what I'd been expecting, so I took a deep breath and crossed my fingers, praying that my plan would still work.

"On your mark, Darling."

She watched the fight for a moment longer, then turned around and pitched the stone at me.

I swung and connected dead on.

"Blam!" Frank shouted, and the Repel-powered impact sent the light item arcing through the air and down toward Goon.

"Okay," Darling said. "Explain."

"It's a rock," I said, as if that clarified everything.

Darling squinted at me. "Is that supposed to help somehow?"

"Drop the K," Frank said.

She paused. "What?"

"R, O, C, Roc," I said as the stone arced over the sands, landed atop a dune, and rolled down to an eventual stop right behind the rear ranks of the players who were absolutely demolishing Akura.

"You know that my vast powers are restricted, right?" Frank said.

"Uh, yeah?" Darling said.

"So when I led bird boy to that stone, I told him it was a rock."

A familiar cry sounded over the ocean, and a winged shadow appeared on the eastern horizon, backlit by the rising sun.

"What I really wanted to say was that it's not a stone at all—it's an egg that belongs to Givora, the Scion of the Desert Wind, a three-headed buzzard that's been hunting for its lost brood for centuries, and now that the water's back and it's eroding the dunes its old nest has been exposed and that's where we found it, but since my dad's a huge dick with a deep-seated fear of my general omniscience I had to settle for trying to hint at the existence of a mythical bird to get around my restrictions." He took a deep breath. "Oof, that was hard to get out in one."

Darling stared at him, then at me, then back to him, eyes widening the entire time.

The creature barreled toward us across the sky, flying low above the ocean, shrieking as the sparkling water swelled and foamed beneath it.

I inspected it.

**{Givora, Scion of the Desert Wind} (Level 19 Legendary Beast)**
**HP: 6,000,000/6,000,000**
**MP: 15,000,000/15,000,000**

"You know what's funny, too?" I said. "If you're killing a World Boss or something like Akura and another creature flies into the fight out of nowhere as your target drops below half Health, what are you gonna think is happening?"

Darling hesitated. "That it's the second phase of a fight or something like that?"

"Precisely."

I cut off as Givora roared in low over the dunes, the sand exploding behind it in the same way the ocean had. It flapped its huge wings as it reached Goon and rose at once, hovering in place while the sands beneath it whipped about.

All three of its heads inhaled sharply, then Givora raked the player-packed desert with three tremendous blasts of wind that tore a trio of twenty-foot-deep gouges clear through a dune and left the top of it looking strangely serrated.

Upward of fifty players went flying, and I could almost feel the moment of panic when others turned to counter the incoming monster, loosed a spell, then realized the full magnitude of the threat they were dealing with.

Shouts to disengage immediately and kite the beast away from the city reached me over the clamor, but it was too late: Givora was already taking another deep breath, and the healers that had been keeping Goon's tanks up while they battled with Akura were suddenly drawing aggro from the new, terrifyingly strong arrival.

"Unbelievable," Darling said. "So was Akura just a setup? To get them to engage something stronger without realizing? Or to distract them, or what? I mean, if so, it definitely worked, but..."

I grinned from ear to ear. "Yep, that's all."

"Such a shame that's all it is," Frank said. "Wouldn't it be cool if instead of just some sort of weirdly elaborate targeting ploy, we'd been handed some kind of epic task days earlier?"

I tapped my chin. "Perhaps even a task with a substantial payout for the city. A task that doesn't care who does the killing so long as it gets done within range."

"That would have been incredibly fortuitous."

"Indeed it would. We can only dream of that having been the case because that could have easily turned the tide of the battle. On a totally unrelated note, Darling, you should probably take a careful look at the Legendary Quest for defending the Black Oasis and tell me what you see."

She opened up a menu and swiped around, then her face fell. "Oh man, we were so close. We finished every requirement but the last: still gotta kill one of the Possibility King's Raid Bosses."

I smirked.

"What? What am I not seeing?"

"It doesn't need to be a Raid Boss—the description says a World Boss or a Legend would work just fine." I met her eyes, still grinning. "Or a Lesser Deity. And it doesn't specify that the mob in question has to have anything to do with the prisms or the Possibility King at all: it just needs to be strong, and it needs to die within five hundred yards of the city."

Darling's jaw actually dropped.

Akura was getting worn down remarkably quickly despite the utter chaos Givora was wreaking across the battlefield, but Frank and I weren't finished yet.

I mentally highlighted the vast majority of the Ghostlight Cannons that House had constructed—there were dozens of them in all—and tucked them into my inventory.

And on that prearranged signal, the entirety of the city guard who'd been pacing the walls of the other wards quietly pulled back and began making their way to the Commerce Ward as I'd directed them to do earlier through Darling.

That left a skeleton crew of guild members behind—not nearly enough to represent a true defensive force—but enough to preserve the impression of one, at least from Goon's still-distant vantage point. I'd also left a number of Ghostlight Cannons in place across the other wards in particularly defensible locations, just to add to the illusion.

I wasn't hoping to accomplish much: just to ensure that Goon would lean on their vast numbers to rush the city as a whole rather than throw everything they had at the Commerce Ward.

I turned to Darling.

"Okay, Akura's about to drop. Let's have the rest of the guild log in now."

She tapped the air and went still for a moment, then a sea of green name tags populated the entirety of the Commerce Ward as every available member of Omen popped into the city within its walls, completely out of Goon's field of view.

And with that done, I slammed the many Ghostlight Cannons back into place exclusively atop the walls that protected the Commerce Ward. The effect was absurd: there were so many cannons present that there was only three or four feet between any two of them.

Then I leaned forward on the wall and waited for the alerts to follow, which was a matter of seconds.

**World-first Alert! The Guild {Goon} is the first Guild to defeat {Akura, God of the Sapphire Depths}!**
**Awarding Unique Title: {Of the Deepest Blue}!**

A round of cheers followed from Goon, and they quickly refocused on Givora, though half their numbers were trying to kill the huge creature while many of the others seemed to be trying to lead it away from the designated Siege area.

Then a massive, golden ripple surged out from the very center of the Black Oasis and its four wards.

**Major Ripple Alert! {The Black Oasis} is the first city to finish its Legendary Quest: {In Defense of the Black Oasis}!**
**All existing Defensive Structures will now be upgraded by 2 Tiers!**
**Now calibrating and distributing rewards for all players who contributed to the city's defense...**
**In addition, the following three players have been identified as the greatest contributors to the defense of the Black Oasis, and they will each receive 1 {Cache of the Possibility King}:**
**Third place: {Tyrann, Worshipper of the Dead}**

Second place: {House, Crazy Cat Lady}
First place: {Francis}

Congratulations, you received 1 {Cache of the Possibility King}!
You received {Voucher: Cloudship Motor Kit} x1!
You received {Minor Tower Token} x250!

**Congratulations, you reached Renown Rank XIII!**
**You may now choose 1 of 3 Renown Perks!**

That last bit caught me completely off-guard, but I didn't have time to puzzle it out because the wall beneath my feet flashed gold before rising substantially higher into the air as towers formed all along its length.

The merlons rose in turn, and murder holes formed in the stone through which we'd be able to target the players below from relative safety.

Many of the Ghostlight Cannons had ended up atop the newly risen towers, and they too were shining and shifting in the early morning light.

And when the glow faded, the freshly upgraded cannons were plated with dark iron, their barrels were easily twice as long and three times as wide, and their flared muzzles were lined with carefully placed Soul Gems that were substantially larger and brighter than anything I'd seen so far.

Even the moat had changed: the bottom was no longer visible from atop the wall, and sinister-looking shadows were ghosting beneath the surface while strange, forked fins protruded here and there.

I looked at Frank, wide-eyed and completely baffled by how Francis had even got on the podium, let alone taken first, but a third alert followed before I could ask.

**World Alert! A Hidden Ripple Threshold has been met in {The Black Oasis}, and the {Stonewhisper Dwarves} have officially begun construction on EBO's first Wonder of the World!**

I took that in, head spinning, looked around to make sure nobody who didn't already know about Francis was in earshot, then dropped my voice just to be safe.

"But how did Francis win?"

"Mostly the tree at work," Frank said. "Quest rewards were based on how much you contributed to the defense, and giving the entire zone 5%

damage, healing, and toughness was a massive contribution. Tree belongs to him, and you've been funding the guard as Francis on top of that, and they've been doing work.

"I can't share the raw numbers with you when it comes to contribution levels, but House snagged second because of all the defenses she threw up, especially the cannons, but she wasn't even close to first."

I was about to respond, but another prompt popped through.

**Warning: The Siege begins in 30 seconds!**

Anxiety and excitement rising in tandem, I pulled up the cache I'd been awarded and popped it open. And the result completely floored me.

**{The Crimson Rail} (Two-handed Enchanted Rifle) (Subtype: Railgun)**
**Grade: C**
**Item Level: 75**
**Damage Type: Magical**
**Quality: Legendary**
**Physical Attack: 0**
**Magical Attack: 300**
**Speed: N/A**
**Primaries: +40 Intelligence, +20 Dexterity, +30 Constitution**
**Secondaries: +10% Critical Strike Chance**
**Effect: While this weapon is equipped, your Ravenblast naturally pierces all enemies in its path, and striking an enemy with Ravenblast increases your Critical Strike Chance by 1.5% for 10 seconds, stacking up to 10 times.**

I equipped it immediately. The rifle was black from stock to muzzle, but its entire length was covered in orange and red runes. It was longer than my last weapon by a full foot, and it felt like I was carrying a cross between a sniper rifle and a bazooka.

I immediately went into my profession menu and pulled up an option that I'd unlocked earlier but dismissed due to my relatively low Critical Strike Chance at the time, because all of a sudden that would no longer be an issue while I had that railgun equipped.

Recipe: {Rune of the Gathering Flock} (Consumable) (Awards 0 skill points per craft)
Critical Strikes caused by your Ravenblasts cause you to summon a Circling Raven that will follow you around and expire after 4 seconds. This duration is refreshed upon causing another Critical Strike. Upon gathering 4 Circling Ravens, your next Ravenblast becomes instant regardless of the weapon you have equipped.
Duration: 24 Hours.
Requirements: {Large Soul Gem} x25.

I crafted one of those up immediately and threw it onto my new rifle, then took my old Legendary rifle and broke it down into my Trinket so that I could keep using the Touchstone power that was attached to it, which would stack incredibly well with my latest rune and the power on my Crimson Rail.

**Your Trinket gained the Touchstone Ability {Fated End}!**

{Fated End} (Touchstone Passive)
Whenever your Ravenblast fails to Critically Strike, your next Ravenblast gains a 10% Chance to Critically Strike. This effect stacks up to 10 times. All stacks are lost on a Critical Strike.

I'd been tempted to stick Water Jet into my Touchstone Socket instead because I was worried about losing the mobility the skill offered after having upgraded my pistols, but I needed damage above all else, and the combo potential was too potent to ignore.

And with that finished, I rolled my shoulders, braced the long weapon on the wall, and looked around.

The newly logged-in guild members had moved into their assigned positions at the base of the wall and inside the ward and were awaiting Darling's signal along with the guards who had just arrived. The moat crew was in place as well, standing atop the high walls and encircling the entire Commerce Ward.

Givora was still ravaging Goon off in the distance, and while they'd finally got it together and managed to dedicate a couple of hundred players to face off with the powerful creature, their forces were looking every bit as scattered and confused as I'd hoped they would.

I Overcharged a blast with my railgun, and the weapon put off a low drone that rose in pitch and volume until the sound had heads turning in my direction. Gold lines of power ran up the barrel's length, and the entire weapon trembled in my grip as the spell completed.

"Here we go," I said.

"Let's show them who they're dealing with," Frank said.

"Yeah, let's."

"To be clear, I meant me."

I nodded and shouldered my new weapon. "I know, Frank. Now help me pick the right people to turn into corpses."

"You got it."

**Warning: The Siege of the Black Oasis has officially begun!**

# Chapter Fifty-Four

Goon's initial approach was as I'd expected: a disorganized, leaping, sprinting mob that rushed all four wards with equal fervor, while a sizable chunk of their forces hung back to grind Givora down, which was everything I'd been hoping for from pulling the mob into the siege and then some.

I couldn't fault Goon for that decision either: despite our defensive upgrades, they still had us outnumbered at close to 10:1, and splitting their forces had successfully stopped Givora from rampaging through their ranks at the same time.

But seeing them all in motion again—the better part of a thousand players rushing the wall in an ever-tightening circle that stretched fully around the city—the scope of what we were up against hit home once again, and the rising hope I'd begun to feel as our defenses ramped up and the first few steps of our plan clicked into place was now giving way to wary determination.

Darling stepped up on a merlon and pitched her voice to carry.

"Everybody hold until my mark! Moat crew on the first axe, everybody else on the second!"

Goon was still rumbling in from several hundred yards off, so it made sense to wait, but I was itching to see if the next phase of the plan I'd concocted would work. And when Darling raised an axe into the air—the same icy weapon the Frostcaller had dropped, the one Frank and I had insisted she keep for herself—I took a deep breath and held it.

Cast bars appeared over the players she'd designated as the moat crew, all of whom were already positioned atop the walls and all around the ward.

Ten long seconds ticked by as Goon rushed closer, cheering and screaming like the horde they were, then the first boat popped into the air. Dozens more followed in a wave, then twenty-something Gunboats and half that many Galleys were falling from the walls and slapping down into the moat below, splashing water over the dark sand beyond.

Goon's advance slowed at the strange sight, but not by much.

The moat crew—who had also been designated as drivers—jumped down and swiftly maneuvered their assigned vessels into position, with the Gunboats forming a loose ring around the outer edge of the moat while the Galleys that naturally rode higher in the water hugged the space closer to the defensive wall, all of which left at least ten feet between the far edge of the moat and the nearest vessel.

Then Darling raised her second axe, and the entirety of the guild flooded out over the walls and leaped onto the newly arrived ships, with the melees taking up defensive positions on the Gunboats and the ranged DPS settling on the Galleys while the healers stayed perched on the walls above.

The vast majority of the melees carried deployable cannons, too, and I looked on as almost every member of the group each deployed two naval cannons on the ship they'd been assigned to, all of which House had created and tweaked for battle with anti-personnel rounds.

And this time around, Goon's advance really did stutter, but their momentum carried their foremost players forward regardless, their rear ranks surging despite the gauntlet that had sprung up in front of them and pushing the entire front line into the teeth of our defenses.

I activated Doppelganger and Double Cast it to generate four clones, two to either side, both with identical railguns pressed to their shoulders, long barrels already whining with gathered power.

I tweaked their targets, assigning each of them various players that were approaching from relatively different angles.

The surge finally entered my rifle's 60-yard range, so I exhaled deeply, aimed, then released the first shot of the Siege.

The railgun kicked against my shoulder so violently that it forced me into an involuntary step backward, and the clones beside me did the same as their weapons barked in sequence.

Five sharp explosions pierced the sounds of the incoming rush, and the entire front seemed to stutter once again as five massive ravens flew down off the walls like fighter jets in formation, each of them trailing a series of dark, smoky rings behind them.

The spells punched deep into the enemy ranks, players vaporizing left and right as numbers I'd considered impossible a moment earlier flew above them: normal hits for damn near 2,000 damage, with Critical Strikes that were almost twice that.

I'd expected Goon to pack their front lines with players with Magical Resistance, but that didn't seem to be the case because even my clones were trucking people despite their reduced damage, dropping several of the approaching players into execute range from full Health.

And thanks to my 4-piece set's cleave effect, every single spell splashed even more damage to those in the immediate vicinity and sent tiny dark birds swarming from person to person.

And the best part of it all? With five shots flying at once and punching into such a dense crowd, the rune I'd applied earlier instantly generated four circling ravens.

The birds dove into my weapon as one, and the red runes flared brighter still.

"Gathering Flock just made your next blast instant."

I pivoted and fired again, taking aim at another group with the same result: damage and death on a scale so widespread that Frank started cackling despite the magic involved.

Then all at once, the swarm of players entered the range of the boats and the cannons behind them.

The devastation that followed immediately put the damage I'd inflicted into perspective as the massively upgraded Ghostlight Cannons as well as the vessels beneath them came into play.

Our ships fired first, the Gunboats rocking back in a wave while the Galleys did the same a split second afterward, with many of the larger, closer vessels bumping up against the wall as the recoil from their many cannons drove them back.

A hail of dark, steely projectiles ripped deep into the oncoming rush, dropping players by the score, and our mages and ranged players rained even more death upon the approaching group.

The Ghostlight Cannons brightened in turn, Soul Gems flaring like miniature suns, then a wave of huge, bullet-like rounds blasted out from them and erupted in pale blue domes of fire that spread all across the enemy's front ranks, throwing players into the air with bright flames trailing behind them.

Darling caught my eye, still standing atop the merlon to my left. "You can thank House for this one!"

She took a deep breath and raised her voice. "Motors, go!" She gathered herself and leaped clear across the Galleys below and toward a Gunboat, hair flying behind her, huge axes gripped in each hand.

The moat exploded with greenish light as every Gunboat activated a Soul Gem motor, and the entire fleet of small, nimble vessels started flying clockwise through the moat just as Goon's first arrivals drew close enough to activate their movement abilities.

A good number of them had already leaped or teleported into the air, intent on landing atop the still-firing Gunboats, and maybe a dozen players splashed down into the water as the vessels zoomed away from beneath them and began to circle the Commerce Ward at blazing speeds.

The players thrashed as the fins I'd seen earlier converged, and Frank shouted with glee as a Gunboat thumped right over someone who had been swimming for the nearest Galley and sent them drifting toward the bottom.

But Goon just kept coming, with three or four players available to step forward for every person we dropped, and before long, by virtue of sheer numbers, a sizable group had teleported or leaped onto the carousel of boats and were engaging with the melee players we'd positioned there.

Darling and House were both riding a particularly crowded vessel whose deck House had covered in oil, and Darling was bouncing from target to target, her Health bar blinking red, but she had several shields in place and her Sinister Momentum buff completely maxed out.

She was cutting people down left and right, cleaving through them and filling the air with green slashes, either dropping them where they stood and leaving frozen statues behind or sending them flying off the boat with wickedly strong strikes. House's healing bots whirred above her head, in position but not healing, letting Darling keep her Health low to maximize her damage while her shields held.

2.0 was there as well, peeling players off House and pouncing on anyone who dropped into execute range before Darling could send them flying.

They seemed to have their vessel under control and it was already speeding away, so I released another massive railgun blast and cut several deep lines through the approaching front, procced another instant thanks to multiple crits, and repeated the process while targeting the healers and casters I could reach as Frank shouted them out until my Doppelgangers blinked away.

Once they were gone, I swapped to my new pistols and quickly threw on a piercing rune plus a Rune of Shattering for a bit of added control and went to work from atop the wall, targeting the melee players who'd managed to land atop our first wave of boats with a Gravity Bird, then following up with a blitz of icy ravens from above, revolvers barking in my hands.

"850 and 906. Ooooh, 1,700 crit to the dome! Gunboat approaching to your left, seven enemies on board, gunners are getting overwhelmed!"

I ducked a greenish orb that nearly took my head off, switched to my Dreadflight Cannon, led the vessel a little bit to account for flight time, then fired three ravens in quick succession.

The boat continued forward, and the three diving birds erupted in sequence in a line across the deck. Enemy players went flying, many of them dead before their feet left the deck, and our melees quickly mopped up the rest and cleared the boat.

Everywhere I looked, Goon's forces were absolutely melting beneath the assault, and what melees had managed to board our Gunboats were being focused either by the Galleys behind them or by players atop the wall or even being knocked away into the moat by our own close-combat players, where the beasts beneath the waves made quick work of them.

I ran down the length of the wall, staying low to duck the spells and projectiles that were increasingly flying in my direction; it seemed that Goon's ranged crew was prioritizing the casters atop the fortifications by sending all sorts of AoE effects flying up to zone us out and off: blizzards, meteor showers, tornadoes, and dark clouds that spewed acidic, burning rain.

But it was working. We were actually winning. Goon's numbers still seemed endless, but they were dropping by the dozen, and between the ships and the Ghostfire Cannons, the damage we were putting out was so widespread that their healers couldn't keep up, and ours were practically invincible atop the walls, where they only had to contend with dodging the suppressing fire Goon was throwing up.

We'd taken some losses too—seven players in all, all melees who'd been sent to defend the Gunboats, including Ton—but we'd easily dropped ten or even twenty times that many between the cannons and the boats alone.

"Four healers within range to your left," Frank said, and I felt him indicate the position in question.

I ducked low and put my back to a merlon, then swapped to my railgun and charged up a blast. "Hit me with that direction again?" I said as the spell completed.

He mentally indicated the spot again. "Target the leather-user at the back—purple cloak, black armor, hands glowing green."

I pivoted up and slammed my rifle onto the wall, staying as low as I could while the spells flew around me and bits of metal sparked and pinged off the walls. I found the caster in question right away, at the very edge of my range where the spell would punch insanely deep.

I took aim and fired, immediately dropping back to safety.

Then the ground lit up beneath my feet in four different shades of red while clouds formed and darkened above me.

"Move!" Frank said.

But I was already Clonedrifting sideways and down the wall. The clone I'd left behind exploded, and I heard a round of cheers go up from Goon, probably as they'd assumed the combination of AoE spells they'd dropped on me had done me in instead of my clone.

So it was with great satisfaction that I popped out of drift with four ravens circling my pistols.

Frank motioned at an area of the battlefield to my left. "Two of the casters that just targeted you are lined up in this area, both rocking D-Grade. You've got another instant to burn, don't waste it by leaving your pistols equipped!"

I rose up and switched to my railgun, then sent another line of feathery death punching into the area Frank had indicated, where two casters were indeed lined up in a convenient little column.

They dropped on contact. I ducked low, then hit the brakes and pivoted back the way I had come and was unsurprised to see the area I would have otherwise been in getting lit up with even more AoE effects than before.

I managed to chain a few more instant railgun blasts, the air crackling around me the entire time until I made the mistake of targeting an area that wasn't particularly dense and failed to proc an instant by letting my Gathering Flock stacks drop.

Standing in place was getting risky with the amount of fire being thrown my way—let alone casting for that long in one place—so I ran low to the ground thinking I'd reposition and try to alter the course of the fight somewhere where Goon hadn't already picked me out as a priority target.

A Ghostlight Cannon exploded to my left as I ran along, and my heart clenched in my chest as a second followed in short order. At almost the same moment, one of our Gunboats burst into flames, and another raid frame grayed out in my peripheral: Jukes was officially out of the fight.

I kept moving until I reached the far side of the Commerce Ward—the area that faced the other parts of the city with the dividing rivers between them, where the rope bridges connected the various wards from above—and the sight beyond was a stark dose of reality that I could have done without.

We might have been crushing Goon on a single front, but their vast numbers had swarmed right over the other three, less well-protected wards, and every single Ghostlight Cannon I'd left in place there had been reduced to smoldering piles of metal that were now only throwing dark smoke into the air.

Red nametags were flooding through the rivers below and scrambling up the dunes toward the Commerce Ward, even running across the rope bridges that were hanging low, overburdened by the sheer number of players trying to cross them at once.

I Clonedrifted up off the wall and atop the nearest tower, where I found Nina and Rock skulking within as I'd requested.

"Is it time?" Nina said.

I switched to my rifle and took aim down the bridge. "Blow the others, but give me a second here."

Nina tapped the air, and the other melee users Darling had assigned to the other two rope bridges stepped out of their respective towers and cut the lines that anchored the bridges.

The bridges to either side of us cracked like whips, and all of the players on them fell into the wide gaps between the wards and into the swift-running waters below.

I took aim and sent a Gravity Bird flying down the last remaining bridge. I detonated the spell right in front of their fastest players, yanking many of them off their feet and into the air, causing a huge roadblock about halfway down the bridge's length.

I took aim with my rifle, wound up a cast that felt terribly long, then released it as my Gravity Bird reached the end of its duration.

Then a heavily armored player raised a tower shield high into the air and it flashed, mirror-like.

My raven struck the shield and rebounded, and I faked a look of panicked shock for a moment before I threw up an Illusory Mirror and bounced the spell right back at them.

"Blow it," I said while the raven was still flying.

Nina and Rock went to work on the points that anchored the bridge, and our side of it dropped free as my raven punched through the line of tightly packed players and wiped several of them before they could fall.

"Jealous!" Nina called up. She was already in the air, having hopped off the tower with Rock close behind.

"You got another instant raven if you can find a target fast enough," Frank said.

I shouldered my rifle and aimed around as Goon poured across the other wards and down their respective dunes, eventually settling on blasting a pair of lined-up healers into the afterlife at Frank's suggestion. But well-timed golden shields prevented them both from dying, and the damage I'd dealt was quickly healed away.

More worryingly, the swarm was closing in, and while our Ghostlight Cannons were firing non-stop all around the ward and our boats were still motoring along, cannons flashing, it was impossible to look at the army below without feeling like the writing was on the wall.

I looked to the Royal Ward, hoping for a miracle as the true weight of Goon's forces pressed in. Even with the bridges down and the defensive advantages we had, seeing that many players on the move at once, all heading in the same direction like swarming ants, was absolutely over-whelming to look at.

Even if they ran up and attacked twice as mindlessly as that first wave had, our casters and healers wouldn't have nearly enough Mana or staying power to fight them off. There were just too many of them.

It was impossible.

"Oh man," Frank said in a tone that made me think he'd just reached the same conclusion.

Then a high-pitched whistle sounded from the direction Goon had taken Givora, and the shit officially hit the fan as their train roared up a nearby dune with Sleep grinning like a maniac at the wheel.

I watched in horror as the massive, hundred-foot-long vehicle barreled toward us at terrible speed. Its entire length was covered in players, and given the direction they were coming from, it seemed that Goon had pulled in a wave of reinforcements, siphoning people off Givora and sending them our way.

The great bird was still battling in the distance, ripping the dunes apart with breath after breath, but Goon had already dropped the creature to 85% and its position was steady, meaning they had probably left a sizable force behind to deal with it despite the reinforcements heading our way.

The train whistled again, and Sleep jumped out of the cabin and rolled over the sand while the vehicle continued on without him at a blistering pace. It ramped off a dune and launched into the air, and the engine in front touched back down before the rear carriage had even left the ground.

Goon's charging forces parted to make room for the approaching vehicle, and I wasn't sure what exactly they were planning until it punched through them and the countless players who were riding atop it all dropped free as it approached the moat.

"Incoming!" I yelled as loud as I could. "It's a ram!"

Omen scattered away from a wide section of the wall, and from my elevated position atop the rope bridge tower, I was able to see the moment when the engine car trucked a Gunboat into oblivion, split a Galley completely in half, and punched right into the stone wall.

But thankfully—impossibly—the upgraded wall held, and the massive vehicle crumpled behind the force of the impact, cars smashing into one another over and over again.

But the moat had been breached and the train had created a makeshift drawbridge that Goon was already piling onto, their numbers pouring right over our deadly boats and hopping onto the walls, using the train as an elevated platform.

I stared open-mouthed at the flood of players as they rolled the healers we'd positioned atop the walls, just as they had over Arranthea, easily outnumbering us three or four to one purely with the players pouring up and over the train, let alone with the aid of the hundreds that were still swarming in from every other direction.

"Just keep swinging," Frank said. "All we can do."

"Yeah." I shouldered my rifle and aimed at the section of wall Goon was streaming over, then fired a raven.

The spell dropped a handful of players on the spot, but either the crowd wasn't dense enough to award me with another instant or I'd just gotten unlucky with crits.

I looked to the Royal Ward, and again, there was nothing.

I checked my private messages. Nothing.

I swapped to my pistols for movement and kept the piercing blasts coming one after another, dropping people from forty yards out and freezing others in place, setting them up for kills on the next go, but I felt my shoulders slumping as the raid frames grayed out one after the other, with Zoe and Rock and Nina dying alongside all the others.

The carnage continued, and for the first time since I'd logged into EBO, I realized that I was truly dreading what lay in front of me: watching as the city we'd worked so hard to build up burned to the ground, as the Renown Path we'd developed was rendered useless in a blink.

And worst of all? I'd come to see the guild as friends, especially Darling, and I was exceedingly grateful for that, knowing that I was about to lose everything else, but the prospect of continuing on without Frank was... unthinkable.

It wouldn't even feel like we—I—would be playing the same game without him.

"I'm sorry, man, but looking at the numbers here, I think this is where we part ways," I said. "We'll take some more people with us for sure, but in case I don't get the chance to say it before we drop, it's been a blast. And thanks for everything."

"I guess it really is the end. It's, uh..." He cut off, hesitating, and I thought he was about to continue when a single line of pink text flashed in the bottom-left section of my screen.

It was a message for Francis from Tyrann.

*I don't know how the hell you pulled this off, but damn do you follow through when you promise something. I'm live, so feel free to make an appearance.*

Then there was movement to my left, deep within the Royal Ward.

The doors to Vesuvian's cellar burst open, the doors to his lavish home exploded off their hinges, and players with green name tags burst right out of the windows, glass flying everywhere.

The same scene unfolded simultaneously across two other particularly luxurious houses, and within seconds, the number of defenders appeared to have doubled and then some, and the reinforcements just kept coming, storming out of the Royal Ward and over its smoking walls and down the dune and right into Goon's rear-most ranks, where their healers and ranged players were suddenly and completely exposed.

The Cult of Information had officially arrived, right through the underground tunnel from Highwater City.

# Chapter Fifty-Five

I pumped a fist.

"We've got a chance!"

I jumped off the tower and rolled as I hit the ground, popped back to my feet, and sprinted for the spot where the train had struck the wall.

Goon members were all over the walls and our healers' raid frames were graying out left and right, but I saw Arlann out of the corner of my eye, leading a squadron of guards toward the train along one side of the wall while Sarissa led a second squadron on the other.

The surviving healers parted as the guards approached, and soon both of the NPC squads were glowing with golden shields and other preemptive heals as they closed the distance.

I saw Arlann lower his shield and I gritted my teeth as I approached a set of stairs that would take me back to the top of the wall. I hated seeing him and Sarissa so exposed, but it was what it was.

I took the stairs three at a time while Arlann blurred forward and bowled over ten Goon members with his shield pinned to his shoulder, knocking every single one of them right back off the wall and down into the moat below.

The guards surged in behind him, and the powerful Elites carved a bloody path through the stray attackers their Captain had left behind.

I made it atop the wall, then risked a glance backward to check on our flank. The Cult was still pouring out of the Royal Ward—there were hundreds of them—and I spotted Tyrann sprinting across the dark sands, golden armor shining with a light of its own.

He had a line of buffs that was stacked three rows deep atop his nameplate, and he was running at the very front of the mob.

A great deal of Goon's approaching forces had turned around to meet the new threat, and the two groups ended up meeting down by the rivers that separated the dunes, their ranged groups exchanging fire.

Goon's melee group was fording the river or leaping across it, totally unconcerned with the casualties they were taking in the process, and Tyrann himself was fighting on the front lines, taking an incredible amount of fire at the water's edge.

But he had so many healers focusing on him and shielding him up that his Health bar didn't appear to be moving.

It was strange seeing the Cult with green name tags, and Tyrann doubly so, but the Siege had locked them in as allies for the time being.

I turned back to the fight at hand and sprinted down the wall toward the train. I saw Arlann kick a dagger user square in the chest and send him flying, then Sarissa dropped to one knee right in front of Goon's vehicle.

"Protect her at all costs!" Arlann shouted, and for a moment I feared the worst: that she'd been gravely injured and was going down.

But then she placed a hand to the stone and blue runes sprang up all around her.

Arlann stepped directly behind her and guards fell in from both sides, nearly thirty Elites in all.

I switched to my pistols. Goon was engaging the guards, and the attackers were still pouring into the city by using the train as an entry point.

So once I was in range, I skidded to a stop across the stone, launched a Gravity Bird down the length of the wall and between the guards and the many members of Goon who were rushing to get at Sarissa.

As soon as the spell was out, I switched to my cannon and unloaded all three charges one after another.

I detonated the Gravity Bird while the arcing ravens were still screaming into the air, then added a pair of pistol blasts for good measure.

The black hole erupted and yanked seven or eight people into a dense knot, the two icy blasts I'd sent racing along the wall connected and rooted them all in place, and the three diving birds howled down from above and deleted the entire group save for a pair of heavily armored players who swiveled in my direction—only for a pair of guards to cut them down from behind.

"She's almost there!" Arlann said.

With three more charges in hand, I hefted my cannon over the wall and took aim below, where the last of Goon's reinforcements on this side of the battlefield were clambering up the train.

I fired three ravens at the front of the vehicle, sending each of them arcing high into the air with a gap between them, more intent on zoning the area off and buying time than killing people outright.

Sarissa stood up, her blue robes whipping about her despite the lack of wind. She raised a hand and a massive, two-foot-thick wall of ice sprang up and extended along the outside of our fortifications for twenty feet to either side of her, rising high over the train.

Then she collapsed, and Arlann caught her before she hit the ground.

Just like that, she'd raised the wall enough that Goon could no longer use their train as a platform to help them climb up and over. They were once again left to contend with the moat and the deadly boats riding atop it, though the enormous vehicle had eliminated our ability to keep them moving in a circle, so Goon's forces below quickly transitioned to boarding the nearby Gunboats.

Green slashes pulsed below and to my left, so I swapped to my pistols and surveyed the scene.

Almost directly below me, Darling was fighting off a trio of melee players atop a Galley, her Health still firmly in the red while all three of her opponents were marked with the slashes I'd seen earlier.

House and 2.0 must have been nearby too because two of her Leadfire Turrets were positioned at opposite ends of the Galley, and both of them were lighting the players up from behind as they attempted to corner Darling in the center of the boat with her back to the wall.

"She's low, but she's still got the full five stacks of Sinister Momentum shielding her," Frank said. "House's healing bots are hiding behind the Galley's mast. She's probably watching Darling's shields from nearby."

I raised my pistols and fired off a Dreadful Shot, which sent one of the players that were stalking her fleeing across the deck.

But before I could drop the rest of them, Darling dashed forward faster than I'd ever seen her move before. Both of the remaining players swung in her direction, but she slipped right between the vertical strikes and set her feet, twisted in place, then attacked with both axes in a tight, spinning attack that sent a helix of green light rising all around her.

The slashes I'd seen earlier pulsed, and the two players she'd struck— and the one I'd sent fleeing—died and turned into frozen statues right there on the deck.

Her head jerked up my way, and she raised her ice-blue axe in my direction. I was about to shout down at her, but then I felt something wrap around my waist.

I looked down to find that two large, dark hands had just clasped themselves together near my belly button.

The world went topsy turvy as I was lifted clear off my feet and smashed backward into the stone, pale blue light erupting all around me.

"Arcane Suplex," Frank said. "Silenced for four seconds, your Health at 45%!"

My vision cleared just in time for me to see Sleep grinning over me.

"Hey again, Ned! Been looking for ya since it started!"

He wrapped a hand around my ankle, then spun a hard 180. I whipped up off the ground and flew in a tight circle, then Sleep shifted his feet and brought me down vertically as if I were a living hammer.

I gasped as I hit the stone, all the breath going out of me at once.

"Runecircle Slam, stunned for four seconds, Heart Vessel popped, your Health back to 30%!" Frank dropped his voice to a whisper that was barely audible. "Silence is about to expire."

I lay there on my back, biding my time as Sleep thundered away but Frank was right: the Silence from Arcane Suplex had just run out.

Sleep leaped for a nearby merlon while spinning a 180 at the same time, planted a single foot atop it, then launched into a high moonsault that was obviously going to end up with him belly-flopping on top of me.

But with the Silence gone, I activated Clonedrift to kill the stun. And since I could now drift in any direction, I forced myself to appear right behind my clone, fully upright, with Frank already gripped in both hands, held high and behind me.

The clone raised a pistol from where it lay on its back and blasted Sleep as he fell with an instant, damage-free Ravenblast that stunned him for three seconds.

And I was already swinging, feet planted, Frank arcing up in a vicious, Repel-powered uppercut that caught Sleep fully in the gut at full extension.

"Kablam!" Frank shouted.

I jumped up onto the same merlon that Sleep had launched himself off and threw myself high into the air right in front of my opponent as the big man hit his apex.

I raised Frank above my head with both hands, then Double Cast a second Repel and brought him down on the top of Sleep's head with every ounce of strength I had.

"Kapow!" Frank screamed.

I'd angled the blow perfectly, and the Repel-enhanced attack sent him flying, spiking him straight down and deep into the water below.

Darling stepped to the edge of her Galley just above where he'd entered the water, both axes held high.

And when Sleep's hand shot out of the water and grabbed onto the railing of the ship and the big man attempted to pull himself out to safety, Darling kicked him full in the face with an armored boot and knocked him right back in while 2.0 seemed to appear out of nowhere, prowling behind Darling, metal paws thudding as they struck the deck.

The strange fins converged on Sleep but then scattered for reasons I didn't understand. Then he somehow reappeared on the shoreline of the moat, drenched from head to toe.

He wrung out his trousers with both hands, pointed a flawless smile up in my direction, then ran off while laughing so loudly I heard him the entire way until he vanished over a dune and in the direction of Givora.

I whipped around, surveying the battlefield now that the wall had been fully secured. I still couldn't see House, but three of her healing bots drifted over to me, and I was especially grateful for the healing with my Heart Vessel on cooldown.

Goon's forces had thinned out on this side of the battlefield, so with Sarissa having sealed off the only point of easy access that Goon had and the guard nearby in case her icy wall dropped, I bolted for the other main front, pistols in hand.

A familiar blue axe flew up over the wall and Darling appeared out of thin air, fingers clasping around the hilt. She landed neatly beside me, already running at full speed.

"I've got all of our available vessels circling up and heading around to the other side! We can smash them between us and the Cult, but Ned, what the hell did you do? Why is the Cult helping us?"

"They aren't here for us, but Tyrann has taken a liking to Francis of late, and he wanted to play the hero for his fans as usual, so here he is!" I hurdled the smoldering remains of a Ghostlight Cannon while Darling went around it. "I sent the Cult off to Highwater earlier today with the promise that if they dropped out of the Siege ahead of time as attackers, I'd find a way to put him at the center of the fight. And when he followed through, I pointed the Cult to a tunnel that links the Oasis to Highwater. They were waiting beneath the city before the Siege even started."

"I love it! We might actually have this!"

We rounded a stretch of the wall, and I had to Clonedrift over one of the guard towers while Darling tossed an axe over and teleported back into place beside me.

"Just need to burn them down!" I said. "We just gotta get 'embelow 10% of their initial number, so if we can manage that, we might not even need to deal with the group they've got killing..."

I trailed off as the fight below came into view. The Cult had taken a page out of our book and spawned a huge number of boats into the rivers between the dunes. Most of them only appeared to be lightly armed, but they'd arranged the vessels to form a series of floating platforms that allowed their healers and ranged players to stand atop the water while the melees—including Tyrann, who was glowing even more brightly than before—forged ahead.

And the Cult was actually pushing what remained of Goon back, directly toward our cannons and the many Gunboats that were now drifting into position across the moat high above them.

I lined up my rifle, took aim, and fired. Then again, and again, and again.

The ships erupted with cannon fire as Goon retreated up the hill, our Ghostlight Cannons followed suit, and what melee crew we still had left poured off the boats they'd been protecting and surged across the dunes with a full head of steam while our healers and ranged charged in behind them.

Darling looked from left to right, gave me a gap-toothed smile, then jumped down to join the carnage.

She and the rest of our forces smashed into Goon from behind, tearing into their unprotected healers and ranged DPS while the Cult pressed their own attack on the other side.

Tyrann was an absolute wrecking ball, two- or three-shotting every melee that got in his way while his team of dedicated healers allowed him to shrug off a truly immense amount of concentrated damage.

His own melee crew surged behind him, focusing the people he spared and stunning or slowing them so the mob could keep rolling.

With their healers engaged and supporting fire suddenly absent thanks to our ambush, Goon's frontline crumbled in a wave, and the Cult of Information surged into the gap and started dropping the attackers left and right.

And just like that—with a colossal volley of magic and cannons that was no different to the dozens that had come before it—an alert went out with maybe sixty members of Goon still sandwiched between the Cult and our defensive fortifications.

**Major Ripple Alert! {The Black Oasis} has successfully repelled an attempted Siege!**
**For the next 12 hours, all PVP combat within the designated Siege Zone is explicitly prohibited unless combatants preemptively opt out of the Zone's protective aura.**
**In addition, as the target of a recent Siege, {The Black Oasis} will be protected from the Siege mechanic for five days.**

**Congratulations, you are among the first players to successfully defend against a Siege!**
**Awarding Unique Title: {Siegebreaker}**

But before I could celebrate, a deep, familiar voice sounded from behind me.

"Well played, friend! But I think you dropped something!"

I whipped around, pistols coming up.

Sleep was charging right at me from further along the wall. I tried to fire a Dreadful Shot at him—only to get an error message that reminded me that combat between players was now prohibited.

The big man blew by me; slapped me on the back, then leaped absurdly high into the air and yelled so loudly that his voice echoed over the dunes and cut right through the celebratory clamor that was just starting to rise from below.

"*Cannonball!*"

I watched him fall a hundred-plus feet, utterly baffled as he splashed down between a bunch of the Cult's ships.

Then a huge, winged shadow fell over me, and I understood.

Sleep had dragged Givora all the way back to the Black Oasis.

# Chapter Fifty-Six

I inspected Givora as it flew in and swooped down to my left.

**{Givora, Scion of the Desert Wind} (Level 19 Legendary Beast)**
**HP: 3,767,322/6,000,000**
**MP: 12,075,050/15,000,000**

She passed low over the city, and her deadly tailwind ripped a Ghost-light Cannon from atop the wall and sent it rolling down the dune while a pair of Gunboats nearly capsized in the suddenly turbulent moat.

The automated cannons lit Givora up as she passed, but the beast only had eyes for Sleep, who was treading water in the river down between the dunes and laughing like a madman.

I jumped off the wall, landed on a Galley in a low roll, then bounded onto a Gunboat, leaped off, and bolted down the sands.

"Tanks or off tanks, we need you! The defenses are going to pull that thing into the city if nobody grabs it!"

Jukes must have respawned the moment the Siege ended because he was already there, rolling right down the dune about a hundred feet to my left, sand flying all around him.

"I'm back!" Ton said, his voice sounding from somewhere behind me.

The Cult members had frozen in and across the river, and many of them were staring up at me as I raced down the dune, revolvers pumping at my side. Healers and ranged damage dealers who had just respawned were flooding out of the city behind me even as the cannons continued to boom and the ships peppered Givora with lead.

Tyrann himself caught sight of me then, and the look of pure rage on his face made me laugh despite it all. His name tag as well as those of all the other Cultists had flashed from green to red in a blink now that the Siege had ended, and both their hostility and their intentions were obvious.

For Goon's part, I'd expected them to scatter and leave us to deal with Givora and its aftermath, but they'd actually done the complete opposite: their remaining force of sixty or so were charging right over and through the shocked Cult members and directly at Givora.

And with the Siege over, Goon's dead were respawning all across the dunes and immediately running headlong into the next battle, shouting and screaming at the Legendary beast with every ounce of the ridiculous amount of enthusiasm they'd brought to the Siege.

The great buzzard inhaled sharply and blew a trio of blasts into the river where Sleep was floating. The incredible knockback blasted him straight out of the water, killing him instantly and sending his corpse cartwheeling up the opposite dune alongside three of the Cult's vessels that had been unfortunate enough to get caught in the blast, each of which shattered into bits of kindling upon contact with the sand.

With Sleep dead and gone for the moment, Givora banked a hard turn and made a beeline for the city.

Jukes threw an icy dagger high into the air, almost vertically, and all I could do was pray that it would connect, especially given the level gap between them.

But the spell hit, and Givora banked right back around and came in low, then landed right in front of him.

"Roast that bird!" Frank said, and Omen cheered as Darling and Rock and Nina and House and 2.0 and everybody else rushed to engage, the entire lot of them screaming across the sands toward Givora and the red name tags that surrounded it.

"Turn Givora around!" I called out. "Make sure it's facing one of the other wards when the breath attack hits!"

Ton leaped right over me and landed halfway between Jukes and me. The other melees crashed in—including an ever-growing number of Goon members who were swarming in from every direction.

I swapped out my Rune of Shattering for a Rune of the Caustic Raven, then lit the creature up as Jukes managed to connect with a Hateful Ice and the entirety of the surrounding force began transferring their threat to him.

He rolled right between the creature's legs and got the position right, and the melees scattered to readjust. Spells and cannonfire and Ghostlight bombs filled the air, and the explosions went on and on, a never-ending series of reports that was so bright I was having a hard time seeing Jukes or even much of Givora, despite its size.

Then I spotted Tyrann charging my way out of the corner of my eye, so I started recording.

The Cult snapped out of it and followed his lead, the entire lot of them charging right across the river and directly at me, universally ignoring the players who were streaming by to engage Givora.

The sand around Tyrann flashed gold, then he hurled himself high into the air even as I kept my fire trained on the giant bird. Tyrann's weapons flared with burnished light, and he screamed as he brought them both down on my head.

Or he tried to.

Because while he should have made contact, his weapons vanished from his grip before they tagged me and he landed awkwardly in the sand, staggering sideways.

I cocked an eyebrow at him, grinning as his allies lit the ground up around me with AoEs and sent whole volleys of magic and metal flying directly at me. The AoE spells raged to no effect whatsoever, and the projectiles fizzled out as soon as they hit me.

Tyrann reequipped his swords and rushed back over. He tried to strike me one more time, getting the same result, then it finally seemed to click.

I dropped my pistols into my inventory.

"You ought to read your prompts more carefully, man! Player combat is disabled right after a Siege." I pulled Frank out and activated Repel. "If you wanna hit someone, you gotta opt in."

I swung Frank right at his face.

"Like this!"

"Shablam!" Frank screamed.

I pulled up inches short of Tyrann's face—I hadn't actually opted into combat because I wasn't a complete idiot—but the familiar blow accomplished what I'd been aiming for: it made him flinch, his features contorting in shock, hands going up to shield his face.

Frank cackled in my hand, and within the space of a breath I had nine images of Tyrann floating in my peripheral, all of them of him panicking in high definition as his useless army continued to throw spells and projectiles my way to no avail.

Tyrann recovered, but his face was already flushing beet red. He opened his mouth as if he had something to say, but I rolled right over him as his guild members collectively realized they couldn't kill me and finally gave up.

"Now that you're done playing with Frank, are you guys gonna help us down this thing before it wrecks the Black Oasis, or are you gonna let the whole city burn 'cause an elf you don't like whacked you with a talking axe and crit your feelings?"

He glared at me, eyebrows twitching. He swallowed as if it pained him and pointed a still-glowing sword at my chest. "This isn't over."

I sent two ravens flying right by him, the two caustic blasts flying either side of his head. "Yeah man, didn't need to be said. Can we get some help here or what?"

He gritted his teeth, and I could almost feel the person he really was warring with the narrative he'd been trying to push by helping the Oasis out in the first place.

A narrative that he'd already tarnished by dropping everything to try and kill me while Omen and even Goon rallied to drop Givora.

He turned and ran off without another word, face burning, the Cult stepping in behind him to engage the three-headed beast.

"Seems like you were right, Frank! We might not have been able to hurt him, but you definitely did some damage to his self-esteem."

"Oh you know it! That one's going in the greatest hits album for sure. Working title: Now That's What I Call Frank. Thoughts?"

I laughed. "I love it."

"Not sure it's selling the me part enough but it's definitely a start. Also, Givora's at 61% and falling fast."

I eyed Jukes' Health bar as it repeatedly fell from full to as low as 10% under each of Givora's devastating attacks, but between the healers of Omen and what remained of Goon—and with the newly engaged Cult—he was actually holding his own.

Ton had stepped up as well, expertly tanking one of the other two heads while Goon used an entirely different approach of focusing on the remaining head and having the boss one-shot someone only for the head to pick a new target, rinse, repeat.

And as Givora ticked lower and more and more Goon members

respawned and immediately joined the fight and the Ghostlight Cannons continued to boom and the ships lit the great bird up, it was with an unspeakable amount of relief and levity that I finally allowed myself to believe it was actually going down. That we'd actually pulled it off.

We must have had 700 players on her, then 800, then 900, and the numbers just kept rising as I fired away, feeling lighter than I had in days while Frank cackled at my side as he distributed the still photos he'd pulled of Tyrann's momentary panic to the rest of the guild.

Givora ticked down to 40%, then 20%, then 10%, and while its three-pronged breath attack dropped thirty or forty players every time it used it, it didn't matter, because the bulk of the casualties belonged to Goon and they were happy to respawn immediately and dive right back in.

Givora dropped into the single digits, and the screams and cheers and laughter that went up reverberated around the dunes and seemed to shake the very ground beneath my feet.

Finally, between four dunes that were littered with corpses, Givora flapped her wings one last time and dropped to the sands, right in front of Jukes and Ton at the very heart of the Black Oasis.

There was a brief moment of silence, and the exultant roar that followed reverberated like thunder across the dunes. The celebration was so intense that I got completely swept up in it for a long moment, and Frank and I were both shouting wordlessly into the noise.

But then he gestured at something nearby.

And while there was no way that Omen alone had accounted for 50% of the damage—meaning loot should have been off the table, at least for us—Givora was still sparking orange.

I pushed my way through the revelry, between Cult members who glared at me as I passed—the lot of them were already retreating to their ships, many of them getting battered around and looking annoyed by the countless revelers, while Tyrann himself was nowhere to be seen—and Goon members who didn't seem to recognize me in the slightest but were quick to offer high-fives regardless.

Even House was going nuts, running around and slapping hands with everyone while 2.0 snaked through the crowd behind her.

I reached the corpse, but Sleep was already there, kneeling and grinning, his smile bright against the dark sands.

I put my hands on my hips and pretended that I was just admiring the kill, then mentally looted the single item that I had access to.

{The Heart of the Desert Wind}
Rarity: Legendary
Effect: ??

Sleep's gaze whipped around, then snapped to me.

"There we go. Was wondering when the body would clear. Hope you got something good, man." He stood up. "That was a hell of a fight. Best one so far—no contest."

I tried to play it cool, but Sleep's grin was so warm and genuine that I found myself returning it. "Likewise, man! That was a blast."

Two players in bloody aprons stepped up around me, huge knives in hand.

Sleep rolled his shoulders. "Any chance you can stick around for a minute?"

I looked at Frank. "Revenant should still be several hours out, right?"

"If your estimate holds, yeah. Rifts will be popping back up soon too. We could always stick close to one to be safe, pop through it if we need to."

I rubbed my chin. "I think I've got a temporary solution for that thing the next time around, but that's a good call."

Then I looked up and met Sleep's gaze.

"What did you have in mind?"

# Chapter Fifty-Seven

About thirty minutes later, I was sitting on one of hundreds of fold-out tables directly in front of the wreckage of Goon's train, with House to my left and Darling snoring to my right with her forehead pressed to the table, one hand still gripping a mug of dark beer, while Frank was soaking in the largest bucket of unidentified liquid I'd ever seen.

Mugs and plates that House had already licked clean several times covered the table. Dozens of other dishes had been set around us and directly on the sands, all heaped with scraps that 2.0 and House's many other cats and also Chip were happily digging into.

Most of the rear cars of Goon's train had survived the worst of the impact, and Sleep's guild had thrown open a number of side panels and opened the cars up, exposing the various kitchens within and turning the entire vehicle into one gigantic food truck out of which Sleep and company had been delivering food non-stop.

And at the center of the huge expanse of fold-out tables, Sleep was holding court in front of a seven-foot-tall drumstick that was roasting over an open fire.

One of the cooks that was helping him gave him a thumbs up, so he dipped low and levered the entire thing onto one broad shoulder.

He waddled over to our table, legs bowed beneath the weight he was carrying.

I'd expected him to slam it on the table, but he set it down with a great measure of care.

"First dibs to the victors! Take as much as you want." He jerked a thumb back at the train. "Other one's marinating, but there's gonna be plenty to go around."

I grabbed a clean fork and ripped a chunk free for myself—the skin was crispy, and the meat pulled apart on contact—then grabbed a portion for House and set some onto Darling's plate in case she woke up.

"Can I ask you something real quick?"

"Sure thing, boss. What's up?"

"What the hell happened with Arranthea?"

He laughed so hard he started coughing and doubled over, hands on knees. "Oh, man! That was funny, wasn't it?"

"But what happened?" I repeated.

Sleep pulled his golden goggles down over his face. "Well, you remember when you showed up outside the Blue Fortress? Asked if we'd consider leaving the Oasis alone?"

"Yeah, of course."

"Still the best day of my life," Frank said.

"It's been less than 24 hours, Frank."

"I said still, didn't I? Open your mismatched ears."

Sleep chuckled. "Well, what did I say? No, right? So you hung out for a bit, then started preparing your defenses. Arranthea tried the same thing. Only when I said no, they kept asking." He scratched the back of his head. "I don't like politics, man. I don't like the way people end up pretending to be somebody else when talking to different groups, you know? To each their own, but it's not for me.

"So when someone asks me something, I tell them the truth. And if they keep asking, I tell them whatever they wanna hear so they'll leave me the hell alone, then I do whatever I was gonna do in the first place."

House straightened. "The two-toed man pays no mind to discounts on sandals."

Sleep bellowed a laugh and pointed at her. "I love this girl. She gets me."

House beamed brighter than ever before.

Frank and I shared a weird look at House's comment, but I didn't fully understand what Sleep was saying and I had to know.

"So, wait: you just lied and said you'd spare them if they helped you out?"

"It was worse than that. They wanted to ally up with you guys, then stab you in the back right before the Siege started. Get all the info they could out of you and relay it to us, then switch sides at the last moment." He spat onto the ground. "I told 'em we'd pass on that so they'd leave you guys alone because it wasn't about winning, but that we were happy to have them join our assault in exchange for safety. And when the time came, we killed 'em.

"Kinda thought that was the best fight we'd be getting today to be totally honest with you, but you guys definitely surprised us. But yeah— we'll be blowing them up in about eleven hours if you wanna join. Should be a good time."

"We'll be there," Frank said. "100%."

I glanced down at Frank. "We'll see, but I appreciate the invite. Did anybody else approach you about helping out?"

He looked up at the sky, which I could have sworn had been clear from horizon to horizon just a few minutes earlier but was now chock full of huge, cottony clouds.

"Uhhh… yeah. That Trevor guy messaged me a little ways back. I never responded. Didn't like the way he was talking to me."

I smiled. "You mean Tyrann, right? The streamer."

"That's the one. Guess he had other plans, eh?"

I tucked that little tidbit away for later. "Apparently so, but that's news to me. Thanks for that."

Sleep looked back at his guild members, who were regarding him with hungry eyes, then hefted the huge drumstick back onto his shoulder.

"I should get back to touring this thing through the camp before it gets cold. You guys let me know if you need anything, yeah? And again— that was a damn good time. That was one we'll never forget."

"It really was, and will do! Cheers!"

He headed off.

I eyed the Red Cathedral and the towers that were now totally permanent, three of them reaching well into the clouds above.

"Training Ground will be opening up soon," I mused.

Darling snored, then cut off halfway and snapped upright. "Cloudscape Hunting Grounds!" She squinted around at us, then at the beer she was still holding. "Did I… I didn't miss anything, right? It hasn't started yet?"

I stabbed a fork into the roasted bird, ripped a chunk free, and pointed it at Darling. "No, and you need to get some sleep. Like, real sleep."

She wavered there for a moment and seemed like she wanted to argue, then sighed. "Yeah, I know." She kicked me under the table. "But I don't wanna."

I laughed. "Gotta be ready for the next push! I promised Frank the Worldbranch Throne, and I intend to keep my word, which means we need an extension, which means we need to beat two guilds that are already way ahead of the curve to the next World-first, or we're dead in the water. And if we're gonna pull that off, we probably need our fearless leader to be at least partially awake."

"Yeaaaah. I'm gonna pass on that and go grab another coffee instead. I'll be back in five." She popped away.

House let out a dramatic sigh and scratched her teeth so violently that it was clear she'd been fighting the urge for quite a while.

"I very much regret that Darling has disappeared, but I have a confession to make and I can no longer bear the weight of it."

I popped the chunk of meat into my mouth and groaned as it melted before I could even chew. "Sorry House, I forgot about that! What's up?"

She took a very deep breath. "I have not been completely honest with you when it comes to the origin of my interest in idioms."

I frowned and took another bite. "Okay?"

She swallowed. "Please do not be mad, but I have been using them to test a hypothesis."

"What hypothesis?" Frank said. "Also hey, drop some of that bird in here."

I threw two pieces into his bucket.

"Thanks."

"Yup. So what exactly have you been doing, House?"

"Early on in my attempts to master the English language, I came to the obvious conclusion that, in all likelihood, I would be unable to do so in a reasonable period of time. So I came up with an alternate plan: to fake it until I made it. In other words, to simply speak with confidence that I did not have and assume everything would be fine."

A piece of meat dropped out from between my lips and back onto my plate.

"I therefore set out to test my approach with idioms. In stage one, I purposefully got them wrong and allowed myself to be corrected to avoid raising suspicion. As time passed, I moved onto stage two, where I seamlessly integrated them into my speech and was congratulated for my progress."

She leaned forward. "In stage three, I introduced minor errors back into my expressions, occasionally substituting an incorrect but usable word. And when no one noticed my substitutions, I proceeded to stage four of my analysis, whereupon I constructed my own nonsensical idioms from scratch and sprinkled them into the conversation."

I felt Frank try to slap the table. "I knew it! I knew it I knew it I knew it! If it's not eight feet, don't build it—what the hell does that even mean? I've been going over that in my head for daaaays trying to figure it out. Why isn't it eight feet? Why should it be eight feet? What the hell is it? And why isn't it being built?"

House smiled from ear to ear. "Then why did you not inquire into the meaning of my statement at said time?"

He grunted. "'Cause I didn't wanna be the only one that hadn't heard of the expression. That's a bad look for an all-knowing axe."

"That is precisely my point." House stood up. "If I can make up an entire expression and slip it into conversation without drawing notice or criticism, then I am free to say whatever I want to anyone at any point. Watch this."

She stepped up to the table next to us, and the conversation there died as she continued to stand there, looming over them as they ate.

A heavily armored player was the first to speak up. "Uhhh... Hi. Can I help you?"

House nodded. "I soak toast in milk and throw it at strangers."

The player stared up at her. "What? Do we know you?"

"You do now." She extended her hand. "I am House."

The player gave her a weird look but shook her hand regardless. "Dexter." He nodded at his companions. "That's Crevan, and that's Hiero."

"A pleasure to make your acquaintance," House said. Then she turned on her heel and sat right back down beside me.

"I don't know what just happened," Frank said, "but I am so, so happy about it."

House leaned across the table conspiratorially. "They still do not realize that I am robot."

"True," I said, laughing in earnest now. "But they definitely think you're weird."

"I currently possess twenty-four cats and one unshelled turtle." She leaned even closer. "I am weird, and I am okay with it. But do you see what this means? I can say whatever I want to anyone at any given point, and the worst thing that can possibly happen is that someone thinks I'm strange. There are no rules."

"Well, there are definitely rules, there's etiquette and norms and—"

I cut off as House bolted back over to the table she'd visited earlier, put two hands beneath it, then flipped the entire thing end over end, dishes and all.

"There are no rules!" she shouted, then she took off at a run, arms pinned behind her, her feline army scrambling out from beneath my table and chasing her through Goon's makeshift camp to confused laughter and raucous applause while Chip slowly slimed himself in her direction.

A beat of silence passed between Frank and me.

"What the hell just happened?" I said.

"Ugh. I think it's safe to say that despite our best efforts, we have officially been bamboozled."

I took another bite of bird and shook my head. "No, man. I hate to say it, but I think we just got Housed."

"Don't. Ever. Say that again, especially around her. We already have one name-based verb, and housing people is already a thing. Like the housing crisis—that's a thing that exists!"

"That actually sounds—"

"I know, I know, it sounds so awesome, right? I heard it as soon as I said it. Obviously the housing crisis itself sucks huge balls, but man, what a turn of phrase."

"Yeah. And look at her go! She's definitely weird, but at least she's happy, right?"

"She's got a serious case of the zoomies, so I think it's safe to say that is indeed the case."

I sighed, feeling suddenly content despite the knowledge of the fight to come and the pressure it represented, despite the Revenant and the manhunt, despite Tyrann and everything.

"I dunno if it's just me, but I kinda feel like a dad who recognizes that he did an objectively terrible job raising his child but is nonetheless exceedingly proud of the result."

Grabbing my mug off the table, I bumped it against his bucket. "I'm right there with you, man. The only question is where—"

I cut off as crimson portals appeared between the puffy clouds that had drifted in overhead. There were dozens, maybe even hundreds of them spread out across the sky, spinning like whirlpools above us, and before I could get a word out, a tower the size of a skyscraper had phased into existence about a hundred yards to my left.

I craned my neck to take in its red, glassy span, but its full height was hidden by the clouds. The area that surrounded the tower was stranger still, as the tower's base was framed by neck-high blue grass that looked like it had been ripped out of another reality altogether.

Then a wide door at the base of the tower clicked open, and an alert followed.

**Citizens of EBO!**
**The Thousand Towers have finally begun to arrive, and every tower is bringing a piece of its own reality with it!**
**Later today, the Thousand Tower Tournament will officially begin, and this perpetually changing world will never be the same!**
**Will you band together to conquer these world-ending constructs and claim the fate-altering rewards within them, or will you allow the towers' strange influence to bleed into your world and permanently change the many zones and cities beneath your feet?**
**The choice is yours!**
**And for those brave few who have already been granted access to the Cloudscape Hunting Grounds, your next grand adventure has already started, and to begin, you need only look to the heavens high above. Good luck, and as always, thank you for playing EBO.**

END

# Afterword

Thank you so much for reading *Gilded Ghost*! I hope you enjoyed the many misadventures of Frank and his unworthy sidekick plus House and her numerous cats volume 3, and if so, please consider sticking it to the moon by leaving a review!

I'm already working on the fourth book, but if you'd like more information on the series and my plans for it (including detailed ETAs and daily progress updates on book 4) please join the Discord, where I'm active every day! Updates are also posted on Reddit!

https://www.reddit.com/r/Shadeslinger/
https://discord.gg/H9xs3Vyc46

Finally, if you'd like to read a bunch of FREE short stories and novellas from the other incredible writers at Portal Books (Including an exclusive short story set in the Ripple System universe detailing the origin story of Tyrann and his god), you can do so by signing up to Portal Books mailing list. There is currently over 80,000 words of content that you can download completely free!

https://portal-books.com/sign-up

By signing up you will also be the first to hear about all their titles, including Saga Online by Oliver Mayes, Elemental Dungeon by Jonathan Smidt, God Core by L. M. Hughes, Titan Online by Steven Kelliher, Battle Spire by Michael R. Miller, The Nova Online Series by Alex Knight, Dungeons of Strata by Graeme Penman and many more!

You can also chat with these authors (and find timings for upcoming books) on the Portal Books Discord, checking out their posts on the Portal Books Facebook group or by liking their page.

https://discord.gg/GXBNDGYQqT
https://www.facebook.com/groups/LitRPGPortal/
https://www.facebook.com/PortalBooksPublishing

For more general discussions about the genre, these groups may be useful to you.

www.facebook.com/groups/LitRPGsociety/
www.facebook.com/groups/LitRPG.books/
www.facebook.com/groups/LitRPGGroup/

Get Franked!
-Kyle

# Portal Books Publishing

Portal Books is a digital publishing house that specializes in LitRPG, Dungeon Core, Cultivation and Progression Fantasy. Our mission is to bring you the best possible novels, with professional editing, copywriting and cover design.

We only work with authors who have a real passion for the genres and we think this shows in the novels we publish. We know that the heart of LitRPG is solid games mechanics and ensure every story is based on the kind of game system we ourselves would love to play.

If you'd like to try out stories from the other fantastic Portal Books authors, you can sign up to our mailing list for 80,000 words of FREE LitRPG stories. Whenever we add more, you'll get the update, absolutely free.

https://portal-books.com/sign-up

You can also find us on Facebook. Join our group to stay up to date on all our upcoming books, cover reveals, author interviews, giveaways, promotions and more!

https://www.facebook.com/groups/LitRPGPortal/

We also have a Discord server where you'll have a chance to chat with some our authors, members of the Portal Books team, or our community of readers as a whole!

https://discord.gg/GXBNDGYQqT

For more general discussions about the genre, these groups may be useful to you:

www.facebook.com/groups/LitRPGsociety

www.facebook.com/groups/LitRPG.books

www.facebook.com/groups/LitRPGGroup

Best wishes,

The Portal Books Team

www.portal-books.com